ONE MAN, ONE DAY

A novel

Patrick D. Bonner, Jr.

ONE MAN, ONE DAY

A novel

This is a work of fiction.

Names, characters, places, events and incidents are products of the author's imagination or are used fictitiously and are not to be construed as real. Any resemblance to actual persons, living or dead, events, or locales is entirely coincidental.

ONE MAN, ONE DAY

Patrick D. Bonner, Jr.
125 Half Mile Road, Suite 200
Red Bank, N.J. 07701

First paperback edition – November 2020

Editor – Cathleen E. Bonner

ISBN 978-0-578-22960-7 (print)
ISBN 978-0-578-78123-5 (e-book)

Library of Congress Control Number: 2020919426

Printed in the United States of America.

To my Mom and Dad

ONE MAN, ONE DAY – CONTENTS

Prologue   1

Part One – The Incident

Chapter 1 – Saturday Morning, Blue Skies   4

Chapter 2 – Shrimp Cocktail At Turnberry Park   13

Chapter 3 – Just Before The Blackness Hit   25

Chapter 4 – A Combination Of Two Events   37

Chapter 5 – The Consultation   50

Chapter 6 – Confident About Our Chances   64

Part Two – The Lawsuit

Chapter 7 – J. Hartwell Briggs And The Gunther
           Home Products Corporation   67

Chapter 8 – Hunkered Down At Island PT   76

Chapter 9 – A Summer Decides Upon A Plan   84

Chapter 10 – Dude, Why Us?   91

Chapter 11 – Mr. Sea-Mouse O'Rally   101

Chapter 12 – Everything That Is Wrong With
            This Country   117

Chapter 13 – A Prestigious Position   126

Chapter 14 – Motion To Dismiss For Failure
            To State A Claim   145

Chapter 15 – The Moon Over Mangrove Bay   168

Part Three – The Discovery Phase

Chapter 16 – The National Shrimp Cocktail
                 Defense Team   174

Chapter 17 – Operation Decannulation   187

Chapter 18 – Lower Than A Speck   202

Chapter 19 – When Does Redemption Come?   210

Chapter 20 – #babykiller   231

Chapter 21 – *"With Any Luck, She'll Expire"*   247

Chapter 22 – The Interim Toxicity Report   266

Chapter 23 – A Strategic Move By The Ketchogue
                 Sports And Recreation Committee   277

Chapter 24 – The Interim Toxicity Report 2.0   292

Chapter 25 – A Friendly Little Visit To The
                 Ketchogue Anti-Bullying Specialist   301

Chapter 26 – Twisting Him Into A Pretzel   315

Chapter 27 – A Visit From Richard Nixon   330

Chapter 28 – Keep The Faith   336

Chapter 29 – Can You Imagine Anything
                 So Unimportant?   347

Part Four – The Deposition And Pre-Trial Phase

Chapter 30 – The E.B.T. Of Daniel X. Beers   355

Chapter 31 – The Snowball   376

Chapter 32 – Jimmy O'Reilly Meets Abraham Lincoln   395

Chapter 33 – *"We Will Bury You"*   412

Chapter 34 – It Was Bright Orange   428

Chapter 35 – The Bubbles Just Stopped   430

Part Five - Trial

Chapter 36 – King George   436

Chapter 37 – A Day At A Time   458

Chapter 38 – Bofey Quinn's Public House   463

Epilogue   467

THAT WAS A memorable day to me, for it made great changes in me. But, it is the same with any life. Imagine one day struck out of it, and think how different its course would have been. Pause you who read this, and think for a moment of the long chain of iron or gold, of thorns or flowers, that would have bound you, but for the formation of the first link on one memorable day.

Charles Dickens, *Great Expectations*, 1861

ONE MAN, ONE DAY

PROLOGUE

January 4, 2018 – 10:42 pm
At Home, Ketchogue

So the story goes like this.

When my grandfather was 20 years old, in 1927, he boarded a transatlantic passenger ship called the SS Caledonia, way up in County Donegal. Back then you had no idea if you would ever see your family again so the night before his parents and seven siblings had gathered for what they called a "living wake." They ate and drank and wished him luck and the next day he got on that boat and was gone. The plan was to make a life in America, and his destination was Boston.

The Caledonia's voyage across the Atlantic Ocean was scheduled to take 8 days. My grandfather had scraped enough money together to buy a third-class steerage ticket, which meant that he would share bunk beds in the belly of the ship with three other farmers. He brought a suitcase with him – that's it – and had exactly 25 bucks in his pocket. The Caledonia would make its first stop in New York City before heading north to Massachusetts, and it was there, in South Boston, where my grandfather planned to meet up with an uncle on his mother's side. The uncle was the only person he knew in America, and if my grandfather could somehow make it up to that Irish-friendly neighborhood, the uncle would set him up with lodging and maybe a job. At least that was the plan. But with no way to contact the uncle once he landed, other than in person, who really knew. Plus, my grandfather had never met the man – he didn't even know what he looked like.

But here's what happened.

After taking breakfast each day, my grandfather would sit on a bench on the second level of the Caledonia, staring out the window at the endless miles of ocean, occasionally reading a James Joyce paperback he had stuffed into the pocket of his overcoat. About 4 days in, he decided he needed some air, and so he headed upstairs to the outdoor upper deck of the ship, fighting the chill of the whipping November winds. Standing at the rail, he struck up a conversation with an old man who, as it turned out, knew his father. They had worked together for a short time in the town of Culdaff, the old man said. Then he asked about my grandfather's destination in America and my grandfather told him about the uncle and his plans to settle in Boston. The old man then offered an alternative.

There are plenty of Irish neighborhoods in Brooklyn, he explained, where people take care of their own. You'll be welcome there and you'll easily find a place to stay and plenty of folks who will recommend you for work. The old man also claimed to know some people with contacts in the New York City Fire Department, a friendly landing spot for Irish immigrants in those days. The two then chatted about New York City, the Irish mayor Jimmy Walker, the Yankees and Babe Ruth, and a host of other things about the biggest city in America. My grandfather thanked the man, shook his hand, and the two went their separate ways.

After kicking it around overnight, my grandfather decided the idea made some sense. The thought of living in New York City was exciting. He certainly knew no more about Boston than he did about Brooklyn, and he could always get word to the uncle that he wasn't coming. So why not? The next morning, he went on deck to ask the old man a few questions, but he couldn't find him among the hundreds of passengers on that ship. As it turned out, he never laid eyes on the guy again. Years later he couldn't even remember his name.

But that ten-minute conversation convinced my grandfather to depart the Caledonia in lower Manhattan on November 26, 1927. He began his new life in Brooklyn, became a fireman and raised a family, and those Boston plans faded into history.

When I was a kid my grandfather told that story around our kitchen table more times than I could count. I barely paid attention, never really giving it much thought. He would have a few sips of his Rusty Nail and his face would turn red and in that Irish brogue he would spin that tale, along with many others. I would turn to my brother Will and ask — isn't this the one where he almost moved to Boston?

And then just as quickly I'd forget about it.

But recently I've been thinking about that story a lot. Especially after what happened to Deb. In fact, it's become an obsession and I can't shake it. Nearly every day now I think about my grandfather on the deck of that ship and I just can't get it out my head how different everything would be if he never ran into that old man.

I mean, there were hundreds of people on that boat, right? What were the chances?

PART ONE

THE INCIDENT

CHAPTER 1

SATURDAY MORNING, BLUE SKIES

WHEN YOU THINK about it, all that business with Agnes really got started on Friday, the night before the events at Turnberry Park. Danny Beers was in the kitchen of the old home on West 17th Street, right around dinner time, clearing the refrigerator of some molded-out Chinese food takeout boxes that had been percolating in there for a month, when Agnes walked in with an iPhone in her hands. She plopped down at the kitchen table, buried her chin in her palm, and began sliding her index finger over the face of the phone to check out her older sister Gianna's newest Instagram story. That's when Danny figured he'd ask.

The next morning, Saturday, presented one of two options, he explained. Either they could go to Agnes's softball game over at Turnberry, or they could hit the Roosevelt Field shopping mall for those Puma sneakers the girls had been begging for. With his head pressed forward into the second shelf of the refrigerator, his butt to the room, Danny requested that Agnes state her preference. *Whaddya wanna do kiddo,* he asked, *you pick.* His question echoed out of the fridge, and Agnes shot back a response without taking her face off the iPhone. She wanted to play softball.

And that was it, the decision was made.

The whole discussion took less than ten seconds.

The next morning, Danny stepped out onto his tiny front porch clutching a dark-roast 7-Eleven coffee and a *New York Post*, clad in blue jeans, construction boots and a grey flannel shirt, expecting an early April chill. He wasn't out on the porch a second, though, before a blast of humidity hit him like a punch in the face.

What the hell ... he thought.

He let the screen door snap back against the house with a bang, and after one breath of the sticky air, he pitched the coffee over the porch rail into a row of evergreen bushes.

"Won't be needing that," he said out loud.

He looked up and saw his neighbor waving at him.

"Hey Danny!" she yelled cheerfully.

Diane something, although Danny couldn't produce a last name if you put a gun to his head. Nice lady though, and friendly. Danny waved back.

"You believe this heat?" she called out from across the street. She was spraying a garden hose into a bed of begonias.

"Crazy!" he hollered.

"Opening Day?" she asked.

Danny nodded and smiled, tossing her a thumb's up.

"Good luck," she yelled, "have fun!"

Good luck ...

Well, Danny knew he would need some that day, that was for sure. And he certainly appreciated the gesture. The people in this town were so supportive and had been since the funeral. But sometimes you just wished the whole world didn't know every detail of your family's business. To be completely anonymous again would be a godsend, but what can you do. Can't have it both ways.

"Thanks!" he yelled back.

Danny alighted from the porch and strolled toward his driveway. His beloved Ford F-350 pickup truck sat facing the single-car garage, and Danny climbed aboard. He tossed the empty coffee cup and the newspaper into the backseat, turning an eye toward the house. If he guessed correctly, Agnes was primping in front of the downstairs bathroom mirror right now, making sure that long ropey braid of hers shot perfectly through the hole in the back of her mesh softball cap. The kid was only ten, but man did she know how she liked things. Danny knew they weren't going anywhere until that braid was just right.

Resigned, Danny twisted the ignition key and fired up the engine. Then he poked on radio station 102.3 FM, the classic rock channel. An old Allman Brothers song sprang to life, and Danny smiled. He cranked down the windows to let some air flow through the cab and leaned back into the tattered cushion of the driver's seat. All around him were the sights and sounds of spring – a blazing blue sky, birds chirping, kids playing stickball in the street, a lawn mower buzzing away in the distance. The steamy air was redolent of blooming azaleas and fresh-cut grass, and Danny drew a deep breath through his nose, taking it all in.

He was excited for Agnes today, maybe even a little anxious. It had been six long months, but finally the day was here. The decision they made the night before, Danny considered, was a good one. Through the screen, Danny saw movement in the foyer. That meant Agnes would be out in a minute. He leaned his head out the driver's side window and let that unexpected baking sun warm his face. It felt good, although he braced himself at the painful memory brought on by the strange, unseasonable heat. But he didn't want to let that ugly thought dampen his mood that morning. He was determined to keep things positive for Agnes.

Danny spun the radio dial, and the Allman Brothers gave way to the ESPN station. He gazed through his windshield at the sun once more. Who knows, he reasoned, maybe this crazy heat today didn't have to mean the worst again. Instead, maybe it was a sign that things were going to get back on track. Every year, right after shaking loose the doldrums of those miserable Long Island winters, the approaching summer season would always energize Danny. Lift his spirits. He had lived for all those picnic lunches with Deb and the girls up at the Sound, and those lazy Sunday afternoons lying with the family on a beach blanket down on Fire Island. Body-surfing, Deb in her bikini, the girls digging with pails at the ocean's edge. And later a cold beer on the front porch, watching the fireflies snap away against the nighttime sky. Man, those were the days.

For some reason, even despite the tumult of the last six months, that April morning had that same familiar feel. Sitting there in his pickup under a sweltering sun, Danny felt hopeful again. He couldn't explain it, but it was there. He felt it in his bones. He certainly knew he didn't deserve it, not with the way that whole nightmare had unfolded. But for whatever reason, the intensity of that early spring sun gave him a surge of adrenaline that he hadn't felt in quite some time.

Agnes scrambled out of the house with a Coleman water jug and a softball mitt, and she settled into the passenger seat.

"Sorry, Daddy," she said, placing the jug at her feet.

"It's okay, we got time."

He nodded over her shoulder.

"Seatbelt now, kiddo."

Agnes clicked her belt in and showed a nervous smile.

"Atta girl," Danny said.

A few minutes later they were chugging along through the town of Ketchogue, a tony north shore enclave nestled up against the cerulean waters of the Long Island Sound. They rumbled past the Dunkin' Donuts, Sullivan's Pub, Sons of Italy Hall, and all the other shops and cafes on Route 25A. Agnes, meanwhile, rode the whole way in silence, picking nervously at a split-end at the tip of that long blond braid. Danny tried to engage her in small talk but since he was only getting one-word answers, he just let her be. He knew what was in store for her in about twenty minutes over at the field.

Soon the pickup rumbled into the parking lot of Walter C. Turnberry Memorial Park, over on Ketchogue's east side. Danny located a spot and angled in the pickup. He twisted the gearshift into Park and turned to his daughter, rubbing the back of his hand against her cheek.

"You ready for this?" he asked her.

"Just one second."

"Yeah sure, no problem."

He saw that look again. So often these days, without warning, Agnes would purse her lips, scrunch up her eyebrows, and blow a lifesaving breath of air out of her lungs. All before wiping her hands down her face. She'd look so nervous, the poor kid. Danny knew why, of course, but what a shitty way for a child to feel. He wanted so badly to help her, but you could never ask what was bothering her without her launching into one of those pre-teen eye rolls.

"Everything alright?" Danny tried anyway.

And there it was, the eye roll, right on cue.

"Everything's fine, Dad."

"Ok, great … I mean … good."

There were times, like now, when Danny walked on eggshells with his girls, not knowing exactly what to say. All week he could see that Agnes's anxiety over this day was sky-high, and what a bummer that was, because right now the park was filled with smiling kids all decked out in their softball uniforms. They were running around playfully, carefree, ready for Opening Day. Man did he wish Agnes would just sprint from the pickup and join them. He wanted so badly for her to lighten up and just be a kid, but that pretty much summed up their life these days.

Agnes nodded toward the softball field.

"Look, they're staring at us," she said with a frown.

Danny turned and looked at the softball field.

"Who's staring?" he asked. "Where?"

"Right there," she pointed. "Between the signs."

In front of them a basketball court sat between the parking lot and the softball field. On the far side of the court a chain-link fence ran along the softball field's third base line, and pinned to it was a fat, rectangular blue sign that read "THIS IS A NO PEANUT ZONE." To the right of it, closer to home plate, a smaller sign read only "BULLIES," with a Ghostbusters slice over the word. Through the signs Danny could see the Carvel Lady Mets – Agnes's team – lined up playing catch but looking straight at the pickup.

"Oh, the girls," Danny acknowledged. "I see them."

In short left field the Geico Lady Marlins – the opponents this day – were assembled in right field, far from the parking lot. They were engaged in their own throwing practice, oblivious to Danny and Agnes. But the Lady Mets had definitely taken notice.

"Actually, I don't know if they're staring at *us*," Agnes then commented with a smile, "or, like, this *truck*."

Danny smiled and pinched his daughter's cheek. He looked across the parking lot at all those shiny, high-priced SUV gas guzzlers, sparkling like they had just emerged from a carwash. Then he affectionately patted the dashboard of his pickup. He loved his ol' clunker even though it stuck out like a sore thumb here. The ten-year old weather-beaten rust bucket was tattooed along the driver's side with gold block letters that spelled out "Beers Construction Co." – except that it was missing an "e" in Beers and a "t" in Construction, so that it actually read "B ERS CON SRUCTION CO." His girls were mortified by it and were constantly busting his chops, telling him it looked "ghetto." They would rather he take his wife's Prius, a vehicle he was still making payments on even though it sat most days in the garage.

"So big whup, they're staring," Danny said, moving past the truck joke.

"Daddy, I hate it."

Danny rubbed her cheek again.

"That, uh, really bother you?"

Over the last six months Danny had asked this very question of his ten-year old daughter maybe a thousand times. The Ketchogue School social worker assigned to them had urged him to keep pressing Agnes to talk – about anything, she said. The subject didn't matter. Her feelings, her clothes, tensions in the Middle East, whatever. Danny's job was to ask questions that would trigger a conversation. Just listen, she told him, don't argue or try to fix things. His problem, though, was that he never knew when and under what circumstances to ask these questions. And he always seemed to get it wrong, somehow managing to piss them off.

"It's just embarrassing," Agnes responded, unhooking her seat belt. Her softball mitt was on her lap now, along with the iPhone.

"Okay."

"And you, like, always ask if things bother me. It's annoying."

"Fair enough," he said, silently searching for patience.

Agnes's thumbs then began to fly over the face of the iPhone, pressing buttons that were click, click, clicking away. It sounded like an old typewriter, except it would always be followed by a *whoooop* noise. The whole iPhone thing was another point of contention between him and his daughters, and Danny often wondered why his wife had ever permitted the girls to own these godforsaken contraptions. They were ten and twelve years old and their faces were glued to them night and day. But ever since the funeral Danny figured he had bigger fish to fry, so he quickly made the decision, for better or worse, that this wasn't a battle he was going to fight.

"Who are you texting Agnes?" he demanded.

Fight or no fight, this was another thing the social worker had stressed. Keep on their social media, make sure you know who they're talking to. It's important. But as far as social media was concerned, to borrow an expression from his mother, Danny would admit he didn't know whether to shit or wind his watch. And who could keep it all straight anyway, from Facegram to Twitbook to Instasnap, or whatever the hell they were called. All useless bullshit in his opinion, and yet it seemed to have taken over the world.

"Agnes, who are you texting?" he asked again.

"No one."

"Agnes-"

"No one, Dad!"

"Agnes-"

"Okay! It's Maggie. God!"

"Alright, no problem. Take it easy now."

Agnes huffed, shoving the iPhone into the pocket of her softball pants. She grabbed her mitt and nodded toward the field.

"Yup, still staring at us."

This time Danny didn't even look at the field.

"Agnes, c'mon," he pleaded, "you have to understand, they're all worried about you. They just hope you're ok with everything."

"Yeah I know Daddy."

"Especially because this is your first school thing since, you know, the funeral."

"You don't have to hesitate every time you, like, say the word funeral, Daddy. I know there was a funeral, I was there."

Danny took a deep breath.

"Hey, can we maybe lighten up a little here? Maybe have some fun today?"

Agnes responded with a soft expression that suggested an opening, and Danny decided to go with it.

"I mean, you're playing the Lady Marlins today, right?"

He began playfully poking her in the ribs.

"The horrible Lady Marlins. The evil, cruel, ugly, wart-faced, bad breath, pimply Lady Marlins! Don't you just want to slaughter them? Rip their faces off? Don't you wanna – "

"Okay, I get it, stop!" Agnes shouted with a smile.

She punched Danny in the arm.

"They don't even keep score, weirdo," she laughed, and Danny reached over and hugged his daughter.

And then, to his surprise, instead of pulling away, Agnes launched sideways and wrapped both arms around his neck. Her softball mitt fell to the cabin floor. She was shaking, sniffling back tears, holding on for dear life. She stayed like that for a full minute, her head pressed into his chest. Danny held her tight, trying to soothe her, until finally she settled down. Despite her precociousness, his youngest daughter was still just a ten-year old kid, Danny thought. He should have seen this coming.

"You ok?" he asked. "What's going on?"

"Daddy?" she asked softly, still gripping his neck.

"Yes baby, what is it?"

She let him go and leaned back in her seat, wiping her face.

"There is something bothering me, I guess."

She was looking down at her hands, her eyes still moist.

"Oh yeah?"

This was good. Progress.

"What's up?"

"You're gonna think this is dumb."

"No, no ... tell me."

"It's just that, uh, like, I don't know."

"Agnes, go on, please."

"Well, at the last softball game I played, like last year I think?"

"Yeah, that's right."

"Mom was here. Sitting in one of our beach chairs. Like, over there." Agnes pointed to the outfield. "She was wearing those sunglasses you gave her for her birthday."

"She was, yeah," Danny said. "The Ray Bans."

"Every time I got up to bat, she'd like smile and wave at me."

"Yeah, she did that all the time, right?"

"Yeah she did."

Agnes took a deep breath and stared through the windshield.

"I don't know, I was just thinking about that on the way over here," she said. "That Mom won't be here today. Stupid I guess."

Danny adjusted himself in his seat.

"Would you rather drop all this and go to the Mall?" he asked.

Agnes shook her head no, and Danny put his hand to his daughter's cheek. He looked into her eyes, those sparkling blue ovals under those beautiful wavy streaks of blond hair – another gift from her mom.

He grabbed both her hands and smiled.

"Agnes, what you just said? That's not stupid at all. It's great you remember that. It's the little memories that keep Mom alive for us, right?"

Danny leaned over and kissed her on the forehead.

"I'm really glad you told me that. So proud of you."

Agnes smiled. She stared out the windshield again, watching the activity out on the field, and Danny let her be. Then, suddenly, Agnes took a breath and slipped on her softball mitt. She punched a fist into the glove, like she was ready to play ball, and Danny felt a weight come off his shoulders. He couldn't believe how his daughters' moods could change like that, going from high to low and back again in the blink of an eye.

Out on the field, the Lady Mets were assembled near home plate now. Behind the backstop a collection of blooming locust trees was swaying with that unexpected humid breeze whistling across Turnberry Park.

"Okay, I'm ready!" Agnes announced with a beaming grin.

"Wait, you're ready?" Danny responded.

"I'm ready!"

"Oh man, she's ready! I love it! Fourth grade softball, Saturday morning, blue skies, who's better than us?"

"Nobody!"

"And what're we gonna do to these Lady Marlins today?"

"Rip their faces off, Daddy."

"That's my girl. Let's go."

CHAPTER 2

SHRIMP COCKTAIL AT TURNBERRY PARK

DANNY WAS HUNKERED down in short left field, leaning on the top rail of the chain-link fence as the clocks rolled 1 pm. The sun continued its blazing assault, beaming down as if it had something to prove after the brutal winter that just passed. Danny adjusted the brim of a Yankee cap he had pulled over his thick salt and pepper hair, shielding his face from the blistering rays, as beads of sweat rolled down his back.

Out on the field the game was in the bottom of the third inning with the Lady Mets at the plate. It had been laboring on for nearly an hour and a half when the tiny Lady Marlin pitcher uncorked a pitch that went rolling against the dugout fence, a good fifteen feet from the plate. The pitch scattered a group of Lady Mets in their batting helmets, waiting their turn at the plate. They skipped over the pitch like they were jumping rope.

"Good eye, Beatrice!" came a yell from somewhere in the crowd when the batter elected not to swing. "Not your pitch!"

"BALL FIVE!" yelled the umpire.

Danny turned to the person standing next to him – a tall, angular splinter of a man, maybe early forties, dressed in a nylon blue Nike sweat suit with a matching mesh runner's cap. He had a thick sturdy head of jet-black hair with a blue-tooth contraption attached to his left ear, and he was swigging from a 20-ounce bottle of Poland Spring water.

"Excuse me," Danny said, "did he say … ball five?"

He had to look almost due north to eyeball the man, owing to his impressive height.

"Aw, yeah, dude," the man replied, gesturing toward the pitcher's mound. "After the second inning if there are too many walks they give the pitcher eight balls for a walk."

"Eight balls?"

"League rule," said Dodge. "They don't want the pitchers

getting too upset if they're walking too many batters. It's like … a traumatizing thing."

Before his wife passed Danny worked most Saturdays and never made it to these games, so he didn't know the rules. Debbie had kept him apprised of only the basics – the girls played softball, had uniforms, and played Saturday games. Beyond that he was clueless. He'd see the girls late Saturday afternoon and ask, hey how was the game, and he'd get back the monosyllabic grunt of a response, "good," before they would thrust their faces back into their iPhones.

"BALL SIX!" yelled the umpire, who had to walk the ball back to the mound. The last delivery by the Lady Marlin pitcher had sailed straight up in the air and landed like a hand grenade halfway between the pitcher's mound and the plate.

Beatrice pounded her bat on the plate, ready for the next pitch.

"Hey, you're Dan Beers, right?" the tall man asked, guzzling some Poland Spring again. He pulled his cap off and wiped his forehead. "Man, it's hot out here isn't it?"

"Yeah, sure is," Danny said.

The two shook hands.

"Dude, I'm Dodge Brewer," the man said. "Glad to meet you."

"Same here," said Danny.

But Danny knew exactly who Dodge Brewer was – he didn't need the introduction. The Brewers were one of those high-profile couples that had their hand in just about everything going on in the town. Whether it was 5k runs, bake sales, car washes, fundraisers, whatever, the Brewers were either running things or somehow involved. They lived over in Starboard Estates, the most prestigious development in Ketchogue, at the end of the cul-de-sac on a two and a half-acre plot that backed up to the Long Island Sound. Their house was one of the biggest in town, a point that Dodge was known to accidentally on purpose slip into casual conversations.

And of course, Danny also knew Cindy Brewer, Dodge's wife, as did everyone else in Ketchogue. Cindy was a six-foot tall statuesque stunner with a body that looked like she just dropped off the cover of the *Sports Illustrated* swimsuit edition. She had represented New York in the 1999 Miss America pageant, and to say she was something of a legend in this town was putting it mildly.

When she strolled down Main Street in Ketchogue in sunglasses and shopping bags, with those long legs and curvy hips, the woman had men walking into fire hydrants.

"Actually, dude, my wife Cindy and I were at the wake."

Danny recalled the whole receiving room turning and staring when Cindy walked in that day. It was quite the scene.

"Yeah, that day was a blur, but thanks man."

"No problem, dude," said Dodge. "And sorry about that whole thing. That really blows."

Danny shrugged his shoulders.

"What're you gonna do."

"BALL SEVEN! Count 7 and 0!" the umpire yelled. This time the pitch landed somewhere in the vicinity of home plate.

"Good eye, Beatrice!" yelled someone in the crowd again.

"Great pitch Chelsea!" yelled another parent. "Keep working!"

"Hey, so what exactly are the rules here? How do they play these games?" Danny asked Dodge, wiping some sweat from beneath his chin.

"Yeah, dude, okay, so this is how it works," said Dodge. "They play six innings, and every kid gets to bat. Doesn't matter how many walks or outs, they go through the whole lineup. That way it's fair."

Dodge tucked the Poland Spring bottle under his arm and reached into his Nike pants. He pulled a 30-gram Muscle Milk chocolate protein bar from his pocket – Danny could see the name of it in block letters across the wrapping. He ripped it open and took a big fat bite of it, continuing with his mouth full.

"After three innings they take a break and have a snack and a drink. Snack moms take turns. You want to be careful the kids don't get too taxed without some rest, so snack time is like a halftime."

Danny nodded. He turned toward the outfield, where five girls sat cross-legged in the grass. One outfielder had her chin in her palms, elbows on her knees, and another had managed to sneak an iPhone out there and was thumbing away. A third player was tossing her mitt in the air and playing catch with herself. In the dugouts the kids were all either sitting or lying on the benches. It didn't seem like rest time was necessary, but who was he to judge.

Danny then ran his eyes along the line of parents leaning on the chain-link fence. He noticed that their level of interest didn't really suggest Game 7 of the World Series either. Nearly every one of them was working their thumbs over the face of some hand-held device. This was the Rec League, the lowest level of competition at this age group, and was mostly for children who weren't very good athletes. The game was like watching paint dry, but Danny understood the parents were all here for their kids.

"And everyone scores a run," Dodge continued. "It's really good for their self-esteem."

Danny looked out at the Lady Marlin pitcher, who was about to uncork another pitch. Then he noticed something strange. The little girl wore a red batting helmet with a full facemask, and she had two large rectangular plates strapped to the front of her body. One was across her midsection and the other across her chest. They were made of hard plastic and secured by four nylon straps that stretched around to her back. She also wore sets of elbow pads and knee guards. With all that equipment encumbering her limbs, she was walking like Frankenstein, Danny thought. She looked like she could survive a ground assault in Baghdad.

"What are those plate things?" Danny asked. "On her chest."

"Aw yeah, dude, okay, so the bottom one is the FUG Wrap."

"The, uh …," Danny lowered his voice, "fuck wrap?"

"No, no, dude, FUG Wrap, F-U-G," he said. "It stands for Fallopian Uterus Guard. It's just for girls' sports. Studies show that if a player gets hit below the navel with a ball hit at a certain velocity, it could cause serious damage to reproductive organs. They're pretty new, the FUG Wraps, but Ketchogue's really good about being ahead of things, you know, with sports technology and shit. So all the pitchers wear them."

"Oh, got it. Never heard of those."

"Like I said, dude, they're new."

"And the one on the chest?"

"Dude, that's the heart plate. Those have been out there a while. Same thing, studies show that if a player gets hit directly in the chest? With a batted ball hit at a high rate of speed? Dude, it can kill you. Especially if it hits in the split second between the beats of the heart. It's actually happened once or twice. You know, somewhere in America."

"Really."

"Yeah, so in girls' softball all the players who pitch have to wear the FUG Wrap and the heart plate, and we make them also wear the helmet and the elbow pads and knee pads."

"Got it. I didn't know any of this."

"Dude, plus, there's the liability. You don't want to mess with that. This way the players are safe and the town is protected. Everyone wins."

"And in terms of ... do they, you know, keep score?"

"Aw dude, c'mon, no way. You can't tell a kid she's a loser. Hashtag no brainer."

"BALL EIGHT! TAKE YER BASE!"

This time the Lady Marlin pitcher tossed a pitch that went backwards over the top of her head. It rose up like she had released a helium balloon, landing with a thud near second base. Beatrice promptly ran to her coach, handed over the bat, and sprinted down to first base, smiling like she just won the lottery.

Just then Dodge's iPhone beeped.

"Dude, gimme a minute," he said.

He began thumbing out a text.

"Here's Cindy, she's pulling in. She's the snack Mom today."

Dodge turned and looked towards the parking lot.

"Hey I gotta go. Great meeting you again. Follow me on Twitter, okay? Dbrewer75."

And with that Dodge was off.

RIGHT THERE BEHIND them, over in the parking lot, a black Mercedes Benz G-63 AMG SUV rolled into Turnberry Park before backing into the handicapped spot near the entrance to the baseball field. Cindy Brewer hopped out dressed head to toe in a sexy little number from the *L'Etoile* tennis collection, which didn't really look like it was ever used much for tennis. The outfit revealed a delicious set of curvy hips, a pierced navel centered on tanned six-pack abs, and about a mile and a half of incredible Pacific Health Club-shaped legs. The whole thing was a sight to behold, and as Cindy exited the Mercedes, there wasn't a male neck at the chain-link fence that didn't crane rearward for a viewing.

Cindy shut the driver side door and pressed a button on her key ring, which automatically raised the SUV's rear door. Then she planted her feet on the blacktop, locked her knees, and whipped her head down toward the ground. In the same motion, she thrusted it back up again, flipping her thick auburn hair over the top of her head so that it fell perfectly into place. She then pulled some manner of hair tie off her wrist and quickly formed a ponytail. Almost simultaneously she motioned toward the baseball field.

"Dodge!" she called, waving him to the Mercedes.

"Come help me with this box."

Dodge was already into a jog and headed toward the parking lot. He was bouncing on his toes in perfect running form as he cruised around the adjacent basketball court, arriving at the Mercedes just as the bottom of the third inning ended. The Lady Mets coach, a father of one of the players, presently was assembling the girls behind the home plate backstop in preparation for snack time. Someone had placed a fold-out rectangular table in that area, and on it were some paper plates and a styrofoam cup filled with plastic forks. The girls collected their Coleman water jugs and took a seat in the grass under the locust trees, which were giving some relief from the unseasonal heat choking Turnberry Park.

Danny watched all of this from his spot in short left field along the chain link fence. As snack time got underway and the girls were congregating behind home plate, the parents began to form circles, chatting or thumbing away on their iPhones. But Danny stayed by himself, his back to the fence, leaning on his elbows. Debbie's closest friends didn't have a child on the Lady Mets team and so Danny didn't know this group of parents very well. He thought a few of the women may have attended the wake and funeral and could have been friendly with Debbie, but he wasn't sure.

Over by home plate, Dodge and Cindy arrived at the fold-out table. Dodge had a yellow rectangular box in his hands and Cindy carried a white plastic bag with an emblem of a red lobster on it. Even from his position about thirty yards away, Danny instantly recognized the inscription on the side of Dodge's box. It read "LENNY'S SEAFOOD MARKET," and if you lived anywhere near Ketchogue you definitely knew the place. Lenny's was considered the high-end gold standard for seafood anywhere near these parts. And everyone recognized their boxes, with that distinctive lettering together with those two large clamshells – Lenny's trademark.

Danny was a big fan and had carried quite a few of those boxes home; he loved their flounder, salmon, soft shell crabs, oysters, scallops, all of it.

Dodge placed the box on the fold-out table and pulled two large plastic containers out of it. He placed them side by side as Cindy dropped the bag and addressed the girls.

"Okay Lady Mets! Mr. Brewer has a nice surprise for us today!" She grabbed one of the containers.

"You girls know Lenny's Seafood, right? So guess what? For snack time today we have beautiful fresh shrimp from Lenny's!"

Cindy turned to look at Dodge, who was clapping his hands and smiling. But the Lady Mets all sat there like wax figures, not moving a muscle. Cindy's enthusiasm would not be contained, however, and she told them, "C'mon girls, everyone grab a plate, you'll love this shrimp, trust me. It's a real treat!" And then one by one the girls all lined up with plates in their hands. Dodge shoveled out a few shrimps to each player as Cindy spooned a dollop of cocktail sauce onto their plates.

"Okay girls," she instructed, "take your fork and dip the shrimp into the cocktail sauce. Lenny's sauce is the best."

Over by the fence, Danny stood with another father named Gary Snyder, a chubby bond trader with a mop of black hair and a jowly inner tube of flesh underneath his goatee. He had arrived in a navy-blue Villanova University pullover and was now sweating right through the thing. Snyder had hired Danny about a year earlier to gut and re-do a bathroom, and as the girls were gathering for snack time Snyder had ambled over, seeing Danny alone, and had offered his condolences. At the same time Danny was keeping an eye on Agnes, thinking about their earlier conversation and hoping she was fitting back into the group after so much time away from all these school activities. He was comforted when he saw her sitting in the grass with two other girls, the three of them talking and laughing and adjusting one another's braids.

After some small talk, Danny gestured toward the Lady Mets.

"So, uhh, shrimp cocktail for snack time? Not bad."

Snyder chuckled, and nodded toward the group.

"Hey man, it's the Brewers. Whadja expect, twinkies?"

Danny laughed.

"First off," he responded, "when I played Little League, you asked for a snack? You got cuffed in the head."

"Yeah, right?" Snyder nodded. "I know man, me too."

"But then again, Lenny's Seafood is the best, right?"

"Oh no question," Snyder laughed.

He hooked a thumb in the general direction of Cindy Brewer.

"You know what though?" he asked in a lowered voice, "just between us kids, the snack mom over there could serve me whatever she wants."

Danny looked over at Cindy, who was pulling the hair tie from her ponytail and shaking the thing loose. The full batch of her perfect locks went spilling back onto her shoulders. Then she tapped Dodge on the arm and without a word handed the hair tie to him. Dodge instinctively grabbed it and snapped it onto his own wrist, as if the two of them had choreographed the move. Dodge had now removed the Nike jacket and had it tied around his waist, revealing a four-percent body fat, lean muscle, whey-protein-shake physique, complete with those blue veins running through the spray-tanned bulging biceps.

Was this Ketchogue, or Beverly Hills?

Danny turned back to Snyder.

"Yeah, I hear you, man," he laughed. "I hear you."

BY THE TIME the top of the fourth inning began, right after Dodge and Cindy had broken down the snack area and stored the fold-out table back in the rear of the Mercedes G60, the intensity of the afternoon sun was overwhelming. Most of the parents were either fanning themselves with whatever they could get their hands on – newspapers, t-shirts or whatever – or had relocated behind the backstop in the shaded area under the locust trees. It was now roughly quarter after two o'clock, and anyone who had arrived in jackets or pullovers that morning now had those sweaty garments either tied around their waists, like Dodge, or balled up under their arms. Their faces were red and glistening and quite a few of them had left the sideline to seek relief in the air-conditioning of their SUVs, the motors of which could now be heard humming away in the parking lot.

What the hell had happened to spring, Danny wondered. Less

than a month ago, in early March, a snowstorm had shut down the Long Island Railroad and kept the kids home from school. Now it felt like they were living in the goddamn Sudan. Back on the diamond, the Lady Mets were in the field. The Lady Met pitcher, a stout little fireplug named Daphne, with meaty cheeks and a bubble belly, frankensteined her way out to the pitcher's mound. She was loaded up with the helmet, facemask, elbow pads, knee pads, FUG Wrap and heart plate. She wore all of that over her size Adult Large Lady Met softball shirt and a pair of shin-length nylon softball pants. Under this blazing sun, Danny remembered thinking, you might as well have wrapped her in cellophane and stuck her in a steam room.

Once she was settled on the hill, Daphne leaned back and hurled a pitch toward home plate. But with the sheer weight of all the body armor, her toss was a sidearm-whirl type of thing, like you see from an Olympic discus thrower. The pitch sailed over the head of the catcher and umpire and went *ching!* against the chain-link backstop fence.

"BALL ONE!" called the umpire, followed by a collective eye roll from the parents huddled under the locust trees. They all began snapping glances at their watches, silently furious with the ring of sweat forming under their armpits. Others were standing with their arms crossed, praying for mercy behind a pair of Ray Bans. When the Lady Mets coach, a father by the name of Pete Briscoe, yelled out, "Good pitch, Daphne, bear down now!" you could actually hear one of the parents mutter "Jesus Christ."

Danny was near third base leaning on the chain-link fence again. He was shielding himself from the blinding rays by jamming the bill of his Yankee cap further down near the bridge of his nose. His flannel shirt was now in a ball on the grass at his feet, and he wore only a very damp sleeveless t-shirt – what he and his friends called a "guinea-t" – with his shoulder tattoos turning pink under the angry sun.

The next series of events would forever be burned in Danny's memory – the umpire calling out BALL TWO! ... the parents angrily shifting in their stances and crossing their arms ... Daphne staggering around on the mound, attempting the next pitch, pulling her arm back a few times to throw, but not releasing the ball ...

Coach Briscoe calling out "Daphne, are you okay?" … several parents pocketing their iPhones and stepping closer to the field – curious, concerned, worried … Daphne dropping down on one knee, struggling to get back up, and then suddenly collapsing down sideways onto the mound … the ball rolling a few feet away … Daphne lying flat on her back, with all of her limbs extended, not moving a muscle … then all hell breaking loose, with parents screaming, leaping over the chain-link fence and sprinting toward the mound … a horde of people in the middle of the diamond, the words "DAPHNE! DAPHNE!" roaring across Turnberry Park … the Lady Mets and Lady Marlins shrieking and crying … frantic parents struggling to get Daphne to sit up … one of them pulling out a cold yellow Gatorade and feeding it to Daphne as the hefty girl sat on her rump on the pitcher's mound, surrounded by over a dozen adults, her face purple and her black hair soaked when they removed the batting helmet and facemask … and then a collective sigh of relief and a round of applause when they finally got her to her feet and began walking her slowly toward the dugout.

And somewhere near the end of all that commotion is when Danny heard the soft voice of a tiny Lady Met player. She was standing to his right.

"Mr. Beers," is all she said.

But Danny's eyes, along with everyone else's, were lasered in on Daphne, who was sitting on the dugout bench now, nursing the Gatorade and taking deep breaths between sips.

Danny ignored the little girl.

"MR. BEERS!" she repeated, this time with some urgency.

"Yes," Danny finally responded, distracted.

He was angled toward home plate, the little girl facing him.

"I'm sorry sweetheart, did you say something?"

And then all she did was point.

Not exactly behind him, but over Danny's left shoulder, far away from the direction of Daphne and the panicked parents and crying players.

Toward the outfield.

And that's when Danny saw her. It was Agnes.

She was lying on her side in the grass in centerfield and looked like she had fallen asleep. The left side of her face was planted in

the grass, her right arm out in front of her, and her right leg swung
over her left one. She didn't appear to be moving. Her softball mitt
was a few feet behind her, abandoned in the outfield grass. Before
you could blink an eye, Danny called out, "what the fuck!" and he
leapt over the fence, sprinting like all living hell toward his daughter.
He was on her in a second.

He was screaming "AGNES! AGNES!" who knows how many
times, and in a flash he was on his knees, gently rolling her over
onto her back.

What he saw horrified him.

Agnes's face was severely swollen, like it had been inflated with
a bicycle pump. The lines of her cheekbones had all but
disappeared. Both her eyes were slits and there were red welts all
over her neck. And her tongue, for God's sake, it was big and fat
and poking through her swollen lips like it was a tortoise peeking
out of its shell.

Danny drew a deep breath that almost caused him to pass out.

"C'mon baby, talk to me! Agnes! Talk to me!"

He leaned down and pressed his face against her cheek. He
could barely hear her shallow, labored breathing.

"Jesus, no! No!"

And then a scream came from behind him.

"SOMEBODY CALL 911!"

Suddenly a group of parents was surrounding him.

"Oh, Jesus, please!" – from one of them.

"C'mon, Agnes, wake up!" came another voice.

"CALL 911!" Danny heard again.

Danny put a hand under Agnes's neck and wiped the sweat
from her forehead. Who knows how long it took, but suddenly two
paramedics were sprinting toward them. One of them was hauling
a large grey box with a red cross on it. A third paramedic was pulling
the ambulance onto the outfield grass, with red flashing lights
lasering across Turnberry. Then the first two paramedics were on
their knees tending to Agnes, and from somewhere came a gurney.
Danny was standing a few feet behind the two paramedics, his body
shaking, with two sobbing women he didn't know gripping him by
the elbows.

How long had she been lying like that in the outfield grass? Five minutes? Ten minutes? He had no idea.

"YOU THE FATHER?!" screamed one of the paramedics as they lifted Agnes onto the gurney. His look suggested terror, fear.

Danny nodded, barely able to breathe.

"We're gonna be jammed in here – you got a car?!"

They were sliding the gurney into the back of the ambulance.

"I'll go with you!" Danny gulped.

The paramedic eyeballed his partner, his face frozen in a state of indecision. Without a word, the partner shook his head from side-to-side.

The first paramedic nodded to Danny.

"Better if you follow us," he said.

With that they were off. The next thing Danny saw was an ambulance pulling off the softball field, with lights and sirens blaring away.

Inside, his ten-year-old daughter.

His little baby girl.

He sprinted to the F350.

CHAPTER 3

JUST BEFORE THE BLACKNESS HIT

BY THE GRACE of God, Danny somehow managed to avoid an accident as he roared his way to Pembleton Memorial Hospital. He tore out of Turnberry Park and serpentined south through Ketchogue, racing through stop signs until he reached Route 25A, the main thoroughfare running east-west through Long Island's north shore. He skidded to a light at a corner looking to head east, but there were several cars in front of him, so he made a mad left into a Dunkin' Donuts parking lot and cut the corner. Then he swung a right out of the lot into oncoming traffic, barreling down Route 25A with a fury.

If there were cars in front of him, he went around them into westbound traffic. If there were red lights, he went through them. On the straightaways, with no traffic, Danny topped 90. Somewhere in the town of East Norwich, he pulled around two plodding Toyotas in the left lane by jumping the curb onto the grass divider before landing with a thud back onto the roadway. The cargo in his rear cabin was shifting with violent metallic crunches with every twist, turn and tire screech.

Finally, there it was – Pembleton Memorial Hospital on the north side of the road. But where was the Emergency Room? Where? Danny spotted it on a blue sign – EMERGENCY ↑ – but where the hell was the entrance to the parking lot? He cast his eyes all around him and saw there wasn't a spot to be had anywhere on the streets. The lot would be his only choice, if he could only find a way in. The lot was boxed off by curbing on all three sides, with the hospital itself forming the final plane of the square. The entrance was nowhere in sight.

Danny circled the entire hospital and found himself back on Route 25A heading east again. And now he was stopped dead in traffic, the sweat exploding from every pore in his body. He was frantic. He jammed twice on his horn, pounded on the dashboard, but nothing was moving. Three minutes … and the cars moved an inch … another three minutes … and then another inch, and Danny thought his chest would explode.

To his left, beyond the curb, there was a thick row of low-slung evergreen bushes marking the boundary to the parking lot, and he knew he had no more time to waste. In a flash he cranked the steering wheel hard to the left and jammed on the gas pedal. His left front tire jumped the curb and then the other three wheels followed, rocking and rolling the F350 and sending the tools and equipment in the rear cabin flying against the right side of the truck. Danny then tore through the bushes, having to press and press on the gas as the truck churned and struggled to break through. Dirt and grass and leaves were flying everywhere. He bounded down into the parking lot and screeched into an open spot, twisting off the engine and wrestling his way out of his seat belt.

Just then Danny heard a *zzzt zzzt* noise and felt his cell phone buzzing in his right rear pocket. The shitty little gizmo was a hand-me-down iPhone from his 12-year-old daughter Gianna – Danny would take her old one whenever Debbie got the girls an upgrade. On his way barreling out of Turnberry Park, Danny had managed to make two phone calls – one to his brother Will, and the other to his father-in-law Henry Mahoney. His voicemail messages were simple – Agnes got hurt, get to the hospital, now.

This sure as shit was one of them returning the call.

Danny jumped out of the F350 and yanked the damn phone out of his faded Levi's. *Zzzt. Zzzt. Zzzt. Zzzt.* He squinted at the display screen – 4% battery life left. The sweat was now dripping off his nose. His heart was beating like a drum. The display screen read, "HENRY," and Danny pushed a green button.

"Henry! Henry!"

"Where the hell are you?"

Henry's voice was low but direct, like he was trying to avoid being heard. "We're in the waiting room. Will and me."

"I'm outside – "

"Then get your ass in here."

"How is Agnes?!" Danny choked out.

"Don't know, Dan, we just got here."

"Did you call Gianna?!"

And that was another thing. Danny was worried sick Gianna was going to hear about this whole thing before he got a chance to call her. If anything bad happened to Agnes, Danny knew, Gianna would be crushed. The two of them were as close as sisters could be – they shared clothes, did one another's hair, laughed together and still slept in the same bed. Danny would find them in the morning fast asleep with their arms wrapped around one another. He would have to get to her soon too, because these damn Lady Mets would start sending twits, or twats, or tweets, or whatever they were called, any minute.

"No," Henry said, clearly annoyed, "was I supposed to?"

"I'm comin' in," Danny replied, running between parked cars.

He punched the red "end" button and decided to hammer out a quick text to Gianna as he continued his sprint across the parking lot. But what would he tell her? No, don't give any details in a text, he decided. For now, just tell her to call. Danny's chest was heaving as he tried thumbing out the text message "*Call me immediately*," but with his fat sausagy fingers, and the damn auto-correct function on this thing, it came out "*crawl bees in media*," and Danny clicked send.

"Goddammit!" he screamed, and then he tried again.

"*crab me in medical*," he sent her this time.

"Shit!"

Zzzt, zzzt, buzzed his phone, an immediate response.

"*?? what the heck!!*" Gianna wrote, and then Danny gave up. He stuffed the phone into his back pocket and bolted into the hospital.

BY THE TIME Danny burst through the doors of the Emergency Room at Pembleton Memorial Hospital, about thirty-five minutes had elapsed from the moment they loaded Agnes into the ambulance at Turnberry Park. To Danny, it seemed like an eternity. He had no idea where she was or who was treating her, and no clue what the hell had happened. And that face, my God, he had never seen anything like it. He was praying she was okay and wasn't scared. He just had to find her and get by her side.

To make matters worse, the ER was a frantic, chaotic scene. Danny entered by slapping a small blue square on the wall outside and running through a set of automatic double doors. He jogged into a hallway that was filled along the left side with three or four gurneys that had patients hooked up to yellow IV bags. The massive waiting room was immediately to the right behind a floor-to-ceiling glass partition. The place was bursting at the seams with patients and families waiting to be seen. There were rows and rows of wooden chairs with blue cloth cushions that seemed to go on forever, and overhead, in each of the corners, several oscillating fans were blowing away. But you couldn't hear them over the buzz of the sneezing, wheezing and moaning patients, scores of them, who were filling every one of the seats. To Danny it looked like a scene from *Night of the Living Dead*, and the thought that his little girl was lost somewhere in the middle of this medical clusterfuck shot a pang of fear into his stomach.

Danny rushed to end of the hallway and entered a wide-open space that had a large open square of desks in the middle, topped with about a dozen computer screens. Inside the square was a collection of doctors and nurses all dressed in blue, running around like chickens without heads. Some were sitting at the computers oblivious to the chaos around them. Behind the square men and women in scrubs were running here and there, pushing wheelchairs or gurneys or running with clipboards.

Someone grabbed Danny from behind, and Danny wheeled around and saw his brother Will. Behind him stood Henry.

"Will, Jesus," said Danny, hugging him.

Danny then turned to his father-in-law.

"Henry," he said curtly, looking directly up at him.

The reason Danny needed to look up was because Henry Mahoney was about six foot nine with medicine ball shoulders the width of a doorway. The man was so large he cast a shadow, and even at age seventy-three he still looked like he could lift a Pontiac over his head. His Marine Corps-style buzzcut was steel grey, and his face was as red as a tomato, fronted by a bulbous nose filled with spider veins. He had a bony forehead ridge that jutted out over the rest of his face like an awning. And that menacing look of homicidal rage – not just presently but the same one that never left him – was one that could halt a platoon in its tracks. When people met Henry Mahoney they often drew back, thinking he wanted to hurt them.

"'Bout fuckin' time," Henry said to Danny. "What took you."

Henry wasn't asking a question, so Danny didn't see the need for an answer. Will then turned to Danny, who was soaking wet and breathing heavy, and nodded at him.

"Whadja do, run here? Jesus."

"No, it's just … the heat," Danny said, craning his neck around. "This place is a goddamn zoo – you guys get any word on where she is?"

Henry then took a step closer.

"Hey Dan, how about you tell us what the hell happened."

Danny dug two palms into his eyes, running his hands down his face.

"Look, Agnes collapsed at her softball game today. They took her outta there in an ambulance. I think maybe she got heat stroke, or she's dehydrated or something."

"Shit," Will said.

"I gotta find out where she is, so just gimme a minute."

"How serious is it?" Henry asked.

"She didn't look good, Henry, I can tell you that."

"Then go find her," Henry directed.

And then he gestured to the entire ER. "And let me know if these people need some encouragement answering questions."

Danny nodded back and scanned his eyes across the room. They landed on a counter to the right with a sign – "Triage Nurse, *Enfermera De Triage*" – which had a line of people about a dozen deep. There was another check-in counter near the waiting room with maybe two dozen more people lined up there. There were no notices anywhere telling you what line you needed to be in and not a person anywhere you could ask. The people on the triage line all seemed to be hurt – the guy next in line was an old geezer in a wheelchair, vomiting into a Kentucky Fried Chicken bucket – but the people in the waiting room looked like they had just fallen out of a *M*A*S*H* episode too, so where the hell were you supposed to go? And if you came to this place by ambulance – God help you – did you need to wait in *any* of these lines?

Danny marched back to the waiting room and found Will and Henry, and they hustled back to the area with the open square.

"Do me a favor and get on this line," Danny told Will, indicating the triage line, "I gotta go find someone who can tell me what's going on."

"Yeah, no problem, I got it," said Will.

"Place is a disaster," Danny answered.

Danny's panic was now ripping his stomach apart, and his breathing was deep and labored. He had to find Agnes and get to her side – he had to. To his left he saw a set of double doors marked "AUTHORIZED MEDICAL PERSONNEL ONLY," and Danny made a beeline for them. He was going to burst right through and find his daughter. He had just turned toward the triage line to see how far up the queue Will had landed, when Henry, who was milling about near the open square, put two fingers in his mouth and whistled. The toot caught Danny's attention. Henry was waving Danny toward him, and Danny rushed to his side.

"Let's go," Henry commanded, and in a minute the two were moving quickly down the hallway. Up ahead, near the patient waiting room, a pair of paramedics was pushing a gurney, flanked by a doctor and two nurses. Behind them was a police officer. Henry was headed right for him, and before he knew it Danny was standing beside Henry as he addressed the officer, a young dark-haired man about Danny's height.

"Excuse me, officer," Henry said, offering his hand. "I'm Henry Mahoney."

"Afternoon. Officer Pazulli."

The officer looked straight up at Henry, puzzled. You could see he was taken aback by the sheer size of the dinosaur before him. Danny had seen Henry introduce himself like this to police officers once or twice before, and he knew that if it was anyone else, like Danny for example, any officer would respond with a "whaddya want" or a "stand clear." But Henry for obvious reasons had a knack for dragging the politeness out of people.

"Retired from the job," Henry told him, "ten years now."

"Oh yeah? Where from?"

"77th in Brooklyn, detective ... homicide."

"Great. How 'bout that."

"Hey, I could use a favor. You got a minute?"

"Yeah, uh, sure," the officer hesitated, searching for the gurney he had entered with. "Whaddya need?"

"My granddaughter is in here somewhere," Henry said, "but

we don't know where. She got here by ambulance."

Henry put a hand on Danny's shoulder.

"This is her father Dan. Her name is Agnes Beers."

"Good to meet you," Danny said, and the officer shot him a dismissive nod. "Right," he said to Danny.

"Think you can head in the back and see where she's at?" Henry continued. "We're gettin' kinda nervous over here. I'd really appreciate it."

The officer looked again at the gurney, and then he took a gaze around the entire emergency room.

He snapped a glance at his watch and turned back to Henry.

"Whadja say her name is?"

"Agnes Beers, ten years old."

"I'll be right back. Wait here."

Less than two minutes later, the officer marched back out the double-doors trailed by a heavy-set black nurse who seemed to be walking with a purpose. She was dressed in blue scrubs over a pair of green rubber clogs, carrying a clipboard. She followed closely behind the officer, and when the two of them came to Danny, Henry and Will, the officer said, "take care, good luck," and walked right out the door.

The nurse marched directly up to the men – she appeared anxious, nervous, and clearly in a rush, something Danny pick up on immediately.

"Who's here with Agnes?" she asked firmly.

"I am," Danny shot back, stepping toward her.

"Are you the father?"

"Yes, Danny Beers. Is my daughter alright?"

"Mr. Beers, we've been looking for you for a while now. Didn't you come with the ambulance?"

"No, I came … no I didn't."

"Well, fine. Mr. Beers, I am Wanda Priestly, I'm a nurse here in the ER. I need to know exactly what Agnes ate today."

Nurse Priestly clicked a pen and lifted a clipboard that held a sheet with a lot of columns and boxes and a good amount of notes. There was something about her demeanor that was off, Danny thought. She seemed to be on a mission, like she had been sent out with a task. There was no exchange of pleasantries, no bedside

manner to her at all. She was looking at him intensely, directly in
the eyes.

"What she ate," he said, trying to remember.

"Yes, what did she eat today? Please."

Danny hesitated. He tried to remember the entire day, starting
from when he woke Agnes up that morning. Before that he had
taken a run to 7-Eleven, and then he sat in the kitchen reading the
New York Post. Agnes came down, they sat together at the kitchen
table, Danny eating Cap'n Crunch in a Hello Kitty bowl, and then
he made Agnes –

"Waffles," he said, remembering. "For breakfast she had Eggo
toasted waffles. With butter and syrup, if that matters."

"Anything else?"

Now it was coming back to him. Over the waffles they talked
about her recent Social Studies test. Something about the explorer
Henry Hudson. She was eating her waffles and drinking –

"Iced tea. She had a can of Arizona iced tea with the waffles."

"Is that it?"

And then he remembered.

Snack time at Turnberry. Dodge and Cindy Brewer. The hair
flip thing. The box from Lenny's Seafood Market.

"She had shrimp cocktail – at the softball game."

"What the hell, really?" Will responded, and then Henry
followed with, "Fuck is wrong with you?"

Danny wanted to jab back but then he noticed that the nurse
was scribbling frantically. Without skipping a beat or looking up
from the clipboard she asked him, "How many?"

"Don't know. They gave 'em to the kids for snack time," he
continued, eyeballing Henry, "maybe two or three, I'm not sure."

"Has she had shrimp before?"

"Before when, today?"

"Yes, Mr. Beers, before today, please," she said impatiently.

"I really don't know – maybe. I don't know."

The unspoken message in his answer was clear, at least to
Danny and Henry. Had Debbie been here, they both knew, she
would have delivered precise details on whether Agnes ever had
shrimp at any time in the past. Like dates, times and probably even
what she had as a side dish. These were the specifics on which

Danny, as the father, just never focused. For a split-second Danny could see an expression on Henry's face that could actually be described as sadness, before it quickly disappeared.

Nurse Priestly clicked her pen and pointed toward the doors marked "AUTHORIZED MEDICAL PERSONNEL ONLY," to the left of which were a few unoccupied benches.

"Do me favor and wait there by those benches, okay?"

"Hey," Danny said to her abruptly, "is my daughter okay?"

"Mr. Beers, have a seat. A doctor will be out to see you shortly."

"Hey, can't I go back and see her?" Danny pleaded.

"Not yet," The nurse said. "It'll be a few more minutes. Please go wait by the benches."

SOMETIME OVER THE next half hour, Will's wife Janet arrived with Gianna in tow. Gianna stumbled into the ER shaking with a pair of bloodshot eyes and Janet's arms wrapped around her. Danny guessed correctly that Gianna would hear about the incident on Twitter, and that is exactly what happened. Right after Danny had instructed her to "*crawl bees in media*" and to "*crab me in medical*," Gianna logged into her Twitter account and saw the trail – there were dozens of tweets that read "*get well soon Agnes, love u #agnesbeers*," or "*hope your ok Agnes #scary*," or "*thoughts and prayers to agnes beers and family #staystrong #loveuagnes*," or similar sentiments. When Gianna saw them, her heart sank. She dialed her father, getting only voicemail on his battery-drained phone. Finally, she got a hold of her Aunt Janet and the two of them hastened to the hospital.

Gianna was sitting on her father's lap now, with Danny's arms wrapped around her waist. Will and Janet were sitting next to each other on an adjacent bench. Janet's fingers were webbed together under her chin with her elbows on her knees, with Will resting his head up against the wall with his eyes closed. Nobody was saying a word, but Henry was making everyone a nervous wreck. He was pacing back and forth with his fists clenched, cursing under his breath. Danny's thought was that if you threw a silk robe on the man you would swear he was about to go fifteen rounds with Joe Frazier for the Heavyweight Championship of the World. Meanwhile, nothing was helping to alleviate the pressure in Danny's chest; he was still breathing heavy and silently pleading with his lungs to pump more oxygen.

And so they waited.

Ten minutes, fifteen minutes, twenty, thirty and then forty-five, with at least a dozen instances of the double-doors flying open and all of them rising in anticipation only for it to be yet another gurney or wheelchair having nothing to do with Agnes. And then finally, after maybe an hour had passed, long after Danny had stopped asking the group what the hell was taking them so long, out walked a doctor in blue medical scrubs.

He was about thirty-five, a little taller than Danny but rail thin with dark olive skin and deep-set brown eyes. He pulled a blue surgical cap off a scalp filled with black peach fuzz.

"Is there a Mr. Beers here?" he asked in a thick Pakistani accent.

Danny launched off the seat and rushed to him.

"Doc, what the hell is going on? Is she okay?"

"You are Daniel Beers?"

"Yes. Doc, what's wrong? What happened?"

"Mr. Beers, my name is Doctor Naison Padmanabi. I am an attending physician here in the Emergency Department."

"Right. How is my daughter? Where is she?"

The doctor looked over at Danny's family. He fixed his eyes on Gianna, and then he pointed to an area closer to the waiting room.

"Can we perhaps take a step over here to talk?"

"Yeah, sure," Danny said.

Will winked at Janet, who promptly gathered Gianna and sat her on the bench. Danny walked over with the doctor, followed by Will and Henry.

"Mr. Beers, I treated your daughter Agnes when she arrived here today."

Danny nodded at him.

"Your daughter suffered a very severe case of anaphylaxis this afternoon, brought on by an allergic reaction."

Danny shook his head, his eyebrows knotting up. He did not expect to hear this – he had all but convinced himself that Agnes just got overheated out there, like Daphne. But of course, he couldn't explain that hideous swelling in her face. And that word he just used –

"Anaph – ," he tried to repeat, swallowing hard.

"Anaphylaxis," the doctor repeated. "It is a very serious allergic reaction. In Agnes's case it was a physiological response to the shrimp we understand she ate today. But of course, we did not initially understand that because we were unable to find you when Agnes arrived here. So we made some medical decisions based on the information before us."

To that Danny didn't say a word. He could feel Henry's look burning a hole in his back, but he didn't dare turn around.

"Sir, were you aware that Agnes has an allergy to shrimp, or to any type of shellfish?"

"No," he replied firmly, "no I wasn't."

The doctor made a note on a pad he was carrying.

"Is that why she looked like that?" Danny asked. "Her face all swelled up?"

"Indeed, yes. In fact, Agnes's symptoms were very pronounced. They were very severe. I understand that this went undetected for a period of time at the baseball field. That is unfortunate."

Again, Danny didn't respond. The image of Agnes lying helpless in centerfield while everyone was distracted by the Daphne imbroglio came vaulting back into his brain. He could hear his chest releasing choppy bursts of carbon dioxide.

"As a result," the doctor continued, "Agnes was in anaphylactic shock when the paramedics got to her. The significant edema, or swelling, that accompanied that condition caused her airways to be blocked off. In the ambulance, Agnes unfortunately went into cardiac arrest."

Those words – *cardiac ... arrest* – nearly knocked Danny off his feet. Suddenly he felt weightless. A wave of nausea ran up his esophagus and settled in his throat.

"What the fuck!" he yelled.

The doctor moved toward Danny.

"Mr. Beers, we were able to revive Agnes," he said, "but I must tell you that her brain was deprived of oxygen for a not insignificant period of time. I'm afraid we had no choice but to medically induce coma, and right now we have her on a ventilator."

The color immediately drained from Danny's face. A cold sweat washed over his entire body and the room began to spin. The images in the ER blurred into a speckled white light, and Danny felt his knees buckle.

Henry screamed "FUCK!" at the top of his lungs, and then he punched his giant fist directly through the Emergency Room wall.

"She's in, she's in a - a - a - coma?" Danny somehow managed, as his eyes rolled to the back of his head. Then, as he was falling into the arms of his brother Will, Danny heard the last words of Dr. Padmanabi, just before the blackness hit –

"Mr. Beers, you may want to get your family's affairs in order."

CHAPTER 4

A COMBINATION OF TWO EVENTS

THAT AFTERNOON, THE staff at Pembleton Memorial Hospital formally admitted ten-year-old Agnes Beers as a patient, wheeling her into an ICU room on the third floor. Danny stood at her bedside that first day, his body numb. Minutes turned to hours, hours to days, and days to weeks, and by the time late June came around, Agnes had been lying in that room for slightly over two months, with little or no change in her condition.

At home, alone with Gianna, Danny viewed his life now as divided into two periods – the time before Agnes's accident, and the time after that day. He would rise each morning thinking about checking off some meaningless items on a pointless to-do list before rushing over to Pembleton, and before long, his life settled into a monotonous routine with a singular focus – his ten-year-old daughter. First thing in the morning he would call the oldest of the three Mexican workers he employed – a man named Carlos, who seemed to live his entire life in a grey hoodie under a Chicago Cubs baseball hat – and give him the schedule of assignments for the day. Carlos would then pick up Arturo and Miguel, wherever they lived, and the four of them would meet at the job site. Once they were organized Danny would head back home and scoop up Gianna. Together they would head over to the hospital and remain there for the rest of the day.

And that was pretty much it for the entirety of that spring.

In the week after Turnberry, Danny barely left the hospital. He slept on the floor there every night, right next to Agnes. He spent his days attending to whatever the nurses suggested – combing Agnes's hair, reading to her, massaging her arms, rubbing her hands, or adjusting her legs and feet – whatever it took to keep the circulation going. At times he would play a loop of One Direction songs, Agnes's favorite, on an old iPod that Gianna had rigged up. He wasn't sure if any of this was helping, but he always had to be doing *something*, had to keep moving. The alternative was to sit and watch while nothing really happened, and that would drive him insane, he was sure of it.

So he stayed and ate out of the vending machines and brushed his teeth down the hall in the men's room. In Agnes's hospital room there were wires, tubes, hoses, computer monitors with constant beeps and hisses, and scratchy voices over the intercom. People scurried through the hallways twenty-four hours a day. All of it was so overwhelming, and Danny's thought was that with all the chaos in this place it was a shame that they sent sick people here, because this place will kill you.

After about a week, when he couldn't keep his eyes open any longer, the nurses finally convinced him to go home at the end of each day and make an attempt at a decent night's sleep. There was nothing he could do here during the night, they told him. They would take good care of her while he was gone. When he finally agreed, Danny spent his evenings sitting alone in his family room with the lights out, nestled into his La-Z-Boy recliner, the only illumination being the yellow glow of the streetlamp outside spilling through the window curtains. He would just stew there, staring straight into nothing. He couldn't even bring himself to turn on the TV for fear that he would click his way to something he enjoyed, in which case the guilt would overwhelm him, knowing that Agnes was lying unconscious in a hospital bed while he was watching ESPN SportsCenter, for fuck's sake.

So instead he would try to engage Gianna in a few minutes of idle chatter, but the events in the hospital were so draining for each of them that going to separate rooms when they got home wasn't such a bad idea. Gianna would retreat to the bedroom she shared with Agnes and sit cross-legged on the duvet cover with her laptop open and a pair of earbuds plugged into her head, the ever-present iPhone in her hand.

Sitting alone in the family room, Danny's brain would run in circles. So many thoughts would go through his mind, and the sheer energy it took to process them all sometimes gave him a splitting headache. But the one theme that dominated the chaos between his ears was *why* – what exactly did his daughter do to merit this fate?

Was it his fault? Punishment for something he did? Did this

have anything to do with Deb?

There had to be an explanation. He had to make sense of this. Six months after burying his wife and being left alone to raise two pre-teen girls, here he was spending every day at the bedside of his precious ten-year-old daughter, who did nothing more than dress that day to go play some goddamn softball. There was a prison sentence for that? Hell, at her age, she was more excited about how the new uniform matched her eyes – *doesn't it Daddy?* – than anything having to do with playing a sport. Did she really deserve this? This? And how about Gianna? First her mother and now Agnes – her pain must be unbearable.

To Danny, the agony of watching Agnes in that hospital bed was excruciating. The machines, the hoses, the monitors, all hooked up to his baby girl. And about ten days into her hospital stay the doctors said that Agnes could no longer remain on the ventilator. They would have to remove it, they advised, but since Agnes would remain comatose, she would need breathing assistance. She would have to be trached.

A goddamn tracheotomy.

So Danny and Gianna sat in the waiting room while they *cut a hole* in Agnes's throat. They attached a breathing hose so she could get a steady flow of oxygen. They also put in a feeding tube, which they had to install by once again slicing into her tiny little body. Danny felt helpless. It was just brutal, beyond words. If Danny could change places with her right now, he would often think, put his ass in that bed and cut that trach into his throat, screw it, he would do it in a heartbeat.

Alone in his living room each night, Danny's thoughts would inevitably wander back in time, to when he first laid eyes on Debra Mahoney, his future wife. The scene was so vivid in his memory after all these years, and up until Agnes's accident, he would remember it fondly as the day his life had changed forever for the good. It was a day that propelled him from a loser on his way to nowhere to a man whose life had purpose, meaning. But since that day at Turnberry Park, thinking back, the concept that played over and over in his mind was how he met her that day by sheer dumbass luck. It should never have happened.

It was the summer of 1999, he was thirty years old and living in a studio apartment in West Babylon, grudgingly resigned to his bachelor status, when he found himself rolling out of the old Oak Beach Inn, or OBI, down near Gilgo Beach on the south shore. He had spent the day with some buddies drinking Long Island Iced Teas and Miller Lites while overlooking the ocean during Sunday Happy Hour. He had a sun-roasted face and a sizzling buzz, and just before he and his friends were about to hit the parking lot on their way out the door, heading home, he turned to them and said, "hey, hold up a sec, I gotta hit the head."

And then that was it.

One split-second decision later, just a moment taken to deal with a basic function of human life, and everything changed for him forever. Because when he walked back out of the men's room door, a mere eight minutes later, he ran directly into an old grammar school classmate he hadn't seen in close to twenty years.

"Holy shit," he shouted over the bar hum, "Jen Annunziato?!"

He was wearing a pair of $4.99 sunglasses he had picked off the rack at Spencer's Gifts at the Walt Whitman Mall, along with an Elvis Costello concert t-shirt. The Crosby Stills and Nash classic *Suite: Judy Blue Eyes* was playing over the OBI's sound system.

"Danny Beers?" she smiled back, "Oh my God, how are you?"

They gave each other a clumsy hug and exchanged a couple of patented "what're you up to's" and "you look great's." Jen told him she was married to a phlebologist, and Danny told her he was doing "the same old shit, just working construction." They both laughed and smiled and then Jen finally turned to her companion, standing just behind her. She said, "oh, jeez, so sorry – Dan, this is my college roommate Debbie Mahoney. She's from Centereach."

And bingo, that was it. It was over for Danny, right then and there. He couldn't believe the sight – tall with a runner's body and a waterfall of wavy blond hair spilling down her shoulders. And my God that smile. He took one look at her and decided to head back inside to buy them both a drink. But in a matter of minutes Jen put two and two together and headed home. Danny and Debbie sat on barstools and talked until the sun went down. Danny felt like he had known her all his life.

Before he knew it, someone had pressed the fast-forward button on his life and he was sitting in the Labor and Delivery

Room at North Shore University Hospital in Manhasset, five years into a marriage that meant everything in the world to him. His Air Jordans were covered in blue surgical booties and he was holding a newborn baby, his second daughter, a little girl they would name Agnes after Danny's grandmother. What he did to deserve such luck, such happiness, he had no idea.

As he sat in his living room with the lights out that spring, and then into summer, blanketed by the silence, it struck Danny as a strange thing that if he had only decided to hold his kidneys that day and head out to the parking lot to catch his ride, like his friends were busting his chops to do — *"aw c'mon, man!"* — none of the events that had transpired over the last six months would ever have happened. He most certainly would have missed Jen, and he and Debbie would never have met. There would be no Debbie Beers, no marriage, no two-bedroom cape in Ketchogue, no garage filled with construction tools, no family room littered with naked, headless Barbie dolls, no peanut butter and jelly on the doorknobs, no basement shelves filled with game boxes of Chutes and Ladders, Operation, Twister, Yahtzee, Sorry!, Junior Monopoly, Candyland, Clue, Stratego, Barrel Full of Monkeys and Life, no monthly payments to the orthodontist, no plastic bins stuffed with Bratz and American Girl dolls and their broken body parts, no Junie B. Jones books, no mortgage payments, car payments, truck payments, insurance co-pays and deductibles, and a hundred other bills.

And of course, no Gianna and Agnes. The two of them would pop like a bubble, just like that, never setting foot on this planet.

And him? Where would Danny have wound up?

He remembered a friend of his at the time telling him how easy it was to get a job as a blackjack dealer out in the Las Vegas casinos. The girls were unbelievable, and screw this Long Island shit man, let's get out of here, did he want to go?

Danny was toying with the idea, he remembered, actually considering it, but who knows if he would have pulled the trigger.

And anyway, then he met Debbie.

Best day of his life. Or so he thought.

As the summer approached and the nights sitting in quiet contemplation piled on top of one another, the sitting around and worrying and getting no answers from these goddamn doctors was beginning to drive him up a wall. And that, in turn, was giving birth to a deep frustration and an overwhelming sense of powerlessness, eating away at him and burning a hole in his acid-filled stomach. He really had to do something, anything, to move the ball forward and help Agnes if he could.

And then at some point what took root as a possible solution to all of this was the thought that he should call a lawyer to talk about Agnes. Not to hire one, but maybe just a consultation. A meeting just so that he could get a bit of advice as to whether he and the family had any legal rights that maybe they weren't pursuing. Initially, right after Agnes's accident, the thought had never occurred to Danny, not even for one second. But a combination of two events that took place within a few days of one another in late June had put a bug in his ear about it.

The first was a random conversation he had outside Ketchogue Bagels on Main Street one Sunday morning. This place was the most popular bagel joint on the north shore and every Sunday morning the line would spill out the door and run all the way down the sidewalk past the frame store, Paula's Hair Salon, Tony's Pizza and all the way down to Paws & Claws at the corner. Danny was somewhere in the middle of the pack when he felt a couple of pokes on his shoulder. He turned around and it was one of his neighbors, a woman who had lived five doors down from Danny and Debbie for over ten years, a friend of Debbie's in fact. She may have even been in his kitchen a few times. But of course, Danny couldn't remember her name if his life depended on it.

"Hey Dan!" she said, pecking his cheek, "how's everything?"

"Heyyy! How're you?"

Debbie had warned him on multiple occasions that when you greet people in this town with a "hey there!" or a "what's up chief?" or a "how's it goin' boss?," or something similar, it's a dead giveaway you don't know their name, you're not fooling anyone. But there was nothing he could do about it. Seemed to be getting worse now that he was fifty, too.

"How's Agnes?" the woman replied sympathetically, and then without waiting for a response she said, "we're so sorry, Dan. If there's anything we can do, by all means, please."

The sun was bright in the sky that morning and there was a

steady warm breeze blowing down Main Street. Danny pulled the bill of his Yankee cap tighter down over his forehead.

"Hey thanks, I really appreciate that."

Was it Kim? Kathy? Kerry? It definitely started with a K.

After a few minutes of small talk, the woman changed the subject back to Agnes. Then, out of the blue, she said, "hey, if you need the name of an attorney, Dan, you know with Agnes? I mean, maybe you have a name already, but I just wanted to let you know that my brother-in-law is an attorney in the city. It's Pete's brother, Bill. I could give you his name and contact information. If you want, I mean it's up to you. Let us know and I can email you."

And that was the first time the thought had ever entered his mind. This Kim, Kathy, or whatever K her name was – Kayla? Karen? – had presented the brother-in-law offer to him as if it were *expected* that he'd be calling an attorney – *maybe you have a name already* was what she said, as if the matter was obvious. Up to that point he hadn't given it a moment's thought. He felt guilty about it, because the conversation suggested there was something he should have been doing for Agnes all along.

But a lawyer? About what?

He couldn't imagine what a lawyer could do or say about any of it. No lawyer could help his daughter get off that breathing machine and feeding tube. The whole notion was confusing to him, and as he was standing there in line on Main Street, he decided to file that little nugget away and give it some more thought at another time, maybe in a few days.

Another woman walked by, heading toward the end of the bagel line. She stopped and greeted Danny's neighbor.

"Hey Beth!"

Ah, Beth, Danny thought. There's no K in Beth.

The second event happened a few days later.

It was Wednesday night just around dusk and Danny was standing at the kitchen stove with a dishtowel thrown over his shoulder. Gianna was in her bedroom after a long day at the hospital. Danny was cooking hamburgers in a skillet and boiling some Kraft macaroni and cheese when the doorbell rang. He lowered the flame on the burgers and jogged to the front door with a spatula in his hands.

Standing on his doorstep were Dodge and Cindy Brewer.

Dodge wore khaki shorts with a pair of untied running sneakers, the laces spilling over the sides, and a Princeton University Crew t-shirt. His arms were crossed with his eyebrows lowered. He wore a hardened expression, like he had something on his mind. Parked at the curb was a black BMW with its driver's side door open and the engine running, which to Danny was a clear sign that whatever they were doing here, they didn't intend to stay very long.

Cindy was next to Dodge in jeans, beach flip-flops and a white t-shirt, and she was holding a plastic bag in her hands. Her face was without a hint of makeup, and she had the remorseful look of someone about to go into a Confessional. She looked like she had been crying. When Danny opened the door, the two of them stood there a moment in silence before Dodge finally spoke up.

"Hey dude," he offered simply.

"Dodge, Cindy."

Dodge jabbed his chin over at Cindy. Without unfolding his arms, he said, "Cindy's got something to say."

Danny looked back toward the kitchen.

"Come in a minute," he said. "I got something cooking inside."

Danny hustled back and turned the flame off the burgers. Then he went back to Dodge and Cindy, who had stepped inside and were standing in his small foyer.

"Nice digs," Dodge said, looking around.

"Thanks," Danny responded, "so what's up?"

"Well," said Cindy, "Dodge and I were talking the other day and I filled him in on something I'm kind of embarrassed about. We came by tonight to talk a minute."

"That's right, dude," Dodge offered.

"I was going to call," Cindy said, "but I really wanted to speak to you in person."

"Sure," Danny said curiously, "of course."

"It's about the softball game," Cindy said. "At Turnberry."

Danny braced himself.

"Okay," was all he managed.

"See," she continued, "I was just so busy that morning."

"Crazy busy, dude," Dodge said.

"And I was the snack mom for the girls that day."

"You remember, right dude? That Cin was the snack mom?"

"Yeah, sure," Danny said.

"And then I had to drop Charlotte off at her lax game. You know my Charlotte, right?"

"She's friends with Gianna," Dodge assisted, leaning forward, in a tone that suggested that Danny needed the clarification.

Danny nodded.

"And then I had to deliver all these papers to our accountant," Cindy labored on, "who is on the complete other side of town."

"It was April, dude, tax time."

"We were also having this issue with the security system, you know, at the house?"

"Been giving us a problem since the time we had it installed."

"And it took me about forty-five minutes to set the alarm!" Cindy said, her voice rising.

"Just crazy dude. Should sue their ass."

"And then I barely got out of there, and I was just … frantic!"

Danny's head was turning back and forth like he was at a tennis match. He was looking up at these two freakishly tall people and trying to follow their incoherent babblings. What in the love of Christ was the point here? He had a couple of burgers on the stove turning into hockey pucks and really needed these two to get on with it. But then Danny noticed that Cindy's eyes were welling up, and Dodge was rubbing her back.

"So anyway," Cindy continued, taking a deep breath, "you see, thing is, I never made it to Lenny's Seafood Market that morning."

"We're really sorry, dude."

"And I really wanted to, because I wanted the girls to enjoy my turn as snack mom. I thought it would be a nice treat. Plus, I had already told a few of the other Moms about it. But by the time I got everything done that morning, I just didn't have time to get there."

Suddenly the two of them were quiet, Cindy looking down at her flip-flops with her chin in an apologetic slump. Dodge was still rubbing her back, silently nodding at Danny.

Danny was confused.

"Wait a second," he said, shaking his head to clear the cobwebs. "I don't understand. Didn't you bring a box from Lenny's with the shrimp in it? I thought I remember seeing that."

"We had that box in our pantry, dude."

"From another time," Cindy told him.

"And she just used it to carry everything."

"But ... wasn't there shrimp in that box?" Danny countered.

"Yes," Cindy answered him.

"And that came from ... where?" Danny asked.

"Shop-Rite, dude."

"Shop-Rite," Cindy echoed.

"Huh, okay," Danny concluded. "Shop-Rite."

He had no idea why they decided to tell him this now, after all these months. But a feeling lingered that maybe there was a larger point here. He decided to press on, hoping to bring an end to this bizarre meeting.

"So let me see if I understand," Danny tried to summarize, "you bought the shrimp from Shop-Rite, and then ... what ... you put it in a box from Lenny's Seafood Market and told everyone it was from there?"

"Hey, I just found this out yesterday, dude."

"Oh, like that matters!" Cindy shouted, slapping her thigh. She still held that plastic bag. Dodge quickly backtracked, adding only, "sorry, hon, you're right."

Cindy turned back to Danny. "I had a few bags of shrimp in our freezer," she confessed, "and we quickly thawed it and brought it over in the Lenny's box. Look, Dan, I'm not proud of this and I'm really sorry."

Danny laughed a bit and shook his head.

"I mean ... why? Not that it really matters, but why?"

"I was just embarrassed I was bringing something from Shop-Rite," Cindy revealed. "When I couldn't get to Lenny's in time, I guess I didn't know what else to do. I didn't think it would matter."

"Cin," Dodge interrupted, "show him the bag."

"Yes, here you go," Cindy followed, "this is the bag the shrimp came in."

Cindy handed over the plastic bag that was in her hand the whole time. It was one of those Ziplock frozen food bags and was colored red, white and blue in equal size one-third stripes. The brand name "Phillips" was across the top, and right underneath were the words "Cooked Shrimp." Right below that, in much smaller font, the bag said "Peeled – Tail On," and down on the bottom were the words "Thaw, Serve."

Danny looked the bag over and wondered again what the point of all this was – so big deal, they bought a bag of crappy frozen shrimp from Shop-Rite and billed it as top-shelf shit from Lenny's. Ridiculous, yes, but really … not the crime of the century.

"I threw that in our pantry after Agnes's accident thinking she got food poisoning, Dan, and that I would give it to you. But then after I heard she was allergic I didn't think anything of it anymore. Anyway, I told all this to Dodge last night and he said we should give you the bag."

"Dude, in case you want to give it to your lawyer or something. We just figured you should have it."

Danny looked again at the bag. He flipped it over and saw the standard nutritional chart along with a few shrimp recipes. Then it was almost as if he were looking right through the bag, holding it in front of his face. He was searching for something to say. He wanted to be nice, because the Brewers had showed up to the hospital a few times and had even sent a huge bouquet of flowers about a week after the incident. Danny had also dropped Gianna off at their house a few times to hang out with Charlotte, which was a welcome respite that allowed him to run some errands. But it also meant that there were plenty of opportunities for them to tell him this, and now it appeared that the only reason they hadn't – or that Cindy hadn't – was because she was embarrassed to be serving Shop-Rite frozen shrimp as the snack mom at a 4th-grade girls' softball game.

Christ, Danny thought to himself. People can be so strange.

"Well, thanks, I appreciate you being honest."

They both nodded. Then Dodge grabbed Cindy's hand.

"But it doesn't really matter, right?" said Danny. "I mean, a shrimp allergy is a shrimp allergy, no matter where it comes from."

"That's right dude."

"And I'm the one who should have known about it and said something. So, I don't think it's a big deal."

"Thanks, Dan," Cindy followed. "I feel so much better."

"Good," Danny said, "and your secret's safe with me."

Danny then winked at them, and their faces instantly displayed relief. They both smiled. Danny knew they didn't have the nerve to ask him to keep this little scandal under wraps, but he also knew it probably meant a lot to them that he did. The whole thing made him want to laugh.

"And by the way, dude, if you ever need anything – "

"Oh absolutely," Cindy trailed him, "anything you need, really."

"Thanks guys … I appreciate it," Danny replied, hooking a thumb over his shoulder, "but hey, I gotta get dinner on."

"You got it, dude."

And with that they were gone.

Soon Danny was back at the stove putting the final touches on the burgers and mac-and-cheese, replaying the conversation in his head. On the one hand there was the whole Lenny's Seafood thing, and how silly that was. But on the other hand, there were those words by Dodge, when he explained why they had brought the bag – *in case you want to give it to your lawyer or something*. It wasn't until Danny was back at the skillet trying to save the burgers when the words struck him. He immediately thought of Kathy … er, Beth … at Ketchogue Bagels the previous Sunday. It occurred to him that everybody in this town had expected that he would, or already had, contacted a lawyer.

Why hadn't this seemed as obvious to him?

And then after mulling it over for a week or so, on another one of those nights sitting alone in the darkness of his family room, with Gianna on her bed and plugged into the world of social media, Danny decided he would make a few phone calls. Who it would be, or what law firm, he really didn't know. All he wanted was a consultation, a discussion, a meeting. An attorney with whom he could float a few ideas, ask a few questions. No commitments, just a cozy little chat. How could that possibly hurt?

He didn't know where the whole thing would go, but the very thought that he finally decided to do something that he would be in control of, well, it gave him a tremendous sense of relief and comfort. For the first time in months it didn't feel like there was an elephant standing on his chest, his lungs pinched in a vise, and instead the air began to flow in and out of his pipes with ease.

That night, after dinner, with Gianna up in her room, Danny went to his refrigerator and popped open a can of Coors Light. He opened a cabinet in his family room and pulled out an old vinyl record album from a collection sitting in a cardboard box. It was one of his favorites – *The Freewheelin' Bob Dylan* – and with the lights turned down he dropped the needle on the second track, *Girl From The North Country*. He listened as the crackling sound of needle against vinyl filled the tiny room. Nestled in his La-Z-Boy, Danny let Bob Dylan's familiar twangy voice and harmonica wash over him as the beer entered his bloodstream. The song reminded him of Deb, and suddenly his eyelids felt heavy.

Danny placed the beer can onto an end table and leaned his head into the soft cushions of the La-Z-Boy. He closed his eyes, sucked in a breath through his nostrils, and in a minute he fell into the deepest sleep that had come to him in months.

CHAPTER 5

THE CONSULTATION

WHEN JULY ROLLED around, the first thing Danny did was jump on the Internet and run some Google searches for lawyers located in Ketchogue. In addition to the offer from his neighbor Beth, Danny had received a few other suggestions of attorney names and numbers, but all of those were out of the question. Danny didn't want anyone locally to know he was even thinking about pursuing this path. That meant that his own homework would have to suffice. Danny loved Ketchogue and Debbie had loved it even more, but this was a small town where everyone knew everybody else's business. And while Danny couldn't give a fiddler's fart what anyone thought about him, for Gianna's sake he didn't want the whole town talking. Plus, he wanted to make his own decision about whom he would talk to, and he was a long way from hiring anyone. It was also possible he wouldn't hire anyone at all.

From the Google searches Danny launched into the websites. He quickly learned that all these damn personal injury lawyers were basically clones of one another; it was as if there were one web-design guy out there who catered to nobody but lawyers. The firm name always would be at the top of the site in an eye-popping bolded font – **Ruth Gehrig DiMaggio & Mantle LLP** – with the words "**Attorneys at Law**" printed underneath in smaller type. Then there would be a photograph or image alongside the firm name that served as the website's background, like a city skyline or the scales of justice or a couple of smiling jackasses in navy suits. Right in the middle there would be both an "*EN ESPANOL*" button that would convert the entire website to Spanish if you so desired, and a big fat 1-800 number that was as subtle as a steel-toed kick in the shin. The number was always something related to bodily injuries that would stick in your memory in case you were too damn lazy to write it down, like 1-800-MAIMED$, or 1-800-GETPAID, or 1-800-HEADCAVEDIN, or something in that vein.

Then most of the websites would ask you if you've been "*hurt or injured in an accident*," or whether "*an injury has changed or affected or devastated your life*," and if that were the case then they would offer you "*free consultations!*," tell you that "*we don't get paid unless you do!*," and explain that their lawyers "*have decades of experience in personal injury law*." To convince you they would then list all the areas in which they exceled, like automobile accidents, negligence, bodily injury, medical malpractice, pedestrian accidents, truck, bus and motorcycle crashes, brain injuries, dog and animal bites, bicycle crashes, nursing home abuse, gas explosions, gun accidents, sports injuries, spinal cord severs, worker's compensation disputes, burn injuries, brain trauma, swimming pool and diving board injuries, and hit and run, and slip and fall, and the list went on and on – the point being that no matter how you managed to fuck yourself up, we'll find some sorry ass sonafabitch to sue.

By the time Danny finished reading all these websites he felt like he just got off the Tilt-A-Whirl at the annual Ketchogue Italian Feast – he was dizzy, nauseous and needed to lie down. These people weren't ambulance chasers, he decided, they were ambulance ... *bounty hunters*, and they were all the same. There was just no way he could select one of these bloodsuckers from the list or tell the difference between any of them.

There would have to be another way.

So he abandoned the Google search method and began to make drive-by visits to lawyers' offices that were located around the Municipal Court at Boro Hall, down near Ketchogue Terrace, the central town center that intersected with Main Street. He'd walk down Main with a cup of coffee in his hand, a newspaper tucked under his arm, peering into the windows of these small legal offices and making judgments about them based simply on the way they looked. It wasn't very scientific, but he felt a thousand times more comfortable laying his eyes on these places than he did reading about them on the websites. He must have passed a dozen of them on the first day without entering a single one, and on more than one occasion he came close to dropping the entire idea.

Then, on a blistering hot morning in early July, Danny spotted a small law office located on the second floor above a donut shop.

He saw something up there that appealed to him – exactly what he could not say. Maybe it was the fact that the office had curtains in the windows along with a large *New York Islanders* banner – strange things for a lawyer's office. Also, unlike a lot of these firms, this one didn't seem to have too much foot traffic. Danny couldn't decide if that was a good or a bad thing but there definitely was a noticeable absence of people running in and out of the goddamn place with those bullshit neck collars and arm slings, or hobbling in and out on crutches, as if the first thing these people do when they run their car into a fire hydrant or fall off a bar stool blind-shittin' drunk is to call a lawyer to see who the hell they can sue.

Anyway, as Danny looked above the donut shop that morning, there was something up there, he could just sense it, so he went back home and looked up the attorney that belonged to that office. He learned that it housed a solo practitioner by the name of Nicole I. Anzalone. She had no website, something that endeared her to Danny even more.

And then Danny decided he would pull the trigger.

He called to make an appointment, which a secretary named Cassie said he could have about three days later. In the meantime, she asked, would he send any materials he had that would be relevant to the discussion. Danny couldn't think of anything other than the plastic bag that Cindy Brewer had dropped off, so Danny hand-delivered the thing the next day.

A few days later, Danny sat in the small waiting area of a two-room law office belonging to this attorney, Nicole Anzalone. He sat in the tiny vestibule for almost half an hour trying to make sense of a newspaper called the *New York Law Journal*, and when the secretary finally ushered him in, he saw this Anzalone lady sitting alone on a chunky leather office chair in a freaking shoebox of an office. She was wearing a bright red cardigan sweater over a pair of blue jeans, in the middle of summer no less. She had dark black wiry hair that looked like frayed brillo – it was flat on top and jutted out from her temples on both sides. She was sipping from a styrofoam Dunkin' Donuts coffee cup and her bare feet were propped up on a dark brown desk. She had red toenail paint that matched her cardigan, and Danny wondered if that was intentional. Also, pressed to her ear was a black telephone receiver that looked like an old rotary phone from a 1940s Humphrey Bogart movie.

Danny took a seat in front of Anzalone's desk, wondering what the hell he was getting himself into. He reminded himself he was there for a consultation only. In all likelihood he'd be out of there in a matter of minutes. In addition to this place being freezing – there was an AC window unit humming away – the place was a mess. The room was cluttered with piles of books, paper piles, case printouts and IKON document boxes, with discarded legal pads strewn randomly about.

Danny looked around and took it all in.

Over Anzalone's head, on a wall filled with framed kids' drawings, Danny noticed a Hofstra Law School diploma. Behind him, against a wall, there was a plaid loveseat sofa choking with piles of documents secured with black binder clips. To his left was a small window from which Danny could see the Boro Hall building, once he peeled back those curtains that had drawn him up here to begin with. Danny rose and moved toward the window to get a better view, and Anzalone twice snapped her fingers at him, motioning with the "siddown I'll be just a minute" sign.

Some nerve, Danny thought, fighting the urge to leave. But in a few minutes Anzalone hung up and introduced herself.

"Mr. Beers, I'm Nicole Anzalone, the –e is silent," she said. "It does *not* rhyme with baloney."

To his great relief, Danny was immediately taken aback by her charm. She was smiling, looking him right in the eyes. The first thing he noticed was her height, or lack thereof. There was no way she was any taller than five feet, tops, Danny figured. He had to lean down to shake her hand. She also had a glowing pair of bright blue eyes that looked like they had 60-watt bulbs lit up behind them, as if they were on fire. They shined like a couple of china dinner plates, and she drove them right into Danny in a way that caught him so off guard he couldn't return the stare, hooking his chin down and staring at his shoes.

"Have a seat," she finally said.

Danny plopped down onto some antique-looking dark brown chair covered in plastic. Everything about this place was dark and brown and if it weren't for the single window allowing some light in you would think you'd been sentenced to solitary confinement.

The conversation started with some small talk – how Danny got there, whether he had trouble finding the place, did you take 25A? Can you believe how hot it's been? And blah blah blah. After a few minutes Anzalone turned the conversation to business.

"Well anyway," she said, leaning back in her chair, "I got the plastic bag you sent, the Phillips frozen shrimp bag. Thanks for sending that."

"Yeah, no problem."

"And I did a little homework after I got it. As I'm sure you know, your daughter's condition received some local press coverage, so I'm not surprised you're here. Tell me, how is Agnes doing these days?"

To Danny, it seemed like he had answered that question so many goddamn times over the previous three months that he could no longer remember whether his answer to it bore any relationship to Agnes's actual condition. When she first arrived in the ICU, the question would shoot a hot flash of panic running through his body. It would jump-start his heart into a set of palpitations so severe he thought the thing would fly right through the wall of his chest. He'd choke out an answer back then, drawing all kinds of apologies and offers for help. He had long ago lost count of how many "if-there-are-anything-I-can-dos," he had received.

But recently, Danny felt none of that.

The trays of ziti had stopped coming after about a month, along with the phone calls and texts, and when he got to the point of having told people about Agnes's condition for what seemed like the millionth time, a deadening routine set in, and then, inevitably, an immunity grew. To ask him about it now, Danny wouldn't flinch.

"Not much change," he'd shoot back in knee-jerk fashion, "but thanks for asking."

But every once on a while someone would ask the question with a sincerity that penetrated Danny's immunity, bringing back those heat flashes and heart palpitations. Like now, the way this Anzalone just asked it, with a look of subtle pain on her face, driving those blue china dinner plates right at him again.

"Well, there's been no change really," he said, drawing some air. "And I'm not sure there ever will be. I don't know if this makes any sense, but it's like she's asleep but not really. She just lies there.

Sometimes her eyes are half open, but most times not. It's like her face is painted and set in a frame on a wall. Never speaks, never makes a sound. And all the time you just hear that sucking sound of that breathing machine, constant, non-stop. Whooosh in, whooosh out, you know? Can drive you crazy sometimes."

Danny let a nervous laugh go and felt a heaviness seep into his chest, like the feeling you get when you sprint up a flight of stairs. He was staring down at his shoes again. It'd been months since he spoke to anyone about Agnes with any real substance, and for Christ's sake he couldn't remember ever having told anyone about how the sound of that machine drove him crazy. It made him want to climb the walls in that hospital room sometimes and scream as loud as he could to make the freaking thing stop. But damn if it didn't feel good to sit in front of this Anzalone, this tiny little creature-attorney he didn't know from a hole in the wall, and let out a little bit of that frustration. This meeting was beginning to feel like he was seeing a shrink, not a lawyer.

Danny looked up from his shoes.

"Anyway, the doctors say there's a chance she'll never wake up, that this is the best I can ever expect. And then in the next breath they tell you she can make a complete recovery, as if the whole thing never happened. They say we have to be patient and stay positive. I tell you, if I gave answers like that to my customers, I'd be on the unemployment line."

"Well that all really sucks, Mr. Beers. I'm very sorry – I can't imagine how difficult this must be for you."

"Well, thank you, I appreciate that."

"But I guess you came in here to talk about whether you have a case, right? So let me see if I can answer that for you, okay?"

"Okay, sure."

This was what he had been waiting for, and as Anzalone flipped open a yellow legal pad, pointing down to a sheet of handwritten notes, he could feel the anxiety burning his stomach.

"This what I know, and some of this I got from Agnes's Facebook page and the newspaper articles I read."

"Yes, my daughter Gianna set that page up after the accident."

"If I leave anything out, you can just fill me in, okay?"

"Absolutely."

"So Agnes was playing softball in a recreation league run by the Town of Ketchogue," Anzalone began. "This was in April. She was wearing a Ketchogue recreation softball uniform – hat, pants, the whole kit and caboodle. All issued by the town, right?"

"Yes."

"The game was played at Turnberry Park, a town park, and was supervised by your daughter's coach, who was selected by the Town Rec Committee to be in charge, correct?"

"Yes, Pete Briscoe, correct."

"About halfway through the game they had snack time, which is something they do as a matter of routine. There was a snack mom assigned by the coach, who again was acting on behalf of the town. All right so far?"

"Yeah, right on the money."

"And who was the snack mom that day?"

"Lady by the name of Cindy Brewer."

"Dodge and Cindy Brewer – those Brewers?"

"Yup. That's them."

Anzalone flipped over the first page of her legal pad and took another swig from the Dunkin' Donuts cup.

"I've heard of them," she said, putting the cup back down onto the desk. She pointed down at the next page of her notes.

"Okay, next thing is they give her shrimp at snack time."

"Yeah, well, they all got it."

"Who all?"

"The girls, all the kids."

"Okay, but that was the snack, the shrimp, correct?"

"Correct."

"And it was given to all the kids by Cindy Brewer."

"Yeah, and Dodge. I mean they both gave it out."

Anzalone scribbled on her legal pad. She leaned back in her leather swivel again, her bare feet back on the desk. She had a pair of reading glasses perched at the tip of her nose, and when she looked at Danny, she would fire those blue china plates right over the top of them.

"Okay," she went on, "but the Brewers were assigned by the coach, who was hired by the Town Rec Committee, correct?"

"Correct … I guess so."

"And Agnes ate some of the shrimp?"

"Yes, she did."

"And you saw her do so?"

Danny paused a moment. Shit, did he actually *see* Agnes eat the shrimp? All this time that question had never even occurred to him. He recalled she had a plate in her hand, she was in line with everyone else …

"Yeah, I think so," he said, " … yeah."

"Okay, this bag, the Phillips frozen shrimp bag."

"Yes."

"Where'd you get it? You see it that day?"

"No," Danny said, and he decided right there he wouldn't recount the entire bizarro shit-show conversation he had with the Brewers that night. Instead, he gave her the abridged version.

"The Brewers gave that to me recently. The day of the accident they told everyone the shrimp came from Lenny's Seafood Market, if you can believe it, but it turns out they bought it from Shop-Rite in the frozen food aisle and just brought it in a Lenny's box."

"Huh," she said, scribbling notes again, "strange."

"Yeah, sure was."

"So the Brewers gave this bag to you?"

"They brought it to my house, correct."

"And they told you the shrimp came from a bag *like* this?"

"No, no, they said that was the actual bag."

"The actual bag," she repeated, still taking notes.

"Correct," Danny confirmed.

There was a rhythm to their conversation now, a flow to the back and forth that Danny was enjoying. He really liked saying the word "correct" to some of these questions; it sounded legal, official, like he was in one of those *Law & Order* episodes.

"And at the hospital they told you she went into anaphylactic shock as a result of a shellfish allergy, am I right?"

"Yes, that's correct."

Danny lowered his head at that one. The memory of that day came flooding back and felt like a punch in the face. He rubbed his cheeks with both hands, and when he looked back up, Anzalone had pulled her feet off the desk and was sitting in her swivel chair, leaning forward.

"You okay?"

"Yeah, fine."

"Okay," she continued, flipping over a sheet of notes. "Let me tell you this, Mr. Beers."

Danny looked back up at her.

"I've done a little research on this bag of yours. I've looked to see whether there have been any problems or incidents involving this product, and whether there have been any lawsuits. This may come as a surprise to you, but your daughter is not the only person that this has happened to. With Phillips frozen shrimp, I mean."

Danny straightened up a bit. The comment itself wasn't anything controversial because having a shellfish allergy wasn't all that uncommon, but she definitely caught his attention.

"Actually, they told me at the hospital it was pretty rare for it to be as severe as what happened to Agnes."

"Well, they're right, but ... well, let me start with this. The Gunther Corporation sells the Phillips frozen shrimp brand, okay? Gunther is a publicly traded company worth approximately twenty billion dollars. I'm sure you've heard of them?"

"Well, yeah, sure, I think everyone has, right?"

"Right, and here's what I've learned," Anzalone said. "Starting maybe a year ago or so, for reasons no one knows yet, there's been a spike in lawsuits against Gunther for these bags of shrimp. Now that doesn't make sense. According to the FDA, in the United States, something like two percent of adults and about four or five percent of children suffer from food allergies, and about a hundred and fifty people die each year because of them. These numbers aren't huge when you consider the size of the U.S. population, so what that calls into question is why this company is getting so many lawsuits. You with me so far?"

"Yeah, uh, yes."

"So if you compare Gunther's sales with the people out there who have allergies, and then cut that down by the limited number of people who may purchase their product, which isn't a lot, they should get, what? One or two lawsuits every five years or so? Tops?"

"And how many have they had?"

"Twenty-one currently in the courts," Anzalone said abruptly. "All filed within the last six months."

"Twenty-one," Danny repeated, "that's, uh, that's a lot, right?"

"Sure is. Somethings going on there, in my opinion. It doesn't make sense that so many have been filed in a flurry recently."

Danny's shifted in his seat.

"And you think this is related to what happened to Agnes?"

"I can't be sure of it, but I would take a bet. And here's another thing. There is a federal statute out there called the Food Allergen Labeling and Consumer Protection Act, or FALCPA. It was passed in 2004. The Act requires food manufacturers under certain circumstances, but not always, to put labels on foods containing known allergens, like shellfish and shrimp. I'm sure you looked at that bag of yours. There was no label there about allergies. No warnings at all."

"Right," Danny repeated. His heart was beating faster now. "So, what exactly are you saying?"

"Well, Mr. Beers, I can tell you that last year, Gunther Home Products Corporation sold over fourteen million bags of Phillips frozen shrimp. *Fourteen million.* So God knows how many people like Agnes are out there. All I know is that cases continue to be filed nationwide, although if you also filed a case, it would be the first in New York, as far as I can tell."

Danny swallowed hard.

"The first?"

"Yes, Mr. Beers, the first, or at least it looks that way. And if I were you, I wouldn't wait. When cases pile up like this, companies like GHPC have an incentive to settle. But the settlement pot in situations like this is only so big. The key is to push the case to trial. And given Agnes's condition, I would make a motion for trial preference. That means we would ask the court to put us on the trial calendar right away. If they do, there's even a chance we could get your case to be the first nationwide to be tried, which is good because there would be an even bigger incentive to settle. They do not want to risk getting hit with a jury verdict, not in New York, Mr. Beers."

"But we could be the first trial?" Danny asked.

"Well, we're getting way ahead of ourselves," Anzalone said, settling Danny down, "but given what I know about the other cases, that's a possibility. The other cases don't appear to be moving too quickly. Maybe Gunther is dragging out the discovery process, but who knows. But I would press like hell to get the case to trial, and I think I'd get it done. Of course, that assumes we get trial preference. But I'll get our case to a jury in under a year. Trust me on that one."

Danny felt overwhelmed. He looked over at this attorney Anzalone, stared again into those blue china dinner plate eyes, and wondered how anyone could be so confident, so goddamned sure of herself. She seemed very smart and competent, Danny thought, but what exactly was her motivation here? Danny was conflicted. He had no idea whether she really gave a shit about his family, and whether she understood that he woke up every day worrying himself sick about the girls, wondering how the hell he was going to provide a stable home for them in a way that was even remotely close to what Debbie had given to their children. After all, Danny reminded himself, this woman was a lawyer – a *lawyer* for God's sake. If you had nothing left in this world but a square of toilet paper to wipe your ass with, Danny always believed, these people would take a third of it without a moment's hesitation. She was probably looking across her desk at him, at this very minute, drooling over the potential for a big fat contingency fee courtesy of a construction worker with a brain-dead kid.

Thing is, you could never be sure about people.

But this tiny little lady sure was impressive, really knew her shit. And Danny really wanted to believe in something good these days, he really did. He was desperate to break free of the pain, the tears, the hospital room smells, and the whooshing of that breathing machine, for just a day or two. And this Anzalone woman seemed honest. Maybe she wasn't like all the rest. Danny wanted to believe she cared.

But then there was the little matter of the money. Will and Janet, and especially Henry, who had as much admiration for lawyers as he had for child molesters and would tell you he wasn't sure which group of degenerates was lower down the ethical food chain, had warned him that filing a lawsuit could wind up costing him a boat load of cash, even on a contingency fee basis. And money was something that Danny sure as shit didn't have. Plus, Agnes's doctors were still telling him after all this time that this was just freak luck, that unless you knew she had a shrimp allergy there was really nothing you could have done, so what the hell was he looking up a lawyer for? And then there was always the chance he would lose, and then what? What would happen then?

Did he really want to put his family through the trauma of a courtroom trial? The time, the aggravation, the stress?

Wasn't it best just to try and move on with his life?

Sitting there in this cramped law office, with this tiny little dwarf of an attorney, with that fuzzy hair jutting off the sides of her head, Danny was getting a bad feeling about the whole thing – a negative vibe that was growing. Something was telling him to get out of there, to run like hell, that he had made a wrong decision coming in here this morning.

"Well, Ms. Anzalone," Danny finally said, "I want to thank you for seeing me today. But I just don't know. I realize I'm the one who made the appointment, but I'm just not sure if we're the lawsuit type of people, you know what I mean? Seems to me that people sue for everything these days, and you know, I just don't want to be in a situation where – "

"Mr. Beers," Anzalone interrupted, folding her hands on her desk. She was looking him right in the eyes again, this time without the smile. "Can I be blunt?"

"Uh, yeah, of course."

He didn't know where this was going, but he straightened up in the chair. She stared hard at him, her eyebrows crossed.

"Let me explain a few things that I'm sure nobody has pointed out to you, okay?"

"Sure."

"The reality of your situation is this, Mr. Beers," she began. "You work for your own construction company, you make in the neighborhood of forty-two grand a year, at best, if I'm guessing correctly, and according to that Facebook page, you let your health insurance lapse. You have two little girls to raise on your own, and probably don't have much more than a couple thousand dollars put away for their college education, if you're lucky. At some point the hospital is going to demand that you move Agnes out of there, if they haven't already, and then how in God's name are you going to care for her?"

Anzalone leaned forward again, folding her arms.

"So you are currently staring down the road at hundreds of thousands of dollars in medical expenses and nursing care, perhaps millions," she said, "which you obviously can't afford and have no idea how you're going to pay. And since no one seems to be able to tell you how long Agnes will live, or when she will get better, or *IF* she'll get better, you have no clue when it will all end. Weeks, months, maybe years, who knows. You can apply for Medicaid to cover part of this, but you won't even be eligible for that until you've paid down your assets to virtually nothing. And in the meantime, *you* are responsible, Mr. Beers."

Anzalone sat up straight and jabbed her pen right into his face.

"*You* sir, no one else. And the bills will keep piling up. Am I making myself clear?"

Anzalone threw the pen down onto her desk and leaned back in her chair, still maintaining the stare straight into Danny's eyes.

"Look Mr. Beers, I've seen this situation a hundred times, and I can tell you what it means. You'll probably lose your home, for starters. I doubt you have any equity in that place anyway, but you can basically kiss it goodbye. In the next six months you probably are looking at personal bankruptcy, the loss of your business, and the only home your daughters have ever known. And despite all that, Agnes may stay in the *exact same condition* she's in today."

Anzalone emphasized those words with three soft claps of her hands. She then paused a moment to let all that hang in the air.

"Do you understand, Mr. Beers?" she finally asked. "You want to re-think whether you're the – how did you phrase it? The *lawsuit kind of people?*"

Danny exhaled a thick gust of breath.

"Oh God," he said.

His chest felt tight again and he dropped his face into his hands. Of course, he knew this news would come one day, this notion that someone would come knocking on the door demanding to know how he was going to pay for Agnes's treatment. It had been hanging over his head for months now, like the sword of Damocles, but he didn't want to confront it, didn't want to face facts.

"What am I gonna do?" he muttered.

"Well here's your answer," Anzalone shot back. "This case is your only way out. Nobody can guarantee you a victory, of course, but it seems to me that Gunther with all its billions of dollars ought to be held responsible for what they did to Agnes. This lawsuit has the potential of making you financially secure for the rest of your life, and the rest of your girls' lives, not to mention providing your daughter with the best medical attention available, and maybe some measure of dignity. Quite frankly, Mr. Beers, in my opinion you can't afford *not* to bring this lawsuit. Whether you hire me or somebody else, I'm afraid you really have no other choice."

TWO WEEKS LATER, on a humid morning in mid-July, Danny Beers walked up the steps to Nicole Anzalone's above-the-donut-shop law office and gave her the authority to sue one of the biggest and most powerful corporations in the world.

A few hours later, Anzalone electronically filed the summons and complaint in the case of *Agnes Beers et al. v. Gunther Home Products Corporation, et al.,* duly paying the one hundred forty-five dollar filing fee and collecting her case number, which the system assigned as 18-67675. She stuck her head out the office door and called to her legal assistant Cassie, the only other employee of the firm.

"Cass, I just forwarded you a PDF of the complaint in this new Beers case," she yelled. "Email it to the editors at the *Ketchogue Advance* and the *New York Post.* I gave you their email addresses."

Anzalone rose and shut her door, and then she plopped back down onto her leather swivel chair. She re-read the complaint, every word of it, and then silently prayed that the editors would take note of the monetary demand she had included in the very last paragraph, just above her signature. In her lawsuit against Gunther, Nicole Anzalone had asked for 50 million dollars in compensatory and punitive damages. And if she could get six members of a jury to agree with her, Nicole Anzalone, the solo practitioner from Ketchogue, Long Island, who made roughly the same salary as her client Dan Beers, would get to keep forty percent of it.

Anzalone placed the Complaint in the corner of her desk, leaned back into her leather chair, and shut her eyes.

CHAPTER 6

CONFIDENT ABOUT OUR CHANCES

July 24, 2018 – 5:42 am
At Home, Ketchogue

So last year after Deb died this social worker started coming to the house to speak to the girls, and she's been a big help. Her name is Katelyn and she's gotta be no more than 25. I thought it would be a one-time thing, but they really connected with her, so I asked if she could stop by once in a while, especially after everything with Agnes, and the school said sure. One day as she was leaving I asked a bunch of questions and off-hand I mentioned I should take notes about her answers. She suggested I start writing things down for myself, in addition to just notes, and I asked like a diary? And she said no, call it a journal. Write down what you're thinking and then after a few weeks go back and read it. It helps to give you perspective she said.

I'm not much of a writer, but I used to jot things down a long time ago. Just notes, lists, ideas, things like that. Then last year Gianna showed me how to get on Deb's old laptop, and so I started using this now. Anyway, now I'm writing things out, and it helps. I got a lot to say, a ton of stuff I need to get off my chest. I hope this journal thing can provide that opportunity, and so from time to time I'll give it a shot.

Anyway, there's been a big thing recently – I filed a lawsuit about what happened to Agnes. Me – a lawsuit. I can hardly believe it myself. I was nervous about Gianna finding out about it on social media so the other day I knocked on her door and went in and told her about it. She was curious and asked a lot of questions. We sat in her and Agnes's room and I couldn't help but look around. Me and Deb worked hard on that room and we decorated it all in pink and white and I installed wainscoting, custom crown molding and shelves and cabinets. The girls filled them with books, stuffed animals, photos, mementos and dozens of other trinkets that they shared. Deb loved that room, and sometimes it's tough for me to go in there.

Anyway, after we talked about the lawsuit, me and Gianna had a good talk about Agnes, and it was long overdue. I have been thinking a lot about how I can divert her attention from everything, think of ways for her to go out and have fun, because she's taking on too much in this house, almost as if she's trying to replace what Deb did. Making schedules, cleaning – it's crazy. It's too stressful for her. She's only 12 years old. Her friend Charlotte Brewer has a birthday party coming up soon, and I am really looking forward to her having a day when she can get away from things.

I also told Henry about the lawsuit the next day, because he was here nosing around and wanted to know where I was when I was visiting with the lawyer Anzalone, who is representing us. He kept pressing, and so I told him. Henry's reaction was to roll his eyes and ask me how I could get involved with one those scumbag piece of shit ambulance chasing parasites. His words, not mine. You could try to explain things to him, but it wouldn't matter. I'm getting a little tired of the way he talks to me, I'm a goddamned 50-year-old man. It was that way when Debbie was alive but now that she's gone it's gotten so much worse. I'm not sure where his hostility comes from, but recently I've been wondering if maybe he suspects what really happened with Deb. Maybe he doesn't, I really have no idea, to be honest. The truth is that I've never uttered a word about that day to anyone. I've never come clean, if those are the right words, so there's really no way he could know. But I think about it every day.

I think at some point I'm going to use these pages to lay it all out. I'm not sure though, but maybe. My hope would be to gain some of the perspective that Katelyn was talking about. I'll think about it, that's for sure.

But in the meantime, I'm excited about this lawsuit I have going on now, as of about a week ago, and what it possibly can do to help my family. This Anzalone is a smart lady. She seems tough, the type of person you can't push around. She has a ton of experience and really believes in our case.

She also seems confident about our chances.

And right now, that's good enough for me.

PART TWO

THE LAWSUIT

CHAPTER 7

J. HARTWELL BRIGGS AND THE
GUNTHER HOME PRODUCTS CORPORATION

IN THE NORTHWEST corner of Orange County, at the point where Interstate 84 crosses the Delaware River to begin its long westerly crawl through Pennsylvania, the global corporate headquarters of the Gunther Home Products Corporation sat on a sprawling one hundred and thirty-two acre campus in the township of Port Jervis, New York. Unlike most corporate headquarters, this campus lacked the typical concrete structures and gridded roadways; instead it was adorned with burnt-clay brick buildings on green rolling hills, with flowering dogwood and magnolia trees dotting the landscape. The place looked more like an elite New England college than a manufacturing company.

The main entrance was located just off Route 209, and when you entered past the mammoth blue and white sign that read "GHPC – HQ," you came upon a security booth set up in the style of a lakeside cottage, except for the red and white security gate lowered across the shining blacktop driveway. Past the booth there was a narrow two-way winding road lined with crisp white Belgian-block stones and thickly blossoming oak trees that seemed to reach to the heavens.

About a half-mile down, at a clearing, the road terminated at the main GHPC building, which rose up like Emerald City. It was a glistening 14-story LED-lit eco-friendly glass structure that looked like it had been bathed in Windex, radiating sunbeams across the open greens. Out front there was a massive circular driveway about the size of a high school running track, with a man-made freshwater pond in the middle. The pond contained a huge ceramic fountain that had a dozen halogen lamps burning at its base. Next to those were six water nozzles set to a timer, such that every two minutes the fountain would blast a plume of water over fifty feet in the air.

Today, around seven-thirty on a steamy morning in late July, a black Cadillac Escalade with tinted windows cruised past the security booth and eased its way down the twisting roadway until it came to the circular driveway. Two roads circled around the main building to rear parking lot A, which spanned the length of a football field, and the Escalade took the first of those roads and moved to the rear of the building. From there another road jutted out from the parking lot and led back to nearly three dozen other buildings and towers filled with thousands of employees, all doing the business of the Gunther Home Products Corporation.

The Escalade creeped its way to the front of Building 17, a smaller glass structure located in the northern part of the corporate campus and came to a stop. A driver in a black sport coat stepped out and pulled open a rear door, promptly depositing a small bookish man with tortoise shell glasses and a light grey suit in front of a set of twin revolving doors.

The man was Stewart J. Handler, a Harvard Law School graduate who several years earlier had been Chairman of the Corporate Department for the New York City law firm of Foster Tuttle & Briggs LLP, an eight-hundred lawyer firm that Handler had joined as a first year associate attorney back in 1982. Handler was now Gunther's General Counsel and Building 17 was where you could find the Gunther Legal Department, consisting of 112 attorneys working exclusively on GHPC legal matters.

Handler entered through the revolving doors and took a private elevator up to the sixth floor, the highest floor in this building. As was standard operating procedure, his Executive Assistant, a 50-ish woman with red hair and liver spots named Joyce Doggins, greeted him near the elevator with a black coffee and a daily agenda. Handler grabbed both items, tucking the agenda under his arm as he wrapped his hands around a coffee mug. He marched past dozens of lawyers and paralegals already present and toiling away in offices and cubicles, eyeballing the agenda, with Doggins astride him step for step. Handler then settled in behind the desk in his mammoth corner office, from which he could see the Delaware River twisting its way south between Pennsylvania and New Jersey.

Sometime later that morning, near noon, Doggins scurried back into the office with a document in her hands, which she waved at him like a flag. Handler was peering down at the time at a memorandum that his Deputy Assistant General Counsel had drafted, which laid out the national Gunther legal budget for the approaching month of August. It listed over a hundred and fifty law firms across the country. Gunther's legal battles involved every conceivable subject matter that entangled any massive manufacturing conglomerate, including contract disputes, distribution deals, labor and employment cases, product liability cases, insurance coverage battles, patent and trademark actions, banking matters, government investigations, mass tort actions, personal injury cases, and various other business-related litigations and legal matters. Handler's job, in addition to keeping over a hundred lawyers in line, was reporting to the Board of Directors, keeping his enormous legal team humming and under budget, and like everyone else, doing his part to keep the Gunther stock price moving north.

As Doggins entered, Handler looked up at her over the top of his reading glasses, placing his pen onto his desktop.

"What is it Joyce?" he calmly asked.

"Summons and complaint. First New York case."

"Another shrimp suit?"

"Yes sir."

"Jeez, okay. How many does that make?"

"Twenty-two. Third one on the East Coast."

"What's the injury?"

"Very severe, I'm afraid."

"Oh boy," Handler said.

"Ten-year old girl by the name of Agnes Beers," said Doggins. "She's been in a vegetative coma since April."

"My God. What's the family situation?"

"Father, an older sister. Sister's twelve, according to the filing."

Handler shook his head.

"Which firm? Do we know them?"

Doggins flipped to the last page of the complaint.

"Looks like a solo … in Ketchogue, New York."

"Ketchogue?" Handler asked, "where is that?"

"Long Island. Name is Nicole Anzalone."

"Anzalone, Anzalone," Handler said, searching his mental rolodex. "Never heard of her. Where'd they file, Suffolk County?"

"No, Bronx."

"Bronx, well that's not good. Email it to Hartwell Briggs ASAP, okay? Ask him to call me when he gets a chance."

"Absolutely," Doggins said.

"You know the drill, get FT&B to do the usual workup. A full background check on this Anzalone, as well as on the Beers family. Let's also get copies of the complaint to our medical team and have them start getting the ER and hospital records. I want the complete medical review as soon as we can get it."

"Will do, Mr. Handler."

"By the way, did we order lunch yet?"

"Yes, Carmine's sir. Chicken parmigiana heroes."

"Okay, great. Thanks Joyce."

"Welcome," she responded, and she was out the door.

Handler pushed aside the litigation budget memo and began reading the Complaint that this attorney Anzalone had filed. He could see she was from that Long Island town called Ketchogue, and in the section of the complaint entitled "Parties," Handler read that the Beers family was from the same town. Maybe she's a family friend, Handler figured. He then flipped back to the front of the Complaint, and at the top, above the caption, he saw the court where Anzalone had filed – "SUPREME COURT OF THE STATE OF NEW YORK, COUNTY OF THE BRONX."

He smirked at that one.

"Nice try," he said with a chuckle.

Handler knew that every personal injury lawyer in the world, no matter where they were from, tried to get their case into the Bronx in New York City if it was at all possible. The Bronx's demographics were not favorable to corporate defendants in personal injury cases, and everyone in the legal world knew it. The jury pool up there consisted of mostly blue-collar working-class people, and the generally accepted rule of thumb was that they handed out money like Hari Krishnas passing out pamphlets in an airport. You could get injured in Timbuktu and even the lawyer you hired over there would try to get the case into the Bronx if she could do it. On the other hand, when you were a defendant, if you had any basis for it, you tried everything in your power to change venue and get the case the hell out of there. Handler hadn't finished reading the complaint and already he could see the first battle taking shape.

When Handler got to the last page, his eyes landed on something called the Wherefore Clause, just above the signature block for the attorney Nicole Anzalone and below a header entitled "Prayer For Relief." In the Beers complaint it read:

```
WHEREFORE,  Plaintiffs,  and  each  of  them,
respectfully  request  that  this  Court  enter
judgment  in  favor  of  Plaintiffs  and  against
Defendants,  and  each  of  them,  on  each  of  the
causes  of  action  set  forth  herein,  awarding
Plaintiffs  the  amount  of  Fifty  Million  Dollars
($50,000,000.00)  in  compensatory  and  punitive
damages,  pre-judgment  and  post-judgment  interest,
reasonable  attorneys'  fees  and  costs,  and  such
other  and  further  relief  as  the  Court  deems  just
and  proper.
```

Handler shook his head as he removed his reading glasses, tossing them down onto his desk. He pinched the bridge of his nose.

"Fifty million," he scoffed, "of course, why not."

He placed the Complaint neatly on a pile of documents in the corner of his desk. The pile was about a foot high and contained only legal complaints filed against Gunther in seemingly thousands of federal, state and local jurisdictions around the country.

"They're all alike," he said aloud, "every one of them."

He stood, buttoned his coat, and headed out the door in search of a chicken parmigiana hero.

ABOUT EIGHT MONTHS earlier, back in November, Stewart Handler had placed a phone call to a lawyer named J. Hartwell Briggs, an old Harvard Law School classmate and the Senior Partner over at the Foster Tuttle & Briggs law firm in midtown Manhattan. When Handler left the Firm a few years earlier to run Gunther's massive Legal Department, Handler and Briggs had remained close, which only solidified the relationship between Gunther and the law firm. Gunther had always been a top client of the Firm, but with Handler in charge now it would stay that way for years to come. Currently FT&B handled virtually all of Gunther's outside litigation, and for cases involving big time dollars and class actions that could really affect the corporate bottom line, FT&B served not only as trial counsel but also as National Coordinating Counsel, overseeing the many law firms that Gunther hired to represent them around the country. In short, any lawyer or law firm that Gunther retained anywhere in the country reported first to J. Hartwell Briggs, and ultimately to Stewart Handler. With both the litigation and corporate work that FT&B handled for Gunther, the company was putting over 70 million a year into the law firm's coffers.

When Briggs took the phone call back in November, Handler explained that he wanted to retain Briggs in connection with a potential series of personal injury lawsuits that would probably arise out of a problem the company had with a brand of theirs called Phillips Frozen Shrimp. Handler explained that the company was beginning to receive reports that consumers were going into anaphylactic shock at a much higher rate than would be expected based on their sales. He explained that a person needed to have a pre-existing shellfish or shrimp allergy for such a thing to occur, and therefore anyone with such a condition could avoid injury simply by not using or purchasing the product. But something strange seemed to be going on, and Handler wanted Briggs and FT&B to get to the bottom of it. Why they were getting so many reports and legal complaints was a mystery, and Handler was intent on getting the problem resolved.

"Lemme see if I unnerstand the problem here, Stewart," Briggs said in his Tennessee drawl. "Y'all are sayin' that these little bitty shrimps can get people sick even after havin' 'em in they mouths only a coupla seconds?"

"Well, yes, Hartwell, that's the way it works," Handler explained. "If they have an allergic condition and they eat the shrimp they can experience those symptoms. But they would have to have an allergy."

"Well now, Stewart, what has that got to do wit' us? Certainly we didn't afflict these people wit' any type a allergy."

"No, we didn't, but for some reason we've had an increase in reports of anaphylactic shock over this particular brand. It's a real head-scratcher, to be honest. We are looking into it."

"Well, was there a recall?" Briggs asked.

"No, there wasn't. The company at one point considered placing a warning on the retail bags but for whatever reason they didn't do it. And that was even before these reports."

"Innerestin'. Lemme ask yew – what are the numbers on sales?"

Handler hesitated a moment and took a breath.

"Hartwell, we've sold over fourteen million units."

"Fourteen meeyan. Hot damn."

"Yes, indeed."

"Well," said Briggs, "that explains the company gettin' its knickers inna twist then."

"No question. The timing on when the warning was considered, versus when we first learned of the reports, is a real concern. We're still gathering information on that front."

"Well, I tell yew what, Stewart," said Briggs. "I'm gone personally brand the ass 'a the fella who decided not to issue a recall, I can tell yew that. Any lawsuits filed yet?"

"There've been a few, yes. We have the complaints and we'll get them to you. But we're expecting more."

"Yes, yew can bet on that."

Briggs then pulled his receiver off speakerphone.

"Stewart, have your staff get those complaints over here right away. We'll dig in and advise on the proper course. We also gone interview the company scientists to see what they have to say. I'm sure they must have some answers 'bout why these people are all gettin' sick."

"Yes, of course, we will do that."

He paused a moment as he was taking notes. "Let me know what else you need, and we'll get it right over to you."

"Sure 'nuff," Briggs said. "Let's keep in touch on 'dis one. Gone be one big doggie."

"Yes, sir," Handler replied, and he hung up the phone.

About a week later, Briggs called Handler after he had reviewed the complaints and had met with his staff. Briggs had assembled a twelve-member legal team, and they dug in on the legal research and devoured the complaints. They wrote thick memoranda to Briggs advising him on all relevant points and authorities.

Briggs took Handler through his notes and commented on some of the legal issues, and then he laid out what he, Briggs, believed was the path forward on these cases.

"Stewart, I've given this situation some thought, and here's what we gone do. We here at the Firm gone coordinate the cases nationwide. Every lawsuit that gets filed, yew send the complaint directly to me, no matter what state it come from. We'll take care of harrin' local counsel, and we'll try the cases."

"Okay, great," Handler said.

"First thing we gone do is some scientific testin'. What's the name of our Research Director?"

"It's Fred Barker. Dr. Frederick Barker."

"Well, we gone have ol' Fred do some lookin' into these shrimps. He gone tell us what the problem is, if they's any problem a 'tall. He gone do that under your supervision, at the direction of counsel. Unnerstood?"

"Yes, understood."

"We'll also need to assemble a panel a' experts to review the toxicity issues, and hopefully there's a defense on the science. We'll point back to these consumers too, Stewart, 'cause how the hell we supposed to know they have an allergy? Yew take ma point?"

"I do, absolutely," Handler said, scribbling notes again. "Thanks Hartwell, this all sounds right on target."

"And one other thing," Briggs said. "Lemme make a point here. May sound too early to be thinkin' 'long these lines, but I've seen these types a cases a meeyan times. They pile up, and pile up, and the worst thing yew can do is incentivize these ambulance-chasin' scumbag lawyers."

"Yes, agreed," Handler said.

"Now, I know we have ourselves a potential problem here," Briggs said, "and I don't know where this all gone go, but based on the numbers yew tellin' me, we can be lookin' at a pile a these cases. Mebbe thousands."

"I know, Hartwell, it's a mess right now."

"That's what yew got us for. Yew make sure yew tell the board."

"I will, of course."

"And yew also make sure they know we need to *fight*, Stewart. Yew start settlin' and it'll be like cockroaches crawlin' out from every nook and cranny lookin' to shake us down. I know from experience it's the worst thing yew can do. Yew take ma point?"

"I do, Hartwell, yes indeed."

"We have ourselves a strong defense, Stewart. If yew know yew's allergic, what yew eatin' our shrimp for? Yew just don't buy our product, plain and simple."

"Correct."

"So right now we can forget 'bout settlin' any a these cases. That is just off the table. Yew file against us, we goin' to *war*. A trial victory for Gunther in the first one a these cases could ward off potentially thousands of additional lawsuits."

"Excellent," Handler said firmly, "this is excellent."

"So here's what we gone do," Briggs summarized. "We gone pick the right case and push it to trial. No matter what kinda settlement is offered, we try that very case. We get it before a jury and we take a verdict. And then we take that verdict and we show every single one a these otha plaintiffs' lawyers they gone take *nothin'* for they clients if they decide to press on. It's gone be balls to the walls, as they say, but we really have no otha choice."

"No, we certainly don't."

"So are we agreed, Stewart? No settlements?"

"Yes, Hartwell agreed," Handler said. "Again, thanks so much."

CHAPTER 8

HUNKERED DOWN AT ISLAND PT

BACK IN KETCHOGUE, right around the time when Joyce Doggins was waving the Beers complaint at Stewart Handler, Nicole Anzalone parked her Honda Civic on Main Street beside a storefront with a blue awning called Island Physical Therapy. It was early on a Wednesday morning, and Anzalone already had the windows zipped up and the air conditioning blowing since the outside temperature gauge on the Honda read 93.

Anzalone crawled out of the Honda with a laptop case in hand and fed a few quarters into a meter before heading into Island PT. She greeted a woman at the Front Desk who was staring into a computer monitor.

"Hey Steph," Anzalone said in a familiar tone. "He ready?"

"No, not yet," the woman, Stephanie, responded, "probably another ten minutes or so."

"How'd he do today?"

Stephanie turned to look through a slide-over window.

"Oh, he had a great day!" she hollered, loud enough for those on the other side of the window to hear. Then in a lowered tone to Anzalone, she said, "He can't wait to tell you about it!"

In the back room were the physical therapists who treated CP patients – cerebral palsy – on Wednesday mornings. Anzalone's son Justin was seven years old and had been coming to this facility for just over a year. Anzalone loved everything about this place. Justin had shown significant improvement since she signed him up here at the urging of his neurologist. The place was out of network and was costing Anzalone a thick penny, but she couldn't ignore the progress. Plus, they treated him with so much compassion there was no other place she would even consider. The one-hour sessions would routinely run to almost an hour and a half, at no extra charge, if the therapist and the patient were making progress, so Anzalone would always bring her Apple MacBook to kill some time while she waited out the extra minutes. The place also had Wi-Fi, another perk that allowed Anzalone to get some work done.

"That's great, can't wait," said Anzalone.

Anzalone took a seat in the small waiting area fronting Main Street and opened her MacBook. She connected to Island PT's Wi-Fi and began checking her email. There was one from a company called Service by Gervis, Inc., which Anzalone used for service of process jobs in her cases. The email confirmed they had successfully served the Beers lawsuit on the Gunther Home Products Corporation that very same day. Anzalone closed the email and leaned back in her chair, gazing up at the ceiling.

Well, she thought, game on. This was now an official lawsuit. She would probably receive a call from a defense lawyer in a matter of days.

Hunkered down at Island PT, Anzalone thought about what the next six to twelve months of her life were going to look like. They weren't going to be easy, that was for sure. The Gunther Corporation was represented nationwide by one of the most powerful and respected law firms in the world – Foster Tuttle & Briggs LLP – and that would be the firm that likely would be taking her on, given that she filed this lawsuit right in their backyard. How she was going to handle the workload this case would require was beyond her. That law firm could throw ten, fifteen, even twenty attorneys and paralegals at this case without even blinking an eye, and all of them would be working eighteen hours a day. They would be billing the file even more if they happened to dream about the case when they slept.

All Anzalone had was herself and Cassie, who was more concerned about who was getting the final rose on *The Bachelor* than she was about any legal matters going on at the Anzalone Law Firm. Some solo lawyers would even consider turning the case down. But how does a PI lawyer say no to a ten-year old kid in a coma?

Well, you don't, Anzalone knew. Any lawyer in her situation would descend upon a comatose ten-year old quicker than a starving lion tossed a bloody antelope. If you are lucky enough to get retained you push the case as hard as you can, no matter who is on the other side. Such cases had the potential to pay what amounted to a monster yearly bonus, but they were also risky because they were straight contingency, which meant that for every hour you spent hammering away on them you were pushing aside the real estate closings, DWIs, worker's compensation cases, INS matters, and the other meat and potatoes stuff that kept a reasonable flow of cash coming in the door. And the rent, payroll for Cassie, her and Anzalone's health insurance, firm supplies and credit cards, not to mention her mortgage, car payment and the bills for Justin's medical appointments – none of that was going away.

But on the upside, every instinct she had told her that Gunther would eventually settle. If she could be a royal pain in the ass to these people maybe they would ask for a mediation – an out-of-court meeting before a neutral where the parties discussed settlement. Sometimes, in the one-off liability cases, companies would fight you until the bitter end, but in the situation where a company screwed up and faced dozens or even hundreds of lawsuits, they would always buckle under the weight of the cases and the potential for massive liability, and eventually they would settle. This is exactly what happened with the asbestos, tobacco, breast implant, and a hundred other mass tort cases.

Anzalone saw these shrimp cases going in the same direction.

She tried not to think of what a settlement could mean to her, but it was difficult. Maybe a new wheelchair for Justin, a modern one that enabled him to control it a little more and give him some additional freedom in his movements. Or a wheelchair-accessible van to get him around. Perhaps even some regular home care without Anzalone having to haul him everywhere. And depending on the size of the settlement, maybe they could move into a small home, in a decent neighborhood, maybe near a park, without having to navigate a flight of stairs.

On a lighter note, maybe it could provide a chance to get away for a few days and escape the mind-numbing boredom of her daily routine. Was it too much to ask to spend some time in the sunshine, maybe down in Jamaica, falling asleep on a lounge chair with a paperback face-down on her belly?

But all of this was a long way off – she had just filed the damn lawsuit and any settlement could be months or even years away, a trial date even longer. But did it hurt to dream?

Once she had connected to the Wi-Fi, Anzalone googled the

name "J. Hartwell Briggs," the famous lawyer who could very well be on the other side of the Beers case. Whether he would actually appear in court on a case like this was another story – it was more likely that the firm would assign a junior partner and an army of additional cronies. But a mere five minutes of research revealed to her that Gunther was Briggs's personal client. He and his law firm handled almost all their legal work, spanning the entire country. Anzalone therefore assumed that J. Hartwell Briggs – *the* J. Hartwell Briggs – would be involved in her case somehow.

Anzalone peered over Stephanie's shoulders, and seeing no sign of Justin, she looked down at her Google search results. The first was a Wikipedia page for Briggs. Anzalone clicked on it, and when it opened Anzalone began scrolling down and reading …

J. Hartwell Briggs
From Wikipedia, the free encyclopedia

Jethro Hartwell Briggs (born August 14, 1945) is an American lawyer and politically active businessman from Creeksburg, Tennessee. Politically a Democrat, Briggs was the United States Attorney for the Southern District of New York who prosecuted cases against New York's Mafia families and corrupt Wall Street executives in the late 1980s. He was lead counsel in a sensational prosecution that resulted in a RICO conviction against NY mob boss Carmine Saccente …

Anzalone certainly remembered that Carmine Saccente trial.

She was in high school at the time but remembered the photo on the front page of the *New York Times,* Saccente in handcuffs and Briggs next to him with his arms crossed.

She remembered reading about Briggs getting death threats from mobsters, and she recalled being in awe over what it must be like to rise to that level of success.

Anzalone shifted in her chair and looked past Stephanie toward the backroom again. There were a few PTs running around but no sign of Justin, so she kept reading.

Her eyes drifted over to a box that said "Contents," which was on the bottom of the first page. She clicked on "Early Life" and read some of the snippets …

Early Life

Briggs was born in Creeksburg, Tennessee, at the foot of the Blue Ridge Mountains. As a child, Briggs attended the prestigious Grantly Kernan Boarding School in Knoxville, a 150-year old institution that boasted some of Tennessee's former Senators and Governors. By the time Briggs was in the third grade, he could already recite more than a dozen Shakespearean sonnets, was assisting the 8th grade teachers in giving algebra lessons and had mastered the clarinet. By 7th grade, young Hartwell was taking summer advanced mathematics courses at the University of Tennessee. After his four years at Grantly Kernan, J. Hartwell Briggs was Valedictorian at Columbia University, graduating with a degree in political science. It was then on to Harvard Law School, where he served as Editor-in-Chief of the *Harvard Law Review,* finishing 2nd in his class.

Anzalone raised her eyebrows at the Columbia and Harvard blurbs, in a kind of "not too shabby" sentiment. She then stood to see if there was any sign of Justin. She could see him in the back – he appeared to be working through some rail exercises, which Anzalone recognized as the last set in his normal routine. She sat and continued reading …

Legal Career

Following Harvard Law, Briggs served as a Law Clerk to Justice Arthur Goldberg of the U.S. Supreme Court. From there his rise in national legal and political circles was meteoric. After a stint in private practice, he was appointed by President Carter, at age of 37, as Solicitor General, arguing dozens of cases before the Supreme Court. In 1987, Briggs was named U.S. Attorney for the Southern District of New York. By the time he left his post in the Southern District, rumors were rampant that he would accept the Democratic Party's nomination for Governor of New York. Thereafter, the law firm Foster Tuttle LLP brought him in as a partner, taking the extraordinary step of renaming the firm and adding his name.

Just then Anzalone heard a humming noise coming from her right, and she quickly snapped the laptop shut. She shoved it back into her laptop case and stood just in time to catch Stephanie pushing a wheelchair out the door of the physical therapy room. There was Justin, smiling away, with his black hair and beautiful hazel eyes. He was nestled into the wheelchair with his head tilted slightly to the left but resting in between the pads of a cushioned headrest. His left arm was pulled tight against his chest, and his left hand, which trembled, was balled up into a fist, except for his index finger, which was pointing down toward his lap. His right hand was working the lever on the wheelchair's remote control.

"Here he is Mommy!" Stephanie exclaimed.

"Hey buddy!" Anzalone said.

She placed both hands on his cheeks, kissing his face.

"Hi Mommy," Justin responded. When he spoke, he would shake his head back and forth, focusing on the ceiling, but never losing the smile.

"He did great today, Nicole, he really did," said Stephanie. "Five to seven steps unassisted between the balance beams."

"Really!" Anzalone yelled, tousling his hair, "is that right?"

"All by myself," said Justin.

Anzalone kissed him again. She wrote out a check and then negotiated the wheelchair out to the Honda. She and Stephanie then loaded Justin into the backseat and secured his seatbelt.

"Thanks Steph," she said, giving her a hug, "you're a doll."

"You bet, Nicole."

"See you next Wednesday."

Then they were off, headed back home where Anzalone would work for the day at her kitchen table. She never made court appearances or saw clients on Wednesdays so that Justin could have his time at Island PT. The time alone in her kitchen, without client phone calls and having to reprimand Cassie about surfing the Internet, allowed her to catch up on paperwork. And of course, Wednesday nights were reserved for NA meetings. Those she would never skip.

During the drive, Anzalone let her mind drift back to the Beers lawsuit, the Gunther Home Products Corporation, and their hotshot lawyer Briggs, with his thick Wikipedia page and impressive list of credentials. She wondered what they must have been thinking when they received the summons and complaint out there at their Port Jervis headquarters today. Well, they wouldn't worry about litigating against the likes of her, right? Most likely her complaint had been tossed into a pile for the routine ho-hum nothing-to-see-here processing by a Gunther legal machine that just kept spinning its wheels and churning away. The case would be a single line item on a legal budget as thick as a phone book and dealt with in due course. Just another sedan coming off the assembly line, Anzalone figured. When it was all over the Gunther legal team would forget it ever existed.

But for Anzalone this case was everything. If she could beat these people, either at trial or by forcing a settlement, maybe she could live with what had happened to her career. Or more accurately, what she had done to it. Maybe if she could take these people down, in some small way she could hang her hat on such a victory and know that she hadn't thrown it all away. That maybe she was worth something as a lawyer after all.

When does redemption come?

At what point is a person truly forgiven?

Tough questions, and ones she asked herself constantly. A victory in this case could go a long way to answering them. It wouldn't make up for everything, of course, but at least this was an opportunity, a chance to prove something to herself. She couldn't let it slip through her fingers.

Anzalone pulled a U-turn and drove west on Route 25A, blending in amongst the vehicles creeping past the storefronts. She looked in the rearview mirror and saw Justin crammed into the backseat of her crappy little Honda Civic. The thing had over 112,000 miles on it and needed an oil change along with a set of brake pads, but right now she couldn't part with the 600 bucks she knew they would bang her for in parts and labor. She then conjured up the image of the third floor no-elevator walk-up townhouse she was about to haul Justin up to when they got home in about fifteen minutes. How she was going to carry him up three flights of stairs when he got older was a mystery.

Anzalone took a deep breath and ran a hand down her face, letting her reality sink in. She hadn't taken that vacation in over four years, hadn't been out on a date since forever, had a plate in her right shin from a prior running accident that still occasionally sent shock waves of pain through her leg, and recently an MRI had revealed a herniated disc at L3 that she would have to ignore for the foreseeable future. She was forty-five years old, and even though she worked almost seventy hours a week, she had exactly $7,387.87 in the bank, most of which was being held hostage by the next round of monthly bills. Well, something would have to give.

At a stop light Anzalone turned toward the backseat.

"How you doin' buddy?" she asked, "everything okay?"

"Happy today, Momma."

"Me too," she smiled. "Me too."

The light turned green and Anzalone hit the gas.

So Briggs had mastered the clarinet when he was in the third grade, huh? And he could recite Shakespeare too – woopdedoo. Big-time, powerful attorney, former Solicitor General, potential future Governor …

Well fuck him, she nearly said out loud.

These people will settle if she played her cards right.

They just had to.

CHAPTER 9

A SUMMER DECIDES UPON A PLAN

A FEW WEEKS later, over in Manhattan, in the law firm run by the world-famous attorney J. Hartwell Briggs, a young and impassioned law student named Seamus P. O'Reilly was camped out in his office up on the 39th floor of FT&B Tower, which sat majestically on Park Avenue just down from the Helmsley Building. O'Reilly was dressed impeccably, decked out in a banker's grey Brooks Brothers suit and gold Joseph Abboud tie. He even had one of those matching hankie squares peeking out of his breast pocket. The whole ensemble cost him roughly the same amount as his first week's salary, but in O'Reilly's humble opinion it was well worth the expense, a feeling he confirmed for himself each time he looked in the mirror.

Right now, it was just after 10:30 on a sunny August morning, roughly twenty minutes after O'Reilly had shown up for work that day, and there he was, nestled comfortably into the soft leathery cushions of his hi-backed office chair. His hands were folded behind his head, and his gleaming black Johnston & Murphy wingtips were plopped down onto his back credenza so that his back was facing the office door. And at that moment, on that day, the man was feeling so good, so incredibly jazzed about the point to which his short legal career had advanced, and where he knew it was going, that his chest was just swollen with pride, bursting in fact, puffed out from here to about Cleveland.

For the entirety of that summer, O'Reilly felt as right as rain sitting in that hi-back. He loved his job, loved his office, loved the Firm and everything about it. He loved being a law student, loved telling people he was on the cusp – roughly a year away in fact – of being a full-fledged member of the New York State Bar. Most days, like today, O'Reilly would take a moment or two to shut his office door and throw his feet on that back credenza to sit and think about where he was and how he had gotten there. Before you knew it, he would be wearing a shit-eating grin under his thick mop of fire-engine red hair. The smile would then graduate to a giggle each time he would plop down onto that black leather seat cushion and listen to it hiss with the impression of his buttocks.

O'Reilly was now into his fifth week as one of seventy-six Summer Associates at FT&B, all of them between their second and third year of law school. The Firm had heavily recruited all of them, and they each had stellar credentials. To land a summer job at this law firm, O'Reilly knew, you had to be among the best. With his hands folded behind his neck, facing back toward the window, O'Reilly ran through a mental checklist of his accomplishments – third in his class at Manhattan Law School. Managing Editor of the *Manhattan Law School Law Review*. The offer for the Summer Associate position here at FT&B.

It was all so exciting. If he successfully completed the Summer Associate gig, the firm would make him an offer for a permanent job, commencing after graduation, that paid him a healthy six-figure salary. The job offer would come at the end of August when the entire Summer Associate class, O'Reilly included, would be heading back to their respective law schools for their third and final year. You had to be among the best even to be considered for the spot, and O'Reilly was right in the thick of things. Sure, he thought, there was the little matter of his law school, Manhattan Law, or MLS as they called it, not being a tier-one school. According to most rankings, it could not really piss with the Ivies. So maybe MLS wasn't Harvard, Yale or Columbia, which is where most of these Summers (as they were called) attended, but what about Yitzhak Schwartz, O'Reilly thought, the brilliant Constitutional Law professor at MLS, himself a Harvard grad? Didn't he once say that the top five percent at MLS could compete with the best at Harvard or Stanford? Schwartz had definitely said that, the little bastard. O'Reilly was sure of it.

O'Reilly whirled his leather hi-back around so that he was facing his desk. He promptly planted his elbows around a document that had delivered a surge of adrenaline when he received it the day before. The thing had arrived in an inter-office envelope, old-school style, and still had his heart pumping. It was a memorandum from the Chairman of the Firm no less, none other than Mr. J. Hartwell

Briggs, who was as big a muckety-muck as you would ever find in any law firm anywhere. The typewritten part of the memo listed all the upcoming Summer Associate social events on the calendar that summer – nights at the opera, box seats just over the home dugout at Yankee Stadium, tours through the Metropolitan Museum of Art, orchestra seats at the hottest shows on Broadway, and countless three-hour lunches at the City's most expensive restaurants – all recruiting tools, carrots dangled to convince the Summers to come back to the Firm as lawyers after graduation.

O'Reilly was pumped about all of that, like everyone else, but right now the only thing on his mind was that memo. Because Briggs, to O'Reilly's disbelief, had jotted a personal handwritten note in the margin of the memo directly to him, Seamus P. O'Reilly of all people. He nearly passed out when he saw it –

To Mr. Seamus P. O'Reilly, Esq. –
Looking forward to our wine-tasting event.
Hope to see you there! JHB.

And there it was – agenda item number three, which Briggs had circled in ink. A wine-tasting party here at the Firm. A function, if you will. A black-tie event that very night in the C. Barton Foster Conference Room, up on the 45th Floor, promptly at six o'clock.

O'Reilly didn't know who the hell C. Barton Foster was or why they would name a conference room after him, and nor did he give a shit. The point was that the only *living* name partner of the Firm, a legal legend, had taken the time to write him a personal note and was *looking forward* to meeting him that very night.

Looking forward to it, he was. Hartwell fucking Briggs.

O'Reilly looked down at the note again and read it aloud – "Mr. Seamus P. O'Reilly," he beamed, puffing his chest to Cleveland again. And then he focused in on his name – *Seamus.* It looked so good on the page. Just the sound of it triggered an avalanche of goosebumps cascading down his arms.

Seamus, he said silently. What a great name.

Gaelic for James. Pronounced *shay-mis.*

He recalled the decision he had made at the beginning of the summer to insist that everyone call him by that moniker. It was indeed the right call. The name was so cool, so worldly. O'Reilly had gone his whole life as "Jimmy," the son of a New York City fire captain from Queens, but who the hell would figure that out in this place? You get a job here and everyone assumes you crawled out of a Connecticut prep school. You can't swing a monkey wrench around this place without hitting a Preston or a Kipton or a Sumner right on the bridge of the nose, so why should he be any different? Yes sir, here he would be called *Seamus*.

Quirky, cool, intellectual – *Seamus*.

Seamus P. O'Reilly, Esq. Attorney-at-law.

Jesus, was that perfect or what?

O'Reilly fingered the memo again and wondered whether any of the other Summers had also received a handwritten personal note from Mr. J. Hartwell Briggs. It certainly was a head-scratcher. Why would Briggs, of all people, write a note to *him*? A random act maybe? Perhaps.

But then something else occurred to him, something that made that surge of adrenalin running through him go nuclear. It was very possible, O'Reilly had surmised, that Briggs wrote the note after setting his eyes on something that O'Reilly had written roughly a week earlier. It was a spectacular legal memorandum, in O'Reilly's opinion, that he had submitted to the assignment partner who doled out work to the Summers. The memo was a legal research exercise they assigned him, requiring that he analyze political asylum issues on behalf of a Tibetan monk, a *pro bono* client of the Firm. O'Reilly had spent about three weeks writing it to make sure it would sing, and in his view the goddamn thing was so brilliant, so intuitive, that he had taken a chance and several days earlier had emailed a copy to Briggs.

The memo had concluded that the poor hapless monk's very life was in danger in certain volatile regions of China, and based on those facts, and on a detailed explanation and analysis of applicable law, O'Reilly had opined that the man had a substantial likelihood of success on the merits of his political asylum application here in the United States. O'Reilly saved it as a PDF attachment and clicked "send" on the email to Briggs, and a mere 72 hours later the Briggs handwritten note appeared in his office mail tray. How could that be a coincidence?

Certainly, this potential international crisis was of critically high importance to a politically connected man like J. Hartwell Briggs. Briggs's sense of fairness and justice had been offended just as strongly as had O'Reilly's. And Briggs most certainly shared O'Reilly's sense that this client of the Firm deserved to be treated with the utmost dignity and respect. Yes, he had gotten the memo alright, O'Reilly concluded, and now Briggs more than likely wanted to discuss it tonight over a glass of vintage Chardonnay. And *that's* why Briggs was "looking forward" to the event in the C. Barton Foster Conference Room, and *that's* why he had written the personal note to O'Reilly and no one else. How else to explain it?

And so O'Reilly decided upon a plan.

Tonight he would march purposefully into the C. Barton Foster Conference Room and he'd corner Briggs. As soon as he saw an opening he would get right to the memo. From there, who knew what could happen. Perhaps Briggs would arrange a meeting with U.S. immigration officials. Maybe O'Reilly would be next to Briggs at the press conference following their inevitable victory in federal court. The possibilities were endless.

His intercom buzzer sounded, and O'Reilly slapped the speakerphone button.

"Yes Sondra," he said to his secretary, or "Administrative Assistant" as she reminded him more than once.

"Hey, I'm goin' to lunch now. That, uh, copasetic with you?"

"Yes Sondra. That would be preferable."

Sondra hung up without another word.

Preferable – he loved that one. He had settled on that word and was now using it whenever Sondra called about lunch.

And right now, O'Reilly had some lunch plans of his own. Earlier that day he had received an e-vite to any Midtown restaurant – to be selected by the invited Summers – from a senior associate named Roger Barnette, who had copied it to another lawyer named Tracy Berkowitz. O'Reilly was relieved, because the number of lunch invitations you received was constantly the talk among the Summers. The lawyers at the Firm arranged these meals in order to get to know them all, and the last thing you wanted was to be seen sitting alone in your office during the lunch hour while the other Summers were out being wined and dined.

O'Reilly dialed another Summer named Chase Wadsworth, a

law student from Yale who wore bowties and spoke like the Kennedys, which O'Reilly though was a bit strange.

"Chase – you see the e-vite from Barnette?"

"We just read it, Seamus."

"I'm thinking Thai," said O'Reilly, "that place in Soho."

"Oh God, not Thai," moaned Wadsworth. "What about Ethiopian?"

Ethiopian ...

Gun to the head, O'Reilly would tell you what he really wanted was a cheeseburger. With good old-fashioned, rubbery, yellow American cheese that comes in those plastic peel-off wrappers. And a plate full of greasy fries and a bottle of squeeze ketchup. He offered up Thai but that was only because if you suggested cheeseburgers around this place they would recoil in horror, like that movie scene when they peel back the curtain to reveal The Elephant Man. Plus, O'Reilly had a vague understanding that people starved in Ethiopia. He wasn't even sure he could find it on a map, never mind tell you what those people ate.

"We know a great place on the West side. Any objections?"

WE know a great place – that was another curious little idiosyncrasy about Wadsworth. The guy had a funny habit of constantly speaking on behalf of a group – everything was "we" this and "we" that, when in fact he was only referring to himself. Who the hell talks like that, O'Reilly wanted to know. If he ever tried to pull that crap in his neighborhood, they would beat him over the head with a manhole cover.

"No objections," relented O'Reilly. "By the way, you busy with any assignments these days?"

And that was another thing. O'Reilly was upset with himself for even asking that question. All anyone around this place ever talked about was how busy they were and how great the "feedback" was – a tiring verbal competition among the Summers that completely drained him. O'Reilly was hoping it was all bullshit, because as far as feedback was concerned, O'Reilly wasn't getting any. Plus, how can everyone be so busy and getting all this feedback with a daily routine of three-hour lunches? It was beyond him.

"Oh my God," Wadsworth answered, predictably, "we're getting killed. But the feedback has been sensational. You?"

O'Reilly was just as guilty. Before he answered, he scanned his desk and saw only the Briggs note and a copy of the Tibetan monk memo sitting next to that day's *New York Post,* folded open to Page Six. There was a blurb in there about Kim Kardashian and her prodigious rump, and O'Reilly couldn't wait to read it; he was saving it for after lunch.

He was embarrassed to give his answer, but he did it anyway.

"Busy as hell, Chase," O'Reilly fibbed. "Getting killed here. But unbelievable feedback though. Ridiculous, stupid feedback –"

"Right," said Wadsworth. "We'll see you in the lobby at 12:30."

"And WE will be there," O'Reilly answered.

O'Reilly hung up the phone and hunted his desktop for his brand-new pair of Warby Parker eyeglasses with the thick black frames that made him look like a hip Clark Kent. They coordinated perfectly with the eyeball-shaped frames worn by all the women around this place, which O'Reilly thought made them look like the evil villainess Catwoman from the 1960s Batman TV show he and his brother Tom liked to watch on Netflix. O'Reilly slipped them on his head now, adjusting them behind the ears. They were a perfect fit.

He then glanced at his watch – 12:21 pm.

Great, he thought, perfect timing. We'll be back from lunch by 3:30, which gives me plenty of time to change into my killer tuxedo.

For J. Hartwell Briggs and the wine-tasting event. The C. Barton Foster Conference Room. And the Tibetan monk memo.

It was all happening, just as he had planned. He grabbed the Briggs note again and smiled. *You mofos want to talk about feedback?* he thought. Just wait 'til tonight. This will be a great day.

And maybe with a stroke of luck the Ethiopians serve cheesecake.

Seamus P. O'Reilly, attorney-at-law.

He buttoned his suit jacket and was out the door.

CHAPTER 10

DUDE, WHY US?

THE BREWERS DECIDED to hold Charlotte's birthday party at their home, located in a section of Ketchogue called Starboard Estates. While Danny and Debbie's two-bedroom cape was jammed in on West 17th Street, over in Ketchogue's "West Side," the Starboard Estates community sat further east and north of Route 25A. The West Side's grid of streets and avenues were filled with capes, post-war ranches and split-levels on postage-stamp properties; Starboard Estates, on the other hand, was a private, gated neighborhood with seven shingled beach-style mansions on two and a half-acre plots. You needed a couple of bucks to live at the Starboard. The Brewers' home was at the end of the tree-lined cul-de-sac, their backyard flowing into the Long Island Sound.

Danny and Gianna were in the F-350 and rumbled up to the Starboard Estates security booth at about two o'clock on a Thursday afternoon. Danny's plan was to drop Gianna off and then meet up with Carlos, Arturo and Miguel at a job site before heading over to the hospital. Gianna wore a white knee-length dress with a pattern of blue and yellow flowers, along with a white bow in her hair. She had a birthday present, wrapped in pink paper, resting on her lap as Danny lowered his window at the security gate. There was a man there, smiling away, dressed in a security uniform that made him look like he was captaining a yacht. He wore a white sailor's hat over a navy-blue outfit – shorts, knee-high nylon socks, and a short-sleeved buttoned shirt with silver anchors on his sleeves.

"Good afternoon, welcome aboard!" the guard chirped, sliding open a glass door. "How can we help you today?"

"Hi, Danny and Gianna Beers," Danny answered, stifling a laugh. "We're here for a birthday party at the Brewers."

The man then checked their names on a clipboard and sent them through with a salute and a brief set of directions.

Danny and Gianna weaved their way past the estate homes,

with their rolling manicured lawns and sprinkler systems, until they reached the end of the cul-de-sac. The Brewers' long winding driveway was lined with faded bluestone pavers, accented with a long row of yellow begonia plants that shined brightly against the plush green front lawn. Danny slowed the pickup and snaked his way up to Dodge and Cindy's five-bedroom mansion. Up near the front entrance there was a circular driveway centered with thick yellow forsythia bushes, and on the porch steps there were two large ceramic planters overflowing with purple impatiens flowers. Tied to each planter, and soaring into the air about fifteen feet, were a half dozen helium-filled birthday balloons, pink and white, each one as big as a medicine ball.

Right now the circular driveway was filled with about a half-dozen SUVs, and Danny pulled the F-350 behind one of them. He and Gianna stepped out of the truck and a dapper young man, no older than twenty, approached them dressed in blue shorts and a white golf shirt. He smiled and said his name was Max, and he asked Danny if he could he valet the truck for him. Danny told him no, he was just dropping his daughter off and he'd be out in a minute.

Danny and Gianna walked into the Brewers' massive foyer and immediately came upon Dodge and Cindy. Dodge was clad in khaki slacks and a white button-down, and Cindy was in a coordinating pair of tan capris with a white polo shirt. They stood with their arms around each other, smiling, greeting the guests as they arrived. Danny could hear the bustle of a group of twelve-year-old girls somewhere behind them.

"Hey guys!" said Cindy as they entered. "Welcome, welcome, welcome! Come on in!" She stepped forward toward Gianna.

"Gianna, how are you?!" she asked, giving her a hug. "Thank you *sooo* much for coming. Charlotte is so excited you're here!"

"Me too," Gianna smiled.

"Can I take that for you?"

Cindy pointed to the present Gianna brought – a pair of shorts that Gianna picked out herself at an Abercrombie store in a neighboring town. Danny had no idea if the gift was appropriate, but he decided to go with Gianna's instincts on this one.

"Sure," Gianna responded, "it's a birthday present."

"Oh, you're such a doll!" Cindy chuckled.

Cindy took the present and placed it onto a large pile of boxes and cards on a nearby table. Gianna was beaming now, and Danny's heart warmed. She really needed an outing like this, and the Brewers were helping to get the day off to a good start.

As Cindy and Gianna walked over to the gift table, Danny took a glance around the foyer of the Brewers' home. Danny assessed it was as big as the entire first floor of his house. The floor was a gleaming white and black mosaic of Spanish ceramic tiles, the walls filled to the twenty-four-foot ceiling with custom wainscoting. On the left there was a sweeping staircase, at least eight feet wide, which curved about forty-five degrees to the second floor, where an open landing led to the bedrooms. A huge glass chandelier hung over the four of them. Behind Dodge there was a massive archway wrapped in thick molding, through which Danny could see the waters of the Sound in the distance. There were also several people in black pants and white shirts scurrying back and forth with trays and other party items; from a quick count there appeared to be a staff of at least eight workers.

Cindy grabbed Danny's forearm.

"I'll bring her in and get her settled," she said, "be right back."

"Sure, thanks Cindy."

"Would you like something to drink, Dan?"

"No, thanks, I actually gotta run."

Gianna turned over her shoulder and waved to her father as the two were walking through the archway. Danny blew her a kiss and told her "see you in a little while," and then she was around the corner and gone. When it was just the two of them, Dodge stepped forward to Danny, reaching into his back pocket.

"Hey dude, a little housekeeping," he said abruptly, pulling out a document that had print on both sides.

"Need your John Hancock, dude," Dodge explained. "We sent this by email to everyone, but I guess maybe you didn't get it."

Danny took the paper and glanced at it. Without his reading glasses it was difficult to make out the fine print, but after his eyes adjusted, he could clearly see the header that read "MUSICAL CHAIRS WAIVER." There were a few paragraphs that began with the word "Whereas," and as Danny was mumbling the words in his head, speed-reading them and holding the document further from his face so that he could see it, his eyes went further down to the bottom, where he was able to focus on one particular paragraph: *"I CERTIFY THAT I HAVE READ THIS RELEASE OF LIABILITY AND I SIGN IT OF MY OWN FREE WILL."*

Danny stared at the document, confused, as Dodge was holding a pen out toward him.

"I'm sorry," Danny said, "this is a little tough to read without my glasses, but … is this … is this a release form?"

"It is, yes."

"And, I'm sorry, what's this for?"

"Aw, dude, yeah, so the kids are playing musical chairs today. That was in the email. But like I said, looks like you didn't get it. Anyway, the form is pretty standard, you know, from the lawyers. They insist on it. It's also required for the homeowner's policy. This way everything's transparent in terms of the legal issues and whatnot. And everyone's protected."

"I see … but … this is for musical chairs?"

"Aw yeah, dude, absolutely."

"Right," Danny said, looking back down at the document. Dodge was still holding the pen out toward him. The front door swung open and a woman hustled in holding the hand of another partygoer. The kid broke free, plunked her present down onto the pile, and made a beeline straight through the archway.

"Hey Bev!" Dodge said to the woman, leaning in for a cheek kiss, "how are you, okay?"

"Great. Five o'clock pickup, right?"

Bev was rummaging through her handbag.

"Yep, five o'clock," Dodge confirmed.

"Here you go," she said, handing over a signed version of the Musical Chairs Waiver.

"Great," Dodge said, eyeballing the document. "Thanks, Bev."

Dodge then waved the document at Danny before placing it on a pile in the corner of the table that held the gifts.

"Hey, I gotta run," Bev said, "see you at five."

When she was out the door, Dodge strolled over and stabbed the pen at Danny again.

"See dude, like I said, it's pretty standard stuff."

This whole thing once again reminded Danny how

disconnected he was to the world that Debbie had lived in, where there were school events, birthday parties, sports practices, games, play-dates, after-school activities, and a whole host of other functions that required extensive interaction with parents, kids, school officials, coaches, and countless other people. He simply didn't know the rules or how any of this worked. He couldn't remember Debbie ever saying anything about having to sign a piece of paper to attend a birthday party, but then again, why would she? She oversaw that part of their life and he wasn't involved. But he clearly had a lot to learn. He wanted to say something to Dodge, point out the absurdity of the whole thing, but instead he tried to remind himself that the smile he saw on Gianna's face a moment ago was all that mattered.

He grabbed the pen from Dodge.

"Right here?" he asked, pointing to the form.

"You got it, dude."

Danny signed the form, handed it to Dodge, and headed back out the door to the F350.

MEANWHILE, ON THE other side of the house, Gianna was having a blast in the Brewer's backyard. She spent the afternoon running around with the girls, smiling and laughing, and playing in and among the various activity stations that Dodge and Cindy had set up back there.

As you walked into the backyard through the massive French doors of the Brewer's Great Room, and down the stairs on the north end of the infinity pool, there was a large red Bouncy Hut, powered by a generator, stationed out on the grass on the west side. Currently four or five girls were jumping around in there. Past that there was a face-painting station and another generator-powered rubber slide about ten-feet high. On the east side there was a table where the girls could get their hair braided or corn-rowed, and closer to the infinity pool there was a section roped off for pony rides. There was a different party person – all adults – hired to run each of the stations, and in the middle of the grass there were three clowns on 10-foot stilts juggling red balls. Dodge and Cindy also had Taylor Swift songs blasting out of rock speakers situated within the pool landscaping.

Dodge spent his time that afternoon playing with Charlotte and the kids, walking from station to station out in the backyard. Gianna took part in each of the activities with all the girls. Later they danced to Taylor Swift in front of the pool house at an open area near the outdoor fireplace and kitchen. Then they played musical chairs, with Dodge laughing and controlling the tunes. As the afternoon wore on Gianna was so preoccupied with the girls, the stations and the music that she gave no thought to Agnes, a result that Danny was hoping would occur.

As the five o'clock pick-up time approached, Cindy was sitting inside the house at an island in the kitchen. She was there with two other Moms, each cross-legged on a stool in front of a glass of Robert Mondavi Chardonnay. In front of them was a platter filled with a ring of crackers and a thick wedge of creamy Brie de Melun.

"I started two weeks ago," Cindy said, her fingers rolling the stem of her wine glass. "I'm part-time, three days a week."

She snapped a cracker and pinched a small dollop of brie.

"It's really going well so far, I'm just so excited about it."

"Well, I don't know what to say except congratulations," said one of the ladies, a woman named Miranda. "That is just great — good for you!"

"Cin, fantastic," offered the second woman, Nancy. "Really happy for you. Here, let's toast to that!"

The ladies clinked their wine glasses.

"Thank you, guys," Cindy told them with a smile. "It's not like we need the money, obviously, but this is just a great way for me to get back into the working world, now that the kids are in school."

"Oh absolutely," Nancy said.

"Right?" Cindy agreed, "especially since it's just three days."

"So what do you do?" asked Miranda, taking a sip of wine.

"Well, okay, so my title is Assistant Director of Diversity and Inclusion. We call ourselves the D&I group."

"And you're with a company?"

"It's a law firm actually. In midtown. Kramer, Kelly, Burgess, Barry and Roth. They do bond work for Dodge's company, that's how I heard about the opening. Do you guys know them?"

The two women nodded no, but still maintained a polite smile. Cindy lifted the Mondavi bottle and topped off all the wine goblets.

"So anyway, ladies, that's my news, that's my story! Just so glad I can share it with you guys," she giggled. Then she asked, "But what is new with you guys? C'mon, you have to fill me in here, I feel like I've been hogging the conversation!"

Cindy brought her wine glass to her lips, but before she could take a sip, a tremendous crashing sound came from the area of the archway and the foyer, causing the three ladies to jerk their shoulders upwards. It sounded like glass shattering, and the women simultaneously placed their wine glasses on the island and stood.

"What was *that?*" Cindy said, and she was on the move toward the foyer. Miranda and Nancy followed. As they walked, Cindy could hear voices coming from just past the archway. At first, she thought they were just part of the ambient noise emanating from the partygoers, but then as she neared the archway, she heard someone yelling.

"Ma'am, you can't come in here!" a male voice hollered.

When Cindy entered the foyer, she came upon one of the workers kneeling over a spread of broken lunch plates. There were shards of ceramic chunks littered all over the foyer's tile floor. She also saw Max, the young valet in the golf shirt. He was standing next to a third person; someone Cindy didn't recognize. It was a heavy-set woman, about forty, with a short-cropped bob of rust-colored hair. She was dressed head to toe in a light blue Adidas sweat suit and had two large envelopes tucked under her right arm. Cindy could also see that the front door was ajar.

"I'm sorry, Mrs. Brewer, I told her she couldn't come in, but she marched right past me," Max told her, nodding to the woman. "And she just knocked HIM over!"

Max gestured toward the worker, who was picking up the larger pieces of the broken ceramic plates with his index finger and thumb.

"No, no, don't do that," Cindy instructed, "you'll cut your hands. Let's get a broom."

"Sorry about that, didn't see him," the woman said flippantly, extending a hand down toward the worker. "That's my bad."

Cindy turned abruptly toward the woman.

"I'm sorry, can I help you with something?" she asked.

"Hope so. You Cindy Brewer?"

"Yes, and who are you exactly?"

"Not really important," the woman said.

She pulled out one of the envelopes and handed it to Cindy.

"This is for you."

"What is this?" Cindy asked.

Cindy looked at the face of the thin manila envelope and saw the words "**Private and Confidential**" in large bolded letters. There was no return address. She assumed it had something to do with Dodge's business, and so she tapped Max on his back.

"Please go out back and get Mr. Brewer," she said.

But Dodge suddenly appeared behind them. He was standing just past the archway with Charlotte, Gianna and about fourteen other kids. The girls all had their hair in tight, fresh cornrows, and several of them, including Gianna, were wearing orange and black face paint with stripes that made them look like tigers. All of them were holding ice cream cones with rainbow sprinkles, delights that Dodge had just scooped for them at a station near the pool house.

Dodge sensed the tension in the room, and he walked over to Cindy. "What's going on babe?" he asked his wife.

The woman then stepped toward Dodge.

"You Dodge Brewer?" she asked, and at that precise moment, Danny entered the open front doorway, accompanied by three other women – parents who like Danny were arriving for the five o'clock pickup. Danny stepped inside first, and Dodge greeted him.

"Hey dude," he said, distracted.

"Hey everyone," Danny responded, "it's five, right?"

"Yeah," said Dodge, "be with you guys in a minute."

Dodge turned to the woman in the sweat suit.

"I'm Dodge Brewer," he said. "I'm sorry, who are you?"

"A person you're never going to see again, so don't sweat the name," she said, offering the second envelope.

"Dodge Brewer, this is for you," she said loudly, making sure everyone in the foyer heard it. The woman then formed both her index fingers into gun pistols. She fired the imaginary weapons, one each at Dodge and Cindy.

"Bang … bang," she said. "Dodge and Cindy Brewer – you've been served."

She then wheeled around and marched right past Danny and out the front door to the Brewer's home. Justin followed her out, and as he walked through the threshold, three other parents entered for pickup time.

"Hey everyone," one of them said.

The girls had moved against the wall near the table of presents in order to avoid stepping on the ceramic shards. They were standing with their ice cream cones and animal faces and cornrows, smiling away. The parents who had witnessed the bizarre scene with the woman in the sweat suit, including Danny, were mumbling to one another as Cindy tried to make light of the situation.

"Well, that was odd!" she exclaimed with a smile.

Dodge peeled off into a corner and ripped open his envelope. Cindy turned her back to the parents and looked at Dodge.

"What is it?" she asked in a lowered voice.

Then she faced the parents again and told them to watch where they were stepping. She waved over another worker, who carried a broom and a dustpan.

"Sorry, everyone," Cindy said to a few parents who had just arrived, "we just had a little accident here."

Dodge pulled out a thin document from the torn envelope. He held it in front of him and began to read.

And his eyes ran down the page, his expression morphed slowly from a matter-of-fact business-like gaze, then to mild curiosity, and then to one of deep concern, his eyebrows crossed.

"What the …," he finally muttered, just audible enough for everyone in the foyer to hear. Then he looked directly at Danny.

"Dude, you *sued* us?! Over Agnes?"

Dodge handed the document to Cindy, shaking his head. Cindy's eyes glanced over the page, and her eyes popped open.

She shot a look over at Danny.

"Dan, is this … a lawsuit?"

"Dude, I'm shocked," Dodge said.

Danny stood there frozen, his back against the foyer wall. Every pair of eyes in the room was on him. The place was uncomfortably silent, except for the clinking and scraping sound of the ceramic shards being brushed over the Spanish tile floor. Danny felt his chest tightening, wondering what the hell Dodge was talking about.

He looked across the room for Gianna. When their eyes met, Danny's heart nearly stopped. It was difficult to tell through the tiger face, but Danny could sense Gianna's terror. He couldn't believe what was transpiring here. The truth was that Danny had no idea if he had sued the Brewers, but the realization that he may have done so, and that proof of that fact was right there in Cindy Brewer's hands, was suddenly very apparent. How had this detail eluded him in his conversations with the attorney Anzalone? He had no clue what to say or how to respond, and so he stood there motionless, unable to speak.

"Dude, why us?" Dodge finally asked. His tone was soft, almost defeated, but Cindy was not nearly as diplomatic.

"You sued us for *50 million dollars*?" she yelled, gesturing to the document. "Dan, I don't even know what to say!"

A few parents gasped. And then Charlotte Brewer, standing next to Gianna, suddenly turned to her.

"You sued my *parents*?!" she yelled. "And you, like, *came* here?!"

One by one the girls started moving away from Gianna and gathering around Charlotte, until Gianna stood completely by herself. The parents also drifted away, moving toward Dodge and Cindy. Danny could see Gianna's bottom lip quivering and he realized he needed to get his daughter out of there. He would straighten all of this out with Anzalone, find out what the hell was going on, but he had to save poor Gianna, who was crying now. Danny darted across the foyer and grabbed the ice cream cone from his daughter's hand. He looked around for a place to put it down, until Cindy finally stepped forward.

"I'll take that for you," she said curtly.

Danny handed her the cone and grabbed his daughter's hand.

"I'll try to find out what's going on," he said to Dodge.

"Maybe it's best you leave," Cindy said.

Danny looked around the room and saw that all the other parents were staring lasers at him, some of them with their arms crossed. The girls, with their cornrows and ice cream cones, were wrapping their arms around Charlotte, silently fuming at Gianna.

"C'mon, let's go," Danny said to Gianna, who was shaking.

The two bolted out of the foyer and made a beeline to the F350.

CHAPTER 11

MR. SEA-MOUSE O'RALLY

THAT SAME AFTERNOON, Seamus P. O'Reilly, law student and FT&B Summer Associate, strolled merrily down Park Avenue under sunrays that were beaming down against the midtown skyscrapers. He was full to the gills with zilzil tibs, lamb key wat, gored gored with mitmita sauce, and several other delicious Ethiopian dishes that he, Wadsworth and his other lunch companions had ordered for the table and passed around family-style. O'Reilly washed it all down with several goblets of strawberry wine, which had now routed its way through his circulatory system and left him a tad bit light-headed, but happy.

Soon O'Reilly was pushing through the revolving doors of the massive three-story atrium lobby of FT&B Tower. He nodded to a few security guards in maroon coats, swiped his employee ID card through the security gates, and marched toward the elevator banks. Before he knew it, O'Reilly was back up on the 39th floor hallway, sauntering past rows of crystal vases filled with fresh-cut yellow tulips and perched atop the secretarial stations lining the interior of the corridors. He cruised into his spacious office, pushed his door closed, and then flung his jacket over the top of his leather hi-back office chair.

Then he stole a look at his watch – 3:51 pm.

Not bad, he thought – a three-hour lunch. Very respectable.

O'Reilly collapsed down onto his hi-back and scanned his desk. As things currently stood, O'Reilly didn't have a pending work assignment and should be placing a call to the summer assigning partner to let him know he had time on his hands. But that would only result in someone giving him a call, possibly with some emergency, and the last thing O'Reilly wanted was to be digging into Westlaw after four o'clock for some inane legal research work. Not when the C. Barton Foster Conference Room and J. Hartwell Briggs were awaiting him for an in-depth discussion of Tibetan monks and political asylum issues. No, that phone call, and any crapola related thereto, would have to wait.

In the meantime, O'Reilly had one more item to check off his to-do list, and he still had to eyeball the Tibetan monk memo as a refresher before changing into his brand-new ass-kicking tuxedo. So time was a-wastin'. The final item was a call to his brother Tom, which O'Reilly had been putting it off since he received the Briggs note. But now he would just have to bite the bullet. He poked his speakerphone button and dialed.

"81st Precinct, Sergeant O'Reilly," a voice answered.

"Tom, hey it's me, Jimmy."

O'Reilly pressed the phone against his left ear and inserted an index finger into the right one. He could barely hear Tom over the buzz of a busy police precinct.

"Oh, so now you're *Jimmy* again?" Tom snapped in a smartass tone. "I heard the bow-tied boys over there are calling you *Seamus.*"

"That is my name, right?"

"Yeah, well, better than Shit-For-Brains I guess. Anyway, what's up? We're clearin' homicides over here."

"Yes, well," O'Reilly stammered, "about the Yankee game – "

"Right, so here's the deal," Tom interrupted. "Meet me at Stan's Bar at six-thirty. Right across from the Stadium. I got the tickets so you should go right there, it'll be easy. And oh, if you're late again? I'm tellin' you right now, I'll taser your ass, I'm not fuckin' around."

"Well, that's what I was calling about," O'Reilly said, and then he heard a crashing noise.

"Goddamnit, hold on a second," said Tom, and the phone went silent. In a few moments he came back on the line, and O'Reilly could hear someone screaming in the background.

"8-1, O'Reilly."

"Tom, it's me."

"Hey Jimmy, I gotta go, man, some crazy broad's in here with her kid screamin' bloody murder. I'll see you at 6:30 – "

"Tom, hold up a sec," O'Reilly yelled, looking toward his door. He was hoping no one in the hallway could hear him.

"What? C'mon, what?"

"Tom, I can't make it tonight."

"What?"

"I'm sorry, something just came up here," O'Reilly said meekly.

"Jimmy, it's four o'clock, when were you gonna tell me?"

"I'm sorry, I didn't realize – "

"You didn't *realize?*"

"I'm sorry."

"What possibly just came up you didn't know about? I paid for the ticket, Jimmy, I don't even know if I can get rid of it now!"

"I know, but it's something I just have to be at tonight – "

"And you just found that out now?"

"Tom, I know," O'Reilly said, "I shoulda called you earlier ..."

"Jesus Christ," Tom moaned, "whatever, man."

"I'm sorry, but it's an important Firm function – "

"A *function?* I should punch you in the face just for saying *that.*"

"Tom – "

"Look bro', I gotta run."

"Tom I'll call you Friday night, okay?"

"Yeah, thanks for nothin' ... *Seamus.*"

O'Reilly flinched as his brother slammed down the phone, his shoulders thrusting upward. That was rough. The four or so goblets of strawberry wine from the Ethiopians eased that conversation a bit, but O'Reilly felt guilty as hell about it. With all the excitement when he got the Briggs note, and then the news about the wine-tasting ... function ... well, the whole thing had slipped his mind. Tom had a right to be angry but at the same time there was just no way to explain to him about important things like fine wine, functions, Tibetan monks, Ethiopians and feedback.

He would just have to put the whole matter out of his mind. He was about to embark on what could very well be the most important night of his short but successful legal career, and this was no time for distractions.

He grabbed the Tibetan monk memo and ran his eyes down the pages, looking at the case cites, the statutes, his analysis and the conclusion. He was comfortable with all of it, didn't need to read another word. He could discuss every issue cold. Even the name of the monk – *Mr. Dawa Jamyang* – which earlier had escaped him, was now burned into his memory.

He was ready.

Giddy with anticipation, O'Reilly slapped his hands together and checked his watch. Ten minutes after four. A little early, but there really was no reason to wait. He leapt to his feet and grabbed a large black garment bag that was hanging on the back of his door. He laid it down onto the floor behind his desk and pulled the zipper the full length of the bag – *zweeeeeep*. He then reached inside and unveiled his masterpiece – a black Stafford Essential tuxedo, only ninety-five bucks online from the JC Penney website. Then he reached under his desk for a small navy-blue gym bag. He opened it and dumped the contents onto his desk, taking inventory.

Black socks, check.

Fresh white t-shirt, check.

3-Pack of fresh new BVDs, check.

Great, he thought, it's all here. O'Reilly had decided that everything on his body was going to be brand spanking new tonight, and that if nothing else positive happened, he at least would be heading into this function feeling like a king. The tux was a perfect fit, and the new socks, underwear and t-shirt would make him feel spectacular. O'Reilly grabbed the gym bag and tux and headed for the door, intending to head down the hall to the Men's Room, but then suddenly he stopped …

Suddenly the thought of those tiny bathroom stalls entered his mind. He wondered how the hell anyone could change their clothes in such a tight confinement with the toilet jamming into your legs. Unless of course you stand outside the stall in the center of the bathroom, but that is always a little weird when someone you don't even know is standing at the urinal and there you are, changing your clothes. So no, you would have to change inside the stall, and with O'Reilly being – how do you put it – not exactly a small man, and with the possibility that his Stafford Essential could touch those dirty bathroom floors, well, the decision was actually easy.

In a heartbeat, O'Reilly decided he would get dressed right there in the privacy of his own office. This way, he said to himself, I'll come busting out looking like a million bucks. Then I'll cruise into the C. Barton Foster Conference Room and get some serious feedback – *you mofos want to talk about feedback?* – from none other than Mr. J. Hartwell Briggs.

O'Reilly dropped the gym bag and hooked the tux onto the back of his door. He walked to his back credenza and lowered the

Venetian blinds. He kicked off his shoes, and after a confirming look to the office door lock, began to get undressed. He pulled off the Joseph Abboud tie, unbuttoned the white cotton oxford, then stripped off the t-shirt. Topless, he stuffed the garments into the gym bag, and then he undid his belt buckle, dropping his suit pants to the floor. With a kick and a flip, he caught them in the air. Then he rolled them into a ball.

"LeBron, from three!" he said aloud, taking a jump shot and dumping the pants onto one of the twin Andover chairs facing his desk. Now, he thought, for my crisp new BVDs. He yanked his underwear to the floor, pulled them off and then jammed them into the corner of his gym bag … and that's when he heard them.

Footsteps.

Initially, he thought those feet were heading down the hall. Maybe they belonged to a firm messenger, or to a member of the cleaning staff. But then the noise grew louder. Suddenly O'Reilly heard a pair of wingtips plant themselves just outside the cherry-wood door to his office.

He braced himself, his eyes widening.

Oh shit – the door …

In a panic, O'Reilly glared at the door's gold-plated latch panel.

A vertical latch – that means it's locked, right?

He could hear someone grabbing the door handle –

OR IS HORIZONTAL LOCKED?!

O'Reilly saw the doorknob twisting – the gold latch moving – then he heard a "click" as the door was slowly moving inward …

Holy Jesus, Mary and JOSEPH! NOOOO!

And then O'Reilly, purely out of instinct, leapt from behind his desk and made a mad dash for the door, hoping to push it closed. But he knew it was hopeless. The immutable laws of physics – the science of bodies in motion – told O'Reilly there was no way he was getting to that door before it opened. Resigned, he stopped dead in his tracks. He was now caught in front of his desk, about four feet from the office door, facing directly out toward the hallway.

The door swung open and in walked Dexter C. Morgan, co-chairman of the Firm's corporate M&A group. The Summer Associate assigning partner. In front of him was Seamus P. O'Reilly, Summer Associate, motionless and facing the hallway, wearing nothing but two black polyester socks, a Timex wristwatch, and a pair of Clark Kents.

Morgan froze in place, struggling to comprehend. He was still holding the door handle.

With little else to do, O'Reilly made what he would later regard as one of his many poor decisions that day. Looking Morgan directly in the eyes, O'Reilly straightened up and stood at attention – belly sucked in, shoulders thrown back, feet together – and then he lifted two fingers to his forehead, giving Morgan a salute. Like a soldier in some sicko porn movie with a military theme, O'Reilly would later dread.

"Mr. O'Reilly!" stammered Morgan, "Jesus Christ!"

O'Reilly was speechless.

"You look, uh, BUSY!" Morgan yelled, his eyes focused on the office carpet. "I'll come back later."

He then turned and fled down the hallway. O'Reilly, meanwhile, had to say something. Anything. His eyes widened again, and then for some reason he thought of Wadsworth, and his sophisticated manner of speech, and he managed to blurt out, "Mr. Morgan! WE can explain!"

But Morgan was gone.

EXACTLY TWO HOURS later, up on the 39th floor, streams of glowing yellow rays from a baking August sun were bursting through the windows and angling in against the desktops. O'Reilly stood at the elevator bank adjusting the knot on a black silk bowtie, wiping a pool of sweat from his forehead. His armpits were dripping, and his face was now a deep maroon.

Clearly, O'Reilly thought, poking the "up" arrow button, Morgan's unexpected entrance was a setback. And that's just how he would have to think about it – it was a setback. Nothing more. But as much as he would try to convince himself that it was no big deal, he could not shake the sinking feeling of regret that was gnawing away at his abdomen right now. For the love of God, why the hell didn't he lock the office door? There was so much wrong with this scenario, so many potential pitfalls, that O'Reilly was losing count. The worst part was not that he had been seen standing there in his birthday suit with his funny business on full display, although even O'Reilly himself was cringing at the sight that poor Morgan had been forced to endure. His bulbous gut, the sagging man-breasts … good God, would he ever get in shape? But O'Reilly didn't care about that – what bothered him most was the sheer madness of it. A full Monty, and in his *office* no less. How? Why? There was really no way to explain it. And my God, what was with the *salute*? It was just an impulse, a reaction. But bizarre, he knew it. What could Morgan possibly be thinking?

Whatever it was, it wasn't good. The man had fled like he was running from a gunman. Man was this delicate.

O'Reilly's first impulse had been to dress and run to Morgan's office to explain. But then he hesitated, sitting and running the whole thing through his head, and before you knew it the window of opportunity had closed. The time had come to head upstairs to the C. Barton Foster Conference Room. So now it was too late. What should he do now? What?

The more he thought about it, the worse it got. O'Reilly's head was spinning. Morgan, would he tell anyone? Of course he would, that rat. He now imagined that everyone in the Firm would be talking behind his back tonight, in hushed circles, with their damn wine glasses, shifting their eyeballs to one another to silently indicate *"right there, he's the one."* The rumors were probably flying around the Firm right at this very minute.

Maybe he should go home. He could tell Briggs he got sick or something. Or that his grandmother died. Or maybe he could fake an aneurysm. Or maybe –

Christ, get a hold of yourself, he thought. Stay calm. Everything will be fine. Just head into the Boston C. Farter Conference Room, or whatever the hell it was called, and mingle. Slap on your Clark Kents and talk about things you know, things in your comfort zone. Like feedback. And Tibetan monks. And Ethiopian dishes, and –

Suddenly O'Reilly heard a *ping!* and the plastic arrow above the elevator bank lit up in glowing white. His heart began to thump again, and he nearly leapt out of his now flaming tuxedo. He couldn't believe how jumpy he was, how bad he was sweating. As the elevator doors opened, he drew a breath and stepped inside, his hands folded in front. He was staring down at the floor. He leaned over to punch the number 45 on the panel but he saw that it was already lit up. So he moved against the back wall, still with his chin lowered. He could feel the presence of another human being in the elevator, but he didn't dare look up.

My God, he thought, what if it was Morgan? Or one of Morgan's cronies over in M&A. He kept his eyes glued to his wingtips. Just as the doors closed, the man turned to O'Reilly.

"'Scuse me," he said. "Mighty fine tuxedo yew have there."

O'Reilly slowly turned his head.

"Yew headin' upstairs for some wine?" the man asked. "Goin' that way myself. The name is Hartwell Briggs."

O'Reilly looked up from his shoes and saw none other than J. Hartwell Briggs standing before him, with a big, yellow, toothy smile. He was extending a paw toward O'Reilly that was as big as a catcher's mitt. Physically speaking, Briggs was colossal. He had a gleaming, bald head the size of a bank safe, and he was wrapped in a tuxedo that O'Reilly figured could blanket the State of Wyoming. O'Reilly looked at him and noticed what appeared to be straw protruding from both nostrils. He stuck out his hand, and Briggs, who practically filled the elevator, gripped him to the elbow, pumping furiously.

"Mr. Briggs!" he stammered, his body quivering from the handshake.

And then O'Reilly couldn't contain his excitement. A huge grin swept across his face, and just like that all the images of his troublesome run-in with Morgan disappeared from his mind. Here was J. Hartwell Briggs, the legend, right here in this elevator, shaking his hand. Oh man how great was this? The firm had promised that all the Summers would at some point get to meet the great Briggs, but O'Reilly never thought his turn would come in an elevator. O'Reilly wasn't sure if his feet were even touching the ground.

"Really ... meet ... to glad you sir!" he stammered.

"Yes indeed."

"I mean meet ... to nice you!"

"Yes, same here son."

"I mean NICE TO MEET YOU!" O'Reilly corrected. "Really nice ... and meet ... to glad you, Mr. Briggs!"

"Yes sir," Briggs smiled, "nice to meet yew too."

Briggs forcibly extracted his hand from O'Reilly's grip. He

punched the "close" button on the elevator, and the doors drew in. O'Reilly laughed at himself for a second and made an introduction.

"The name is O'Reilly, sir," he said, beaming.

And then suddenly a light went on in Briggs's eyes.

"Oh sure!" he bellowed, slapping O'Reilly hard on the back.

"Yew must be Mr. Sea-Mouse O'Rally," Briggs said confidently. "I've heard mighty fine things about yew Sea-Mouse!"

O'Reilly stared back, confused. *Did he just say … Sea-Mouse?* He wasn't sure. It could have been the accent. But he did say it twice. Better to correct him.

"Actually sir," coughed O'Reilly, "it's pronounced *Shay-mis* – "

"I tell yew wut, Sea-Mouse," Briggs said, "yew gone really enjoy this little wine-tasting party tonight. We do this every year. Folks really look forward to it, sincerely. Myself included."

Briggs sank two thumbs into his cummerbund, while O'Reilly searched for words. *He just said it again – Sea-Mouse. Let's try this again.*

"Sir, actually, it's an Irish name and – "

"Personally, I don't go in for the wine, Sea-Mouse, I'm a Kentucky bourbon man," Briggs said, cutting him off. "Where I come from wine is for the lady-folk. I know that's not very politically correct these days, but yew catch my meanin', right Sea-Mouse? Yes sir, sure like to have me a nice tumbler filled wit' bourbon, but I ain't the one makin' the rules."

Briggs was laughing now, gesturing with his colossal hands. O'Reilly was staring at him with a look of terror, like he was viewing a horror movie. This couldn't be happening.

"How about it, Sea-Mouse? Yew drink wine?"

There was no mistaking it now. The man had just called him Sea-Mouse, for the sixth time in under a minute. *Sea-Mouse.* Like a mouse … in the ocean, he guessed. Did such a creature even exist? Oh, the humiliation. And O'Reilly understood what had happened, because it wasn't the first time someone had butchered that first name. It happens when you read it, O'Reilly knew, like when you see it written down, but you've never heard it spoken. But no one had ever said Sea-Mouse. Jesus Christ, Sea-Mouse.

Just then, an idea – the Tibetan monk memo. The reason you were looking forward to this event in the first place. Mr. Dawa Jamyang. Get to the memo, thought O'Reilly, which Briggs obviously loved, and get to it fast. And then segue from that to a correction of the first name. There was a *ping!* again, and the elevator opened on the 42nd Floor, but no one stepped in.

"Mr. Briggs," O'Reilly said confidently, with the doors opened, "I guess you and I need to discuss a very important topic tonight. Right sir?"

O'Reilly winked at him with a knowing smile. Like the two of them shared some sort of a secret. Briggs's facial expression changed, and he gave O'Reilly a curious stare.

"Oh yeah? What's that Sea-Mouse?"

The elevator doors then shut.

"Mr. Dawa Jamyang, sir," said O'Reilly. "And his legal status here in these great United States."

O'Reilly puffed his chest a bit. In his mind, he was fully prepared to knock out of the park any questions that Briggs might have about Mr. Jamyang and his important political asylum application. But then Briggs pointed his chin upward, trying to recall the name.

"Hmm, Mr. Jamyang ..."

He was rubbing his chin, and then he turned to O'Reilly.

"Our ambassador to South Korea?"

O'Reilly swallowed hard.

"No sir, Mr. Dawa Jamyang. From the memo?"

"What memo?"

"The memo I sent you sir, the one on – "

"Yew know what Sea-Mouse, now that I'm in private practice, I confess I sometimes don't follow our ambassadors and the important work they doin' on behalf of our blessed country – "

"No sir," O'Reilly said, interrupting him now, "no, no."

O'Reilly was panicked, and he was sweating again.

"Sir, Mr. Jamyang is a monk. He's a monk – from Tibet."

"A what?" Briggs responded quizzically, and then he actually starting giggling. "Did yew say a *monk?*"

O'Reilly just stared at him.

"Sorry, son, I ain't never heard a no *monk*," he said, this time with a big bellowing laugh. "'Magine that, a monk!"

Then, another *ping!* and the doors opened on the 45th floor.

"Well, here we are Sea-Mouse!" Briggs said, landing another

blow to O'Reilly's spine. "Whaddya say we have ourselves a few shots a wine?"

Briggs extended a hand out the elevator door.

"After yew, Mr. Sea-Mouse O'Rally!"

A MOMENT LATER, O'Reilly entered the C. Barton Foster Conference Room. The place was enormous, running the length of the west side of the building facing Park Avenue. It had a ceiling that vaulted up three floors, and windows on the south side that gave glorious views of midtown Manhattan, the Freedom Tower way downtown, and the eastern part of New Jersey near Newark. But O'Reilly presently had no taste for the views, or anything else for that matter.

The place was abuzz, packed with FT&B lawyers and Summers, and O'Reilly eased himself in among a sea of tuxedos and evening gowns, trying his best to be inconspicuous. The lights were set dimly to a cozy glow, and soft jazz music was playing somewhere from hidden speakers. The lawyers were all standing in circles holding sparkling yellow and crimson goblets, laughing, sipping and swirling behind their Clark Kents and Catwomans. It was a time for socializing and networking, a time to make yourself known, but O'Reilly wanted to be anywhere else but here. He could not remember the last time he felt so dejected, so insignificant. Briggs hadn't read the Tibetan monk memo after all. And he didn't even know O'Reilly's goddamn name. Based on Briggs's pronunciation, you'd think O'Reilly had been named after some freakish amphibian profiled on Animal Planet – something called a Sea-Mouse.

Well, why *should* Briggs know his name? thought O'Reilly. Who the hell was *Seamus P. O'Reilly* anyway? Just some nudist quack from Manhattan Law School, that's who. He *deserved* to be called Sea-Mouse. After all, wasn't it a *stupid* name? O'Reilly silently mouthed it with disgust – *Seamus*. Who in their right mind would name a red-blooded American kid Seamus? Ridiculous. His goddamn potato-eating, freckled-faced, red-nosed, Mick parents; couldn't they have named him – Ned? Gary? Wayne? Something normal at least. He would go to the county clerk's office and file for an official name change first thing in the morning.

O'Reilly took in the sight of all these high-powered lawyers from all these incredible law schools. Why was he even here? Why? What idiot had offered him this job? Most graduates from MLS went on to file dog bite cases or to comb ERs for herniated discs – they didn't land in places like FT&B. How the hell was he supposed to compete with the Harvards and Yales of the world after coming out of a legal nursery school like MLS? Yitzhak Schwartz is a babbling idiot.

O'Reilly moved to the center of the room and looked around to get his bearings. He jammed an index finger between his throat and bowtie, gasping for breath. He could not be more uncomfortable, he decided, if he was napping on a bed of nails.

Suddenly O'Reilly sensed he was standing completely alone, without a drink in his hands, so to avoid the social awkwardness he hunted the room for a conversation partner. Anyone would do. His eyes landed on a short man with a thick dark mustache carrying a tray of yellow wine goblets, dressed in a tuxedo very similar to O'Reilly's. He wore sneakers, had a white cloth draped over his arm, and a nametag that read "Roberto.".

Perfect, thought O'Reilly. *What I need is a good stiff belt.*

O'Reilly approached the man, smiled, and introduced himself.

"Hello Roberto," he said, pointing to the nametag. "I'm Seamu – uh – Jim. Jim O'Reilly. May I?" he asked, gesturing to the tray.

"*Si* sir," said Roberto in a thick accent. "Theez eaze a white burgundy, a 1996 Chevalier-Montrachet Bouchard Pere."

Yeah – blah, blah, blah, thought O'Reilly, swooping up the goblet. In a series of gulps, he downed its contents. Then he plunked the goblet down onto the tray and grabbed another. He gave it a few chugs, and O'Reilly could feel the booze swiftly entering his bloodstream, chasing the strawberry wine from the Ethiopians from several hours earlier.

"Roberto, you and me are going to be very good friends tonight," said O'Reilly, after another gulp from the goblet. "So where ya from?"

"*Mehico*, sir," said Roberto.

"*Mehico* – excellent."

"*Si*, sir," Roberto answered.

O'Reilly blew out a sigh of relief. The air conditioning in this airline hangar of a conference room was now bringing a hint of comfort. He killed the remainder of the goblet and wiped his chin.

"Well Roberto, let's drop the *sir* stuff. Call me Jim."

"*Si*, Mr. Jim, sir."

"Hey you know what?" O'Reilly then said, draping an arm over Roberto's shoulders. "I'm gonna ask you a favor."

O'Reilly wiggled his empty wine glass.

"If you see me with a dead soldier in my hand tonight, would you instantly replenish me with another beverage, Roberto? Would you do that?"

"*Si*, Mr. Jim, I will do that."

"Excellent," said O'Reilly.

He promptly high-fived Roberto and lowered his lips to the next wine goblet, giving it a wet, sloppy sip. In less than a minute it was gone.

And then over the next few hours, moving from tuxedo circle to tuxedo circle, O'Reilly murdered eight more goblets, and then nine, maybe ten and possibly more. Every time he got to the bottom of one, there was Roberto, delivering another. Before he knew it, O'Reilly could feel his armpits returning to milder temperatures. The river of sweat that had been running down his spine, soaking his tuxedo jacket, was now as dry as a cactus. The wine was beginning to burn a couple of maroon circles into his cheeks, but other than that, O'Reilly was feeling ... *gooood.* Suddenly the room was the perfect temperature, his tuxedo was comfy, and his shoes were as cozy and cushiony as bedroom slippers. His entire being was blanketed in an uninhibited feeling of euphoria.

There was a moment, halfway through the event, when O'Reilly realized he should have called it a night. But then at some point he passed that critical threshold from reason to non-reason, and before he knew it, there was no looking back. And the wine goblets kept coming. And then he was in a zone.

To hell and back with his brother Tom and his frickin' York New Yankees. And Morgan, that Non-Knocking Intruder. And Wadsworth with his bowties and Kennedy voice can go to H-E double toothpicks. And Briggs, the Ethiopians, JC Penney, Tibetan monks – screw 'em all.

It was now well past nine p.m., and with the room still jam-packed with tuxedos and evening gowns, and the buzz of conversation still thick, O'Reilly tipped his next goblet to no one in particular and buried it in one voluminous gulp.

A short while later, O'Reilly looked hazily to his right and noticed a familiar collection of tuxedos standing near the corner of the room. It was Wadsworth, along with a few of that day's lunch partners. And holy shit there was J. Hartwell Briggs. For the previous twenty minutes he had been walking up to tuxedo circles and just standing there, but then he would leave when the group would give him those funny stares – what was wrong with these friggin' people? And so when he saw Wadsworth and the rest of the crew they were like a buoy in an open sea, a life raft, and he decided to make his move.

"Bliggs, ya bashtard," he said aloud, "where ya been all night?"

With a saliva-soaked grin, O'Reilly wobbled his way over to Briggs's circle, his legs now silly putty. The march over to them and the image of what he must have looked like would be one of the horrifying memories that would survive the night and haunt him the next morning. Presently a single shirttail dangled below the front of his tuxedo jacket, and his Clark Kents sat askew on his nose. He was spilling some yellow wine onto the hardwood floor of the conference room, but he simply didn't notice.

As he approached the circle, he stayed hidden behind Briggs and his enormous bank safe head, but close enough so that he could make out the chatterings of the group. Then he thrusted himself into Wadsworth, pushing him forward. Briggs noticed the shove and turned to O'Reilly.

"Hey there Sea-Mouse," he said, "where ya been boy?"

O'Reilly's unsteady legs caught the attention of everyone in the circle. He wiped a backhand across his mouth.

"Does everybody here know Mr. Sea-Mouse O'Rally?" Briggs asked. But then Wadsworth gripped O'Reilly by the upper arm.

"Seamus!" he whispered, "we need to get you out of here *now!*"

But O'Reilly would have none of it. He waved Wadsworth off.

"What're you, what're you, what're … yoooou," he said, trying to form a question, and then he stumbled backwards. Wadsworth managed to grab him behind the waist so that he didn't keel over. O'Reilly regained his balance and gestured to Wadsworth.

"What exactly are yoooou … trying to inseminate … there

Wadsy-worth?" he garbled, and then he turned to face the group.

"Missa Biggs!" he said, knees buckling. "Missa – *hiccup* – Biggs."

O'Reilly had an index finger in the air now, and he turned and faced Wadsworth, leaning so close their noses were almost touching. Then he turned back to the group. He was wobbling back and forth while the entire circle fell into complete silence, their mouths agape in utter disbelief. Wadsworth was biting down on a fist to keep from laughing out loud, and then finally Briggs, noticing O'Reilly's condition, had had enough.

"Sea-Mouse," he said sternly, holding a crimson goblet, "perhaps it's time we call yew a taxicab. That okay wit' yew?"

"Abso-LUTELY," yelled O'Reilly, and after a moment of wobbling, his eyes scanned the group. Through his fog, he noticed everyone looking at their shoes. Briggs removed a handkerchief from his breast pocket and wiped his face. Because Seamus P. O'Reilly, Summer Associate, recalling the blow that Briggs had delivered to his back when meeting him in the elevator, had just returned the favor, emphasizing the word "Absolutely" with a gargantuan wallop to the back of Briggs's neck, which in turn triggered a ferocious jolt of the crimson goblet he was holding. Red wine was now dripping down Briggs's face, as well as Wadsworth's Clark Kents, and the pleated tuxedo shirts of three other lawyers.

Pathetically, O'Reilly didn't recognize this, and he continued.

"Hello, McFly? Anyone home? Why's everyone so quiet?"

O'Reilly suddenly became aware of the pained expressions on the faces of his colleagues, and the realization of what had just transpired hit him like a cannonball. The color drained from his face and his sweat glands exploded. Everything he worked for, all the late nights, the sacrifices –

My God what have I done?

He brought both hands to his open mouth and began to shake. He could feel what little remained of his Ethiopian lunch begin to rise in his esophagus, and in a state of sheer panic, with cold sweats creeping up his arms, O'Reilly decided he needed to get the hell out of there. He turned, wide-eyed, and searched the room for the one friendly face he could count on – "ROBERTOOOOO!" he shrieked, and with that O'Reilly bolted toward Roberto, who was standing about ten yards away. His back was to O'Reilly, holding a fresh platter of yellow goblets slightly to the right of the entrance to the conference room.

As he ran, O'Reilly lost his footing and stumbled forward, his heels snapping upwards. Briggs called out, "Sea-Mouse, yew get back here boy!" but O'Reilly couldn't stop.

Just as Roberto turned in recognition of the voice belonging to his new friend, O'Reilly pitched forward and hit Roberto full speed, ramming his shoulders into Roberto's midsection while wrapping both arms around his waist.

Roberto and O'Reilly hit the floor.

Upon impact, the wine tray flipped into the air, scattering the goblets like bowling pins. They crashed down and sprayed glass shards and wine all over O'Reilly, Roberto, and the beautiful hardwood floor of the C. Barton Foster Conference Room.

CHAPTER 12

EVERYTHING THAT IS
WRONG WITH THIS COUNTRY

VERY LATE ON a Friday afternoon, Anzalone received a few missed calls and a voicemail from her client Dan Beers. The man was irate. He was demanding to speak to her immediately. She didn't see the calls or listen to the message until the next morning, Saturday, and she dialed him back from her kitchen with a knot in her stomach. Justin was sitting at the table making a disaster out of a bowl of Fruit Loops as she punched in her client's cell number. When they finally connected, Danny was still in a panic, screaming at her through choppy bursts of breath.

"Ms. Anzalone, I had no idea we were suing the Brewers!"

"Mr. Beers – "

"Jesus Christ, these people were friends with MY WIFE!"

"Mr. Beers, hold on a second – "

"Why the hell would we sue *them*?!"

"Let me explain – "

"We gotta drop this case, Ms. Anzalone!"

"Mr. Beers, just relax a second, okay? Please – "

Danny asked her to hold, and he began taking gargantuan gasps of oxygen while coughing uncontrollably. Anzalone heard him choke out, "I'm gonna have a heart attack," and then Danny finally put the phone back to the side of his head.

"Ms. Anzalone, we were at the Brewers yesterday," he managed. "For a birthday party. And some process server walked in and handed them the lawsuit while me and my daughter were RIGHT THERE! With parents and kids looking at us like we were a bunch of lowlife scumbags. It was fucking humiliating for Gianna! She's been crying all night!"

"Mr. Beers, I'm really sorry, but – "

"So you gotta tell me, who else did we sue? I gotta know."

"Listen," Anzalone responded, finally getting his attention, "you're obviously upset. Can we meet over at my office?"

Danny agreed.

He drove over in the F350 and screeched into a spot in front of the donut shop. He jammed the transmission into Park and bounded up the stairs. In a few minutes the two were settled into Anzalone's office, Danny pacing while Anzalone sat in her leather swivel chair. Danny turned down an offer for coffee and got right to the point. He just wanted answers.

Anzalone tried to explain, but she thought the easiest way to go through this was to show him a copy of the complaint that she had filed in court. She excused herself and went out to a metal file cabinet near Cassie's desk and pulled a copy that had an electronic file-stamp, along with her signature. She went to the copier and stuffed it into the top feeder. When the machine spat a copy out, Anzalone handed it to Danny.

"Let's just go through it one defendant at a time," she said.

Danny sank into an office chair and stared at the caption on the first page of the complaint:

```
SUPREME COURT OF THE STATE OF NEW YORK
COUNTY OF THE BRONX
_____

DANIEL X. BEERS, AS PARENT AND GUARDIAN
OF THE INFANT AGNES BEERS, AND AGNES
BEERS, INDIVIDUALLY,

PLAINTIFFS,

V.

THE GUNTHER HOME PRODUCTS CORPORATION,
THE KETCHOGUE SPORTS AND RECREATION
COMMITTEE, REGINA WARTHAM, BRUCE DIXON,
MOSHE WAGSHUL, THE TOWNSHIP OF KETCHOGUE,
PETER BRISCOE, SHOP-RITE USA INC., DODGE
R. BREWER, AND CYNTHIA L. BREWER,

DEFENDANTS.
_____
```

Well there it was. Danny read it and it took his breath away. All told, in addition to the Gunther company and Shop-Rite – and who gave a shit about them? – Danny had sued six of his neighbors. His *neighbors*, right there in Ketchogue. He had also sued the town and the Rec Committee, along with its three chairpersons – Regina

Wartham, Bruce Dixon and Moshe Wagshul. They all lived in Ketchogue and were volunteers; they had kids at the Ketchogue elementary school.

Danny couldn't believe it.

The fact that he knew some of these people was mortifying. Like Regina Wartham for example. Danny knew her to say hello and she knew Debbie well. She had been to both the wake and the funeral and had even dropped off a huge basket of breakfast muffins, bagels, and ground gourmet coffees about a week after the burial. He had never gotten around to writing thank-yous to a lot of people, Regina included, and now here he was sticking a 50-million-dollar lawsuit up her ass. There was no way her family could deal with a legal matter like this – she was a special education teacher in Manhasset, a few towns over. She worked with autistic kids if he remembered correctly. She didn't have fifty million dollars. Probably didn't have a thousand dollars.

And then there was Bruce Dixon. Bruce was an electrician with a monster bubble-gut who looked like he had swallowed a keg of Budweiser. He walked around in a pair of ball-hugging bicycle shorts he had no business wearing, knee-high tube socks, and a "Dixon Electric" baseball hat, whenever he wasn't donning items from the Trump campaign. Most people thought he was an unrelenting hardass who had elbowed his way onto the Rec Committee just so that he could run every little kid's sport with the intensity of the NFL playoffs. But he had thrown a few jobs Danny's way and so Danny had no problem tolerating the man, although he could forget about any more referrals now, that was for sure. Plus, a guy like that, who knew everyone, could make your life miserable in a small town like Ketchogue.

Danny didn't know Moshe Wagshul at all, but he most certainly was a volunteer like the rest of them.

And then there was Pete Briscoe, Agnes's coach. My God, that one really hurt. Danny didn't know what he possibly was going to say to him the next time he saw him. He was friendly with Pete and had even played on the same men's softball team with him. Danny had installed the deck on the back of Pete's house, the two of them devouring a six-pack of Heineken on it the day it was finished. About six months before Debbie passed, they went out for burgers and beers with the Briscoes on a Friday night. Their daughter Chelsea was the one braiding Agnes's hair that day at Turnberry, just before snack time. These people were friends for God's sake, not foes. How could he *sue them*? How?

Danny next wondered if he had run into any of these people since they got this complaint thing, and if so, whether in his oblivion he had unintentionally smiled and waved at them as if he were sticking it in their faces. He couldn't be certain. Regardless, there was no way he could ever face them again, no matter what the outcome. He couldn't imagine what they must now be thinking. About him, Gianna, Agnes.

Danny tossed the complaint down onto Anzalone's desk.

"I don't know what to say." He ran both hands through his hair. "I can't tell you how bad this is for us."

"I understand Mr. Beers, so let me explain if I can."

"Okay," Danny told her, "but first I just wanna say something here. I appreciate what you're doing for us, I really do, and I apologize about all the yelling. But I got into this thinking we were trying to pull some cash out of some huge company that would never even notice it was missing. The Gunther company. To help me pay the medical bills. That's what I thought. I didn't know about Shop-Rite, but they don't really matter."

Danny shifted in his seat.

"I was not aware we were going after people in Ketchogue. Friends, neighbors. People I see in town. People my daughters hang out with. Who I do work for sometimes. So it's very embarrassing for me and my family. Plus, how are they even responsible? Pete Briscoe was just the Coach. The guy signed up so he could spend some time with his daughter. And the Rec Committee? None of those people were even there."

"Mr. Beers, before we even get to those questions, let me just clear up one thing between me and you. Is that okay?"

"Yeah, what's that," Danny stated. It wasn't even a question. He just wanted her to start explaining why she never told him he basically was trying to bankrupt the town. That this lawsuit would make him Ketchogue's Public Enemy Number One. His neighbors would now treat him like he had an infectious disease, you could put that in the bank.

"Well, first," Anzalone said, turning to her computer, "I am looking at an email I sent you about a week after we first met. The email attached a draft complaint and I said in the email that, assuming we go forward, this would be the complaint we would file. I asked you to read it and let me know if you had any changes. Do you remember that?"

Actually, he did remember that. Fearing Anzalone had emailed him, Danny had spent an hour trying to locate the computer's password. The thing was Debbie's and he never went near it. He tried asking Gianna, yelling from the kitchen up to her bedroom, but she just screamed back "no clue!" without even waiting for him to finish the question. He turned the house upside down and finally found the password written on an index card at the bottom of the kitchen junk drawer – Debbie had written "passwords" at the top and a few dozen were listed. He felt a pang of sadness when he saw her handwriting, but that was quickly overtaken by a mounting frustration when none of the passwords worked. He was typing and hitting "Enter," over and over again, and out of frustration he almost threw the monitor through the kitchen window.

When Danny finally discovered the right one for the computer, he next had to find the one that opened Debbie's Gmail account. He eventually got through to the inbox, he remembered, but there were about 437 new, bolded emails, and then about fifteen different pop-up boxes were flying all over the screen, obscuring his view of the Gmail account. He began x-ing out of all of them and then was so mentally exhausted from the whole exercise that when he finally located Anzalone's email he typed back "ok" without even reading the attachment, i.e., the complaint. Then he popped open a can of Coors Light and collapsed on the couch.

"And as you can see," Anzalone continued, turning her flatscreen so that Danny could see it, "you wrote back 'ok'."

"I see that. I remember that now."

"So when you came back and gave me authority to file, I assumed you understood the path we had chosen. And then after we filed, I sent you the final copy – the one we filed in court. Did you not see that?"

No, he didn't. Because Danny never looked. He was too busy shuttling back and forth to the hospital for Agnes, taking care of

Gianna, trying to keep Carlos, Arturo and Miguel gainfully employed, and dealing with a hundred other things. He had no time to log onto a computer to read some legal mumbo-jumbo he couldn't understand a fucksworth anyway. So no, he didn't read the damn thing.

Danny wiped both palms down the sides of his face.

"Ms. Anzalone, what's next? Where do we go from here?"

Anzalone took a breath herself.

"Look Mr. Beers, let me first assure you of something, okay? You have to understand there's likely an insurance policy for every defendant we sued. Here's how it works."

Danny listened intently.

"The Town assembles the Rec Committee, the Rec Committee hires the Coach, and the Coach assigns the snack mom. Dodge assisted Cindy Brewer and served Agnes the shrimp. So Agnes was at an official town function that day and all those people were agents or representatives of the town. There's bound to be insurance covering the town and every one of those people. We'll find that out for sure in discovery. But in order to increase our chances for a recovery, I want to be able to make claims on as many insurance policies as possible. And these policies will assign and pay for everyone to have lawyers, so all their legal bills will be paid. That's not even true for you. No one is paying me unless we win."

This made some sense. Danny was beginning to feel at ease a little. Not much, but a little. He said nothing, and Anzalone, sensing that she was making a connection, continued.

"And another thing is this – if we do win? All those people will be indemnified by the policies. That means that the insurance companies, not your neighbors, pay the damages that any jury might award us. In effect, we sued the insurance companies, not the individuals, you can think about it like that. We're not trying to bankrupt anyone. No one's trying to take anyone's home. I don't know if Gunther or Shop-Rite have policies, but those are corporations. They have the money to pay a judgment, believe me."

Danny felt a sense of calm wash over him.

"Maybe I can explain all this to the Brewers," he said.

"I wouldn't advise that," Anzalone responded. "We're in litigation now, and anything you say to them can be used against you. It's best if you simply don't speak to them about the case."

Danny nodded. All of this made sense. He recalled the first meeting he had with Anzalone, when she walked him through the reasons he had to file a lawsuit. He remembered how she laid things out in a way his simple mind could grasp. This little woman had a knack for making things easy to comprehend, that was for sure. And if he could describe it the way she just did it was something he could probably sell to anyone in town who asked him about it. Maybe he could even explain it to the Brewers, Pete, Regina, Bruce and Moshe, whoever he was. And as far as the cold shoulders and the criticism he'd likely be getting, he could endure all of it, just so long as it was directed at him and not his family. He could put up with it, take it all on for the sake of his girls. Nothing would shake his faith, his resolve, his commitment to making things right for Agnes.

But the one thing that Danny couldn't endure, what Anzalone couldn't undo, was the pain that Gianna currently was going through. That was a wound that would take a while to scar over. The look of terror on her face when all those parents and kids separated from her in the Brewer's foyer was brutal to see. She was utterly humiliated, at a time when she was most vulnerable. How could he subject her to something like that? The guilt was overwhelming. By the time they got home, with Gianna sobbing in the passenger seat of the F350, the orange and black face paint looked like a mudslide soaking down her cheeks. She ran to her room and slammed the door and wouldn't let him in.

Danny thanked Anzalone and descended to the street. He would head home now and try to explain things to Gianna, make her understand.

It was not going to be easy.

OVER THE NEXT few weeks, Danny and his family were shut out by the Ketchogue masses, ostracized in the manner that Danny expected. Gianna was barely communicating with him; he had no idea what was going on with her. He just knew she was sad all the time, and nothing more. When word got around that he had filed the lawsuit, and had sued people who lived in the town, a lot of people naturally developed mixed feelings about it. But if you took a poll, there'd be a majority anti-Danny. On the one hand they felt bad for Agnes, sure, but they mainly sympathized with the people sued. For most, the whole thing just didn't sit well.

And that sentiment only got worse after an article about the lawsuit appeared in The Ketchogue Patch in September. The next day the Associated Press picked it up and it ran online nationwide. One day Danny got a call from Will, who asked, "Jesus, did you see that article?"

Danny told him, "No, what are you talking about?"

Will said, "Log onto Deb's computer and go to yahoo.com."

With Will's assistance, Danny navigated to the headline:

Yahoo! News
Ketchogue LI Man Sues Gunther Corp., Neighbors, For $50M

The article was written from the perspective of the Ketchogue parents, and its theme was greed. It barely mentioned Agnes and what she was going through. But it explained how people had volunteered their time to help the town's children and were thanked for it by being placed on the business end of a fifty-million-dollar lawsuit. Regina Wartham gave a quote:

"These have been trying times for us since we got word about the lawsuit. We are just scraping by financially and the possibility of going to court over this has caused more stress for us than you can possibly imagine. We're sorry about Agnes but my family wasn't there and had nothing to do with the incident."

Then, down at the bottom, Danny read the reader comments. These were brutal – words like "greedy," "outrageous," "thieves," "ridiculous," were sprinkled throughout all of them. One person suggested that the courts should terminate Danny's parental rights. Another person said he should be arrested. Yet another wrote that he and his family represent "everything that is wrong with this country." Danny felt like his insides were falling out as he read.

After that the scuttlebutt inside the bagel store, the hair salon, the pizza places, around the bar rail at Main Street Pub, and along the sidelines of the soccer, baseball and lacrosse fields, was that Dan Beers didn't need to sue these people, he could have just gone after the Gunther company, the bastards that sold the shrimp. If he had to sue anyone at all. And when the article reported that Agnes had an allergic reaction with Danny in attendance, a lot of people were scratching their heads – wait a second, the father was *there*? At the field? Why didn't he stop her from eating the shrimp if he knew she was allergic? Some others – not many but some – understood that point but didn't necessarily agree. What if it was your kid in a coma? What would you do?

But in the meantime, the calls and referrals to Beers Construction Company were drying up faster than a damp rag in the desert. By late September Danny had nothing going on but a kitchen re-do that Carlos could handle with Miguel, and with no other major jobs scheduled he could no longer keep three people on. He had to let Arturo go.

Then after Labor Day, there wasn't a single additional online donation to the GoFundMe site that Will and Nancy had set up. Most people figured if he was suing for fifty million and got anywhere near that amount, he'd be fine. What no one knew was that the $33,567 the site had generated had all been forked over to the hospital. Then when Danny paid the September bills a few weeks ago he did so with a pair of shaking hands. He still owed the hospital over $130,000 and they were constantly telling him he would need to pay up or take Agnes home. He was juggling the accounts and holding off creditors, but the bottom line was this – he was broke. There were no two ways about it.

If things didn't pick up soon, he would need to look into taking a second job.

CHAPTER 13

A PRESTIGIOUS POSITION

NEKKED?"

"Yes sir."

"In his office?"

"Yes."

"Are ya sure?" Hartwell Briggs asked, dumbfounded.

"Oh, I'm quite sure, sir," Dexter Morgan answered.

"'Cause yew witnessed it, Morgan? That what yew sayin'?"

"Yes sir, I certainly did," said Morgan. "I walked in on him and there he was. Standing there in his birthday suit."

Briggs was scratching his chin as the room went silent. Then he crossed his arms, shaking his head in thought. He looked around the conference room at the three other lawyers attending this meeting of the FT&B Personnel Committee. They were taking notes on legal pads, listening as Morgan gave Briggs the blow by blow. After Morgan finished, each one of them looked back up at Briggs, who was processing Morgan's story. No one said a word while Briggs sat there contemplating.

Finally, Briggs slapped his paws down onto the conference room table.

"Well, I tell yew what," he said. "It ain't unheard of."

"*Excuse* me?" Morgan responded, dumbfounded.

"I know ya have ya doubts, Morgan, but I'm tellin' yew, it ain't unheard of."

"But sir -"

"So help me, I once knew a falla liked to hunt pheasants nekked. Honest injun'. Lived down the road from me and my daddy. He'd go out in the woods wit' his rifle and he'd be wearin' nothin' but huntin' boots and a coonskin cap. Some folks are like that. Bat-shit crazier'n a raccoon drownin' inna tarpit, yew ask me. But like I said, it ain't unheard of."

"But Mr. Briggs," answered Morgan, "this wasn't in the woods, or in a tarpit. It was here in our offices. In our law firm."

"I take ya point. But I'm just sayin' – it ain't unheard of."

"Well I think it needs to be *addressed* sir," Morgan pleaded.

Briggs looked at the ceiling, contemplating again. Then he turned back to Morgan. "Okay Morgan, lemme ask. What *'xactly* was he doin'?"

"Doing sir?"

"When yew walked in. What was he *doin'*?"

"Well, it seemed to be some manner of ... military exercise."

"*Military* exercise?"

"Yes sir, a military exercise. I opened the door and he was standing there like an army private or something. And, well ... he was saluting me. Hand up to his forehead. Feet together. Facing out toward the hallway."

Briggs's eyebrows shot up.

"Sa-lootin'?!"

"Yes sir. No mistaking it."

"Did he *say* anythin'?"

"Nothing, not a word."

"And he was wearin' what? Anythin' at all?"

"No, absolutely nothing," Morgan said. "Not a stitch of clothing."

Briggs scratched his head.

"Well hot damn," he said, "that ain't no army private I ever heard of. He a veteran a' some sort? Mebbe got himself a case a post-treematic stress disorder?"

"No sir, nothing like that," said Morgan. "We looked at his resume, which we have on file. It's just a very strange and troublesome situation."

The lawyers all looked at each other as Briggs began playing finger drums, shaking his head in thought.

Finally he threw his hands up.

"Well, I'm atta loss," he said. "Anyone wanna add anythin'?"

To Briggs's right, an attorney named Rebecca Cavanaugh, a partner in the Tax Department, spoke up.

"Well," she said, "just that there also was an incident in the conference room that same night. At our wine-tasting event."

"Well I can address that," Briggs said, pointing a finger in the air. "There was indeed an incident. The young falla showed up there drunker'n a sailor on New Year's Eve. Was full to the eyeballs wit' moonshine, or wine, or whatever we were servin' up that night. And then off he went, sprintin' cross the room, jus' runnin' and hollerin' like a wild dog. Before yew knew it, he up and tackled a Mexican falla, like he was playin' linebacker for the Volunteers, back there at UT. I wouldn't a believed it myself if I hadn't witnessed it wit' my own eyes."

"My goodness," Morgan said.

"And lemme just say," Briggs continued, pointing at the others, "that nobody supports the Mexican-'merican people more'n I do. Any attack on those hard-workin' people is an attack on all of us, yew unnerstand? So I'm not condonin' it."

Everyone in the room nodded. Cavanaugh leaned back in her chair and drew a breath. Then Morgan spoke up again.

"Well, sir, I think we've kicked this around long enough. I move that we terminate his relationship with the firm. I believe we have to fire him, Mr. Briggs. To me this is an easy call."

"I would second that," Cavanaugh chimed in. "The office debacle was bad enough. For example, if a secretary walked in, we could be subject to a hostile work environment claim. So, there's that. But the conference room incident was terrible too – we worked things out with the catering company that supplied the worker who got tackled, so there won't be any lawsuits, but it's the potential that we're concerned about here. If the man had been seriously injured this could have been a disaster."

"Exactly," Morgan agreed.

Briggs looked around the room.

"Anyone else?"

Nobody said a word.

Briggs began scratching his chin again as the group awaited his next move. You could tell they were all treading lightly here, hesitant to say anything that would cross Briggs. It was a bold move by Morgan to suggest the firing without first clearing it with Briggs, and Morgan let go a sigh of relief when Cavanaugh backed him up.

They all now stared at Briggs, who was deep in thought.

"Lemme ask y'all somethin'," Briggs finally said. "When do we make our job offers to the summer class?"

Briggs was referring to the job offers the firm would make to the Summer Associates for permanent positions as lawyers after they graduated from law school. With offers in hand, the Summers would return to their respective law schools in the fall and finish their third and final year of school before returning the September after graduation to begin work as full-time lawyers. O'Reilly and all the other Summers had been focused on their August "offers," and not much else, the entire summer.

"We are due to make the offers tomorrow," said Morgan.

"And outta the seventy-six Summers we got on board, how many are gettin' offers?"

"Well, seventy-five sir. O'Reilly is the only question mark. I mean theoretically, instead of firing him, we can simply tell him he's not getting an offer, and then he's out of here as soon as the summer program ends, which is next week. I guess we can do that."

"Yes, true," Cavanaugh interjected, "but personally I would let him go today. I think we just cut ties and terminate him. That would send a message that this program is not a joke. That you can't just – well, look, we've been over it and over it. That'd be my vote."

"It's my preference as well," Morgan promptly answered.

"And the others?" Briggs asked, turning to the other two lawyers on the Personnel Committee. "How yew votin'?"

Briggs then received two additional votes to terminate the employment at Foster Tuttle & Briggs LLP of one Seamus P. O'Reilly, Summer Associate. So other than Briggs, the vote was unanimous. Briggs then nodded to the group, stood, and began pacing back and forth at the head of the conference room with his hands folded behind his back, his chin pointing to the ceiling. Morgan was sitting silently with his arms crossed as Cavanaugh and the others were anxiously tapping pens on their legal pads.

Briggs strode a full circle around the table and finally plopped back down onto his chair. He planted his elbows on the conference room table. All eyes were then on Briggs, because even though this group had taken a vote, every one of them knew that J. Hartwell Briggs had the final say on this matter, and all other matters, and that this here meeting of the Personnel Committee was by no means subject to the democratic process.

"Well, I 'preciate everyone's input, I rally do," Briggs said. "But

Jacob Horowitz, the Dean over at Manhattan Law School? He's a friend a mine. And a friend of the Firm. And as yew all know, I agreed as a favor to him to bring one student from MLS into our summer program, 'cause we ain't never harred nobody from that law school, bein' it ain't a top tier school. That student turned out to be this O'Rally falla."

Briggs leaned back in his chair and crossed his arms. He looked up at the ceiling again, pondering the fate of Seamus P. O'Reilly. The truth was that Morgan and Cavanaugh and the rest of the Personnel Committee had fired associate lawyers and paralegals and other staff members for a lot less than what this O'Reilly character had pulled. They rarely sought input from anyone outside the Committee. But when it came to firing a member of the Summer Associate class, and the potential public relations impact that could have on the Firm's recruiting efforts, they would always consult with Briggs. And so Morgan, Cavanaugh and the others sat and awaited the verdict. Finally, Briggs placed both his palms on the conference room table and looked them all in the eyes. He had made his decision.

"Well, I tell yew what. I just can't tell ol' Jake we far'n the one falla we ever brought in here from MLS. He wouldn't 'preciate that, even if I told him the boy was tryin' to turn this place into a drunken nudist colony."

Morgan and the others nodded, disappointed. They had made their case and there was nothing more they could do. At the end of the day, this was Briggs's call and they all knew it.

"But lemme ask," Briggs continued, "am I right that the Summers who attend the local schools here in the city will work part-time a few days a week during they final year a school?"

"Well, that's correct," Morgan told him. "Once we give them job offers at the end of the summer, we give them the option of continuing to work here on a part-time basis during the school year. Assuming they go to school locally, of course. Most of them take us up on it and we find it to be very profitable. We bill them out at a first-year attorney rate, which for most matters is about $475 to $525 per hour, and we pay them $60 per hour. Even on a part-time basis they typically give us about thirty hours a week with minimal overhead. So, if you run the numbers, with approximately thirty of our Summers attending local schools, we clear close to $400,000 a week in gross profits just on the part-timers."

"Right, and this O'Rally falla, bein' he's a local too, he'd be in that same category, correct?"

"Well yes," Morgan hesitated, "theoretically, that's correct."

"Okay then," Briggs concluded, smiling, "here's what we gone do. Y'all leave this falla to me. I'm gone rehabilitate the boy."

Briggs then shifted in his chair.

"Y'all mighta heard that we been retained to represent a longstandin' client of the Firm – the Gunther folks – in a whol' buncha product liability cases comin' down the pike. Ko here gone be my right-hand man. Ain't that right, Ko?"

Briggs gestured over to another member of the Committee, a litigation partner named Yang Hsue Ko, who right now was thumbing through emails on his smartphone. Ko was jolted to attention, and he quickly placed the phone down onto the conference table as if he'd been caught passing a note in math class.

"Yes, that's right," he agreed, "that's correct."

"And where we at on things there, Ko?"

"Well, right now we're working closely with the client to identify and collect documents, and it's pretty much a massive undertaking. We anticipate quite a few of these cases, and currently we're assembling a team to index and review them – "

"And so we need bodies, is what Ko is sayin'," Briggs said, cutting him off. "And this O'Rally'd be perfect for this shindig. Give us all a chance to eyeball the falla doin' some real work."

Briggs then rose to his feet.

"So assumin' this boy can keep from goin' nekked, and he lays off the sauce, we gone bring him on as a lawyer next September. Meantime, he gone be under the watch of me and Ko here, workin' on the Gunther Home Products docs. And I tell yew what, that boy so much as remove his necktie, I'm gone innerduce ma foot to his ass. So help me God."

Everyone in the room began scribbling notes on their legal pads, trying to keep pace with Briggs, who was lecturing now as if he were at a podium during a Congressional debate.

"So we gone make this O'Rally falla a job offer," he continued, his voice rising now and his yellow teeth glowing through a smile, "and this way we report that one hunnert percent of our Summers received offers for full-time employment wit' the Firm. And we gone put that on our website. For the whole world to see. Right out there on the 'ol Innynet."

Briggs opened his palms and faced his team.

"And that, ladies and gentlemen, is the way it's gone be."

Morgan and his team immediately dropped their pens and broke into a round of applause, with smiles filling the room. Briggs was nodding to all of them, soaking in the adoration.

"Thank yew, thank yew," he told them, and when the applause finally died down, he asked them, "where's this boy at right now?"

"He's just down the hall, waiting for us," Morgan answered.

"He is?"

"Yes sir, I asked him to report here. Quite frankly it was for the purpose of letting him go. But I think we've made a courageous decision here today, and I for one am fully in support of it."

Everyone in the group nodded in agreement, and there was another round of applause, with smiles all around and a couple of thumbs-up thrown in. It would then be recorded in the minutes that the FT&B Personnel Committee, after discussing an "employment issue," had made a unanimous decision to present Summer Associate Seamus P. O'Reilly with an offer for a permanent job with the firm. Moving forward, the minutes would state, O'Reilly would be working directly for Hartwell Briggs and Yang Hsue Ko on the Gunther Home Products Corporation product liability cases, until further notice.

"Righty then," said Briggs, "no time like the present. Go get that boy and bring him in here. Let's get this thing done."

Ko rose and bolted through the conference room doors.

On the morning after the wine-tasting event up in the C. Barton Foster Conference Room, O'Reilly woke up in a fog in his Park Slope, Brooklyn studio apartment, with his medulla oblongata still drenched in alcohol, like a soaked sponge. He was face down on his double bed with his right leg dangling over the side and his arms splayed out, looking like he had fallen out of an airplane. He was still dressed in his Stafford Essential tuxedo, except that his shirt was open to the navel and caked somehow in dried ketchup. The bowtie was nowhere to be found. For some unexplained reason, his sheets, mattress pad, comforter and pillows were rolled into a ball and thrown into the corner of the room. He was lying on a bare mattress, and there was a massive drool spot under his cheeks.

O'Reilly pushed his face off the mattress and felt a pain between his ears that suggested someone had drilled a hole in both of his temples. Despite the drool patch, his mouth was as dry as a cactus and his throat burned with acid. The first thing he saw through his blurred vision was his beloved pair of Clark Kents, which were jammed up against his headboard in a twisted, mangled state. One of the lenses was missing and the other was shattered and covered in a mysterious sticky substance that O'Reilly believed was maple syrup, although the source of that would forever remain a mystery. The left earpiece was broken in two and the right was bent in a frightening direction – it was a miracle the damage hadn't also resulted in a skull fracture. The mere fact that he was alive gave him the sinking feeling he had somehow dodged a bullet.

O'Reilly then sat up and fought off a wave of nausea as the room began to spin. He saw that only one of his shoes was on – the other foot was bare. How the hell was that possible? The sock and shoe presumably were with his bowtie, wherever that was. In a panic he then groped in his pants and pulled out his wallet, and upon inspection, quickly learned that it had nothing in it but an ATM receipt for a $200 cash withdrawal taken at 12:37 am. Where the hell did he do that? Where? He had no clue. He vaguely remembered a taxi ride home and an irate driver slapping him awake when they got to this apartment. The man obviously had rolled him to get his fare, and then had helped himself to a jackpot.

When O'Reilly finally pushed himself off his mattress, he enjoyed about a minute and a half of blissful ignorance during which he stood dizzy and peeing at the toilet with no recollection of where he had been the night before. All he knew was that his right hand was throbbing and the back of it was scraped and bloody; it appeared to have been worked over with a cheese grater. Did he fall maybe? Who knew. O'Reilly then zipped himself up and stumbled over to the sink to run his hand under the water. He caught sight of himself in the mirror, his orange hair an electrified, post-hurricane disaster, and right then and there, whammo, the whole scene came flooding back into his memory.

"What the fuck, no," he said suddenly, and then he ran and sat on the edge of his bed, frantically accounting for every last second of every single conversation he had up in that conference room. Or at least the ones he could remember.

Jesus Christ, he panicked – Morgan and the naked salute – he had almost forgotten about that. And then the wine-tasting event, you've got to be kidding me. He recalled wobbling his way over to Briggs's group. Then there was a fuzzy image of him calling them all McFly, perhaps whacking Briggs on the back of the neck. Did he really do that? Did he?

And then – oh my God – he remembered …

Roberto. Wine glasses shattering.

Holy shit, no. Oh Jesus no.

O'Reilly ran back to the bathroom and vomited.

Later that morning O'Reilly slinked into the Firm. He eased into the crowded elevator with a reddened mug that felt like it was on fire. He had a mouthful of cotton, bloody eyes, a blinding headache and a pair of trembling hands. The booze from the night before and the Listerine he had gargled made his breath smell like peppermint schnapps. Worse, he was pouring sweat, agonizing over what everyone in the elevator was thinking, all of them pretending to be glued to their *New York Times* or *Wall Street Journal* foldovers.

That day, and for the next three working days, O'Reilly did nothing but sit in his office waiting for a call or an email, anything. But there was nothing – not a word from Morgan, nothing from any lawyers looking to hand him work, and no emails with lunch invitations. Even Wadsworth hadn't returned his calls. Sondra seemed to be a co-conspirator as well, because in the last three days she hadn't bothered to intercom him to let him know she was going to lunch, and therefore O'Reilly couldn't respond that it would be "preferable" that she go.

So O'Reilly stayed cloistered in his office like a hermit. Each morning, he logged into Yahoo! News or ESPN.com, waiting for the phone to ring. Calling and asking for an assignment, which he knew he was supposed to do if he was idle, was absolutely out of the question because that meant having to call Morgan. Should he email him instead? Send him a smoke signal? O'Reilly was exhausted from mulling it over. He had been through about thirty drafts of a proposed email, all of which he had now deleted.

In the meantime, the freeze-out was killing him. Absolutely driving him insane. When the afternoons rolled around O'Reilly would be so hungry he could hear his stomach growling, but there was no way he was leaving that office for lunch, and of course the Firm cafeteria was out of the question. By day three, the solitary confinement had him begging for the guillotine. That he would be fired seemed a certainty; it was just a matter of when, and by whom. This was torture, pure and simple. In O'Reilly's view, those Guantanamo detainees had nothing on him.

And then finally, on the afternoon of the fourth freeze-out day, the phone suddenly exploded and the mere sound of it was so unexpected that O'Reilly almost had a heart attack. He jolted back from his computer screen and looked at the caller ID panel sitting atop his Meridian phone set, and there it was – MORGAN, DEXT x8338. One ring, two rings, three rings – should he let it go to voicemail? Purely out of instinct O'Reilly almost punched the speakerphone button and thank God he didn't. In an instant he caught himself, took a deep breath, and picked up the receiver.

"Hello," he coughed, "Seamus O'Reilly speaking." Three days later and his dehydrated larynx still sounded like paper crumbling.

"This is Morgan," the voice warned in response, in a tone typical of an undertaker. "Dexter Morgan."

"Mr. Morgan," O'Reilly coughed back, "how are you?"

"Mr. O'Reilly, please report to Conference Room 24B. We'd like to have a word with you."

"Sure," O'Reilly said in a defeated voice. "I'll be right there."

"Give us fifteen minutes. Bring your personal belongings and firm ID card with you. Is that enough time, or do you need more?"

O'Reilly's heart sank, and he closed his eyes.

"No sir, I can make it."

"Thank you," said Morgan, and that was it.

He hung up the phone with a thud.

Down there on the 24th floor, O'Reilly sat on a sofa in a dimly lit hallway under a collection of framed wall paintings. At his feet was a gym bag filled with the few items he had stored in the office that summer – a mitt he used at a softball outing a few weeks earlier, a pair of running sneakers he had tossed under his desk, a framed 5x7 photograph of him and his parents at his SUNY Buffalo college graduation, and of course a copy of the Tibetan monk memo, which O'Reilly decided he would keep as a memento. His firm ID swipe card was in his breast pocket.

Other than those items he had nothing – he was ready to be escorted from the building.

For an hour O'Reilly stewed there ruminating about his career. What was next for him? He would return to law school for his third and final year in about two weeks, but where he would go from there was the big unknown. No big firm would hire him now, of that he was sure. Before the C. Barton Foster Conference Room incident, there were rumors flying around the Firm that all the Summers were getting offers, which meant that after they canned O'Reilly's fat ass, he would be the *only one* who didn't. Just try explaining that in a job interview. Go ahead, tell them how you managed to fuck up a cushy Summer Associate gig when everyone in the world knows your main job responsibility was to successfully order mint-jelly lamb kebabs off an Uzbekistan restaurant lunch menu, for Christ's sake.

Running all the options through his head, O'Reilly thought that maybe he would drop the whole law thing, avoid the debt of the final year, and go in another direction. In that regard, he wasn't completely without options. He had a cousin Hughie, out in East Northport, who was blind in one eye and was missing two fingers on his left hand as a result of a forklift accident. Hughie had used the lump-sum worker's compensation settlement to start a mildly successful water-sprinkler business out there. O'Reilly had visited him one time and noticed a peculiarity – on account of his one-eyed depth-perception issues, Hughie was firing the sprinkler heads on his own front lawn directly into the street, soaking the Hyundais parked at the curb. O'Reilly had made a mental note that maybe he needed some help. Perhaps it was time to give him a call.

O'Reilly had his elbows on his thighs when a partner he recognized from the Firm website approached.

"Afternoon, I'm Ko," the man said. "Yang Ko."

"How ya doin'," O'Reilly responded, rising to his feet. The attorney Ko nodded toward the conference room.

"They're ready for you now. Follow me."

Soon O'Reilly was pacing down the hallway feeling like the convict from *Dead Man Walking*. He entered through the double doors of the conference room right behind Ko and immediately saw Briggs along with a group of three other lawyers that included Morgan. They were sitting in front of legal pads. So with Ko there were five of them, which meant they were doing this by way of a full firing squad. O'Reilly's heart jumped when he saw the group, but he was so resigned to his fate that he quickly settled down when Briggs addressed him.

"Sea-Mouse! Welcome! Have a seat right down there."

Briggs pointed to a chair they had placed at one end of the long cherry-wood conference table. He sat at the head, at the far other end, directly across from O'Reilly, flanked right and left by his four henchmen, two on each side in a sort of half-moon arrangement. Morgan sat just to Briggs's left with his arms crossed and his nostrils flared. It was too difficult to meet his stare, so O'Reilly focused on the others and nodded.

Once again, Briggs had addressed him as Sea-Mouse, but what did it really matter at this point? Taking his seat, O'Reilly decided there was no use correcting him. Briggs wouldn't remember it anyway. Plus, they were just about to pink slip him, his career was in the shitter, so as far as O'Reilly was concerned, Briggs could call him Sea-Mouse or Ocean-Rat or whatever the hell he liked. He was out of there in about eleven minutes.

"Well now, Sea-Mouse," opened Briggs, "how'd yew enjoy your summer wit' us here at the Firm?"

"Fine, sir," said O'Reilly. The question caught him by surprise. A funny way to begin a firing, he thought. Briggs seemed happy to see him – man these people were strange.

"I, uh, you know, I really enjoyed it sir, and – "

"Well I tell yew what. We rally enjoyed havin' yew, Sea-Mouse. Some lawyers 'round here had some mighty fine things to say 'bout yew son."

Briggs was smiling, and O'Reilly stared back, confused. He was waiting for the "but," which he figured was coming any second.

"Well, Sea-Mouse, as yew know," Briggs continued, "'round this time a year we decide whether to make offers to our Summers for permanent employment wit' the Firm. Before y'all head back to law school for your final year. And at this point we've now made our decisions on all y'all, and that's why we brought yew in here today. Yew unnerstand?"

"Yes sir, I do." He placed his gym bag on his lap, ready to head for the lobby elevator.

"Before we discuss your situation," Briggs went on, "perhaps we can provide a lil' constructive criticism. That alright wit' yew?"

Constructive criticism? What was the point? But fine, whatever.

"Yes, of course," O'Reilly said, shifting in his seat.

Briggs then rose to his feet and began pacing back and forth behind the other lawyers.

"Yew know, Sea-Mouse," he opened, "this profession of ours – lawyrin' – can get mighty stressful sometimes. Mighty stressful. And everybody got they own way a relaxin'. And mind yew, relaxin' is important. It can get a falla refocused, ready to take on the difficult work we do for our clients."

Briggs had his hands behind his back, with his chin pointed in the air.

"Now take yours truly for example. As far as relaxin' goes, I like me some fiddlin' on the ol' clarinet. Been playin' since I'm knee-high to a show pony. And even though I don't rally get much time to play no mo', I tell yew what, when I can break that ol' thing out, I get real energized-like. Just sets me at ease. Yew know what I'm sayin' Sea-Mouse?"

O'Reilly nodded. *Relaxing* – where was this going?

"And I got me a granddaughter, name's Becky. Lives down there in Nashville wit' her Momma and Daddy. And she like to do that hot yoga thing. Yew ever hear a that Sea-Mouse? Hot yoga? Some sorta new-fangled exercise I'm tol', where yew stretch yourself in a room 'bout a hunnert twenty degrees. Wind up sweatin' like a whore in a Confessional. Just pourin' outta yew. Sounds like torture to me, Sea-Mouse, but Becky tells me it's very relaxin'. Very relaxin' indeed."

"Yes sir," O'Reilly managed, utterly confused. He wanted to say something, or ask a question, but Briggs would not break stride. And no one else in this room was saying a word.

"Then I suppose there's meditation," Briggs continued.

"Plenny a folks are doin' it these days, 'specially out in California, where they got all types a hippies and freaks and whatnot. So help me, I was at a conference in San Diego, and sure 'nuff, there was a whol' gang a them out there on the beach first thing inna mornin'. I'm tellin' yew there was nally forty of 'em. Just sittin' out there on they mats. Injun-style. Meditatin' away under the mornin' sun. Looked pretty relaxin', I 'spose, if yew enjoy that kinda thing."

The other four lawyers were now either scribbling randomly on their legal pads or had leaned back in their chairs to stare out the windows overlooking Park Avenue. The attorney Ko was thumbing away on his phone. But the one thing they weren't doing any longer was paying attention to Briggs, and O'Reilly himself was wondering whether the man had gone insane and nobody had the nerve to point it out. O'Reilly had come in here expecting to get fired, and now he wasn't so sure. And there was no interrupting Briggs.

"I guess ma point, Sea-Mouse," Briggs rambled on, "is that everybody got they own way a relaxin'. Everybody jitterbugs to a different tune, so to speak. Which brings me to yew."

Suddenly Briggs stopped his pacing and crossed his arms. His demeanor swiftly changed, and the smile was gone. He lowered his eyebrows and looked O'Reilly directly in his eyes.

"To put it bluntly, son, I unnerstand that in your private time, yew like to strip down to the bare ass that God gave ya, and then run yourself through some US Army-style calisthenics. Now ... I ain't never heard a such a thing. But like I said, everybody jitterbugs to they own tune. So I ain't judgin' Sea-Mouse. I ain't judgin'."

O'Reilly's jaw was now hanging open, his face frozen.

Jesus, you've got to be kidding me. He actually thinks –

"Mr. Briggs," O'Reilly tried to interject, "Mr. Briggs – "

"But yew gotta unnerstand," said Briggs, ignoring him, "we got to keep up appearances here. And if some employee, like a female God forbid, were to walk in and see yew standin' there ... wit' everything yew got ... just hangin' and wigglin' like nightcrawlers on a fishhook ... well, it could put the Firm in a bit of a pickle. Yew take ma point Sea-Mouse?"

"I do sir, but if I could just – "

"So whether it's nekked army exercises, or hot yoga, or meditation, or fiddlin' on the ol' clarinet, or whatever, we gone do our relaxin' on our own private time. And between these walls? We gone do the difficult work our clients deserve. We unnerstand each otha Sea-Mouse?"

There was nothing more O'Reilly could say. Explaining anything would be like talking to a wall. Plus, something short of a miracle seemed to be happening here, and O'Reilly was feeling a surge of adrenaline. Was it possible he wasn't getting fired? Was that even possible? O'Reilly thought about apologizing, giving them the standard bullshit about not letting one bad naked, drunken day mar an otherwise impeccable summer performance, and blah blah blah, but there was no way he could pull it off with any degree of sincerity. Instead he decided just to let it ride and respond to Briggs and hope for the best.

He looked everyone in the eyes with a confident smile.

"We certainly do, sir," he said.

"Well alrighty, then! Now we gettin' somewhere!" Briggs gestured toward Morgan. "Mr. Morgan, take it away."

Morgan nodded back and thanked Briggs. He looked down at his legal pad and flipped over the first page. Then he turned the legal pad face down and addressed O'Reilly, who wanted to leap in the air and pump his fists. O'Reilly couldn't imagine what Morgan was about to say.

"Mr. O'Reilly," Morgan began, a smile creeping across his face, "on behalf of the Personnel Committee and the Firm, we would like to make you an offer to join us here at Foster Tuttle & Briggs as an Associate Attorney following your graduation from Manhattan Law School next June. We really enjoyed your work here and think you'll be a magnificent addition to our team. We hope you will accept and come aboard."

And there it was. He wasn't getting the ax after all. O'Reilly was floored. Elated. Over the moon. He couldn't believe it. How had this happened? How? Why? What manner of mental gymnastics had the five of them undertaken to arrive at this bizarre decision? What factors led these people to the maddening conclusion that the Firm was somehow better off with him *inside* its walls then out? O'Reilly couldn't fathom.

But of course who gave a flying fart. If he had heard correctly through his frisbee-sized ears, Morgan had just told him that he was getting an offer to be an *attorney* at the firm. An attorney. O'Reilly's heart was pounding so fast it felt like a jackhammer. He nearly leapt out of the chair to run and kiss Morgan, but then he caught himself, quickly concluding that such an act was a bad idea, considering the circumstances surrounding their last encounter. So he opted instead for an enthusiastic yet curt reply.

"Thank you, Mr. Morgan, I accept," he blurted out.

"Well, hold on a second," Morgan responded, laughing a bit. "You should know that the offer comes with a few conditions."

O'Reilly's breathing was trying to catch up with his pounding heart. He wanted the meeting to end so he could run to his office and scream.

"Well okay," O'Reilly said back to him impulsively, "shoot."

He immediately regretted that response. But he was so shocked, so overwhelmed by what he had just heard, his tongue and his brain were in a temporary disconnect. As his "shoot" hung in the air, O'Reilly glanced at Briggs, whose lowered eyebrows quickly put O'Reilly in his place.

"Of course," he stammered, "uhh, you said, conditions … sir?"

"First," said Morgan, all business now, "we don't yet know what the first-year salary will be for next year, but I can tell you that this year our first-year attorneys made $175,000 in base pay. There is also a lucrative benefits package that includes health insurance, dental, 401(k), and a few other things, but you will be getting a letter that outlines all of that."

Beautiful, O'Reilly thought.

He would have accepted the job for half that amount, and anything they added on top was nothing but chocolate cream pie. O'Reilly said nothing to this, and just kept smiling at all of them. He was hoping he didn't look like a deranged maniac.

"Second," Morgan continued, "you should know that every Associate position here at the Firm requires a yearly minimum of 2400 billable hours. And let me stress – that number is a *minimum.* Although your performance evaluations will include both the quality and the quantity of the billables you log, billing anywhere under 2400 is a red flag to us that you are not carrying your weight. But again, all of this will be outlined in your offer letter."

"Yes sir, I understand."

O'Reilly wasn't fazed by that in the least. The billable hour requirement was a well-known fact of life at big New York City law firms and O'Reilly didn't care one wit. He could easily run the math – he needed a minimum of 200 billables a month to keep them happy. Fifty a week. O'Reilly could do that standing on his head. *What else you got Morgan?*

"And third, our offer is conditional on you passing the New York State bar exam next July. And to be clear, we expect you to pass on your first attempt, which is something that is important to the Firm and to our clients. If you, or anyone else, were to fail the bar exam, we would meet with you to go over the circumstances of why you were unable to pass, and while it does not necessarily mean we will rescind the offer, we can tell you that short of an illness or something similar, we would likely recommend you search elsewhere for a job. Is that clear?"

"Very clear, sir."

If Morgan was trying to intimidate him, the man was 0 for 3. O'Reilly had no doubt he would pass the bar exam on his first try. In fact, he planned on getting started on his studies in January of his final semester. He wasn't leaving anything to chance. And following graduation in May he would take his bar exam materials and hole-up in his apartment Howard Hughes-style – the pajamas, the long ZZ-Top beard, the whole nine yards – and devour the stuff night and day. He'd be as prepared as anyone when the time came.

The bar exam – *pssht*. This was a so-called "condition"? Morgan was making him laugh.

"And finally," Morgan concluded, "given that you are a local student, Mr. O'Reilly, we would like you to participate in our part-time employment program beginning in September. Assuming your schedule allows, this means that we want you working at the Firm whenever you are not in class or studying. We offer this opportunity to most of our local students, who are all from either NYU or Columbia, am I right Rebecca?"

"Yes, all of them," Cavanaugh quickly replied.

"Right, and virtually all the local students take us up on this program, which is strictly voluntary. However, in your case, Mr. O'Reilly, we are requiring it as a condition of your offer. We want you in the program as a way for us to further evaluate your work. It would start in September, roughly a week after the Summer Program ends. We'll want at least 30 hours a week, which you may need to do on weekends, since – "

"Morgan, if I may," Briggs interjected.

Suddenly Briggs was on his feet. He must have sensed O'Reilly's confusion and decided to clarify things. And O'Reilly was indeed confused. He knew that local students worked part-time at FT&B during their final law school year, but he never heard it being a condition of anyone's offer. Plus, Morgan had just made it clear that he, O'Reilly, was the only one being put to a further evaluation. What a buzzkill. The smile quickly vanished.

And another thing suddenly occurred to him – this would also put a serious damper on O'Reilly's plans for the fall. He had only six more classes to take before graduation, three per semester, and had arranged his schedule so that he'd be taking them all on Tuesdays and Thursdays. He'd have three workdays, plus the weekends, completely off. And last week at the Clearview Park Golf Course under the Throg's Neck Bridge, O'Reilly had lipped out a six-inch putt on eighteen for a 112; in September he was planning to spend most of his off-days trying to lower his handicap to about a +36. Now it looked like he'd be working and would be under a fair degree of scrutiny. Maybe Morgan was 1 for 4.

"Sea-Mouse, yew look a little unsettled, so lemme see if I can explain," said Briggs. "See, I'm here to inform yew 'bout a prestigious position we created just for yew here at the Firm. A very prestigious position indeed."

Briggs took a step closer to O'Reilly.

"Sea-Mouse, I am pleased to announce that we are hereby namin' yew as the newest member of the National Shrimp Cocktail Defense team. You gone be an integral part of our operation."

O'Reilly wasn't sure if he heard that one correctly.

"The, uh, National … Shrimp Cocktail … Defense Team?"

"Yew betcha," said Briggs. "The National Shrimp Cocktail Defense Team. Yew gone be workin' wit' some mighty fine lawyers, helpin' us defend some important cases for a major client. We gone give yew all the details but suffice it to say that yew gone be workin' under the tutelage of ol' Hartwell Briggs, reviewin' some very important documents. In a very prestigious position here at the

Firm. What yew say to that Sea-Mouse?"

Briggs was staring at him with that big toothy, yellow smile, his arms crossed and his chin pointing to the sky again. O'Reilly had no idea what the shit a National Shrimp Cocktail Defense Team could possibly be, but for Christ's sake, he did say something about reviewing documents, including on weekends. A thirty-hour a week document review assignment while juggling law school classes, and right under Briggs's nose, as a way of further evaluating his credentials for a permanent job. O'Reilly's initial enthusiasm was going into the shitter in a hurry.

And then something else hit him – he'd be the guy named Sea-Mouse who works on *shrimp cocktail* cases. Can you imagine the confusion around the Firm? Oh, the embarrassment. What would they all say to that one? What is he, they'd ask, some sort of half-assed maritime lawyer or something? O'Reilly wanted to disappear.

"How 'bout it, Sea-Mouse?" asked Briggs. "We got a deal?"

O'Reilly felt cornered. What choice did he really have? Start interviewing at other firms? Yeah, good luck with that one. The man had student loan debt that rivaled the gross national product of Portugal. He desperately needed the money. Plus, he had already leapt out of his chair a moment ago and accepted. There really was nothing else to do. He was going to be a member of the National Shrimp Cocktail Defense Team, whatever the hell that was. Were there uniforms? Hats?

Whatever, this was a done deal.

"Uh, sure," O'Reilly managed. "Yes sir, uh, we have a deal."

"Well hot damn, that's mighty fine news! Congratulations Sea-Mouse! Yew gone be one helluva fine addition to our team, son. And we all gone keep our eyes on yew and see how yew do in this new prestigious position. Then we gone see where that takes us."

Briggs beat a retreat to the conference room door, but then he abruptly turned and pointed a finger at O'Reilly.

"Meanwhile, we all gone keep our clothes on, and we gone lay off the hooch on compn'y time. Yew take ma point Sea-Mouse?"

"Absolutely, sir."

"Well alrighty 'den."

CHAPTER 14

MOTION TO DISMISS FOR
FAILURE TO STATE A CLAIM

THERE'S NOTHING LIKE the Civil Division up in Bronx County. If you've never been up there you don't know what you're missing. The crowded dockets, the rude and irritable court officers, the frazzled, impatient judges with bullshit detectors constantly on high alert, the cut-throat lawyers who'd sue Mother Teresa if they discovered she had a spare nickel, and not a damn thing "civil" about it, well, the place was a trial lawyer's dream.

At least that was Anzalone's humble opinion. She loved the place. Occasionally she would land a case up there, or would file one herself, and she was never more excited about her job. The case would get her out of Ketchogue and into a world where real litigators and trial lawyers went at each other with a vengeance. She even enjoyed the travel – in fact, she considered it a mini-vacation whenever she could shake loose the daily Ketchogue drudgery and make a court appearance up there. She'd hunker down on the Long Island Railroad in one of those three-seater benches and slide over against the window with a coffee and scone in hand. She'd power down her iPhone and grab three newspapers from the station newsstand – the *Post*, the *Times* and the *Wall Street Journal* – and sit in perfect solitude, catching up with whatever was going on in the world. There'd be no law practice, no Justin and his wheelchair, no broken down Civic, no having to reprimand Cassie about surfing the Internet, no bills or mortgage payments, and most importantly, no complaining clients. From the time Anzalone left her apartment in Ketchogue to the time she would land at the Bronx courthouse, about two-and-half hours would typically go by. Anzalone wished it were twice that time.

On a Monday evening in October, Anzalone called Danny at home to walk him through how things would work the next morning in court. She explained that not too long after the process servers had done their job, the defendants filed a pile of motions and the court was now hearing oral argument on all of them. The first motion, she told Danny, was a motion to change venue. In that one, every defendant signed onto a joint motion claiming the case had no business being in the Bronx. They wanted it moved back to Nassau County, where Ketchogue was, and where Danny lived and where Agnes got hurt. Danny figured they were probably right about that one, because even he had wondered what they were doing up there in the Bronx. But he was praying his side would win that motion. With the case up there, it wasn't right in everyone's faces in Ketchogue.

But the second group of motions was the one that really worried him. Every single defendant had filed what Anzalone called a motion to dismiss "for failure to state a claim." Danny asked her to repeat that, and then he wrote it down. In those, each defendant wanted his lawsuit dismissed immediately. They were telling the court that his lawsuit had no legal merit whatsoever and could be booted out of court for good. And that was before they got to taking any discovery, or even had a trial.

"Can the court really do that?" Danny asked, perplexed.

"They can," Anzalone answered. "The court will read the complaint and assume – at this stage of the case – that every fact we stated in there is true. Then they will determine if those facts state a valid *legal* claim under New York law. If so, the court denies the motion and we go forward. If not, they dismiss the case, and we are out of business."

"Just like that?"

"Yes, Mr. Beers, just like that."

Anzalone told Danny that none of the parties to the lawsuit would be present in court the next morning and reminded him he didn't need to attend; it would just be the lawyers. She could fill him in afterwards. But since he wasn't going to get any sleep anyway, he figured he'd get dressed and meet her there. Plus, he really wanted to see what was happening in this case for himself, especially if they were going to throw him out on his ass. He'd sit in the back and observe, just blend into the woodwork.

The next morning, Tuesday, Anzalone arrived at the steps of the Bronx County courthouse at about ten after nine under a gunmetal grey sky. When she got to the courthouse, Dan Beers was already waiting, sipping a Dunkin' Donuts black coffee about halfway up the courthouse steps. He was wrapped in a blue and orange *New York Knicks* jacket and was scrunching his shoulders to shield himself from the chilly autumn winds whipping down Grand Concourse. Anzalone climbed the courthouse steps, waving hello as she ascended, and Danny greeted her with a handshake.

"You ready?" Danny asked.

"I'm ready," Anzalone nodded back. "You wanna go inside?"

"Sure," Danny said, and in they went.

THE COURTROOM WAS on the third floor of the Bronx County Supreme Court building. Anzalone entered Part 23 – belonging to Justice Elisa G. Fuentes – through a set of wide double doors, and Danny followed. The courtroom was massive, with deep brown mahogany walls and ornate carvings that ran up more than twenty feet. You entered the courtroom roughly in the middle, and to the left were rows upon rows of benches that made up the gallery. On the far side opposite the double doors there were six twelve-foot high windows that overlooked East 161st Street, and right now they allowed for daylight to wash over the room. To the right behind the wooden rail were counsel tables, the jury box and the judge's bench, which was perched up so high that the lawyers probably had to look straight up to speak to the judge. Everything in there was dark brown, and there were two massive chandeliers hanging over the counsel tables, providing even more light than what was currently streaming in through the windows.

As the two entered the courtroom, Danny cast his eyes upon a sea of lawyers. There had to be over a hundred in there. They were littered throughout the expansive gallery, some sitting there casually reading the *New York Post* or the *Times* or digging through legal files they had spread out on the benches. Many were standing in groups of three or four, chatting away about this, that or the other thing, or discussing their cases, and still others were walking purposefully up and down the gallery's center aisle, for whatever reason. The wall along the near side of the room, opposite the windows, was lined with people staring at smartphones.

To the right, beyond the bar rail, Danny saw a collection of court personnel gathered to the side of the judge's bench near the windows. There was a foldout table pressed against the gallery rail on that side. A middle-aged woman with short brown hair and reading glasses sat at the table, and on the other side of it, beyond the rail and running toward the back of the courtroom, was a long line of lawyers holding files or hammering away on phones. They were checking in for their cases, and the woman was marking them off on a sheet. The buzz of conversation in the room was so loud that Anzalone had to raise her voice to Danny.

"Sit right over there," she instructed, pointing to one of the benches in the gallery. "I'm gonna go check in."

In a minute Anzalone was in the line against the windows. Danny took a seat alongside the center aisle, right in the middle of the room. He watched the ebb and flow of the lawyers sauntering up and down the aisle, and he momentarily took comfort in his anonymity as the masses moved around him without even throwing him a glance.

To his right, a heavy-set lawyer with thick, buttery cheeks and jet-black hair, dressed in a dark blue suit, walked up with a fat legal file under his arm. He was wiping sweat from his forehead as he stopped beside Danny.

"RODRIGUEZ VERSUS THE CITY!" the man screamed out, trying to catch his breath. "ANYBODY GOT RODRIGUEZ?"

Danny looked around. Nobody was even acknowledging the man, and yet he was screaming over the mayhem of the courtroom.

"YO! Right here!" another man called out.

Danny turned and the second man was walking up the aisle with a "think I really give a shit?" expression, his smirk the first thing that Danny noticed. He wore a grey suit and a red tie whose knot landed somewhere in the middle of his chest. He was wearing running sneakers and he looked to Danny like he hadn't shaved in three days.

"Who ya got?" he moaned to the heavy man.

"Plaintiff. You?"

"I got the carrier. For the co-defendant. You got a demand?"

"Yeah, it's in the file, two hundred k. What, you don't read?"

The man in the sneakers looked around.

"C'mere," he said, nodding over to a corner, "let's talk."

The two then drifted away, and then Danny gazed around the room again. A man in a brown suit walked by carrying what looked to Danny like a human spine. Another lawyer ambled by carrying a poster board, maybe a trial exhibit. Danny couldn't tell.

Suddenly, a woman in a black leather skirt and white top was in the aisle beside him. She was also carrying a thick file and she yelled out, "MENENDEZ VERSUS ALBRIGHT CONSTRUCTION! ANY COUNSEL HERE ON ALBRIGHT?"

But before anyone could answer, one of the court officers near the judge's bench stepped forward and pushed his way through the small gate that separated the counsel tables from the gallery. He had a rosacea-filled florid face and was clad in black pants and a white uniform top. He had a buzzcut and a 9-millimeter semiautomatic pistol strapped to his hip. He planted his feet firmly on the ground as the gate slammed shut behind him, and with his hands on his hips he shot a roar across the courtroom.

"HEY SHAAAA-DUUPPP!" he bellowed. "EVERYBODY SHAAAA-DUUPPP!"

He pointed to the double doors leading out into the hallway.

"YOU WANNA TALK, TAKE IT OUTSIDE IN THE HALLWAY! KEEP IT DOWN OR YOU'RE OUDDA HERE!"

The officer then walked calmly back through the gate and settled near the conference table. He was chitchatting with the other court employees. To Danny's surprise, hardly anyone in the room even looked at the officer when he began screaming. It all seemed very routine. The only effect was that the buzz in the room diminished to the point where Danny could hear newspapers being ruffled and voices being cleared. A few people took the officer's suggestion and headed into the hallway.

Anzalone reappeared and plopped down next to Danny. She dropped her files onto the bench.

"Okay," she told him, "we're all set. Everyone is signed in."

"Everyone?"

"Yes, for our case," she clarified, looking around the room. "I don't know who they all are, but we'll find out soon enough. We're number 37 on the motion calendar, so we'll be here awhile."

Danny looked at his watch. It was nearly ten minutes to ten, almost twenty minutes after this hearing was supposed to start. Anzalone didn't seem concerned, but he figured he'd ask anyway.

"Was this supposed to start at 9:30?"

"Well, yes, but it never starts on time. The judge usually graces us with her presence about 10:30 or thereabouts. She's got 68 motions on her plate today, so I hope she gets started soon."

Anzalone smiled and winked at him, and then she pulled a stack of documents out of a maroon file folder.

"Plus," she said, hooking a thumb toward the line of lawyers, "lots of people are still signing in."

Danny followed her direction and saw the lawyers still queued up at the conference table. He couldn't believe the mayhem choking this place, couldn't wrap his mind around the fact that this was how they ran a New York state courtroom. He took a deep breath as Anzalone thumbed through the stack of documents on her lap. She held a yellow hi-liter and was wiping streaks through a set of notes on a legal pad. Like everyone else she was oblivious to the disarray of the entire operation around her. The hum of conversation in the courtroom rose again, and in a minute, it was back at full force, taking over the room and creeping all the way up the mahogany walls and beyond the enormous chandeliers.

Danny looked to his right and watched a woman walk up the aisle past him. She had light brown skin and wore a set of tight cornrows. She was wrapped in a drab green trench coat that went just past her knees, and below that she wore shin-high white athletic socks and a pair of orange track shoes. She was carrying a white plastic bag that Danny could see contained a bottle of apple juice and a banana. She didn't look like a lawyer, but then again, this entire place didn't meet any of the preconceived notions Danny had about courtrooms. When the woman got to the front of the aisle, he expected her to take a right and head out through the double doors, but then the court officer stepped forward again and opened the gate for her. She glided through it and nodded to all the court employees, marching through a door marked "CHAMBERS."

Instead of easing the gate closed, the court officer stepped forward again, planted his feet and lifted his chin.

"EVERYBODY SHAAAA-DUUUPPP! LAST WARNING, YOU WANNA TALK, TAKE IT OUTSIDE!"

The hum of conversation diminished again, and the court officer took his place among the employees near the foldout table. With Anzalone still marking her notes and the room still cluttered with lawyers walking around, or filling the gallery, or signing in, Danny cracked open a *New York Post* he found abandoned on the bench when he sat. In a short while he checked his watch again – 10:42 am. Just then Danny saw the thick brown door to the room marked CHAMBERS swing open, and out stepped the woman in the cornrows, this time wearing a black robe. The court officer promptly slapped his hand three times on the foldout table. *Fwap! Fwap! Fwap!* He planted his feet, just like before, but this time he screamed, "ALL RISE! THE HONORABLE JUSTICE ELISA G. FUENTES PRESIDING!"

OVER THE NEXT hour, Danny sat and listened to dozens of lawyers argue their cases before Justice Fuentes. There were all types of lawsuits represented – personal injury cases, contract disputes, construction site accidents, malpractice claims, and a host of other problems that the masses were bringing to this courtroom for resolution. Anzalone had explained that this was a motion calendar, which meant that the court today would not be resolving the cases, like at a trial. Instead, Justice Fuentes would only be dealing with some minor dustups that the lawyers couldn't resolve themselves as the lawsuits were chugging along. Most of these had to do with what Anzalone described as the "discovery phase" of the case. They involved pissing matches over who was supposed to produce what documents, or answer what questions, or sit for which depositions. Danny found a few of these interesting, and he was paying rapt attention. The lawyers were all tough-talking and street smart and Justice Fuentes was no-nonsense. Danny liked her. She wasn't putting up with any crap from these attorneys. When she'd heard enough of the bickering, she would make her ruling and shoo the lawyers away.

Sitting in the witness box right now was the woman who had been checking in the lawyers at the conference table. Her job was to call out the names of the cases, and she did so in a raspy, phlegmy voice that sounded like she smoked four packs of unfiltered Camels a day. When she barked out the case names the lawyers would rise from their locations back in the gallery and move through the small gate to assemble at the counsel tables. If the lawyers didn't immediately come forward she would yell, "SECOND CALL!" and swiftly move to the next one. "You snooze you lose" was the rule here – you had to be on your toes in this place.

To the woman's left was another long table that contained piles upon piles of documents in thick stacks, bounded together by fat rubber bands. Most of the documents had blue backings, and each time the woman called out a case she would grab one of the stacks and drop it in front of Justice Fuentes. They landed with a thud, like someone had beaten a bass drum. Danny leaned over to Anzalone and asked about the stacks.

"Those are the motion papers filed by the lawyers," Anzalone whispered, "they're mostly briefs and affidavits with exhibits."

Danny just nodded.

"Typically, a judge and her staff will read those before oral argument. But not Fuentes. As you can probably tell, it looks like she hasn't read anything."

And how could she? Danny thought.

There were over sixty motions on today and in each one of them the lawyers had filed what looked like a pile of phone books. Fuentes had three motion days per week in her courtroom, according to Anzalone. So these motions were like tidal waves that never stopped coming, and Danny could do the math. If she had to read all the papers filed in all these cases, it'd take her … what? A month? A year? He couldn't imagine.

So instead of actually reading these motions, the judge would unsnap the rubber bands and peruse them while she was listening to the lawyers rant and rave. She'd ask them a bunch of pointed questions, and as soon as she had heard enough of the bullshit, she would shut them down, issue a ruling, and run their asses out of court. Sometimes she would tell them she was "reserving" her ruling and that they would get a written decision at some point. Each case on average was taking less than fifteen minutes, and yet these document stacks must have taken the lawyers weeks to prepare, at God knows what cost. Just so they could sit on the judge's desk wrapped in bungee cords.

What a system, Danny thought.

And then it hit him – she would be deciding *his* case in the same manner, wouldn't she. In the next half hour, he would learn his and Agnes's fate. The thought that he could be thrown out of here today after fifteen minutes of a bunch of lawyers yelling back and forth, just so Justice Fuentes could move on to the next dozen or so cases, the next phone book stack, the next motion calendar … well, Danny was scared for his life.

The woman with the scratchy voice suddenly called out, "NUMBER 37, AGNES BEERS VERSUS GUNTHER HOME PRODUCTS CORP. CASE NO. 18-67675. COUNSEL PLEASE STEP FORWARD."

Anzalone tapped Danny on the knee. "Here we go," she said, and she headed for the front of the room.

DANNY WATCHED AS the woman in the witness stand went over to the conference table. She grabbed three meaty stacks of documents and dropped them on the judge's desk. Like all the prior cases, each one was at least a foot high, but here there were three of them.

"My, my," Justice Fuentes said when she saw the stacks. "I guess everyone did their homework on this one."

She peered over her reading glasses and watched as the lawyers on this Beers case approached the gate that led to the counsel tables. On all the prior motions there were two or three lawyers who appeared and argued the cases. But not on this case. Here the entire courtroom watched as an army of lawyers in blue suits moved toward the front of the room.

During the morning Danny had picked up that typically the plaintiff's lawyer would take the counsel table to the right near the jury box, and the defense lawyer would take the other table. Indeed, when Anzalone moved through the gate she settled in front of the jury box. The defense lawyers filed in after her. Danny thought they looked like sedans moving through a toll booth. One by one they began congregating around the counsel table opposite Anzalone.

Danny counted as they walked through – one, two, three … in all there were seventeen of them. When the last one entered and the gate swung closed, there was a large crowd gathered at the defense table. Anzalone stood by herself on the other side.

Justice Fuentes pulled off her reading glasses.

"Wait, are you all here for *this* case?"

The lawyers all nodded in affirmance.

"Well that's just great," she moaned, pulling the rubber bands off the first stack. "Let's see what we have here."

She began reading the first page of one of the documents, and then she looked up and nodded at Anzalone.

"You're plaintiff's counsel I'm guessing?" Then she gestured to the full throng of defense counsel. "You're responsible for all of these people?"

There then came a collective laugh from the gallery, and Justice Fuentes was smiling. Anzalone smiled back at her.

"Yes, Your Honor, I am," Anzalone said.

"Well, okay then, let's first get your appearance on the record, and then maybe you can tell me a little bit about this case and why we have a full platoon of lawyers at the defense table."

Back in the gallery, Danny moved to the edge of his seat. He could feel the moisture on his palms and under his arms.

Well this was it, he thought. Game time.

In about ten minutes he could be walking out of here with no lawsuit, no potential recovery to help Agnes. Or he could have himself a whopper of a legal action that would soon kick into high gear. It was one or the other. An eerie silence fell upon the room as the lawyers lining the walls and the gallery were craning their necks to see what this one was all about. All eyes were on this tiny lawyer standing all by herself at the plaintiff's table.

"Thank you, Your Honor," Anzalone began, "my name is Nicole Anzalone, Law Offices of Nicole I. Anzalone, located at 435 Ketchogue Terrace, Ketchogue, New York."

Anzalone let that hang in the air. The judge was taking notes as Anzalone spoke, and Anzalone waited until she could look the judge directly in the eyes. When Justice Fuentes finally shot a stare at her from over those reading glasses, Anzalone continued, speaking in a booming voice that belied her diminutive stature.

"Your Honor, I represent the plaintiffs in this case," she said. "My client Agnes Beers is a ten-year-old girl who has been in a persistent vegetative coma since April. She currently is at Pembleton Memorial Hospital on Long Island kept alive by a tracheotomy and a feeding machine. I believe she is likely to be discharged soon, not because of her health, but because of the family's inability to pay. I also represent her father, Mr. Daniel Beers, who happens to be here in the courtroom today."

Anzalone turned around and across the expanse of the massive courtroom her eyes met Danny's. Danny didn't move, only because he had no idea what to do. When Anzalone mentioned his name, Danny froze. At the same time, nearly every person in the courtroom was searching for the father of this girl whose lawyer just announced was in a coma.

"Your client is *here?*" asked Justice Fuentes. "Where is he?"

"In the back, Your Honor." She turned again toward Danny.

"Mr. Beers, where are you?" the judge asked, searching the room behind the counsel tables.

Every head then turned toward the middle of the courtroom. Slowly, a middle-aged man in a blue and orange *New York Knicks* jacket rose to his feet. He was holding a baseball cap in his hands, which he had placed over his heart. As Danny stood, he brushed his hand over his hair to improve his appearance.

"Mr. Beers," said Justice Fuentes, "come up here and sit with your attorney."

Danny stepped out into the aisle and walked toward the judge's bench. The only sound in the room was the squeaking of Danny's Timberland work boots on the courtroom's tile floor. He made it to the front of the courtroom and pulled open the wooden gate, letting it bang shut. Then he walked over to Anzalone and stood next to her.

"There you go, and thanks for being here today," said Justice Fuentes. "I'm very sorry about your daughter."

"Thank you, Your Honor," Danny coughed meekly. He then pulled on the front of his *Knicks* jacket.

"I'm so sorry, I didn't know," he said apologetically, barely above a whisper. "I woulda worn a suit … I have one."

"It's fine Mr. Beers. Have a seat please."

Justice Fuentes pulled a document from one of the stacks and began flipping the pages of it, one after another. She turned her head to the defense side of the room and addressed the lawyers.

"Ok then, who has a motion on today? Who wants to start?"

At that question, a thirty-something Asian lawyer stepped forward to a lectern that was on the left side of the defense counsel table. He opened a thin black blinder and addressed the court.

"Good morning Justice Fuentes," he opened, "my name is Yang Hsue Ko, and I'm a partner in the law firm of Foster Tuttle & Briggs LLP, based in midtown Manhattan. My firm represents the defendant Gunther Home Products Corporation."

Judge Fuentes pulled off her reading glasses.

"Well, well, Foster Tuttle & Briggs! How about that?"

There followed a low rumble of laughter from the gallery. Justice Fuentes was smiling, but when the laughter didn't subside, she twice rapped her gavel down, without losing her grin.

"I'm sorry," she said, "but we don't get the white shoe firms up here too often. So, you'll have to excuse my surprise. But what a pleasure. Welcome to the Bronx, Mr. Ko."

"Not at all, Your Honor, thank you," said Ko. "It's a pleasure to be here."

"And it's a pleasure to have you." She then pointed to the first document stack. "So, Mr. Ko, is this going to be a short story or a long story?"

The attorney Ko was a tall man with a youthful appearance, dressed impeccably. He wore a dark grey suit, a white shirt and a patterned royal blue tie. Danny hadn't noticed him before, but once he stepped to the lectern and opened his binder, Danny could see how impressive a figure he was cutting. He most certainly looked and spoke more professionally than any of the lawyers that Danny had watched over the last hour or so. If Danny didn't know any better, he would have guessed the man was a U.S. Senator. You could see how comfortable he was standing there in a courtroom arguing for his client. It was unnerving to say the least.

Danny prayed that the rest of the gang over there wasn't as sharp as this Ko character appeared to be. Plus, the judge had just greeted Ko as if he were a U.S. Ambassador arriving for a diplomatic mission. This wasn't starting off very well. Danny shifted his attention back to the lectern.

"Your Honor," Ko began, "I am here on two motions. The first is a Rule 3211 motion to dismiss. It is our position that the plaintiff's complaint fails to state any viable legal claim and must be dismissed as a matter of New York law. If Your Honor grants that motion, as we think you must, the case is over and you need not consider the second motion. But if Your Honor denies that first motion, we would collectively ask that you hear and grant the second motion, which is being made on behalf of all defendants. That second one is a motion to change venue –"

Justice Fuentes wasted no time in interrupting.

"Hold it, Mr. Ko, what's the claim here? Let's begin there. Why is your client being sued? Gimme the two-sentence synopsis."

"Sure, Your Honor" Ko answered calmly. "The plaintiff alleges that she ingested a product that my client sold – a brand called Phillips frozen shrimp – and that she had an allergic reaction to it. She alleges she went into anaphylactic shock and is now in the present physical condition reported by Ms. Anzalone."

"Ok, thank you for your brevity. So, she ate your shrimp and suffered an injury from it, and she's been in the hospital since April. That's the allegation. And on this motion, at this early stage of the case, I am required to accept those allegations as true, correct?"

"Yes, Your Honor you are."

"All we are doing right now is testing the *legal* sufficiency of the plaintiff's claims, and we are not arguing or deciding facts, correct?"

"True, Your Honor."

"And I am required to read the complaint as broadly as possible and resolve any ambiguities in favor of the plaintiffs, right?"

"That's right, Your Honor."

"In fact, if I find *any* possible valid legal claim under New York law, I am required to deny your motion, correct Mr. Ko?"

"Yes, that is the correct standard, Your Honor."

"So what's the problem, sir?" Justice Fuentes asked, more aggressive now. "Why isn't what Ms. Anzalone said in the complaint enough?"

"Your Honor –"

"I'm guessing the plaintiff has alleged claims for negligence, strict products liability, failure to warn, etcetera, etcetera, the usual panoply of claims we see in all of these complaints, am I right?"

"Yes, Your Honor, but –"

"So the plaintiff has alleged duty, breach, causation and damages. Sounds like a valid lawsuit to me. So again, I ask you, what's the problem Mr. Ko? Why is Gunther and its 800-attorney law firm taking up what precious little time a lowly civil servant like me has to offer?"

Danny watched all of this with awe. He had settled in and felt more like an observer, with no stake in the game, as if he were watching the whole thing on the History Channel. Justice Fuentes was so sharp, and her tone so aggressive, but this Ko just wouldn't be flustered. He was meeting her aggression with calm and poise, and Danny half wished, just for a moment, that the guy was on his side. Right now, the gleam of confidence in his eyes was intimidating. He had the look like he knew he was right and at any minute he would convince you of that fact.

"Your Honor, it is a question of proximate cause," Ko answered. "Allow me to explain."

"Please do, Mr. Ko."

Justice Fuentes lifted her pen, and Anzalone did the same. Ko's lurid voice radiated into every nook and cranny of the courtroom.

"The plaintiffs here allege that Agnes Beers was given shrimp as a snack during a town-sponsored softball game," he said. "They allege she had a preexisting shellfish allergy, and that when she ate the shrimp, she had an adverse reaction, thereby suffering her injuries. Her main claim is for failure to provide a warning. But to be clear, there is no allegation that the shrimp was defective or tainted in any way. Agnes, sadly, simply should not have eaten my client's product, or any other shellfish product. But the key here, Your Honor, was that the father, Mr. Beers," and with that Ko shot a glance over at Danny, "was in attendance that day. Paragraph 27 of the complaint makes clear that Mr. Beers was present at the field *before* the town and its representatives provided the snack to Agnes. So that means one of two things is true Your Honor."

Ko then stepped from one side of the lectern to the other. The courtroom seemed to be hanging on every one of his words.

"Mr. Beers, Agnes's legal guardian, either did NOT know his daughter had a shellfish allergy," he explained, "or Mr. Beers DID know she had an allergy. Under either circumstance the plaintiffs cannot recover, because they will not be able to prove that any conduct on the part of the defendants – negligent or otherwise – was the proximate cause of Agnes's injuries."

Ko then paused a moment and rested his hands on the lectern. In all the prior cases Justice Fuentes had barely taken a breath and had fired questions at the lawyers, almost as if she were cross-examining them. But when Ko was speaking Justice Fuentes's head was down, and she was frantically scribbling notes. She was letting him go on, and even Anzalone seemed to be captivated by his presentation. Her pen was now resting on top of her notepad and she was listening along with everyone else. The point was obvious to everyone in the room – Ko was making a lot of sense, and the judge seemed to be listening.

"Go on, Mr. Ko," said Justice Fuentes.

"Let's take the first scenario," Ko continued, "that Mr. Beers did *not* know his daughter had a shellfish allergy. The main legal claim in this complaint is that Gunther negligently failed to warn that eating the shrimp could cause an allergic reaction. But in the circumstance that Mr. Beers had no knowledge of a shellfish allergy, what difference would a warning have made? Gunther could have provided the biggest and boldest product warning, but if one is unaware she is allergic, one has no reason to modify her behavior in the face of a warning. Consequently, a *failure* to warn has no impact, and cannot cause any injuries."

Justice Fuentes was back to scribbling on her pad again. Danny looked over at the sea of defense lawyers and saw that several were eyeballing him. Their stare suggested blame, judgment, contempt. The father was there, they seemed to be repeating, right there with his daughter. He apparently did nothing to help her. And he's suing *us?* Outrageous. Danny's mouth and throat were now bone-dry, and his hands began to shake. He placed them on his lap and focused back on Ko.

"The second scenario, Your Honor," he continued, "compels the same result. If Mr. Beers *did* know his daughter had an allergy, then there simply is no need for any warning at all. New York law is clear that a product manufacturer or distributor has no duty to warn of a product's potential dangers where the risks are open and obvious. Here, under scenario two, assuming Mr. Beers knew that his daughter had a preexisting allergic condition, all that would have been required to avoid the plaintiff's injuries would have been for Mr. Beers to prevent his daughter from eating the shrimp. Sadly, he did not do so. But regardless, any failure to warn had no role in causing these injuries, and the case must be dismissed."

When Ko was finished Danny could hear rumbling throughout the courtroom. The lawyers in the gallery waiting for their cases apparently had an opinion about what Ko had just presented to the court, and if Danny could guess, they agreed with him wholeheartedly. The whole thing made sense to Danny and confirmed what even he believed when the first suggestion had been made to him to consult a lawyer about this whole disaster. It also brought front and center something that Danny had long feared – that his role in this incident would be the target of the defendants. They would be pointing the finger of blame at him.

But of course what did it matter now – Ko was brilliant and Fuentes was going to dismiss his case. Danny was sure of it.

Ko and Justice Fuentes batted questions and answers back and forth for another five minutes, and then Justice Fuentes instructed him to sit.

"I want to hear from your adversary," she said.

Anzalone promptly strode to the lectern on her side and dropped her notes on top. She launched directly into her argument.

"Your Honor, all of that speculation and guesswork is very interesting," she began, "and I'm sure Mr. Ko will do a very nice job explaining all of that to a jury when this case eventually gets to trial. New York law is clear, however, that the question of proximate cause is nearly always one for the jury and should not be decided on a motion to dismiss at the beginning of the case. And while Mr. Ko focuses on what *Mr. Beers* knew, he conveniently ignores what his *own client* knew. In that regard, I direct Your Honor's attention to paragraph 36 of our complaint."

Justice Fuentes placed her reading glasses atop the bridge of her nose again and flipped pages. When she found her place, she pointed a finger in the air without looking up.

"I'm there," she said, "go ahead."

"As you can see," Anzalone continued, "in that paragraph we allege that Gunther knew that its product could cause *severe* allergic reactions and resulting injuries. Not just normal or typical allergic reactions, but severe ones. We further allege that notwithstanding that knowledge, Gunther still neglected to provide a warning. In the following paragraphs we further claim that Gunther was aware of a spike in allergic reactions with respect to this particular brand of products and still did nothing to warn the consuming public, or perhaps issue a recall. Under New York law, at this stage of the proceedings, those allegations must be accepted as true and are more than adequate to survive a motion to dismiss."

"But Mr. Ko is not arguing a duty to provide a warning," said Justice Fuentes. "He's arguing causation. He's saying that any such warning on the bag of shrimp would have been futile, given his two scenarios, which seem to me to be correct. Are you suggesting there's a third scenario?"

"I'm stating that he and his client are speculating," Anzalone responded. "What Mr. Beers knew or didn't know, what all of the other defendants knew, and how each of them would have reacted in the face of a clear warning about the product's inherent dangers, are all facts that will be determined during the discovery process. We are a long way away from those findings. Right now, the only question is whether we have sufficiently alleged a viable claim under New York law, that's all. And clearly we have."

The attorneys then went back and forth, with Justice Fuentes firing questions and the lawyers swatting them away with answers. They each were citing to cases, giving numerical citations, and using legal phrases that Danny couldn't make heads or tails of. Justice Fuentes was so smart, Danny thought, and Ko was terrific. But Danny saw that Anzalone was equally as good, and man was she prepared. She knew the facts of every case the lawyers quoted, and when Fuentes asked about them, Anzalone recited them cold, explaining why they were or weren't relevant.

Ko had the last word, but soon the judge showed her palms.

"Okay, enough," she said. "I'll hear from your co-defendants."

The lawyers for the town of Ketchogue, the Sports and Recreation Committee, the individual members Regina Wartham, Bruce Dixon, Moshe Wagshul, the Coach Peter Briscoe, and of course Dodge and Cindy Brewer, all took their turns arguing for a dismissal. But Anzalone was prepared, and she methodically explained why their motions had no merit. In their official capacities they plied Agnes with a snack, and she was now in a coma. And if they weren't acting in their official capacities, they personally were responsible for their negligent acts. Anzalone cited cases to support her arguments, chapter and verse. Period, end of story.

Further, she noted, the Brewers had lied to everyone and announced the kids were getting seafood from a renowned institution – Lenny's Seafood Market – when in fact she was feeding them garbage from the frozen food aisle at Shop-Rite. They were all liable and responsible for these injuries, Anzalone argued, and she would prove it. All she had to do at this stage was state a legal claim, and Justice Fuentes wasted no time in agreeing.

One by one she denied their motions.

Then the attorney for Shop-Rite stepped forward, a man named Neil Acton. He wore aviator eyeglasses over a bulbous, red nose that looked to Danny like someone had been chewing on it. He spoke softly, and Justice Fuentes had to admonish him three times to raise his weak voice. But he made a very convincing argument, at least to Danny, that his client did not manufacture or package any of these shrimp products, and that all it did was "bring it in the back door and sell it out the front door." He said that Shop-Rite made no alterations to the product and that under New York law, as a retailer, it had no responsibility for any warnings. Anzalone tried her best, but even Danny could see that she was struggling to piece together a coherent argument.

"Ms. Anzalone, stop, I've heard enough," Fuentes finally said. "The defendant Shop-Rite Inc.'s motion to dismiss is granted, and the case against that defendant is dismissed with prejudice. Mr. Acton, you'll submit an order for my signature?"

"I will, Your Honor, thank you."

He gathered up his papers, scooped up his trench coat, and made a beeline through the double doors and was gone.

"Anyone else?" Justice Fuentes asked.

Yang Hsue Ko stood. "No, Your Honor," he said, "except we do have an additional motion, the one for change of venue, which all defendants have signed on to. And given Your Honor's ruling on the non-Gunther defendants' motions, it appears Your Honor will need to hear that one."

She picked up her pen again, glancing at a wall clock.

"Well, have at it, Mr. Ko."

Ko then pressed that Agnes's injuries occurred in Ketchogue, she currently was in a Nassau County hospital, all the defendants other than Gunther were located in Ketchogue, which was also in Nassau County, and all relevant documents and evidence from the plaintiffs' side were also in Ketchogue. For the convenience of all the parties, including the plaintiffs, Ko argued, the case should be transferred out of the Bronx, which had no relation to the events in question. Once again Danny thought Ko was masterful, but then Anzalone met his challenge.

"Your Honor, this really is an easy one. Under New York law, venue is proper in any county where any party can be located. In my opposition papers I have clearly demonstrated that Gunther has a distribution center right here in the Bronx. That center is where the Phillips frozen shrimp brand was collected and stored and then shipped to the food stores on Long Island, including Shop-Rite. Mr. Ko knows this. Quite frankly, I'm surprised they filed the motion."

Justice Fuentes turned to the defense table.

"True, Mr. Ko?"

"Well yes, Your Honor, we do have a Bronx distribution center, but –"

"Well that's good enough for me," she said. "Assuming I do not grant your motion, looks like you'll be here in the Bronx. Welcome aboard."

Then she turned to Anzalone.

"However, Ms. Anzalone, if the court grants the Gunther motion and dismisses Mr. Ko's client, and with Shop-Rite gone, that leaves only the Ketchogue parties, am I right?"

"You are, Your Honor."

"And in that instance, you're not going to stand there and tell me I should keep this case in the Bronx, at least not with a straight face, am I correct, Ms. Anzalone?"

Anzalone didn't hesitate. "I won't do that Your Honor."

"So that leaves us with the Gunther motion, correct?"

"Yes, Your Honor."

"Okay, the court will stand in recess for five minutes."

The judge stood, and the buzzcut court officer jumped to his feet. "ALL RISE!" he screamed, and Justice Fuentes retreated through the door marked CHAMBERS.

DURING THE SHORT break the defense lawyers congregated for a quick strategy session out in the hallway, but Danny and Anzalone stayed at the counsel table. Danny had a million questions, but the only one he wanted answered was this – what did Anzalone think of their chances?

"I'm not sure, to be honest" she said, not very confidently. "This is unusual, her taking a break like this. Maybe she wants to read over one of the briefs, but who knows. Let's just keep our fingers crossed."

"You know, if she lets Gunther out, I'm not sure I wanna go against only the people in Ketchogue. We'll need to talk."

Anzalone shrugged her shoulders.

"We'll know in a few minutes," she answered.

This wasn't the answer that Danny wanted, but at least it sounded honest. He leaned back in his chair and let the hum of the courtroom wash over him as Anzalone cracked open a newspaper. Time seemed to be standing still, and in a strange way, over the next ten minutes or so, Danny felt calm. There was nothing he could do to help himself here, nothing he could do or say that would change the outcome. If Justice Fuentes tossed him from her courtroom today, he would just have to figure things out.

But all of that changed in the next second. Danny looked up and saw Justice Fuentes strolling back from her chambers. The buzzcut officer slapped the desk again, and the pounding snapped Danny back to reality.

"ALL RISE!" he yelled, and everyone launched to their feet. Every lawyer in the courtroom was now hanging on Justice Fuentes's decision, as if they were watching the final scene of a movie. The judge took her seat at the bench as Danny stuffed his shaking hands in his pockets. His heart was pounding, and he could barely feel his feet on the floor. There was a wave of nausea rising in his intestines.

"Be seated," said Justice Fuentes. "Thanks for your patience."

Then she delivered her decision.

"The Complaint here alleges that plaintiff Agnes Beers is a ten-year-old child currently in a coma as a result of ingesting a shrimp product packaged and sold by the defendant, Gunther Home

Products Corporation. Plaintiff has alleged claims that include causes of action for negligence, strict products liability, failure to warn, and intentional and negligent infliction of emotional distress. The defendant Gunther has filed a Rule 3211 motion to dismiss, essentially arguing that plaintiff's complaint is legally deficient because plaintiff will not be able to prove a causal nexus between the defendant's conduct and the plaintiff's injuries. Under New York law, however, the court is required at this stage to accept the plaintiff's allegations as true, and it does so today. As such, and in full consideration of the arguments made by Gunther's very able counsel, Mr. Ko, Gunther's motion to dismiss is hereby denied."

The judge placed her notes down and looked over at Anzalone.

"Ms. Anzalone, you will submit an order for my signature?"

"Yes, Your Honor, I will."

And there it was, just like that.

Danny jerked his head sideways, toward Anzalone, but her face was expressionless. She looked to Danny like she had expected this exact result, as if anything else would have been the surprise, not her victory. Danny shot a look over at Ko, who was at the lectern writing on his legal pad. It all seemed routine to these lawyers, but Danny wanted to scream. He let out an audible gasp, an involuntary blast of carbon dioxide that forced its way out of his constricted lungs. The resulting noise sounded like a sneaker squeaking on a gymnasium floor, and it could be heard throughout the entire courtroom. Sensing his relief, Anzalone placed her hand on his forearm and then patted him on the back.

"I'm sending this case for a Preliminary Conference to establish a schedule," the judge said, "and I want this case to move. I don't like cases with so many lawyers involved because all I get are requests for delays. But that's not going to happen here. All of you people will cooperate. That better be clear. And Ms. Anzalone, let me explain something to you."

Justice Fuentes pointed her pen and shot Anzalone a stern look over her reading glasses.

"You've obviously taken on a beast of a case, and as you can see from the other side of the aisle, you are clearly outnumbered. This is not going to be easy for you or your client, but I expect you already know that. I just hope you know what you're doing. You should also know that I'm not going to be cutting you any breaks. Not one, and you better get that straight. You're going to stick to the schedule, and if that's too difficult for you ... tough cookies. I'm not going to have this case drag on past our deadlines. Do we understand each other?"

"We do, Your Honor, thank you."

"Good then." Justice Fuentes waved the back of her hand to all the lawyers. "All of you, please clear out now."

Justice Fuentes then turned to the woman in the witness stand.

"Call the next case please."

And that was it.

Danny wanted to throw his hands up to declare victory, but Anzalone abruptly grabbed her document folder and stood.

"Let's go," she said, and the two of them hurried out the door.

OUT IN THE street, at the base of the courthouse steps on East 161st Street, Danny and Anzalone stood in a brisk October breeze as the taxis and traffic chugged by them. They moved a few paces down the sidewalk beyond the courthouse steps, and then behind them they saw the defense team file out, a full platoon of trench coats and briefcases. Ko shook a few hands and then he climbed into a Lincoln Town Car at the curb.

Under the midday clouds, Danny let the cool air fill his lungs. He felt as if a piano had been removed from his back. He was soaked in sweat and yet he was freezing. Then he told her how stressed he felt in there.

"And I wasn't the one on my feet. Can't imagine how you felt."

"Well, Mr. Beers," said Anzalone, "you kind of get used to doing it and it becomes routine. But as the judge said, we certainly have a big case in front of us. We're a long way away from where we want to get to, but today was a big first step. Gunther is in it for the long haul and could face a trial in the Bronx. They won't like that, so the first battle goes to us."

"Well, you really did a great job in there."

"I appreciate that."

And just then Danny's cell phone rang.

He pulled it from his Knicks jacket.

"I think this is the hospital," he said.

"Hello? Hello?"

"Dan," came a voice, "it's Marion, from Pembleton Memorial."

"Yeah, Marion, it's me, what's up? Everything alright?"

It was Agnes's head nurse, Marion Barnes. She led the hospital team tending to Agnes all these months and for that reason she and Danny were on a first name basis. Danny knew her well enough to judge the tone of her voice, and he didn't like what he was hearing.

"Dan, you need to get here as quickly as you can."

"Marion, Jesus Christ, what's the matter?!"

"Where are you? Can you get here soon?"

"Shit, Marion, yeah, but is she alright?!"

What Danny felt then was terror. Shear, unadulterated terror – in its purest form. He felt it in his bones, in his blood, in his flesh, and at the sound of her voice he felt weightless, as if he wasn't standing on his own feet anymore. It hit him as soon as he saw the hospital telephone number appear on his phone and in an instant there was no lawsuit anymore, no Justice Fuentes, no attorney Ko, nothing except for the image of his little girl in that hospital bed.

But then he heard Marion giggle.

"Dan, Agnes is awake!" she said.

Danny's heart jumped and he couldn't speak. He was dizzy, and for a moment he thought he would fall.

"She's awake!" Marion continued, "and she's looking around the room! I'm sitting next to her and I'm holding her hand! And she's squeezing it right back! I think she needs Daddy ..."

Danny couldn't believe what he was hearing.

"Dan are you there?! You hear what I just said?!"

"Yeah," Danny finally choked back, "yeah, I'm here!"

"How quickly can you get here?"

Without another word, Danny began sprinting down East 161st Street.

CHAPTER 15

THE MOON OVER MANGROVE BAY

October 19, 2018 – 11:02 pm
Ketchogue, Home

So Agnes woke up the other day. She's awake. Her eyes are open, and she can't speak because of the trach but she's awake. So maybe my prayers have been answered, maybe somebody up there is looking after the Beers family after all. Deep down my worst fear was that she would never come out of that coma. I know we have a long haul in front of us but over the last 2 days I've been able to breathe. Not much, but a little.

Meanwhile, I've decided I'm going to keep this journal thing going. It feels good to write all this shit out once in a while. I should have done this a long time ago, like years ago. It's like seeing a shrink, but free. Anyway, it's Friday night and its late and the girls are sleeping, and I'm meeting Carlos at a job at about 12 tomorrow, so I have a few minutes before I hit the sack.

Well guess what's been eating me alive recently – money. It's all I think about. My business is doing shitty there's no sense sugar-coating it. I'm getting my ass kicked. Most of this is my fault and I know that. After Deb died, I let a lot of shit go because I was so goddamned depressed that I wasn't more on top of things. I had no clue what bills we paid and to who and some days I couldn't even get out of bed never mind start digging around the house looking for who got paid what. And if I'm being honest back then I even thought of having Will and Janet take the girls for a few months because I had no idea what to do with them. Pathetic when I think about it. But one of things I let slip at that time was the health insurance premiums which I didn't pay for months. So the policy eventually lapsed and when Agnes got hurt, I had nothing. Been kicking myself for it ever since.

A few months ago I signed up for one of the Obamacare plans, but I have a big fat $4000 deductible that applies across the board for just about everything so right now I'm paying a ton of money out of pocket. I'm behind on the PT bills and a few others and I owe the hospital over

150 grand. Those unpaid bills along with a hundred others are on my credit report and I don't even want to know what that number is right now. I don't think anyone would loan me a nickel. Next week I've decided I'm gonna go see if I can find some extra work tending bar over the weekends. I'll need Henry and Will to help out with Gianna but Henry for one will do it. He'll make some smartass comments to me but he'll do it.

These are the times when I really miss Deb, times like now when I feel like everything is spiraling out of control. She had a way about her that was calming for me. Not that she was a pushover or anything like that because she wasn't. What I mean is just that Deb was in charge of everything in our house. She knew where every dollar went and made sure everything was paid on time and had the place as clean and organized as an Army barracks. She ran all of our schedules and knew who had to be where and when including me. And she still brought so much joy and happiness into the place. What can I say, she was my best friend. How do you ever replace that?

I'm not saying everything was perfect between us because it wasn't. We used to get on each other's nerves like any other couple and man did we have our fights. But when I look back on it now I can see that it was all just a matter of her wanting everything organized as a means of coping with how much she worried about shit all the time, and how much I made that worse for her because I couldn't see what the cause of all of it was. She was always worried about the girls, constantly, like every day and night, but it wasn't money and bills and practical stuff it was all emotional and mental things, stuff I was just clueless about. It was like she could see inside their heads and knew what they were thinking and what was bothering them. Then she'd take all of that on herself and it would turn her inside out. She'd never share any of that with me but instead the way she'd deal with it was by doing shit around the house like vacuuming three rooms, spraying and wiping counters, painting the hallway, cleaning out the garage, or a hundred other things. And of course, I had no sense of what the problem was, and I'd tell her cut the shit and relax and you're always complaining, take a breath and calm down, or something stupid like that. Funny thing is, now that's me. I regret not seeing all that at the time. I can see now that all I did was add to her angst. I could have been a help, but I wasn't.

Anyway, I think the way that Deb was had a lot to do with Henry and the way she was raised. Henry is from Brooklyn and his father, who was also named Henry, was off the boat from County Mayo. He came over here in the '30s, Henry's father that is, and moved to Boerum Hill. Henry grew up on those Brooklyn streets and was a tough dude even as a kid. He became a cop as a young man, I think, because he's got this sixth sense about law and order and rules. It's in his blood. Back then you just did not mess with Henry Mahoney. Can you imagine running into him on the streets? I've met a few of his old partners and boy did they have a couple of stories. I guess Henry saw too much bad stuff on the job and that made him want out of the city, so he moved the family out to Centereach and that's where Deb was born. Henry was a tough father too, Deb told me all about it. Like I said, he had his rules and if you lived under his roof you didn't break them. Plain and simple.

I met Deb on a Sunday out at an old Long Island bar called the OBI, down in Babylon on the beach. What a great place that was. It's closed now but those Sunday happy hours were a blast. Anyway, we were a little older than most couples when we met and so I guess a little more set in our ways. After I got to know her a bit, I learned that Deb had a lot of Henry in her when it came to the rules but had none of him when it came to being a happy person. Deb had Henry's sense of law and order and her mother's love of life and sense of humor. Perfect combination if you ask me.

After we'd been together for about six months, I took Deb back to the beach in front of the OBI, the place where we met, and I proposed to her. Back over the bay the sun was setting and it was October so we were alone on the beach with a bottle of wine and a blanket. One of the top ten greatest days of my life no question. I remember everything about it, from how cold the sand was on our feet to the flowered dress Deb was wearing with that white cotton sweater over it to the cool autumn breeze blowing off the ocean. I'm fifty and when I think back on my life, as you tend to do at this age, that day sticks out as one of the best I can ever remember.

In fact, I got this thing I think about a lot, and it goes like this – see, when you're 80 or 90 or something and you know you're at the end of your rope, you'll look back on your life and you'll remember maybe ten particular moments, maybe not even ten maybe only five, when you were the happiest you've ever been. And then all the other meaningless days just kind of blend together in your memory. And I can tell you the moments that fall into that category for me and they're not the ones you would expect like the day my kids were born for instance, although I will never forget those days of course. They were incredible life moments but until I was holding those healthy babies in my arms I was anxious as hell because I didn't want anything to happen to Deb and the babies and by the time it was all over and nature had taken its course I was more relieved than anything else.

Instead, for me the day I would pinpoint as number one happened earlier than the kids. See, me and Deb got married in June, about eight months after that day on the beach at the OBI. Our wedding was really a great time. Will was my best man and my Mom was there before she passed. It was modest by most weddings but that was only because we went low budget on the reception and saved for a great honeymoon in Bermuda. We flew there on the Monday after our Saturday night wedding and Deb brought her flower bouquet with her to the airport. After we checked the bags I went up to the counter because I wanted to ask how long it was before boarding and just for kicks I told the flight attendant that we had just gotten married and I turned around and pointed to Deb and her bouquet. Then I asked, was there any chance we could get upped to first class for our big day and honeymoon? The lady laughed a little, told me congratulations, and then she started clacking away on her keyboard. Then all of a sudden she said sure here you go. The machine spat out two first class tickets and I ran back to Deb like a kid at a carnival. We sat up there in first class on the two-hour flight and laughed the whole way there.

When we got to Bermuda we checked into this place called Kensington Beaches where all the staff spoke with British accents and ran around in navy blue shorts and knee high socks and safari hats like that guy Jim from the old Mutual of Omaha's Wild Kingdom show. The place was incredible it was right on this peninsula where the ocean was on one side and an inlet called Mangrove Bay was on the other. We had a cottage all to ourselves surrounded by palm trees and it sat about 15 yards from the ocean. That first day we threw our stuff in the room and sat on the beach for a few hours and then in the afternoon we went back to the room and made love and took a shower and then we went off to dinner. We got a seat right in the middle of this lively restaurant that was part of the resort and we each had one of those fruity rum drinks and we ordered some seafood. While we were waiting, sitting there with our sunburned faces, there was this Calypso type song playing on the rock speakers and right near us was a gazebo with a bunch of palm trees surrounding it. Leading out from it was a little walkway that went down toward the bay. We had a few minutes before our food arrived and so I asked Deb to dance.

She smiled and grabbed my hand and we walked over to the gazebo and stepped out onto the walkway. She pressed her face into my chest and wrapped her arms around me and I did the same to her. I looked up and there was this enormous full moon lighting up Mangrove Bay, shining on the water like it had been placed there just for us, just for that dance. We swayed back and forth to the music and I remember thinking how absolutely lucky I was to be in that moment, right there, dancing with this beautiful girl under the moon over Mangrove Bay. And I knew even then I wanted to freeze that moment, hold it there and make it last, because I was old enough to know that life just didn't get any better than that. We were just married and had our whole lives in front of us and I'm sure Deb could have found a ton of other decent guys to spend her life with but there was no way I could possibly do any better. I had this amazing person come into my life by some incredible stroke of luck at a time when I really had no feel for where my life was going. And at that moment I was the happiest I've ever been. When I look back when I'm 80 or 90 or a hundred, like I said, that moment is number one.

Anyway, that big fat moon that hung over Mangrove Bay that night has become a thing for me, something I always think about. The moment came and went, just like that moon rose and fell. The whole thing was just so temporary. And of course, it's all gone now. That moon, Debbie, our lives together – all gone. But just the thought of it motivates me and reminds me not only of the happiest day of my entire life but also what I want to regain. Maybe it won't be a dance with a beautiful girl, but it'll be something else that I can give my kids. Some measure of happiness that they can define for themselves.

I'm going to get them through this dark period of our lives. Somehow, some way I'm gonna do it.

I'm not going to sit around and piss and moan and feel sorry for myself. I don't know how it's going to get done but it will. Just mark my words. See, you have to have faith in this world. You have to have hope. Because, really, what else is there?

Well shit it's late – it's after 1 am, and I gotta get to bed. I'll be checking back on this thing soon, I hope.

PART THREE

THE DISCOVERY PHASE

CHAPTER 16

THE NATIONAL SHRIMP
COCKTAIL DEFENSE TEAM

L OUIS BRANDEIS.
    Benjamin Cardozo and Oliver Wendell Holmes Jr.

Thurgood Marshall, John Marshall Harlan and Antonin Scalia.

And of course, Abraham Lincoln, James Madison, Learned Hand and Felix Frankfurter.

These were just a few of the brilliant constitutionalists who had so profoundly inspired O'Reilly that he had taken to law school like a duck to water. With tears in his eyes, and fire in his heart, O'Reilly had devoured all their speeches, all their essays, and all their appellate and Supreme Court opinions. The precision in the language, the depth of the legal and analytical reasoning, the fight for the cause of those less fortunate – it all blew O'Reilly away. It had ignited in him a burning ambition and sent him into law school ready to take on the world. He had long resolved, with unbridled determination, to follow in the footsteps of these legal titans and make his mark in this dignified, honored profession.

Yes, by the grace of God, O'Reilly was going to bring righteousness and justice to the United States of America.

He would right wrongs, and let freedom ring, from sea to shining sea.

He would make a real difference in people's lives.

He would take on corporate greed, expose wrongdoers, and bring down fraudsters, scammers and liars. And if there were anyone in this great country of ours – anywhere – who didn't have the economic means to take on the good fight, they could simply contact Seamus P. O'Reilly, Esq., and there you would find him, fist in the air before a bank of microphones, screaming for justice for the downtrodden, the lonely, the oppressed.

Yes sir, Seamus P. O'Reilly would commit his career, his very life, to striking fear in the hearts of those who would seek to take advantage of the tired, the poor, the huddled masses – anyone yearning to breathe free. Upon entering law school that was his mission, his *raison d'etre*, and may God have mercy on the soul of anyone who stood in his way …

And now here he was – the lowest-ranking junior shit-heel member of the National Shrimp Cocktail Defense Team. Let me repeat that, he would say to himself –

The National … Shrimp Cocktail … Defense Team.

How had it come to this? How had he fallen so low?

It was now November and only three months earlier O'Reilly had been soaking in the comforts of his cushy Park Avenue office, logged onto Westlaw and eyeball deep in caselaw interpreting the U.S. Immigration and Naturalization Act. He was working tirelessly as an FT&B Summer Associate to aid the plight of a poor defenseless monk whose basic human rights had been so egregiously violated, he had been forced to flee Tibet with angry Chinese officials nipping at his heels. If it was the last thing he would do, O'Reilly decided back then with a gritty resolve, he would help this man obtain refuge in these great United States, even if it meant the anxious monk had to sleep on O'Reilly's futon, and eat his Apple Jacks, until he found some decent room and board.

And now?

Well, now O'Reilly's fat ass was in a warehouse in Secaucus, New Jersey, of all places, plowing through boxes upon boxes of documents from the Gunther Home Products Corporation, relating to frozen shrimp for Christ's sake, at a clip of eleven hours a day.

Was this what he went to law school for? For *this*?

There was nothing about this situation that pleased O'Reilly, nothing at all. And it all started with the commute from Park Slope, Brooklyn, out to the infected bowels of Secaucus. O'Reilly's day would start with a half-mile walk from his studio apartment past the brownstones on First Street until he got to 4th Avenue, where he would turn right toward the Union Street subway station. There he would hop the R train to Manhattan. That took him fifteen lumbering stops through Brooklyn to midtown, where he would get off at the 34th Street Herald Square station. He would then weave his way through the hordes and the mayhem near Greeley Square, turning right down 32nd Street until he got to Penn Station.

Once he descended into the guts of Penn, O'Reilly would plow his way through the sweaty masses to the Eighth Avenue side and board a New Jersey Transit train on the Montclair-Boonton line, getting off at the Frank R. Lautenberg Secaucus Upper Level stop. But that only put him on the other end of Secaucus from where the warehouse was, so O'Reilly had to walk ten minutes over to Secaucus Junction, where he would catch the 129 Bus toward Secaucus Plaza. From there, the final leg of the journey was another half-mile walk to the warehouse over on Meadowlands Parkway. The Firm made clear to O'Reilly that they expected him to arrive no later than 8:00 am and that he'd be working *four days a week* – Mondays, Wednesdays, Fridays *and Saturdays* – digging through the Gunther boxes.

On the first day of his new assignment back in early September, O'Reilly left his Park Slope apartment at six-thirty am, grabbed a dark roast coffee and a chocolate chip muffin from a Dunkin' Donuts on Seventh Avenue, but then with all the changes and switches and delays, he didn't arrive at the warehouse until 9:10 am. He had to let three R trains go by at the Union Street subway station before he could cram his way onto the fourth one, and then the jam-packed subway train stopped between Atlantic and DeKalb Avenues without explanation for almost fifteen minutes, during which a man with dreadlocks and Mike Tyson face-tattoos kept hitting him in the back of the head with a guitar case. Once he arrived at Herald Square, O'Reilly sprinted down 32nd Street and down the stairs into Penn Station. He just missed the Montclair-Boonton line NJ Transit train, bounding down the steps to Track 9 to watch the red taillights disappear into the tunnel. He then waited twenty-five minutes to catch the next one.

O'Reilly was frantic during each leg of the trip, checking the time on his iPhone about three hundred times. When he finally arrived at the warehouse, he was tense and sweating and completely out of breath. He met immediately with a Senior Litigation Paralegal named Manuel Perez, who instructed O'Reilly to call him "Manny." Manny was a short, skinny man in his late thirties with a heavy Hispanic accent and a receding hairline. He oversaw the entire Secaucus operation, and he greeted O'Reilly in a pair of blue jeans and an untucked short-sleeved Ralph Lauren polo shirt over black

Nike basketball sneakers. O'Reilly was dressed in his Brooks Brothers ensemble – dark grey suit, white shirt and gold tie – except that he had lowered the tie a bit to get some air.

O'Reilly shook Manny's hand, and then wiped the sweat from his forehead. Manny looked back at him and shook his head.

Then he said, "Bro, we start here at eight o'clock sharp, okay? Not 8:01 or 8:03 or 8:05. And it sure as shit ain't ten after nine."

"So sorry," said O'Reilly, "the trains were so delayed."

"Then you leave earlier, bro," Manny said.

"Yeah, absolutely," O'Reilly told him, "I definitely will."

"You're over an hour late, *amigo*."

"Yes, like I said, I'm real sorry."

"They have these things called cell phones now – you think maybe you could make a call and let us know?"

"Oh right, of course. I should have –"

"Common courtesy, *muchacho*."

"I'm really sorry."

"*Hombre*, this how it gonna be the whole time? If so, you maybe should tell me now."

"No, I just had a tough first morning. Came here from Brooklyn."

"Don't matter to me if you came here from Dublin with a box of Lucky Charms, *comprende*? We start at 8 am. Sharp."

"Absolutely. Understood."

"So we cool?"

"Yes, no problem. Won't happen again."

"Good. Better not." Manny looked him up and down. "And boss, I'd lose the suit. There's no AC in this building. You're gonna wanna be in a short-sleeved shirt maybe."

"Oh right, 'course. I didn't know."

"It's September and we still sweatin' our *culos* off in here."

"Thanks. That's a good tip."

"Let's go bro, follow me."

The next working day, Wednesday, O'Reilly decided he would get a jump on things and so he set his alarm for 5:30 am. He left his apartment right at six, a half-hour earlier than the Monday before. He hit the Dunkin' Donuts again and hustled over to the R Train. He timed it beautifully and strolled onto the first train into the station. Then he made it to Herald Square without incident. Before he knew it, he was into Penn Station and on the next NJ Transit train to Secaucus, which pulled out of the station only four minutes after O'Reilly got there – perfect. But then the train sat in the tunnel for the next forty-five minutes because "switch problems" were causing extensive delays on all trains in and out of Penn Station "until further notice." The train announcer came on the intercom and thanked everyone for their patience and for riding New Jersey Transit and told them to have a nice day. O'Reilly got to the warehouse at 8:20 am.

"What the fuck, bro!" Manny said to him as soon as he walked in, "you shittin' me? Was I not clear with you the other day?"

"Manny, I am so sorry, I –"

"*Hombre,* do I gotta make a call about you?"

"No, definitely not –"

"Bro, your first two days? After what we talked about?"

"I know. I –"

"*¿Eres estúpido o algo?*"

"I think I know what that means. I'm not stupid –"

"*Amigo,* let's go over it, let me see if I can help you. How long you spendin' in the shower?"

"Manny –"

"You hittin' the snooze button? How many times? *Tres? Quatro?*"

"I may have hit it once –"

"Layin' your clothes out the night before?"

O'Reilly took a deep breath. "I hear you loud and cl –"

"See where I'm goin'? We really need to be having this conversation?"

On the third workday, O'Reilly wasn't taking any chances. He set his alarm for 4:30 am, hit the snooze button once purely out of reflex, and left his apartment at ten after five. He was so nervous about oversleeping the alarm he barely got a wink, tossing and turning and finally falling asleep around 2:45 am. When the alarm rang the second time he bolted from his bed. As he bounded down the stairs from his apartment with his eyes burning, First Street was pitch black except for some early lights glowing from the brownstones. He decided to skip the Dunkin' Donuts and he sprinted to the R train. Then he made every connection and arrived at the warehouse, bathed in sweat, at 6:47 am. The entrance was locked and the building was completely dark. The sun was barely up and this section of Secaucus was virtually abandoned at this hour with nowhere to grab coffee or breakfast, and so O'Reilly sat on the concrete in front of the entrance with his back against the glass doors, his backpack on his lap, his stomach growling away. Manny was the first to arrive at about 7:40 am.

"Yo! The Irish Mafia is in the house!" he shouted with a smile. "*Amigo*, that's more like it. I knew you could do it."

And so O'Reilly fell into a routine. On each Secaucus day, he would rise at 4:30 and after showering and dressing would make it to the warehouse sometime before seven am. It wasn't ideal but if he left any later he would likely run into transit delays and miss the 8 am start, which would do nothing but incur the wrath of Manny. It was better to get there early and build in an hour for delays, which were painfully common. About two weeks in O'Reilly ran into another NJ Transit nightmare and arrived at the warehouse at 7:59 am. He burst through the doors like an Olympic sprinter breaking the tape in the 100-meter dash. Manny eyeballed him and pointed up at a clock on the wall near the entrance.

He said simply, "playing with fire, *hombre*."

Meanwhile, the operation at Secaucus was as efficient an exercise as O'Reilly had ever witnessed, and O'Reilly attributed all of that to Manny. The firm had rented out the 80,000 square foot warehouse specifically for this document review exercise, which they expected would last at least the entire fall. After the first few shrimp cases landed on Gunther's doorstep, Briggs and Handler decided that the firm needed to get its arms around all of the documents that Gunther was in possession of nationwide that potentially could be called for in the discovery phase of these growing lawsuits. The task would be a significant undertaking, because without knowing specifically what the plaintiffs' lawyers would be demanding, or how many cases they would be dealing with, or what all of the claims would be, the company had to cast as wide a net as possible to account for every possible relevant document. Briggs was determined that he and his legal team would know exactly what was in these records, no matter what the volume, such that they could identify any potential Achilles heels well before the documents had to be turned over to these blood-sucking vampire plaintiffs' attorneys in discovery.

After Briggs and his team consulted with the Gunther people, they quickly learned that not only were there millions of pages of possibly relevant records located in many different Gunther offices and locations across the United States, it was also the case that the vast majority of these went back several decades and therefore were not in electronic or computerized form. So in a massive document collection exercise that went on throughout the summer, the hard copy documents were identified, copied, boxed, indexed and shipped from dozens of Gunther locations to Secaucus, where Manny would log them in and place them on the many rows of racks in the warehouse.

When the collection phase of the exercise was complete, the Secaucus warehouse was filled with approximately 2,400 banker's boxes containing somewhere in the neighborhood of 4.8 million pages of Gunther documents. They related to every subject area that possibly could be relevant to the growing number of shrimp cases, including Gunther corporate structure, product marketing, company advertising, product labeling, warnings, government regulation, compliance, and quality control, all having to do with the Phillips frozen shrimp brand.

Inside the warehouse, FT&B had assembled a legal team consisting of seven junior lawyers in their first through third years at the firm, fifteen paralegals, and one part-time law student coming off his recent Summer Associate gig – a guy they called Sea-Mouse. The job of the team – dubbed the National Shrimp Cocktail Defense Team – was relatively simple. Every single page in every single box needed to be reviewed. And summarized. And categorized. And coded. And ranked for sensitivity. And then scanned into a computer database called LawDocs.

Once all the documents were loaded into the database, the entire program would be fully searchable. Thus, when Gunther received a document request from any plaintiff's lawyer, in any state, in any case, the FT&B attorneys working the cases over in New York could simply log onto LawDocs, toss in some search terms, and immediately print out every single document that was responsive to the request. And because of the previous work of the National Shrimp Cocktail Defense Team, the lawyers in New York would know the details and legal impact of every document they produced and would be miles ahead of the plaintiffs' lawyers.

When you entered the Secaucus warehouse through the glass doors, there was a set of stairs to the right that led up to a large open room with about twenty workstations, or cubicles, where all the paralegal document reviewers sat. O'Reilly was assigned a cubicle way in the back, and his view was that of a wall of cinder block. His cubicle was against a 12" steam pipe that ran vertically from the first floor up to the 20-foot high ceiling. The pipe for some reason was sizzling hot to the touch and would clink all day long, sounding as if someone were inside banging away with a hammer. And Manny did not lie, the place was a sauna, which was only made worse by the suffocating heat that radiated from the steam pipe. O'Reilly would be in a sweaty lather no later than 8:15 every morning and was convinced he would look like an Ethiopian marathoner by the time this gig was over. The desk in O'Reilly's cubicle, like all of them, had a 27-inch state of the art Apple iMac computer on it but no Internet connection and no phone, which in and of itself was a clear message. Here you wouldn't be making calls or doing any research. You would be reviewing documents and loading them onto the computer, and nothing else. O'Reilly would have to use his iPhone if he needed to make a call, except that there was no signal where he sat next to the blistering hot steam pipe. He would have to walk out the front door down on the first floor, out of the view of Manny.

On O'Reilly's first day, after his late arrival, Manny led him down a hallway on the first floor where the seven associate lawyers sat in tiny, cramped offices. This area was markedly cooler than the rest of the warehouse and the lawyers sat at small silver desks that had telephones. Manny introduced O'Reilly to a third-year lawyer named Ralph Burgess, a thirty-year old with John Lennon glasses and a horseshoe ring of black hair that circled his bald head. Burgess spent ninety minutes training O'Reilly on LawDocs, how to code the documents, and some of the issues that would come up in the cases. After that, Manny sent O'Reilly back to his cubicle with a banker's box containing 2,000 pages of documents.

"Get goin' bro, and don't fuck up," he instructed. "We have four months to get this project completed. *Hombre*, that's 2,400 boxes in four months, which means I gotta get about 100 boxes from your Irish ass, and I only got you four days a week. Plus, it looks like you got a thing about showin' up late, so automatically I'm behind the eight-ball with you. So, *amigo,* dig in and get moving. You feel me?"

"I do Manny," O'Reilly said dutifully.

"Good," answered Manny. "When you're done with that box you come and see me. Then you grab another one."

The first thing O'Reilly did when he got back to his desk was read the complaint in the recent New York shrimp case. Burgess had given him a copy of it when he was finished with the LawDocs tutorial. He explained that the plaintiffs had filed the case up in the Bronx and that the court had recently denied Gunther's motion to dismiss and for change of venue, which meant that proceedings in that case would start to move now.

O'Reilly read the complaint filed on behalf of a ten-year-old girl named Agnes Beers, who lived with her father and sister on Long Island. The Beers kid apparently was in a coma. Sad, but the family was suing for fifty million dollars, which O'Reilly thought was ridiculous. Surely the father was to blame here – he had to know his daughter had an allergy to shrimp, and he let her eat it anyway. And if he didn't know, what kind of a father was he?

That first day O'Reilly tossed the complaint down and began digging into the first Gunther box from Manny. He lifted half the documents out of the box – roughly a thousand pages – and made a pile to the right of the computer. In no time the papers were crispy and warm to the touch with the blistering heat from the steam pipe.

O'Reilly pulled the first document off the pile and saw that it was stamped on the lower left-hand corner with the alpha-numeric code GUNTH.157.355.1435.006257433. Burgess had instructed him that all the numbers following the "GUNTH" had significance – they stood first for the Gunther office location from which the document had been collected, then the Gunther company department, then the individual employee who had provided the document, and then finally the document number. All this information would need to be typed into LawDocs.

O'Reilly's task was to read the document and provide a maximum three-sentence summary, no more, using as many key words as possible from a list that Manny provided to all the document reviewers. After that, O'Reilly would have to enter as much identifying information that was available from the face of the document, such as its date, author, subject line, title, number of pages, recipients, those given a courtesy copy, etc. Finally, O'Reilly had to code the document to a set of subject matters to which it could be relevant, and then he had to rate its "sensitivity," which meant that he had to give it a rating on a scale of 0 through 6 – six being the most sensitive – based on his evaluation of how the document could hurt Gunther or help the plaintiffs in the lawsuits. If he rated the document a three or higher, there was an additional field in which he had to provide a written explanation of why the document was so important.

The first document that O'Reilly pulled was dated April 1, 1982 and was titled "MINUTES OF THE MONTHLY MEETING OF THE MANAGEMENT COMMITTEE." The document was so old and yellowed O'Reilly at first thought he had stumbled across the Magna Carta. He looked at the office location code – 157 – and went to his chart; the document was from a Gunther plant in Tempe, Arizona. 355 stood for "Executive Management." O'Reilly loaded all the preliminary information into LawDocs, and then he read the nine-page, single-spaced document, which clearly had been written on an old typewriter. There was an extended discussion about the fact that an army of striped whipsnakes recently had been seen slithering across the executive parking lot, terrorizing mid-level managers when they arrived for work every morning. The minutes droned on about whether the Committee should approve a $2,467.43 cost for some company to come and set traps. Unanimously approved, with a note that several of the Committee members parked in that lot and knew from personal experience that you had to slam your car door and sprint to the office entrance, bouncing up and down on your toes, as the whipsnakes snapped away at everyone's pant hems. The writer had spelled it "TOSE."

Then there was a discussion about a pipe that burst about a week earlier in the women's bathroom on the third floor, sending a torrent of water pouring into a conference room on the floor below, soaking the staff. The Committee unanimously approved an $18 per employee dry-cleaning allowance and the hiring of a construction outfit to do the repair. O'Reilly read all of this and wondered why this particular document was collected in the first place. What did this possibly have to do with these lawsuits? Nonetheless, he entered all the required information into the database, and in the summary section he entered *"snakes, flood - irrelevant."* Neither of those words was on the key words list, but what did it matter with this one. He gave the document a sensitivity rating of zero.

The second document was also entitled "MINUTES OF THE MONTHLY MEETING OF THE MANAGEMENT COMMITTEE," and this one was dated March 1, 1982. Curious, O'Reilly went to his pile and flicked the edge with his thumb. Almost the entire pile was meeting minutes, going back in time. O'Reilly then lifted the pile and pulled the document on the bottom. It was another set of minutes from the management committee, this one dated November 1, 1974. What did these documents have to do with the shrimp cases?

Maybe he didn't understand the instructions here. He glanced at the paralegals sitting nearby, and every one of them had Skullcandy or Beats by Dre headphones on – O'Reilly could hear the bass drums pumping out of each person's head – and so he headed down the stairs and found Manny, who had his own private office on the first floor, in the hallway where the seven associate lawyers sat.

The door was open, so O'Reilly knocked on the doorjamb.

"Hey Manny, got a minute? I have a question."

Manny was working at a computer terminal, his fingers clacking away on the keyboard. He ogled O'Reilly over a pair of reading glasses, and then pulled them off and tossed them on his desk.

"He has a question," he said with some irritation. "He's curious."

"Yeah, just a quick one."

"Tardy and curious. Lethal combination."

"Sorry, I was just –"

"Well, you are really starting out as a royal pain in the *culos*."

O'Reilly said nothing in reply as Manny tossed his glasses down onto his desk. He began rubbing his eyes with his palms.

"Ask away, *amigo.*"

"So I was just wondering. If a document is clearly irrelevant, I mean, if it has nothing whatsoever to do with anything related to these lawsuits, do we even need to enter it into LawDocs? For example, I'm looking at meeting minutes from the 70s and 80s, for an office out in Arizona, and they're talking about whipsnakes and dry-cleaning, and – "

"*Hombre, hombre,* hold up a second," Manny said. He was pinching the bridge of his nose. "This work boring you already?"

"No, no, it's not that, it's just that –"

"Look, *muchacho,* we got our procedures here, *comprende?*"

"I understand –"

"I mean, I don't know how they do things over in County Cork, but we been at this for a month, and over here in Secaucus we got rules. *Las reglas,* you know what I'm sayin'?"

"Yes, I do –"

"Okay, you do. And so now you jumpin' on a moving train and you want to start telling the conductor how to run the railroad?"

"No, Manny, I just –"

"I mean, *hermano,* please."

"Ok, right. I get it, but –"

"Boss, *yo creo que tu yo estamos comenzando con el pie incorrecto,* you agree with me?"

"Huh?"

"The wrong foot," he snipped. "You and me – we're getting off on the wrong foot I think."

"I, uh –"

"So let's me and you pretend you didn't just come down here. Is that copasetic?"

"Yeah, sure," said O'Reilly. "No problem."

"Good. I'm glad it's no problem."

Just then Manny's phone rang, and he snatched up the receiver.

"Manuel Perez," he said, cramming the phone between his ear and shoulder. He looked at O'Reilly and pointed to the ceiling, mouthing the words – *Hombre, go back upstairs.*

O'Reilly nodded at him and fled.

Back at the steam pipe, O'Reilly plopped down into his chair and loaded up LawDocs. He turned over another page of meeting minutes and began entering the data into the computer. All around him the paralegals were dutifully doing the same, but with all those headphones strapped to all those heads, there was no communication among any of them. Shit, O'Reilly thought, is this the practice of law? Is this really how it works?

CHAPTER 17

OPERATION DECANNULATION

S HE'D BEEN LYING on her back since April and it was now the day before Thanksgiving. Miraculously the family had prevented any bedsores, but that was only because of their vigilance. Each day they took turns adjusting her and readjusting her in the bed. Around the clock they would massage her feet, calves, thighs, hips, hands, forearms, shoulders and neck. Religiously they bathed her, washed her hair, applied moisturizers and lotions. Every day she glowed with a rosy hue and smelled like lilac or jasmine or some other pleasant fragrance. Sometimes on weekends Gianna would put her makeup on and tell her how beautiful she looked, hoping she was hearing her. Every one of them – Danny, Gianna, Will and Janet, and Henry – took their turns in the rotation. They were there at the hospital, every day without fail. They talked to her, read to her, played her favorite songs. At times they would carry on entire conversations right around and over her, as if she were listening in and participating. During the night shifts when they couldn't be there the nursing staff would take over, headed by Nurse Marion, and if everything wasn't perfect when the family got there in the morning, they knew they would hear from Henry.

Despite all the help, Danny would tell you there was no greater pain than watching his daughter lying in that hospital bed. The week of Debbie's wake and funeral was close, but that whole nightmare began and ended over the course of five days. Then Debbie was buried and all that was left were the painful images and the longing for her. But this was going on for seven months now. Every day Danny had to endure seeing his little girl in a helpless state. The tubes, the hoses, the machines, the beeps – it was all unbearable. His heart ached so badly it hurt to even breathe. But no matter what, Danny had resolved that he was going to see his daughter out of this mess. He was going to do whatever it took to get her healthy again. There were days when he doubted his strength, moments when he wondered if he was going to make it through it all. But for the most part his determination was growing stronger, not receding.

And so every day, regardless of whatever else was happening, Danny was beside her in that hospital room. When he was alone, he would spend hours holding her hand, combing her hair, kissing her forehead or caressing her cheeks. He would talk to her, assure her everything was going to be okay, tell her about his day. He'd fill her in on the most meaningless details, let her know if it was raining or if the sun was shining, or whether there was traffic getting there that day. Sometimes he would just sit and stare at her, and before he even realized it, he could feel the tears coming. But then he would catch himself and he'd remind himself to be strong.

Knock it off, man, he'd say. Cut the shit.

Complaining or feeling sorry for yourself doesn't help anyone or anything. And it was critically important for Gianna to see her father as a strong, believing, positive, hopeful person. She had to be able to rely on him, that much he knew. That was something he could control.

As the months dragged on Agnes's vital signs were getting stronger, according to the doctors, but her eyes had closed about three weeks into her stay and had remained that way. It was a concern to them; they couldn't explain it. Then one day Danny was walking out of court with his attorney and he received a call from Marion, explaining that Agnes was awake and was looking around the room. Danny rushed to the hospital like a madman and had Janet grab Gianna to meet him there. He burst into the room and alighted to her bedside. He placed both hands on her cheeks, smiled, and with their noses an inch apart he said, "Baby, it's me. It's Daddy. I'm right here." And there they were, those beautiful blue ovals, right where he had last seen them. Her stare was fuzzy and unfocused, but Agnes was awake. She couldn't speak, but she was awake.

It was now two weeks later, and this morning Danny and Gianna arrived at the hospital at seven-thirty. Danny called Gianna's school and phoned in her absence and then they jumped into the F-350. When they arrived Will, Janet and Henry were already waiting in the lobby. Will and Janet were hip to hip on a bench, but Henry was pacing, as was his custom. When Danny and

Gianna entered, the five of them darted for the elevator bank without so much as a greeting. In no time they were on Agnes's floor standing at the nurse's station, waiting for the doctors. Nurse Marion was there, and she handed Danny some forms to sign.

"This is a big day, Dan," she told him, patting him on the back, "you ready for this?"

"Ready as I'm gonna be," Danny shrugged, handing her back the forms, "just hope everything goes okay."

"It's gonna be fine. Trust me, you'll see how easy a procedure this is. We've done it a million times."

Danny and his crew then took a seat in a waiting area just down the hall from Agnes's room. It was a familiar spot; Danny had slept many a night on the hard-plastic seats there. None of them needed to say a word, because the tension in the room was thick. They all wanted this over with as quickly as possible. At least Henry was now sitting, thought Danny, which settled everyone a little. He was reading a magazine he had lifted off a table. Danny then filled everyone in on what was going to take place.

"They're preparing her right now," he concluded. "Then we can all go in."

"How long does it take?" Janet asked, "the decannulation?"

"I think just a few minutes, if everything goes smooth. Let's just keep our fingers crossed."

"Everything's gonna go fine," Henry chimed in. "These people are professionals, they're not gonna fuck it up. Stop worrying."

Danny looked over at Will, stifling a smile.

"They're not gonna fuck it up," he silently mouthed, out of Henry's eyeline. Will laughed, and then Danny glanced over at Gianna, who apparently had caught his comment. She had her hand over her mouth and was giggling. Danny threw his arms around her.

"Grandpa's right," he teased her, "what're you laughing at?"

"You said a bad word."

"Don't tell on me."

Just then Nurse Marion arrived.

"We're all set," she said enthusiastically, "Operation Decannulation! Everyone ready?"

OVER THE LAST month or so Danny had attended several meetings with the hospital administration about Agnes's condition, her stay there, and the financial considerations surrounding all of it. They were not painting a pretty picture. His debt was climbing and was now solidly in the six digits. They were making it clear that room and board there wasn't free. He was making some meager payments whenever he could, but right now even those dollars were coming from a stash that technically wasn't his to hand over. Danny was a business owner whose customers paid him in cash or check, so there were no tax withholdings taken from his pay. Instead he made quarterly estimated payments and like all self-employed people he would square up with The Man on April 15. But these days Danny was taking the hospital money from his separate tax account.

He made no estimated payments in June or September and had no idea if he'd be able to make one in January. When April 15 came around in about four and half months, if things stayed the same, he wouldn't have a nickel to pay Uncle Sam. He resigned to worry about it later, but it was an issue for him to say the least. The bottom line was that on top of everything else Danny had a growing tax problem that was keeping him awake at night. There were also letters from collection firms filling his mailbox. The simple fact was that not enough money was coming in the door, especially after the fallout from that Yahoo! News article.

Danny explained all of this to the hospital administration and tried talking them into a payment plan. But their answer was always the same. We tried that Dan, and you've missed the payments. We're very sorry. You'll have to make other arrangements for Agnes. Then suddenly Agnes was conscious, and the consensus medical opinion was that she was ready. They were going to remove Agnes's tracheotomy in a procedure called a decannulation. A few days after that, assuming she could breathe on her own, as they expected, Agnes was going home.

After Marion collected the Beers family from the waiting area, she escorted them into the room where Agnes lay. They had moved Agnes from her regular room into one of the procedure rooms and right now in addition to Marion there were two other nurses present. They were dressed in dark purple medical scrubs and wore surgical masks secured behind their heads. They had on light blue latex gloves and had stethoscopes and hospital employee ID tags draped around their necks. Marion positioned Janet, Will and Henry at the foot of the bed and then she led Danny and Gianna next to Agnes's head. All of them wore masks.

"Okay Agnes," Nurse Marion said loudly, stroking her hair, "we're gonna get that terrible hose out of your throat now. Then we'll put this mask on for you, okay sweetheart?"

Marion was speaking for the benefit of the family, and everyone knew it. She was holding up an oxygen mask that would go over Agnes's nose and mouth when they removed the trach. Agnes wasn't reacting to what she said, but her eyes were open.

"It'll help you breathe easier," she assured them all.

Danny hooked an index finger on the top of his mask and pulled it down. He leaned over and kissed Agnes on the forehead. Then he snapped his mask back on and stood as close to her as he could. He held onto the bed rail and took in the sight of his daughter. Agnes was lying at a 45-degree angle and had a long clear plastic tube attached to her throat through a surgical incision. The tube went all the way down into her bronchial passages. It was connected to a white plastic brace that fit just under Agnes's chin and had at its end two brown pads that lay hard against the front side of her neck. A rubber strap secured the device to her esophagus. From there, a blue flexible hose ran from Agnes's throat along the side of the bed to a breathing machine. That was the box that had kept Agnes breathing and her brain functioning over the last seven months as she lay there in a state of unconsciousness.

To Agnes's immediate left there was yet another machine with a blue digital screen that beeped and had numbers that would change by the second. Next to that was a gurney with two IV bags that were draining something into Agnes's wrist. There were various other plugs, wires and hoses that ran across Agnes's chest and stomach, but Danny couldn't tell what any of them were, and he had stopped asking weeks ago. Right now, he wanted this over with as quickly as possible.

Nurse Marion pulled a long suction tube from a machine on her side.

"Okay kiddo, let's get some of that stuff out of your mouth."

Often, as Agnes laid motionless, a considerable amount of saliva would accumulate in her mouth, and right now Marion placed the tube between Agnes's lips. That sucking sound filled the room. Danny rubbed Agnes's arm and looked into her eyes. They were still slightly unfocused, and Danny wondered whether she realized what was happening. On the one hand he hoped she did because that meant only progress from a cognitive standpoint, but on the other hand he wouldn't mind if she wound up having no memory of this ordeal at all.

He wanted so badly to change places with her. He'd do anything to make that happen.

"Oh, that feels good, right baby?" Marion said as she suctioned, trying to keep things light. "Gets all that yucky stuff out, right?"

Suddenly Agnes was gagging. Her face turned red and her eyebrows scrunched, and Danny gripped the bed rail tighter.

"She's okay, everyone!" Marion assured, "that's very normal."

One of the other nurses then began reading Agnes's vital signs. "Blood pressure 132 over 74," the nurse said calmly. "Pulse 116. Saturation a 99."

"Great numbers," said Marion. "You're doing great Agnes."

The other nurse was adjusting the blue flexible hose, while the third was marking items off on a clipboard. Marion was moving all the other hoses and tubes. The suction tube was still sucking away as the breathing machine was whooshing up and down. The nurses were full into it now, and Danny took a deep breath. He looked down the end of the bed at Will and Janet, and the two of them were locked arm in arm. Henry was standing behind them, towering over the room with his arms crossed. His eyebrows were lowered almost underneath his eyeballs, and Danny's thought was that if something goes wrong here Henry is going to kill someone.

"Is she okay?" Gianna asked Danny behind her mask.

"She's doing great," Danny assured her.

Marion then snipped the rubber strap that went around Agnes's neck. She pressed her finger down onto the white plastic device over Agnes's throat, and Danny could feel a surge of adrenaline.

"Almost done!" she informed the room. She disconnected the flexible hose that was attached to the device on Agnes's throat. Agnes gagged again and it looked like she couldn't breathe. Her face turned dark red. She started moving her head from side to side with a pained expression that shot a chill right through Danny's body.

"Jesus Christ," he said, taking a step backwards.

"Oh Daddy," Gianna moaned, and she was crying. She gripped Danny's arm and sunk her head into his chest. The second nurse launched forward with the suction hose and cleaned out Agnes's mouth, her left index finger still pressed against Agnes's throat.

"Is she okay?" Danny asked, and then he looked to his right. Will had his arm around Janet, who had both hands over her mask and face as if she were watching a horror movie. Henry still had his arms crossed but now he was pacing back and forth again.

"She's fine guys, don't worry," Nurse Marion said. She placed a hand on Agnes's cheek. "I know, Agnes, this is awful, but we're almost done."

The other nurse walked behind Agnes and gripped her by the shoulders with her left hand. In her right had she had a clear plastic oxygen mask ready to strap onto Agnes's face.

"Here we go," Marion said, "I'm going to pull this tube now."

Danny wondered again if Agnes understood any of these instructions. He couldn't tell if she was scared but he was praying she wasn't. He hoped she understood that her family was right here by her side. The second nurse was now holding Agnes steady by the shoulder, trying to stabilize her body. Nurse Marion leaned forward and pinched the device attached to Agnes's throat.

"Out it comes, baby, ready? One … two … THREE!"

And then, in the next instant, Marion pulled on the small hard plastic device that had been attached to Agnes's throat since April. Agnes's face turned a deep crimson again, and Marion pulled out the tube. A short beige rubber hose, about six inches long, popped easily out of Agnes's neck, and just like that, Operation Decannulation, as Marion had called it, was over. Agnes was off the breathing machine.

She was drawing oxygen on her own.

"You did it!" Nurse Marion declared, "great job Agnes!"

The other nurse quickly placed the oxygen mask over Agnes's nose and mouth, while Marion taped a strip of white medical gauze over the hole in Agnes's throat.

"Ninety-nine percent!" the third nurse then read off a machine, and then all three nurses were clapping.

Right then, Gianna abruptly separated from her father and

ripped her mask off. With tears in her eyes, she lowered herself down to her little sister and placed her cheek against the right side of Agnes's face, her right hand against Agnes's left ear.

"Way to go Agnes!" she yelled across the room.

"Thank God," Henry then bellowed.

Will and Janet came around the bed and hugged Danny, whose heart was pounding. He blew a great blast of air out of his lungs.

"Well how about that?" he said, looking around at everyone.

Then he rubbed Gianna's back and smiled. It wasn't until he looked back at Henry when he realized he was crying.

"Okay, that's enough of that," Henry said when their eyes met.

Danny ignored him and looked back at Agnes. The nurses were adjusting and moving hoses and equipment again, and Danny could see that Agnes's eyes were searching the room. Then they landed on Danny. She was squinting, almost as if she were trying to figure out where she was.

And then Danny sensed something that no one else in the room had noticed. Something only a father could see. Agnes was trying to say something. She was slowly lifting and then lowering her right hand, but she was moving her fingers with purpose.

"Marion," he said, "look."

Nurse Marion diverted her attention from the hoses and equipment and moved closer to Agnes's head. She leaned down toward her, but Agnes was now without question looking directly at her father. Danny brought his face down to her, and he knew. He didn't need any medical opinion on this one. He knew his daughter, her expressions, and exactly what she wanted. He hadn't seen any clarity in her eyes in half a year, but it was there now.

Agnes wanted her father.

Without seeking permission, he gently eased the oxygen mask from Agnes's face. He placed his cheek against hers.

"What is it, sweetheart?" he asked her softly.

And then in the next instant Agnes smiled.

She coughed and swallowed hard, but then she smiled again.

And then for the first time since that terrible day at Turnberry Park, Agnes spoke. It was a low, soft, crackling whisper, spoken through a raw and sore throat, but everyone could hear it.

"Daddy," she whispered, looking at her father.

"Daddy," she rasped again.

"Yes, baby," Danny said back, tears welling in his eyes again. He wrapped his thick hands around her face.

"I'm right here sweetheart," he assured her.

ABOUT THREE HOURS later, the family was in a diner on Route 25A. They took a booth by the front window overlooking the parking lot. After the nurses had settled Agnes back in her room, they convinced Danny that the girl was exhausted and needed to sleep. Henry chimed in and told everyone they should leave her the hell alone, and hasn't she had enough bullshit for one goddamn day. He commanded that they all go grab a bite before Danny and Gianna needed to head back there.

So off they went.

After they were nestled in a booth a waitress came over and handed out menus. She wrote down their drink preferences and then returned to take their orders. Danny could barely eat but he made sure that Gianna had a full plate. She ordered a burger and French fries and asked her father if she could get a chocolate shake.

"Of course," Danny agreed.

Then the others placed their orders, and Henry went last.

"Bowl of Manhattan clam chowder and those oyster crackers," he instructed, snapping the menu closed. "Bring me the check."

Over the next half hour, the family ate in silence. Gianna occupied herself by staring at her iPhone. Will and Janet tried to make some small talk about the weather, but Henry just sat there with his elbows on the table and his hands webbed under his chin.

There simply wasn't much to say after what had transpired in the hospital room. Everyone was mentally and emotionally exhausted. Danny felt both relieved and terrified – on the one hand Agnes had finally spoken, but on the other hand he was certain that when he returned to the hospital that afternoon, they were going to discuss a date certain for Agnes's discharge. It would be within a week, and then she would be home under his care exclusively. He broke that news to the family over lunch. The feeling he had a mountain to climb under the weight of a thousand pounds would just never go away.

Henry shoved his empty clam chowder bowl to the center of

the table and looked at his watch. He pointed across at Gianna.

"You need this one with you this afternoon?" he asked Danny.

"No, not really," Danny answered.

"Then why don't I take her home. Been a long day already. I'll sit with her until you get back."

Danny put his hand on top of Gianna's.

"That okay with you?" he asked her.

Gianna nodded. Danny could see she wanted to go home and he didn't blame her. What a day it had been for her.

"Good," Henry said.

He flipped three twenty-dollar bills on the table.

"Take care of the bill," he said.

Henry and Gianna then headed out the door. Henry's 2009 Mercury Grand Marquis was parked in one of the front parking spots that Danny could see from the window, and he watched as Henry opened the passenger door for Gianna and helped her in. Henry was about as friendly as a rabid porcupine, Danny would always say, but may God have mercy on your soul if you crossed one of his granddaughters. She was safe with him.

"Hey, I'm gonna head out too," Janet then said, shimmying across the booth. "Got a lot of work to do for tomorrow."

Danny understood. Tomorrow was Thanksgiving and Will was hosting his in-laws. Danny slid out of the booth and stood, and Janet wrapped her arms around him.

"This was a huge day, Dan," she said, her eyes still moist.

"Yeah I know," he said back, "but we got a long way to go."

"I know, but we're all here for you," she assured him, kissing him on the cheek. "And we'll stop by tomorrow, promise."

The statement sent a quick chill through Danny, with the reminder that there would be no Thanksgiving for him and Agnes. Will and Janet had insisted that Gianna go to their house to hang out for the day with her cousins, Will's three kids, but Danny wasn't leaving Agnes alone for a minute. He'd be right by her side.

When Janet left it was just him and Will, which Danny was happy about. It had been a while since he had a chance to sit and talk with his brother. The waitress came by and asked if they needed anything else, and Danny ordered a coffee. Will then nodded toward the parking lot.

"Fuckin' Henry," he laughed. "Dude's a piece of work."

"He really is," said Danny, "but I gotta tell you, he's been an incredible help this past year. First after Deb, and now with Agnes."

Danny shook his head.

"It's gotta be rough on him too, I figure, you know?" he asked.

"Yeah, sure," Will said, "no question."

Will took a sip of his Diet Pepsi.

"But how are you, man?" he asked. "How are you making out?"

Danny placed his elbows on the table.

"Not good, Will," he answered.

"What's wrong, besides the obvious."

"I'm lost, man," said Danny. "I have no idea how to raise these girls, none whatsoever. I'm flying by the seat of my pants. Thing is, Debbie did everything for them. Everything. I was just … I don't know, I was just *there*. I don't mean I was an absentee father or anything, but when they needed anything they went to her, not me. And now I have to fill that role and I gotta tell you I'm really messing it up. Even before what happened to Agnes."

"Aw, c'mon man," Will said, "you're being rough on yourself."

"No, I'm not, I'm being honest. It's like the whole world changed and no one told me. The girls need help and I don't know anything about these phones, this social media stuff, what's going on in their schools, their friends, how to handle all this girl drama and emotional shit, it's overwhelming. Everything that Debbie did for them just ain't gettin' done. I'm trying, believe me, but I'm not replacing her. It's more like there's a hole there for them."

Danny paused for a moment and shook his head.

"And when Agnes got hurt, I don't know, Gianna didn't deserve that."

"You're doing alright," Will offered, "just remember no one's had to go through what you've been dealing with, brother, no one."

Danny leaned back against the booth and crossed his arms. The waitress swung by and dropped a cup and saucer in front of Danny, who began shaking out a sugar packet. He dumped it in and brought the cup to his lips and sipped. Then he leaned back again, staring across the diner.

"Hey Will," he finally said, "you remember the story about how our grandfather got over here from Ireland, back in the '20s?"

"Think so."

"C'mon, you remember," said Danny, "he's twenty years old and he gets on a ship from Londonderry up in County Donegal and he's in the bowels of that boat to New York for eight days, right? And sometime during the trip, just by chance, he meets this old guy up on the deck while he's staring out across the Atlantic Ocean. He strikes up a conversation and it turns out the guy knows his father, our great grandfather. Ring a bell?"

"Yeah, okay, I know the story."

"So after the ship goes to New York, the plan is he's staying on and headed for Boston and that's where he'll live. He's supposed to meet someone up there, an uncle or some shit, who's maybe arranged an apartment for him, and so he's going to be a Southie. Live his life in Boston. But then this guy, his father's friend, he tells him to go to Brooklyn, and he sells him on it. So Grandpa mulls it over and at some point he decides he'll go to Brooklyn. He doesn't know anyone in the entire country, but he changes his mind and he goes and settles in New York. Just like that."

"Yeah, like I said, I know the story. So what's the point?"

"The point? I've been thinking about that a lot lately."

"Why? You're freakin' me out."

"I don't know, I've just been thinking about it. Did it ever occur to you that if he never runs into that guy, you and I don't exist? We just never … *exist*. Poof, gone. He moves to Boston and never meets our grandmother. Our own mother never exists. And I never meet Debbie and Agnes never goes through this whole ordeal. But the decision that one man makes on one day … it changes everything. It alters the course of humanity, Will. And not just in a simple way. In an unbelievably profound way, you know? I mean, there were what? Hundreds of people on that ship? Why did he run into that guy? Why?"

"Christ, I don't know – fate? Who knows."

Danny waved him off.

"I don't believe in that. Fate - what's fate? It doesn't exist. The answer is that it's random, and that's what drives me nuts. But I know this – you take that one day out, or you take that one decision and you alter it, and so much of the world goes in a completely different direction. So many decisions I've made, big and small, got me to where I am right now. If I only knew, you know? One man, one day – you can do anything, even when you don't mean to. It's scary, if you ask me."

Will shifted in his seat.

"Well now you are *definitely* freaking me out," he said.

Danny laughed.

"Sorry," he said, throwing his palms up. "But you leave a man alone too much, and he gets to thinking. That's not a good thing."

"Jesus Christ!" Will replied, and then the two enjoyed a hearty laugh. The waitress then swung by again and asked Danny and Will if they need anything else. Danny said no, and Will agreed. Danny checked his watch – it was time to get back to the hospital.

"Tell me," Will then said, trying to change the subject, "how's everything with the business?"

"Well that's another thing," said Danny. "That article on Yahoo was a killer. It really hurt. I'm like a criminal in this town now. People seemed pissed. I haven't had a referral in months."

"Yeah, me and Janet picked up on that, we feel terrible."

"Brought it on myself though, I guess, right?"

"Well, what about that? What's going on with that lawsuit?"

"Well, it's moving ahead, but I don't where it's going. The defendants recently tried to get the whole case kicked but a few weeks ago the court denied their motions. We're going forward, but Will, I gotta tell you, you had to hear the lawyer for the other side."

"You were there?"

"Yeah, and I'm glad I went. Because the way this guy explained everything to the court – I almost forgot whose side I was on. He basically told the judge that there was no case because if I knew Agnes had an allergy to shrimp then I shoulda done something to stop her from eating it. And if I didn't know, how were they supposed to know? I mean he put it more professionally than that, but that was the gist. And I'm listening to him and I'm saying, you know what? He's freakin' right."

Danny shook his head.

"A father's supposed to protect his kids, Will. If you're not doing that, what are you doing?"

Will hung his head a moment, and then he took a sip of his drink. He looked back at his brother.

"Well, the part about how *they* could know she was allergic, I have to be honest, that occurred to me too. But what do I know? What's your lawyer say?"

Danny shrugged his shoulders.

"She says we have a case."

"Good, so you have a case. What're you worried about?"

"Will, I'm not so sure. Not after what I heard. But I don't want to say that out loud."

Will then smiled at him.

"Well, you remember what the Irish say about that, right?"

"No, what?"

"*Is binn beal ina thost,*" Will answered.

"Mom used to say that, right?" Danny said, smiling back now.

"Yeah, she did."

"What's it mean again?"

"Silence is golden, or as Mom used to put it," and Will then put on an Irish brogue, "keep your fooking gob shut."

The two of them laughed.

"But anyway," Danny continued, "bottom line is I gotta get something out of that case, because I'm on fumes over here. After the Yahoo article I was thinking of dropping the whole thing, but then the GoFundMe account dried up and now I'm tapped out. I owe that hospital over a hundred grand."

"Holy shit," Will said bluntly.

"Yeah, no kidding," Danny said. "I'd sell the house but that'd only net me about 20k, maybe. But you know what? Somehow, some way, I'm gonna figure it all out. I'm not letting anything happen to my girls."

"Dan, anything you need, me and Janet got your back, always."

"I appreciate that, I really do," Danny answered, "and when Agnes comes home next week I'm sorry to say I'm gonna have to take you up on that. I mean, you saw her right? She's awake now and conscious, but just barely. She's got a long way to go. A long, long, long way to go. I have no idea what her future holds."

Will gave him a sympathetic smile.

"Yeah, I know," he told his brother.

"You're only as happy as your saddest child, Will," Danny said, shaking his head. "Never more than that, my man."

Suddenly, from out in the parking lot, Danny and Will heard a tire screech, which caught the attention of everyone in the diner. Danny looked and saw Henry's Mercury skidding to a stop in the handicapped spot near the diner entrance, almost crashing into a thick hedgerow near the diner's front wall. Then he saw Henry ripping off his seat belt, his red face filled with a rage that was surprising even for him. Gianna was in the passenger seat, sobbing.

"Christ," Danny muttered, and in a second he and Will were on their feet headed toward the diner exit. Danny pushed open the glass doors and was on the diner's front steps just as Henry was marching up the walkway.

"There you are," Henry said to him in a fury. He was motioning him in with his index finger. "C'mere, right now."

Henry marched back down the walkway toward the Mercury.

"What's going on?" Danny demanded, trailing Henry.

Henry held out what Danny recognized as Gianna's iPhone.

"What the fuck is this?" asked Henry.

Danny grabbed it and looked at Gianna. Her face was soaked in tears. She looked at her father with terror in her eyes.

Danny then looked down at the phone screen. It was opened to a Twitter page. Up at the top was that little blue bird, and on the left there was a blank red square where Danny surmised a photo should be. The name of the person who had sent the tweet that Danny was about to read was one that Danny didn't recognize, only because it wasn't a name at all, just a series of letters and numbers.

But right there in the middle of the page Danny could see what had sent Henry into a tailspin. When he read it his heart stopped:

HCRTP45 @hellcat   2h
#giannabeers @giannabeers I hope you fucking dye, go sue someone else u ugly little bitch

Danny slumped down onto the concrete edge of the walkway and let his hands, which held the phone, drop between his knees.

"Oh my God," he said simply.

CHAPTER 18

LOWER THAN A SPECK

O'REILLY WAS HAVING lunch at a local Secaucus diner with Ralph Burgess, the lawyer who had trained him on LawDocs. Burgess had asked O'Reilly if wanted to "get off campus" for an hour, and O'Reilly's first instinct was to ask if Manny had to officially bless the outing. Burgess advised him it was fine. He told him the diner had some great dishes and O'Reilly would like the menu. With his eyes glazing over after weeks and weeks of plowing through Gunther boxes, O'Reilly was grateful for the invitation. But Burgess made clear – unlike over the summer, you pay for your own lunch now. The gravy train is off the rails, permanently.

When they got to the diner, the two settled into a red leather booth. Burgess was dressed in a blue golf shirt and dark dress slacks, O'Reilly in a pair of khakis and white button-down shirt with the sleeves rolled up. The blast of air conditioning in the diner, and its contrast with the stale swelter in the warehouse, felt to O'Reilly like he was getting a massage.

O'Reilly quickly learned that Burgess had also been a Summer Associate at FT&B, just like O'Reilly, and had joined the firm as a full-time lawyer after his graduation from NYU Law School. Burgess had opted against the part-time work during his final year and spent his time studying for the bar exam. He lived in Teaneck and therefore had a relatively short drive to the warehouse every morning, which he told O'Reilly was a welcome, albeit temporary, respite from the commute into New York. O'Reilly then explained his arduous journey every morning from Brooklyn, and Burgess just waved him off.

"Look, no one's shedding any tears over your commute."

"Oh, I know. I was just saying."

"Just wait 'til you get back here next September."

"Yeah, so I've heard."

"You think it's bad now? Let me tell you something. I graduated second in my class at NYU and was Editor-in-Chief of the NYU Law Review. I had job offers from twelve different firms in the City. But I chose this place, and since I started three years ago? I've done nothing but document productions. All in massive cases."

"Oh man."

"Oh man is right," said Burgess.

O'Reilly leaned in. He definitely wanted to hear about this.

"The first one was out in Lincoln, Nebraska," Burgess continued. "I started at the firm on a Monday and had two days of orientation. They flew me to Lincoln on *Wednesday*. We were representing a company that manufactured those farm irrigation systems, you know, the ones you see out there in cornfields and shit? A few members of the management team were embezzling funds and so the Board decided to conduct an internal investigation before the lawsuits landed. It was a public company. Anyway, we were out there eight months, in a fucking internal conference room with no windows. Seven of us, and a couple of paralegals. You know what there is to do in Lincoln, Nebraska on a weeknight? Try nothing. You know what there is to eat out there? Try even less."

"Oh, God, that sounds awful."

"Awful is right," said Burgess. "And we just had a baby at the time, but I came home only on weekends. I'd walk in and my own kid had no idea who the fuck I was. I'd hold her and she'd scream like I was a kidnapper."

"Ouch. I'm really sorry."

"Ouch is right," Burgess went on, "'cause when I got back from lovely Lincoln it was on to another document production, but at least this one was in New York. We were representing an accounting firm that the SEC was just shitting all over, hitting those guys with subpoena after subpoena because a couple of their top guys were ... how shall we say it ... 'cooking the books' for this hedge fund they were working for. Total shitshow."

Burgess shifted in his seat.

"Anyway," he continued, "the firm was asked to respond to a single subpoena, and then before you knew it a bunch more came in and we were in there reviewing everything you could possibly think of, including the writing on the side of the fucking toothpaste tubes. That one went on a year and a half – an entire year and a half

– while the government investigation was going on. And in the end four of the fuckers from that firm pled guilty to fraud. They're currently at Club Fed doing ten years a piece."

"Jeez," O'Reilly offered.

"Jeez is right," countered Burgess. "So all I did was review documents. Twelve to fourteen hours a day, six days a week. After that it was some more document productions in a bunch of smaller cases, but the hours were basically the same. Until these shrimp cases came up and I got the engraved invitation to the Secaucus warehouse. This one will go until February or March, if Manny keeps cracking the whip."

Burgess started cleaning his John Lennon glasses with a napkin.

"Funny, isn't it?" he asked, smiling. "Representing a company that sells frozen shrimp? Ever think this is what you'd be doing as a lawyer?" He shrugged his shoulders. "Whaddya gonna do."

O'Reilly shook his head in the sympathetic manner of someone given news of a death. He felt silly about how he had opened this conversation talking about his Brooklyn commute. At least he currently had his Tuesdays and Thursdays, when he only had three hours of classes followed by a few hours of study time in the MLS library. By comparison, those days were like mini vacations. By five pm he was having a beer with classmates, while Burgess was settling in for another six hours of document review.

The waitress arrived and the two placed their order – O'Reilly a grilled chicken sandwich and fries, Burgess a turkey club.

"Let me ask you," said Burgess, passing the menu to the waitress, "what did they have you do over the summer?"

O'Reilly was almost too embarrassed to answer. The image of the three-hour lunches, strolling in at ten-thirty, out by four-thirty, and all the wasted worry over "feedback" – while Burgess was getting shelled by enemy fire in the trenches – well, he couldn't bring himself to even tell him. But Burgess must have sensed his hesitation, because he had a knowing smile on his face and told O'Reilly, "go ahead, you can say it."

"I was working on a political asylum case."

"Oh, a political asylum case," Burgess laughed. "For who? Tell me, exactly who was seeking political asylum?"

O'Reilly could feel his face reddening, as if someone were

holding a Bic lighter to his cheeks. He felt like a kindergartener.

"It was, uh, you know, a monk. From, uh, Tibet."

Burgess threw his head back and laughed.

"A Tibetan monk!" he roared. "A fucking monk!"

"Yes," was all O'Reilly could muster.

"Oh man, that is rich! Let me guess, this monk wasn't the CEO of … I don't know … say, an Exxon subsidiary in Tibet, for example, right? So this wasn't an hourly rate client?"

"No, it wasn't."

"A pro bono case."

O'Reilly wanted to disappear.

"Yes," he confessed.

"So you were working on a pro bono case seeking political asylum on behalf of a Tibetan monk – how long you do that for?"

"A while," O'Reilly told him, "weeks."

Burgess gave him a smirk.

"Most of the summer," O'Reilly confessed.

"Try the *whole* summer. And they had you write a memo, right?"

O'Reilly just nodded.

"It's alright," Burgess said, still giggling, "I'm just busting your balls. But that is funny. My summer they assigned me to a pro bono death penalty case. Some shitbag down in Louisiana stuck up a Mom and Pop store – a shoe repair joint for God's sake – and then shot and killed the owner, who was 80 something. Then he locked the wife in the backroom and set fire to the place. Real fucking boy scout. Anyway, we were arguing over evidentiary violations, about whether color photographs should have been shown to the jury. What the Christ, right? That shitbird had no shot, and we lost the appeal. The whole time I'm on the case I'm thinking, if anyone deserves the death penalty, it's this piece of shit, you know?"

"Wow, that actually sounds really interesting."

"Yeah, it was *interesting*," Burgess smirked, throwing up finger quotes. "I did that for almost the entire ten-week summer stint, researching and writing up memos for three hours a day, and then lunching and going to baseball games. Just like you."

O'Reilly just nodded. The waitress arrived with their lunch plates and the two began digging in.

"Look," Burgess said, chewing on a fry, "let me help you out, my man. You seem lost, so let me tell you how things really work."

"Oh great," O'Reilly answered. "Absolutely."

"Here it is, okay? The Summer Associate stint is fantasy island," said Burgess, "we all know that. They lure you in and give you the cushy office and a meatball assignment you can easily knock out of the park. They just want to see if you're someone they want around here on a regular basis, have a pulse, and can put pen to paper on some basic legal issues. Then when you get back after your final law school year? They pound the hell out of you. I had my own office as a summer, and now as a lawyer I share a shoebox with two other third years. When I'm there, that is. Ketchup."

O'Reilly passed the ketchup bottle, paying rapt attention.

"But you gotta understand the economics of a big law firm before you jump in here. You gotta understand what you're signing up for. Otherwise you'll lose your mind. Salt."

O'Reilly slid the salt over, and Burgess sprinkled his fries.

"As a junior associate, Sea-Mouse, say in your first five years at the firm, you are nothing but a speck of dust, okay? You're a pawn. A spoke in the wheel. Lower even – you're an ant crawling in the grass. A meaningless grain of sand on the beach. Sweat on the balls of a slug. You're a dime a dozen, and they can replace you like *that*."

Burgess violently snapped his fingers into O'Reilly's face. Then, with a mouthful of fries, he pulled his iPhone and opened the calculator app.

"But you're also an asset," he continued, "and that's why you exist. Because on the one hand you're a fixed cost, okay? But you're also an hours-eating billing machine. You literally shit money."

Burgess was poking his iPhone with his index finger.

"So, let's say as a first year they pay you a $175,000 salary – pretty nice, right? And with health insurance, secretary, overhead and all the rest of the happy horseshit, you run them $225,000 a year. Okay fine. So now let's say you bill 1500 hours for the year at $450 per hour. Do the math – that's $675k. You whack off the $225 grand you cost them, and you've just made them $450 grand."

"Wow," O'Reilly said, "nice."

"Nice is right," said Burgess. "But why should they be satisfied with 1500 hours? Why only 450 grand in profit? That's nothing. What if they got 2000 hours out of your pathetic, useless ass? That's

900 grand in fees. But your fixed-cost status doesn't change, see? You *still* cost them just $225,000. So now when we back out your $225? You've made them $675,000. And we can keep going."

Burgess was still poking his calculator app, getting excited now.

"Let's go 2500 hours. At $450 an hour that's a million one hundred twenty-five grand. One point one two five! That's 900 thousand in profit, just from *you*. Now multiply that by 700 associates. That's *630 million* into the firm's coffers! And that's just the associate hourly work – you still got the massive corporate deal fees and of course the partner hourly billings. Most of those guys are going out at over a *thousand dollars per hour.*"

"A thousand an hour?"

"Yeah, a thousand," confirmed Burgess. "So, you see the deal here? The firm's only reason for hiring you is to suck as many hours out of you as they possibly can, because every one of those hours after your 225k is profit. Pure profit. Get it?"

O'Reilly was following it now. He was getting the picture.

"So that's what you do my friend," said Burgess. "It's why you exist. To eat, sleep, shit and bill hours. Nothing more."

Burgess shoved another french fry into his mouth.

"That's all big law firms are, Sea-Mouse, they're salesmen. They sell billable hours. And *you*" – Burgess stabbed a finger right at O'Reilly's nose – "have a lot of them. What you don't have is a life."

Burgess chomped into his sandwich and continued with a mouthful of turkey and rye bread.

"So the firm will drag every single one of those hours out of you until you can't give them one single more," he said. "And in three- or four-years' time you'll crawl out of here on your hands and knees. You'll have a pale face, black bags under your bloodshot eyes, rotten coffee breath, and sleep deprivation so bad you'll barely even know your own fucking name. And guess what? As you're crawling out the door begging for mercy, there'll be a platoon of fresh new graduates with fat student loans stepping on the back of your neck to take your spot."

Burgess wiped some food debris from his chin.

"You getting the picture Sea-Mouse?"

O'Reilly sighed, and stared across the diner. He had taken a few bites of his chicken sandwich but had lost his appetite. This entire conversation was making him depressed.

"Ralph, let me ask," he said, looking at Burgess now, "how many hours did you bill last year?"

Burgess didn't hesitate.

"Thirty-three hundred and forty-six," he shot back. "I was billed out at $525 per hour. So they pulled in $1,761,900, just on me. I cost them about $250k, which means they made $1,511,900 on my work. And yes, I have the numbers memorized."

"And it was all document production work?" asked O'Reilly. "Have you ever been to court?"

Burgess scoffed.

"Court?! What's *court*? No, we don't go to court, Sea-Mouse. Maybe four or five litigation partners get to go to court, everyone else works in their offices. We are litigators, sure, but going to court is really not what we do. I had some small legal research assignments here and there but well over ninety percent of my work was on document productions."

"What about depositions? Ever attend any of those?"

"Rarely. There's a chance I'll be attending the deposition of the father in that Beers case, the one up in the Bronx. But for the most part, no."

"So why do you do it? It sounds so awful."

"Oh, it sounds awful, does it?" Burgess shot back. "Well it is awful. It sucks. But if you can find me another job that'll pay me 200 hundred grand a year, you let me know. In the meantime, I have $175,000 in student loans between college and law school, a jumbo mortgage out in Teaneck, and a wife and a kid and another one on the way. So I'd love to be out there making the world a happy place where Tibetan monks can have their shits and giggles, but right now I have a couple few bills to pay."

"Right, of course," O'Reilly managed. He felt his face getting red again.

"Plus, this place has a strict seven-year partnership track," informed Burgess. "It's called up-and-out. If you don't make partner at the end of your seventh year, they boot your sorry ass out the door. But the vast majority of the associates around here hightail it out of this place after three or four years. They just can't take the hours anymore and they split. My first-year class started with seventy-two new lawyers – you know how many will be left going into year seven?"

O'Reilly shook his head.

"Five or six, tops. And I plan on being one of them."

"Wow."

"Wow is right," said Burgess. "And from that small group maybe two or three will make partner. If you can hang in there you have a chance. And that's when you can start being a real lawyer, going to court, taking depositions and making all the strategic decisions in the case. You know what the partners here make?"

O'Reilly shook his head no.

"Last year the profits-per-partner came in at *$3.2 million a head*. I don't know about you, Sea-Mouse, but three mil a year is worth suffering through a few document productions."

O'Reilly didn't respond. He leaned back and looked around the diner. So this is what it was all about – suffering through the drudgery of mindless tasks that any paralegal with a certificate could do, for the possibility of making millions after seven years. And having no life at all because you're chained to a desk – or in O'Reilly's case a steam pipe – for six or seven days a week. O'Reilly knew the hours at big law firms would be arduous, but he was under the impression he'd be using his law license (once he got it) for the greater good, or to change people's lives. Man was he mistaken. He was now sad he'd taken up Burgess's offer for this lunch.

O'Reilly leaned forward just as the waitress dropped the check.

"So I'm just a speck, huh?"

Burgess lifted the check and began eyeballing it.

"Lower than a speck," he said, without looking up.

"Sweat on the balls of a slug?"

"Worse. *Dust* in the sweat on the balls of a slug."

O'Reilly crossed his arms just as Burgess pointed to the check.

"It's twenty-two bucks with tip, Sea-Mouse," he said, snapping his fingers. "Let's go, pony up."

CHAPTER 19

WHEN DOES REDEMPTION COME?

OVER THE LAST six months Justin had been complaining about his left arm. Anzalone ignored him for a few months but then she could see the change with her own eyes.

Ever since he was a baby, Justin would always hold his left forearm tight against his chest with his left elbow fanned out like a chicken wing. He would ball his left hand into a fist with his index finger pointed at his lap. The PT techs would work it over every Wednesday, straightening and massaging the arm and extending the fingers, almost as if they were untangling a twisted telephone wire. But then they would let it go and his arm would recoil back against his chest. Recently, the index finger was pointing in the direction he was looking, which meant that his arm seemed to be rotating inside out. At night he would wake up crying and all Anzalone could do was hold him. Eventually she took him in to see a specialist and they ran all kinds of tests and took multiple x-rays. The other day a nurse called and told her to come in, they wanted to talk.

The appointment was set for a Saturday in early December, and after that Anzalone planned to take Justin to hunt for a Christmas tree. Last year she started what she hoped would be a tradition – she and her parents had loaded Justin into the Civic and drove out to a Christmas tree farm in East Northport. A worker tied a six-foot Douglas fir to the roof, and then Anzalone and her parents drank hot chocolate with Justin by an outdoor fire. They had such a good time they vowed to do it again.

Right now, Anzalone was camped out in the waiting room of an orthopedic surgeon named Surie Gubash, M.D., a doctor she and Justin had never seen before. Anzalone was more than a little anxious about what she could hear sometime over the next hour. Not just about Justin, but also about her finances, the ever-present albatross. Today they were getting the news about whether Justin needed surgery and she was praying the answer was no. She hated that money had to be a consideration when you were talking about a potential operation for your kid, but that was her reality, those were the facts. Maybe with a stroke of luck they would tell her he could continue with physical therapy and the problem would resolve on its own. Maybe. That would be the home run. But with the way her silver plan on the New York Obamacare exchange worked, an operation would mean three grand out of her pocket – money she currently didn't have.

Up on the wall a clock read ten minutes after eleven, so they were now forty minutes past their ten-thirty appointment. Justin was asleep in his wheelchair. She dumped a magazine onto an adjacent table and put her elbows on her knees, looking at the pattern in the waiting room carpet. She knew the deal here – in a short while they'd call her name and then the two of them would spend another twenty minutes in the little room before the doctor finally came in and gave them something less than four minutes of his time. Welcome to modern medicine.

At times like this, Anzalone had time to think, process, ruminate. Melting in a waiting room was one of those dead zones in life, like sitting in traffic or standing in line at the DMV, when the mind had nothing to do but reflect, and nowadays those dead moments always seemed to take her backwards – to her past. She would look over at Justin, like right now, and run through the events of her life over the last fifteen years and she'd feel something that was not supposed to be associated with someone you love so much. And that emotion was regret. Sometimes she'd repress the very idea of it, but in time she came to believe that it was better to be honest and confront such feelings head on.

The truth was that Justin should never have come to exist. It was hard not to think about that fact. She certainly loved him with all her heart; that wasn't the point. There was just the inescapable truth that if life had proceeded in the manner she had expected, and had followed the natural trajectory it was on, poor Justin wouldn't be here. It was really that simple.

Sometimes Anzalone would try to step out of the whole thing and attempt to look at it as if she were just some casual, non-involved observer. She'd try to be an objective third person and tell the tale with no emotion, no judgment, no scorn. She would become a narrator and do it chronologically, starting at the beginning. And when she simply laid out the facts it didn't seem so bad, maybe because when she had told the story between her ears so many times, the shock of it simply faded and it became like an old scar. Then she would begin to approach something that resembled understanding, perspective. It felt good to do it this way – therapeutic in a way. But then inevitably that dead zone would get interrupted before she could make it through the entire script – they'd call her name at the DMV, or the traffic would start moving – and it'd be over.

Right now, with Justin sleeping and a waiting room filled with patients who had arrived before she did, Anzalone closed her eyes and rested her head against the back wall. She folded her arms and let her mind drift, backwards, first to college, and then to law school, and then her graduation with her parents there – Carmine and Mary Anzalone – so proud. She recalled how excited she was to land her first job at that Garden City defense firm – Buckley, Sullivan Doyle & Finch LLP – and how she had risen swiftly through their ranks after obtaining defense verdicts in a few high-profile medical malpractice trials. She thought about her beautiful Cape Cod in Rockville Centre, her dream home, and that jet-black Audi A4 she was so proud to drive. And then she thought about the fact that she was a mere few months from being elected to the partnership at Buckley Sullivan when the whole thing came crashing down on her.

And of course, all of that focused her mind on Suchek. Sebastian Aloysius Suchek – the man she was going to marry. She wondered where he was these days, what had happened to him. Was he still playing guitar, doing his gigs? She thought about that beautiful Christmas Eve night, when he proposed to her in front of her whole family, and how right after the holidays …

AND CONTINUING ON *through the winter, she and her mother had stayed busy with details of the wedding. It was planned for the fall. Suchek was taking on as many gigs as he could and was stuffing away every extra cent. He had also turned over his apartment lease at the end of the year and moved into her cape. All the extra cash that wasn't going to rent was being saved for the honeymoon. They were both so excited. Meanwhile, she stayed swamped at*

Buckley Sullivan. The firm made its partnership decisions each year in September, and so after seven years of hard work she was in the home stretch. Everyone in the place considered her a shoe-in. Life could not have been better.

Shortly after the engagement she began to envision what the wedding pictures would look like and decided her wedding dress would be a size zero. She was a tiny little person to begin with but had resolved that her current size four was unacceptable. So right after the New Year she had started jogging. She hated it at first and could barely make it around the block from her cape. Her calves would be burning with lactic acid as she limped into the office each day. But after about a month her running became somewhat of an obsession. Over time, she couldn't make it through a day without it, whether it was a short jog or a long relaxing run. She got in shape, got her legs under her, and before long she was busting out three to four miles a day. Suchek wasn't much for exercise and so she would go on these runs solo, and before long she was a complete convert to the religion of running. She'd pop out of bed before the sun came up and fly out the door. She enjoyed the peace and solitude of the roads at just before six a.m. and found that it cleared her head and got her day started in a positive way.

In May of that year, she signed up for the Rockville Centre Memorial Day Fun Run, a 5k race that raised funds for the town's elementary schools. On a pleasant Sunday morning with slate blue skies and temperatures in the 50s, she showed up in a pair of ankle-length running pants with a light pink Nike jacket. The run was a little over three miles – nothing to it – but she was hoping to turn in a competitive time. Suchek told her he'd meet her at the finish line and take her out for breakfast.

At the starting line she settled in the middle of the pack, with the more competitive runners up front. She was stretched and warm and ready to go. She had decided to go with a heavy metal playlist for the run and she hit the play button before stuffing her iPod into a pouch that was Velcro-ed onto her upper arm. The opening guitar lick and thumping bass drum from AC-DC's You Shook Me All Night Long *came ripping through her earbuds, and she started bouncing to Brian Johnson screaming about a fast machine. Just then the gun sounded, and she was off. She got right into her pace and about a half-mile in she found her rhythm. She reached the perfect heart rate and was cruising. She felt light on the road and took easy strides as the spaces between her and the other runners opened. A woman in an orange jacket in front of her looked to be moving at about her pace, and so she used her as a marker. She stayed behind her about ten paces, constantly looking down at her watch.*

At the first mile marker she checked her time. She had just ripped off a 7:09. It was fast for her, but she felt strong and so she decided to overtake the woman in the orange jacket. She pushed hard and in about a quarter mile she passed her. She kept up the quicker pace for a while and then settled back down into a more typical rhythm. Her breathing was steady and she seemed to be barely touching the road, so she decided to quicken her stride again. She was moving with ease and blew through the second mile marker at 13:57. She now had a shot at breaking 21 minutes – an average of sub-7-minute miles. She'd be thrilled with that time, so she decided to go for it. She sucked some oxygen into her lungs and began to push.

About an eighth of a mile later she was moving as fast as she'd ever gone. She felt some heaviness in her chest and some weight in her thighs but otherwise she was strong. If this was a five-mile race she could never run at this pace but on a 5k it was possible. Before long she was alone on a residential road that would take her to the turnoff heading to the finish line at the elementary school. There were cheering homeowners sitting on beach chairs along the sidewalks, and she could feel the sweat rolling down her back. She felt great and looked down at her watch. She was at 19:17, but up ahead she could see the turn. There were people stacked up at the corner waving her in.

She was almost home.

Suddenly two runners rumbled up behind her. At about midway through the second mile she had ripped the earbuds out and stuffed them into her jacket pocket and so right now she could hear their footsteps pounding on the pavement. She looked over her left shoulder and saw them coming. They were young – early 20s she guessed – and they were really moving. There was plenty of room on the road for them to pass her but because the right turn was coming up, they were hugging the right shoulder of the street. In a moment they came right up on her, and one of them yelled out, "on your left!"

She raised her left arm quickly to acknowledge she heard them. She moved slightly to the right. She was now directly up against the curb. Before she knew it the two runners overtook her, and when they did, one of them brushed against her left shoulder. It wasn't very hard, but the contact was enough to send her onto the grass between the curb and the sidewalk. The difference in the terrain caused her to lose her footing, and she began to fall forward. For a second she thought she was going to nosedive straight down, but then she regained her balance, jumped back onto the roadway and was moving again.

And then, suddenly, her running career came to an abrupt end. It would be the last time she would ever run anywhere, even to get herself out of the rain.

Instead of concentrating on the road she was looking ahead at the twenty-year olds. She was running as hard as her legs could carry her, something just short of a sprint. She wanted to catch these two, but if she couldn't at the very least she wanted to recognize their clothing. Because after she got through the finish line she fully intended to find them in the crowd of runners grabbing bagels and bottles of water and offer a bit of polite advice – how about an "excuse me" next time, and don't let it happen again.

She looked ahead, taking a mental picture of their sneakers and jackets. Her legs were pumping and she was flying down the road. For that reason, she didn't notice a ten-inch deep pothole in front of a driveway about a quarter mile from the finish line. She stepped directly into it and her right leg caved. She heard a sickening crack and before she knew she was face down on the pavement.

She rolled over onto her backside and felt her forehead. She had driven her head into the roadway and her palm was now soaked in blood. Then she looked down at her leg, and what she saw almost caused her to pass out. Her right leg was broken midway between her knee and ankle, and as the leg descended from the knee, it turned grotesquely to the left directly at the point of the break. Her right foot was underneath her left calf. She felt a burning, stabbing pain shooting up her leg and she began taking huge gulps of breath. She frantically pulled her running pants to expose her leg, and that's when she saw the jagged edges of her tibia and fibula sticking through her shin. Her blood was dripping onto the roadway. She fell backwards and screamed.

A moment later there was a crowd surrounding her telling her to lie back down. Several people were screaming for someone to dial 911. A woman then rolled up a sweatshirt and put it under her head. The pain was overwhelming, and she felt waves of nausea running up her throat. She was suddenly ice cold and she slammed her fists down onto the roadway. Then she leaned over and threw up. A minute later an ambulance appeared. The beams of its spinning red lights were ricocheting off the front windows of the homes aligning the street. The EMTs wrapped her leg in an air cast and mounted her onto a gurney as police officers kept the growing crowd at bay.

An hour later a team of surgeons wheeled her into surgery. They placed a gas mask over her face, and she was out …

A NURSE CAME into the waiting room.

"Sylvia Metzel?" she called. An old lady struggled to her feet. With the help of her husband, a walker and an oxygen tank, she crept toward the medical rooms.

Anzalone checked her watch and glanced over at Justin. He was still asleep. She put her head against the wall and closed her eyes …

When does redemption come?

At what point is a person truly forgiven?

When can you say you've made amends, cleaned the slate and moved on, regardless of the lives you shattered and the anguish you caused? No one goes through life mistake-free, she would be told, you're human and you make errors in judgment. And when you act upon them those actions have consequences. But you atone with sincerity and ask to be absolved and eventually peace will come.

But what about the shame? What about that? Is there anything more painful and enduring than shame? When does it end?

All of these would be interesting philosophical inquiries, Anzalone had resolved, were it not for the fact that there were actual people involved. And there were days over the ensuing years when she would lie in the converted basement of her parent's house, trying to fall asleep on a pull-out sofa, and truly ponder these questions. Really think about them. She read books about them, took seminars, sought counseling and wrote in journals. She even tried something she hadn't done in over twenty-five years – she prayed and dragged herself back to the Confessional.

And in the end … nothing.

None of these so-called professionals and philosophers and theologians had any more of a leg up on these metaphysical ponderings than she did. Because despite all the psycho-babble, the answer, over time, became as clear to her as the nose on her face.

When are people truly forgiven? When does redemption come? The answer is never if can't forgive yourself. In that case the shame lives on like a malignant growth, and redemption is nothing but a pipe dream. You wear your regret like an old tattoo.

She was almost finished …

THE OPEN, COMPOUND *fracture that she suffered to her right leg that day in May required six hours of surgery. At first the doctors thought she was going to lose her leg, but then they installed a metal plate and twelve screws and sewed up the incision with fourteen staples. They wrapped the wound in gauze and gave her a leg brace that she wrapped tight with Velcro straps. It ran from her ankle to about mid-thigh.*

Under the insurance guidelines, the hospital discharged her a mere forty-eight hours after her surgery. Suchek was there to help. He lifted her off the hospital bed and eased her into a wheelchair. Then he pushed her into an elevator and rolled her through the lobby. When they got out to the Audi, Suchek and Carmine lifted her into the passenger seat. She was in tears from the pain. Suchek drove her home and got her into bed.

On Wednesday of that week, a Buckley Sullivan partner named Jimmy Doyle called and told her not to worry about anything at the firm. He'd heard about how bad the injury was and said everyone was thinking about her.

"Just heal up, Nicole," he told her. "Take your time and let me know when you feel better. If we have any questions about your cases we'll call and ask, but in the meantime, you just rest and we'll see where you're at next week."

That day and for the rest of the week she lied in bed and barely moved her leg. Suchek played nursemaid, running errands and bringing meals. Meanwhile, she could barely sit still because the pain in her shin during those first few days was unbearable. It felt hot at the spot of the incision and a dull, heavy ache pulsated through her bones. It felt as if someone were pounding down on her shinbone with a sledgehammer every time her heart took a beat. It was running up her thigh and into the small of her back, and after a few days it was combined with a blistering headache. For the first four days post-surgery she didn't sleep a wink and was frantic. The Advil Liqui-gels she was taking weren't doing a damn thing. The pain was getting worse. Something had to be done. So one morning she called her doctor and waited, and then she called again. Eventually a nurse called back.

"Did you fill the prescription for the pain?" the nurse asked.

No, she told her, she didn't. In her post-surgery fog, she had forgotten all about it. She couldn't believe she hadn't thought of it earlier. She quickly hung up and begged Suchek to find the plastic bag with the drawstring that the hospital gave her upon discharge, the one where she stuffed all the paperwork they made her sign. Remember it? Please, get it quick she told him. He searched the kitchen and finally located it. Sure enough, right there amidst all the other documents, she found a prescription for Percocet 10/325. She handed it to Suchek and implored him – Jesus Christ, drive down to Rockville Centre Family Pharmacy and get this thing filled. In a half hour he was back. She screwed off the top, shook one of the pills into her palm, and downed it with a bottle of Snapple Diet Iced Tea.

And that was the day that her life changed forever.

In fact, if you pressed her, she could tell you the day, the hour, and within a few seconds, the exact minute.

It didn't take more than twenty minutes for the medicine to circulate through her system. When it did, she was blanketed in a warm glow that washed over her whole body. The stress of the injury and the office and the wedding and anything else that may have been going on in her life completely disappeared. She felt euphoric and at peace. Everything was going to be okay – her injury would heal and get better; it would all be fine. There was nothing to worry about. She was sure of it. She was calm and felt a sense of unbridled happiness. As far as the pain in her leg was concerned, it wasn't simply that the drug took it away, but more to the point, it made her feel like she didn't care about it any longer. Her tormented restlessness disappeared but at the same time she didn't want to sleep. Instead she lied in the bed in a vacant, tranquil fog with half a grin on her face, staring at the walls and ceiling. She had the sense that she was hovering there, not even touching the sheets. It was nothing like she had ever felt before in her life, and from the moment she took that first pill, as her blood was carrying those narcotics to every limb in her body, she couldn't imagine not having this feeling again.

She wanted it to stay. She wanted it to linger.

She wanted it to be permanent.

Suchek came in with a tray that held a sandwich, chips and a Diet Pepsi.

"Here you go. Made some lunch."

"Heyyy big guy," she said.

Her eyes were fixed on the ceiling.

"Want this on the nightstand?"

"Just leave it … anywhere … I'll eat it … later."

"Oh my God," Suchek observed, "you're wasted."

And she was. Suchek made a joke about it but it was true – she was in a fog and was out of it. Suchek eased the door closed and let her rest.

That afternoon, around 4pm, her shin was throbbing again. And on that first day, out of curiosity, she downed another pill. The next morning, as soon as she woke, she took another one. Then she swallowed another after her lunch and a final one before bed. After each pill she would return to an opioid-drenched stupor and lie in bed in a state of blissful oblivion. By the third day Suchek insisted she follow doctor's orders and move around the house on her crutches. So she made her way downstairs to the living room, clumping down one stair at a time. Breathless, she plopped down onto the sofa and rested her leg on an ottoman. Within fifteen minutes she told Suchek her leg was on fire.

So she took another pill.

The next day she was due to start PT. When she arose that morning Suchek assisted her in and out of the shower, which was a difficult task because the leg had to be wrapped in a full-length plastic bag that had a rubber seal at the top to prevent water from leaking in. She showered balancing on one leg and then dried off and got dressed.

Then she and Suchek were in the car.

"I have a massive headache," she complained from the passenger seat.

Suchek nodded. He helped her inside and an hour later he returned to assist her home. As soon as she got in the door, she downed another pill and then collapsed on the sofa. She took another one after dinner. Then one more the next morning …

"IS THERE A Richard Castiglione here?"

This time the call came from behind the slide-over window. A man in blue coveralls with the name "Richie" stitched to his breast pocket stood and slogged his way toward the backrooms. Anzalone opened her eyes and checked on Justin.

Then she closed them again …

ABOUT A MONTH post-injury Suchek received a call from the PT center. A technician explained that he was listed on the forms as the emergency contact.

"Hey, listen," the tech told him, "just a head's up here. You may want to suggest to Nicole that she wait until after our therapy sessions to take the pain killers. She comes in here on Queer Street and we don't really get anything done. I've told her a few times now, but maybe you can get the point across."

Suchek thanked him politely and hung up. The guy hadn't said it directly, but his subtle message was clear. She was taking too many of these things. It seemed to be her sole focus when she got up every day. It had been going on for over a month now. Suchek would have to say something, maybe ask her whether she needed them anymore. But it was difficult – she would hobble down the stairs every day like a grouch and would swear the pain was so bad that she couldn't take it one more second. Then she'd swallow a pill and for the rest of the day she'd be smiling and barely speaking and lying around and not doing much of anything else. When he told her about the conversation with the technician, she barked at him and fell asleep.

The next Monday she was due to return to work. Suchek would drive her there. She was snapping at him while she was getting ready, and Suchek was running here and there dutifully following every instruction. They finally got to the car and had just turned north onto Peninsula Boulevard when she popped open her handbag and pulled the top off the prescription bottle.

"My leg is throbbing," she said, and she washed a pill down with a Starbucks Grande Pike.

Three hours later Suchek received a call from Jimmy Doyle.

"You need to come and get her. She seems a little out of it today."

So Suchek picked her up and she didn't make it back into the office for the rest of the week. Instead, it happened that another prescription bottle was nearing the bottom and she was already warning that she wanted it refilled. She called her doctor's office and they refused to do it over the phone. They told her she needed to come in. She pleaded for an appointment as soon as she could get it, and they gave her one on Thursday.

At the appointment the doctor examined her and told her that he didn't see anything wrong with her leg. It was progressing nicely. The swelling was gone and the incision was almost entirely healed. Quite frankly, he told her, I'm surprised you're feeling any pain at all. With your physical therapy you should be walking without the assistance of a cane.

Well I'm not, she pleaded, and the pain is still very intense. It's affecting my life. Could there be a problem with the plate? Maybe there's a problem with the plate. It doesn't feel right. I'm sure there's a problem with it. They took an *x-ray, and the doctor reported that it looked perfect. There were no problems at all. But he agreed to write her another prescription. So she got her pills.*

Over the next month it was the same routine. She would start the day snapping at Suchek and after she took her pill she would be comatose on the couch for the rest of the day. It was affecting her body clock too because now she was waking up at about eleven at night, just as Suchek was going to sleep. He would hear the television humming downstairs sometimes at three in the morning.

At the end of that month, on a Monday, she made another attempt to go back to work. This time the office called by ten o'clock in the morning. It was Rachel, the Office Manager, who delivered the same message — Suchek needed to come and get her. She wasn't right and probably needed to rest. That afternoon Jimmy Doyle called and told Suchek he and some of the partners were concerned. The word he used caused Suchek's heart to jump; he said that she appeared "impaired" and shouldn't have been in the office in such a condition. He said he knew she was still in a lot of pain, but she really should just stay home until she was fully prepared to return to work. Could he make that point clear to her? Suchek said he would.

And that is when the screaming matches began. Suchek would insist she needed to stop taking the pills and she would explode. "YOU THINK YOU HAVE ANY FUCKING IDEA WHAT YOU'RE TALKING ABOUT?" she would shriek, "IT'S MY FUCKING LEG!"

Suchek would tell her — calm at first, and then he would yell back himself — that she ought to try getting through the day without taking anything. The pain couldn't possibly be that bad. She roared back at him and told him he was wrong, and then she began insulting him. She called him names, told him he was useless and dumb and that he had no ambition and how the hell did she ever get mixed up with some guitar-strumming going-nowhere hippie. And then she'd take her pill and she would be flat on her back on the sofa again, staring at the ceiling.

When the next prescription bottle was about to run out, she was frantic. She called her doctor's office demanding an appointment. The plate had to be brushing against a nerve because the pain was overwhelming, she said. The office staff told her the doctor would get back to her when he could, and then finally Suchek received the call. The doctor explained that he had seen this a thousand times and that it was obvious she was now dependent on the pain killers and that he would not write her another prescription, it was out of the question. If she was truly in that much pain, which he doubted, she could make an appointment with a pain management specialist. In the meantime, he suggested that if she were smart, she'd stop taking anything stronger than an Advil.

When she got that news, she and Suchek were screaming at each other so loudly the neighbors could hear it. The woman across the street was standing at her doorway with a cell phone in her hand, ready to call the police. But then she slammed the front door and with her cane in hand she began clumping to her car. Suchek yelled from the door.

"Nicole! Where are you going?!"

"Fuck off!" she yelled back, and she screeched down the street.

Twenty minutes later she was at the Emergency Room. Yesterday she fell down the stairs, she lied, and banged her leg badly on the bottom rung. She recently had an operation and now she feared she damaged the plate they had inserted because the pain had become unbearable. They took an x-ray and told her it was fine, there was no need to worry. Keep ice on it and you should be okay. Then she asked if she could have something for the pain. Right after the operation they had given her ... what was it called? Percocet 10/325 maybe? She claimed she couldn't remember exactly but anyway that really seemed to work. Maybe they could give her some of those? They said that's fine, and they wrote her a prescription. She went immediately to the pharmacy.

In the next few weeks, she made one more attempt to return to work and this time Jimmy Doyle greeted her in the reception area. He took one look and told her, Nicole, no dice. Go home and get yourself straightened out. In the meantime, we are putting you on a leave of absence. Your cases have been reassigned and when you get yourself well again maybe give us a call. You know how everyone feels about you, especially me, but that injury was more serious than any of us really appreciated and the most important thing is that you recover and get well.

And with that she was out the door at Buckley Sullivan ...

ANZALONE DIDN'T REALIZE it, but she was crying. Her eyes were closed as a tear rolled down her cheek, settling on her neck.

There was an old man sitting next her.

"Excuse me," he said softly, "are you okay?"

Anzalone opened her eyes and smiled.

"Yes, I am, thank you."

"Tough day?" he asked.

Anzalone nodded. The old man patted her arm ...

OVER THE NEXT *several months things spiraled downwards. She was in a fog most of the day and was up most of the night. She and Suchek were screaming at one another daily, and Suchek, beside himself, had resorted to calling Carmine and telling him exactly what was going on. Carmine sped over there with his wife. They knew something was wrong with her, but that day they couldn't believe the sight of their daughter. She had lost close to fifteen pounds and had dark circles under her eyes. Her mother was in tears, and Carmine demanded she get some help. She told them both to fuck off and to get out of her house. Suchek was shocked, mortified. She slammed the door behind them when they left. They didn't understand her, they never did, not her whole life, she told Suchek, and how could they, her own parents, say those things to her? Can you believe that? Can you? She didn't want either of them over here ever again, do you understand me? Do you?!*

Nicole, Suchek said to her, baby please.

The arguments moved past the pills. She was going four or five days in a row without a shower and looked horrific. Suchek told her she should be in a hospital and she threw a plate at him. She stopped paying the bills and Suchek had to take them over. She had no income now and with the money he earned he couldn't afford the mortgage and the bills and didn't know what they were going to do. She wasn't lifting a finger around the house and when he wasn't cleaning the place was a mess. And currently Suchek had no idea what she was taking, but the very thought of it was scaring the life out of him. He would hear her leave in the middle of the night and return about an hour or so later. He would demand to know where she was, and she would scream back at him.

The truth was that when the final prescription was about to run out, she had jumped on the Internet and navigated through to some nefarious websites. She wound up with a cell phone number for a guy named Clay who had agreed to meet her at the train station over in Hempstead. He'd be in a blue Chevy Cruze and would park near the newsstand. One night she hit an ATM and took out two hundred dollars and met the guy at three-thirty in the morning. She paid him for a number of oxycontin tablets. She took one right there at the train station and Clay just shook his head and laughed.

"I'll see YOU in a few days," he said, and he pulled away.

She then fell into a routine and every two weeks or so she would meet Clay at the train station in the middle of the night. She needed to take more and more of the oxycontin tablets to get herself right and she was blowing through her cash. Finally, Suchek told her if she didn't get some help he was going to move out and she at first screamed at him but then told him she'd consider it. She loved him and didn't want him to leave. She resolved to stop taking the pills, but then she hid Clay's stash in a plastic bag that she stuffed through a hole in the sheetrock in the back of her closet.

She bit the bullet and didn't touch a pill for three or four days. She was sweating, itching and her heart was pounding. Then she told Suchek she couldn't believe how badly her leg hurt and there was definitely something wrong with the plate. It had to be impinging on a nerve and they had clearly committed medical malpractice when they did the operation. She was going to call the doctor and let them have it. Maybe she would sue. At a minimum they had better give her another prescription for the pain.

"For God's sake, Nicole, it's not the damn plate!"

She lifted a lamp off the living room table and threw it across the room, and it shattered against the fireplace mantle. And that's when Suchek had had enough. He quickly packed a bag and in a minute he was bolting for the door.

"Where are you going?!" she raged, violently flipping over a coffee table.

But Suchek left without a word, shutting the door behind him. She limped to the front door, pulled it open, and watched as he sped down the street.

With Suchek gone, she met regularly with Clay and took two or three oxycontin tablets a day. She would be passed out in her living room, sometimes on the sofa, sometimes on the floor, for almost the entire day. Carmine came by one day and pounded on the door, but she hid and wouldn't answer. Finally he left. Her sister came over a few times with her husband and she did the same thing. Meanwhile, she was barely eating and had dropped to about ninety-seven pounds, which looked waifish even on her five-foot frame. She'd wake up near midnight and would be wired most of the night. As soon as the oxycontin tablets wore off her entire body would ache, and she would itch from head to toe and she'd be bathed in sweat. It had to be from the surgery, she would reason. After-effects from the surgery. She was sure of it.

Two weeks after Suchek left she heard a racket one morning and went to the front door. She looked through the glass side panel and saw a man loading her Audi onto a tow truck. She watched expressionless as a long steel cable attached to the Audi's rear axle pulled it onto the truck's flatbed. The driver pulled down the street and disappeared. She collapsed back onto the sofa.

A few nights later she pulled the plastic bag from the sheetrock hole. It had two pills left, and she began to panic. She dialed Clay and he answered, saying, *"same time, same place baby."* Sometime in the middle of the night she called a cab, and before the driver arrived, she downed the remaining tablets. They swiftly entered her bloodstream, and in less than ten minutes she felt some relief. But it wasn't enough. She needed more. She could barely walk, but she had to get to Clay. When the driver arrived, she staggered out, cane in hand, and hobbled into the cab.

"Hempstead train station," she mumbled in slurred speech to the driver, a woman with blond dreadlocks, *"but first the ATM at Bank of America on Franklin Street."*

"Right," the driver answered suspiciously. *"Uhh, you sure about this?"*

"Please," she answered, *"just go."*

When they got to the ATM, she stumbled out of the cab and nearly fell over as she stood at the outdoor machine. She was barely coherent enough to punch in her PIN, but when she did — three times — the machine indicated insufficient funds in her account. She opened her purse and saw that it had nothing in it but a single twenty-dollar bill. And then she began to cry. She *would have to figure something out, make some kind of deal with Clay. He would have to listen to reason, cut her a break. She hobbled back into the cab. Go, she said to the driver through sobs, please just go.*

"Lady, how about I just take you home, whaddya say? It'll be no charge."

"Just drive," she snapped back, wiping her nose. And then in a minute she was out cold. When they got to the station, she sensed the car come to a stop and she opened her eyes. She felt like there was a thousand-pound load on her shoulders and she could barely keep her head from tilting forward. She was taking long draws of breath through her nose and was trying desperately to keep from falling unconscious. It was approaching four o'clock in the morning when she stepped from the cab. She handed the driver her last twenty-dollar bill and when the woman asked if she wanted her to wait, she said no, she could go. The driver shook her head and left.

She was at the regular meeting spot but there was no blue Chevy Cruze. In fact, the place was abandoned. She took a seat on a bench and was fighting fatigue, fighting sleep, with every ounce of her strength. She just wanted to meet Clay and get back home.

Suddenly a pair of headlights turned a corner. They pulled slowly into the parking lot and came to a stop right next to her. She got up and limped to the driver's side. She saw another man there, younger than Clay, with a shaved head and tattoos running down his neck. Clay eased the driver's side window down and looked at her, shaking his head.

"No car?" he asked with a smirk.

She shook her head no.

"Probably fucking sold it, right you junkie?"

She didn't say a word.

"So you gonna just stand there, you got the bills?"

She shook her head no again. The winter air was freezing her ears but she barely felt the sting. Clay looked at her with disgust and hooked a thumb toward the back seat.

"Get in the back while we talk, I'm freezing my ass off."

She pulled open the rear passenger door and climbed in. She wasn't sure if she could stay conscious much longer, but she managed to tell Clay she didn't have any money. She was good for it next week, she promised. Could she have maybe three or four pills, just to get her through a few days? Clay just laughed.

"Fuck you think this? I'm running a business here girl. Plus, I'm out of your usual shit anyway. I'll be back in supply in about two days."

Clay then popped open the glove compartment.

"But I do got this," he said.

Clay then showed her ... that thing. That terrible medical instrument. She looked at it and she knew. She nodded at Clay, and then she began to reason with herself. It'll just be this one time. Maybe that will get me through. She never wanted to go this route but what choice did she have? He said he was out. So yes, she would take it, she told him, but could they please work something out about the payment? Please. I understand you'd be doing me a favor, she told him, but please, if you could just —

"Tell you what," Clay said.

He nodded at the man in the passenger seat.

"Here's what we're gonna do. I'm gonna cut you a break. See, it's been a while for my man here, if you know what I mean. Been more than a little while, in fact," and the two of them laughed. "So, we figure maybe he'll just slip in the back with you, know what I'm saying? You can make your payment in trade. You cool with that girl?"

Before she said a word, she had it in her hands and rolled up her sleeve. The man with the neck tattoos opened the front passenger door, threw it shut, and climbed in the back. She dropped it to the floor and her head went backwards. She was falling in and out of consciousness, and then she realized she was lying down. The man was on top of her and smelled like cigarettes. He was grunting, bouncing up and down, and in a minute it was over. She woke up to an image of Clay tapping her on the cheek.

"Yo, you need to get dressed and get the hell out of my car," he said.

About six hours later, the loud crack of a police stick jolted her upright. She was sleeping in a fetal position on a bench inside the train station.

"Move it, you can't sleep here," the officer told her. She shielded her eyes from the blinding daylight, fighting the urge to throw up.

"Let's go," the cop said again, "get up and get out of here."

She looked around for her cane, but it was gone. A young couple stared at her, the girl shaking her head. She stood and limped to the doors.

A few weeks later, she was on her sofa, sobbing and shaking, her body radiating pain and sweat and chills. She hadn't eaten in a day and a half and barely had the strength to get to the bathroom. She was nearly frozen because there was no heat or electricity in the house. She knew she had hit bottom, that her very life was at stake.

So she called Suchek in tears. She begged him to come over and stay with her. She told him she knew she needed help and if she got counseling and went into rehab was it possible they could get their lives back together? Was that possible? She told him she'd do anything to make things right.

"I don't know, Nicole," he told her, "I don't know."

But she begged and pleaded and the next morning he was there. She arose eagerly from her bed and got in the shower, the first one in over a week. When he arrived she met him at the doorway. She was dressed as prim and as proper as she could make herself up, and yet Suchek still noticed the change.

"My God, you look like shit, Nic. You really need help."

She agreed. They talked for hours, and in the end she told him she would go to an in-patient rehab facility. Suchek told her it was the only way he would even consider trying to get their relationship back on track. She said she'd do anything to make that happen. If that's what it took then she was all in, she was ready. He admitted he still loved her and cared for her and that her getting healthy was the first step in the process. If she could do that then maybe they had a chance. But he made no promises.

The next day she packed her bags. There was a facility out in Suffolk called Inspirations and Suchek called and made the arrangements. Then he and Carmine drove her out there. They got her admitted and they told her they would see her in thirty days. The first thing the staff did was give her a complete physical and admit her into the Detox portion of the facility. She went to sleep that night in a tiny room on a bed that was no bigger than a cot, but she didn't care. She felt encouraged, hopeful, that maybe this long nightmare was over. At 8 a.m., the following morning, a nurse's assistant woke her. They told her to get dressed and head to the facility Director's Office.

She walked in and there was a nurse along with the Director, a woman named Beth. They invited her to sit. The nurse handed Beth a piece of paper.

"Nicole, do you know you're pregnant?" Beth asked.

She swallowed hard. For a fleeting moment, sometime over the last month, the thought had crossed her mind during yet another wave of nausea. But it quickly passed, and she moved on. She unwillingly conjured the image of the night at the train station with Clay and the man who, try as she might, she could not even put a face to. He was nothing but a blur lost among the haunting images of that evening's terrible events.

She didn't say a word. Instead she began to shake as tears rolled down her cheeks. The nurse walked her back to her room. The next day she told them she needed to make an emergency call. She wanted to call Suchek; she just had to speak to him. But it was strictly against the rules and they told her she had a choice – she could wait until she was out of Detox or she could check herself out and make all the calls she wanted. Your choice, they said, and good luck to you.

She decided to wait.

About a week later she couldn't wait any longer. She called Suchek and told him the news. She was hysterical on the hallway payphone, standing there in a pair of grey sweatpants and a t-shirt, in bare feet. She said she had made a horrible mistake, and could he come and see her so they could talk this out. Could he please?

"Aw Nicole. I'm so sorry for you, I really am."

They both knew they hadn't been together in many months, and that it couldn't possibly be his child. Suchek told her he didn't see the point in a visit.

It was over, for good this time.

"I really wish you luck, Nicole," he said, and he hung up the phone.

It would be many years before she would either see or speak to him again.

What happened over the next year occurred with little emotion. When she was released from rehab she moved into her parent's basement, because the bank had foreclosed on her cape. She wasn't there a week before she was hit with a Notice of Hearing from the New York State Ethics Commission for a potential disbarment based on a charge of stealing client funds. About a month earlier, she had received a call from an old client looking to pay a small overdue bill, and in her desperation, she told the client to cut her the check. She'd give it to the firm, she lied, and then she deposited that money into her personal bank account. The client never got a receipt and called the firm demanding answers. The firm figured things out in the blink of an eye and made a full report to the Commission about their former colleague.

At the hearing a few months later, at which she fully expected to lose her law license, she stood at counsel's table, representing herself, in a pair of jeans and a white blouse that swelled out over her baby bump. Her mother and father sat in the gallery, with Carmine's arm wrapped around his wife, who was in tears. She admitted her guilt, explained her plight, and didn't spare them a single detail. Jimmy Doyle, of all people, appeared unexpectedly as a character witness, and to her surprise the Commission did not disbar her. Two-year suspension, provided she make full restitution and attend counseling.

Then, the following July, she gave premature birth to a five pound three-ounce baby boy she named Justin. They told her right in the delivery room there was a problem, and in a matter of hours they gave her the diagnosis. Justin had cerebral palsy. His life would be met with untold challenges. They gave her the name of some specialists and they sent her and Justin home …

"NICOLE ANZALONE?" THE nurse called. She was holding the door open with her hip. Anzalone's eyes were still closed but she sprang to attention and stuck a finger in the air.

"Right here."

She got behind Justin's wheelchair and followed the nurse through the hallway. They came to a room marked "4" and the nurse led them in.

"The doctor will be right with you," she said.

Anzalone pushed Justin in and turned his wheelchair to face the door. She stroked his hair and kissed him on the forehead.

"How are you, Justy?" she asked softly.

"I good Mommy how you?"

Soon Dr. Gubash entered in a waist-length white coat and reading glasses. Skipping pleasantries, he popped an x-ray into the light board on the wall and flicked on the electricity behind it.

"Ms. Anzalone, this is the picture we took your last visit," he opened, pointing to the x-ray with the stem of his glasses, "the epiphyseal plate, or the growth plate, in the radius bone of Justin's left arm for some reason has closed. We can't really explain why, but it has. The ulna bone, on the other hand, which is here," he ran the stem of his glasses down the other arm bone, "continues to grow, as one might expect for a boy of his age. The result is that Justin's arm is beginning to twist, or corkscrew is a better way to describe it. He's probably in a lot of pain, and if this condition progresses, as we believe it will, it will affect his shoulder joint, if it hasn't already."

Anzalone didn't respond. Instead, she put her arm over Justin's shoulders. Dr. Gubash flicked off the light and sat on a counter.

"I highly recommend this be addressed as quickly as possible."

"And this gets addressed how, doctor?" she asked gravely.

"We address it surgically, Ms. Anzalone."

Well there it was. They were headed for surgery.

Anzalone thanked Dr. Gubash and rolled Justin out to the Civic. The poor kid would not understand why he would be in so much pain, and the thought of that made her sad. Anzalone would comfort him and get him through it, but meanwhile, how she was going to pay for this procedure remained a mystery.

Once settled in the Civic, Anzalone thought about her little law firm and this Beers case that was beginning to overwhelm her. It wasn't bringing in a cent. The defendants, led by that massive FT&B law firm, recently served her with document requests, demands for bills of particulars, requests for authorizations and medical records, requests for expert disclosures, and a few other demands, and drafting the responses to all of them and collecting all the evidence was taking time, a lot of it. The firm was sending her letters threatening the court's intervention because of her delay. She also had to draft demands of her own, and she was twisting in the bedsheets at night sweating over how she would be able to review all the information and documents that the other side would produce to her. Without question she would need to hire a temp lawyer and pay that person for the work.

But where was that money possibly coming from?

Of course, on the surface, nothing really had changed about the potential for this case to bring her what would amount to a large recovery and fee, so in the end it could all be worth it. But there was one little nagging inconvenient fact that the other side would eventually discover, and one that Anzalone, in the privacy of her own mind, was really getting worried about. And that was this – the Beers kid was getting better.

Her doctors recently removed the trach and she was home now and on the mend. It was a funny thing about these damn personal injury cases, Anzalone knew, that they always seem to bring a certain moral tension to the surface. Being a mother with a special needs child, she naturally was happy that Agnes's condition was improving. But on the other hand, that only meant the value of their case was plummeting. You felt guilty even thinking about it in those terms, but that was just the reality of it. Agnes Beers had a long way to go and perhaps would always have some cognitive impairment, but that was an unknown right now, and only time would determine that fact. In a year she could come skipping into the courtroom reading an algebra textbook, and Anzalone's demand for $50 million would make her look like a fool.

As a result, Anzalone was waking every day to a sense of dread. Maybe Gunther would have no interest in settling and would push for a trial. She had little appetite for a long, drawn-out case, not against a firm like Foster Tuttle & Briggs, and certainly not against J. Hartwell Briggs. But if that's what it took, if that is what she had to do, Anzalone was determined. She would make her own goddamn redemption, one way or the other. She could look at this like she was a seventh grade Pop Warner team taking on the Dallas Cowboys, or she could take stock of herself and fight. If she could get this case into settlement discussions, she resolved, she'd convince those hotshot lawyers they could lose.

And if she had to try the case, she would stand up before that jury and take her chances.

Anzalone and Justin were on the Long Island Expressway now, on their way to her parent's house, where she would give them the news about the next hospitalization for their grandson. In the meantime, with Justin sitting quietly in the backseat, and traffic creeping along in front of her, Anzalone leaned on the steering wheel and finished her story …

BY THE TIME *Justin was four, she decided to move out of her parent's basement and get on with some semblance of a life. She was 40 and raising a child and it was time. She'd been attending NA meetings regularly and working as a waitress at two different restaurants, and she got the bug to get back to the practice of law. She applied for reinstatement and New York State re-issued her a law license. With the help of Carmine, she and Justin found a little townhome in the small village of Ketchogue, up on the north shore. It was going to be a fresh start, and she was excited about it.*

As far as a legal job was concerned, she knew that no firm would hire her, and she really didn't want to work for anyone anyway. So she hunted the ads for some cheap office space, without much luck at first. But then one day she was in a donut shop grabbing a coffee and out of curiosity she asked the owner about the space up there on the second floor. Before she knew it, she had worked out a modest deal with the owner and over the course of a weekend she cleared boxes and other garbage out of the place and set up some desks. In the next week she sent out announcements about the opening of a new law firm, which she would call The Law Offices of Nicole I. Anzalone, solo practitioner…

CHAPTER 20

#babykiller

"DUDE, YOU REALLY think this is gonna work?"

"Yes, I'm quite certain, Mr. Brewer," whispered Moshe Wagshul, his fingers webbed under his chin.

"I gotta tell you, dude, I'm dubious," said Dodge. "Sounds like a longshot."

"Why's it a longshot?" Bruce Dixon chimed in, irritated. He was nodding his fat-filled chin over at Moshe. "He does this shit for a living, chief."

Bruce was trying to be calm but you could tell he was barely containing himself. His body language suggested nothing but disdain for Dodge Brewer, which was being made worse by the fact that Dodge was directing all his questions and comments to Moshe, as if Bruce didn't exist. The tension in the room was thick. And unlike Dodge and Moshe, whose shoulders were slumped with their chins lowered to avoid being heard, Bruce's posture was erect and confrontational. Right now he had both palms planted on the table in front of him.

For his part, Dodge didn't think much of Bruce Dixon either and really believed he'd be stopping by tonight for a quick chat alone with Moshe. But then he walked in and there was Bruce Dixon, all teed up like a high-schooler ready to take on anybody in the lunchroom.

Undaunted, Dodge went on.

"Well, it makes no sense, so I'm telling you, I'm dubious."

"Well, I'm sorry you're *dubious*, but it makes sense to me."

"Please, keep your voices down," Moshe instructed.

Dodge then leaned in toward him.

"Dude, just tell me how it plays out."

Bruce snapped right back at him.

"For fuck's sake, did you not listen to him the first time?"

"I did, dude," Dodge said dismissively, and then to piss off Bruce, "and I'm dubious."

"You're dubi – Moish, explain it to Mr. Princeton here one more time."

The three of them were sitting in Moshe's 3-bedroom split-level home over in the central district of Ketchogue. That neighborhood backed up to the West Side, where Danny Beers lived, but the realtors would tell you the central district was a step up in both value and prestige, even though the houses basically looked the same. They were all small capes or split-levels on postage-stamp-sized properties. They were built in the late 40s and early 50s right after the War when first generation New York City immigrants were expanding out to build suburbia and replace the duck farms on Long Island. The neighborhood was situated just north of Route 25A, which was only about a hundred yards from Moshe's backyard. In the summer, on Sabbath Saturdays, Moshe and his family would open the windows and could hear the cars rumbling back and forth.

Right now, at the Wagshul kitchen table, under the dimmed lighting from a stained-glass chandelier, the three of them were knuckled down in conference. Bruce was wearing a *New York Jets* sweatshirt and a "Make America Great Again" baseball hat, the kind with the mesh backing and the plastic snap-on fastener. The hat looked about three times too small for his massive head. He was sipping from a can of Mountain Dew with his beer belly pressing against the edge of the Wagshul's family table.

"Thank you, Bruce, I am happy to explain," Moshe answered, ignoring Bruce's predilection for calling him "Moish." Moshe had corrected him a few times in the past but now seemed to have given up on it.

Moshe pressed his thick-lensed eyeglasses against his face with his index finger and laid his skinny forearms on the table.

"But I will ask you to lower your voices please."

Moshe said that last part looking at Bruce, who simply nodded and showed him a palm. Moshe Wagshul, member of the Ketchogue Sports and Recreation Committee along with Bruce, was about thirty-five but looked to be in his early twenties. He was razor thin and wore a short-sleeved white shirt under his baby face of pink freckles. There was a thick eyeglass case stuffed into his breast pocket and a black yarmulke topped his tangled mop of strawberry hair. The glasses he wore were thick and heavy and looked as though the weight of them could snap his scrawny neck. There was a Mac laptop on the table near his elbows, open to a Twitter page. The ambient light from the laptop was glowing in the half-lit room.

Dodge leaned in again to get the lowdown from Moshe about this idea they had about how to set things right in the Beers case. Or at least that's how Moshe described it. Dodge went from the office straight to Moshe's house and so he was decked out in a navy-blue Dior suit with a maroon tie, which was hanging about an inch below the top button of his white cotton oxford. It was just past eleven o'clock on a Tuesday evening, and the three of them were speaking in lowered voices over a bowl of kosher pretzels. What Moshe and Bruce were telling him about how to deal with the Beers litigation didn't make any sense, so Dodge had arranged this meeting – with Moshe he thought – so he could get some answers.

"It is called a twitter-bot," Moshe explained.

"Yeah, that's what you told me, dude. And this is relevant to our case how exactly?"

"As we explained, Mr. Brewer, we were very successful the last time with the hashtag 'agnesbeers.' If you recall, we put out a series of tweets and retweets that raised a lot of sympathy for the volunteer board members. We then referred to them on an anonymous blog and the Ketchogue Patch picked up the story. We used a second twitter-bot to spread that article, and then the big article appeared on Yahoo News with Ms. Wartham's quote. We wrote and placed that statement. We were able to engineer a development that was enormously helpful to our situation."

"So Wartham's in on this too?" asked Dodge.

There was a touch of smartass in his tone, and Bruce, who was beginning to lose his patience, picked up on it right away.

"*In* on it? Fuck's that supposed to mean?"

"Exactly what it sounds like, dude. She's the President of the Committee. She know about this or not?"

"Maybe," Bruce answered protectively.

"Gentlemen, please," Moshe interrupted, "allow me to finish."

Dodge then turned to Moshe, waving off Bruce.

"Dude, just get to it. What's a twitter-bot?"

"Okay," Moshe began, "you're familiar with Twitter, I take it?"

"Uh, yeah, dude, I am."

"Well then, a twitter-bot is a computer program one writes to produce automatic posts on Twitter. They come in various forms. You see them a lot with spam and with advertising, for example. Or they allow you to retweet certain messages or to respond to certain hashtags and phrases automatically. Again, this is done without human intervention. You write the program and Twitter just responds to it, sending out your messages. For example, in 2016, twitter-bots were used very effectively by both the Clinton and Trump campaigns to get political messages out."

Dodge let all that hang in the air a moment as he absorbed it. Moshe had the calm, disaffected look of a mad scientist, like he was cooking up some evil plot to destroy the world. It was beginning to freak Dodge out a little. He didn't know the man very well and didn't really understand where all of this was going, but he was getting the sense he had made the wrong decision coming here tonight. He looked at them both again, right and left, as if he had just met them, and then he faced Moshe.

"Dude, what do you do again? I mean, for a living …"

"I'm the IT Director for a commercial leasing agency."

"Right," Dodge nodded back.

Then Bruce leaned toward Dodge and added, somewhat sarcastically, "Net, net, he works with computers, okay guy?"

"Yeah, that part I got, dude."

"Well, so now you know."

Dodge turned back to Moshe.

"Ok, dude, they're programs that allow automatic tweets. I get it. What's the point?"

Both Moshe and Bruce smiled at that comment, as if they were dealing with a child. Moshe adjusted himself in his seat and webbed his hands together, looking directly at Dodge.

"Well, Mr. Brewer, the point is as follows," he patronized, "twitter-bots can be used for benign purposes, of course, but they can also be used as a weapon. They are a modern-day form of warfare, you see. They allow you to artificially increase social-media traffic and create the appearance that there is a consensus of public opinion moving in one direction, when in fact there may not be. For example, you can use twitter-bots to have anonymous twitter accounts follow certain twitter users, creating a false appearance of popularity. Or you can use them to send waves of tweets and re-tweets advocating for one side of an issue. By flooding the cybersphere with your message, or with information that attacks your enemies, you can change the way people think. Before you know it, the perception becomes the reality, and society reacts accordingly. This is one of the methods used by ISIS to gain new recruits. And it is one that we will use as the next step necessary to bring an end to this very dangerous and ill-advised lawsuit."

"So we're like ISIS," Dodge muttered softly to himself.

"We're not ISIS, smart guy," Bruce responded, but Dodge ignored him again, focusing on Moshe.

"And you really think this is gonna work with Beers?"

"It worked very successfully the last time, Mr. Brewer."

"I'll remind you the guy is toxic in this town after that Yahoo article," Bruce added, "but he hasn't exactly dropped the case yet, has he?"

"And so we feel we must increase the pressure," Moshe added.

Dodge had his elbows on the table now, his fists pressed into his cheeks. He looked at them both, his eyes rotating back and forth as if he were at a tennis match. If it were up to him, he simply would let this lawsuit take its course. It was a legal matter, a simple business transaction. Something you add to the expense sheet and you cost it in. But for these guys it was a big deal and Dodge understood that fact. If they were coming up with a way to get rid of the entire lawsuit, well, he was all ears, because his lawyer fees were coming out of his own pocket. But the whole thing wasn't sitting well with him; it just had a bad flavor to it. This Moshe dude was a strange bird and Dixon was a meatball with the IQ of a ball peen hammer. Sitting at this kitchen table was giving him the creeps.

Moshe and Bruce stared at him now, waiting for a comment.

"Well, like I said," Dodge finally responded, "I'm dubious."

"Yeah, you mentioned that," Bruce said.

"The guy, Dan Beers," Dodge continued, "I don't know, I feel bad for him. The dude's just a construction worker."

"He's just a what?!" Bruce yelled, his voice now piercing the Wagshul kitchen. "And I'm just an electrician, Brewer! And he fucking sued me for 50 million dollars!"

"Mr. Dixon, your language, please …"

"And I wasn't even at the field that day chief – "

"Mr. Dixon …"

"But Beers *was* there, with his own goddamn kid – "

"Mr. Dixon, please …"

"And now I gotta worry about being bankrupted? Well screw him, Brewer, and up yours too! Maybe you got 50 million sitting in an offshore account in the Caymans somewhere, but I don't. Do you know I had to cough up FIVE GRAND to these shyster defense lawyers to cover the deductible on the town liability policy?! That was a real kick in the balls, okay? I'm sure you got that much in your Gucci wallet right now, but me and Moish over here had a little trouble parting with it. So excuse me if I'm hurting people's feelings, but I'm gonna play a little hardball, and if you don't like it, or it makes you *dubious,*" Bruce threw up some finger quotes, "I don't really give a shit!"

Moshe placed a hand on Bruce's forearm, but Bruce swatted it away. He lowered his voice and went on, "Look Brewer, you're here as a courtesy to let you know what's happening, but it's happening, okay sport? So, either you're in or you're out. Make a decision."

Bruce began stretching his neck, rotating his head in a circle, trying to twist the stress out. Dodge let him simmer for a moment as Moshe shot a glance to the stairs leading up the bedrooms, hoping Mrs. Wagshul wouldn't appear to throw them all out.

"Okay, dude, you made your point."

"Yeah, I did."

"Anything else, dude?"

"Yeah, in fact there is," Bruce added, but this time in a hushed voice, leaning forward over the table, "how about we all acknowledge the big pink elephant in the room and point out that it was you and Miss America who fed the goddamn kid *shrimp* … *fucking* … *cocktail* at a little girls' softball game. But it was me and Moish and Regina, who weren't even there, who got the lawsuit shoved up our asses."

Bruce jerked a thumb toward the ceiling as he made that last comment, and Dodge just nodded. The point was a good one. There were quite a few nights when he sat up, unable to sleep, knowing that it was he and Cindy who put the Beers kid in the hospital and caused all of them to get sued. He thought he warded off the lawsuit when he brought the shrimp bag over to Dan Beers's house, but then the guy had the nerve to send a process server sauntering into his foyer during his daughter's birthday party. When that happened, screw it, the gloves were off. Beers threw the first punch and Dodge had to defend himself. And he had to help these people defend themselves too, and that basically was the only reason he was here tonight. If there was a chance to get the whole case kicked, he couldn't be a barrier to that result. They could not afford an adverse jury verdict against them.

Plus, what had transpired with the insurance coverage in this clusterfuck of a lawsuit was complicated. There were separate policies issued to the town of Ketchogue and the Committee by two different insurance companies, and every one of the defendants, other than Gunther, had tendered their defenses to these insurers. But both carriers denied coverage to Dodge and Cindy; Dodge, they determined, was simply unaffiliated with either the town or the Committee in any official capacity. Similarly, they determined that the "snack mom" was a volunteer role that had not been sanctioned by the Town or assigned by the Committee and was not entitled to coverage. The individual members of the Committee – Bruce, Regina and Moshe – were being defended under the Committee's policy, but each had been required to pay $5,000 as part of the deductible on legal fees, and the policies had a $250,000 liability cap. This presented a real threat of exposure to these people; it could mean financial ruin.

The coach, Pete Briscoe, was covered under the Town's policy, which didn't have a deductible, and of course when that became known it launched Bruce into a tirade of expletives at the next Committee meeting, screaming bloody murder. As far as the lawsuit was concerned, the lawyers protected their clients by hurling cross-claims against everyone they could – Bruce sued Moshe and Regina, Moshe sued Regina and Bruce, Regina sued Moshe and Bruce, and everyone sued the Brewers, the Committee, the Town and the

Coach. The fingers of blame were pointing in every direction. And, of course, everyone pointed directly at the nose of Danny Beers. The whole thing was a tangled, legal mess.

After Bruce had emphasized the jamming of the lawsuit up his ass with the jerk of his thumb, Dodge turned again to Moshe.

"Okay, dude, I'm in," he said, waving the white flag. "What's next?"

Moshe didn't hesitate. He leaned in and spoke in a whisper, like he was revealing a Top-Secret CIA operation.

"I am releasing the next twitter-bot tomorrow," he coldly advised. "It will automatically shoot out tweets every five minutes with the hashtag *'agnesbeers'* once again, but this time they will include a second hashtag. And then every time either hashtag appears, the bot will retweet it exactly thirty more times in four-minute increments, all from different anonymous Twitter accounts. Every tweet and retweet will contain a series of rotating comments that are favorable to our cause, and all of them will refer to the terrible, tragic incident that recently took place, along with a photograph of that unfortunate event. The photograph, together with the rotating comments and the new hashtag, will all be targeted to bring social media attention to the fact that we volunteers are being ruthlessly attacked. They will all deflect attention away from the condition of the girl."

"And you think this will put pressure on Beers to drop the entire lawsuit?"

"Enormous pressure, Mr. Brewer," Moshe said confidently, with his mad scientist demeanor. "I expect the new hashtag to trend within a week. When that happens, it will be on every national news outlet in the country. People will be outraged. And then I, of course, will give a statement."

"Je-sus," Dodge responded.

"Fuckin-A right," Bruce kicked in.

Dodge then stared across the Wagshul kitchen, taking all this information in. It sounded extreme, and unnecessary, but he didn't feel like he had any say here. Then he snapped his attention back to Moshe, focusing on something that Moshe had just said.

"Wait, did you just say – what's the second hashtag?"

Moshe didn't hesitate. His smile was sinister, and he looked Dodge right in the eyes, straightening him up in his seat.

"Hashtag *babykiller*," Moshe reported coldly.

Dodge's eyes shot up, and he looked over at Bruce.

"Dude … *baby* killer?"

"You heard him," Bruce deadpanned.

"Christ, okay baby killer. And dude, what tragic incident?"

Bruce and Moshe looked at each other and smiled.

Bruce pushed his prodigious belly from the table, and then he and Moshe stood.

"Let's go," Bruce said.

A FEW MOMENTS later they were circling around to Moshe's backyard. The property was small and protected, and Bruce led the march down a narrow driveway that had an unpainted 8-foot picket fence to the left and a collection of four brown Rubbermaid garbage cans shoved up against the house on the right. On the rear boundary to the Wagshul property, and running around to the west side, there was a continuous row of thick arborvitae bushes that soared to almost fifteen feet, blocking any view of the neighbors' homes, thereby ensuring some measure of privacy for the Wagshul family. In the left corner of the yard, at the end of the driveway, there was a sizeable detached two-car garage that had a strip of concrete to the right of it. Moshe's beige 2012 Pontiac Montana minivan was parked there. With the rear and west side arborvitaes, and the garage to the left, the minivan could not be seen from the street.

The three men gathered near the passenger side of the Montana. Moshe stood next to it wrapped in a coffee-colored winter parka with a fur-trimmed hood, which was pulled over his head for protection against the December chill. His coke-bottle glasses were peeking through the hoodie, and he had a can of black spray paint in his hands. Bruce seemed oblivious to the cold and wore nothing but the *New York Jets* sweatshirt, but with the multiple layers of subcutaneous fat thickening his gut, arms, chest and neck, it didn't seem to make any difference. He pulled his Trump hat further down over his forehead, more for the purpose of hiding his face than for anything related to the weather. The result was that a straw-like patch of silvery hair jutted out from the back of his head.

Dodge, in his Dior suit and tie, together now with a dark blue shin-length overcoat, stood looking at Moshe, shivering from the cold. Moshe was shaking the spray can, with the rattling of the metal spray-can ball the only sound in the backyard.

"Dude, what the hell you gonna do with that?" Dodge asked him. His frozen breath was clouding up in front of him.

Bruce had his arms crossed and had a creepy smile on his face.

"Watch and learn there, Mr. Ivy League," he said. He pointed his chin at Moshe. "Take it away, Moish."

Moshe promptly lowered to one knee and continued shaking the spray can. He was facing the passenger slider door of the minivan. He popped the top of the can, and then he sprayed out the following words in script letters across the side of his own family's minivan:

Baby Killer Jew #agnesbeers

When he was finished, Moshe stood and gathered himself next to Bruce. The two of them stared at Moshe's handiwork for a few seconds and then they simultaneously turned to Dodge, who was standing with his jaw hanging open. Then for nearly a minute nobody spoke. Finally, Dodge raked a hand through his hair and left it on the back of his neck.

"Dude, you have got to be shitting me," he said.

"Terrible, ugly, sad turn of events, Mr. Brewer," Moshe responded. "A horrible unfortunate incident that should never have occurred. It is bad enough that these community volunteers have had their time and commitment to the children of the town rewarded with a fifty million dollar lawsuit, but now they are being viciously attacked ... with anti-Semitic slurs no less ... and their personal property vandalized."

Moshe nodded at the now defaced minivan and shook his head.

"When will it end, Mr. Brewer? Why are these volunteers even in this lawsuit? It is a dastardly attack on innocent people. And to call them killers of babies? It is outrageous."

Moshe took a step closer to the minivan. "These people have suffered enough," he told Dodge. "The case has exacted a great personal toll on these volunteers – emotionally and financially. The prospect of losing everything has caused tremendous stress in their lives, and now this." He nodded to the minivan again. "The lawsuit must end."

Moshe reached into the pocket of his parka and pulled out an iPhone, handing it to Bruce. Bruce began poking buttons and then he held it out in front of him, his arm extended. With his right hand he snapped a series of photographs, all showing the minivan from front wheel to back. The automatic camera flash lit up the nighttime backyard in a series of short, choppy electronic bursts.

Dodge didn't know what to say. He was trying to mask the adrenaline surge rushing through his body right now, but his heavy breathing, evidenced by the small balls of frozen smoke spilling from his open mouth, was giving him away. He now saw very clearly where all this was going. A shitstorm was going to rain down on Dan Beers, that was for sure. The next few days were going to be interesting. Would Beers cave and drop the case? Who the hell knew. But regardless, Dodge made a vow that in the coming weeks he would stay as far away from these two as he possibly could.

With the whole thing now in play, and nothing he could really do to stop it, Dodge simply nodded over to the minivan.

"Dude. But that's your car."

"Yes," said Moshe.

"You got a deductible on your auto policy?"

"It is washable paint, Mr. Brewer. It will come off."

"Ah, got it dude. Smart."

Bruce then handed the iPhone back to Moshe.

"So Moish," he asked, "you think pretty boy here is still dubious?"

ABOUT THIRTY-SIX hours later, and approximately six hundred yards away, Danny was in his living room over on West 17th Street, sitting on the plaid-green sofa located underneath the front bay window. He had his arms wrapped around Gianna, who was crying. She felt beaten, defeated, frustrated, and Danny was trying to comfort her. Henry was with them, pacing back and forth again, holding a pink iPhone. His head was nearly scraping the ceiling. He watched helplessly as Gianna's shoulders convulsed up and down, sobbing against her father's chest.

"She has no idea who's doing this?" Henry demanded.

"None."

"And you neither?"

"Course not," said Danny. "How would I know?"

"She's your kid Dan. How many is this now?"

"I think it's the third," Danny said.

"Fourth," choked Gianna, her face stuffed into Danny's chest.

"And this hellcat person – fuck's that mean anyway? Any idea?"

Danny shook his head no. He made a hand motion for Henry to lower his voice because Agnes was home now, sleeping upstairs in her room.

"Gianna? No clue what this is about?" Henry demanded again.

"No," she sniffled back.

Henry eyeballed the iPhone, shaking his head. There before his eyes was the latest tweet directed at Gianna.

> HCRTP45 @hellcat   30m
> #giannabeers @giannabeers maybe yur looser father shud drop lawsuit before someone slices you up u little whore

Henry let his right hand drop to his thigh. He turned and walked toward the foyer. There was something about this whole Twitter situation, going on for months now, that wasn't making any sense. Danny and Gianna kept telling him it likely was some kid at Gianna's school who set up a fake Twitter account and was making her life miserable, but that just didn't have the right feel. It sounded like bullshit. And for twenty-eight years as a New York City police officer – twenty-one of them as a homicide detective – the one thing that Henry Mahoney had become an expert in was bullshit; he could spot it a mile away. He was so accustomed to people lying to him, from the victims to the family members to the perps to the bystanders, as well as the witnesses, lawyers, prosecutors, judges and every other person associated with the criminal justice system, that Henry simply got to the point where he assumed people were lying unless it was plainly obvious that they weren't. To Henry it was part of human nature. You'd ask them a question and if they had any reason whatsoever, they'd tell you bullshit.

And this Twitter thing with Gianna sounded like bullshit.

Henry wished it were true that it was some kid at school because that sure as shit was an easy cure. You'd deal with that situation the way you dealt with any schoolyard bully, the way that Henry dealt with scumbags on the street for the better part of twenty-five years. Gianna was only twelve but he'd send her into that school with a roll of quarters in her little fist, teach her how to grip it so that it wouldn't crack her metacarpal bones, and get her to walk right up to whatever little Twitter fucker was sending these tweets, and crack the little shit right between the eyes, busting his nose right across his gutless face and making it leak blood for an hour. That would help anyone give a good long think to what a stupid idea it was to piss off Gianna Beers. That would end the whole ordeal.

But this wasn't a kid, Henry was sure of it. This lawsuit his son-in-law had going? And that Yahoo news article? It didn't seem like things a kid would tweet about. And why to Gianna? No, these were going to Dan *through* his daughter. And it was working, because every single kid in Gianna's school and all her friends were seeing these things, Gianna was humiliated by them, and the stress was eating Danny alive.

Henry took a step toward the sofa and held the iPhone out.

"Here," he said to Gianna, "take it."

Gianna took the phone and wiped her nose with her father's sleeve. Henry pointed at Danny.

"I'm gonna look into this situation, make a few calls."

"Who are you calling?" asked Danny.

Henry waved him off.

"Never mind that, just leave it to me."

"Henry, please, if – "

"You want *this* to continue?!" Henry barked, gesturing to Gianna. And then suddenly his attention was diverted through the bay window and out onto Danny's front yard, where the sun was shining down on a frigid Thursday morning. All at once Henry could see two events happening at the same time. Parked at the curb was a white van with its slider door fully open to reveal a collection of black boxes, tangled wires, cords, cameras and small television monitors. The emblem "News Channel 12" was on the side. Stepping around the van from the street side was a tall angular man wrapped in a hooded parka with a TV camera mounted on his right shoulder. He was struggling to keep pace with a short, attractive black woman in a red overcoat and black heels, with a microphone in her hand, marching up the Beers's front lawn.

At the same time, Henry could see a tow truck with its flatbed fully descended and laying halfway upon the Beers's driveway. A fat man with a *New York Rangers* skullcap had a thick chain in his hand and had just exited the truck. Henry saw him hooking it to the undercarriage of Danny's Prius, which was parked on the driveway with its rear end exposed to the street.

"What the fuck is this now?" Henry asked.

As Danny twisted his head around to look, Henry nodded to the street and instructed – "You better get your ass outside."

In a flash Danny was on his feet, staring out the bay window. As soon as he saw the Prius being hauled onto the flatbed, he knew. He hadn't made a payment in months and multiple notices from the leasing company had piled up in one of the kitchen drawers. One of the items on his to-do list had been to place a call to those people and ask if a partial payment could ward off the repo man, but with everything else going on the whole thing had slipped through the cracks. The sight of the flatbed on his driveway now was a punch-in-the-gut reminder of his oversight.

"Aw shit!" he yelled out, and he was out the door. Just as he was making a beeline for the fat man, maybe to reason with him, maybe throw him a twenty to pull the damn thing off the rack, suddenly there was a woman standing in front of him blocking his path. She was stuffing a microphone in his face. Behind him a bright light popped on from a TV camera mounted on some guy's shoulder. Danny held his hands up to shield his eyes.

"What the fuck," he said, as the woman was yelling questions.

"MR. BEERS, DID YOU HAVE ANYTHING TO DO WITH THE ATTACK ON MOSHE WAGSHUL?"

"Excuse me? Attack on who?"

"ARE YOU AWARE YOU'RE BEING INVESTIGATED FOR A HATE CRIME? THAT'S A FELONY, ARE YOU AWARE OF THAT?"

"What the hell are you talking about?" Danny responded, still shielding his eyes from the glaring light of the TV camera. The woman was now positioned directly between Danny and the tow truck driver, and as Danny leaned to his left to get an angle toward the driveway, he could see the Prius being pulled backwards onto the flatbed.

"Hey, just a minute! Please!" he yelled.

And then: "ARE YOU RESPONSIBLE FOR THE ANTI-SEMITIC SLUR ON MR. WAGSHUL'S PROPERTY?"

"No ... what?! ... No!"

The light from the camera was getting brighter and Danny struggled to see the Prius. He tried walking around the woman but with each step he took she countered with a move blocking his path. All the while Danny was shielding his eyes from the blinding light of the camera.

Suddenly Danny could feel his chest tightening. Despite the below freezing temperatures, his face was on fire. He felt dizzy and light-headed, and he began taking huge gulps of breath.

"Get outta my way!" he barked, and then he yelled to the truck driver. "Hey, can you wait ONE MINUTE PLEASE?!"

His chest felt like it was in a vice, with sharp pains radiating down his left arm. The woman stepped in front of him again.

"ARE YOU RESPONSIBLE FOR THIS ATTACK SIR?"

"Back the fuck up!" Danny yelled.

The woman now held a large color photograph and was shoving it into Danny's face. Danny glanced at it and saw what looked like a minivan with some words spray-painted across the passenger door. Then he felt another stabbing sensation in his chest when he read the word "Jew." The man in the parka had the camera about ten inches from Danny's head, and the microphone was almost touching his nose. Danny swatted it away. Every breath he took now felt like he was swallowing shards of glass. He grabbed his throat and felt his knees buckling.

"PLEASE!" he screamed to the truck driver over the scraping sound of the gear crank. The Prius was just about fully loaded.

"THERE ARE PEOPLE SAYING YOU SHOULD DROP YOUR LAWSUIT. HOW DO YOU RESPOND?"

"Get the hell off my property!" he yelled, and then Danny bolted around the woman and sprinted up to the fat man, who had a red box with a lever in his hand. The man was pulling back on the lever and causing the thick chain hooked to the Prius to pull it aboard the flatbed.

"C'mon!" Danny pleaded, "I'll pay for your time!"

"Back up, mister, it's on the bed, nothing I can do."

Danny could hardly catch his breath and the pain in his chest was now overwhelming. He could see white lights sprinkled in front of him and suddenly he dropped to one knee, clutching his chest. His face turned from a pale white to a deep maroon.

"Oh shit," he choked out with his eyes closed. His arms were crossed directly underneath his chin as he gasped for air.

"Goddamn it," he managed, and then Danny collapsed directly at the feet of the man in the Rangers cap. The cameraman flicked off the light as the woman in the red dress made a slashing motion across her neck.

"We got what we need?" she asked.

"Yeah," he nodded back, staring down at Danny.

The woman turned to the fat man.

"He's all yours," she said, and they made a beeline for the van.

"To hell with that," the fat man responded, "I'm outta here."

By this time the Prius was completely loaded onto the flatbed. The fat man jumped into the tow truck's cabin and twisted the starter key, and the engine roared to life. In a second he was off, bounding out of the Beers's driveway and down West 17th Street.

Henry then came sprinting from the house. He grabbed Danny by the shoulder and flipped him over. Danny was unconscious, with a few blades of frozen grass pinned to his face.

"Jesus Christ," Henry said.

He looked into Danny's eyes, which were dead and at half-mast.

"Dan," Henry said firmly, "get up."

He was tapping him lightly on the face. Danny wasn't moving.

"DAN!" he yelled.

There was no response.

CHAPTER 21

"WITH ANY LUCK, SHE'LL EXPIRE"

EVEN THOUGH IT was mid-January, remnants of the holidays were still sprinkled throughout the cavernous C. Barton Foster Conference Room. On the mahogany ledge overlooking Park Avenue, which ran the entire west side of the building, there was a long row of red poinsettia plants, maybe fifty of them, sitting upright and perky in black ceramic pots. Against the southwest wall there stood a fifteen-foot Christmas tree decorated with twinkling lights and fat red Christmas balls the size of grapefruits. Empty boxes encased in red, green and silver holiday wrapping sat at its foot, and to the left and the right of the tree there were gold Menorahs with glowing yellow bulbs arranged on corner tables.

Right now, a few minutes before 10 am on Martin Luther King Jr. Day, Seamus P. O'Reilly, former Summer Associate and now third-year law student, took it all in as he stood at a deep-black granite countertop built into the wall on the direct opposite side of the Christmas tree, which was about a football field away. O'Reilly turned and looked at the tree and the holiday decorations all the way across the room, and then he gazed up at the ceiling, three floors above. Despite his ample frame, he felt small in this place.

At the countertop, O'Reilly spooned some diced fruit from a large glass bowl onto a small breakfast plate. Then he poured himself a coffee from a tube-shaped silver urn before ambling over to the brown conference table, which was about fifteen yards in length and one of three situated end-to-end in the C. Barton Foster Conference Room. A pile of documents sat neatly arranged in front of each hi-backed leather chair, and when O'Reilly sat down, he pulled off the rubber bands holding his stack together. Some paralegals had organized the stacks for the strategy meeting about to take place between the FT&B legal team working on the shrimp cocktail product liability cases and the General Counsel of their billion-dollar client, the Gunther Home Products Corporation.

Meanwhile, the fact that O'Reilly felt uncomfortable in this place, sitting there alone at the conference table with his coffee and fruit plate, was certainly an understatement. He felt very much like a serial killer returning to the scene of one of his gruesome homicides. Looking right and left, O'Reilly recalled the fuzzy images of his booze-filled performance back in August, after which he assumed his career was over and that he'd never get a chance to work as a lawyer. Over there, by the double-door entryway, is where he recalled tackling that poor Mexican man. And all of that after getting caught *in flagrante delicto*, as Black's Law Dictionary would define it, right there in his office.

Good God, what a day.

O'Reilly glanced inconspicuously around the room and wondered if any of these people remembered that night, or him for that matter. It was probably wishful thinking they all forgot about it, and even if that were the case, his presence there would be a brutal reminder.

Isn't he the guy that ....

O'Reilly suddenly felt hot. He didn't expect to be invited to this meeting and now wondered whether he should leave. But Ralph Burgess had called him and told him it would be good for him to attend. O'Reilly had been sweating beside the steam pipe out there in the Secaucus warehouse since September, Burgess explained, and had read so many Gunther documents, logged so much information into the LawDocs database, that his head was in a constant state of data overload. It was time for a break. Burgess figured he had earned himself a field trip. But then this morning Burgess emailed him and told him he was taking MLK Day off as one of his floating holidays and wouldn't make the meeting. He offered O'Reilly good luck and told him to let him know how it went. O'Reilly only got that message as he was getting off the elevator just now. Did anyone here even know he would be attending?

As ten o'clock hit the lawyers started filling the room, dressed in navy blue or banker's grey corporate getups. They greeted each other with cranky nods and curt hellos and then robotically grabbed some coffee, fruit or mini-muffins at the countertop before dutifully seizing a seat at the conference table. As all of this went on, O'Reilly kept his head down, sipping some Starbucks breakfast blend from a navy-blue FT&B ceramic coffee mug. He was trying not to be noticed, but that was always difficult for him with his mop of bright orange hair. Right now, he was pretending to read one of the documents from the stack in front of him. He had carried a legal pad with him as a prop, and every few seconds he would jot some notes down about absolutely nothing whatsoever.

In a few minutes there was a buzz of conversation from a horde of maybe twenty lawyers who had arrived. O'Reilly then felt a nudge, and when he looked up, he saw Manny Perez.

Manny had a plateful of grapes and pineapple chunks and a mug of coffee along with his own stack of documents, which was tucked under his right arm. He was standing at the seat next to O'Reilly. O'Reilly was relieved to see him, and he rose to greet him.

"Manny, how are you?!"

"*Hombre*, you clean up well," Manny said with a smile, nodding at O'Reilly's suit.

"Not bad yourself," O'Reilly responded. It was the first time he had ever seen Manny in a jacket and tie. It was also the first time Manny had ever smiled at him.

"But *amigo*, don't get used to this," he said. "On Wednesday I need you back rockin' the free world at your steam pipe."

O'Reilly laughed.

"Thanks, Manny," he said.

O'Reilly relaxed a little having Manny there. With Burgess AWOL, the lawyers no doubt would wonder who O'Reilly was, and now sitting next to Manny at least he had an answer if anyone asked.

Just then, all heads turned to the double doors to the conference room's entrance as three men entered. They marched in single file and in the front leading them was J. Hartwell Briggs, in his familiar majestic stride, with his hands behind his back and his chin in the air. Right behind Briggs was a man O'Reilly had never met but certainly knew – Mr. Stewart Handler, a former partner at FT&B and current General Counsel of the Gunther Home Products Corporation.

Bringing up the rear was the litigation partner Yang Hsue Ko, the lawyer who was running the day-to-day aspects of all the shrimp cases. The three entered the conference room like generals marching into a War Room, and the moment they did the conversation buzz came to an abrupt halt. If anyone was at the countertop buffet, they quickly took a seat at the conference table.

Briggs settled in at the head of the table and Stewart Handler sat to his left. Ko dumped some documents in front of the chair and darted over to the countertop for a mug of coffee. All eyes in the room then turned to Briggs, who officially opened the meeting.

"Good mornin' everyone. I wanna first thank y'all for bein' here today. Please everybody join me in greetin' Mr. Stewart Handler, the man who runs things over at the Gunther Corporation."

The room then launched into a round of polite applause, as if Handler had just sunk a putt. Handler politely waved them off.

"Stewart, lemme first make some innerductions. And then I'm gone turn it over to Mr. Ko, who gone take yew through our progress so far."

"That would be great, Hartwell, thank you."

"Course, if yew have any questions, please jump right in."

"I will, thanks very much."

Ko was back at the table now and he handed Briggs a binder, which Briggs placed in front of him on the conference table.

"As yew know, Stewart,' he said, flipping a page, "our defense team is divided into three divisions – the west coast, central, east coast teams. Of course, Mr. Ko and his gaggle a lawyers oversee every one of the cases, no matta where they get filed. And Ko reports directly to me."

"Yes," Handler stated dutifully.

"Over here," Briggs went on, gesturing to his right, "we have our team coordinatin' the west coast cases, workin' wit' local counsel. That team is headed up by Ms. Chelsea Parker, seated right over there."

A thin woman with a short crop of blond hair rose halfway out of her seat and smiled politely at Handler. Four or five lawyers seated in her vicinity joined her by nodding in unison.

"Yes, Ms. Parker," Handler said, "we've spoken by phone."

"Then there's our central cases team, run by Mr. Eric Schwartz, who's doin' a bang-up job. Mr. Schwartz? Ah, there he is."

Briggs pointed with an open palm to a jowly man with thick black hair and furry eyebrows, surrounded by another group of four or five lawyers. Schwartz stuck an index finger in the air, and Handler nodded.

"The third group is our east coast team, which is run by Ms. Andrea Corning and her cohorts here in New York. Ms. Corning? Where yew at?"

A heavyset woman wearing a pair of what O'Reilly would call Catwoman eyeglasses rose slightly and smiled. She too sat amongst a small ring of attorneys making up her team.

"Ah, Ms. Corning," Briggs said.

O'Reilly was furiously scribbling notes now, this time for real. All this information was new to him, from the three divisions to the identity of the lawyers running each team – he realized what a cocoon he'd been living in all these months out in Secaucus. He felt settled in and was comfortable now that the meeting was well underway, but then Briggs suddenly shot a look in the general direction of him and Manny.

"And finally, we have our representative from the National Shrimp Cocktail Defense Team, which as yew know, is coordinatin' our national document collection efforts. Right over here is Mr. Manny Perez, who in a few minutes gone update us on how things are comin' together out there in the Secaucus warehouse."

And right on the word "warehouse," Briggs's eyes landed on O'Reilly, and his eyebrows shot up. That he hadn't noticed O'Reilly's presence until that point was obvious, and a smile spread across his face. Any hope that O'Reilly had about blending into the polished mahogany woodwork here instantly vanished, as Briggs pointed directly at him.

"And accompanying Mr. Perez, Stewart, is one of our crackerjack law students we have workin' here at the firm. The young falla is helpin' us wit' our document review while he finishes up his schoolin'," he said, smiling directly at O'Reilly. "Stewart, please welcome Mr. Sea-Mouse O'Rally. Sea-Mouse, young falla, I'm glad yew could make it."

O'Reilly felt his face light on fire. He glanced around the conference table and saw they were all smiling, stifling giggles, as if he were back in third grade. These weren't friendly or welcoming smiles either, or at least that is how O'Reilly felt. To him, they were condescending smirks meant to patronize him. They were laughing at the pronunciation of his name, humiliating him. He was the most junior person in the room and they were treating him like a child. It was bad enough that he had corrected Briggs on several occasions and the guy just couldn't – or wouldn't – make the adjustment, but now he was doing it in front of a room full of people. It seemed to O'Reilly like it was intentional, and he was pissed. After four and half months at the steam pipe, mindlessly shoving square pegs into square holes like some circus monkey, he was getting to the point where enough was enough. He nodded his head and lifted his pen, not making any eye contact with Briggs or anyone else.

O'Reilly now felt that he didn't belong here, that he didn't want to be here. He'd get more respect working at McDonalds for Christ's sake. Manny must have sensed something too, because when everyone's attention turned back to Briggs, he elbowed O'Reilly in the ribs.

"*Hombre*, just forget it," he whispered.

O'Reilly nodded back, looking down at his legal pad.

Briggs went on with his introductions and summaries, but it was all just background noise to O'Reilly. He was drawing spirals onto his pad, not paying attention to anything. But then suddenly he heard Briggs introduce Manny again, and Manny shoved his hi-back rearward and stood to address the room. He had a legal pad in his hands with a few pages flipped over the top, and he spoke in a forceful voice.

"Thank you, Mr. Briggs," he opened.

"As you all know, we started our document collection efforts back in February of 2018 and that continued into the spring. By May we collected and indexed over 2,400 boxes containing almost five million pages. Our team began the review of those documents on June 1. Over the summer, however, as our document review was progressing, and after we re-evaluated our collection protocols, we broadened our searches and that resulted in an additional 950 boxes, or approximately 1.9 million more pages, that arrived in Secaucus and needed to be reviewed."

O'Reilly once again was scribbling notes and taking down all this new information. The scale of the Secaucus operation was no surprise to him, but hearing these numbers brought front and center the fact that he was nothing more than a cog in a very big wheel.

He recalled his lunch with Burgess that day over the summer when Ralph told him he was merely … if O'Reilly remembered correctly … *"dust in the sweat on the balls of a slug."* A completely expendable, replaceable, fungible, meaningless component part of a massive legal machine.

A slug whose name they couldn't even get straight.

At the same time, O'Reilly was impressed with Manny's stage presence and demeanor. He didn't appear nervous at all, and it seemed to O'Reilly as if Manny had been doing these presentations for years. Manny wasn't a lawyer but he certainly looked like one, standing up there and addressing this team of accomplished attorneys. O'Reilly could envision him in a courtroom before a jury. Manny was also watering down his accent and sounded more like a news anchor rather than the guy ripping him for being a few minutes late out there in Secaucus. O'Reilly felt a surge of pride and was glad to be with him today.

"As of yesterday, we've reviewed 2,746 boxes and summarized them into the LawDocs database. That is approximately 5,490,000 pages. Those documents are all categorized, coded, scanned and fully searchable. We have approximately 630 boxes left to review, or about 1.25 million pages. But those materials are from smaller corporate departments that are less likely to yield responsive documents for the lawsuits. So as far as we are concerned, we are prepared to begin making document productions immediately."

Manny placed his legal pad onto the conference table and folded his hands behind his back. Briggs jumped in with a question.

"Manny, when y'all think yew gone be finished?"

"Mr. Briggs, we will be completed with the review by the end of March. You can be assured I will keep the team focused and on track. At that time all documents will be loaded into LawDocs, and then we can begin the process of reviewing them for privilege and confidentiality. But we expect that exercise to go much more quickly, as we will identify those documents using search terms rather than by a manual review of hard copies. And, of course, we can always review the documents for those issues at the time of production in any particular case, once we identify the documents that are responsive to the document requests."

Briggs crossed his arms and smiled, turning his head to Handler. "Well, Stewart, any questions for Mr. Perez?"

"None. Thank you Manny, that was excellent."

"It really was, thank yew Manny," Briggs added, and then he winkled at O'Reilly.

"And thank yew too, young Mr. Sea-Mouse O'Rally."

This time O'Reilly didn't blink. He stared straight at Briggs and didn't care who may be laughing. He had an urge to get up and leave now, because the portion of the meeting regarding the goings-on at the Secaucus warehouse was over, but Manny sat back down and picked up a pen, so O'Reilly did the same, although his enthusiasm for this meeting was gone. He wanted to get back to his steam pipe and think. He was not needed or respected here, and he knew it.

Briggs next spoke about some administrative matters relating to the shrimp cases, and then he turned it over to Yang Hsue Ko. Ko stood and walked over to a lectern situated on the side of the conference table near the Park Avenue windows. One of the lawyers on the opposite side rose and went to the light panel, and suddenly the room was dimmed.

Ko had a laptop in front of him and with a small key he clicked a button. O'Reilly watched as a white screen lowered from a mahogany-wrapped eave that hung over the buffet countertop.

Ko tapped his index finger and a PowerPoint image appeared:

FOSTER TUTTLE & BRIGGS LLP

PRESENTATION TO GUNTHER HOME PRODUCTS CORPORATION

PHILLIPS FROZEN SHRIMP – PRODUCT LIABILITY CASES

JANUARY 16, 2019

Ko then turned and faced Handler. He explained that he would be taking Handler through a summary of the lawsuits and presenting a strategy for moving forward. He told Handler that if he had any questions at any time, to please let him know. Handler agreed, and Ko plowed forward.

"Stewart," he began, "we now have 67 nationwide shrimp cases officially filed and served on Gunther. Although the first few cases were filed on the respective coasts, the majority are now with the central district team, which has 36 of them. All 67 have been filed within the last year. Before that, over the previous ten years, Gunther had a total of seven product liability lawsuits filed against it relating to its frozen shrimp brand. And Gunther won every one of those suits; they were either voluntarily dismissed or we won them at the summary judgment stage or at trial."

As Ko spoke, he continued to pop his index finger down onto his laptop. Each time, a different slide would appear on the massive screen descending from the mahogany eave. Together with the information about the cases, which was bolded and in dramatic font, there were small images blended into the background of each slide, either the scales of justice or a U.S. map with the three districts represented in different colors, so that the entire presentation was easy to follow. Ko was impressive, at least to O'Reilly. He had the look and feel of a TV news anchor or politician and spoke with great command.

"In terms of a litigation strategy," Ko continued, "we would like to speak today about three particular cases that are in a more advanced stage. We feel that all three present a unique opportunity for Gunther to secure a trial victory, which we could then use as a deterrent to all the other cases that are out there, and to any new attorneys thinking of suing us."

As the slides moved up and down the screen, O'Reilly was back to his furious notetaking again. His head was spinning with all the data being presented. As Ko spoke, O'Reilly understood why Burgess had invited him here and at last he was grateful. Burgess knew this meeting would give O'Reilly some context to the work he was doing, and although he still wanted to take a Billy club to Briggs over the whole Sea-Mouse thing, at least he found this part of the meeting interesting.

Up on the screen, a slide appeared that read, "*Recommendations.*"

"Now, with regard to the three cases," Ko said, "we are going to highlight one of these for discussion today, and we will get to that case in a moment. But more generally, the plan here is to delay the proceedings in all the other cases nationwide, to the best of our ability, and at the same time aggressively press forward with these three cases, which are further along. If we can secure a victory in one of those cases, we can then discuss a more global strategy of resolving all the lawsuits. But with an overwhelming victory in our pockets, we will negotiate in those cases from a position of strength. But let's first discuss these three cases."

Briggs, who had been sitting with his arms crossed and nodding along with Ko, suddenly addressed Handler.

"Any questions so far, Stewart?"

"No, Hartwell, none. This is all very clear."

"Very well then. Ko, please continue."

"The first is a wrongful death action pending in Texas," Ko went on, tapping the laptop and revealing another slide. "Forty-seven-year-old Dennis Jenkins ate our brand at a friend's house back in March while watching an NCAA Tournament basketball game. He reported to the partygoers that he wasn't feeling well, and he left. Found deceased in his car on the side of the road several hours later. He apparently pulled over halfway home and expired. Mr. Jenkins had two high-school age children and was a welder. Income $63,500 for 2018."

As the images continued to roll up and down on the big screen, O'Reilly listened and took notes just like everyone else. Ko went on to describe the facts of the Jenkins case, including what the family knew about his allergies. He also discussed the potential damages that could be awarded if Gunther lost the case. He went through their calculation of his past lost wages, future lost wages, hospital expenses and funeral expenses, as well as what a Texas jury could award for any pain and suffering he may have endured.

"Fortunately," Ko summarized, "Mr. Jenkins, according to the medical records, appears to have expired quickly, so any pain and suffering will likely have been brief. Mr. Jenkins's estate is being represented by the Norman Fuller firm in Dallas. As you know, they are a preeminent personal injury firm and are very successful."

"Indeed," Handler answered, and Briggs nodded.

O'Reilly wrote the words *"p&s brief; Norman Full attys"* onto his legal pad. He suddenly felt numb. There was a strange matter-of-fact quality to this presentation that just didn't feel right. He knew they weren't here to mourn the loss of this Jenkins sap. They had a case to defend and were only doing their jobs. But they were speaking about the guy like he was nothing more than a financial figure on some ledger sheet. They said the man *expired*, like he had a "sell by" date tattooed on his ass. Could you imagine, O'Reilly thought to himself. You're a 47 year old father, raising kids and paying your taxes, not bothering anyone, and you go to watch a hoops game with your buddies, you pop a couple of shrimp into your mouth, maybe down a few Heineken Lights or something, and the next minute you wind up dead in a frickin' Honda hatchback on the side of the road somewhere in East Bumfuck, Texas. And then they sum up your life in a matter of minutes on a couple of slides up here in the C. Barton Foster Conference Room, for Christ's sake, noting that it was "fortunate" that you kicked so quickly.

O'Reilly snapped to attention and focused back on the screen.

"The next case," said Ko, "is the Holly Erickson case pending in Des Moines, Iowa. 64-year-old female, unmarried and no children, teaches 19th Century British literature at a local community college. Hospitalized for three weeks and made a full recovery. Her damages therefore are not as potentially exorbitant as we have seen in other cases. Also, there is a real issue in that case as to whether she actually ingested our brand of frozen shrimp. Evidence exists that she also purchased a competitor's brand at or around the time of her incident, so we may have a defense based on the product itself. Ms. Erickson is represented by attorney Jack Kaufman, another accomplished PI attorney."

Ko clicked his way through some additional slides about the Erickson case, including its procedural posture, the results of a few discovery motions, and how much money the woman racked up in hospital expenses while laying on her back for three weeks with tubes and IV needles sticking in her every which way from Sunday. Ko also revealed that "Plaintiff" – that is how he referred to her – ate her shrimp on a Sunday night, together with a glass of chardonnay, while sitting in her pajamas watching *Homeland*. She was found unconscious by a fed-up apartment neighbor who was banging on the door to demand that she turn the damn TV volume down. The man wouldn't accept her silence as an answer and called the super. The two of them found Gunther's next "plaintiff" lying between her couch and coffee table in a puddle of vomit, although Ko called it "a considerable volume of expectoration."

"The final case," Ko then instructed, "is the Agnes Beers case, which is pending right here in New York City. Filed in the Bronx, motions to dismiss and to change venue denied. Plaintiff is a ten-year-old girl from Long Island who ingested the shrimp at a town softball game. She experienced anaphylactic shock and was in a coma for a period, but we understand she's been discharged and is now at home. We do not yet know her current condition, but we certainly will be conducting an independent medical examination very soon."

Ko clicked to a slide that read "AGNES BEERS, ET AL V. GUNTHER HOME PRODUCTS CORPORATION, ET AL – TRIAL STRATEGY". He pointed a pen at the screen and turned to Handler.

"It is this case, Stewart, the Beers case, which we suggest we prioritize among the three. We recommend we take a firm no settlement position on this one, unless of course they will settle for nominal litigation costs. Short of that, we would like to take this one through summary judgment, and if necessary, trial. For the reasons we will make clear in a moment, we feel that this particular case is one that we can win, and can do so decisively."

O'Reilly's ears perked up, as the meeting was now becoming interesting. He loved the strategic part of these lawsuits. Handler, Ko and Briggs were lobbing questions and answers back and forth and O'Reilly was jotting everything down, learning more facts about the case. He recalled that back when he first appeared at the warehouse, they gave him the Beers complaint to read as background material, but the meeting now was going into much greater detail.

Ko clicked his laptop again and another slide appeared. He explained that what was now up on the screen were the reasons why they believed they would be victorious in the Beers case.

"First," he explained, "there is the Beers's attorney, a woman by the name of Nicole Anzalone. She is a solo practitioner based in Ketchogue, Long Island, the same town where the Beers family lives. The best we can surmise is that perhaps she is a family friend. As you are aware, Stewart, these shrimp cases have piqued the interest of many high-profile plaintiffs' attorneys and yet the Beers family has selected a complete unknown among the plaintiff's bar. She has no associates or attorneys in her office and no employees other than a legal assistant who answers the phones. And from what we can tell, her general practice consists of only a small percentage of plaintiff's personal injury cases."

"Interesting," Handler answered, "and very odd."

"Certainly is," Briggs agreed.

Ko clicked another slide and what O'Reilly saw appear on the screen caused him to draw in a breath. The slide's header read, "NICOLE ANZALONE, ESQ. – BACKGROUND," and it contained some very personal information about the Beers's attorney. O'Reilly sat up a bit and then leaned over the table to see past Manny's left shoulder, because Manny himself had also leaned forward for a better view.

"As you can see," Ko explained, pointing to the slide, "Ms. Anzalone is experiencing significant personal and professional difficulties, financial and otherwise. First, back in 2009, Anzalone was temporarily suspended from the practice of law for the offense of stealing client funds."

Ko paused and looked around the room, letting that revelation hang there and penetrate the ears of all in attendance. If he was hoping for a reaction from Handler, he soon got it, because Handler's eyes widened, and he too locked eyes with everyone around the conference table.

"What the hell!" he exclaimed. "That is just terrible!"

Handler's bulging eyeballs scanned the room, looking for sympathetic faces to share in his outrage. He landed on Briggs.

"Shockin', Stewart," Briggs responded, shaking his head.

"Where do they find these people?!" Handler shouted again. Every head in the room was nodding along with him.

Ko pointed to the screen again.

"It gets better," he reported. "As you can see, Ms. Anzalone appeared at a disciplinary hearing with respect to that charge and admitted to a drug dependency. The New York Commission suspended her for two years. She did not seek reinstatement until 2014. Our information reveals that she worked as a waitress during the period of her suspension."

"My God!" Handler snorted.

Everyone in the room shifted in their seats and shook their heads in disbelief. There was also a low rumble of conversation that followed Ko's announcement. But O'Reilly had something else on his mind.

How did Briggs's team find this information out?

Maybe it was a matter of public record, but O'Reilly wasn't sure. And perhaps investigating the background of plaintiff's attorneys and using the information to evaluate the strength of your case was par for the course when you defended personal injury lawsuits. Maybe O'Reilly was being naïve. But the fact of it felt sleazy to him. Like it was below the dignity of the lawyers in this place.

Ko was still pointing up at the screen.

"Ms. Anzalone also has some very serious personal financial issues," he instructed, "and because she is the sole owner and principal of her law firm, those financial difficulties run to her professional life as well."

O'Reilly stared up at a list that summarized the attorney Anzalone's dismal financial status. The slide didn't paint a pretty picture – there were credit card debts, mortgage payments, car payments, small business loans, and a host of unpaid medical bills for the care and treatment of her seven-year old son who, according to Ko, suffered from cerebral palsy. Cerebral palsy for God's sake. Ko reported it without emotion, like he was giving a weather report. O'Reilly couldn't believe what he was seeing. It was obvious they had run a complete background check on this lawyer and had managed to dig up some very private information. O'Reilly looked over at Manny, who had his head down, scribbling away.

"Her son's condition," Ko trudged on, "is severe and takes a significant amount of time away from her legal practice. Quite frankly, it is highly questionable how she possibly has the time to handle a case of this magnitude. But regardless, unlike in many of the other cases, all of this gives us a meaningful advantage in terms of time, manpower and resources. We have a tremendous opportunity here that we must exploit to our benefit."

When Ko finished O'Reilly looked over at Handler and Briggs. The two of them shared a determined, business-like expression. Ko's slides impressed them both and you could see Handler's confidence growing in his A-team group of lawyers. Ko was doing a fabulous job of explaining how they were going to utterly manhandle this dancing-on-the-edge-of-bankruptcy, once-suspended, solo-practitioner mother of a cerebral palsy kid, and his client loved every minute of it.

O'Reilly felt like he needed a shower.

"Second, apart from the Beers's lawyer, there is Mr. Daniel Beers himself, the girl's father. He is also a named plaintiff. And like his attorney, Mr. Beers is also in extremely dire financial straits."

Ko clicked another slide and similar information appeared – a repossessed car, missed mortgage payments, a failing construction business, unpaid medical bills, the works. Ko informed the group that Mr. Beers made approximately $36,000 last year. He reported that both Beers and his lawyer were likely desperate for any kind of a recovery and would settle even for nuisance value – pennies basically – if FT&B were to offer it. He advised that based on these facts they should remain relentless and keep the pressure on them by demanding action in the lawsuit and filing motions to which this Anzalone had to spend money and time responding, whatever it took. And he informed Handler that regardless of anything else, Beers and his attorney were unconnected to any larger consortium of plaintiffs' attorneys, were out there on their own, and were simply too small a legal team and lacking in any meaningful resources to put up any kind of a fight.

Ko informed the assembled group that Beers and his attorney could be "annihilated," and that this was the case to push forward on and win. Handler kept nodding as Ko plowed on.

"Our third point, Stewart, relates to the facts of this particular case. Now, we know we have an injured ten-year-old child here, and we are in the Bronx, a notoriously bad venue for defendants. But the undeniable fact is that Mr. Beers was with his daughter that day at the softball field. He was in attendance, watching the game. He knew prior to her ingesting the shrimp that she was about to eat a shellfish product. And yet he did nothing about it. In this regard, we have run mock cases and test samples through VerdictNow, our jury consultants, and that fact scenario tests extremely well. Jurors almost universally do not appear willing to award any money to an injured child where the parent falls down on the job and could have prevented the injury. And that for sure is what occurred here."

O'Reilly thought Ko was right about that fact. That was something that always gave him pause about the Beers case. The father apparently was right there with his daughter and let her eat the shrimp. O'Reilly figured that meant he didn't know the kid had a shellfish allergy. And if that were the case, what good would a warning have done? This probably was a good case to take to trial if you were Gunther. O'Reilly couldn't imagine the Beers family and their solo attorney winning this one.

O'Reilly looked around the room at the twenty-odd lawyers attending this strategy meeting. He again took in the massive scale of the C. Barton Foster Conference Room, with its ornate tin ceiling three floors above. He looked at the three mahogany conference tables stretched end-to-end, surrounded by countless leather chairs, each one of which probably cost a couple grand. O'Reilly started counting all the lawyers and then he did some quick multiplication. With Briggs and Ko billing out at over a thousand dollars an hour and the more senior attorneys here going out at $950, this here two-hour meeting, including the preparation time for the lawyers and their elaborate slides and the background investigations, was going to cost Gunther approximately $70,000, best O'Reilly could figure.

Roughly twice the amount that Beers, the poor schlub, made last year. The guy had no idea what a major ass-whipping he was in for. But this meeting certainly was making that clear.

Handler interrupted Ko.

"What are we talking about in terms of the non-economic damages and future medical expenses on this one? It seems that if there were ever a verdict here – and I take your point that such a circumstance is extremely unlikely – the damages could be significant. Am I wrong?"

Briggs jumped in.

"Yew are not wrong, Stewart. That's certainly a possibility, although extremely unlikely as yew say. But assumin' we did lose at trial, Ko, what numbers are we lookin' at?"

Ko took Handler through what he believed could be the dollar value of an adverse jury verdict in the Beers case. He clicked through slides that gave various scenarios of liability percentages spread among the various defendants and calculations of the plaintiff's past hospital expenses and medical bills. Then Ko discussed FT&B's calculations of what the future medical expenses could possibly be for the care of Agnes Beers during the remainder of her lifetime. Ko was methodical and precise as he presented the medical issues, the costs, the interest rates associated with a verdict, consumption rates, and all the other methodologies that went into calculating how an award of future damages is made under New York law. It was this calculation, he explained, that created a great unknown for Gunther. There was no way to know how and whether the ten-year-old child's medical condition would improve over time. And as he mentioned earlier, they had not yet conducted their own medical examination.

And then Ko gave an answer to a Handler question that nearly knocked O'Reilly out of his seat. O'Reilly watched as Handler leaned forward on the conference table.

"So with the severity of her injuries, the future medical expenses for the Beers girl could be a very large figure, is that correct?" asked Handler.

"Yes," Ko responded flatly, "but you must remember that the young plaintiff was in a coma for a very long period of time, and right now we do not know her present condition."

Ko then shifted his stance behind the lectern.

"With any luck" he said, "she'll expire."

There it was, that word again.

Expire.

This time about a kid.

As it hung in the air an awkward silence filled the room. Most of the lawyers' heads were focused down onto their legal pads as they pretended to jot down notes. Even Briggs shifted in his chair a bit. Handler just stared straight at Ko, looking for him to finish answering his question.

O'Reilly, meanwhile, was looking around the room intently, trying to gauge everyone's reaction. After his initial shock, he was more sad than angry at the comment. Sad that he was here, sad that he was part of this crew. He shook his head and didn't really care who saw it. Manny leaned in close to him.

"*No bueno,*" he whispered, nudging O'Reilly in the ribs.

Finally, Briggs broke the prickly silence in the room.

"What Ko means," he said cautiously, "is that if the child tragically were not to survive her terrible ordeal, such an event would cut off any future medical expenses, for which Gunther would no longer be responsible. It's a simple fact 'bout the damages calculations, Stewart, we certainly ain't rootin' for the young child's demise now. Yew unnerstand?"

"Yes, of course."

"That correct, Mr. Ko?"

Briggs was smiling now.

"Yes, correct, Mr. Briggs."

"Excellent, then," Briggs concluded, "there yew have it."

And then Briggs leaned back in his chair as his grin spread across his face. The smile grew into a chuckle, which then grew into a low laughter. In the next moment the room exhaled, and everyone joined in, including Handler. Then the group of twenty-odd attorneys had a good roar. Even Ko managed a smile as he waited to click the next slide.

O'Reilly wasn't sure if this was just a matter of Briggs having broken the tension in the room, but O'Reilly couldn't laugh about it. Perhaps this was gallows humor, and nothing more, but there was an injured kid here who had been in a coma and her father and lawyer clearly were not able to help her. O'Reilly didn't think they had a case and fully believed that Gunther had a right to defend itself, but that defense ought to be based on the facts and the law and nothing else.

As the laughter subsided, O'Reilly shot a look over at Manny, and their eyes met. O'Reilly knew right away that Manny felt the same way as he did. He leaned close to O'Reilly again and whispered, "*Amigo* ... assholes."

Ko next explained that FT&B was about to make its main document production and would be dumping several hundred thousand documents into an online password-protected confidential dropbox that Ms. Anzalone could log into from the comforts of her Ketchogue office. It was a substantial production, one that would stand up to any attack. The not-so-subtle message that would accompany the enormity of it was clear – there was no way Anzalone could review all this material prior to when depositions would start or when dispositive motions would be due. Or prior to the end of time, for that matter. It would require a massive amount of time, money, resources and manpower, and she was lacking in all four.

But she asked to dance with the big boys and O'Reilly figured she deserved what she got. It was not their job to make things easy on her. Instead, FT&B was going to keep the pressure on her and her client. Big-time, balls-to-the-wall, unrelenting pressure. In the very case that the Gunther Home Products Corporation selected among dozens for all-out war. This Anzalone lady was really in a world of shit.

O'Reilly flipped over the pages to his legal pad and stuffed it into his briefcase. Ko kept talking and clicking slides but O'Reilly wasn't listening.

CHAPTER 22

THE INTERIM TOXICITY REPORT

BACK IN SECAUCUS, O'Reilly's seat next to the steam pipe had become the envy of every document reviewer on the National Shrimp Cocktail Defense Team. February's snow and freezing winds had arrived with a vengeance, and it was so bone-chillingly cold inside the warehouse that you could see your breath frosting up. The document reviewers were wrapped in thick winter parkas and skullcaps and were blowing warm air into their hands as they continued to plow through the never-ending tidal wave of Gunther boxes. O'Reilly, on the other hand, was sitting comfortably in a golf shirt and for the first time ever was enjoying the heat radiating from the steam pipe. His second floor, jammed-in-the-corner cubicle was warm and toasty, and now considered prime Secaucus real estate.

Despite that single pleasure, O'Reilly was feeling anxious about his future at FT&B. As the long President's Day Weekend approached, he had been robotically logging documents into LawDocs since September – six long months for four days a week at eleven hours a clip, and on top of that doing the hellacious commute back and forth from Park Slope. He had taken only occasional days off for exams or whenever Manny would grant him a day's parole, like last month when he attended that strategy meeting in Manhattan. And yet despite this dedication, not a soul from the main office ever checked in on him. There were no phone calls or emails from anyone in Personnel or from the Summer Associate Program asking him how it was going, did he need anything, thanks for the effort, or whatever. If it wasn't for the Firm's direct-deposit payments into his TD Bank savings account every two weeks, like clockwork, he would seriously question whether they knew he was alive.

Of course, Burgess had warned him that everything would change once the summer was over and that he'd transition from a pampered Summer Associate to *Dust in the Sweat on the Balls of a Slug*, but O'Reilly didn't think it would be this drastic. He also remembered what Briggs had promised when he sent him out here – that it was a "prestigious position." That turned out to be a cruel joke. The whole thing was so unnerving. Back in the summer, at least he felt like a contributing member of the FT&B legal team, even though his only task had been to protect the interests of a Tibetan monk. But this warehouse work?

Any moron with a sixth-grade education could do it.

Trying to be hopeful, O'Reilly thought that maybe this was the way it was for all the former Summers working part-time now, but if he was being honest, he doubted it. From what he had heard, those students were all in cozy Park Avenue offices doing legal research assignments and dining in the firm's subsidized cafeteria. O'Reilly, on the other hand, was banished to Secaucus breathing Jersey factory fumes and eating dirty water dogs and yellowed sauerkraut from a cart run by a blind man named Raul. At the firm you signed for your free lunch and ate gourmet entrees with shiny silverware and embroidered napkins. O'Reilly, on the other hand, constantly had to remember to bring the only currency the sightless Raul would trust as payment for the hot dogs – singles.

Meanwhile, up at the steam pipe, it was back to LawDocs. On this Monday, O'Reilly had a lukewarm coffee and a banana nut muffin in front of him as he polished off a box from the Saturday before. How many did this make now? He had lost count, and what did it matter anyway. He saved his database entries and neatly placed the documents back into the box. He headed downstairs, arriving at Manny's office with the box in his hands.

"Got another dead soldier here," he droned. "Where do you want it?"

"*Hombre*, nice job," said Manny without looking up. He was reading the *New York Post*. "Just leave it there. I'll re-shelve it."

"Righty then," O'Reilly said, dropping the box.

Manny nodded to the area behind O'Reilly.

"Next one's in the hallway, I got 'em stacked for you."

"Got it. See you later."

In the hallway O'Reilly saw a line of about a dozen boxes that Manny had pulled from the shelves and set against a wall for whatever document reviewer happened to wander down the stairs next. O'Reilly grabbed a random box in the middle of the line and slogged back to the steam pipe. Like he had done about a hundred previous times, O'Reilly flipped open the box top, grabbed the first few hundred pages out and formed a stack to his right. The documents in this box were all in folders filled with about 100 or so pages, and O'Reilly opened the first one and began reading.

Right away, O'Reilly could tell he had pulled a box from the Gunther Legal Department. The first document was labeled with the alpha-numeric code GUNTH.001.015.0006.011368131, and O'Reilly pulled his chart. Sure enough, the number 001 stood for the company's global headquarters in Port Jervis, New York, and 015 was the code for Legal. O'Reilly braced himself when he saw that the employee number – 0006 – was the code for Mr. Stewart J. Handler, the company's General Counsel.

The first document in the pile was part of a folder that contained documents relating to the company's application to trademark the name "Phillip's Frozen Shrimp," and O'Reilly dutifully began logging each document into LawDocs. The basic information was the easy part; the challenge on all of these files would be whether they would be subject to the attorney-client or work product privileges and therefore not subject to discovery in the various lawsuits, given that they were from the Legal Department. If so, O'Reilly would need to mark the documents as potentially privileged, and later, when the document review exercise was over, a team of lawyers would go back and make final privilege calls. The last thing he wanted to do was let a privileged document from Handler's files slip out and wind up in the hands of a plaintiff's attorney, which could be a potentially career-ending screw-up. So O'Reilly needed to be careful.

In about two hours he was finished with the first folder and he placed it back into the box. Then he grabbed the second one. This folder was a little thicker and contained mostly pleadings from dozens of slip and fall lawsuits based on accidents that happened in various Gunther distribution centers. When he was finished with that folder, it was about 12:20, and so O'Reilly grabbed his coat and headed out to Raul's hot dog cart.

In a few minutes he was back in his cubicle with three lukewarm rubbery dogs sitting in stale bread and smothered with yellow mustard squeezed from a small plastic packet. O'Reilly devoured the first one in two bites and washed it down with a raspberry Snapple Iced Tea. Then he flipped open the next folder and flicked the edges with his thumb. It contained mostly FDA statutes and regulations streaked with different colored highlighters. They also contained handwritten notes that O'Reilly assumed were jotted there by Handler.

But the first document in the folder was different. It was a single-page memorandum with an attachment written by a man whose name O'Reilly had never seen before, which was unusual given his title – The Director of Scientific Research at Gunther, Dr. Frederick T. Barker.

O'Reilly's first reaction was that it was now February and he was only seeing this man's name for the first time. Strange. In any event, O'Reilly cast his eyes down on the first page of the document and read:

MEMORANDUM

PRIVILEGED & CONFIDENTIAL
ATTORNEY-CLIENT COMMUNICATION

To: Stewart J. Handler, General Counsel

From: Dr. Frederick T. Barker, Director of Scientific Research

Date: November 22, 2017

Re: Phillips Frozen Shrimp Brand – Interim Toxicity Report

        Stewart:

        As we discussed, and as you requested, attached is the Interim Toxicity Report that our team prepared. The findings speak for themselves. Please let me know when you would like to discuss next steps. As indicated, we are prepared to confirm results in January. Happy Thanksgiving.

        Fred

The covering memo from Barker was stapled to another document, a formal report from the Gunter scientific research department. With the third of Raul's dogs now in his hands,

O'Reilly read the attachment. By the time he got to the bottom of it he could feel his heartbeat quickening.

The attachment was labeled "**INTERIM TOXICITY REPORT –
NOVEMBER 22, 2017 – PRIVILEGED & CONFIDENTIAL**" and appeared to contain the results of some scientific testing that the Gunther Research Department had performed on certain batches of the Philips shrimp brand. It was from the "DEPARTMENT OF SCIENTIFIC RESEARCH AND QUALITY ASSURANCE," and up at the top, in the right-hand corner, was that name again – Dr. Frederick T. Barker, Ph.D. O'Reilly first scanned the document, but once the substance of it began to sink in, he started again from the top.

There first was an "Abstract" section that explained that *"GHPC SRQA conducted toxicity testing with respect to the concentration of sulfite preservatives as expressed in parts per million (ppm) on sixteen batches of Phillips frozen shrimp,"* and that such testing took place during three days in November of that year. The scientists had used something called the modified Monier-Williams distillation-titration procedure, whatever the hell that was, to determine the presence of five different chemicals in the shrimp – sulfur dioxide (SO_2), sodium bisulfite ($NaHSO_3$), potassium metabisulfite ($KHSO_3$), sodium metabisulfite ($Na_2S_2O_5$), or sodium sulfite (Na_2SO_3). The sixteen batches tested, according to the report, were samples from other batches that had been *"sold for consumer purchasing."*

The section about a third of the way down was startling, and O'Reilly read it with his mouth filled with hot dog chunks:

Summary/ Conclusion - Significantly high levels of sodium sulfate (Na_2SO_3) were determined in all sixteen (16) batches of tested product. Some levels exceeded 1600 ppm. All sixteen batches had levels that exceeded 1150 ppm. Under applicable FDA regulations, sulfite levels may not exceed 100 ppm and labeling requirements apply after product sulfite levels exceed 10 ppm. Historically, Philips brand frozen shrimp are treated with trace amounts of (Na_2SO_3) as a preservative and therefore product is exempt from labeling requirements of 21 C.F.R. 101.100(a)(4). Defective batches noted herein most likely resulted from breach of treatment procedures and failure of QA testing. Follow-up testing to confirm results to be performed during January.

And if that weren't enough, O'Reilly then read the final paragraph of the document, which ended at the bottom of the page:

Recommendation - Class I Product Recall recommended upon affirmance of results. Product batches at noted elevated levels present a reasonable probability that exposure may cause serious adverse health consequences or deaths. Product with levels at > 200 ppm present significant health risks for sulfite-sensitive asthmatics. Class I Recall should implement nationally at level

And that was it. O'Reilly flipped over the document to see if it continued on the back. Then he picked up the folder and spread open its contents. Where was the rest of the document? The report ended in the middle of a sentence – *Class I Product Recall should implement nationally at level* ... – but O'Reilly couldn't find the other pages anywhere in the folder.

He pressed the document against his desk and read it again. It hardly mattered where the other pages were, because the implications of this thing were enormous. The report appeared to confirm that Gunther had tested sixteen batches of its Philips frozen shrimp and concluded they had been treated with unsafe levels of preservatives called "sulfites." O'Reilly had by now read plenty of information about shrimp products and knew that nearly all sellers of frozen shrimp, including Gunther, treated their products with sulfites in order to preserve their coloring and texture. The FDA considered them safe assuming the amounts used were small, or "trace." Treating shrimp with sulfites was no big deal.

But according to this document, the Phillips brand had been exempted from FDA labeling requirements, which meant that Gunther didn't need to provide a product warning label because the sulfite concentration in Phillips shrimp was less than 10 "parts per million." Anything above that number and your warning obligations kicked in. Concentrations of this stuff in excess of 200 ppm presented real health risks. It didn't take a genius to figure this one out – Gunther's own testing showed that the sulfite concentrations in every batch of shrimp they tested were through the roof – over 1150 ppm and in certain instances in excess of 1600 ppm. Worse, the document reported that the cause of this disaster was a "*breach of treatment procedures and failure of QA testing*." O'Reilly knew enough to understand that a single "batch" of product would correlate to many thousands of bags of shrimp. The Report contained results of sixteen batches. This meant that the amount of hazardous product that had found its way into grocery store freezers across the country had been ... *enormous*. O'Reilly zeroed in on that one line in the Recommendations section – "*Product with sulfite concentrations at noted levels presents a reasonable probability that consumer exposure may cause serious adverse health consequences or deaths.*"

Holy shit.

It also said "sulfite-sensitive asthmatics" were particularly vulnerable. Was this what led to all these lawsuits?

Could that be true?

O'Reilly thought back to the meeting last month in New York. That case they were going to push to trial – the Agnes Beers case, the one up in The Bronx. Was it possible the kid ate shrimp loaded up with sulfites? Her lawyer filed a case accusing Gunther of failing to warn about shellfish allergies. How that case had survived a motion to dismiss O'Reilly would never know. But her complaint never mentioned sulfites, and for that matter neither did any of the other lawsuits, as far as O'Reilly knew.

O'Reilly took in the weight of all this information. Dr. Barker's recommendation was for the company to conduct a "Class I Product Recall," and O'Reilly remembered from his second year class in Administrative Law what that meant – Class I recalls were for products that could cause severe health consequences or kill people. They were a very big deal; they were expensive and caused a public relations nightmare. They impacted stock prices and companies hated them.

O'Reilly knew that Gunther never issued a recall – but why not? What happened? There were so many questions. Did Barker ever issue a Final Report? The Interim Report discussed further testing in January. Did it ever happen? Whatever the answers were, this document was dynamite. The Beers's lawyer – the one who Ko joyfully reported had been disbarred and was on the verge of bankruptcy – well, she was going to shit herself when this hit her desk. FT&B was preparing to make its document production in the Beers litigation in about a week and this would be an explosion.

O'Reilly quickly entered all the relevant information into the database. He gave the document the highest possible sensitivity rating – a 6 – which was the first time he had ever given anything higher than a 3. The advanced rating required that he provide a further explanation and O'Reilly summarized the document with as much detail as possible in the LawDocs field designated for that purpose. He then filled in all the fields that required him to assign key words to the document so that it was sure to come up in any subsequent searches for responsive documents. Finally, O'Reilly had to indicate whether the document was privileged.

He looked back at the covering memorandum that Dr. Barker wrote and saw that it was stamped with the words "Privileged & Confidential." The Interim Report contained the same label. Suddenly something occurred to him – why was this document in the company's legal files instead of in its scientific research files? Why was Dr. Barker sending this report to the General Counsel?

O'Reilly was sure there was an explanation for this but in the meantime, he considered his task a simple one. The covering memorandum was marked "Attorney-Client Communication" because Barker was writing to the company's lawyer, Handler, so O'Reilly would mark that document as privileged. But the separate Interim Toxicity Report contained scientific research findings and any lawyer worth his salt knows that such a document does not contain legal advice and is therefore not privileged. He marked it accordingly – non-privileged – and clicked save.

O'Reilly wiped mustard from his mouth, guzzled down the remainder of his raspberry Snapple, and bounded down the stairs to find Burgess. This was way too big for him to simply log in the document and move to the next one; he had to run this quickly up the food chain.

Down in his first-floor office, Burgess was leaning back in his chair with his wingtips perched on his desktop. O'Reilly entered breathing heavily, waving the two-page memorandum at him.

"Ralph, you have to see this!"

Burgess was reading a document of his own and never took his eyes off it. Instead, he silently pointed to a chair on the side of his desk. When he was finished, he turned to O'Reilly.

"Okay, whaddya got Sea-Mouse?"

"Ralph, I found this in the files of Stewart Handler, the GC!"

"Yeah, I know who he is."

"It's a report written by the Director of Scientific Research reporting that the company mistakenly treated a number of batches of shrimp with sulfites, at dangerous levels. Way above what the FDA allows!"

"Treated them with what?" asked Burgess.

O'Reilly pointed to the middle of the page.

"Sulfites, look, the batches were *actually sold*, and got into stores. And right after that we've got all these lawsuits! This is crazy! The fucking guy – Barker – recommended they do a product recall – "

"Sea-Mouse, relax," Burgess interjected, motioning his hands down. "Take a deep breath and gimme the damn document."

O'Reilly placed it onto Burgess's desktop.

"Look, it's labeled as an 'Interim Toxicity Report'."

"I can read," Burgess interrupted. He grabbed the document and leaned back in his chair, running his index finger down the page. When he was done, he flipped the document over to the other side.

"Where's the rest of it?" he asked.

"That's it," O'Reilly answered.

"Whaddya mean that's it, this is an incomplete document."

"That's all that's there. In the file I mean."

"Well, it ends in the middle of a sentence."

"Yeah, I saw that, but what did you think of the first page?!"

"O'Reilly, look," Burgess cautioned, "let's not get excited, we need the rest of the report. Did you see if it's in the box you pulled?"

"I looked quickly; I didn't see it. But Ralph, for shit's sake, the sulfite levels were 1600 parts per million and every batch was over 1150. That's tens of thousands of bags out there in the market. It can cause health issues or deaths at anything over 100 ppm, which the FDA doesn't even allow. Companies have to provide warnings at levels over 10, and Gunther never provided sulfite warnings on this shit – I mean ever."

"Right, I get it, but – "

"Barker says it was caused by a treatment error. That's a manufacturing defect under New York law. There's no way the plaintiffs' lawyers know about this, do they? I mean, I've never seen manufacturing defect claims in any of these cases, have you?"

"Uh, yeah. I mean no. Or maybe – fuck I don't know." Burgess was getting frustrated. "Did you log this in?"

"Of course."

"Okay, so we're good, right?"

"Well don't you think somebody should know? This has to be produced pretty soon. In the cases I mean. Like in that Beers action in the Bronx, and maybe in the Jenkins case down in Dallas. This'll be a game changer, don't you think?"

"Yeah, fuck, alright," Burgess relented. He blew out a breath of irritation. "Tell you what, give me a copy of this, and make sure the rest of the document isn't sitting in the file, okay? Ko sure as shit will ask me that and I don't want to sit there like a dumb-fuck."

"Absolutely."

"And just make sure your LawDocs entry is comprehensive, because they are going to log in and pull it up."

"I will, I mean I did," O'Reilly said dutifully.

"Okay, great job," said Burgess, handing the document back.

"Should I give a copy to Manny?"

"No. Give me a copy and stick the original back in the file."

"Great," O'Reilly answered.

O'Reilly then jogged over to the first-floor copy machine and hastened back to Burgess's office. He handed a copy of the two-page document to Burgess and then, back upstairs, he went through the rest of Handler box page by page. There was no sign of the remainder of the Interim Report. O'Reilly went downstairs and reported that to Burgess.

"Okay, thanks, I got it," Burgess said. "Again, great job."

O'Reilly gave him a thumbs-up with a smile spread across his face. Then he headed back upstairs to the steam pipe.

THAT NIGHT, ON the commute back to Park Slope, O'Reilly felt a surge of pride about his discovery. There was no question that Gunther's entire defense in these cases could change based on this disclosure. If the company negligently over-treated these shrimp batches with dangerous levels of sulfites and failed to do a recall once they made their discovery, then in O'Reilly's view the company would have to settle all these cases. At what cost, he could only imagine. O'Reilly figured he'd be getting a call soon from New York thanking him for the find. Can you imagine if one of these paralegals had stumbled on this document?

O'Reilly conjured up the image of them sitting with their headphones on, barely paying attention. They would have ranked this with a sensitivity of 0 and stuffed the document back into the box without fully understanding what they were reading. Thank God the box had landed in his lap.

For the last leg of the ride home, with straphangers filling the subway car back to Brooklyn, O'Reilly thought about how Briggs and Ko would deal with his document in court. It would be fascinating to see what happens next. And to think he had something to do with that …

Of course, it was curious how they didn't know about it already. O'Reilly thought about that – Barker had sent the memorandum and report to Handler and told him, "the results speak for themselves." So Handler obviously has known about this testing for some time.

How could Briggs and Ko not know? And why wasn't this brought up at the strategy meeting last month?

Hmph.

O'Reilly made a mental note to ask Burgess about it on Wednesday.

CHAPTER 23

A STRATEGIC MOVE BY THE KETCHOGUE
SPORTS AND RECREATION COMMITTEE

THE KETCHOGUE BORO Hall building sat on the northeast corner of Turnberry Park, at the intersection of Dowling Street and Freeman Avenue, just across from the softball fields. When you entered through the main entrance, you walked into an open circular rotunda that had a skylight at its roof three floors above. The rotunda had shining hardwood floors and soft yellow walls that contained framed portraits of every Ketchogue mayor dating back to 1812. You could follow the portraits chronologically around the rotunda and see how the thick bushy muttonchops and high collars of the 19th century gradually transitioned to the modern look of navy-blue Brooks Brothers suits and power ties. There were little gold plates at the bottom of each portrait that listed the names and years of service in office, and sadly, the dates of their demise. The portrait of the current mayor – The Honorable Woodrow Travis, an enormously popular public official known affectionately as Mayor Woody – was last in line, right by the main doors.

As it so happened, one of Mayor Woody's first official acts in office was to fill a vacancy for the Presidency of the Ketchogue Sports and Recreation Committee, which was the arm of the Boro Council responsible for organizing and running all of the town's recreation sports. The job opened after a man named Saul Grasberg dropped dead of a massive heart attack while jogging through Turnberry. They found him face down under a bench in Nike sweats and sneakers, with an iPhone in his right hand and a *Stone Temple Pilots* song still spilling out of the earbuds. He was 41 and had three kids who played sports in the town, and out of respect for him and his family, the job sat vacant for some time while his wake and funeral went forward. But in Sullivan's Pub on Main Street that year, immediately following the Annual St. Patrick's Day Parade, with a third or fourth mug of Guinness in his hands and a green derby perched atop his balding pate, Mayor Woody handed the job to his next-door neighbor, a 44-year old divorcee named Regina Wartham.

With the Clancy Brothers blaring away, Regina had pinned Mayor Woody up against a dartboard that afternoon. She told him – with her nose practically pressing up into his chin and her index finger poking his breastplate – how much she would love the assignment and what a great job she would do. Since they had been friends and neighbors for so many years, and mostly to get out from under her unrelenting assault and get a fifth mug of Guinness in his belly, Mayor Woody offered her the job on the spot.

And Regina, for her part, was eager to accept it. She currently was raising three sons in this town and it was her third one, Remy – a skinny fifth grader who was something of a computer whiz and liked *Star Wars* movies – for whom she really wanted this gig. If you asked her, Regina would tell you that if she accomplished nothing else as President of the Rec Committee, she was going to make these sports and recreation activities more open and accessible to the kids who weren't star athletes. There were many kids who just wanted to make a team and feel part of something, even though they had little interest in anything related to sports. Her Remy was first in line. There was no way Regina was going to let him or any other of the so-called nerdy kids be mistreated – no way in hell. Poor Remy was constantly on the receiving end of some brutal teasing by the popular sports kids and Regina was determined to stop it. If that meant she had to shove her way onto the Rec Committee, so be it.

And that was the thing about Regina that everyone in Ketchogue fully understood. When she wanted something done, she sprang into action, and if that rubbed people the wrong way, she really didn't give a shit. She could not care less what people thought about her, that was her attitude, and she was proud of it. She wasn't willing to take no for an answer once she set her mind to something, and she would never let anyone push her or her family around. Her true friends accepted that about her, and everyone else could kiss her ass.

Once named President of the Committee, Regina decided she was going to rule it with an iron fist. She had an opportunity to do some good, make some needed changes, and she wasn't going to pass that up. Mayor Woody technically had authority over this Committee, as did the Boro Council, but Regina would make sure that everyone understood that confronting her about anything would be so completely exhausting it simply wasn't worth the effort. The role therefore would give her the power to change the way these activities would be played, under what conditions, and according to what rules, and she was intent on making things fair for everyone, including her Remy.

And as far as the actual sports were concerned, well, Regina had never played one in her life, so what did she know about it, and what did it all really matter anyway? The purpose of this Committee, as far as she saw it, was not about organizing sports, it was about helping children. She had three of them and therefore considered herself an expert. She did not need a bunch of dimwitted jocks telling her how to raise kids or what was best for them.

And so it was that on the third Thursday of every month, in the small conference room on the first floor of Boro Hall, President Regina Wartham hosted the monthly meeting of the Ketchogue Sports and Recreation Committee. Its three executive members – Regina, Moshe Wagshul and Bruce Dixon – were responsible for setting policy at these meetings. There was a wider group of eight other non-executive Committee members who ran the day-to-day aspects of the sports, but their job, unofficially, was to listen to Regina and carry out her policy decisions. There wasn't anything about recreation sports in Ketchogue that Regina didn't control.

At just before seven p.m. on the date of the February monthly Executive Committee meeting, Bruce and Moshe walked into Boro Hall and entered the small conference room, where Regina was already present. By and by the other non-executive members strolled in and peeled off their winter coats and jackets. Everyone greeted each other politely before settling in at the conference table. Regina called the meeting to order at 7:03 p.m., and then she pulled a small stack of papers from her Louis Vuitton shoulder bag. She had typed up the agenda for the meeting, as she always did, and she passed it out now to the group. There wasn't much on the table for discussion this month, but Regina knew that even the few items listed would trigger some conversation. Bruce Dixon in particular was a royal pain in the ass and she was sure he would be a problem tonight – there was nothing really unusual about that. But she would put him in his place the way she always did.

The first agenda item, Regina announced, had to do with the Recreation basketball season, already underway.

"I understand the coaches are making the kids run sprints, and they're calling the sprints '*suicides*,'" she reported. "That's the word they're using – suicides. Paul, is this correct?"

Regina looked over at a young father named Paul Tatum, who ran the Rec basketball program. Paul was roughly 6'6" with shoulders the size of Thanksgiving turkeys. He had played Division III basketball at Amherst College and the Committee thought he was a logical choice to organize the town's basketball season, but Regina presently had other thoughts.

"Uh, yes, that's probably correct," Paul said defensively.

"Suicides," Regina deadpanned.

"Yes."

"They're saying that to *kids*?"

"Yeah, they are," Bruce Dixon jumped in. He had both hands planted on the conference table and was about three seats from Regina, who sat at the head. The room was small, and with Bruce's prodigious belly nestled against the conference table, his wooden chairback was pressed against the side wall of the room.

"What's the problem?" Bruce asked.

"It's horrifying, that's the problem," shot Regina. "Suicide is no laughing matter. Our coaches shouldn't be referring to it casually."

"Casually?" Bruce snapped back.

"Yeah, casually. I want it stopped, and the coaches reprimanded. Or maybe we'll have their heads examined. This is awful. I can't believe I have to explain this."

"Regina, please," said Bruce. "The term 'suicides' is part of the language of the sport and has been for a hundred years. It's a tough basketball wind sprint, so they've been called 'suicides' for as long as anyone can remember. They use that term at every level. Paul, is that right?"

Paul Tatum nodded back quickly, shifting in his chair. He was trying his best to blend into the background and wanted no part of this debate.

"Exactly," Bruce said at Paul's nod. "Regina, it's a common term. Maybe for this sports-related stuff you should defer to the people with knowledge, like Paul here."

Regina tossed her pen down.

"Defer?" she asked him sharply.

"What's next on your list?" Bruce asked dismissively. "Let's move on."

But Regina would not move on.

In the end it really didn't matter to her how this came out, in terms of the words that were used, because if it were true that the term was always used in the sport, as Bruce had said, and Paul had confirmed, it probably would not affect the children at all, which was her main concern. But to Regina there was a much bigger issue here. Bruce not only was challenging her authority, he was questioning a decision she had made, and doubting her judgment, in front of a group of people. And as far as Regina was concerned, that in and of itself was unacceptable. Once that happened, nothing else mattered to her but winning. No one – not now or ever – would get away with doing that to her. She was not going to let Bruce Dixon or anyone else disrespect her.

They debated the topic a few more minutes until everyone could see Regina wearing Bruce down. They all knew it was only a matter of time before he caved. Agitated, Bruce turned to Moshe, who right now was doodling on his agenda sheet.

"For Christ's sake, Moish," Bruce pleaded, "you're sittin' there like a goddamn quadriplegic. You got two cents you want to add?"

Moshe shoved his thick eyeglasses against his face with an index finger. "Yes, well," he said, clearing his throat, "let me say this. The point that the term suicide is potentially traumatizing is, of course, a fair one. If we could avoid it, perhaps we should do so."

"Oh, for Christ's sake."

"But at the same time, Regina," Moshe continued, "Bruce is correct that the term is fairly ubiquitous in the sport. Consequently, I would not reprimand our coaches. Do you have an alternative term to suggest?"

"Safeties," Regina responded quickly.

"Safeties," Bruce repeated with a roll of his eyes, "Jesus Christ."

"Bruce, is that a fair compromise?" Moshe asked.

"Moish, the *kids* call them suicides!"

"Kids follow the leadership of adults," Regina retorted, "so the word will be dropped. I don't want it to come out of the mouths of our coaches. Frankly, I don't understand your objection."

"I explained my objection."

"Well, it makes no sense to me. Does it to anyone else?"

Regina looked around the room, as did Bruce. Not a person spoke, or even moved. They all looked down at their agenda sheets and lifted their pens, pretending to take notes. Regina didn't wait a second more.

"There you have it," she said to Bruce.

"Fine," Bruce relented, "we'll call them 'safeties'." He snapped some finger quotes, and then he adjusted the bill on his "Make America Great Again" cap. "And if the coaches say 'suicides' we'll give 'em detention and make them sit in a corner. What's next?"

Regina made a note on her agenda sheet. Maybe this was just a small dispute, but Regina had won again and had swatted away any challenge to her authority. She had won because she would never accept losing to anyone, under any circumstances. Winning was what defined her and gave her purpose. No matter what the circumstances, no matter how small the battle, Regina Wartham was going to come out on top. You could bet the ranch on that.

Over the next half hour Regina brought up a few more points for "discussion," but like all the prior issues these were really matters that Regina had already set in motion prior to the meeting. She was just giving everyone, including Bruce and Moshe, the news of her decisions and how she wanted everything carried out. Eventually Bruce stopped speaking altogether – he sat there with his arms crossed.

Finally, Regina got to the last agenda item – the status of the Beers lawsuit against the Committee and its members. Except that this one was not on the sheet. Bruce, Moshe and Regina had agreed privately that the monthly meeting was a good opportunity to speak informally about where things stood, without the lawyers present.

"We have one more item to discuss," Regina reported, after the meeting had been dragging on for ninety minutes, "but we are going to do that in private session with just the Executive Committee."

She thanked everyone for coming, and the eight non-executive committee members hurried out the door, collecting their iPads and personal items and bolting as fast as they could to the parking lot.

With only the three of them remaining, Bruce took the lead. He settled at the head of the table and began with a softer tone that he hoped would signal a truce of some sort to Regina. They needed to be on the same side when it came to this lawsuit.

"Well, you saw what happened with the twitter-bot thing we did, right?" he asked. Regina nodded affirmatively.

"It really worked, I gotta hand it to Moish over here."

He patted Moshe on the back.

"Twitter just exploded over it and the comments were overwhelmingly on our side. It all made Beers look like a money-grubbing ingrate who injured his own kid and then sued his neighbors over it. And the anti-Semitic comment thing – did you both follow that? The bots even suggested that *Beers himself* was involved – again, Moish, great job. It was brilliant. It's been two months and there are still comments every day."

"Well, I'm still a defendant in the case," Regina reported.

"As am I," said Moshe.

"And I want out," Regina followed, "which was the point of that whole thing."

"Well, like I said, it worked," said Bruce, "I'm hearing whispers he's thinking of dropping us."

"Whispers?" Regina asked.

"Yeah, whispers, rumors," Bruce said, "that he might drop us."

"I heard he had a heart attack," Moshe interjected.

"No, apparently it was a panic attack," Bruce answered. "He supposedly collapsed when a reporter showed up at his house over the Jew comment."

He patted Moshe's back again.

"Moish, no offense."

Moshe waved him off.

"Well, I heard about the collapse," Regina said back, "and I read the articles. They were very critical of him."

"Exactly what we were hoping for," Moshe said.

"But the whispers, the rumors," Regina backtracked, "is he dropping us or not?"

"I don't know that for sure," Bruce answered, "but that's what I'm hearing. Obviously, I haven't spoken to Beers. I was hoping it would all be resolved before the depositions came up, but who knows. Did you both get scheduled for depositions?"

"Yes, indeed," Moshe answered, "I am noticed for April."

"Me too," said Regina.

"Yeah, me three, shit," Bruce answered, shaking his head.

Regina then changed the subject slightly.

"Look, the Committee's lawyers – Cornstein, Shapiro & Betz – are making our document production to Beers's lawyer in a week or so. I know you're both dealing with your personal lawyers on that, but on behalf of the Committee, I'm collecting the documents they asked for and will send them to Cornstein. If you have anything at home, I need it. Can you get me that stuff by Monday?"

"Sure," said Moshe.

"What the hell do they want?" Bruce asked.

"Just anything related to the Committee. Meeting minutes, agendas, personal emails you have that discuss Committee business, things like that. Cast as wide a net as you can."

Bruce started shaking his head again.

"The fuck does all this have to do with this kid eating shrimp, when none of us were even at the damn field?" he asked. "This whole thing is ridiculous."

"Well, we agree on that," Regina responded, "but we still need the documents. Just send me what you have by Monday."

They both nodded.

Soon Bruce and Moshe packed up their papers, slipped on their coats, and were out the door. Regina was then alone in the conference room. She had some business to attend to – an important final task that she would not leave to anybody else. She hadn't told Bruce and Moshe about it, or anyone else for that matter, but tonight was the night.

Regina looked out the conference room window and watched as Moshe and Bruce got into their cars and drove out of the parking lot. Then she shut the conference room door and tested its lock. She lowered all the window shades and marched purposefully to the back of the room.

There, against the wall, was a long brown credenza with six file cabinet drawers. Inside, in various stacks, all bound together with thick rubber bands and black binder clips, were reams of documents going back over the last three years, all placed there by Regina and Mr. Saul Grasberg, her poor departed predecessor. There were bids for contracts relating to the softball and baseball fields, budgets for the various sports, insurance forms and applications, and tons of other documents.

And in that cabinet, Regina knew, was where they also maintained the Parent Authorization forms.

These were the sheets that the parents filled out and signed giving permission for their child to play sports in Ketchogue. They were due, under the Committee's rules, by July 15 of the summer before school began in September, and they would cover all the sports for the upcoming scholastic year. These were the forms that were the target of Regina's concerns this night.

Back at the credenza, she yanked open the third cabinet on the right and reached way in the back. She pulled out a rubber-banded stack of Authorization forms about a foot high. If the Beers family had filled out a form for Agnes, it would be in this pile. Of course, it was possible there would be no Beers form at all, because her Committee typically would allow a kid to join a team even if the parent missed the deadline and never handed in a form. If the parent came by with the $35 fee at some point, the kid was in. Also, when the Committee members collected these documents at the registration desk in the rotunda at Boro Hall on sign-up day, they did so as each parent walked in the door, making one big unorganized pile. So the forms were not in alphabetical order. This meant Regina would have to go through them a page at a time.

But she didn't care if it took her all night.

With the pile in front of her, she flicked the edge and wondered how many documents were in the stack. She was aware that Beers's lawyer had requested that the Committee produce *all* Parent Authorization forms relating to girls' softball, and this here stack precisely met that description. She could easily stuff the pile into a Federal Express box and ship it out to Cornstein Shapiro and let them separate out the softball forms. Hell, that's what the insurance company was paying these lawyers to do anyway.

But there was no way she was letting Dan Beers win. If there was evidence in this stack that would hurt her case, she wanted to see it. She wanted to know what it said. So Regina would go through the stack on her own. She reached into her Louis Vuitton handbag, pulled out a Diet Pepsi, popped the top, and began turning pages.

As she expected, the documents were in no particular order, and she made no effort to separate anything out.

After a half hour, as her eyes were glazing over and she'd been through several hundred forms, Regina turned another page, and finally, about four inches down into the stack – there it was. Her heart began to pound as she read the form that Debbie Beers had filled out on the due date.

Just like all the others, it contained the caption "KETCHOGUE SPORTS AND RECREATION COMMITTEE," and was entitled "PARENT/ GUARDIAN AUTHORIZATION FORM." Debbie Beers had dutifully provided all the relevant information – she wrote "Girls Softball" on the line labeled "Sport/ Activity," and had jotted in their home address, cell phone numbers for both parents, and her email address. She signed it, dated it and had handed it in, just like everyone else.

Regina leaned back in the chair and eyeballed the document – every word of it. Regina and Debbie had been friends, and when Regina thought about it, knowing Debbie, there should never have been any doubt that she completed that document on time. In fact, it was even possible Debbie had handed it to *her* – on the bottom she noticed her own initials, indicating that the Beers family had paid the $35 entry fee.

Regina held the document up to the halogen ceiling lights and read Debbie's entries again. It was chilling to see her handwritten words there in blue ink – it gave Regina the sense that Debbie was alive, or at least had been. She was a mother, just like her, and had filled out this sheet in the normal course of her life, taking care of her kids, getting them involved in things and making them happy. It was so sad she was gone.

But all of that was in the past. In the wake of her untimely death her husband had sued *her*, Regina. After that she felt as though nothing else mattered. Debbie was dead and their friendship no longer existed – those were the facts. And Dan Beers simply was not going to disrespect her or her family, no matter how sick or injured his kid was.

As far as the lawsuit was concerned, well, right there on the form was the kicker. Debbie had written words that made Regina sit up in her chair:

> Agnes has a mild shellfish allergy.
> She is also slightly asthmatic.

Regina shook her head. Why Debbie would even write such a thing on a permission form for girls' softball was beyond her. Who could possibly think that mattered? How could she know that Cindy Brewer, with her long legs and power tits, would be assigned as the snack mom and would show up with *shrimp cocktail* at one of these softball games?

Well, it didn't matter now, because Regina knew what the lawyers would say about this document. She had attended the initial meeting with them and all they talked about was "notice." Did the Committee or any of its members have "notice" the kid was allergic? There was "actual notice" and "constructive notice," and Carl Betz, the lead attorney from that firm, explained the legal implications of both terms until Regina's eyes had frosted over. She understood the point, but to emphasize it further, Betz had asked each of them directly – did *you* know Agnes Beers was allergic to shrimp? Was there anything in writing? Did anyone have prior notice? Those questions were the key to the entire case, he explained, and if the answer to any of them was yes, then serving up a plate of shrimp as an official act by the town was a problem. If not, and there was no notice, Betz made clear this whole thing fell on the father.

Regina leaned forward and placed the Beers form onto the conference room table again. She rested her elbows left and right of it, with two fists in her cheeks. She read the document again, from top to bottom, and then leaned back, looking up at the ceiling.

Another thing Betz said was that the insurance covered her up to a certain dollar amount, called policy limits, and after that *she* potentially could be responsible. And it could be millions. She was the President of the Committee and had the most to lose, that much was clear.

But Regina never lost. Not now, not ever. This, in fact, would be an easy decision.

She stood and wrapped those thick rubber bands back around the stack of forms. They would all go into the Federal Express box to Cornstein, Shapiro & Betz.

But the Beers form was headed elsewhere.

Regina left the conference room with the document in one hand and her key ring in the other. She marched down the hall to one of the administrative offices and shoved the key into the lock – as President she had access to certain rooms at Boro Hall and she planned to make use of one of them this very night.

Before she entered, she looked up and down the hallway. The place was empty, it being well after 9 pm. Regina knew that the only people around right now were the late-shift officers sitting over in Police Headquarters, on the other side of the building.

She slipped into office and shut the door. The office was small – there was a metal desk with a few small cactus plants in tiny terracotta pots, a desktop computer with yellow sticky notes pressed to the top of the screen, a stand-alone bookshelf on her right, and a bunch of boxes stacked in neat rows on the left.

In the far-right corner, there was a garbage can.

And perched on top of it was a shredder.

Regina cast her eyes down onto the Beers Authorization form again and looked at those words, the ones written there by Debbie Beers, Agnes's mother – *Agnes has a mild shellfish allergy; she is also slightly asthmatic.*

Pity, Regina thought. She never wanted it to come to this, but what choice did she have?

"Oh well," she said out loud, and she slipped the form into the mouth of the shredder. She pressed the "Go" button and the shredder instantly sprang to life. Its teeth grabbed the document and sucked it in.

Just like that, in an instant, it was gone.

Regina had won. Again.

She locked the door and went back to the conference room. A few minutes later she was in her minivan heading home to her kids.

ON THAT SAME night, across the rolling greens of Turnberry Park, up there on the second floor over the donut shop, Anzalone sat in her cramped law office with a single sheet of paper in her hands. It was a printout of an email that an associate lawyer at Foster Tuttle & Briggs named Andrea Corning had sent her a few hours earlier, indicating that the firm had finally delivered, on behalf of Gunther, its document production in the Beers lawsuit. The email contained a password and a hyperlink to an online dropbox that Anzalone could click into, enter the password, and view the documents that Gunther had produced to her.

This was part of the modern era of paperless document productions in litigation these days, which allowed parties to gather, collect and review documents from the relative comforts of their offices. You could search, sort and view them all on your computer screen with the assistance of a software program and print out only what you wanted. It saved a lot of time and took mercy on the trees.

Anzalone had already clicked on the link and the page was right there on her screen, with a blinking cursor inside a box, waiting for her to type in the password. She'd been staring at the screen for several minutes, looking back and forth from the password on the printed-out email to the screen prompting her to enter it. The truth was that she really did not want to see what was in this dropbox. If it turned out to be a few thousand pages she could handle that level of volume, but if the volume was any greater, Anzalone didn't know what she would do. She would need to enlist some help, but where was that money coming from? And on top of it, there wasn't much time – depositions were starting in a matter of weeks.

Anzalone looked out the window and saw the streetlights glowing on a vacant Main Street. A few cars straggled by, but it was late and cold and most normal people, with normal lives, were home nestled comfortably in front of their televisions, with maybe a fire blazing away. Anzalone wanted desperately to do the same.

Resigned, Anzalone blew out a burst of air, entered the password and closed her eyes. When she opened them, she saw a little circle spinning. Soon the circle disappeared and dozens upon dozens of Adobe pdf icons began popping up in neat rows of eight across. Anzalone scrolled down, and there appeared to be no end to them. They went on forever.

Her heart began racing. She began clicking open the pdf icons, and nearly every one of them ran on for hundreds of pages. This meant her worst fear was confirmed – this document production was massive. She quickly jumped onto her email and typed in andrea.corning@ftblaw.com, and cranked out an inquiry to the lawyer at Foster Tuttle & Briggs who had sent the documents. With shaking hands, Anzalone wrote: *"Andrea – thanks for the email and for Gunther's production. I was hoping you could tell me – how many individual documents did you produce, and what is the total volume in terms of pages?"*

It didn't take more than three minutes for a response.

Anzalone heard her inbox chime, and there was the reply from Corning: *"Ms. Anzalone – we produced 181,343 documents, which consist of 1,574,211 pages. The documents are all bates-stamped. We believe our production is comprehensive and responds fully to Plaintiff's document requests."*

Anzalone swallowed hard.

Of course, Corning had completely misinterpreted her question; she apparently took it as a challenge to the completeness of their production, when Anzalone in fact had intended exactly the opposite. She wanted to know why the production was so large, but it really didn't matter.

There was no way she could review all these documents, not in a lifetime. There were over 1.5 million pages for God's sake. She thought of it like a novel – she could plow through a 400-page crime thriller in roughly a week, and if her math was correct, this was about *3,750 novels.* She had about a month to get through them before depositions began. Even if she ignored all her other clients, there was no way she could complete the work.

On top of everything else, there was Justin. The poor kid had just been through a horrific operation on his left arm and was bolting awake in the middle of the night, screaming from the pain. It was killing Anzalone to watch him in agony like that, and of course there was no way to explain it to him. The operation had cost her over three grand and now she wasn't getting a wink of sleep. She asked her father, Carmine, to sit with him one night so that she could get some shut-eye, but the task was so exhausting for him, at his age, that Anzalone didn't feel right asking him again.

Anzalone clicked "Log Off" on the dropbox. Then she dialed her client, Dan Beers. His voicemail kicked in, so she left a message.

"Mr. Beers," she said, "this is Nicole Anzalone, calling on the Gunther matter. I know it's late, but can you please give me a call? There's a few matters I'd like to discuss with you."

Anzalone dug her palms into her eyes and yawned. Maybe she would have to go into these depositions without reviewing all the material, which in any other case would be malpractice, but what choice did she have?

Of course, there were other pressing issues she needed to address with Dan Beers. Lately the publicity over the case was horrendous, especially with the recent incident of someone writing the word "Jew" on the car of one of the defendants, who happened to be orthodox. The calls and emails she received after that event were among the worst she had ever experienced. Anzalone privately prayed that her client had nothing to do with that situation, as the press articles were suggesting.

And now these documents, my God. The time, money and resources that would be required … Anzalone needed to think. She needed to find a path forward that would work. She also had to have a tough conversation with her client.

But right now, she had no clue what to tell him.

CHAPTER 24

THE INTERIM TOXICITY REPORT 2.0

O'REILLY CRUISED INTO the warehouse on the first Monday in March sporting an outfit that contrasted sharply with the Brooks Brother suit he wore on his first appearance there back in September. Since that time, with Manny's silent approval, the corporate getup slowly transitioned to the casual, unkempt look of a lumberjack.

This morning O'Reilly wore a pair of wrinkled brown Billabong corduroys over a set of Timberland work boots, with shoelaces dangling, together with an untucked, thickly lined tan flannel shirt. His unruly mop of red hair was barely restrained under a Yankee cap, and the unshaven rusty scruff on his cheeks – which glowed with the orangey color of Cheese doodles – was about a quarter-inch thick. The flannel's only purpose that day was to get him warm and snugly to Secaucus, but soon after his arrival, O'Reilly peeled it off and sat next to the steam pipe in a SUNY Buffalo Women's Basketball t-shirt – a gift from a power forward from St. Louis who O'Reilly dated for a month during his sophomore year. Presently, O'Reilly's muffin-top hairy belly had about fifteen pounds of blubber swelling out below the bottom hem of the t-shirt. It wasn't law firm attire, but who cared out here.

Meanwhile, the casual style of his wardrobe matched O'Reilly's sunny disposition these last few weeks. According to Manny, the National Shrimp Cocktail Defense Team, in all its glory, mercifully was coming to an end, probably in about six weeks or so, and O'Reilly was giddy as he counted down the days. He felt like a manslaughter convict on the brink of parole. Plus, spring was on the way, some warm weather was coming, and the Blessed High Holy Mother of All Feast Days – St. Paddy's Day – was right around the corner. His Tuesday/ Thursday classes at MLS were a piece of cake and his final exams would be a breeze. Law school graduation was only a few months away and he had a full-time job waiting for him in September, here at FT&B, which was a great relief when you considered that many of his classmates were struggling to find employment. Also, because this Secaucus work paid him some decent bank, his August plans with his brother Tom were now set in cement. The two would be spending a few vacation days on the links at the Lahinch Golf Course in County Clare, over in the motherland, and that was going to be a helluva lot of fun. The only real ball of stress out there for him right now was the July Bar Exam, but once that behemoth got in his rearview mirror, the rest of the summer would be like a slice of heaven.

On top of all of that, he reminded himself, there was that juicy little document discovery from a few weeks ago, that Interim Toxicity Report he had stumbled across in the files of the General Counsel. O'Reilly was sure that sucker would blow the cover off these lawsuits, once it got public. Digging that thing up made O'Reilly feel like he had unearthed a T-Rex thighbone on an archeological dig. He was quite pleased with himself and the buzz hadn't eased off since. He felt then, as he did now, that he had really contributed to the team.

Of course, it surprised him a bit when he never heard another word about it after his impromptu meeting with Burgess, but so be it, he had decided, just let it go. He didn't want to appear too much like an amateur fishing for compliments. So he was more than happy to keep his head down, his mouth shut, and just do his time until Secaucus, the warehouse, the steam pipe – all of it – was a distant memory.

That's why the last thing he needed was what happened that morning, shortly after he arrived.

When O'Reilly checked in, at roughly 7:45 am, he strolled past Manny's office, giving a rap on the doorjamb.

"Manuel, ol' chap," he said lightly, for some reason in a British accent, a knapsack thrown over a shoulder. "What is shaking, my good man?"

Manny was, as usual, glued to his computer screen, his fingers clacking away on the keyboard. It was his custom to ignore O'Reilly and this morning was no different.

"*Hombre,* get going," he said, nodding to the ceiling. "I wanna get out of this hellhole as badly as you do."

"Need a box, homes," O'Reilly said, snapping his fingers. "Polished off another one on Saturday. Who's better than me?"

"*Amigo,* a lot of people."

O'Reilly tossed a chin over his shoulder.

"Hallway?" he asked.

"*Si,* hallway." Manny was biting into an egg sandwich. "Let's see if you can knock an entire one off in one day," he garbled with a mouthful.

O'Reilly shrugged his shoulders.

"I'll try my best."

"*Amigo,* try harder than that," said Manny. "You do your best and we'll be here 'til Christmas."

A few moments later, O'Reilly was settled in his cubicle with a stack of documents from the new box piled up to the left of his keyboard. He had a 20 oz. 7-Eleven coffee steaming away on his desktop and had just logged into LawDocs for what felt like the millionth time. He entered his password and was just about to click on the button for a "New Document," but before he did, he decided to pull up the entry he had recorded for the Interim Toxicity Report a few weeks back. There was something sticking in his craw about it, and he'd been thinking about it ever since that day he ran into Burgess's office, waving it at him like a madman. He wanted to read his entry again, really for no other reason than to satisfy himself that he had adequately explained its significance and hadn't sugarcoated it in any way that would make them overlook it. Based on the silence over the last few weeks, he had half a mind to go speak to Burgess about it, maybe ask why the whole thing seemed to have been swept under the rug, but the guy was just so impatient whenever you walked in on him …

Well, O'Reilly wanted to be sure that any shitty write-up he may have provided wasn't the reason why no one had ever mentioned the document to him again. That's what was on his mind that morning. So he logged in and searched for the LawDocs record relating to it. In a flash it was on his screen.

He couldn't believe what he saw.

"What the hell," he said.

He leaned in closer to the screen.

"What ... the ... HELL," he repeated louder, his eyes growing wider. He was staring at the screen, trying to make sense of what he was reading. The document entry looked completely different from what had had submitted.

"I don't believe this ...," he said.

His first thought was that he had made a mistake and had pulled up the wrong document. But he lasered back in on the screen, and sure enough, this was his entry. For the Interim Toxicity Report.

He ran his eyes along each data box that made up the entry, and then the next thing he noticed was that someone had changed the sensitivity rating to a 0. Or at least O'Reilly assumed that was the case. Because as sure as the sun rose in the east, O'Reilly had recorded that document as a 6. He was *sure* he did. *Positive* in fact. Six was nowhere near zero on the keyboard so O'Reilly was confident *he* hadn't made the mistake by tapping the wrong number. In fact, he specifically recalled being so excited about his find that he stared at that number – 6 – for a full ten minutes, with his heart thumping, before clicking save on it, just to be sure he had it right.

It was the first document to which he had ever given that rating.

So yes, someone had changed it purposefully. They gave the document a zero. A *zero*.

Those fuckers. Those sneaky little bastards.

O'Reilly couldn't believe it.

He then scanned his eyes down to read the explanation section, the one that required you to expound on why you rated any document higher than a three. O'Reilly had written four paragraphs about it and had even cited some New York Court of Appeals cases. It had taken him nearly three hours of editing and re-writing to get it just the way he wanted. He had read that section over, like what – ten times? Before finally submitting it?

Well it was all gone now. Deleted. Purged. Finito.

The entire section was blank – exactly what you would expect when a document was rated a zero.

O'Reilly could feel his blood boiling.

He next scanned down and found the box for the privilege designation. And sure as shit, someone had marked the Interim Toxicity Report as a *privileged* document. They recorded that it was protected against disclosure by the attorney-client privilege. It would never be given to plaintiffs' lawyers in discovery. How could that be? How? It was scientific research and contained no legal advice. O'Reilly had even thought, at the time, that it was a stretch calling the cover memo a privileged document, the one that the Scientific Research Director had sent to Handler, the General Counsel. But O'Reilly had designated it as privileged anyway, but that was only because it originally was marked that way in big bold letters. However, he was careful to point that out to Burgess, in case they wanted to change it back.

But the Report itself? No way.

O'Reilly had thought long and hard before he marked that as a non-privileged document, and he was confident he could defend the decision. There was no question, in O'Reilly's mind, that under the New York discovery rules the Report had to be turned over in these damn shrimp cases. Once that happened, and this sulfites disaster got leaked, FT&B and Gunther would have a difficult time – no, an *impossible time* – explaining that away before any judge or jury. The only question was how quickly the lawsuits would settle. So now to protect their sorry asses, they had gone ahead and ... *they*. O'Reilly paused and repeated the word in his head. He wasn't even sure who the hell "they" were.

Who did this? Burgess? O'Reilly wanted to know – now.

In a flash, he grabbed the arms on his ergonomic meshed-backed office chair and launched himself out of his seat. But then something else struck him. Something even more important, something that caused him to spin back around and plop down into his seat again.

The Beers case. The one with the 10-year-old comatose kid up in the Bronx, or out on Long Island, or wherever the hell she was from. The case they earmarked for trial. They had just produced documents in that case, didn't they? Did this Report get sent? Obviously not if it was marked privileged, but O'Reilly had to see it for himself.

He leaned in toward the computer screen so that his nose was about an inch away. He navigated down to the "Production" entry box. And sure enough, a big fat "NO" was staring right back at him. It was almost as if the computer was giving him the middle finger.

"No, asshole," it seemed to be saying, "we did NOT produce the document." Goddamn, this was infuriating.

LawDocs had a sorting function and O'Reilly hastily clicked some buttons. He saw that FT&B had produced over 180,000 documents in the Beers case, but the Interim Toxicity Report was not one of them. Well, that certainly was going to make things difficult for that Beers attorney, wasn't it? That over-matched two-bit hack of a lawyer who had stolen client funds – she would have no clue what really happened. No clue her client likely was in a coma because of a massive overdose of sulfites, not from some allergy. If Beers only had a *slight* chance of winning to begin with, the poor sonofabitch had absolutely *no shot* now.

Jesus, the dishonesty, thought O'Reilly. The mendacity.

He wanted to scream. But first he wanted an explanation.

In a fit, he slapped two hands down onto his desktop and rose to his feet. The slam of his paws shook the entire cubicle and caused a few of his document-reviewer neighbors to pull the earbuds out of their heads and give him a quizzical stare. But O'Reilly didn't care – he raced past all the second-floor document reviewers and bounded down the stairs, two steps at a time, and in a minute he was flying into Burgess's office.

"Ralph, what the hell is going on?!" he yelled, giving Burgess no context whatsoever. Burgess was leaning down over his desk with a pencil in his hands, his nose buried into the *New York Times* crossword puzzle. O'Reilly's abrupt entrance startled him, and he jolted upright.

"Sea-Mouse, Jesus ..." he said. "You scared the shit outta me."

"I want to know what happened!" O'Reilly roared, pointing up at the ceiling. He meant to indicate his computer, and the entry for the Interim Toxicity Report, but Burgess's expression revealed he had no idea what O'Reilly was talking about.

He then noticed O'Reilly's untied work boots, scruffy face and ill-fitting SUNY Buffalo t-shirt, and said, "Christ, my landscaper dresses better than you."

But O'Reilly was having none of it. He yelled back, "Don't change the subject! What happened?!"

"What happened where? What're you talking about?"

"What am I talking about?!"

"Yeah, what're you talking about?" Burgess then stood. "And why are you yelling?" he asked.

O'Reilly ripped off his Yankee hat and raked a hand through his hair. His heart was pounding, and right now he was so angry he felt like grabbing Burgess by the neck and pressing him up against the wall until the man started giving up answers.

"The goddamn REPORT!" he yelled, pointing at the ceiling.

"Seamus, what report? What're you – "

"You KNOW what report!"

"Hey man, take a deep breath," Burgess pleaded.

O'Reilly's adrenaline surge had him nearly hyperventilating now. He fully understood he needed to calm down. Maybe Burgess wasn't playing dumb and really didn't know what O'Reilly was talking about, but then again maybe he did. Either way, O'Reilly just needed to get his point across. He *needed* to. He wanted to do so calmly, but for whatever reason, he just couldn't. The months of petty torments and insults had been piling up on him and there wasn't much more he could take. He had endured the mangling of his name, the brutal commute, the agony of the steam pipe, Manny's dictatorship, the boredom of the work, Raul's rubbery weaners – all of it – but there was no way he would tolerate dishonesty. And in his gut, that's what O'Reilly felt was going on here. It was the last straw. That big Zero staring back at him on the sensitivity rating – the NO regarding production – the deletion of his written explanation ... how dare they.

Well screw this, he decided. He let Burgess have it.

"FUCK OFF, you don't know what I'm talking about!"

"Hey! Seamus –"

"The Interim Report!! WHO CHANGED MY ENTRY?!"

Burgess took a few steps backward, and rolled his chair between he and O'Reilly, who now had thick blue veins running down his neck.

"Oh, that," Burgess said back defensively.

"Yeah, THAT! WHO DID IT?!"

"I did! And calm down!"

"You?! Why?!"

"I was told to do it, that's why!"

"What?! By who?!"

"New York, okay?" Burgess said. "Now keep it down."

O'Reilly became aware that he was pacing a step forward, and Burgess a step back, with each exchange in their conversation. Burgess looked fearful, and realizing this, O'Reilly stood still and lowered his arms. His chest was heaving with every breath, and his face was still on fire. But he wasn't finished with Burgess.

"What do you mean New York?" he coughed out.

"They logged in and saw your entry and told me to do it," Burgess said tentatively, with the demeanor of someone talking to a hostage-taker. He was showing his palms. "I don't know what to tell you."

But O'Reilly was incensed. He pointed at Burgess.

"I'll go to the press," he warned. "I'll go to the FUCKING PRESS!"

"No, you won't," Burgess shot back. He dropped onto his seat again. "You do and you'll never work again, okay ... *Sea-Mouse*? You forget who your CLIENT is?!"

"This ain't right, Ralph!"

"The fuck you know about document productions anyway?"

Burgess was suddenly emboldened and losing his temper with O'Reilly. This miserable little ... underling ... standing there dressed like a homeless bum, wasn't even a lawyer. Who the hell was he talking to?

"Where do you get off telling me, or anyone else, how to run things, huh?" he yelled. "Go back upstairs and do your job."

Suddenly O'Reilly heard a rumbling to his left and he turned to face the door. There was Manny, standing at the threshold.

"*Hombre*," he said, "what's with all the noise?"

O'Reilly wheeled around and faced him.

"Manny, are you in on this too?!"

Manny looked over O'Reilly's shoulder at Burgess, confused.

"The Report," Burgess deadpanned. "He just read the entry."

Suddenly Manny's demeanor changed, and he slumped his shoulders. He stared off to the side, looking like he had been caught stealing money from a tip jar. He wiped a hand down his face and stared at O'Reilly, not saying a word.

"Manny? C'mon man," O'Reilly said with some desperation.

Manny didn't respond, but his eyes met with O'Reilly's.

"Aw Manny. *You* knew about this?"

There was another pause, and finally Manny took a deep breath. He crossed his arms and looked directly at O'Reilly.

"Never mind that," he said. "None of your concern. Orders from On High, *muchacho*." Then he was snapping his fingers. "Let's go, back to the steam pipe, *amigo*. I'm behind now because of you."

O'Reilly's eyes widened and he could feel his chest tightening, his blood boiling, his head about to explode. There was an injustice happening here, and he couldn't let it go. Maybe this Beers family shouldn't win this case, but the fight had to be fair. He thought about that meeting back in January, when they had singled out the Beers family for annihilation and had revealed all that private information about the family's lawyer, information they should not have had. It made him feel sleazy then, the same way he felt now.

He couldn't be a party to this. They had to understand.

O'Reilly clenched both his fists and gritted his teeth. He was standing between the two of them – Manny at the door, and Burgess at his desk – with his head bouncing back and forth, looking at them both. Well, this was it. He couldn't take it one more second. If they wouldn't listen to him, if they couldn't see the wrongful nature of their fucking little conspiracy, he would let them know exactly how he felt about it. O'Reilly then wheeled around and looked directly into Burgess's eyes. Suddenly that line came back to him …

Dust in the sweat on the balls of a slug …

Well.

In a flash, O'Reilly grabbed one of the visitor's chairs stationed next to Burgess's desk, lifting it over his head.

"FUCK … THIS!" he screamed, and he threw it as hard as he could against the warehouse's cinder block wall.

CHAPTER 25

A FRIENDLY LITTLE VISIT TO THE
KETCHOGUE ANTI-BULLYING SPECIALIST

WHAT'S THAT SHIT all over your face?"

Danny was at the edge of the sofa under the living room bay window, spraying Windex over the metal rods and faux-leather seat cushion of Agnes's wheelchair. He was wiping it down with a paper towel with one eye angled toward the foyer, at the front door, through which Henry had just entered. Henry marched in and that was the first thing out of his mouth. No pleasantries, no greetings, just a typical Henry shot across the bow.

Henry shook the rain off his windbreaker, spraying the droplets out onto the porch. Then he pulled the front door shut and flipped the jacket over the back of the La-Z-Boy.

"It's a rash," Danny answered him, without looking up.

Gianna was sitting on the sofa to Danny's right, with an iPhone on her lap, watching a show called "Kate Plus Eight" on the TLC Channel. Danny had half a mind to tell Henry to curb the language a bit, but he knew it was pointless. The man was an enigma – he'd commit murder for his granddaughters, but he'd swear like a longshoreman in their presence. It was something they all had gotten used to, without much choice. That included Gianna, who would hear these words and not even flinch.

Danny was now on one knee, next to the wheelchair, continuing the spraying and wiping, hoping Henry would keep his mouth shut.

"It's on neck too," Henry further observed, leaning around Danny to get a better view. He started moving toward the kitchen. "Looks like you got the AIDS."

"It's all over my body," said Danny. "Mostly on my back."

And that was true. Several weeks ago, a small red patch the size of a dime had appeared on Danny's left temple. Then it grew and spread down his cheeks. It moved across his forehead and onto his neck and it was now all over his chest and back and down his arms. It was red, itchy and blistery, and at times painful. Danny had elected to ignore it, hoping it would go away, but that strategy was failing. Still, there was no way he was parting with the couple hundred bucks he knew they would ring him up for with a doctor's appointment. An ointment of some sort from a pharmacy would have to suffice.

Of course, to make matters worse, the rash was not his only medical concern these days. Danny was sure an ulcer was burrowing its way through the lining of his stomach, which burned like he had swallowed a jalapeno pepper and some battery acid. He had taken to starting each day with a glass of whole milk, which was helping a bit, but if things continued in this manner, he'd have to bite the bullet and go see a doctor. Presently he was waking up in the middle of the night with his head spinning in circles with worry – over Agnes's health, Gianna's mental state, and of course their finances. He knew the rash and the stomach pains were likely symptoms of that angst. And once awake, it was all over; there was no way he was falling back sleep. Most nights he'd get up and head downstairs, tiptoeing so as not to wake the girls. Then he'd plop down onto the sofa and read a magazine or watch TV with the sound off, hoping sleep would come. He wanted desperately to get one night when he slept all the way through to the morning, but that didn't seem possible right now.

"How the fuck you get it?" Henry hollered from the kitchen.

He grabbed a Coors Light from the fridge and popped it open. Then he walked back into the living room, ducking his head under the archway.

"Don't know," Danny answered.

Henry leaned down over Danny's shoulder.

"Christ, look at you," he said.

Danny shot an irritated look up at his father-in-law.

"Agnes is sleeping," he said softly, lowering a palm to the floor. He was referring to the volume of Henry's voice, which without much effort on Henry's part could reach an octave level that Danny didn't consider human. The man's regular speech decibels could rattle windows.

"You going in?" Henry asked, in a lower tone this time.

He plopped down onto the La-Z-Boy, drawing a sip from the beer can. Danny jabbed his chin at Henry.

"A little early, ain't it?" he asked, referring to the beer.

Henry waved him off.

"You make an appointment? Fuck you waitin' for?"

Danny focused on the wheelchair, scrubbing the front rails.

"It'll go away. I got some cortisone cream from Duane Reade."

"Right, smart move," Henry said sarcastically. He crossed his right leg over. "Meantime, you look like a goddamn burn victim."

Henry then looked over at Gianna, who was sitting with her arms crossed, her head leaning back into the sofa cushion. The phone was face down on her lap. She was staring up at the ceiling, moping Henry thought. It occurred to him she shouldn't be home at this time of the morning. He placed the beer down onto the coffee table in front of him.

"What's with her?" he asked.

"I let her stay home today."

"Why? Shouldn't she be in school?"

And with that Danny drew in a breath. He was trying to avoid the topic with Henry, because he knew the man would lose his shit over the whole thing. Danny really did not want to deal with him over it, but there didn't seem to be any way around it now.

He crumpled up the Windex-soaked paper towel and tossed it down onto the coffee table. Then he stood and grabbed the phone from Gianna's lap. He flipped it over, pressed some buttons, and handed it to Henry.

"This is why," he said.

Henry accepted the phone and pulled a set of reading glasses from the breast pocket of his flannel shirt.

He held the phone up and read:

> HCRTP45 @hellcat   17hrs
> #giannabeers @giannabeers u don't lissen
> drop the lawsuit bitch not gonna tell yu again

Gianna was staring at her grandfather with a look of frightened anticipation. Henry tossed the phone onto the sofa and stood. Predictably, he began circling the La-Z-By with his fists clenched. Then he turned and faced Danny, who was now sitting on the sofa.

"How many is it now?" he grunted through clenched teeth.

"I don't know," Danny said, "five or six."

"Who is it?!" Henry yelled at Gianna. "You must have a clue!"

Gianna shrugged her shoulders.

"Fuckin' A," Henry blasted, throwing his hands up.

"Henry, just take it easy – "

"Well, what's the plan, Dan?!" Henry then screamed.

In fact, Danny did have a plan. Over the last week, out of curiosity, he had jumped on Google and typed in some search terms hoping to find a way to deal with this growing problem. He stumbled across some articles that discussed what the so-called experts termed "cyber-bullying," which to Danny's shock was fairly common. He then went to the Ketchogue Borough School's website and learned, much to his surprise, that there was something called a Bullying and Harassment Policy in effect. Based on his reading, it appeared that it could apply to this whole situation with Gianna. It seemed like he could get the school involved and maybe get them to investigate. It was a start at least.

Today his "plan" was that Gianna was staying home to tend to Agnes while he paid a friendly little visit to the Ketchogue Anti-Bullying Specialist, who apparently had an office at the school. In fact, his plan was set a few days ago, and he was headed there right after he finished cleaning the chair. Meanwhile, yet another missive had arrived last night from Hellcat, whoever that was, making Danny's plan all the more urgent.

Danny explained all this to Henry, who promptly ripped his windbreaker off the top of the La-Z-Boy.

"I'm going with you," he shot at Danny.

"Henry, it's not necessary," Danny retorted.

"Fuck that, I'm going with you," Henry said again. "Let's go."

DANNY AND HENRY pulled into the parking lot of the Ketchogue Borough School at just before noon. The school was a red brick building fronted with a half-moon blacktop driveway and a flagpole. Next to the flagpole, under the words "Ketchogue Borough School," a bulletin board notified of a "St. Patrick's Day Dance, Friday, March 17," and Henry and Danny stormed past it, headed for the front entrance of the building.

After being buzzed in through the school's front doors and signing in on a sheet of paper at a desk just past the electronic security station, Henry and Danny made a beeline into the first floor Main Administration Office. As soon as they entered a bell went off, triggering a change of periods. The classrooms promptly emptied, and hundreds of kids flooded the hallways with bulging backpacks strapped across their shoulders, talking and walking and laughing and marching toward their next scholastic session. Danny could see all this through the windows of the Administration Office as he and Henry approached a counter, behind which were three desks in a room filled with metal file cabinets. To the left were a set of windows that overlooked the front half-moon driveway, and to the right another set of windows overlooked the hallway where the kids were rolling by in waves.

As the two approached the counter, an elderly woman with plump cheeks and a red sweater tied over her shoulders, with a bun of grey hair and dark reading glasses hanging over her neck, stepped from behind a desk and greeted them, asking if she could help.

"Thanks, I hope so," Danny said, his hands on the countertop, "my name is Dan Beers, my daughter Gianna is a 6th grader here."

"Yes, of course, Gianna Beers," the woman repeated softly with a smile, indicating her familiarity, "a lovely girl."

"Thanks very much. I appreciate that."

"My name is Mrs. Finnerty," she said, "I knew your wife Debra, she was one of our more involved parents, we all loved her here."

"Thanks," Danny said again, "that's very nice of you."

Mrs. Finnerty then noticed Danny's face and neck.

"My goodness, did you get too much sun?"

"No, it's just a little rash," Danny answered.

"Right, well. How can I help you Mr. Beers?"

Danny had never met this woman before, but her warm greeting was comforting and helped Danny relax. He thought perhaps her tone would also set Henry at ease, in which case there was a chance they would get something accomplished here today.

Danny gestured over to Henry. "This is Gianna's grandfather, my father-in-law Henry Mahoney."

Henry leaned down to shake the woman's hand, but his ever-present glare and lowered eyebrows straightened her up a bit.

"Well, well," Mrs. Finnerty said somewhat uncomfortably, taking Henry's giant paw, "I see where Gianna gets her height."

Henry released her hand in silence, nodding back with a stern expression. Danny could see Henry was in no mood for pleasantries, so he got right to the point.

"Mrs. Finnerty, I understand a Mr. Nicholls works here?"

"Yes, Mr. Preston Nicholls is our Bullying Specialist."

"We'd like to see him if we can. Hopefully he's in today."

Mrs. Finnerty's face registered a look of surprise.

"Oh, my. Is there a problem Mr. Beers?"

"Well, there could be, yes. But we're hoping it's nothing and that maybe he can help us. Is he in?"

Mrs. Finnerty paused to don her reading glasses, balancing them at the tip of her nose. The silver chain dangled in loops near both her ears. She dutifully pulled a clipboard from a shelf that sat underneath the counter and ran her index finger along the page attached to it. She had the clipboard raised so that Danny and Henry could not see the sheet. When she got to the bottom she looked up at Danny.

"Mr. Beers, do you have an appointment today?"

"I do not, but I hope that's not a problem – "

Before he could finish, Henry stepped abruptly to the counter, brushing against Danny's right shoulder and bumping him slightly to the side. The countertop landed somewhere near the top of Henry's thighs, and the sheer size of the man caused Mrs. Finnerty to take a step backwards, if for no other reason than to get a better angle as she looked up at him.

She pulled off her reading glasses as Henry spoke.

"Look, Mrs. Finnerty," he said testily, "is he back there? Maybe you can tell him we just need five minutes of his time."

Sensing Henry's agitation, Danny placed his right arm in front of Henry's abdomen.

"Henry, please," he said, but Henry was having none of it.

"Dan, excuse me," he said curtly, looking down at Mrs. Finnerty again.

"If you could, tell him we're here please," Henry directed.

Mrs. Finnerty placed the clipboard onto the countertop.

"Mr. Mahoney, I'm sorry, but Mr. Nicholls usually sees people by appointment – "

"Excuse me, ma'am," Henry interrupted, his patience growing thin. "This guy Nicholls is here to assist parents I assume, and Dan here is Gianna's father. I'm the grandfather. We're taxpayers. My daughter volunteered her time here as a parent. There's an issue we'd like to discuss with him, it's important. So if you could, tell him we're here and that we'll only take a few minutes out of his precious schedule. I appreciate it."

The tension in the room was thick, and Danny blew out a breath. Once again Henry had managed to make what could have been a polite meeting denigrate into an unnecessary confrontation. Sensing Danny's discomfort, Mrs. Finnerty, whose demeanor had now taken on an official status, apparently got the message that Henry wasn't taking no for an answer, and so she reluctantly slid the clipboard underneath the counter and gestured toward a row of hard plastic chairs on the wall behind Danny and Henry.

"Gentlemen," she said in a monotone, "have a seat, I'll see if he has time for you today."

ABOUT TWENTY MINUTES later, Mrs. Finnerty reappeared from a doorway at the far end of the Administration Office. Danny couldn't imagine where she had been all that time, but Henry's warm and fuzzy greeting certainly could not have helped things. It seemed to Danny that she was letting them stew there a while in order to send a message, and Danny could see that it was driving Henry up a wall. With Henry pacing back and forth in front of him now, looking intermittently at his watch, Danny's angst over this meeting was doing nothing but getting worse.

As she re-entered the room, Mrs. Finnerty walked directly to her desk and sat, instead of coming to the counter. Then, without looking at them, she said, loud enough for them to hear, "Mr. Nicholls will see you now – down the hall, third door on the right."

Without another word she turned to her computer screen.

Henry then bolted from the Administration Office and marched purposefully down the hallway with Danny a pace behind. The hallway was a bright corridor with a brown tile floor and shining cinder block walls painted with a yellow hi-gloss. The walls were filled with rows upon rows of colored drawings of tigers, lions, giraffes and other animals, all on white paper sheets and held there with masking tape. Along the top of the walls near the ceiling, on both sides, there were shiny four-leaf clovers connected by long strings of yarn.

In a minute Danny and Henry were standing at the closed door to an office that had a window facing the hallway. The blinds were drawn, apparently to block any view of the interior of the office. Beside the door, about halfway up the wall, a small black rectangular plaque had the words "P. NICHOLLS" slid into a small mounted metal holder.

Henry wrapped on the door with his giant fist, and after a few seconds a weak male voice behind the door told them to come in.

 Danny entered first. He came upon an enormously rotund man in an inflated blue plaid shirt and maroon tie, with giant bubbles of fat attempting to leak out of every available escape route that the man's wardrobe allowed. He wore a goatee sprinkled silver and had a headful of wiry grey hair, with thick unruly sideburns that appeared as though no one had paid any attention to them in years. He was stuffed in behind a desk that was cluttered with documents, newspapers and smeared food wrappers, with roughly six or seven empty Pepsi cans laying haphazardly on top. The desk was jammed up against the wall to the right, with Nicholls's stomach roll spilling onto and under the desktop. The front of the desk was facing the back wall, such that Nicholls's ample back was facing the hallway and the window above him, his view toward the rear of the office. Danny thought it was a strange way to arrange the furniture – it seemed like the place was set up exactly backwards.

Currently there was no light in the room other than what was being directed toward the middle of Nicholls's desktop from a small banker's light with a metal string hanging from it. There was also the ambient light radiating off of Nicholls's computer, which Danny noticed hadn't been touched in a while, because there was a screensaver of a frog on a lily pad, with moisture droplets all over it, rotating back and forth on the screen.

Danny and Henry moved to the back of the room and turned and faced the desk. Nicholls flicked a switch on a wall and the room lit up a bit. Without looking at them, Nicholls pointed to the visitors' chairs.

"Gentlemen, have a seat," he said flatly, placing a James Patterson paperback face down onto the debris scattered across his desk. The first thing that Danny noticed when he sat was the pungent stench of unwashed feet, which Danny knew was coming from Nicholls, because he could see a pair of unattended docksider loafers sitting under Nicholls's desk.

Without a word, Nicholls pulled open a drawer and took out a plastic bag of Dorito's corn chips, which he promptly ripped open. He began to pop Dorito chunks into his cavernous mouth.

"What can I do for you?" he said without emotion.

Danny took a seat, but Henry stood. After Danny made introductions, he launched into an explanation of why they were there. He reported that his daughter currently was the victim of some cyber-bullying, and he took Nicholls through the whole series of events, from the lawsuit, to the incident in the Brewers' foyer, to the tweets coming from Hellcat, with their threats and attempts at harassment and intimidation, all directed at Gianna and using her name with a hashtag. He explained the emotional damage it was inflicting on his daughter, and how it was affecting her schoolwork and her friendships and social life. He concluded by telling Nicholls that if there was anything that could be done, if there was any way to find out who was doing this, he and his family would be grateful.

Nicholls listened to all of this in silence, without expression. Danny noticed that the man was not even looking at him when he spoke. Instead, his stare seemed to be fixed on the back wall. All the while, he kept picking Dorito chips out of the bag and stuffing them into his mouth.

When Danny finished, Nicholls crumpled up the Dorito's bag and dropped it onto his desktop. He then held a single finger in the air and promptly reached into a desk drawer, pulling out a thin black binder. He dropped it onto a mess of papers, pushing aside a few soda cans, and then with his orange-crusted fingers he began turning pages. When he found his spot, he addressed Danny with his head down.

"The Board of Education prohibits acts of harassment, intimidation, or bullying of a pupil," he read in a perfunctory monotone. "A safe scholastic environment is necessary for students to learn and meet our high academic standards. Harassment, intimidation and bullying has no place in an academic environment, and all administrators, teachers, faculty and staff must take all appropriate measures to bring an end to all disruptive or violent behaviors within their school community to ensure that all students treat each other with decency, civility and respect."

"I understand, thanks," Danny said. "That's why we're here."

Nicholls turned a page, just before he popped an index finger into his mouth, licking off the residue of the Dorito chips. When he was done, he wiped the finger on the side of his pants, and then he began reading again, once more without looking up at either Danny or Henry.

"Are either of you the natural, foster or adoptive parent, legal guardian, or surrogate of the pupil?" he droned on, "and if the parents are divorced, do you have legal custody, and if so, have your parental rights with respect to the pupil ever been terminated by a court with appropriate subject matter jurisdiction?"

Danny looked over at Henry, whose face was getting red. His arms were crossed, staring down at Nicholls. Danny knew what that look meant, and he turned to Nicholls, trying to get his attention.

"Mr. Nicholls, we just went over that," he said, "I'm Gianna's father and Mr. Mahoney here is her grandfather."

Nicholls turned another page. He pointed his fat orange-stained finger at the page again.

"Were the referenced electronic communications that allegedly formed the basis for the report of bullying and/or harassment and/or intimidation reasonably perceived by the pupil to be motivated by any trait inherent in the pupil, such as race, gender, color, religion, natural origin, sexual orientation, gender identity, or a mental or psychological condition?"

As Nicholls read the question, his voice inflection never changed. It was flat and without emotion, and Danny slid to the front of his seat, alternately looking at both Nicholls and Henry.

"No," he answered sharply, "I just told you what happened. I think it has to do with the lawsuit we filed, but what difference does that make?"

Danny and Henry looked at one another again. Henry's hands were now dropped to his side, his back tensing up. He took a step closer to the desk and was now directly alongside Danny's chair.

Nicholls turned another page.

"If the alleged bullying and/or intimidation and/or harassment takes place off school property," he read, "does the pupil reasonably believe the offending acts would place the pupil in reasonable fear of physical and/or psychological and/or emotional harm such that the acts or alleged acts will affect the pupil's scholastic and/or academic performance?"

"Uh, yes," Danny answered forcefully. "I just told you that."

Danny rose to his feet. He sensed, correctly, that if he didn't get this man's attention quickly, Henry was going to intervene, and if that happened, they would have a problem. He leaned over Nicholl's desk and tried to angle himself between Nicholls and Henry, placing himself directly in the man's line of vision.

"Look, maybe you can put the binder away so we can just talk."

But Nicholls ignored him. He turned another page.

"Does the pupil – "

"Her name is Gianna," Danny interrupted, looking back at Henry. "Stop calling her *the pupil.*"

But Nicholls ignored him again.

"Does the pupil have reason to know the identity of the alleged aggressors, such that an administrative entity can apply necessary remedial measures to the alleged offense and/or offenses?"

"No, we went *over* that," Danny said, getting more impatient. "We don't know who is doing this, that's why we need your help."

And then suddenly Nicholls folded his hands in front of him, as if he were praying. He looked up from the binder, blowing out a sigh. But his face was still angled toward the back wall, and he made no eye contact with either Danny or Henry. He wore an expression that suggested frustration, impatience, as if Danny's mere presence was an annoyance.

"Well, what do you want *us* to do?"

"Excuse me?!" Danny responded.

"If *you* don't know who is doing this, sir, how are *we* supposed to know?"

Danny shook his head and looked up at Henry.

"What?! Don't you conduct an investigation?!"

"I'll ask again – what exactly are *we* supposed to do about it?"

"Look into it! Ask questions, speak to the kids!"

Danny couldn't believe the obstinance of the man, and he was all set to lay into him. But before he could Henry stepped abruptly to his left, nudging Danny toward the wall. His eyes were lasered in on Nicholls.

"We're not the FBI," Nicholls went on. "We don't have infinite resources to run down every rabbit hole, especially if *you* can't even tell *us* if this is a school-related incident."

"Are you kidding me?! Don't you HAVE to get involved, after what I just told you?!"

Nicholls licked his index finger again and turned another page. "Does the pupil – "

"Hey!" Danny then yelled, rising to his feet, "STOP THAT!"

"Does the pupil – "

"Mr. Nicholls! Look at me!"

"Does the pupil – "

"I'm telling you right now – "

And then, in that moment, Henry slapped his giant left hand down onto Danny's right shoulder and shoved him aside. In the same motion, he gripped the top of Danny's chair and violently threw it backwards with one sweep of his massive arm. He stepped against the desk, such that the desktop was roughly at his knees.

He thrusted an index finger right at Nicholls's nose.

"YOU FAT FUCK!" he screamed, leaning down over Nicholls, "PUT THAT BINDER AWAY!"

Nicholls, startled, looked up at Henry, his eyeballs wide. For the first time Danny saw something on his face that resembled emotion – which very clearly was fear. The man seemed shocked at Henry's outburst, and he leaned back in his chair, almost as of the wind from Henry's breath had blown his massive frame backwards.

Nicholls hastily grabbed a pair of eyeglasses that were lost somewhere in the mess in front of him, placing them on his face. He stared up at Henry with a look of utter shock.

Henry's face, meanwhile, was now as red as a beet. Both his fists were clenched. Danny panicked, and he grabbed Henry's arm.

"Henry!" he yelled, but Henry yanked it free.

"YOU HEAR ME!" Henry blasted again, "PUT THAT FUCKING THING AWAY!"

"Hey, you can't speak to me like that!"

Nicholls's face turned white as he tried to wiggle out of the seat, but the manner in which he had wedged his gigantic torso in between the desk and the window was making that impossible, especially since Henry was pressed up against the desk, forcing it further into Nicholls's gigantic belly.

"Henry!" Danny pleaded again, "calm down!"

"ARE YOU GONNA HELP US OR NOT?" Henry shrieked.

"No, I'm not!" Nicholls yelled. "I will not help the pupil – "

And with that, Henry violently swiped his giant left arm in a ferocious backhand, which knocked Nicholls's binder, along with a pile of papers, soda cans and other debris, flying across the room. The mess sprayed against the wall to the left side of the office.

"CALL HER THE PUPIL ONE MORE TIME!"

Wedged in now and with nowhere to go, Nicholls frantically tried to push the desk backwards to extricate himself from between the desk and window. But Henry only pressed harder against his side of it. Nicholls had no chance of escaping, and his eyes widened with fear. Danny grabbed onto Henry's left arm with both hands.

"HENRY!" he yelled, but Henry easily shook himself loose.

"I'm calling security!" Nicholls yelled, and he reached to his right for his phone. But before he got his hands on it, Henry grabbed it and ripped it off the desk. He threw it hard to the floor behind him, and with both fists he grabbed Nicholls by the front of his blue flannel shirt.

"YOU SONOFABITCH!" he screamed, just as a bell went off, piercing the room and the hallway beyond it.

With both of Henry's vise-like hands full of flannel shirt, just under Nicholls's chin, Nicholls managed to reach to his right. He grabbed the string to the blinds on the window behind him. He yanked it down, and the blinds zipped up to the top of the window casing. Danny saw a hallway filled with students rolling by in both directions, with their backpacks and books and binders. Seeing this, he grabbed tighter onto Henry's right arm.

"Henry, stop it!" he yelled, but there was no way he could break him free. Henry had Nicholls by the shirt and was shaking him, snapping the man's head frontwards and backwards, banging it up against the glass.

"HELP ME!" Nicholls screamed, "SOMEBODY HELP ME!"

Danny looked through the window, which he thought was about to shatter, and saw well over two dozen school kids, out in the hallway, holding smartphones upright in their hands. Their eyes were as wide as saucers, and they were screaming and pointing into Nicholls's office. Each phone had a small glowing light on the back of it, capturing the image of this giant man with fistfuls of Mr. Nicholls's flannel shirt, smashing his head against the window.

Just then Henry raised his right hand in the air and balled it up into a fist. His left hand was still underneath Nicholls's chin, with about a foot of shirt fabric clenched in it.

As Henry lined up his fist, Danny launched himself between Henry and Nicholls, just as Henry's right fist drove down toward Nicholls's face. The punch landed directly into the back of Danny's neck. A second later three security officers came flying into the office. As Danny rolled off Nicholls, with his back directly over the desktop, the officers wrestled Henry to the ground, landing against the back wall of the office with a thunderous crash.

CHAPTER 26

TWISTING HIM INTO A PRETZEL

T HE NIGHT AFTER the chair-hurling incident, Tuesday, O'Reilly received an email on his iPhone from a woman at FT&B by the name of Bridget Fitzpatrick-Goldberg. He had never heard of her, but he could see, right there at the bottom of her signature block, that she was Assistant Executive Director of the firm. Her instructions, copied to several attorneys, including Burgess and Yang Hsue Ko, were clear – O'Reilly was not to report to Secaucus the next day. Instead, they were summoning him to a meeting in New York, to commence at 11:00 am sharp. He was told to report on time.

When O'Reilly heard the ping on his cellphone that night, indicating the arrival of Fitzpatrick-Goldberg's email, he was lying on his futon in his Park Slope studio, his eyes shut, pressing a cold can of Miller Lite against his forehead. The room was dark, but his 60-inch Samsung smart TV was blaring away – some reality show about a bunch of over-sexed couples locked in a beach house. Ordinarily O'Reilly would be glued, but right now he wasn't paying any attention. He read the email, tossed the phone back down onto his coffee table, and laid his head on the futon again. The beer went right back up against his forehead.

That morning, O'Reilly had attended his three classes over at MLS and dutifully scribbled his notes, but his head was nowhere near the classrooms. All he could think about was that chair from the day before. And why he had thrown it against the wall, screaming at Burgess. How could he have lost his temper like that? For the second time in under a year O'Reilly had committed an act that he was sure was going to get him fired. This time it seemed a certainty. And this was a problem. The job recruiting period was over, this being March, and graduation was only a few months away. Any big firms hiring first year lawyers for September had already made job offers the previous August, so their first-year classes were full. If this gig at FT&B fell through, he'd have no chance anywhere else. None. And man did he have loans to pay. Holy crap did he need a job. Unless he could talk his way out of this one, he was *screwed*. It hurt his head just thinking about it.

The next morning O'Reilly rolled out of the rack early, and the first thing he did after his shower was drag a razor across his cheeks and chin. His sink filled up with chunks of orange fur, which had been percolating on his face for nearly three months now. He next got dressed in office-appropriate attire and hastened over to Dick's Barber Shop on Seventh Avenue. It was an old-fashioned barbershop with the spinning pole out front, and O'Reilly climbed into the chair and told the man to make it short. They wrapped a blue sheet around his neck and started buzzing and snipping away. In about fifteen minutes he walked out into a breezy March morning with a fresh haircut that would make the Marines Corps proud. He headed to Grand Army Plaza and boarded the number 2 train into midtown Manhattan.

At roughly 10:45 am, O'Reilly entered the lobby of FT&B Tower on Park Avenue and swiped his way through the electronic security gates. In a few moments he was sitting up at the 44th Floor reception area reading the *New York Law Journal*, smiling back at a blond-haired receptionist parked behind a black marble reception desk, upon which sat a humongous bouquet of pink tulips. The room was softly lit and eerily quiet, like a funeral parlor. O'Reilly was fidgety, nervous, anxious, jumpy – whatever word you wanted to use – and his heart was racing even more than it should have, owing in part to a Starbucks vente Sumatra that he should not have had on an empty stomach before arriving here. The bitter liquid was now mixing with his anxiety-induced acid reflux, making it feel like he had swallowed lava. Half a dozen times he got up, tossed the newspaper down onto the little rectangular coffee table that was stationed between the two facing corporate-looking sofas, and paced in a circle with his arms crossed. Then he would sit back down and read the *Journal* for another minute before getting back up to pace around the sofas again.

The thing was, unlike during the summer, and quite apart from the other New York-based Summer Associates doing part-time work, O'Reilly no longer had an office here, so there was nowhere to put him while he awaited this meeting. He had a seat next to a steam pipe out in the swamps of New Jersey, and nothing more. So there he was, pacing back and forth in the lobby like some visitor at his own law firm. It was yet another indignity, another little screw-you to remind him what his status was in this place. Maybe this will all get better when he returned officially as a lawyer in September, O'Reilly silently hoped. Perhaps then they would treat him with a little more respect. Unless, of course, he was getting shit-canned today, in which case all bets were off. That was a distinct possibility.

The receptionist then motioned to him as O'Reilly was taking another trip around the sofas. Her face was lit up by the glow of the computer flatscreen in front of her, the brightest light in this room.

"Would you like water or coffee or anything?" she asked.

She spoke slightly above a whisper, like some announcer on the Golf Channel. O'Reilly looked over and for the first time noticed how attractive she was. She was probably mid-thirties with bright green eyes and a gleaming set of pearly white choppers, probably the beneficiary of an expensive dental bleach, O'Reilly figured. Under different circumstances, O'Reilly knew he'd be right over there making small talk and flirting, but right now he was in no mood. Even the smallest things were irritating him. She was wearing a telephone headset, a high-tech looking black metallic number, with one of those microphones that came from the area of her left ear and landed in front of her mouth. Even that was ticking him off. What, he thought, is she guiding in a 747 for a runway landing, for Christ's sake? Why is she wired up like a goddamned air traffic controller? Why –

"Nah, I'm good, thanks," he said finally, telling himself to relax.

"No problem," she smiled back.

O'Reilly began rubbing his stomach, trying to soothe that lava ball burning a hole down there. He looked at his phone – 11:18 am.

"Excuse me," he said, "did they say 11 am?"

He was pointing at his wrist, even though he wore no watch.

"Uh, I'm not sure. Would you like me to call someone?"

"No, that's okay. I was just wondering."

"No problem," she smiled again.

A few minutes later, after some more pacing around the sofas, the telephone in front of the receptionist suddenly chirped with a series of electronic beeps. She poked a button and webbed her fingers together.

"44th Floor," she said softly, hands-free, "how can I help you?" She then looked over at O'Reilly.

"Yes, he's right here," she said, giving O'Reilly a thumbs-up. And then, "yes, of course."

She clicked a button again and twisted the mouthpiece down.

"You know where Mr. Briggs's office is?" she asked.

"Uh, yeah, sure," said O'Reilly.

"Go right ahead," she said, nodding down the hall.

BRIGGS'S OFFICE WAS shaped like a trapezoid and was one of four corner offices just like it up there on the forty-fourth floor, the highest level of offices below the conference rooms, which were up on 45. At FT&B Tower, all the lawyer offices were external with exterior-facing windows, and the four corner offices on each floor had that trapezoidal shape, fanning out wide against the windows. Briggs's office was also on the desirable southwest side, with panoramic views of downtown Manhattan. At that height you could clearly see the Empire State Building and, way in the distance, the Freedom Tower and New York harbor.

When O'Reilly arrived, he saw that the office was fronted with two thick mahogany double-doors that swung open barndoor-style, and given that they were spread open now, O'Reilly had nothing to knock on when he appeared at the opening. It was the first time he had ever been in this office, and he gazed around a moment before anyone noticed his presence. The office looked more like a living room than a lawyer's workspace, at least to O'Reilly. The walls on the left and right sides of the office were adorned with burnt umber wainscoting that ran up about four feet, and above that there was paisley wallpaper dotted with a line of thickly framed pastoral paintings of soldiers sitting on horses in open fields. The floor was a soft brown hardwood and in the middle of the room, right in front of O'Reilly, there was a mustard-colored patterned area rug that had to be twenty feet wide. To the left, against the wall and facing the center of the room was a great big cherrywood desk the size of a small boat, with two brown chairs with maroon leather seat cushions in front of it. There was an old-fashioned banker's light and a desk blotter on the desktop, but nothing else, not even a computer, O'Reilly noticed. To the left of and slightly behind the desk, in the far corner, stood a large black marble bust of Abraham Lincoln, perched high on a cherrywood end table, making it appear that our sixteenth president had been charged with the task of keeping an eye out for anyone entering the room.

Once at the double-doors, O'Reilly looked to his right and saw Briggs sitting on a chestnut leather sofa, which was situated in front of a floor-to-ceiling bookshelf filled with bound hardcover legal reporters. He was sipping from a coffee cup, balancing it on a saucer he held in the palm of his left hand. In front of him there was an antique-looking coffee table, upon which sat a bowl filled with apples and pears, and on the other side of it there was an identical sofa that currently housed Yang Hsue Ko and Dexter Morgan, who O'Reilly knew was on the Personnel Committee. O'Reilly gulped, thinking that a representative present from that body was not a good omen, to say the least. Right now the entire room was lit up by the sunshine pouring in from the massive windows on the far wall of the office, and the three men were chatting comfortably, each with a right leg hooked over their left knee, leaning back into the sofa cushions. It was Briggs who first noticed O'Reilly, and as soon as he did, he placed his coffee cup and saucer onto the coffee table and rose to greet his guest.

"Ahh, Seamus!" he said enthusiastically. "Welcome there young falla! Come on in."

Ko and Morgan also stood, and O'Reilly cautiously entered the room. He shook their hands and Briggs then offered him a seat on the sofa across from him. Morgan and Ko took their seats and crossed their legs again, as did Briggs, but O'Reilly sat on the edge of the seat cushion, his elbows resting on his knees.

The first thing that struck O'Reilly as he entered was that Briggs had addressed him as Seamus – not Sea-Mouse. Progress, he thought. O'Reilly had been prepared for a confrontation on that score and was relieved when Briggs greeted him with the appropriate moniker. Maybe someone had finally corrected him, perhaps Ko or Morgan. Of course, the other possibility was that Briggs had been mangling his name intentionally all that time, but

O'Reilly didn't want to believe that was true. Anyway, the man now had it right – this was a good start.

Once they were settled, Briggs spoke up.

"Well, Seamus," he said, "I suppose yew be wantin' to know why we brought yew in here today. Am I supposin' correctly?"

"Yes sir," O'Reilly answered. He was sitting on the sofa next to Ko. The living room feel to this meeting, with all of them sitting on sofas with a coffee table between them, made O'Reilly feel awkward and out of place.

"Yew want sump'n to drink?" Briggs asked, in a tone that O'Reilly thought suggested a police detective about to question a perp under a set of hot lamps. "Coffee, water or anythin'?"

"No sir, but thanks."

Briggs then dug in.

"Well then, Seamus," he said, "lemme get right to the point. I unnerstand yew were involved in an incident out there in Secaucus. Lost your temper, I'm tol', and mebbe threw some furniture, did some hollerin' at your bosses. That true?"

O'Reilly was too mentally exhausted to be nervous or intimidated, and he certainly wasn't going to defend his own actions. What he wanted was to get to the Interim Report and the reasons why they seemed to have buried it. If that meant he had to cop to throwing a chair or two, he was fine with it.

"Uh, yes sir, it is true," he said, in a somewhat defiant tone.

"And yew think that's proper behavior, Seamus?"

Briggs had his coffee cup and saucer back in his hands now. He was sitting at the edge of the sofa, like O'Reilly, while Ko and Morgan were leaning back with their legs crossed. O'Reilly noticed that Morgan had a legal pad on his lap, taking notes.

"No, sir, I certainly don't," O'Reilly said. "But I was upset about something I thought wasn't right. Something that happened with one of the documents I found."

"Well, let's put the documents aside a moment, Seamus," Briggs said flatly, very much in control. "What 'xactly am I supposed to tell the folks out in Secaucus 'bout you continuin' to work out there? Yew tell me."

"I understand, sir."

"Yew see the position yew put me in? Put all us in?"

Briggs waved a hand to Morgan and Ko.

"I do sir, I get it," O'Reilly answered.

"You unnerstand we can't run a shop under such circumstances, am I right, Seamus?"

"I understand, sir, but I'd like to talk about the document I mentioned, if that's okay."

"Well, what about it?" Briggs asked.

"Well, I think it should have been produced."

"Oh, yew do, do ya?" Briggs countered, his eyebrows rising. He started laughing, and right on cue Ko and Morgan joined in.

"Well that's very innerestin'," he said. "Did yew follow protocol, and mention that to Burgess, your boss?"

"I did, yes."

"And so when yew didn't get the answer yew wanted," Briggs asked rhetorically, waving a hand again, "yew decided to hurl a chair against the wall? Do I have that correct?"

"Sir, I understand – "

"Yew take ma point?"

"I do sir, and I apologize, but – "

"Which brings me back to ma question, Seamus. What 'xactly am I supposed to tell the folks out in Secaucus? 'Bout yew workin' out there?"

A silence then gripped the room as O'Reilly cast a furtive glance down at his wingtips. Briggs's point was a good one, of course. O'Reilly was kicking himself for the way he addressed the whole issue, had been regretting it ever since. But this meeting here – it seemed designed to overlook the bigger picture. And that was something O'Reilly couldn't let happen. He had an opportunity to make his point, and no one at the warehouse – not Burgess, not Manny, not any of the other lawyers, and certainly not a single one of the dozens of document reviewers out there – cared one wit about whether a document got produced and what its impact might be. They were punching a clock and simply didn't give a shit.

O'Reilly looked past Briggs's head to the windows over Park Avenue, to the incredible Manhattan skyline, to the sunshine streaming in through the windows. Then his eyes drew back inside, to the Abraham Lincoln bust over in the corner, and to Briggs's mammoth desk. It was a wonder how he got here, working with

these people. It occurred to him that he'd come a long way since
the C. Barton Foster Conference Room back in August. Back then,
he would never have had the lemons to confront these three, would
never have had the nerve to question anything about the way they
conducted their business. But things had changed. He had changed.

He needed to get some answers.

He looked back at Briggs and stared directly into his eyes.

"Mr. Briggs," he said, breaking the silence, "I don't mean any
disrespect, I really don't. Whatever you tell them out there is fine
with me. And I do apologize for my conduct. But we ought to be
speaking about that document. As you probably know, I marked it
with a sensitivity of 6 and wrote up a detailed explanation of why it
was so important. Gunther appears to have conducted testing
showing that certain batches of their shrimp were mistreated with
sulfites, by mistake, at very dangerous levels. This explains the
spikes in the lawsuits the company has received. It also explains the
injuries, particularly in that Beers case. It also – "

"Hold up a minute there, Seamus," Briggs interrupted with a
smile, "let's all take a deep breath and relax."

It wasn't until Briggs's comment that Seamus realized how
agitated his voice was getting, rising as he went on his rant. He drew
in some air, as Briggs had suggested, and rubbed his palms across
his face. It felt good getting his point across and they actually
seemed to be listening, but at the same time his heart was now
beating mercilessly. The confrontation was triggering an adrenaline
surge that was making him start to sweat.

"Ko here gone explain some things, Seamus, for your benefit,"
Briggs continued. "As a teaching point, if yew will, 'bout document
productions. Things that – bein' a young falla – yew wouldn't be
expected to know."

Briggs then turned to his junior law partner, who had shifted to
the front of the sofa.

"Ko?"

"Yes, thank you Mr. Briggs," Ko said, jumping right in.

Ko was sitting next to O'Reilly, and he turned to him.

"Seamus, look," he said, "the bottom line is that there are
several reasons why we have no obligation to disclose that
document under the New York discovery rules. At the outset, you

have to understand the difference between responsiveness and relevance. *Responsiveness* and *relevance*, okay? That's a key distinction when you're doing a production, particularly when you are managing a massive amount of material, as we are. Under the rules, we only have a responsibility to turn over what the other side has asked for. In other words, what's *responsive* to their requests. That's the first cut you make. After that, you determine whether what they have asked for is relevant. But the first cut is responsiveness. Do you understand?"

"I do, but – "

"It's not our responsibility to do the other side's work for them," Ko said. "So we don't run around trying to collect and produce materials that no one has asked us to produce. That's number one."

"'Dat's right," Briggs offered.

"But Mr. Ko – "

"Hold it," Ko interrupted, "let me finish."

He was leaning forward with his elbows on his knees now, looking directly at O'Reilly. Morgan was scribbling notes, Briggs sipping his coffee.

"Here, the Beers's lawyer didn't ask for drafts," Ko then stated, "you can clearly see that for yourself in their document requests. And the document you are referring to is unquestionably a draft. It is marked as an interim report, and the document makes clear that the company intended a final. Therefore, that report is not a final document, it's a draft, and so it's not *responsive* to their requests."

"Correct again," Briggs said.

"OK, but – "

"The report you mentioned was also a single page document?"

"Yes, it was, but – "

"Okay, and it cut off at the end of the first page?"

"Yes."

"Do you know what it says on page two, or three, or four?"

"No, uh, no," answered O'Reilly.

"Of course you don't," Ko concluded, "and neither do I. Which means it's not a complete document. The Beers document requests did not ask for partial documents or incomplete documents. They could have asked for those, as well as drafts, but they didn't. So the document, again, is not *responsive*. Our obligation is to turn over complete documents, not partial documents, because that is what they asked for. Do you understand?"

"I understand but – "

"That is why when we provide written responses to any set of document requests, we always say the same thing – we will only produce relevant, non-privileged documents that are responsive to the requests. Which brings me to the next point, that the document is privileged."

"There were two documents," O'Reilly interjected, "the cover memo and the report."

"And both are protected by the attorney-client privilege," Ko shot back with authority. "The memo makes clear that the research was done for litigation purposes, at the direction of and at the request of lawyers. So, it's attorney work product."

"'Xactly right," said Briggs.

"But Mr. Ko," O'Reilly cut in, finally able to ask a question. "Why was the sensitivity of the document changed to a zero? I had given it 6."

Ko waved him off.

"That's simply for administrative processing," he said. "Helps us keep track of the documents that get produced. No document gets a 6 that's a draft and will never be turned over."

"But what about the other cases?" O'Reilly then countered, "isn't LawDocs for *all* the cases? Haven't even *one* of the other plaintiffs' lawyers in the dozens of other cases asked for drafts or made claims about possible manufacturing defects? And what if they do?"

Ko didn't respond, and instead he simply crossed his arms. He leaned back into the sofa with his eyes fixed on O'Reilly. Briggs placed his cup and saucer down onto the table in front of him, while Morgan, who seemed to be there to serve as a stenographer, as far as O'Reilly could see, was still busy scribbling notes.

O'Reilly then turned away from Ko and looked again at Briggs.

"Mr. Briggs, this makes no sense," he pressed, with urgency in his voice. "We said in that Beers action that the girl had no case because there was no way anyone could know she was allergic. We said that not even the father knew, and if so, how could *we* know?"

"That's right," Briggs answered, "how could we?"

"But why does that matter?" O'Reilly asked, incredulously. "It's possible our over-use of these sulfites was the cause of her injuries. How can we not disclose that?"

"Voluntarily?" scoffed Ko, with some sarcasm. "Even assuming that report is accurate as an interim study, which I do not grant you, the Beers family made no allegations about sulfites. So the document is not relevant to their claims, but you want us to volunteer that information?"

O'Reilly shook his head and pressed his index fingers to his temples. His head was spinning in circles and his frustration level was off the charts. He looked back at Ko.

"Mr. Ko," he said, as calmly as he could, "that interim report stated that multiple batches of the product were accidentally treated with dangerously high levels of those sulfites. Under the law, that's a manufacturing defect. Didn't you tell the court at oral argument that there were no allegations that the shrimp was defective or tainted in any way?"

"And there were no such allegations," said Ko.

"But how *could* there have been those allegations, if they don't have the interim report?"

"The interim report is a draft," Ko reported, "and an incomplete document. And privileged."

O'Reilly felt now like they were twisting him into a pretzel. The logic made no sense to him, and he was sensing this was intentional.

"Can you at least tell me – was there ever a final report?"

"We're not talking about any final report," Ko said back aggressively. "We're discussing the document you were called here to talk about. The one you threw a chair over."

Ko shifted in his seat and turned to Briggs. O'Reilly could see that Ko was getting angry, fed up, and was pretty much finished with O'Reilly.

"Look, Mr. Briggs," Ko said, "are we about done here?"

Briggs rose, and everyone stood on cue, including O'Reilly. Ko pulled out his iPhone and began thumbing out some messages, as Morgan, who hadn't said a word, tucked his legal pad under his right arm. All of this was an indication, at least to O'Reilly, that this meeting was over. O'Reilly had made his points but was even more frustrated than before he entered.

"Gentlemen," Briggs said to the group, "is there anythin' else?"

"Well, yes, Mr. Briggs," Morgan responded, "I think we should all remind Mr. O'Reilly about his fiduciary obligations to our client and about the confidentiality agreement he signed upon the commencement of his employment. Given what he apparently said to Mr. Burgess about contacting the press, I think this certainly needs to be emphasized."

Morgan stared straight at O'Reilly when he said this. He wasn't the least bit hesitant about mentioning it in his presence. O'Reilly had all but forgotten about that comment, but he knew it was said in the heat of the battle. He would apologize and assure them he meant no such thing.

In the meantime, Briggs chimed in on the point.

"Ah, yes, thank yew Morgan," he said, "I'll certainly do that."

Briggs winked at both Ko and Morgan and put his giant paw on O'Reilly's shoulder.

"Gentlemen, leave us now, if yew would," he said, "and let me have a few more words with Mr. O'Rally here in private."

Briggs thanked them both for coming and the group then shifted from the sofas over to the threshold of the double-doors. Briggs shook their hands and both men retreated down the hallway.

A moment later Briggs turned to O'Reilly, such that his back was facing the interior of his office, with the sun shining on his shoulders, casting a shadow into the hallway. O'Reilly was facing him. He was standing slightly to the right of Briggs, and as Briggs crossed his arms to address his young law student, that's when O'Reilly saw them. Sitting right there on the floor.

The boxes.

Looking just past Briggs's left shoulder, O'Reilly had an angle across the spacious office and his eyes connected to a spot down on the floor at the foot of the Abraham Lincoln bust, which was just to the right of Briggs's desk. Way over in the far-left corner of the trapezoid.

Right then O'Reilly – quite by accident – happened to catch sight of three white document boxes sitting on top of one another, in the corner where the windows met the trapezoid-angled wall behind Briggs's office chair. They were situated in a manner that suggested that Briggs didn't want anyone to see them, stuffed behind the Lincoln end table. O'Reilly recognized them immediately, and his eyebrows shot up. He had been through hundreds upon hundreds of these boxes and was intimately familiar with them. He would recognize them from a mile away.

The boxes unquestionably were from Secaucus. From the warehouse – his warehouse. These were the Gunther document boxes that had consumed his life for the last seven months.

As Briggs was beginning to address him, O'Reilly stepped a few inches to the right to get a better angle, trying to be inconspicuous and still appear as if he were looking at Briggs. Through the legs of the end table that held our greatest President, O'Reilly could clearly see the markings on the bottom box, the one on the floor. These were thick black letters and numbers, which contrasted sharply with the bright whiteness of the boxes.

Right there, plain as day, O'Reilly saw the alpha-code GUNTH.001.015.0006. It was written on all three boxes. O'Reilly didn't need to look that code up, not at all. He didn't need to refer to his chart to know what that code meant. Because those numbers were burned into his memory, from the very day he stumbled across the Interim Toxicity Report. The boxes came from none other than Mr. Stewart J. Handler, General Counsel of the company.

O'Reilly's heart skipped a beat. Why were Handler's document boxes sitting in Briggs's office? Why weren't these boxes in New Jersey where they belonged, so that the contents of them could be logged into the LawDocs database? And more importantly, how'd they get here? Manny? Burgess?

"Well, Seamus, young falla," Briggs then said, snapping O'Reilly to attention. "I think we made our point today, and I 'preciate yew comin' in."

Briggs then instructed O'Reilly about his confidentiality obligations and questioned him about his comments regarding the press, and O'Reilly – barely paying attention – offered a perfunctory apology and explained it was just something he said in the heat of the moment and that he didn't mean it, not at all. He convinced Briggs there was nothing to it, and Briggs seemed to accept the comment. All the while O'Reilly had one eye on those boxes.

"Seamus," Briggs then said with a smile, "I'd like yew to take a few days off, take some time to unwind. We all appreciate the hard work yew been doin' out there for the National Shrimp Cocktail Defense Team, and I think yew've earned a little mini-vacation."

Briggs then told O'Reilly to head back out to Secaucus the following Monday. He told O'Reilly that the few days off would do him good, but at the same time they wouldn't tolerate any more temper tantrums. He needed to apologize to Burgess before he returned, if he hadn't already. O'Reilly agreed and offer his apologies to Briggs, promising never to do it again. Briggs waved him off and shook his hand, and in a few minutes O'Reilly was marching down Park Avenue, under the sunshine, on his way to the subway to head back home to Brooklyn.

It was a nice day, so O'Reilly walked all the way down Park Avenue to Grand Central Station. Once there, he swiped his way into the subway system and boarded the Shuttle over to Times Square. He then boarded the next No. 2 train heading downtown.

On the ride home, O'Reilly ran through that meeting over in his head. It was a strange thing, he thought, that three powerful men of their seniority and stature would give that much time to a lowly Summer Associate law student. It was odd they would go out of their way to explain – to him of all people – their supposed justifications for their failure to turn over the Interim Report to those plaintiffs' lawyers. Why him? Why did it matter what *he* thought? He was as low in the pecking order as a person can get, and yet here they were – three of them – trying to convince *him* about the New York discovery rules. It made no sense. It was also a shock, once again, that they simply didn't fire him.

With his head leaning back against the subway windows, the No. 2 train roaring down Seventh Avenue, O'Reilly mulled all of this over in his brain. The only reason to pull a low-level document reviewer on the National Shrimp Cocktail Defense Team into a meeting was because he, O'Reilly, had uncovered the report and made a stink about it, O'Reilly figured. And that got them worried. It made sense that they were very concerned about that document and the possibility of it getting out and made public, which made O'Reilly think that perhaps they never intended for it to be sent out to Secaucus in the first place. O'Reilly recalled that it stood out in the box like a sore thumb, and that no other documents relating to it were in the same box. He remembered thinking that it didn't seem to belong there, like it had been left there by mistake. But now that it was out, Briggs and Ko were obviously scared shitless about what he would say about it. This meant, O'Reilly figured, that they needed to keep him where they could watch him, keep him close. Maybe this was the primary reason for that bizarre meeting, and maybe in a strange way he had himself some job security no matter how many chairs he threw against the wall.

The number 2 train came to a stop at Chambers Street, and O'Reilly stayed in his seat as dozens of passengers jumped off for a transfer, followed by dozens more jumping back on just before the doors slammed shut. O'Reilly was leaning on his knees now, as two passengers jammed into the seats next to him. O'Reilly continued mulling, his head now spinning.

Whatever their reasons were for that meeting, O'Reilly thought, he certainly seemed to have caught their attention. Meanwhile, was there anything he could do about this document? Anyone he could speak to? And where were the rest of the pages of that Report? Was a final study or report ever done, and what were the results?

So many questions, so much uncertainty.

O'Reilly needed answers.

With the two neighboring passengers pressing into his hips, O'Reilly stood and grabbed a pole as the subway train cruised past Wall Street and into the tunnel on its way to Brooklyn. Where all of this ultimately would go, he had no idea. But regardless, O'Reilly was sure about one thing. He was convinced that the answers to all his questions lay in those boxes, up there on the floor in Briggs's office, under the watchful eyes of Abraham Lincoln. And O'Reilly was also glad he had made himself a copy of that Interim Report.

CHAPTER 27

A VISIT FROM RICHARD NIXON

To GIANNA AND Danny's humiliation, Henry's arrest took place right there in the parking lot of the Ketchogue Borough School. The lights and sirens of half a dozen police cars blared away while a sea of middle school kids looked on in horror. The sight of Henry in the back of the squad car, with his hands shackled behind his back, right in front of all those teachers and children, was more than Danny could even believe.

To make matters worse, Danny knew right then that Gianna's social media nightmare was nowhere close to over, a thought soon confirmed by dozens of YouTube videos, all capturing Henry's titanic blow into the back of Danny's neck. At last check, one of those videos – entitled "MIDDLE SCHOOL PARENTS GO WILD!!" – already had over 600,000 views.

Four days after the Henry debacle, Danny, Gianna and Agnes were at a McDonald's over on Route 25A, having lunch after one of Gianna's Saturday dance classes. They were sitting alone in a booth up against the front windows that gave a view of a Red Lobster just across the street. It was a brisk, sunny afternoon, and the three of them still had their winter coats on as the girls ate their Happy Meals. Danny sat in the booth across from Gianna, with Agnes out in the aisleway settled into her wheelchair.

Recently, Danny was getting Agnes out and about whenever he could. Over the last few months her condition had showed some improvement, although she still had a long way to go. She still could not walk unassisted, and so Danny had carried her into and out of the F350 that morning before wheeling her into the restaurant, as was the case whenever they decided on an outing. Her speech was sharpening a little, but she could still only mumble and whisper. Her motor skills also had some promise, although every meal was still a physical challenge for her. In fact, this day was no different. There was a pile of french fries spread out like matchsticks on the table because Agnes could not grip them between her forefinger and thumb. Gianna patiently was placing them back into the red McDonald's box without a word, and then coaching her on how to grab them back out. It was frustrating to watch sometimes, but Danny could see that Agnes's overall dexterity was improving, due in large part – Danny believed – to Gianna's patience and persistence with her little sister.

The three of them had been sitting there for roughly half an hour when the man in the olive trench coat walked in.

He had a short-cropped corporate-looking parted-on-the-side hairdo – jet-black – and wore a pair of dark-framed eyeglasses, giving him the look of a Dick Tracy clone. Nobody noticed him at first, but then Gianna did. But that was only because her focus happened to be angled directly toward the door from which the man had entered. The dining area was half full of customers, and Gianna noticed that upon entering the man stood there frozen, gazing around the room, just before his eyes landed and fixed directly on the three of them. Then he walked purposefully toward their table. When he approached, he confidently pulled a manila envelope from inside the chest area of his trench coat and dropped it on the table in front of Danny, without breaking stride.

"For you, Daniel Beers," was all he said, and then he circled around the room and walked out a side door to the right of the service counter.

Danny snatched up the envelope and turned it over for an inspection. He saw his name, in black capital letters – DANIEL X. BEERS – with no address and no information about the sender. It was sealed across the opening with a thick strip of clear tape.

Danny did not want to alarm the girls, but the drop-off caused his heart to skip. There simply was no way anyone could know they were in that McDonald's. He and the girls had never been there before and had planned the stop in the spur of the moment. That meant they had been followed – a thought that sent a chill down his spine. As far as the package was concerned, he assumed it had something to do with the lawsuit and was dreading what might be in there. He would need to share whatever it was with Ms. Anzalone, that was for sure.

Danny placed the envelope face down and smiled at the girls.

"What's that?" Gianna asked, poking a fry into a small ketchup cup. Danny dismissed the question.

"Nothing," he said, "I'll look at it when I get home."

"Who was that guy?" Gianna asked.

"Don't know," Danny shrugged.

Then to make light of the situation he asked, "but he looked a little like Richard Nixon, didn't he?"

"Who's Richard Nixon?" Gianna asked.

Danny smiled. "Never mind," he chuckled.

Later, at home, with Agnes settled in the living room in front of the TV, with Gianna brushing her hair, Danny sat at the kitchen table with a bottle of water and a box of oyster crackers. He hadn't eaten a thing at McDonalds, which was typical of his appetite these days. He twisted off the bottle cap and took a swig, eyeballing the envelope. He considered not even reading it and simply dropping it off to Ms. Anzalone, but of course there was always the possibility it didn't have anything to do with the lawsuit at all. So he ripped it open, tossing the envelope aside.

Inside was a stack of documents about a quarter-inch thick, and Danny placed them face up on the table. The first document in the stack was a legal document, with a caption that was similar in structure to the documents he had seen on multiple occasions in his own lawsuit. Except this one was not from his case – it was from a different matter entirely.

The document contained a header up at the top that read, "SUPREME COURT, STATE OF NEW YORK, SECOND JUDICIAL DEPARTMENT," and inside the caption, it read, "IN THE MATTER OF NICOLE I. ANZALONE, A SUSPENDED ATTORNEY."

The document was labeled "Decision and Order on Motion," and explained in clear terms, understandable even to a non-lawyer, that the court had suspended Ms. Anzalone – his lawyer – from the practice of law. The "motion" referenced in the document was one made within a proceeding brought by the "Grievance Committee" of the Second Judicial Department, and in the body of the order, it discussed how the motion had been granted, giving the attorney Anzalone a two-year suspension.

Danny read that Anzalone had lost her professional license for stealing client funds, and because of a significant drug dependency, for which she had been ordered to counseling.

The documents were dated several years earlier.

Danny flicked his thumb across the remainder of the documents, pausing on several of them to read the first few paragraphs. They all related to the same disciplinary action against his current attorney – the lawyer on whom his security, and that of his family, currently depended. One of the documents was a transcript of the very hearing in which Ms. Anzalone had been suspended, and Danny read this one intently. At that hearing, Ms. Anzalone had admitted to all the misdeeds cited in the various documents, including her theft of a check from a former client. Danny swallowed hard as he read Anzalone's admission that she had used the stolen funds to fuel her drug addiction. She had also announced to the court at the hearing that she was pregnant and had just been released from a drug treatment center.

When he was done reading, Danny shoved the documents to the middle of the kitchen table and leaned back in his chair. He webbed his fingers behind his neck and stared up at the ceiling. Then he crouched forward to catch a glimpse of the girls inside watching television. His daughter Agnes, now eleven years old, was plopped down in a wheelchair, struggling every day to make it through her daily existence, while Gianna was behind her, twisting her long wavy blond hair into a braid, intermittently kissing her little sister on her neck and cheeks.

Danny popped another cracker into his mouth. He faced the document pile in front of him, placing his hands on the tabletop, drawing in a slow, deliberate breath. For reasons he could not explain, and despite the turmoil that strangled his life these days, Danny felt a calm wash over him, warming his entire body as if he were sitting in front of an open fire.

He had no idea who that Richard Nixon character was or what group of lowlifes had hired him to follow his family into the McDonalds. He had no clue why these people – the lawyers and others associated with the Gunther Home Products Corporation, he assumed – would think they could gain some type of advantage by dropping those documents into his lap. Perhaps the plan was to turn him against his own lawyer, or maybe to force him to drop the case altogether. Maybe they were also the ones behind all the tweets to Gianna, and it wasn't a few nasty and misguided school kids after all. Who really knew.

And more importantly, what did it matter at this point?

Rather than driving a wedge between him and Ms. Anzalone, reading those documents gave Danny hope. Sitting at his kitchen table, Danny felt a resolve and a determination grow in him that he had never previously experienced. Before that day, Danny's hope and faith and trust in the process, and in the possibility of coming out of all of this with his family in one piece, had stemmed directly from his desperation, his frantic need to set things right. But today he did not feel that panic, that sense of hopelessness.

Whatever had happened to Nicole Anzalone back in the day must have been a horrible experience for her, and certainly one that she had inflicted on herself. Whatever choices she had made had set her on a path Danny was sure she had never anticipated. But she had accepted the consequences of her actions and had taken responsibility for her conduct – the transcript of those proceedings made that clear. Somehow, she had risen above it all and came out stronger. That was a person he wanted in his corner; this was a lady with whom he could go to battle.

As far as Gunther was concerned, Danny harbored no anger at all. What he felt was pity. He thought about all the work those people did to get to where they were – all the hours of schooling and studying and working themselves to the bone – only to find themselves denigrated to the pathetic task of authorizing a man in a trench coat to follow a working-class family into a shitty McDonalds so that they could achieve a potential minor advantage in a lawsuit. It was so shameful.

Danny lifted the pile and tapped it down onto the kitchen table to rearrange it in a neat stack. There was a junk drawer behind him under a counter, and Danny pulled it open and found a small binder clip. He secured the documents and placed them back down onto the table.

Danny knew what he had to do now; it was all clear to him. He knew the path he would take his family down, no matter what the outcome. Agnes would get better; he was sure of it. They would reemerge from this hellacious nightmare a stronger family, just like Anzalone had done. The tweets to Gianna, his financial troubles, the re-possessing of Debbie's Prius, that terrible Yahoo article, that anti-Semitic attack on Moshe Wagshul that everyone seemed to be blaming on him, his panic attacks, that horrible rash all over his body, Henry's arrest and the fallout from it, and everything else raining down on him and his girls – none of it mattered now.

Danny was going to get his family to other side. That moon would rise over Mangrove Bay. There was no question about it.

He stood and walked into the family room.

"Ladies," he said with a smile, "what're we watching?"

CHAPTER 28

KEEP THE FAITH

O N FRIDAY, ANZALONE sent Danny an email asking if he had time for a meeting first thing Monday morning. Danny got the email on his phone, and typed back, "sure thing, I'll be there." With Gianna's assistance he had become somewhat adept at email and texting and everything else technology-wise these days, so responding back to her was a breeze.

Danny arrived at Anzalone's office just before ten am, carrying a small leather briefcase he used for his business. He first hit the donut shop on the first floor and bought three extra-large café lattes, one each for him, his attorney and her assistant Cassie. When Danny entered the office, Cassie greeted him with a smile. Danny had his briefcase tucked under his left arm as he entered with the cardboard drink tray in his hands.

"Oh, you didn't have to do that, thank you!" Cassie said.

"It's no problem at all," Danny replied, handing her a beverage.

"She's just on a call," said Cassie. "she'll just be a minute."

"No worries. I have some time."

Danny took a seat, and in a short while he was in Anzalone's office, that dark dungeon he recalled from his first meeting with her last summer. There seemed to be even more paper in the place now, and Danny wondered with a smile whether the documents in there were breeding.

Anzalone first questioned Danny about his face, which caused her to draw back with concern. The condition was now completely covering his entire head with a red, blistery mask.

"It's not contagious," Danny joked, "it's just a rash."

Danny's mood was light that morning, but he noticed Anzalone was tense. She sat leaning forward, her elbows on the desk. She looked straight at Danny with those big blue china-plate eyes, except today they seemed to be encased by a face revealing angst, worry. She told Danny she brought him in this morning to talk about the case, where it stood, and how she regarded their prospects for success going forward. Danny sensed he was not going to like what she had to say, but at this point he could handle hearing bad news. He was prepared for anything.

"Look, Mr. Beers," Anzalone finally said, "I'm sorry to have to tell you this, but I think we both know that our lawsuit has taken some turns that neither one of us anticipated. Unfortunately, these unforeseen events will have an impact on our chances for having any kind of success here. That's why I brought you in, to discuss all this. I'm just not sure we can achieve the type of victory we may have expected when we started out. Bottom line is that we're going to have to adjust our expectations a bit."

"Okay, tell me what your concerns are."

"Well, first," said Anzalone, "you have to understand that with any jury trial, the pool of people who make up the jury inevitably get very curious about the litigants who are there in front of them, and even though they are told by the court not to read anything about the case or the parties, there is just too much information out there in the public domain, and it's too easily obtained. So, in my experience, jurors go home and look you up, there's just no way around it. And I am not sure if you have ever googled your name, Mr. Beers, but for whatever reason, when you do, there are a multitude of unflattering articles that surface."

"Well, yeah, I've seen some of those."

"As have I. And the worst ones on that list – and I'm sure I'm not telling you anything you don't already know – are those that came out last month after Moshe Wagshul's car was vandalized at his house, when someone spray-painted the word 'Jew' on his car."

"I'm well aware of that. It was terrible."

"Yes, so I'm sure you realize the public reaction that triggered, especially on Twitter and other social media sites, and the sympathy it garnered not only for the Wagshul family, but also for the other volunteer defendants, like Briscoe, Wartham and Dixon. This alone could be very devastating in a jury trial, especially – and I'm sorry to have to say this – since many of those articles strongly imply you may have been involved, which I know is just ridiculous."

Danny nodded, indicating he understood.

"But ridiculous or not, Mr. Beers, you have to understand that our jury pool could be sitting there thinking you attacked one of the defendants with an anti-Semitic slur, or you had something to do with it. Unfortunately, this is a bad development."

In fact, Danny had never mentioned it to Anzalone, but that incident had also resulted in two Nassau County detectives arriving on his doorstep, unexpectedly one morning at 6:30 on a random Tuesday. They banged on his front door and asked him to come down to the police station. Danny asked if he was under arrest, and when they told him no, he insisted he would be more comfortable at his kitchen table. They tried to strong-arm him, but he stood firm and asked if he needed a lawyer. The older of the two, a man who Danny thought looked like Clint Eastwood, told him "only if you got something to hide." Danny sat in his kitchen and answered questions for over an hour. When the two finally left, Danny crumpled down onto his La-Z-Boy in a pool of sweat.

"Okay," Danny said, "I get it. What else?"

"Well, there's last week, with your father-in-law's arrest."

"I know," Danny nodded apologetically, "I know."

"Mr. Beers, I'd love to know what happened there, but I guess we can talk about that another time. Right now, we need to focus on how this will affect our lawsuit."

"I understand," Danny said, dropping his head.

"I haven't mentioned this, but my phone has been ringing off the hook from reporters. Twitter is lighting up over that whole thing. The public comments are not only about Mr. Mahoney, but also about you and what they are calling your 'greedy lawsuit.'"

Anzalone used finger quotes to emphasize the point.

"For example, the article in *The Daily News* implied you and your father-in-law went in there intentionally to beat the man up. A man whose job it is to protect people from bullies. I'm sure you appreciate the irony."

"I do, and I'm sure you appreciate that was not the case at all." Danny shifted in his chair. "That was all my father-in-law. But I take your point."

Anzalone explained how all this negative information stays in the cybersphere forever, and that although people may temporarily forget about it once the news cycle changes, a public opinion about

Danny and his family unfortunately may now be set in stone, with no way to change it. Any of it could be pulled up at any time by way of reminder. She explained that it did not necessarily mean potential jurors could not put aside any pre-conceived beliefs, and rule on their case impartially, but the reality that this information was out there was not going to change.

"Okay," Danny responded, "is that it?"

"Well, in all candor, I will tell you that there are some personal issues that I am dealing with, both financial and with my little law firm here, that are making things very difficult for me, unfortunately. My son Justin, who you may know is a special needs child, recently had a surgery that financially was devastating for me. To be honest, the way my insurance works, it cleaned me out, basically. The result is that I am finding it very difficult to fund this lawsuit, which is taking an enormous amount of time as we head into the deposition phase of the case."

"Well, I sympathize with you there," Danny replied.

"And I know the litigation expenses are my problem under our retainer agreement, but I do want to be transparent with you. As we currently sit here, I need an expert witness on the warnings issue, but there is no money to fund it. We can go to trial without an expert on this issue, but we would have nothing to counter the highly credentialed experts that Gunther is going to parade through that courtroom, assuming they don't throw our case out on summary judgment before we even get to a jury. So, I think we are going to have to look at some other options for moving forward, which may include at some point – maybe not right now – but at some point approaching the other side about a settlement."

Anzalone next informed Danny that Gunther and its big law firm recently produced over 1.5 million pages of documents, an enormous amount of material. If there was any evidence out there that Gunther was responsible for Agnes's injuries, she explained, it potentially could be contained within that collection of documents.

"But to review all that information in any meaningful way," Anzalone told him, "would take many months and an army of temp lawyers and God knows how much money, which we obviously do not have."

Danny nodded. He folded his hands in his lap, taking all this in.

"Is that everything?" he asked.

"Well, there's obviously the merits of the case itself, but we have always known that is a concern and a potential roadblock. In your deposition, and at trial, you will have to explain in a convincing manner why you allowed Agnes to eat the shrimp that day, and why a warning on the bag of Phillips shrimp would have changed things, especially since you never saw that bag. So, there's that too."

Anzalone leaned back in her leather chair.

"I'm sorry about all this, but lawsuits are very unpredictable, as you can imagine. I'm afraid we find ourselves in a difficult spot."

Anzalone slid over a legal pad.

"But I do have some positive news," she added, "which I just received on Friday afternoon. I think it may be a way forward for us, and another reason why I brought you in here today."

Danny nodded again, but then he held up a finger, asking her to wait a moment. He lifted his briefcase and placed it on his lap. He then pulled out a thin stack of documents.

"Before you get to that," he said, "there's something I'd like to show you. Something you should be aware of."

Danny passed her the document stack that the man in the olive trench coat had dropped onto his McDonald's lunch table.

"I received those on Saturday," he said.

Then he explained the circumstances under which he had received it. He told her that after Gianna's dance class and in the spur of the moment they had stopped for a bite without letting anyone know. He explained how the man walked in and made a beeline to their table, dropping the envelope before beating a retreat out the door. Finally, he told her he had read through every document in the stack, and now was aware of everything in it.

Anzalone's face was at first blank, expressionless, before a look of sadness washed over her. She calmly placed the documents in a neat pile on her desk and folded her hands. Danny noticed that she had eyeballed only the top document in the pile but hadn't bothered to sift through the balance. Danny next saw an expression of shame, which gave away the fact that she knew all too well what was contained in those papers.

Anzalone stared at Danny with her chin sloped. She looked vulnerable, joyless, and Danny regretted even raising the matter.

"Mr. Beers, I really don't what to say about those," Anzalone said softly, almost in a whisper, nodding over to the pile. "You read the documents, so you know what happened. There's not much I can say to you, other than I'm sorry. I understand completely if you want to terminate me and get another lawyer."

Danny didn't respond. Instead, he adjusted himself in his chair, rubbing his hands down his face, trying to collect his thoughts.

"Thing is, I can't change what happened," Anzalone continued, "and I've never really hid from that time of my life, although I do realize I never informed you about it. I can tell you that I have no excuses for what happened. I can only try to explain it. Bottom line, Mr. Beers, is that I got myself into a situation I couldn't handle, the situation you read about in those documents. Before I knew it, I was hopeless, lost. I hurt a lot of people, and left wounds that will never heal. I live with the shame of that every day. And worse, a lot of people tried to help to me, and I rejected them. I was stubborn, obstinate, and completely unrealistic about the depth of my illness. I decided on a destructive path that cost me everything. I lost my law license, friends, family, and a lot more than that. And I have no one to blame but myself."

Anzalone dropped her head.

"See, thing is – "

Anzalone tried to continue, but Danny wasted no further time in interrupting her. He didn't want to hear her explanation, or for one more second be the cause of the look of humiliation and shame on her face.

"Ms. Anzalone, just stop, please," he said, "you don't owe me or anyone else an explanation."

Danny rose and walked slowly over to the window overlooking Ketchogue Terrace. He peered down at the traffic rolling by and the pedestrians filling the sidewalks. The sun was nearing its midpoint in the sky now, casting a shadow over the buildings across the street. Danny stuffed his hands in his pockets and stood there in silence, while Anzalone sat motionless at her desk. There wasn't a word between them for a full minute, before Danny finally spoke, his eyes glued through the window.

"Weather's starting to turn," he observed.

"Yes, I read that."

"It's gonna be warm soon they say."

"So I hear."

Danny lingered at the window, staring. The only sound in the room was the clacking of Cassie's long fingernails on her keyboard out in the foyer. Danny finally broke the stillness as he pointed with his chin.

"You can see Turnberry Park from here," he said.

"Yes, just the west side of it," she agreed.

"It's a nice view."

"It is, yes," said Anzalone.

Danny put his hands in his pockets again, taking a step even closer to the window. Anzalone leaned back in her chair, allowing Danny to have his moment of quiet contemplation. He seemed to be staring there at everything and nothing at the same time.

"Funny how I wound up in this town, you know?" Danny commented, turning his head toward Anzalone now. He walked slowly back to his chair.

"You know, I'm not from here. Not sure if you knew that."

"I didn't, no," said Anzalone.

"Never would have thunk it – me living here I mean."

"Me neither," Anzalone said.

Danny sat back down in the chair in front of his lawyer, running a hand through his hair. His elbows were on his knees now.

"You know, Ms. Anzalone," he said, "you get to a certain age and you'll have some pain in your life, you know what I mean? Adversity, hard times. Loss. You live long enough, you'll have suffering and sorrow. You can't avoid it, I guess. You'll make mistakes too, and you'll face consequences. I mean, that's life."

"Yes, it is," said Anzalone.

"You'll also have a lot of joy, too, no question. But it's in those difficult moments when you figure out what you're really made of, I think. You find your *character*. What kind of a person you are. I really believe that. Life can leave you as a spiteful, hateful person who turns his back on people, or those hard times can inspire you to be a beacon of hope, a positive force in people's lives, someone people can depend on."

"I know what you mean," said Anzalone.

"You know, I'm really not a religious man," Danny said, "but I've spent a lot of time searching for answers lately, believe me. And recently I read about a concept called God's grace. You ever hear of that?"

"Sure," Anzalone nodded earnestly.

"I never really knew what it meant, but here's what I've learned – see, even though we screw up and do stupid things, we are all still worthy of God's love, or the love of family and friends, even though we don't do anything to earn it. We just get it, simple as that, because as people we are all entitled to respect, and dignity, regardless of our faults. But what we give back for it is faith – faith and hope and belief in each other."

"Very interesting," Anzalone smiled.

"I'm not a perfect father by any means," Danny went on, "and I was not a perfect husband, but that's something I can hang my hat on. I really like that."

"I like that too," Anzalone said, her smile wider now.

"See, there's so much in life that is just so random, so beyond our control. You stop to take a leak one day and you meet the girl of your dreams. Or one wrong turn of a steering wheel and you lose that person forever. Or you decide to go to a softball game, instead of the mall, and your daughter winds up on life support. It's crazy how a single decision, a single event, can have so much impact on your life. How your whole world can change in a split second. You wonder sometimes – why go through everything, if things like that can happen, just like that?"

Danny snapped his fingers, but Anzalone said nothing in response. She was staring at Danny now, her eyes locked in on his.

"But I think what connects everything," Danny continued, "what unites us all and helps to make sense of the randomness in this life, is things like faith, hope. Having a belief in the goodness of people, knowing that you'll always be there for friends, family, your loved ones. Allowing people to depend on you, and never letting them down. And then enjoying everything that life has to offer because you have that mindset. See, that's not random and meaningless, you know what I mean? We can control those things. Now that's something that's real."

Danny turned his palms up.

"To me, that's everything."

"It's a very comforting thought," Anzalone replied, "thank you for sharing that. I appreciate those words, more than you know."

Danny rose to his feet again.

"And that's why I would never terminate you, Ms. Anzalone. Never. And it's why I don't want you to give up on me either."

"I understand, Mr. Beers."

"You and I are in this together," Danny told her, "and we need to have faith in one another. We need to stick together and believe in each other. Look, you said a moment ago that we need to adjust our expectations, right? Well, that's nothing new, that's life. People have to do that every day. But it doesn't mean you give up hope, that you have no faith. I don't know if things will work out here, and maybe they won't at all, but I trust you, and I believe in you. I know what you went through, and I see how you are now, how strong you are, and I'm proud you're my lawyer. I wouldn't want to be working with another person in this world. And fuck those guys and their documents and their petty bullshit and the horse they rode in on. We will find a way – you and me. Somehow, some way, we will find a way. We just need to keep the faith."

Danny stood and offered Anzalone his hand.

"So please, I beg you, don't give up on me and my family," he urged. "Let's put our trust in one another and see where it takes us."

"Okay, Mr. Beers," she said, letting go a soft laugh.

She accepted his handshake with a smile.

"We have a deal."

"Excellent then, thank you. Thank you so much."

DANNY AND ANZALONE took a break, with Danny hitting the men's room and Anzalone making a few phone calls. Cassie went down to the donut shop for some more coffees, and before long Danny was back in his lawyer's office.

"So, about the good news I mentioned," Anzalone said. "This comes from Phil Dornbrook, the lawyer for the Brewers. He called me on Friday."

"Oh, okay," Danny said, "what did he have to say?"

"Well, he's made an offer," Anzalone explained. "But don't get too excited, it's not much. He wants a complete general release for his clients in exchange for a $20,000 payment. He says it's non-negotiable and is a one-time offer good only for a week, although my sense is that we have some flexibility on the timing. He explained that it's an ideal time to make the offer now, before we get into the cost and expenses of depositions, which begin next month. But he said once depositions start, and they incur more legal fees, the offer no longer makes sense and is off the table."

Danny nodded, contemplating.

"What do you think?" he finally asked.

"Well, as I say, it's not much. But it does put about $12,000 in your pocket, tax free."

Danny considered that for a moment. It wasn't a lot of money in the grand scheme of things, but right now it sounded like a fortune. He could get the Prius out of the re-po yard, and pay a few overdue bills, including the mortgage. He could also get a few construction projects underway, and maybe make a few dollars.

"Do you think it's a fair offer?" he asked.

"No, I don't," Anzalone answered bluntly. "The Brewers served the shrimp that injured Agnes, and they never should have done that without asking parents. Snacks should be carrot sticks or pretzels or something, not shrimp cocktail. It was inappropriate, and I think jurors would agree. So $20,000 is not fair, not at all."

Danny nodded.

"But here's what I'm thinking. What if we conditioned acceptance of the offer on either Dodge or Cindy agreeing to testify for us? What if they can state that if a warning label been on the bag of shrimp, regarding allergies, they would not have selected that item as the snack that day? See, that gets us past Ko's proximate cause argument. We can tell the jury that an adequate warning would have caused Cindy and Dodge to alter their plans, thereby shutting down the snack table that day, so to speak. In other words, we can prove that the *absence* of a warning caused Agnes's injuries."

Danny processed that for a moment, intrigued.

"You think they'll do that?"

"I don't see why not. We'll sign a settlement agreement in which they deny liability, they get out of the lawsuit, and our case against the other defendants is strengthened."

"Well, shit, sounds great to me," Danny said.

"I agree with you," said Anzalone.

"And what about the other defendants, the Town, the Committee, and all the individuals? Where do we stand with them?"

"Well, I'm glad you asked. Unfortunately, all those defendants are taking a very hard line in the case. They tell me it's a warnings issue, and that it's all a matter between us and Gunther. They say Gunther's bag never warned *them*, and we never told anyone that Agnes had allergies, and so they feel they have no liability."

"What do you think?"

"Well, first I want to see their document production, which I'm getting next week," she informed him. "They are obligated to turn over all the Parent Authorization forms, among other things, and we will see what Debbie wrote on that document. You told me you're sure she would have filled one out, correct?"

"Absolutely. She was obsessive about that kind of stuff. If they gave her a form, she would have completed it. I'm sure of it."

"Okay, then, we'll take a look at their production, and then we can talk about it."

"Great," said Danny.

"In the meantime, I want to give some thought about how I can get the Brewers to accept my counter-offer. It requires them to testify, and maybe incur some additional costs, which they may not like. We'll see Dornbrook at your deposition, which is coming up in a few weeks, and we can discuss it there. Tomorrow I'll call him and tell him we'll let them know our decision by that date. I'd also really like to see how things shake out with your deposition, see if our case gets any stronger."

"Perfect," Danny said. "That's perfect."

"My other thought, Mr. Beers, is that we hold back some of that settlement money to fund the rest of the lawsuit. Pay for a few experts and other litigation expenses. If you are amenable to that, it'd reduce your take by a few thousand dollars, but as I said, it's a way forward for us. I really would recommend it."

Danny considered the thought, and then nodded his head.

"It does make sense, I agree."

"Good then," Anzalone replied, smiling. "We have a plan."

"I like it," Danny agreed.

CHAPTER 29

CAN YOU IMAGINE
ANYTHING SO UNIMPORTANT?

March 17, 2019 – 5:11 am
Home, Ketchogue, NY

It's St. Paddy's Day today and in years past I'd probably be into my second or third beer by now even though it's 5 in the morning. Christ how things change, right? Instead I'm sitting here writing this stuff down and I got a lot to say.

First off there's this thing going on with Gianna that's keeping me awake nights. Some little shit is really giving her a hard time over the whole social media thing. There's some anonymous twitter account posting the worst stuff about her. The person doing it is a gutless piece of filth and I really wish I could figure out who it is. But we can't and it's becoming a real problem. When I filed the lawsuit and that damn process server showed up at the Brewer's house way back when, well, it was right after that all this twitter crap started. It can't be a coincidence. Henry says he's going to get to the bottom of it and I really want him to back the fuck off but he's just impossible. He's already been arrested over it. I tell you what though, arrest or no arrest, if it turns out to be an adult who's behind this thing instead of a kid God help the fucker because Henry will kill him.

Anyway, Gianna spends most of her time in her room now unless she's hanging out with Agnes. I'm having such a hard time talking to her. None of her friends have been coming over and I don't really know what's going on with them or her. But Gianna is just a great kid and I have to keep remembering that. She cares so much about everything and in that way she is just like Deb. She's very mature, never thinks about herself like most kids that age. Before this twitter thing she'd go to the mall with her friends and ask for a couple of bucks and I'd give it to her and when she'd get back turns out she bought something for Agnes or Deb. Never herself. That's just the way she is. She doesn't deserve this cyber stalking bullshit.

Some time ago I learned another thing I can hardly believe. One of the defendants in my lawsuit is a guy named Moshe who sits on the Rec Committee. He's just some working stiff like me, I think he's some techie for a company near Rockville Centre or so I heard. Apparently his car was vandalized and someone spray-painted an anti-Semitic comment on it. Called him a baby killer jew. They're saying the baby killer part was a reference to Agnes. You gotta wonder about people, you really do. But regardless I feel awful about it. And you should read the shit I am seeing on Twitter. It's exploding or trending or whatever it's called. So many tweets coming in waves all saying what a creep I am for filing this lawsuit. It's unreal. Some are suggesting it was ME who spray-painted his car which is what that reporter yelled at me. But I am being honest when I say that I had nothing to do with it and I don't know who did. God's honest truth.

And then there's everything with Agnes. We brought her home from the hospital back in October and I set her up in mine and Deb's room. I sleep downstairs on the couch now. For three months there hasn't been much change in her which is worrying the shit outta me. There's been a little improvement but I only recognize it when Will and Janet come over on the weekends and tell me what they see. When you are around her every day it's hard to tell. She still can't walk but I take her to PT once a week and it's costing me a fortune but the guy there whose name is Darren tells me he sees improvement but once again I am struggling to see it. He tells me to be patient it just takes time. Everyone is telling me to be patient. I am trying my best but Christ it ain't easy.

The thing that's got me most concerned is her speech. She spoke for the first time in the hospital the day they pulled the trach out of her throat. She just mumbled a few words but it was a great day when she did. Recently she's added some words and phrases but it always sounds like she has a mouth full of peanut butter. We encourage her to speak and help her form words but her preference seems to be to stay quiet. My guess is that she knows what's going on and is frustrated but I really don't know. I wish I did. I wish I could get through to her. I wish I knew whether she is sad, frustrated, angry, or anything else, and that I could help her. But I can't. The frustration is overwhelming.

Meanwhile, I bring her down every morning from the upstairs bedroom to the kitchen for breakfast and I carry her. I scoop her out of the bed with my arms underneath her legs and back and most times she snuggles against my chest. She's little and she weighs like nothing.

I kiss her cheeks the whole way down and she doesn't seem to mind. Then I put her in the wheelchair and bring her to the table. It's just the three of us, all alone. She doesn't talk and then she really struggles with her hands. We are trying to get her to use the fork or spoon but her hands just have no strength. They're like rubber and they've gotten fat like sausages and she has almost no dexterity. Her arms have atrophied and she has no strength in those either.

Gianna is so patient and she talks to Agnes the whole time and carefully places the fork or spoon in her hands and wraps Agnes's fingers around it to help her eat. She tells her over and over, you can do it, there you go, great job, just stay with it, I'm so proud of you. Everything is just so positive and hopeful. And then no matter what Agnes does, there could be food all over the table and all over the floor, she tells her she did an awesome job and that it's all going to get better don't worry about it. Gianna is only 12, she's not an adult, but you would never know it. The kid has more sense and compassion and maturity than any adult I know, that's for sure. I tell them both we have to have faith and hope and stay together and we'll get through this. Agnes smiles at that and then she struggles to say something.

And I'm dying to know what she wants to say. Jesus Christ if there was only some way for me to know what she's thinking I'd give my left arm for it. She moves her lips and then she stops, gives up, and then she tries again but then nothing comes out and then there's this sad look on her face like she feels like she let you down. And then we see tears welling up in her eyes. That's when Gianna runs over and hugs her and tells her it's okay, don't worry, things are going to get better.

And I really, truly believe they will. I have to. There's been so many bad things over the last year but I refuse to lose hope, lose faith. And recently there's been good news – her eyes. Those beautiful sparkling blue blazers she got from Deb. In the hospital they were hazy and unfocused but now they are becoming clearer. They seem to give away the fact that she knows what's going on around her because her face and eyes react to things the way you would expect a normal person's eyes to react. I don't mean normal, I guess I mean healthy. If that means progress, I'll take it.

Well I guess this brings me to what I've been wanting to write for a long time. All week I've been thinking about it. I just gotta get it out because it's about Deb. Maybe I'll tell the girls one day when they're older. Or they can read this. I don't know I'll see. But it goes back some time, maybe a few years ago. I guess that's when I would pinpoint it.

See, back then everything was going great for us it really was. But in hindsight I can see how I was kinda detached from stuff when it the came to the girls. That's where I'll start I guess. Things had just evolved to the point where that was Deb's department and I was so busy working six days a week trying to earn some money, trying to get us ahead. That was my department. Deb would run the house and I'd bring home the money, if you can call it that, because it wasn't much.

But there was always this thing between us where I was always commenting on how much she worried all the time and why won't she just calm down and I'd complain about the way she kept herself moving and organizing shit from the moment she got up. There'd be tension and she'd bark at me about not doing things around the house and I'd bark back that I was working my ass off and blah blah blah. It all seems so trivial now. So unimportant. It's embarrassing to write because it sounds like we were some stereotypical sitcom couple or something but it wasn't like that. We were just two really busy people with two young kids and we had a hectic house and of course money was always tight for us and so we had stress. Not major stress just hectic stress. And with the kids taking up so much of our time we'd plop into bed at night exhausted and we just didn't communicate very well. We'd let things go when we should a talked about them.

So with all of that going on sometimes I would get impatient with everything. I had this tendency to snap out orders or be short with her and the kids especially when things were crazy at work which was pretty much always. I'd have two guys over at a house doing a kitchen remodel and two other guys doing an outdoor deck and maybe two other guys ripping out a bathroom and I'm running back and forth between the jobs and dealing with the customers' complaints and trying to get people to pay me and a hundred other things. And then I'd call Deb on the cell and when it went to voicemail I'd go up the wall.

See, that's where it all started, me getting voicemail when I'd call. Can you imagine anything so unimportant?

I don't know why it would send me into a tailspin but it just would. I had this thing that I was so busy and I wanted her to answer the goddamn phone. Just pick it up you obviously can see it's me calling and if I'm trying to get a hold of you in the middle of the day it's important I'm not calling to bullshit or discuss the weather or the price of peanuts in Timbuktu, for the love of fuck, I'm calling because I need something and I have no time to deal with leaving a message and waiting for you to call me back so just pick up the flippin phone. Or maybe I'd send her a text and then I'd wait forever for a response and in the meantime I'm going nuts because she's not answering me.

And it's funny because that was really the only thing I'd ever get worked up about. I'd go with the flow with everything else. Everyone tells me I'm an easy going guy and I think they're right. But I'd shoot her something and then I'd see those bubbles start to come up on my phone which meant she was texting me back and then the bubbles would disappear and no text would come through. So that meant she got it but simply didn't respond and that would make me crazy.

I remember one morning I started yelling, really losing my shit over the whole stupid, trivial issue. I said something like I'm paying for the fucking thing so I want you to answer me because I have a million things going on. And I cursed, I said fucking. To my own wife. She said relax Jesus Christ if I see your message I answer you and if I don't it's because I didn't see it. And I yelled back bullshit just answer me. And then the same day I was at a job site banging away on some tenpenny nails and it was hot as balls out and we were really behind and a few of my guys were screwing up and I sent a text asking how much we had in the expense account because I had to go to Home Depot to buy some ¼ inch plywood and half these guys are standing there doing nothing and costing me a fortune and when I got nothing back from her I wrote ANSWER ME GODDAMMIT! And I felt terrible because that's no way to speak to your wife. So I brought home some flowers and I apologized especially after what I had said in the morning. Cursing and everything. Just so dumb and pointless.

Well, after that Deb would respond back pretty much right away. I had made my stupid pigheaded point, didn't I, which in the grand scheme of things didn't amount to shit. Like I was someone important. When I saw how upset she was I finally got my head out of my ass and I apologized again. She had things to do too – more important things really. I told her forget it, don't worry about it, get back to me when you can, I'm so sorry.

And I really was.

But see, that was Deb. If it was important to you, if something mattered to you, even though it was dumb, then it mattered to her and she'd do it for you. And so she did after that. When I'd call or text she pretty much got back to me right away. I realize it was all because of what an ass I'd been but to be honest it made things a little easier on me. So at the time I was happy with it.

So there we were back in October and I'm about to head out on a weekend trip to Atlantic City with my cousin Paul – my first cousin on my father's side. Me and Paulie grew up together and lived half a mile apart in Babylon our entire childhood. Every summer our families rented a house together for a week down on the Jersey Shore on Long Beach Island for a little vacation. As kids the two of us would run wild on that beach, swimming, surfing, throwing sand, and sneaking out of the house late at night for a midnight swim in the ocean. We just got so close and we stayed that way. It all ended when my Dad died but that's another story.

Anyway, for the last ten years before Deb passed me and Paulie would spend a weekend down in AC. We never really saw each other anymore except for that one weekend a year, which we would set aside and make a commitment to. We liked staying at the Tropicana because we could always get a decent room price and we'd check in and go to a bar and have a few T&Ts and catch up on the past year and then we'd hit the blackjack tables and it was always such a great time. We gambled but most of all we just laughed. Originally we started going down there on Thursday night and then after a few years it'd be Friday night but that October there was so much going on in the house with the girls and Henry was having some surgery that weekend and Will and Janet were busy so there's no way I shoulda went at all, I shoulda just canceled. Paulie would have understood. Deb was standing in the kitchen making sandwiches and she said to me are you really going?

I could tell she was feeling pretty overwhelmed but she said it more like a plea for help because she knew how close Paulie and me were and she was always so supportive of our weekend away. See, I really hadn't made that many friends in Ketchogue the way Deb had and so I think she always knew how important Paulie was to me especially since he was family. But that particular weekend she had to drive Henry home after his surgery and when she asked me if I was really going I stood there speechless. Henry was there, sitting at the kitchen table, and he said, you gotta be fucking kidding me. Those were his exact words.

Anyway I went. On Friday morning Deb was getting stressed and she let me have it. Not really yelling or anything she just went into her Henry-like organizational stress mode and she laid down the rules. With Henry going into the hospital you don't leave until Saturday afternoon after dance classes, she said, and you're back here the next morning promptly at ten, not a minute later, with bagels for Sunday breakfast, and then I want you to take both girls to the skate park over at Turnberry because I gotta go to the Roosevelt Mall for that sale they're having for new winter jackets and ski mittens, and then you gotta split those logs of firewood you left in a pile in the backyard, and while you're at it Mr. High Roller, will you … and I don't remember everything else, but that's pretty much what she said.

When she was finished I started laughing and then Deb took a deep breath and started laughing too. Before we knew it the two of us were hysterical. And man, that was Deb. I could always get her to see the light side of things and she was just naturally a happy and joyful person so I could easily make her laugh and I did it all the time. But seriously she said, you'll be home? Absolutely I said. It all seemed pretty reasonable to me and so I said yes to all of it and I kissed her goodbye on Saturday about 1 pm and suddenly there was Paulie beeping the horn at the curb. He didn't want to come in because he thought Henry would be there, and Paulie was absolutely scared shitless of Henry.

So I grabbed my wallet and bag and some cash and off I went. Henry already was settled in as an outpatient since 5:30 am getting a hernia repair and I remember thinking Henry is cranky enough as it is without a hernia aggravating him even more and I hope for the doctor's and nurse's sake they don't piss him off. Deb was all set to pick him up about 4:30 pm when the hospital said the anesthesia cocktail would wear off and he'd be ready to go home. Deb would have to help him into the car and I asked how're you going to do that with the girls because Henry is as big as a dinosaur and she said I'll manage and then she let me know it was all arranged that the girls were just going to hang out at a neighbor's house and play until she got Henry settled in and got back home. It was no big deal she said just go and have fun but be back in the morning with the bagels like I said. I said absolutely I'll see you tomorrow. And that was that. I kissed her goodbye and told her I loved her and I left.

And that's where I'm going to stop right now. I hear one of the girls starting to stir.

I'll get back to this when I can.

PART FOUR

THE DEPOSITION
AND PRE-TRIAL PHASE

CHAPTER 30

THE E.B.T. OF DANIEL X. BEERS

WHEN ANZALONE TOLD Danny the date in April when his deposition would take place, Danny felt disheartened – it was one year to the date of Agnes's accident at Turnberry. Originally, the plan had been to recognize the date with a tender moment at home with his family, but now Danny understood he'd be in a conference room somewhere getting eaten alive by a hungry pool of ravenous sharks dressed in $1200 suits. There was nothing he could do about it, so he decided just to make the best of it.

About three days prior, Anzalone had summoned Danny to the office to prepare him for the event. She told him it was called an Examination Before Trial – or an EBT – under New York legal parlance. It was a pre-trial discovery device that allowed the lawyers for the defendants to take testimony that would be sworn under oath and could later be used at trial. It would take place right there in Anzalone's small conference room, next to her office. It would be difficult to jam everyone in there, but Anzalone told him there was no way she was doing this on Briggs's turf, in New York City. The FT&B lawyers would have to come to her.

Anzalone explained that other than the two of them and the lawyers for the various defendants, the only other person in the room would be the court reporter, who would transcribe everything that was said. There would be no judge there, so no one would be able to rule on evidentiary objections. All of those would be preserved and could be made later at the time of trial. For the purposes of the EBT, Danny would be expected to answer all the opposing lawyers' questions unless they strayed into clearly irrelevant topics, or attorney-client privilege matters, or if they began to badger or harass him. She would not let that happen, of course. She also instructed him to listen carefully to each question and answer only that question and nothing else. He was not to speculate or guess and if he didn't recall something, or if he didn't know an answer, then he should say so. She warned him not to volunteer any information under any circumstances – it was up to the Gunther lawyers and the other attorneys to ask the right questions. If they didn't, then so be it.

Danny asked Anzalone how long the whole thing would take, thinking he could plan some work activities in the afternoon that day, but then she told him – it would probably take about seven or eight hours. Danny couldn't believe it. The thought of him sitting there for that length of time, answering questions from trained legal professionals, was only adding to the angst he already felt over the whole ordeal. But he was determined to get through it, so he listened intently to Anzalone's prep questions and instructions, and he took all her advice to heart. When they were done with their meeting, Danny felt ready. He would do the best he could.

The EBT was scheduled to start at 10 am on a Thursday, and Danny rose from his bed that morning at 5:30 am. He woke initially at roughly three-thirty in the morning, twisting and turning and wrestling with the bedsheets, hoping more sleep would come, but then he knew it was pointless. He jumped in the shower, dressed, and then went downstairs to brew a pot of coffee. Janet arrived at about 7 am, as they had planned, so that she could see Gianna off to school and then sit with Agnes for the day and tend to whatever she needed. Over the last several weeks, since the arrest, Henry was not answering any of Danny's phone calls and had not been by that much, and Danny had resolved to confront him about his absence. He was really needed here, and Gianna was asking constantly about him. But in the meantime, Janet was a godsend, as she had been the entire year – Danny didn't know what he would do without her.

When Janet was settled in, Danny fired up the F350 and pulled out of his driveway. He wore a grey sports coat and a blue-collared shirt for his appearance that day. There was a great little place called Chief's Diner up on Route 25A, and Danny had planned a quiet, peaceful breakfast with coffee, a newspaper and his deposition notes, which he would give one more eye to before heading over to Anzalone's office.

Before he knew it, Danny was wedging the F350 into a spot on Route 25A, a short walk from Ketchogue Terrace. A few moments later he was seated across from Anzalone in her tiny office again.

"You ready?" she asked him with a smile.

"I am. I feel good about it, thanks to you. We're gonna keep the faith, you remember?"

"I remember."

She nodded to the wall behind her.

"They're all in there waiting on us," she said, "let's go on in."

In the next minute Danny and Anzalone entered the conference room. It was small and rectangular-shaped and shot off to the right lengthwise when you entered. Directly across from the door was a row of windows overlooking Ketchogue Terrace. Seated with his back to the door at the first chair was an Asian-American lawyer who rose to his feet and gave his name as Yang Hsue Ko. He announced that he represented Gunther in the lawsuit. Danny remembered him from that time in court back in October, when Ko was so impressive before Justice Fuentes. Ko was tall, trim and handsome, and it was intimidating meeting him in person.

Ko next introduced his colleague, a thick-waisted female lawyer with short-cropped dark hair. Her name was Andrea Corning. Anzalone then went around the room and asked for everyone's name and the parties they represented. In total there were eight other lawyers there, all cramped into chairs that were pressed up against the conference room wall to the right and the windows on the far side of the room. As the lawyers identified themselves and their clients, the words went in one of Danny's ear and out the other. There was no way he was going to remember them all, so he simply nodded politely.

Anzalone directed Danny to the seat across from Ko, his back to the windows. Anzalone sat next to him on his left. To Danny's right, at the head of the table, was a woman named Kim Whiteside, the court reporter. Once Danny was settled in, Ms. Whiteside asked Danny to raise his right hand and she swore him in.

Then she told him to state his name for the record.

"Daniel X. Beers," he stated in a sturdy voice.

Well, this was it, thought Danny.

After a whole year he was finally getting a chance to testify and tell his story. The deposition had begun.

Anzalone sat close to Danny with a laptop open in front of her, and with the help of a software program called LiveDeps she could see right there on her screen, in live time, all of the questions and answers that Ko and Danny would be giving. They scrolled down her screen in transcript form, making it easy for her to state any objections to the questions, take notes, or give Danny any special instructions that may be required.

Ko opened the deposition by introducing himself again and stating that he represented the Gunther Home Products Corporation in the lawsuit that Danny and his family had filed. He told Danny he would be asking him questions relating to that lawsuit and that he wanted Danny to give honest answers. Then he gave Danny a set of instructions. He told him to listen closely to all the questions and let him know if there was anything he didn't understand. If so, Ko would re-phrase the question. He told him not to speak over Ko and to let him finish the question before Danny gave his answer. Finally, he told him he could take a break whenever he wanted, but not if there was a question pending.

"Do you understand these instructions?" asked Ko.

"I do," said Danny.

Ko then fired away, opening with some basic background stuff – like where Danny lived, whether he was married, how many kids he had, did he own or rent his home, and on and on. These were all name, rank and serial number type of questions; Anzalone had predicted that Ko would open in this manner. Danny thought these were easy to answer and they set him at ease a bit, relieving some of the tension in the room. He didn't know what all this personal stuff had to do with Agnes getting sick, but then again these were lawyers – their job was to sweat the details.

Anzalone had reminded him that the most important thing he could do here today simply was to tell the truth – something he didn't really need to be told. But it was a helpful reminder about how to keep his focus.

Over the next few hours Ko rambled on with his mundane questions. He went through Danny's employment history from the moment he stepped foot out of Babylon High School. He asked him to describe what he did and what his job responsibilities were. He inquired about Debbie's educational and job history as well. Then he went into an entire line of questioning about their respective roles as parents and how they dealt with their children –

he wanted to know what the kids typically ate for breakfast, lunch and dinner, whether they went to restaurants, and if so, who decided what the kids would order. He asked Danny to list all their sports and activities and to identify each of the coaches, teachers and instructors. He wanted to know if the kids ever got sick, and if so, whose responsibility it was to take them to the doctors' offices. He asked whether the kids were vaccinated, what medicines they were ever given, and whose name was listed as the emergency contact for doctors, school, sports and every other after-school or leisure activity. He went through these activities one by one and had Danny respond to each. He also went through each of Gianna's and Agnes's entire medical history, inquiring about every ailment, sneeze, cough, cut or scrape each of them ever had, what doctor or specialist they saw, and the dates and times of every visit and whether it was Debbie or Danny who had taken them there.

Every once in a while Anzalone, while staring down at her computer screen and the scrolling LiveDeps transcript, would chime in with the same line – "*object to the form, you can answer*" – and Danny would simply nod and provide a response to the question. The other lawyers were mindlessly scribbling notes, most of them with chins resting on palms, elbows planted on the table. All of this seemed like a waste of time to Danny, but he tried as best he could to concentrate and to follow Anzalone's instructions. By the time the lunch break rolled around, which the parties took precisely at 1 pm, Danny's brain felt like oatmeal.

For the break Anzalone ordered in some turkey sandwiches from a nearby deli, and Danny and Anzalone munched them in Anzalone's office as all the other lawyers went out to eat. Danny asked about the point of all these questions and topics, and whether Ko was ever going to get to the real facts of the case. In other words, what happened to Agnes.

"He will," said Anzalone with a mouthful of turkey. "Remember this is discovery – he's making inquiries into areas that he hopes will lead to information that may help his case. You're right that a lot of this is not relevant, but he'll get to the important stuff when we go back in."

And Anzalone was right. Immediately after the lunch break, Ko's questions became more aggressive, his tone now accusatory and adversarial. He seemed to be in attack-mode, and as the questions dragged on, the room was getting hotter. Ko was trying to pin Danny down on matters that Danny knew were not only relevant but went right to the heart of the lawsuit. Anzalone followed along on LiveDeps.

Q.   Mr. Beers, were you aware, prior to the date of Agnes's injury, that she had an allergy to shrimp, or any other type of shellfish, or anything else?

A.   No. No, I was not.

Q.   So just to be clear, you are not saying she did not have any such allergies, you just didn't know one way or the other, isn't that right?

A.   Well, I guess that's right, yes. That was Debbie's department, as we discussed earlier.

Q.   Correct. And because that was Debbie's department, you were unaware, as you stood at the softball field that day, whether Agnes was allergic to anything at all, including shrimp, isn't that right?

A.   Yes, I suppose so.

Q.   You suppose so? Mr. Beers, you either knew about allergies or you didn't - which is it?

A.   I didn't know, you are correct.

Q.   In fact, isn't it true that prior to the date of your daughter's accident, you could not even state whether your daughter had ever eaten shrimp at all, at any time in her life, isn't that correct?

A.   Uh, I'm not sure what you mean.

Q.   Sure you do, Mr. Beers. Prior to Agnes's accident, did you know whether Agnes had ever eaten shrimp at any time in her life?

A.   Uh, I - I don't recall.

Q.   Well let me refresh your recollection.

Ko asked Ms. Whiteside, the court reporter, to mark a document "for identification," and she pressed a numbered sticker onto it. Danny felt his cheeks flush and his face heat up. Ko was really going at him now, and the questions seemed not only to attack his lawsuit, but also his role as Agnes's father.

Ko slid the document in front of him.

Q.   Mr. Beers, I am showing you a set of nurse's notes that we obtained from Pembleton Memorial Hospital.

As you can see, they are dated the same date as your daughter's accident. Do you see that?

A.   Yes, I do.

Q.   And I am going to read an entry made by Nurse Wanda Priestly, who met you in the ER that day. It states, and I quote, "Father unaware of any allergies to seafood or shrimp. Father unable to state whether patient ever ingested shrimp prior to incident." Did I read that correctly?

A.   Yes, you did, yes.

Q.   So, I'll ask you again, Mr. Beers. On the date of your daughter's injury, you could not even state whether Agnes had ever eaten shrimp at any time in her life, could you?

A.   No, I couldn't. I guess you're right.

Q.   You had no idea one way or the other, correct?

A.   Correct.

Q.   And because you had no idea whether she had any allergies at all, and could not even state whether she had ever eaten shrimp at any time in her life, is it fair to state that you never told anyone, at any time, that Agnes had an allergy to shrimp?

A.   Yes, that is fair to say, I guess.

Q.   So to be clear, prior to Agnes's injury, you never informed the Brewers - Dodge and Cindy - that Agnes had any allergies, correct?

A.   Yes, that's right.

Q.   And you never told the coach, Peter Briscoe?

A.   That's correct. I never said that to Pete.

Q.   And you certainly never told that to anyone employed by or associated with the Gunther Home Products Corporation, correct?

A.   Well, as I said, I never said that to anyone.

As far as Danny was concerned, Ko had made his point. Danny simply didn't know what Agnes was allergic to, if anything, and right now he was silently embarrassed about it. By the same token, Debbie never knew what jobs he was doing or what Ketchogue families he was working for, and that's just how they compartmentalized things. But regardless, his testimony meant that the defendants in this case were also unaware that Agnes had an allergy, with the notable exception of the Town of Ketchogue and the Rec Committee. Danny had been adamant with Anzalone that if Agnes did in fact have any known allergies, Debbie would have informed the Rec Committee about it when she filled out the Parent Authorization form. He wanted to scream this fact out loud right now, but Anzalone's instructions were clear – do not volunteer any information and answer only what they ask. Ko did not ask about what the Town may have been told, and so Danny's point was not getting across. This was frustrating, but regardless, this whole line of questioning was making him look like a shitbag for a father.

Ko then turned to the events of that terrible day. He asked Danny to state in his own terms what he saw, and Danny did his best to describe it. He told Ko he was standing along the chain link fence, somewhere between home plate and third base, and like everyone else he was focused in on the girl named Daphne, who had collapsed from overheating. He explained that there was a lot of commotion regarding Daphne and that everyone was really worried about her. Then he explained how another little girl had tapped him on the elbow and directed his attention to centerfield, and it was then that he saw Agnes lying in the grass.

Danny felt tears welling up as he finished. He didn't want Ko to see this, but then he couldn't mask it, and so he wiped his eyes. Ko was tapping his pen down onto the conference room table, his chin resting on a fist. He asked Danny if he wanted to take a break, and Danny declined. Ko had a black three-ring binder in front of him, and he flipped over a page of his notes with a snap of the paper. He adjusted the binder on the table and looked straight at Danny. He then dragged Danny through a series of questions about where he was standing, how far from home plate, the pitcher's mound, the outfield, and on and on, until Danny's head was ready to explode.

Then he began asking about the Brewers.

```
Q.      Mr. Beers, do you recall that Dodge and Cindy Brewer
        were serving the team snack that day?

A.      Yes, it was Cindy Brewer's turn as the snack mom.

Q.      And they did in fact bring the snack, correct?

A.      Yes.

Q.      You were there at the field when Cindy Brewer pulled
        up in their family car?
```

A.   I was, yes.

Q.   You recall seeing her pull in?

A.   Yes, I do.

Q.   What kind of vehicle was that?

A.   Mercedes. A minivan of some sort.

Q.   Okay, and you were standing at the chain link fence
        when she pulled in, correct?

A.   Yes.

Q.   Do you recall what time of day this was?

A.   No, I don't. But it was afternoon some time.

Q.   Were you with anyone when Cindy Brewer pulled in in
        her Mercedes minivan of some sort?

A.   Yes. I was with Dodge Brewer.

Q.   Did you speak with him at that time?

A.   I did, yes. I'm pretty sure I did.

Q.   What if anything did he say as Cindy entered the
        parking lot?

Danny had to think for a second about that question. He
recalled a very long conversation with Dodge about the nutjob rules
of the fourth-grade softball game, and about all the ridiculous,
unnecessary equipment the girls were forced to wear. And then he
remembered what Dodge had said, conjuring up the image of Cindy
in her revealing tennis outfit.

Q.   Do you recall what he said, Mr. Beers?

A.   I remember him saying that Cindy was the snack mom,
        and that he was running over to help her. Then he
        said to follow him on Twitter.

Q.   So he told you Cindy was the snack mom, correct?

A.   Yes, correct.

Q.   And this was before Agnes or any of the other girls
        ate anything during snack time?

A.   Yes, definitely.

Q.   So you will agree that there's no question you were
        aware that whatever it was that Cindy Brewer had
        brought with her that day, it was going to be served
        to your daughter as a snack, correct?

A.   Well, yes, I guess that's right.

Danny felt flush. It had to be a million degrees in that room. He was sweating through his button-down shirt all the way into his grey sportscoat. He lifted the water bottle in front of him and took a swig, just before wiping some sweat from his forehead. Ko snapped over another page of his notes, and Danny answered the next series of questions in a low, subdued tone.

Q.   Mr. Beers, what if anything did you see Dodge Brewer carrying out of the Mercedes after he went over to assist Cindy that afternoon?

A.   Well, he was carrying a yellow box, I believe.

Q.   Was it a box from Lenny's Seafood Market?

A.   Yes, it was.

Q.   Prior to Agnes's injuries, Mr. Beers, were you familiar with Lenny's Seafood Market?

A.   Yes.

Q.   You had ordered from there before?

A.   We did, yes. Me and Debbie.

Q.   So you were familiar with their yellow boxes with the two clamshells, correct?

A.   I was, yes.

Q.   And you knew Lenny's was a seafood market, correct?

A.   Sure.

Q.   Mr. Beers, was Cindy carrying anything from the Mercedes that day?

A.   Yes.

Q.   What was that?

A.   A white plastic bag.

Q.   Did this white plastic bag have markings on it?

A.   It did, yes.

Q.   What kind of marking?

A.   It had a red lobster on it.

Q.   A red lobster. So, as Dodge was carrying the yellow box that you recognized as coming from Lenny's Seafood Market, and Cindy was carrying a white plastic bag with a red lobster on it, what did you think was being served as the snack that day?

Danny felt cornered. He knew Ko was scoring major points here, just as he had done in court back in October. And to make matters worse, now the finger of blame seemed to be poking him right in the eye.

Danny hooked his chin down and remembered Anzalone's instructions. Just tell the truth and keep your answers short. And the truth here was this – there was no question he knew Agnes was being plied with some sort of seafood that day. In fact, he remembered speaking with Gary Snyder, a neighbor, and joking about the fact that the Brewers were serving up shrimp cocktail, and how Snyder had responded with a crack about Twinkies. Danny resigned that he would have to answer the question honestly and let the chips fall where they may. So he told Ko the truth – he assumed the girls were being served some kind of seafood that day.

Ko tossed his pen down onto his opened three-ring binder.

Q.   So Mr. Beers, as you are standing at the chain link fence, and you are watching the snack mom about to serve seafood to your ten-year old daughter, what if anything, as Agnes's father, did you do about it? Did you tell anyone to stop?

A.   No, I didn't.

Q.   Did you tell anyone, for example, "hey, don't let my daughter eat seafood." Did you say that?

A.   No.

Q.   In fact, you never said a word to anyone, and instead you simply stood there and watched as your daughter was served and then ate seafood, right in front of your eyes, isn't that correct sir?

A.   I guess I did, yes. I, I just didn't know.

Q.   You didn't know. Well, who should have known what foods your daughter could safely eat or not eat that day? Whose responsibility was it to know?

A.   Well, as I said, that was Debbie's department with the girls. She would have known.

Q.   But Debbie had already passed, correct?

A.   That's right.

Q.   So Agnes's only parent was you, right Mr. Beers?

A.   Yes.

Q.   And because that was Debbie's department, you as
      Agnes's only parent did not know what foods your own
      daughter could safely eat or not eat, correct?

A.   I didn't know about shrimp. I just didn't know.

Q.   And Mr. Beers, your complaint in this case makes a
      claim for failure to warn, correct sir?

A.   Yes, I believe that's right.

Q.   It alleges that my client, Gunther Home Products,
      should have placed a warning on the outside of the
      Phillips frozen shrimp bag, stating that the product
      could be harmful to people with shellfish or seafood
      allergies, isn't that right?

A.   Yes, I believe so.

Q.   But Mr. Beers, you have already told me that prior
      to Agnes's incident, you did not believe that Agnes
      was a person who fell into the category of people who
      had such an allergy, and therefore could be harmed
      by the product, correct?

A.   I didn't know about her allergy, that's right.

Q.   So you will agree with me, won't you Mr. Beers, that
      any such warning would have been meaningless to you,
      isn't that right?

A.   I guess - well - I guess you can say that, uh, I mean
      - I would not have thought that it applied to Agnes.
      That would not have occurred to me.

Danny asked if they could take a break, and Ko agreed. Danny
and Anzalone retreated hastily to her office, and Danny dropped
into a chair.

"I'm not doing too good, am I?" he asked Anzalone, exhausted.
But Anzalone waved him off.

"You're doing fine," she said, swigging from a water bottle.
"Just keep your answers short, like you've been doing. He hasn't
raised anything we didn't expect." In a few minutes they were back
in the conference room, Danny under oath again.

Ko went on the offensive.

Q.   I want to direct your attention to the time just
      before the young girl named Daphne went out to pitch.

A.   Okay.

Q.   By that time, the game had started again, and Agnes
      had already eaten the shrimp snack, correct?

A.   That's right.

Q.   What you were doing at that time?

A.   Well, I was watching the game, like everyone else.

Q.   And where was Agnes?

A.   In centerfield, like I said earlier.

Q.   Were you watching her?

A.   I'm not sure. I don't recall.

Q.   Mr. Beers, when Daphne went out to the mound to pitch, did you see Daphne walk out there?

A.   Yes, I do remember that.

Q.   And when Daphne collapsed, where were you looking?

A.   I was looking at Daphne, like everyone else.

Q.   And were you still looking at Daphne when everyone ran out there to assist her?

A.   Yeah, sure. Of course.

Q.   You weren't looking at Agnes?

A.   I was not, no.

Q.   In fact, you had to be told by another young player on the Lady Mets that Agnes had fallen, correct?

A.   Yes. I guess so, yes.

Q.   Well, did you see your daughter fall?

A.   No.

Q.   So, Mr. Beers - even though you watched your daughter eat seafood as a snack that day, it never occurred to you to keep an eye on her as she went out to centerfield, isn't that correct?

A.   Well, I'm not sure I would say it like that.

Q.   Well, do you know how long Agnes was lying in the grass out in centerfield before the little girl tapped you on the arm to get your attention?

A.   No, I don't.

Q.   And do you believe that if you had been knowledgeable about your daughter's allergies and medical history, and had been keeping an eye on her while she was out in centerfield, like a father should, that maybe she would not have suffered the full extent of the injuries she suffered? Do you Mr. Beers?

A.   I really don't know, Mr. Ko. I have no idea.

Ko snapped over another page of notes as Danny gulped some more water. Ko was delivering his questions in a loud, booming voice that was bouncing off every wall of the conference room. Anzalone had to object on several occasions, instructing him to lower his tone. But Ko pressed on, his questions getting more accusatory. Danny was feeling the pressure. He looked at the other lawyers and saw nothing but stares of contempt coming back at him. His cheeks and the back of his neck were on fire now.

Ko pointed down at his notes, and this time he launched into an attack on why it had taken Danny so long to arrive at the hospital that day. He pulled out a set of nurse's notes and informed everyone in the room that from the time the ambulance arrived at Turnberry Park, until the time that the Nurse Wanda Priestly had finally found Danny inside the Emergency Room, well over forty-five minutes had elapsed. The ER records stated clearly that without knowing what Agnes had eaten that day, they were uncertain how to proceed with her treatment. The result was a worsening of her condition, in the view of the ER doctors.

Ko was apoplectic as he attacked Danny.

Q.   SO WHERE WERE YOU, MR. BEERS?! Your daughter is in
       the Emergency Room with a life-threating condition,
       and you were … WHERE?! Completely AWOL?! Did you stop
       for lunch or something?!

Anzalone objected that the question was argumentative, and she told Danny not to answer. Ko then re-phrased it. He countered that he simply wanted to know where Danny was and why he hadn't ridden inside the ambulance with his daughter – it was a legitimate question, he said. Anzalone instructed Danny to respond.

Danny tried to explain, but even he knew the answer sounded lame. He testified that three paramedics told him to follow the ambulance instead of getting on board. He said he raced like a maniac to Pembleton Memorial but since the ambulance pulled out before him, he had lost it on the way there. He described how when he finally arrived at Pembleton, he was unable to find a parking spot and had driven right through a row of hedges.

Q.   So, Mr., Beers, let me see if I understand. Your
       daughter is lying there in the hospital, in a coma,
       and the ER doctors have no idea how to treat her,
       because you couldn't - what? Find a parking spot? Is
       that really your testimony?!

Anzalone objected again, but in Danny's mind the point was made. There wasn't a day that went by when Danny didn't regret not getting into the ambulance with Agnes. And the image of her lying in the grass in centerfield, and Danny not knowing how long she had been in that condition, still haunted him in his dreams, every single night.

Ko then went into a topic that surprised even Danny. He hadn't even remembered the conversation to which Ko was referring, and for that reason he had never filled Anzalone in on it, or at least the part that Ko was asking about. But as Ko was going through it, Danny could see Anzalone's expression change.

Q.   Mr. Beers, do you recall a time when Dodge and Cindy Brewer arrived at your house to deliver the Phillips frozen shrimp plastic bag?

A.   Yes, I do remember that, sure.

Q.   And it was during that conversation when Cindy informed you that she had not, in fact, served anything from Lenny's Seafood Market, correct?

A.   Yes, that is right.

Q.   They told you the bag came from Shop-Rite?

A.   They did, yes.

Ko then flipped another page of his notes, and he let a silent pause fill the conference room. He then looked Danny right in the eyes.

Q.   Mr. Beers, during that conversation, did you make the following statements to the Brewers as they were standing in your foyer that day? "A shrimp allergy is a shrimp allergy" and "I'm the one who should have known about it and said something"?

Danny sat there frozen. He did not recall making that statement until Ko had just repeated it back to him. But as soon as he did, Danny remembered. Dodge was in a t-shirt of some sort and Cindy was wearing flip-flops. She was crying, or had been. They were standing in Danny's foyer, with the Brewers' car still running out by the curb. And that's when he said it. He remembered now, clear as day. He had tried to ease Cindy's emotions, saying it as an off-hand remark to let them know he wasn't angry over the whole Lenny's Seafood debacle. But they obviously had turned around and recalled the conversation for Ko here, so that he could throw it back in his face. Danny wanted to tell Ko that he certainly didn't mean the comment as a confession of guilt, which was the way Ko had just presented it. But none of that mattered now. The question Ko had asked was straightforward, and he pressed Danny for an answer.

```
Q.    Sir, please, did you make those statements to the
      Brewers that day? It's a yes or no question.
```

Danny cleared his throat and ran both his hands down his face.

```
A.    Yes, I did.
```

Ko let the answer hang in the air for a full minute, maybe more. He was looking intently down at his notes, turning pages to emphasize the fact that he was not finished here, that he still had more ammunition with which to attack this witness. Everyone else sat there in complete silence, including Anzalone. Danny was dying to ask her what she was thinking, but it didn't take much imagination for him to guess. He had never told Anzalone about that comment, and the reason was that he did not remember making it himself. But the detrimental effect of it felt large right now, and Anzalone's stern expression suggested that she agreed.

Ko next confronted Danny about the attack on Moshe Wagshul's minivan when someone spray-painted the word "jew" on Moshe's car. Ko demanded to know where Danny was that night, and Danny told him he simply did not recall. He asked whether he knew where Moshe lived, and Danny confessed that he did. He also asked whether, as a person in the construction industry, Danny had access to or was in possession of spray paint. Danny scoffed, but told him that he did. Ko then asked him point-blank whether he had any involvement in that terrible incident, and Danny denied it emphatically, and for the first time was animated in his response.

Ko then went off in a different direction.

```
Q.    Mr. Beers, do you recall a news reporter showing up
      at your home shortly after that incident?

A.    Yes, I do.

Q.    The reporter informed you that you were under
      investigation for the attack, did she not?

A.    I guess so, yeah.
```

Q.   And when the news reporter confronted you, accusing
      you of being involved in the anti-Semitic attack on
      Mr. Wagshul, a defendant in this case, isn't it a
      fact, Mr. Beers, that you then passed out?

A.   Mr. Ko, that is not why I blacked out. That had
      nothing to do with it.

Q.   But that happened almost immediately upon being
      confronted with the accusation that you may have been
      involved in the attack, correct?

A.   When you say it like that, I guess that's correct.
      But the two things are not connected.

Danny looked at his watch and saw that it was now a little after 4pm, which meant that he had been answering questions for over five hours now. He was mentally exhausted, his brain just fried, but he told himself to concentrate and to press on.

Ko followed up with an inquiry about Henry's arrest at the school. His questions seemed designed to suggest that Danny and Henry had gone over there intentionally to inflict harm on Mr. Nicholls, the Bullying Director. But at least with this series of questions Danny felt as if he had defended himself adequately. He told Ko his daughter was being bullied and harassed and that he just went to the school simply to ask them to investigate, which was their right. Anzalone allowed him some leeway, but then she told Ko to move on, that the topic was irrelevant.

The EBT lasted another two hours, with Ko spending the time on medical issues –doctors, treatments, specialists, bills, insurance, invoices, how much Danny has spent, how much he owes, and on and on. When it finally ended, and Ko said he had no more questions, and the other lawyers had asked some follow-up questions, Danny was spent. He felt as if he had run a marathon; he had been sitting in that chair for over seven hours.

Back in Anzalone's office, after all the lawyers had left, Danny stood at the window overlooking Ketchogue Terrace, his hands in his pockets, while Anzalone returned some phone calls. There was an unspoken feeling in the room that this EBT had been a disaster for them. When it was over, Ko had slapped his binder shut and said to Anzalone, right there in front of the court reporter and all the other lawyers, "we really need to talk," and even Danny knew what the topic would be.

Ko would demand they drop the lawsuit.

When Anzalone hung up the phone, Danny said to her, "Look, Ms., Anzalone, I realize we didn't have a good day here today, and I'm sorry."

"Mr. Beers," Anzalone responded, looking exhausted herself, "let's not even talk about it right now. I want to take a day to think. We'll wait until we receive the official transcript, and then we can both go over it. We'll assess where we are at that point."

Danny agreed, and a moment later he was out the door.

BUT ANZALONE DID not wait until she received the transcript.

The next day, after reading the notes she had typed into her LiveDeps program, she called Ko, who to her surprise took the call.

"Look," she said, after exchanging pleasantries, "it's no secret yesterday didn't go well for us, and I'm going to be having a 'come to Jesus' conversation with my client. What I want to know is this – would you guys be willing to go to mediation on this case? It seems like a good opportunity to do so, before we start to incur the costs of going forward with all the defendants' depositions."

Anzalone was praying he would agree. A mediation – a meeting before a neutral evaluator who would assist the parties in settling the case – seemed to be her only hope for a recovery. But Ko's response was not promising.

"Not with a $50 million demand, Ms. Anzalone, no chance," he answered. "I will not even take that request back to my client."

"We are past that," Anzalone relented, "my client is much more realistic about where we stand these days, especially after yesterday."

"It's not just his deposition or this lawsuit," Ko shot back, "I hope your client realizes the public perception that is out there about him. I mean, with all the events that have taken place, what does he expect? Attacking people at the school, the incident at the Wagshul's house, all those articles, Twitter?"

"Look, Mr. Ko, I think we both know where we're at," said Anzalone. "We are a long way from our original demand. I think you should tell your client that a mediation would be worth it. I'm confident we can resolve this case for a reasonable sum. And it's not as if you bear no risk at all."

"Well, I'm not so sure after that EBT yesterday," Ko said, "but I'll speak to my client."

As soon as she hung up, Anzalone dialed Dornbrook and made the counter-offer to the Brewers. The deal was the same as she had discussed with her client – they will accept the $20,000 offer and Danny will release the Brewers from the lawsuit in exchange for Dodge and Cindy's testimony that they would not have plied the Lady Mets team with shrimp had any kind of a warning been there on the bag.

"Quite frankly," Dornbrook said, contemplating the offer, "I thought you'd be dropping the case after that shit-bomb yesterday. Does your client have any idea how bad that went?"

"Look, Mr. Dornbrook, this is a good faith counter-offer. It gets your clients out of this case for peanuts. Do we have a deal?"

There was silence on the line, which Anzalone took as a good sign. But that didn't stop her heart from thumping away. She was praying that Dornbrook wasn't going to pull the 20 grand.

"Well, I'll tell you what," he finally said, "I like it."

"Well, that's great."

"I'm going to recommend it," said Dornbrook.

"Excellent."

"Full general releases?"

Anzalone agreed.

"Alright, leave it with me, I'll speak to my clients. Stay tuned."

THAT AFTERNOON, ANZALONE received two emails.

The first came in at 4:57 pm and was from Yang Hsue Ko, who informed Anzalone that he had spoken with his client about the offer to go to mediation. He wrote that while a mediation was possible in theory, as he had mentioned, the plaintiffs would have to formally withdraw the $50 million monetary demand that was in their complaint before Gunther would even consider it. Then they would have to give Gunther a settlement demand that was reasonable and more accurately reflected what Ko described as their "sinking lawsuit."

"Assuming you do so, we would like to discuss where you see the numbers coming out, and what your expectations would be, before we commit to participating," wrote Ko. "As of now, we see any settlement as a nominal one that would have us simply avoiding paying the additional legal expenses we would incur with a trial. If you want us to participate under that framework, perhaps we can have a further discussion."

Well, this wasn't horrible news, thought Anzalone, but it certainly sent a clear message that FT&B believed it was in the driver's seat here. They were telling her they would settle the case at something less than their trial expenses. That was nowhere near where Anzalone saw this case going when she took it on roughly a year ago, but at least it was a start. Or, put another way, it was better than the alternative, which was Anzalone going all the way through trial, at enormous time and expense, and getting her ass booted out of court with a complete defense verdict.

The second email landed a few minutes later and was much more encouraging. It was from Dornbrook.

"Ms. Anzalone, it looks like we have a deal," wrote the Brewers' lawyer. "However, we would like to discuss the 'testimony' portion of this settlement to make sure we both understand what it is that my clients can actually attest to truthfully. And, of course, we will need to prepare a settlement agreement that reflects our overall deal. I will put together a draft. Of course, nothing is final until we both sign the agreement, and we each reserve our rights."

Well, there it was, thought Anzalone.

She had a loose agreement to discuss the possibility of going to mediation with Gunther, and $20,000 from the Brewers. She and her client had discussed funding some experts, but after that deposition yesterday she didn't have a strong sense of what remained of the case. Dan Beers had told her to keep the faith, but it wasn't going to be easy. Anzalone clicked off her computer and stuffed some papers in her briefcase. She grabbed her coat and headed out the door to her Honda, parked out on Main Street.

In a strange way, she was almost relieved that this case was likely nearing its conclusion. She would have to have another frank discussion with Dan Beers and explain how bad that deposition went, but despite that setback, she was determined to press as hard as she could to get the Gunther team to a mediation and hopefully wring a few dollars out of them.

Of course, on the other hand, there was this – if Gunther decided not to make a settlement offer, both she and her client were in big trouble. That much was certain. In the meantime, they were a mere two months from trial, and so time was running short.

Anzalone pulled the Honda out of its parking spot, and as she creeped down Main Street, she ran through a mental checklist of her overdue bills.

If it were not for the Brewers' $20K, which would pay her approximately $4,000 after expenses and taxes, she was sunk.

It wasn't much, but at least she had that.

Thank God for that.

CHAPTER 31

THE SNOWBALL

DODGE, IT'S PHIL Dornbrook, you got a minute?"
Dodge was sitting in his spacious office up on the 38th floor of a building on Avenue of the Americas, which overlooked Radio City Music Hall and NBC Studios, when his cell phone rang. The number looked like the one for his lawyer in the Beers case, so Dodge took the call.

"Yeah, sure dude, what's up?" Dodge responded.

It was roughly quarter after eleven on a Wednesday night, the building getting chilly as midnight neared. Dornbrook explained that earlier in the day he had cut a deal with the Beers's lawyer Anzalone and settled the case with them for 20 grand. Dodge was elated. He had given Dornbrook up to 50 thousand in authority, and now that the guy had gotten rid of this headache for 30K less, well, this was a reason to celebrate. This lawsuit had been weighing on his mind for a while and he couldn't be happier it was over. Dornbrook explained that he might have to provide some testimony, but Dodge didn't care about that. He had given deposition testimony in lawsuits before and it was no big deal. The fact that he and Cindy were being dismissed from the suit was key.

"And that's it, you're done," Dornbrook said. "We are putting together a settlement agreement and then we'll file the stip of discontinuance with prejudice on the e-courts filing system."

"Dude, that's great," said Dodge. "We need to grab dinner soon." Dornbrook agreed, and Dodge clicked off his phone. He tossed it onto his desktop and leaned back in his leather office chair.

Right now he was alone up there in his firm, after everyone else had long since left, staring down at a memorandum he had drafted and would send to investors, tutoring them about the ebb and flow and ups and downs of the stock market – where it was going, where the trends were, how Poseidon saw interest rates fluctuating and the strength of stocks, equities and bonds, and what factors and market conditions would affect it all. Dodge loved writing these brochures because he knew his investors hung on every one of his words and thoughts and insights. He would email these documents out, these formal statements from the Poseidon Capital Partners Investment Committee, to hundreds of clients, and then they would call him, seeking his advice. He loved this part of his job, and when it was time to prepare the next of these documents, Dodge often found himself tied to his desk into the wee hours of the night.

Sometime after midnight, the Investment Committee memorandum was singing, and it was finally time to hit the road. Another long night at the office, he thought, as he printed off copies of the memo for two of his partners and then tossed them onto their office chairs, just down the hall. He was craving sleep, and knew he'd be right back here by 7:00 a.m. to get working on another deal, and so he was anxious to get home.

Back in his office, Dodge stuffed his arms into his suit jacket and then plopped down onto his leather hi-backed chair to check his e-mail one more time before he split for the night. He hadn't checked it in hours, and if anything needed a response, he'd rather get it done before he hit the sack.

He ran his index finger along his trackpad and opened his Microsoft Outlook icon. Then he clicked on the "Send/ Receive" button. Four e-mails appeared. The first was from his lawyer, Dornbrook, confirming the settlement he had just called about. Dodge dragged that into a folder called "Beers Case." The second and third emails were garbage – one was a departure memo from a young analyst from Yale who was leaving for a career writing survey questions for *Family Feud* – and good luck with that – and the third was from a secretary asking if anyone knew a reasonably-priced divorce lawyer in Queens. Dodge quickly deleted both.

The final email was from a college buddy of his named Kevin Anderson, now a bond trader at GPG Investments Inc. in Chicago.

Dodge took a look at the list of names in the "To" field in Kevin's e-mail and realized he had sent it to a group list that included most of Dodge and Kevin's Brown University pals, along with a bunch of other friends that Kevin had added over the years. The subject line of the e-mail read "Take The Quiz!" and there was a jpeg file attached.

Dodge eye-balled his office door and double-clicked on the e-mail, reading it aloud:

Men - test your powers of observation. There is a hot car somewhere in this photo – can you find it? The majority of American men cannot see the car, even after staring at the picture for hours. Try it. Good luck! Kev

Dodge chuckled – typical crap from Kevin, he thought. And then, simply out of curiosity, he decided to play his game. He clicked on the jpeg file, and in an instant a photo appeared that filled his entire 27-inch monitor. It was a picture of a completely naked woman with enormous boobs, smiling away in the sunshine, leaning against a cherry-red convertible BMW, her right foot propped up on a turned-over plastic bucket.

"Jesus," Dodge said aloud, turning toward his office door again. Of course, there was no one there, but the graphic nature of the picture kicked Dodge into protective mode. There was a strict policy at his company, installed by Dodge himself, about having this type of material on your computer. In the last few months, he had reprimanded several of his friends – most often Kevin – about sending this type of stuff to his work email.

In the picture the woman's arms were spread and her face and blond hair silhouetted against a dazzling blue sky. Dodge got the joke – men can't see the car because they look only at the woman. Very funny. Typical Kev, he thought. Dodge rolled his eyes and slid his cursor to drag the email and the photo into the trash bin, but then suddenly he got an idea. It was a thought that came to him in a fleeting second, the kind that pops into your head in a moment of weakness, perhaps because you are tired, or because of the lateness of the hour, or because for whatever reason you aren't thinking clearly. Months later, he would tell you that no, he had no inclination that a simple act that he believed was innocent, trivial, private, and yes … juvenile, would alter the course of his life.

Regardless, in that moment, during that momentary lapse of judgment, Dodge made a decision – *let's have a little fun,* he thought.

A little harmless ribbing, which Kevin of all people deserved.

Instead of clicking delete, Dodge hit the print button and sent the jpeg file of the naked woman to his Canon ImageRunner color printer, located in the hallway at his Administrative Assistant's station. The ImageRunner zipped the photograph out in a heartbeat. Dodge was alone in the hallway as he checked his watch, knowing that at any minute the car he had called to take him home likely would be waiting for him in the street. He grabbed the photo from the output tray, chuckling again at what would be the look on Kevin's face when he saw Dodge's response.

Because the thing was this – Kevin was a relentless ball-buster, and he'd been that way his whole life. All his friends knew it. He'd pick up on that one thing that embarrassed you the most and he'd throw it in your face as often as he could, and most times right in the middle of a crowd, for maximum humiliation. He'd laugh like hell and tell you he was only kidding, but you just wanted to kill the guy sometimes. But that was Kevin, who at the same time could be the most loyal of your trusted friends.

At the same time, mostly by way of payback, Dodge had never let Kevin live down the time when, two years earlier, Dodge had dragged him to the Poseidon Capital Partners Holiday Party and Kevin proceeded to drink half the company's supply of eggnog, along with probably a gallon of scotch. He then spent the rest of the evening stumbling all over the office, his tie swinging down in the middle of his chest, his shirt tails dangling, but worse, also falling all over a shy receptionist that Poseidon employed, a young woman named Gwen Adams, who read the Bible when she had downtime and was not amused by Mr. Anderson's overtures. Kevin wound up sending a note of apology the next day. He was so embarrassed he didn't call Dodge at his office for six months, knowing the young woman would likely answer the call.

With a mischievous grin, and knowing this was a great method to stick something right back in Kevin's face, Dodge sauntered down the hall over to the main reception desk that sat in front of the floor-to-ceiling glass doors just off the elevator banks. He gazed down on the dozen or so personal photographs that the young Ms. Adams kept of friends and family members, all of which were thumbtacked to a softboard hidden underneath the top of the reception counter that surrounded her chair.

Dodge's eyeballs shifted left to right, and then they landed on one photo taken of Gwen and three friends smiling away in the

Jamaica sun earlier that spring. He yanked the thumbtack and thought *perfect — this will do.*

Dodge next hastened down the hallway to the 38th floor "mini-room," which contained the floor's supply of inter-office envelopes and FedEx labels as well as a massive Hewlett-Packard color copier. His first thought was to do this whole thing by way of Photoshop, but who had time for that. And anyway, because the point here was simply to bust Kevin's chops, it didn't really need to be perfect. Dodge punched in his company ID number, placed the photograph of Gwen down onto the glass, and in a second the HP copier spat out a crisp duplicate of Gwen and her friends.

Back at his desk, Dodge took a pair of scissors and carefully cut out Gwen's head. With a tiny scrap of tape, he then secured Ms. Adams's head onto the photograph of the blond woman from Anderson's jpeg file.

Dodge laughed again as he marveled at his artistry, and in a minute he was back from the mini-room copier, this time with a single photograph of a naked white woman, with Gwen Adams's head, leaning against a cherry-red convertible Jaguar.

The whole reproduction took less than two minutes.

Dodge stared down at the photograph, smiling.

Holy shit, he thought, *this actually looks real.*

A moment later, Dodge had successfully scanned the new photo onto his hard drive and had attached it to a response e-mail to Anderson with a subject line that read "Re: Take The Quiz!" Dodge then typed:

> Kev: Funny, but I found a similar picture of your friend and my receptionist Gwen Adams — did you take this (see attached)? Maybe just after you met her at the Xmas Party? Try not to get too excited. Later, Dodge.

Sitting in front of his computer, Dodge stared at the text of his e-mail and for a moment — just a moment — he considered deleting it. He moved the cursor arrow back and forth between the delete button and the send button a few times and then checked his watch. It was now well after midnight and he was tired, his eyes heavy, his brain cloudy. He left the e-mail prompted on his screen while he tossed his suit jacket over his shoulders, and then he grabbed his briefcase. A moment later he dropped back down onto his high-back and thought, *Oh c'mon, dude, it's just a joke.* He clicked the "send" button, and off it went.

About six minutes later, in the back of a Lincoln Town Car, Dodge was feeling uneasy and slightly regretful. He took out his cellphone and dialed Anderson at his office. He got voicemail.

"Hey dude," he said, "Dodge here. It's about one in the morning and I'm on my way home. Anyway, nice quiz you sent today. I failed it, as you might have guessed. I sent you a response . . . and . . . uh . . . I probably shouldn't have sent that. Do me a favor and delete the e-mail as soon as you get it, okay dude? I'm a little nervous about it. You'll see why. `Preciate it man. Later."

Dodge clicked off the cellphone, stuffed it into his jacket pocket, and sunk back into the headrest for a snooze.

AT HALF PAST six the next morning, the trading desk at GPG Investments in Chicago was a hurricane of activity. The firm was located on the 40th floor of a downtown building a block from Lake Shore Drive and offered spectacular views of Lake Michigan. But nobody here had time to notice the views, and certainly not on a trading day. Here junior traders were already sprinting orders back and forth from cubicle to cubicle, getting screamed at by their bosses, who spent most of the time with a telephone crammed between their cheek and shoulder. There were computers beeping, voices booming, phones ringing, all underneath an overhead electronic ticker board that spun stock prices all day long.

At about twenty-five to seven, local time, Kevin Anderson came sprinting into the firm over half an hour late. There'd been an overturned tractor-trailer on the Dwight D. Eisenhower Expressway, and he wasn't happy about it, to say the least. He was gripping a Starbucks grande latte and a copy of the *Wall Street Journal,* and as soon as he arrived at his desk, he dumped the paper down and screamed for Justin Pendrick, the VP that reported directly to him.

"Hey, Pin-Dick," he yelled, poking his computer on, "where are we with Chase?"

"Ten million at 10, closing tomorrow!" boomed the reply, which Anderson could hear over the buzz of the trading floor.

Anderson flipped a thumbs-up to Pendrick, and then crammed a telephone receiver against his face. On his phone he saw a light flashing, and so he dialed his voicemail.

"*Welcome to audix,*" the machine sang in a tinny female voice, "*you have one new message. Message 1, new, from an external number –* "

"Jesus Christ," Anderson moaned, and then he punched the number six, which he knew would bypass the recording and instantly play the voicemail. It was a message from his college friend Dodge Brewer, a private equity guy in New York, received at 11:52 Chicago time the night before.

"*Hey dude, Dodge here,*" Brewer said on the voicemail, "*it's about one in the morning and I'm on the way home. Anyway, nice quiz you sent today. I failed it, as you might have guessed. I sent you a response . . . and . . . uh*"

"Hey Anderson!" Pendrick screamed from six terminals over, drowning out the balance of Dodge Brewer's voicemail. "I'm going 10 mil at 10 with BNY! You want in you got thirty seconds!"

"Wait a second!" screamed Anderson, "Jesus!"

Anderson quickly poked a finger at number three on the telephone pad, and the Audix lady sang, "*Deleted!*" Dodge Brewer's voicemail was gone – Anderson would call him later, maybe tomorrow. Next, he opened his e-mail and saw one from dbrewer@poseidoncapital.com, which he noticed had come in about ten minutes before Dodge's voicemail.

Probably what he was calling about, Anderson thought, and he double-clicked to open it. Immediately a full-screen image appeared of the same naked white lady he had sent out the day before, but this time the girl's head was different. She now had the face of a smiling black woman, and for some strange reason she looked awfully familiar. Anderson then read the text of the e-mail and it hit him – this was the woman named Gwen Adams, that receptionist at Dodge's company who Anderson had tried to pick up one night in a drunken stupor.

"Holy shit," he said aloud. In an instant the embarrassment of that ugly night came flooding back into his memory. Dodge, that fucker, had never let him live that night down, and here he was busting his balls over it again.

But that photo – what the hell, thought Anderson. He stood there a moment staring at it, and then called for Pendrick.

"Hey Pin-Dick, come check this out!"

Pendrick came bustling over, and he and Anderson stared slack-jawed at the photograph.

"Jesus," said Pendrick, "who is that?"

"Chick who works at my friend's company."

"She white or black?"

Anderson shot him a look.

"The picture's obviously a fake, you dumb shit."

"Yeah, huh?"

"Yeah, huh? What're you, retarded?"

Pendrick hooked a thumb back over his shoulder.

"Look, BNY, I gotta make a move here. Whaddya want to do?"

"Gimme a minute," said Anderson. "I wanna forward this."

As Pendrick drifted away, Anderson clicked the "forward" button on his e-mail menu and tabbed down to the "To" field to type the word "boyz," which was a group e-mail list that included fifty-four of Anderson's friends based in New York, Chicago and Boston. A few others were scattered in Florida and in London.

In the text box he typed, "From a friend of mine in New York – definitely worth a laugh."

Anderson clicked "Send," and chased after Pendrick.

LUCY WATTS DIDN'T mind the late hours at Sherrington Partners PLC because the job paid a decent wage in OT. Between the rent she was paying for her one-room West London flat, and the cost of her commute to the firm's offices at Holborn Viaduct, up in London's business district, there was no question she could use the money. She just wished that her boss, an interest rate swap analyst named Nathan J. Crepps, would be more sensitive to her personal time. Like now, for instance, the way he just sat in that office of his, at three minutes past one in the afternoon, after having asked her to stay put until his conference call was over, knowing full well that she had lunch with the girls every day.

Couldn't he once give her a break, let her take lunch in peace?

She could see into his office now, could see the brown wingtips over the royal blue socks stacked up on the desk, and the way he was laughing into the phone, all of which meant that the conference call obviously had ended. But here he was blabbing away on a personal call, completely disregarding the fact that six other secretaries were probably standing down in the lobby right now waiting for her.

Lucy looked again at the clock mounted on the wall above her supervisor's desk, when Crepps finally emerged from his office, oblivious to her lunch hour, which would now have to be crunched down to about forty-five minutes.

"Pardon, Lucy," he said, pulling a jacket over his shoulders, "I'm on my way to a business lunch at the Savoy Hotel, and I'll be back by four."

The married Crepps went to this "business lunch" every Wednesday, at the same hotel, and Lucy had her suspicions.

"Right," Lucy said, glancing at the wall clock again. She was anxious to get moving and was silently begging for him to leave.

"One favor before you go, love," Crepps continued, "I just received the final credit agreement from our solicitors."

Crepps pointed his chin into his office.

"Would you please forward it to the two main bond groups?"

"Certainly, Mr. Crepps," Lucy replied, gritting her teeth.

"Imperative that it goes out straight away."

"Got it."

"Right then, love. Cheers."

As soon as he turned the corner, Lucy shot a text to a co-worker named Gail – "*2 mins, otw*" – and scurried into Crepps's office, pulling up his e-mail inbox. She hastily scanned the e-mail subject lines for anything resembling a credit agreement, when suddenly the computer beeped as a new e-mail appeared, its subject line in deeply bolded letters. The subject title read "Fw: Re: Take The Quiz!" and did not appear to be from any solicitors. Lucy was puzzled. Was this a credit agreement?

Certainly didn't look like one, but there were no other new emails. And this one had a jpeg file attached, and that was the way the credit agreements sometimes arrived. And in any event, who had time to check.

Without reading the text of the e-mail or opening the file, Lucy forwarded it to a group e-mail list entitled "BondGroup-Asia," which included 137 traders based in Hong Kong, Bangkok, Singapore and Malaysia, and to "BondGroup-Europe," a group list made up of 179 traders in London, Munich, Paris, Rome and Madrid. She clicked the send button, and off it went.

Just as her boss had instructed.

On Thursday morning, down in the Cortez Hill section of San Diego, the sun was beating down through the palm trees that crowded the second story office window belonging to Jimmy McManus, the Southeast Regional Sales Manager for Krudson Brands Inc., a national food and beverage conglomerate headquartered in Dallas. McManus was breaking a sweat over his morning coffee because the air conditioning system in this building would not kick on for another hour, at eight.

Right now, on a gorgeous morning in April, McManus was staring open-mouthed at an e-mail he had just received from Kevin Anderson, a college friend who lived in Chicago. He was squinting to see the image on his computer screen, and so he stood and twisted the venetian blinds to block out the sun rays. With the type of guys that made up his sales force, McManus would receive a lot of e-mails like this, but this one was a doozy. With the room now darkened, McManus could see that it was a picture of a naked white lady with a black woman's head, and as far as McManus could tell, staring at it as he did for about five straight minutes, it looked authentic. But this couldn't be real, could it?

The picture had to be a fake. McManus dunked a bagel into his lukewarm coffee.

"Anderson, man, where's he come *up* with this crap?"

McManus thought of another college buddy of his, an old friend named Wesley Preston, a six-foot three tank of a man who McManus shared the backfield with for a season in the Brown University football program. Preston was now the Varsity football coach at a high school in Montgomery, Alabama.

Wes loves this shit, thought McManus, and he decided to send it along. He clicked "forward," and as he began to type the first few letters of the address wesley.preston@conoverhigh.edu into the "To" field of the e-mail, his company e-mail system automatically prompted a memorized group list for its West Coast Sales personnel – westcoastsales@kb.org. When McManus tabbed down to the text field, the e-mail address to West Coast Sales stuck, but McManus didn't notice.

He clicked send and headed down the hall for a coffee re-fill. In less than ten seconds, the e-mail and photograph were delivered to 3,274 KB employees in twenty-four sales regions across California, Oregon, Washington, Idaho, Nevada, Arizona, Wyoming and New Mexico.

CATIE MCWATERS PULLED up a steel fold-out chair in front of a computer terminal in the Bostov Internet Café in central Moscow. She frequented this place, located near the southeast end of Red Square, because it had beautiful views of St. Basil's Cathedral and the only coffee in this city that didn't taste like wall-paper glue. Plus, the computers were faster than the ones at Lomonosov Moscow State University, where she was living for the summer as part of a Stanford University study abroad program. She could also get easy access to her Gmail account.

After logging on, Catie opened her inbox and smiled when she saw a message from tfaviani@kb.org, the summer work address for her roommate Toni Faviani. Boy, did she miss Toni. Toni had missed the cut-off for the program in Moscow by two-tenths of a grade point, or else she'd be here too. Instead, Toni was working as a summer intern at the Krudson Brands company near her home in Albuquerque, New Mexico.

Catie double-clicked on the e-mail and read Toni's message:

You believe this? Came from a KB sales manager in San Diego. Looks like he forwarded it by mistake, and I think they canned his ass. But scroll down and look at the original email from some scumbag in New York, some private equity guy. You want to talk about racist? Anyway, how's Moscow?

Catie opened the photograph, and her jaw hit the floor.

THE ONE THING that Tim Hanratty couldn't understand about his job as an assistant producer at Fairview Productions, an independent film company, was why he had to fight so much traffic to get to it. Hanratty sat in his 2009 Saab 9-3 convertible under a pair of cheap sunglasses on the eastbound Santa Monica Freeway, staring at the back of a Plymouth Voyager minivan packed with a bunch of school kids. They were laughing and giving him the finger.

Hanratty felt the early morning California sun beat down on the back of his neck. In about ten minutes he'd put the top up and crank the AC, but right now, parked behind that minivan, he figured he'd check e-mail on his phone. With the emergency brake pulled, Hanratty navigated his way to his e-mail inbox and saw one from his cousin, Mike Philbus, a CPA in Boston, entitled "Re: Take The Quiz!" Mike never sent anything to Hanratty that could be shown or read to any decent human being, and so Hanratty had to exercise some judgment every time he opened one of his cousin's emails. Where Mike found this stuff Hanratty would never know. The time Mike wasted digging it up was no doubt the byproduct of being bored shitless in a life spent as an accountant, Hanratty figured.

Anyway, Hanratty could see that some guy named Kevin Anderson had sent this one to Mike, who forwarded it on to him. Mike's e-mail read:

Yo Tim – here's a pic of a naked white chick with a black woman's head. Funny shit. Check it out when you get out of traffic. Mikey.

Hanratty laughed at Mike's ability to predict he'd be reading his e-mail while stuck in traffic, and he tossed the phone onto the passenger seat. But then he got an idea. About a month earlier, Hanratty was at a seminar on cinematography in Burbank and sat next to a guy named Curtis Gilson, a short disheveled Australian with a bright orange beard and dirt under his fingernails. Physically speaking, Gilson was repulsive, an appearance that perfectly matched what he did for a living. Gilson told Hanratty that he operated an adult entertainment company based in Sydney, and was in southern California "on business," whatever that meant.

Hanratty thought Gilson was nuts, but he remembered the maniac babbling in that accent of his about an offer to pay fifteen hundred bucks for any type of sicko photographs, which he took the time to describe, that he could publish on one of his company's disgusting websites. Hanratty couldn't see the photograph on his phone, but the idea of a naked white woman with a black woman's head was probably right in this wacko's ballpark. And fifteen hundred bucks was much needed right now. Hanratty was sure he had the guy's card somewhere, maybe in his briefcase.

While steering with his legs and flipping the bird back to the school kids in the minivan, Hanratty located the guy's e-mail address and successfully forwarded the photograph to the other side of the world. It arrived there in less than fifteen seconds.

Two hours later, and approximately 7,500 miles away, at about two a.m. on Thursday in Sydney, Gilson uploaded the photograph onto a website entitled "naughtysecretaries.com," under a heading labeled "New Yorkers." Then he mailed a check for fifteen hundred American dollars to Los Angeles, California.

THE METRO DESK at the *New York Times* was the dream job of many a young reporter, and Paul McWaters felt lucky to be there. It not only got his name in print every day in the Times, but it also got him out on the street, investigating crimes and accidents and domestic disputes and everything else that pumped the heartbeat of this great city. What McWaters loved most though, what really got his blood flowing and helped him spring out of bed every day at five-thirty in the morning, was the pursuit of The Big One. The hunt for the Bahama Mama. That one story that would land on his desk one day, without notice, and whammo! – he'd go A-1.

Because that was the big time for any reporter in Metro, and McWaters and everyone else knew it. Page A-1, top of the fold. The print edition of the *Times* was going the way of the dinosaur, but the Metro Desk reporters still died to get a story on A-1, and McWaters was as determined as anyone.

On Friday morning, at just before nine o'clock, when the night shift copy editors would be heading out the door as the daytime Metro reporters were stumbling in, McWaters was at his desk stuffing an egg and cheese sandwich into his face when his computer beeped with an e-mail from his little sister Catie, a Stanford junior studying in Moscow for the summer. He knew that Catie loved this little Internet café over there and would hang out after classes sending e-mails back to the States.

He opened Catie's e-mail and read:

Hey Woodward (or Bernstein, I forget) – here's a scoop for you. Take a look at the attached e-mail and photo (yuk). A NY private equity guy sent it to 1 single person, and judging from the history, it seems to have made it all over the world. Think this moron knows? Anyway, technology run amok? Hostile/ racist work environment? Lots of angles. Call you Tuesday. Cate.

And with that McWaters's eyes became as big as pancakes. He scrolled down and read the lengthy e-mail history, calculating the way in which it had circulated all the way from New York to Chicago to New Mexico and then to Russia and then back to New York, all in a matter of hours. And then he saw that photograph. The guy's receptionist, for God's sake.

Did she even know? Does *he* know?

McWaters stared dumbfounded at the photograph for several minutes, looking over his shoulder at least three times, and then he clicked a button and sprinted down the hall to the printer. As he ran, a huge smile spread across his face, because McWaters could see this one coming a mile away. It was a story, alright.

A real big story.

TWO HOURS LATER, McWaters was sitting in a conference room with a man named Ted Collins, an assistant managing editor in Metro. The two men had their feet planted on the conference room table as they dialed the general number for a company called Poseidon Capital Partners. After a ring or two blasted over the speakerphone, a woman answered.

"Good morning, Poseidon Capital," she said softly.

"Hello ma'am, Ted Collins and Paul McWaters from the *New York Times*. We'd like a word with Mr. Dodge Brewer, please."

"Oh, I see. May I tell him what this is in reference to?"

"You may," Collins answered curtly, winking over at McWaters. "It's about a story we're running tomorrow on Page A-1 about a racially offensive email and photograph he recently sent. We'd like to know if he's interested in providing any comment."

BY NOON ON Friday, New York time, only thirty-six hours had elapsed from when Dodge had clicked send on his e-mail to Kevin Anderson and climbed into the back of the Lincoln Town Car.

Since then, his e-mail had hit the computer terminals and iPhones of some sixty million people.

As Dodge was chomping down on a turkey club in the company lunchroom, marking up another draft of his Investment Committee memorandum, the text of his e-mail to Anderson, as well as the photograph, was being viewed by a carp fisherman in Reykjavik, Iceland, the president of a bank in the Fiji Islands, a camp counselor with Outward Bound in Oslo, Norway, the owner of a motel in Sao Paulo, Brazil, a sushi restaurant owner in Tokyo, Japan, and the foreman on a timber cutting crew in British Columbia, Canada. And each of those people then forwarded the e-mail.

To a total of three dozen people who also forwarded it.

AN HOUR LATER, at just after 1pm, Gwen Adams stepped out of the elevator on the 38th floor, exiting with three Managing Directors who had been working within thirty feet of her for the last six years, but with whom she had never spoken. She pulled open the glass doors to Poseidon Capital and rounded the receptionist's desk, hastening over to her chair. Gwen was carrying a black shoulder bag that contained a small tupperware tin of unfinished salad, along with a copy of the St. James New Testament Bible, which she read every day on the D train from Brooklyn to Manhattan.

As she approached her workstation, Gwen looked up and saw Rita Fuller, Poseidon's Head of Human Resources. She was with Bill Champlain, the company's Executive Director, and the person to whom all administrative staff, including the receptionists, ultimately reported. Fuller was whispering into an iPhone, and Champlain had a newspaper tucked under his arm. Gwen noticed that the two of them looked nervous, which caused her heart to race a little. When they saw Gwen had returned from lunch, they both smiled, taking a step forward.

But the smile quickly dropped from Fuller's face.

"Gwen," she said gravely, "Can we talk a minute?"

"Certainly," Gwen responded, stealing a glance around the reception area. She saw two other administrative staff people, huddled in a doorway, staring at her with their arms crossed. Gwen noticed that Champlain had twice raked a hand through his hair.

"May I ask, am I in some kind of trouble?"

"Of course not," said Champlain.

A moment later, he led Gwen into a small conference room located near the reception area, across from the company lunchroom. Fuller handed her a copy of that day's *New York Times,* and then Champlain asked her to read a news article that appeared on the front page.

"Brace yourself," he told her coldly.

The article was entitled *"Around the World in Eighty . . . Seconds!"* and had a subheading that read "CEO'S E-MAIL MAY SPUR CIVIL CLAIMS." Confused, Gwen folded the paper over and read.

The article discussed a sexually explicit photograph that the CEO of Poseidon Capital Partners, a man named Dodge Brewer, sent from his computer in New York to a single bond trader in Chicago. The picture had been altered to contain the head of one of his female employees. Initially, Gwen could not understand what all of this had to do with her, but then suddenly she saw her own name – *Gwen Adams* – right there in black and white.

"Oh my God," she gasped. "Mr. Brewer did this?"

Gwen finished the article, which reported that in two days the e-mail and photo had been forwarded to every major city in the United States, all European capitals, all over Southeast Asia, to Moscow, Sydney, the Fiji Islands, India, China, Japan, Scandinavia, South America and Reykjavik, Iceland, and was still being forwarded, according to sources. The article noted the breathtaking speed with which the e-mail had circumvented the globe, referring to it as *"The Snowball,"* stating that it had gotten bigger by the minute since the moment that Brewer sent it. The article conservatively estimated that over sixty million people had already received it.

It stated further that there was no way to know how many more people would get it, and that the reason for the continued forwarding appeared to be a gathering sense of curiosity – not only about the outrageous nature of the photograph, but also about this wealthy CEO of a private equity company who had gone so far out of his way to humiliate his working class minority employee. It further stated that people were now forwarding the email and photograph in connection with some bizarre competition, for the sheer thrill of it – they wanted to see how far around the globe it could possibly go. The article stated that when it popped into your email inbox the challenge was to forward it to ten more friends, with instructions that they do the same. The article also referred to the fact that Twitter and every other social media outlet was calling for this CEO's head on a silver platter. The topic currently was the number one trending hashtag on Twitter - #poseidoncapitalracists.

Gwen next read a sentence that caused her to feel physically nauseous. It said that the photograph – with her face – currently was posted on over a dozen adult entertainment websites and counting. She finished reading the article and turned to Champlain.

"Mr. Champlain," she said with resolve, tears welling in her eyes, "have you seen the photograph to which this article refers?"

"Yes, I have."

"Do you have a copy with you?"

"I do."

"May I see it please?"

Champlain didn't say a word, and instead he rubbed his chin.

"Mr. Champlain, I'll find it myself on the Internet," she said, and then she gestured down to the newspaper, "or perhaps I could call Mr. Paul McWaters of the *New York Times* for a copy."

"No. That won't be necessary."

FOR HIS PART, after shooting his e-mail to Kevin Anderson in the wee hours after midnight Wednesday, Dodge had been strangely insulated from the whole thing until early Friday afternoon, when Cindy called him at the office in tears, absolutely hysterical, telling him she had just received the e-mail and photograph from her own mother, of all people.

Dodge then scurried into his office, hearing commotion out in the hallway. He plopped down into his seat and lifted the receiver.

"Dodge," Cindy choked hysterically, "it's everywhere! It's in the papers, it's on television! Everyone is talking about it. My Mom got it from a friend of hers. Did you really do this?!"

"I don't get it," Dodge answered, a heat flash burning his face. "I sent that thing as a joke just to Kevin in Chicago, no one else, Cin. How'd your mother get it? I don't understand."

"I don't know Dodge!" she responded, blowing her nose. "This is awful. It's so bad, have you seen Twitter?"

"No – I mean, no, I haven't."

Dodge felt a sharp pain in his chest.

"I have to go get Charlotte before she sees this," said Cindy. "You have to go and explain things. Just call me, I'll be here."

Dodge hung up the phone, hyperventilating. He then went to Google and did a search. What he saw almost made him pass out.

Dodge grabbed the phone again and hastily dialed his lawyer.

ON MONDAY MORNING, Gwen Adams stood at a podium flanked with half a dozen microphones at the offices of Willis C. Fairchild, a fiery New York City civil rights lawyer whose list of multi-million-dollar settlements was as long as the Mississippi River. Gwen wore a navy-blue shin-length skirt with a black sweater, over which laid a strand of white pearls. She held her Bible in both hands down at her waist. Standing at the microphones along with Gwen and Fairchild was the Rev. Luscious Calverton, minister of the Revivalist Baptist Church in Flatbush, Brooklyn.

"We are shocked and outraged!" Calverton screamed, pounding on the podium, "that this company, which has not one African-American among its partners – *not one*! – would maliciously and callously defame its most loyal employee, without any regard for her dignity and self-respect! We announce today the filing of a $100 million defamation lawsuit against these evil bunch of wealthy bankers, and this Mr. Dodge Brewer, who was carrying out a longstanding policy of racial discrimination and callous disregard for human decency that has permeated this company for *years*!"

As Calverton spoke, Gwen stood silently next to him, dabbing tears, while Fairchild held a copy of the lawsuit in both his hands, directly over his head. Just like Moses with the stone tablets, thought McWaters, who was taking notes in the back of the room.

THE NEXT DAY, Tuesday, the filing of Gwen Adams's lawsuit was reported in an Associated Press article that ran in every major newspaper across the country, including on Page A-1 of *The New York Times*. The second McWaters article in less than a week also reported that Poseidon Capital Partners had closed its doors on Monday afternoon, after hundreds of investors had pulled their billions of dollars out of the company over the weekend. It also informed the public that Dodge Brewer, the company CEO at the center of this hurricane, could not be reached for comment and had not been seen in the town of Ketchogue, where he lived, since the story ran on Friday.

However, the United States Attorney's Office for the Southern District of New York, with the assistance of the FBI, was actively looking for him.

CHAPTER 32

JIMMY O'REILLY MEETS ABRAHAM LINCOLN

THE 81ST POLICE Precinct where Tom worked was way over in East Brooklyn, on Ralph Avenue, where the gritty streets of Bedford-Stuyvesant blend with those of its Bushwick neighbor. O'Reilly and Tom agreed to meet nearby so that Tom could sneak out for 40 minutes or so during his shift. O'Reilly told him something had come up at work and he needed to talk. He asked if he could meet face-to-face, and that he wouldn't take too much of his time. Tom's response, which was typical, was simply, "this better be good," although that was more of joke than anything else. He told O'Reilly he could spare him a half hour, and O'Reilly jumped at the offer.

They decided on lunch at a place called Clarita's Cafe, a Cuban joint over on Malcolm X. Boulevard. It was a few blocks from the 81st and Tom told O'Reilly to make sure he brought a stuffed wallet. "You're paying little brother," Tom had said cheerfully, "we're gonna eat good with all that blue blood money you're raking in."

O'Reilly was grateful Tom was making the time, so he had no objection. His plan was to explain the whole situation as best he could, but at the same time, he knew it was going to be difficult to get Tom to take him seriously, to acknowledge the importance of the matter. Tom would remind you that he dealt every day with murderers, rapists, arsonists, kidnappers and every other manner of deadbeat and cretin, and for that reason he considered what O'Reilly did for a living as unimportant in the grand scheme of things. It was nothing more than people in expensive suits fighting over money, according to Tom, and when it came right down to it, none of it amounted to a hill of beans. But O'Reilly really needed some advice, and Tom seemed like the logical choice.

O'Reilly got out of an Uber on Gates Avenue on a breezy Sunday afternoon, just around 12:45 pm. He walked directly over to Clarita's. Tom arrived a few moments later in his police uniform.

The two settled into a small booth in the tiny café, and a heavyset woman with olive skin and a dark ponytail ambled over, a smile on her cherubic face.

"Mariposa!" Tom yelled cheerfully, "how are you?"

"Well, well, Sergeant O'Reilly, good to see you again," she said in an upbeat tone. "I thought maybe they promoted you to Commissioner or something, and you forgot about us!"

"Never, Mariposa," Tom assured her. "You know me, I've just been chasin' bad guys."

"Better you than me!"

Mariposa nodded to O'Reilly.

"Who's this? He's a cutie," she asked.

"This mutt? A cutie? Nah, this is my little brother Jimmy, he thinks he's gonna be a lawyer someday."

"Wow, looks and smarts, nice combo. Nice to meet you."

O'Reilly nodded back. "Pleasure," he said.

"Look," Tom interjected, "if you're angling for a big tip, you got the right idea, 'cause he's paying."

Mariposa laughed.

"So what can I get you guys?"

Tom jumped right in.

"Mariposa, we're both gonna have the fried pork chops and we'll split a large bowl of the congri. Make it as hot as you can. Then maybe some of them fried plantains."

"Good choice," Mariposa answered, lifting the menus. "Be just a few minutes." She then pushed her way through a door to the rear of the restaurant, and Tom turned to O'Reilly.

"This place is great," he said, leaning forward on his elbows. "Food's unreal, get ready to eat, little brother."

"Porkchops?" O'Reilly asked. "Whaddya tryin' to give me a heart attack?"

Tom scoffed.

"You got a set a tits on you already," he said, "ain't like you been eatin' salads."

"Yeah, I know. I really gotta lose some weight."

"You'll start tomorrow."

"By the way, what's congri?" O'Reilly asked.

"Rice and beans, spicy," Tom told him, "you're gonna love it."

Over the next few minutes, O'Reilly caught Tom up on his life at FT&B, his work out at the warehouse, how things were going at school, and his plans for graduation and the Bar Exam. Then they discussed the trip to Ireland in August, with Tom announcing that he had purchased a new set of irons along with non-refundable plane tickets. He told O'Reilly how excited he was for the trip, that he was blowing some serious vacation time to go, and that if O'Reilly canceled on him, "I'm gonna cave your head in." O'Reilly swore that would not be the case.

Knowing he had little time left, O'Reilly then brought up the subject of the Interim Report, the reason he had organized this lunch. He explained the circumstances under which the document had landed in his lap and the significance of it in terms of how it could impact the shrimp cases. He told him about the conversations he had with Burgess, Ko and Briggs over the substance of it, and of course his decision to toss a chair against the warehouse wall when he couldn't get any of them to listen to reason. Then he told Tom he really needed his advice on what to do next.

"Well, first off," Tom said, shaking his head, "how in God's name have they not fired you yet? I mean, whaddya gotta do to get canned in that place, shoot somebody?"

"Well, I've thought that several times myself."

"And what are they paying you for that warehouse work?"

"Sixty bucks an hour."

"Jimmy, Christ Almighty, for sixty bucks an hour I'd shovel horseshit. Fuck's the matter with you?"

O'Reilly ignored the comment. He really needed Tom to give him some perspective, because his angst over the whole matter was keeping him up at night. O'Reilly felt he was at a crossroads, that his next decision was critical and could affect his entire legal career. He leaned down over the table and looked intently at his brother.

"Look, Tom, I really need your help here. That report is a very big deal, okay? A person can have an allergy to seafood or shellfish and would need to stay away from a product like this, but you can also be fine eating shrimp, and separately have an allergy to sulfites. Every company treats shrimp with sulfites to preserve the coloring and whatnot, so that's fine, but they use tiny, trace amounts. If you are allergic, the higher the concentration of the sulfites the worse your allergic reaction will be. The document I stumbled across made it clear that the sulfite concentrations in the affected batches were enormous. They screwed up, it was a mistake. But it explains why there was a spike in all the lawsuits."

"Okay, I get it, they soaked the shrimp with sulfites," Tom said, with little emotion, "are there rules about how much you can use?"

"Bet your ass. According to the FDA, if you go over a certain amount, you have to label the packaging and provide warnings."

"And they went over?"

"Ten times over," said O'Reilly, "by a screw-up in the quality control checks. Now they got people in comas, and dead."

"Okay, but if I'm following the plot, you're on *their* side, right?"

"Tom, I'm telling you, I was not supposed to find that document, nobody was. It made no sense it being in the file I found it in, which belonged to the General Counsel – there were no other documents in there that had anything to do with that topic."

"Well, but you *did* find the document, and you followed protocols and went to your bosses, right? And they told you what?"

"They told me what?" O'Reilly asked, frustrated. "Whaddya mean they told me what? They said they don't have to disclose it to the other side, is what they said. Have you been listening?"

Tom webbed his fingers together, elbows on the table.

"I'm listening, Jimmy, and I'm not that jazzed about it," he said. "What am I missing here, what's the problem?"

"What's the problem?!"

"Yeah, Jimmy, what's the problem?" Tom asked, trying to make a point. He leaned forward and looked his brother in the eyes.

"Why's this any of your business?" he asked. "You pulled the document out of a box, and according to you your job was to log it into that database, right? And that's what you did?"

"Of course," O'Reilly answered, flustered.

"But you did more than that, you went to the muckety-mucks and told them about it, even though you didn't have to, am I right?"

"Yeah, you're right, Tom, but – "

"Jimmy, look," Tom interrupted, "you're probably not gonna want to hear this, but you want my advice little brother? Leave it the fuck alone. Let them handle it. At sixty bucks an hour, why do you even give a shit?"

Behind Tom, Mariposa sauntered over with two steaming plates of fried pork chops, one in each hand. She was followed by a food runner in a white apron carrying a large bowl of rice and beans. In tandem they dumped everything on the table, together with two large glasses of ice water. Tom promptly stuffed a white cloth napkin under his shirt collar. He grabbed a fork and plunged it into the first chop in the pile, as O'Reilly shoved his plate to the center of the table.

"Tom, there's obviously a bigger issue here," he said impatiently, "what they're doing isn't right, it's not fair."

"It's not fair," Tom repeated, his eyes fixed on his plate of food.

"That's right, it's not fair, not to the parties in the cases, not to all those injured people, and not …," O'Reilly waved a hand in the air, "to the entire system of justice we have, to be perfectly honest."

Tom shook his head and smirked.

"The entire system of justice?" he asked sarcastically. "Jesus Christ, Jimmy, you're a trip, my man."

He pointed his fork at O'Reilly.

"See, right there. That's always been your problem."

"My problem?"

"Yeah, your *problem*," Tom responded sharply, with a mouthful of meat now. "Your whole life you've been focused on some warped sense of right and wrong you got. You remember when you were a kid, I don't know, about eleven? I'll never forget it – you caught that kid Vinny Campezzi pinching bills out of the Christmas collection envelope at the school, at St. Xavier's. And so you ratted the kid out, went to the Pastor about it, you remember that?"

O'Reilly nodded and crossed his arms.

"Damn right I did," O'Reilly answered. "That money was for victims of that earthquake in Peru. I donated all my paper route money, like twenty-eight bucks. The kid should'na been robbing it."

"Yeah, and so what happened?" Tom asked with a giggle. "Turns out Campezzi was helping his old man pay the damn electric bill, wasn't he? The kid was eleven and he was stealing to help keep the lights on in his house. So what did you do? The next week you gave all your paper route money *to Vinny*. Un-freakin-believable."

"He needed the help," O'Reilly shrugged.

"Jimmy, it wasn't your fight to take on, that's my point!" Tom said. "You don't get it, sometimes you gotta focus on the practicalities of a situation, and just let it be."

O'Reilly rolled his eyes.

"The practicalities?"

"Yeah, Jimmy, the practicalities, the realities," Tom shot back.

He looked at his brother and let a small laugh go.

"See, thing is, you're not actually a lawyer, are you?"

"Not yet," O'Reilly answered.

"And this Gunther company, it ain't your client, is it? 'Cause right now you're just a factory worker without a law license, right?"

"Yes."

"And the lawyers who *are* representing the client, the ones responsible for the cases, they all said you're wrong, and that they did *not* have to disclose that report, and that you didn't understand the rules. They said *they* would handle it, right?"

"That's exactly what they said, but it's all bullshit, don't you get it?" O'Reilly countered, his voice rising now. "These lawsuits are piling up because Gunther made an egregious error and people are getting sick, some dying. This is a public company and they're trying to protect their *wallets*, Tom, because if this information gets out in the public domain the cases will quadruple and the stock will take a nosedive. It ain't right."

Tom then grabbed the handle of a large serving spoon buried in the bowl of congri. He scooped a moundful of it and dumped it onto his plate.

"Look, Jimmy, you asked for my advice," he said, digging into his rice, "and you oughta listen to what I'm about to tell you, okay?"

"Go ahead," O'Reilly answered.

"Drop it, little brother," he said. "Wait until you become a lawyer before you take this kind of shit on, because right now you're just a spoke in the wheel. You don't want to fuck up your career. You got a bright future ahead of you, and you did the right thing. Just leave it at that. Plus, you said you signed one of those confidentiality agreements, didn't you?"

"I did, yes," said O'Reilly.

"So what choice do you have? Let this one go," Tom advised. "You got plenty of time to be a crusader and take on the good fight

when you become a real lawyer and not some half-assed glorified
Walmart clerk like you are right now. In the meantime, I don't know
… maybe you can help little old ladies cross the street, volunteer to
work with blind nuns, go play sports with retarded orphans, shit like
that. It's right up your alley. And then when you pass the bar you
can take on the world's problems to your heart's content."

O'Reilly planted his elbows on the table and buried his face in
his palms. He had no appetite now, and merely watched as Tom
forked gigantic chunks of pork chop into his mouth.

"You're being a smartass," he said, "and not very helpful."

Tom shrugged his shoulders.

"Whaddyagonnado."

O'Reilly stared across the restaurant as Tom devoured the rest
of his pork chop and shoveled forkfuls of rice and beans into his
face. Maybe he's right about the whole thing, thought O'Reilly.
Maybe he had no choice. He did in fact sign a confidentiality
agreement and to violate the terms of that contract would most
certainly be the end of his career. He had gone to the highest levels
within the firm and had voiced his concerns. If in the end it turned
out that Gunther never disclosed the results of that testing, at least
he, O'Reilly, could sleep at night, knowing he did everything within
his power to right that wrong.

But that comment, from his own brother, that he was just a
"spoke in the wheel," well, it was statements like that that were
unacceptable to him. The truth was that the advice Tom was
offering was exactly what he had expected from him, but he needed
to hear it spoken aloud to convince him that he would never follow
it. O'Reilly really didn't know where the whole thing was going, but
"dropping it" was not an option for him. Maybe in the end he would
do nothing more than make one last appeal to reason with Briggs
again, assuming he could even get an audience with him. Perhaps
that was as far as he could take it.

But right now, what O'Reilly wanted was answers. Before he
could make any decisions, O'Reilly wanted a complete picture, a full
set of facts, and then he would tackle this problem analytically, like
a lawyer. And in that regard, he thought about what the information
gap was, what missing pieces of the puzzle currently were hindering
his analysis. And what he didn't know was this – did Gunther ever

prepare a Final Report about the sulfites testing? And where were the missing pages of the Interim Report?

O'Reilly grabbed a fork and stabbed one of the pork chops in front of him. Right there, sitting with Tom in Clarita's Café, O'Reilly made a decision. To get a full set of those facts, to get that complete picture he was hoping for, he needed to know what was laying up there in those boxes, in Briggs's office, at the feet of none of other than Mr. Abraham Lincoln.

There were no two ways about it.

THAT SUNDAY NIGHT, O'Reilly left his Park Slope apartment at precisely 9:45 pm. He marched purposefully down Seventh Avenue, past the shops, cafes and bars, and made a right turn down Lincoln Place, entering the New York City subway system at Grand Army Plaza, up where Flatbush Avenue dissects Prospect Park. He swiped his MetroCard and jumped on a Manhattan-bound no. 4 train.

The subway was light that evening, and so O'Reilly found himself a seat in the middle of the car. He was dressed neutral so that he wouldn't stand out, but at the same time he didn't want to appear like a cat burglar. It was a cool evening in late April, so O'Reilly wore dark blue jeans and deep brown shoes with a denim buttoned-down shirt under a navy-blue sweater. O'Reilly had also pulled a Yankee cap down over his head in order to mute the glow of his orangey skull. If anyone asked him why he was there, he wanted to look like a casually dressed FT&B employee who simply had legal business to conduct on a Sunday night. O'Reilly, however, was banking on the place being empty. If there was one night at the firm where the staff of lawyers and paralegals was skeletal, O'Reilly knew, Sunday was the night. Hopefully he wouldn't run into a soul.

At roughly 10:30 pm, the subway car rumbled into Grand Central Station, and O'Reilly alighted to the platform. He took the escalator up to street level and before long he was out on Lexington Avenue, walking north. The streets were dark and empty, with little pedestrian activity and only a few taxis and cars rolling by. The main entrance to FT&B Tower was a block west, on Park Avenue, but O'Reilly stayed on Lexington. He had no designs to enter the firm through its front doors. If he did that, the swipe of his employee ID card would leave an electronic record of his entrance. Plus, the few security staff there would clearly remember someone arriving so late on a Sunday.

Instead, O'Reilly had other plans.

Back in the summer, sometime in mid-July, Dexter Morgan had sent an email asking if any of the Summers had a few spare hours to assist reviewing documents in an antitrust case, apparently to meet a court-ordered deadline. O'Reilly had jumped at the opportunity. In a short while, he and three other Summers met in the office of a Senior Associate named Jacob Edelstein, who promptly announced that a dozen bankers' boxes were arriving from the client by car down in the street, and would the three of them mind helping him carry them up to a conference room?

Before he knew it O'Reilly was down on the sidewalk on Park Avenue, with Edelstein and the three others, decked out in his suit as the sun beat down and swarms of people marched by in both directions, right in front of FT&B Tower. A Lincoln Towncar pulled up but then quickly swung around to the side street, since no parking spot was available in front of the building. O'Reilly assisted by pulling two boxes from the back seat, piling them one on top of the other in his arms. He figured they would head back around to the Park Avenue entrance, but then Edelstein nodded to a side-street loading dock that belonged to FT&B.

"We'll just go in this way," Edelstein said with a conspiratorial wink, "but don't tell anybody you can waltz right in here, it's a little firm secret." O'Reilly and the three other Summers found themselves walking up a ramp and pushing their way through a heavy plastic sheet with a slit down the center. They landed in the basement of the building and promptly hopped a freight elevator to the lawyer floors above.

With that event still fresh in his memory, O'Reilly headed directly to the loading dock that Sunday night. The back of FT&B Tower abutted Lexington Avenue, and when O'Reilly located the side street, he pulled his Yankee cap tighter down on his head, stuffed his hands in his pockets, and walked slowly up the side street, moving west toward Park Avenue. If nothing had changed, O'Reilly assumed he could enter the building undetected through the loading dock, leaving no electronic sign that he had ever gained access. Of course, there was always the possibility of a surveillance camera back there, but if O'Reilly remembered correctly, there was only one of them in operation, something he had taken notice of at the time of Edelstein's revelation, finding it odd that the loading dock did not have a locked door. Of course, if O'Reilly's memory had failed him, and there was more than one camera, he could always abort the mission and head back to Brooklyn.

At just before 11, O'Reilly approached the loading dock from the east. The side street was unlit and virtually empty, save for a few yellow taxis rumbling west toward Park Avenue. O'Reilly stood along the wall of the building and looked into the loading dock.

Sure enough, it was exactly as he remembered.

The loading dock was an open, dark space, like a garage stall, with a cement floor and cinder block walls. Toward the back there was a four-foot high blue wall topped with a broad stripe painted bright yellow. On the left side, up against the wall, there was a steel walking ramp that landed on top of the blue wall. To the right of the ramp were two parking spaces marked with similar yellow stripes, and up on the loading area, on top of the blue wall, was a platform that ran back into the building. The platform also had thick steel girders running vertically, spaced every eight feet or so. At the rear of the platform there were two steel garage doors that O'Reilly could see were pulled down and secured to the floor with padlocks. But to the right, way up in the back, and completely out of view from anyone standing on the street, was that heavy plastic sheet. It was no more than the width of a regular office doorway.

O'Reilly looked to the ceiling and confirmed his memory from that day with Edelstein. There was only one camera, with a solid red light glowing on top of it, pointed directly at the steel ramp. O'Reilly was on the complete opposite end of the loading area, his back up against the wall. If he stayed that way, moving sideways, he could slip in directly underneath and out of view of the camera, and that is exactly what he did. He pressed his back to the wall and began stepping one foot over the other, out of view of the camera. When he hit the blue wall, O'Reilly jumped on top, landing on his rump. Then he rolled over and stood. He was now behind where the camera pointed, completely out of its range.

Finally, there it was, the plastic sheet. O'Reilly pushed through it and found himself moving down a short hallway. Right in front of him was the door that Edelstein had announced would be open that summer day, and O'Reilly knew this was the moment of truth.

He grabbed the door handle … and pulled it open.

O'Reilly was inside the building.

He was in a wide-open area that looked very much like the loading platform, with cement floors and cinder block walls, and over to the right, in a tight opening, was the freight elevator. O'Reilly moved quickly toward it, but then he stopped dead in his tracks. Up on the ceiling, angled directly at the elevator, was another security camera, one that O'Reilly never noticed that day over the summer. Like the one out in the loading area, this one also had a glowing red light on top. O'Reilly didn't move. He looked to his left, across from the freight elevator and out of range of the camera, and sure enough there was a door marked "Stairwell."

O'Reilly yanked the door open and pulled it shut behind him.

Then he began his march up forty-four flights of stairs, all the way to the 44th Floor, to the office of Mr. J. Hartwell Briggs.

WHEN O'REILLY FINALLY ascended to the 44th floor, he was soaked in sweat from head to toe. His shirt was sticking against his chest and back with moisture, and he could even feel his toes swishing around in his now-drenched socks. His heart was thumping, and his quadriceps and calf muscles were so aching and thick with blood it felt as though he were carrying a piano on his back. Somewhere around floor twenty-five he had removed the sweater and tied it around his waist, and he used it now to wipe the sweat dripping from his face and neck. He wanted nothing more than to shower and go to sleep, but he had come this far and was determined to see this through. All the answers that had been eluding him seemed only a few minutes away.

O'Reilly pulled opened the stairwell door and entered a small alcove between the entrances to the men's and women's bathrooms on that floor. He eased past a secretarial station and was now in the hallway, right near the open reception area. He looked right and left, seeing nothing but the vacant secretarial stations topped with flower vases and stacks of documents. The hallway and reception area were dimly lit, and O'Reilly could see that the perimeter lawyer offices were all dark. To be certain, he took a purposeful march around the entire floor, circling back around to where he had entered from the stairwell. Sure enough, there was no one present on this floor. He was completely alone.

O'Reilly walked back into the alcove by the bathrooms. To the right there was a small copy room that also contained a soft drink machine. He shoved a few dollar bills in and punched a button, and a bottle of water clunked down into the dispenser shoot. O'Reilly twisted the top off and chugged the bottle halfway down.

Well, he thought, it was now or never.

O'Reilly strode to the southwest side of the building and approached the double doors to Briggs's mammoth trapezoidal corner office. The doors were closed, and O'Reilly figured they likely would be locked, and he was right. He gave a tug on the door handle to confirm, and when the doors wouldn't budge, he peered down into the lock mechanism located directly in the center of the two doors. He saw quickly that it was a standard spring bolt, and he smiled as he snatched his wallet from his pocket, yanking out a plastic Visa card. Having a New York City policeman for a brother had some benefits and learning how to card his way through a simple spring bolt had been one of them. O'Reilly slid the Visa card between the doors, pressed it hard up against the sloped side of the bolt, and bent the card sideways. He felt the bolt give just as he twisted the door handle, and in a flash he was inside Briggs's office.

O'Reilly quickly shut the doors and hastened to the left side of the office, over to the trapezoid's wide-angled corner near the windows. He left the lights out, of course, in case some lawyer or paralegal or member of the night crew happened to come by, moving quickly behind Briggs's desk. He next looked down at the floor. Sure enough, at the foot of the Lincoln bust, lay a single Gunther document box from O'Reilly's beloved Secaucus warehouse. It was marked just as he had remembered, with dark black writing over a bright white box – GUNTH.001.015.0006. O'Reilly knew right away it was one of Handler's boxes. In his previous visit there had been two more boxes, and O'Reilly wondered what had happened to them. But that didn't matter now.

O'Reilly plunked down into Briggs's office chair, taking another swig from the water bottle. He tugged gently on the chain of a green banker's lamp sitting on Briggs's desk. The light clicked on, and

O'Reilly placed the bottle down in front of him. Then he leaned down to flip the top off the box. He grabbed a set of documents, about the thickness of a phone book, and arranged them in a pile.

Under the soft glow of the banker's lamp, O'Reilly turned the pages and began reading.

There were reams of documents relating to compliance with FDA standards and regulations, with reports from Gunther scientists, communications between Handler and his legal team about various products that Gunther sold, copies of pleadings in countless cases across the country, and various legal budgets and other financial documents. But there was nothing, as far as O'Reilly could see, about the Phillips frozen shrimp brand. He read on, slowly at first, but soon he was turning the pages quickly as he started to get a sense of what was in front of him. When he got through the first pile, O'Reilly placed the stack back into the box, and then he pulled another phonebook-thick stack. He dumped it onto the desk and continued reading. It was more of the same – all useless, meaningless documents – and O'Reilly's heart sank.

When he got through the second stack, O'Reilly gathered that one up too, and he swiveled Briggs's office chair to the left, leaning down to place the documents back into the box, just as he had done with the first pile. More than half the box remained, and O'Reilly straightened up now, frustrated. He glanced at his watch and looked across the darkened room. To his left, out the window, the office and building lights of the New York City skyline sparkled against the nighttime sky. O'Reilly wondered whether he was wasting his time. His clothes were dry now, and O'Reilly was starting to feel cold. He was exhausted, his eyes were heavy, and right now he was dreading the walk down forty-five flights of stairs, the sneaking out through the loading dock out of range of the security cameras, and the subway ride home, especially at this time of night.

Just then O'Reilly noticed the desk drawer, right there in front of him. Underneath the top of Briggs's desk there was a thin drawer with two old-fashioned handles with a brushed nickel finish, and O'Reilly yanked on one of them. The drawer was locked. He glanced across the room and saw a small armoire that also contained a thin drawer. There was a tiny key dangling in the lock. He walked over and pulled it out. The furniture in here appeared to match, and perhaps the key would work in the drawer to Briggs's desk, O'Reilly thought. O'Reilly then inserted the key into the lock of the desk drawer. He twisted and pulled the drawer open.

Inside there was nothing but a manila envelope, with no markings on the outside. O'Reilly lifted it and could feel the weight of a document. He undid the metal clasp, and what he saw sent a chill through his entire body. The document was entitled, "FINAL REPORT – JANUARY 26, 2018 – PRIVILEGED & CONFIDENTIAL." It was from the Gunther "Department of Scientific Research and Quality Assurance," and as with the Interim Report, it was prepared by Dr. Frederick T. Barber.

O'Reilly felt an adrenaline surge as he read the entire 14-page report. As he expected, the report confirmed the results of the prior testing of the sixteen batches of Phillips frozen shrimp that Gunther scientists had performed in November, as detailed in the Interim Report. The results were *confirmed,* O'Reilly said to himself. Every batch was tainted and mistakenly loaded up with sulfites as a result of a defect in the manufacturing process. The levels in the bags that had gone to market and sold in stores were exorbitant and posed a grave risk of injury and death to anyone with a sulfite allergy. Gunther had failed to label the Phillips product bags properly, and Dr. Barker, once again, had recommended a Class I Product Recall.

A product recall that had never taken place.

O'Reilly was nearly hyperventilating now, staring down at the first page of the report, his hands shaking. What now to do? What? It wasn't clear to him. How could these people withhold information like this? he thought. How could they do this? How? O'Reilly was beside himself. There was no question, in his mind, that something needed to be done about it, but who could he possibly tell about this discovery? Tom? That would be pointless. In fact, O'Reilly knew that telling anyone would require revealing the fact that he had gained unauthorized access not only to the building, but also to the law office of one of the most powerful men in the country. It would mean the end of his career. It would mean never becoming a lawyer.

"Damn it," he said aloud, and he leaned back in Briggs's chair, staring across the room. His eyes were hazy and unfocused as he tried to think, process. What could he do, what were his choices? It hurt his head even thinking about it. There didn't seem to be many options, and in any event, he certainly was not going to make any decisions sitting in this chair. But the one thing he sure as shit *was* going to do was make a copy of it. He would slip the original back into the manila envelope, lock up Briggs's drawer, and then figure out his next steps from there.

O'Reilly leaned forward to rise from the chair, and that's when he noticed the coffee table. The one across the room, situated between the two loveseat sofas. There, on the table, were two short stacks of documents, one on each side. They seemed as if they had been placed there for the convenience of two people sitting across from one another on the two facing sofas. In fact, as O'Reilly looked closer, he saw a legal pad underneath one of the stacks and two pens laying carelessly on the table. Then, over in the corner, O'Reilly saw a sport coat hanging on a walnut-colored coat stand.

Had someone been in here? O'Reilly had no idea. He thought it odd he hadn't noticed the documents or the coat before, and he instantly felt his heart sink. He wanted to get the hell of this place, and he grabbed the Final Report, rising from the chair ...

O'Reilly then heard the feint sound of a "ping!" coming from the area of the elevator banks, down the hall near the reception area.

Then, footsteps ...

He drew in a breath, his eyes as wide as saucers.

"Shit," he whispered, and he stuffed the Final Report into the front of his jeans, pulling his shirt over. Then he plopped down into Briggs's chair again, lowering his head. The office doors were closed, and O'Reilly snapped the chain to the banker's light, darkening the room.

The footsteps grew louder, accompanied by muffled voices. A second later, O'Reilly could hear two humans, chatting away, stop right in front of the double-doors.

Then – the rattling and clinking of a set of keys ...

In a panic, he dropped to the floor behind Briggs's desk. The doors began to open, and O'Reilly, lying flat on his back now, pushed Briggs's chair forward so that it slid into its position underneath the desk. His right side was pressed up against the wall, his head near the bottom of the Lincoln bust but hidden from the view of anyone standing in the office.

A second later, J. Hartwell Briggs and Yang Hsue Ko entered the room. O'Reilly could hear their voices, but he could not see them. He raised his knees slightly so that his massive feet could not be seen sticking out on the left side of Briggs's desk.

"I tell you what Ko," Briggs said, closing the office door, "I'd bet my life I locked that door."

"I don't remember, sir."

"Funny thing, yew get to a certain age, and it's the memory that goes. I remember what ma home looked like when I's a child, but sometimes I walk into a room and I forget why I went in."

Ko chuckled.

"That's very funny, sir."

O'Reilly heard the snap of light switches, and the office lit up under the glow of the halogen ceiling bulbs.

The two men moved over to the loveseat sofas. O'Reilly kept his eyes closed, but to him every beat of his heart sounded like a basketball being dribbled on a hardwood court. He made every effort not to breathe, but at the same time he feared an audible exhale would reveal his presence. Instead he laid there still, not moving a muscle, letting the air seep slowly in and out of his nostrils. His face and head itched from the dried sweat, but he didn't dare lift a hand to scratch.

"I 'preciate yew comin' in here this evenin' Ko," Briggs then said. "I'm travelin' all week, and so tonight's the only night I had."

"It's not a problem."

O'Reilly could hear the two men plop down onto the sofas. He listened as they chatted, first generally about events at the firm, and then about the shrimp cases. O'Reilly surmised, based on their conversation, that they had met earlier in the evening and then went four floors below to Ko's office to look at some demonstrative trial exhibits that were on large poster boards, thereby leaving the documents and legal pads sitting on the coffee table. O'Reilly quickly realized that had he arrived an hour earlier he would have come upon the two of them sitting there pouring over documents.

"Yew think we're ready for this here trial?" Briggs then asked, "we're less than a month from jury selection."

"No question," Ko answered confidently. "We will win this case for sure, sir. The mediation is scheduled for Thursday, and Mr.

Handler has made it clear he'll resolve the case only if this Anzalone will take a nominal offer. But their liens will likely prevent that. There's no way we will offer anything that approaches what they owe. So I think we're going to trial."

"I'll take the lead and you'll second chair it, as we've discussed."

"Of course," Ko said.

"And also, we gone have to – "

And then there was quiet. Neither Briggs nor Ko spoke.

O'Reilly wondered what they were possibly doing, and his eyes widened with fear. He didn't think he could lay there in that position for too much longer, and he was praying that maybe they were finishing up and would simply leave. But they didn't seem to be standing, or moving, because O'Reilly could not hear feet moving, bodies rising, papers shuffling, or anything else for that matter.

Finally, it was Briggs who broke the silence.

"Ko," he said flatly, "that your bottle?"

O'Reilly's heart stopped. His water bottle – *holy shit*. He realized he left it sitting on top of Briggs's desk in his haste to drop to the floor. The realization caused an overwhelming suffocation to come upon him as oxygen rapidly filled his lungs, inflating them to their fullest capacity. He lifted his hands across his abdomen and pressed them over his mouth and nose. With his chest about to explode with a burst of carbon dioxide, O'Reilly was certain he was about to be caught. He thought about simply standing and trying to come up with some bullshit explanation as to why he was laying there behind the desk of the Firm's name partner, but he knew it would be futile. There was nothing he could say. If they caught him in the next few seconds his career was over. It may even mean an arrest.

O'Reilly closed his eyes and prayed. He heard a telephone receiver being lifted, and then dropped into its cradle.

"No, sir, it's not," he heard Ko say.

Then, silence again. O'Reilly heard them stand.

"Mr. Ko," said Briggs, "go downstairs and get security."

CHAPTER 33

"WE WILL BURY YOU"

T HE PLAN WAS for Anzalone to meet Danny on Thursday at 7:30 am, over at Chief's Diner on Route 25A. They would grab a quick breakfast before heading to the Ketchogue train station for the ride into Penn Station, in Manhattan.

The corporate offices of LARS, Inc., the alternative dispute resolution company selected to mediate the Beers case, was located at 2 Penn Plaza, so Anzalone didn't see the need to drive into the City. They could get off the train and go right upstairs, and then descend directly down to the trains when it was over. Privately, Anzalone didn't think the mediation would take that long and was convinced that Gunther would not make much of a settlement offer. But that remained to be seen.

Danny rose early that morning, at about 5 am. He jumped in the shower and threw on a blue shirt and maroon tie under a grey sportscoat and headed out to the F-350 with a soaking wet head. He planned on grabbing a booth at the diner nice and early, but as he chugged down West 17th Street that morning, Danny felt something pulling him south, away from Ketchogue. It was an urge, an undefined compulsion of sorts, but its force was strong. It was summoning him down toward the beaches, to where all of this started. He looked at his watch and figured he had some time.

In a short while Danny found himself rumbling along on the Northern State Parkway heading east. He cruised down the twisting lanes of the freeway, weaving in and out of light traffic, past the soaring evergreen trees and low-slung shrubs, through the towns of Westbury, Hicksville, Plainview and finally Melville, until he reached the ramp for the Sagtikos Parkway. Danny took the exit and headed south. He felt his pulse quicken and he lowered both front windows. The cab filled with whistling cold air as the pickup gained speed. There was little traffic heading south toward the beaches, and Danny had the road mostly to himself.

As he neared the exit for the Southern State Parkway, Danny poked on the radio. An old classic by Tom Petty – *You Wreck Me* – came roaring to life, and Danny cranked the volume. Soon he made the turn onto the Robert Moses Causeway, heading toward the ocean. Presently there was no one in front of him or behind him on the open road. Tom Petty was screeching through the cab – *Ohhhh-ohhhhh! Yeeaaa-aahhhhh!!* – and Danny pressed hard on the gas pedal.

65 ... 70 ... 75 ... 80 miles per hour.

Danny lifted his butt off the seat and was screaming away to the lyrics of the song now. He flew over the Causeway's intersection with Sunrise Highway, and now there was nothing ahead of him but the open roadway and the Causeway bridges spanning the Great South Bay. Just ahead lay Robert Moses State Park and the sparkling beaches of Fire Island. Off to the west, down Ocean Parkway, was Oak Beach, where it all began.

85 ... 90 ... 95 ...100 miles an hour, and Danny hit the bridge. There was nothing right and left of him but open ocean. The F350 was shaking, the engine revving and roaring at a breakneck pace. Danny was practically standing on the gas pedal now. He felt free, peaceful, unrestrained. His heart was racing, the music was blaring at an earsplitting level, with the windows down and the cool ocean wind whipping against his face. Danny was pounding his fist on the dashboard to the driving beat of Tom Petty and his scratching electric guitar, and for that reason he simply did not hear the police siren whining away behind him.

As Danny crossed the Captree drawbridge and slowed the pickup to take Ocean Parkway west, toward Oak and Gilgo beaches, where the old OBI previously sat, and where he once met a girl named Debbie Mahoney while looking over the Atlantic Ocean on a warm Sunday afternoon, Danny finally noticed the spinning police lights in his rearview mirror.

"Shit," he said aloud, and he made the turn onto Ocean Parkway. Then he pulled over on the sandy shoulder, next to a line of low shrubs. He turned down the music as the police cruiser pulled in behind him. Danny watched in his side view mirror as the trooper yanked open the driver's side door and jumped onto the roadway. He was a black man, with a thick neck and shoulders. He slammed the door shut and marched toward the F350, his right hand on his holster. Danny's chest was heaving, like he had just run a 5k. Beads of sweat had formed on his forehead.

The trooper walked purposefully to the driver's side window.

"Hands on the steering wheel!" he shouted as he approached, and Danny quickly complied. In a second, the officer was at the window, looking straight toward Danny.

"Hey guy, you in a rush?!" he shouted.

"So sorry," Danny said through choppy breaths. He had both palms on the steering wheel, as directed, and was lurched forward, trying to draw air into his lungs.

"I'm real sorry," he huffed.

"You realize I just chased you over the goddamn bridge!"

"I didn't, didn't see you," Danny choked out, "I'm so sorry."

"Yeah you didn't see me, 'cause you're going near a hundred," the officer shouted. "License, registration and insurance, let's go."

Danny fumbled through the glove compartment and handed over the documents. The officer snatched them from Danny's hand, and held up the driver's license for inspection.

"Stay here, don't move."

The officer marched back to his cruiser, and Danny watched in the sideview as the cop dropped down into the driver's seat, eyeballing what Danny assumed was his license.

Danny then leaned his head back, trying to relax. He looked ahead, his line of vision following the westbound roadway, that stretch of concrete so familiar to him. In front of him was Gilgo Beach and Cedar Overlook Beach, those beautiful ocean landscapes on which he had spent his childhood. They had barely changed since he was a kid, and right now the ocean breezes and salty air felt calming, serene.

In a few minutes, the officer was back at his window.

"Here you go," he said, handing Danny back the documents.

"Thank you," said Danny, wondering what was coming next. His heart had settled now and he was breathing freely. He was mustering up as much politeness as he could.

The officer crossed his arms, holding a flashlight.

"You're Dan Beers, the guy with the kid, right?"

Danny paused a moment, somewhat confused. It was an odd comment, and Danny didn't know what to make of it. He stared up at the officer, and then shook his head.

"Uh yes sir," he finally answered. "Sorry, yes – I have two girls."

"Your daughter I mean, the one in the coma. You got the lawsuit I read about in the papers. That's you, right?"

"Uh, yes sir," Danny said meekly. "That's me."

"How's she doing? Your daughter."

"Well, getting better, thanks," Danny said, "but not great really, you know, in the grand scheme of things. Just keeping my fingers crossed. Maybe I'll catch a break one of these days."

The officer nodded.

"I'm sorry about that."

"Thanks, I appreciate it."

"Got three girls myself. They're trips, you know?"

"Yeah, no kidding," Danny laughed, tensely, "they really are."

"Wouldn't trade 'em for anything though."

"I agree with that, for sure."

The officer pointed over the F350 toward the bridge.

"So what's up? You flew over the bridge like you just robbed a bank. You okay?"

"Yeah, I'm really sorry. I was just blowing off some steam, I guess. I'm heading to a meeting with a bunch of lawyers and I'm a little freaked out about it. Just wanted to head over to where the old OBI was first."

Danny nodded to the road in front of him.

"Met my wife there."

The officer adjusted his cap.

"She passed too, right, your wife? I read that too."

Danny nodded.

"Yes sir, she did."

"Well, that's tough. How you holdin' up?"

Danny raised a hand to shield his eyes from the rising sun, low on the horizon now. The officer had shifted his stance, sending the sunbeams directly into Danny's face.

"Day at a time I guess. What're you gonna do."

"Yeah, I bet."

The officer stuffed his flashlight into his back pocket.

"Do me a favor, take it easy. Keep it under the speed limit."

"I will, I really appreciate it."

"You flip this rig goin' 90 and there'll be two people in a coma. You don't want that."

"No, absolutely not. And again, I'm really sorry."

"Alright, you take care. And good luck with those scumbag lawyers." The officer tipped his cap.

"Have a safe day," he said.

He wheeled around and was gone.

DANNY ARRIVED BACK in Ketchogue at just past 7:00 am, after spending roughly twenty minutes standing at the shoreline at Cedar Overlook Beach, staring into the vastness of the ocean. When the grey sportscoat wouldn't hold back the frigid ocean winds any longer, Danny trudged through the sand back to the pickup and turned on the heater, rubbing his hands together for warmth. He wasn't sure why he had made the drive, but the whole experience had left him calm and tranquil, even given the altercation with the police officer. Debbie's absence was heavy on his heart that morning – he wanted so badly to tell her about this whole lawsuit thing and get her advice about this mediation, or whatever it was called. But at the same time, he had this sinking feeling that if Debbie were alive, there was no way Agnes would be in her current condition and there'd be no mediation to attend in the first place. Somehow, some way, Debbie would have made sure the whole disaster never happened. It was one more reason for him to feel guilt and shame over the situation his family was in.

When Anzalone arrived at the diner, Danny was already sitting in a booth in front of a cup of black coffee, reading the *New York Post*. He rose slightly to greet her, but Anzalone motioned him back down. She dumped her bag onto the maroon leather bench seat and slid in opposite Danny. The two ordered breakfast from a sullen waitress who barely said a word, silently acknowledging the ungodliness of the hour. Danny ordered an English muffin and oatmeal, Anzalone a western omelet. The two made small talk for a few minutes before Anzalone looked at her watch.

"Well, about the case, and about today," she said. "I guess the first thing to discuss is the Dodge Brewer situation."

Danny nodded. He knew Anzalone would raise the topic, given that it was the lead news story for a few days on just about every network and media outlet in the country. Danny understood the $20,000 offer was probably gone now, but he needed to hear it from his attorney.

"I don't know what to say," Danny confessed. "The whole thing is mind boggling. There was another report about it on Dateline NBC last night."

"I saw that," Anzalone said.

"You know the Brewer's house is for sale now?" Danny asked. "Cindy and the kids moved in with her parents, I heard. Up in Massachusetts or something. I just can't believe it."

"Well, Dornbrook called," Anzalone then reported. And then she confirmed what Danny already knew. "They withdrew the $20,000 settlement offer as you may have guessed. Dornbrook says he hasn't heard from Dodge, only Cindy. And she isn't saying where he is, if she knows."

"The papers say the feds are looking for him."

"They are, he's in some trouble, and his company filed for bankruptcy after all the investors ran for cover."

"Unbelievable," Danny lamented. "I actually feel bad for him."

"Well, I don't. We were counting on that money, Mr. Beers," Anzalone said, getting to the point, "and now with it gone, and the two of them possibly in bankruptcy, it makes no sense to keep the Brewers in the case any longer. We are certainly not getting the testimony from them that we had hoped, and it looks to me like they will simply default. But I'm not sure what a default judgment even does for us. It is just really unfortunate, to say the least."

Danny nodded, pulling off his cap. He took a sip from his coffee cup.

"Where are we with the other defendants?" he asked.

"Nowhere really," Anzalone answered. "We received their document production, and as I mentioned, there were no Parent Authorization forms for Agnes. It looks like Debbie simply didn't submit one. I know you said that was a nearly impossible scenario, but that seems to be the case. We matched every Parent Authorization form against the school list, and only six families in

Ketchogue failed to put one in for their fourth-grade child that year. You and Debbie were one of them. I'm sorry."

"It just makes no sense," Danny said, shaking his head. "Debbie was religious about that stuff. Obsessed with it. I'm just really surprised."

"Well, who knows what happened," Anzalone responded, trying to appease him, "but that unfortunately leaves us with very little evidence that the town, the coaches or the Committee had any notice of Agnes's pre-existing shellfish allergy. I did what I could at their depositions, but I didn't score many points. And yesterday I received their motions for summary judgment. They are all asking the court to dismiss the case against them prior to trial. They claim there is no evidence they knew of Agnes's condition, that you didn't know either, and that under those circumstances they had no duty to act to prevent the snack mom from feeding her shrimp. They claim any warning by Gunther would not have changed anything as far as they are concerned, because not being at the park that day, they would never have even seen it. I will argue that the snack mom was acting as the agent of those defendants, and that anything that Cindy did was done on their behalf, but that is a stretch."

"But we're not arguing failure to warn by those defendants, are we?" asked Danny.

"No, we're not," Anzalone answered. "We only brought a negligence claim against them. We said it was unreasonable and careless to provide shrimp to a fourth grader without first inquiring whether Agnes could safely eat it. Of course, your deposition did not help on that front, because you testified you had no idea she was allergic. The non-Gunther defendants are arguing that such testimony is conclusive evidence that even if Cindy or Dodge approached you, you would not have had any reason to say no."

Danny nodded. He knew this to be true but was hoping Anzalone had come up with another theory for keeping them in the case, some reason to get at the insurance money they had.

"Will those defendants be at the mediation today?" he asked.

"No, their carriers have refused to attend until the motions are decided," Anzalone answered. "It will just be Gunther today."

The waitress arrived with their breakfast plates and the two of them ate in silence. Anzalone then brought up a few points about the mediation and what she expected would go down that day. Danny listened and asked only a few questions. He told her, once again, that they needed to keep the faith and do the best they could.

Anzalone nodded at him. She told him that unless they resolved the case today, they would proceed to trial in about two weeks. She explained that she had hired a warnings expert and had paid him by drawing against the home equity line of credit on her townhome. She reported that the expert was prepared to offer an opinion that had Gunther placed a warning on the bag, it is "likely" that any reasonable person would have heeded that warning by deciding not to provide the product to the children that day. However, she cautioned that she could not offer any assurances that the court would not reject his testimony as improper scientific evidence.

"In a strange way, though," Anzalone further explained, trying to calm him, "without the Brewers present, I can probably avoid dismissal of our case against Gunther by arguing that it's for the jury to decide what Dodge and Cindy would or would not have done, because they will not be there to deny or confirm. Assuming the court does not dismiss our case, it is just a matter of getting those six jurors to agree with us."

Privately, of course, Anzalone was praying that Gunther would make a reasonable settlement offer when they arrived at LARS that morning. And if they did, she would do everything in her power to persuade Dan Beers to accept it. In her mind it was a last-ditch effort to save their case and maybe put a few bucks in her and her client's hands. And if Gunther refused, well … she didn't even want to think about that.

Anzalone shoved her plate forward and shot a look at her watch. Then she began gathering up her things.

"Let's see what happens today," she said, "maybe Gunther will offer something that allows us to settle everything without a trial."

"You'll do a great job," Danny told her confidently, wiping his mouth with a napkin, "I have complete faith in you. Let's be positive about this and see what happens."

THE HONORABLE GEORGE J. Casey was a retired Justice of the Nassau County Supreme Court. He now worked full-time for LARS Inc., a company whose acronym stood for "Litigation and

Arbitration Resolution Services." Its main source of business was mediations, and it employed a roster of "neutrals" – some of which were retired judges like Casey – whose job was to gather litigants in a room and assist in negotiating settlement terms that would obviate the need for a trial. The court system loved mediations, of course, because they functioned like a cardiac surgeon performing bypass on the massively clogged artery of the judiciary's grossly overloaded trial calendar. Every case that settled by way of mediation brought a smile to the face of the trial judge, and George J. Casey, with his reputation for success in these matters, was constantly in high demand. It typically took months to get a date with him, but Briggs had placed a call over to LARS, and lo and behold Judge Casey's administrative assistant found an open day on his calendar.

Danny and Anzalone arrived at LARS at roughly 9:40 am. They entered a brightly lit vestibule with grey walls and a dark blue carpet, with about two dozen chairs filled with lawyers and their clients spread around the perimeter of the room. There was a small reception desk there with a young woman behind it, sitting with a hands-free phone receiver attached to the top of her head. Anzalone went to the desk and checked in. The woman entered their information into her computer and nodded to the chairs.

"You'll be with Judge Casey in Conference Room 13," she announced. "Please have a seat, and we'll call you."

Over in the corner, at the front of the vestibule, Danny saw Ko and the FT&B attorney Andrea Corning standing and chatting quietly with a third woman Danny did not recognize. He and Anzalone went to the complete opposite corner, near the glass entry doors, and stood next to a small end table filled with copies of the *New York Law Journal*. Danny felt like a boxer circling the ring before the bell went off, and he turned to Anzalone, nodding to Ko and his team.

"Looks like the gang's all here," he whispered.

"Yep," Anzalone whispered back calmly, with a smile.

She lifted a copy of the *Journal*.

"Hopefully they brought their checkbook."

"Let's hope so," Danny agreed.

A few minutes later the receptionist yelled "Beers versus Gunther!" across the vestibule, and Danny and Anzalone promptly followed Ko and his crew down a hallway. They marched past a dozen conference rooms filled with litigants and neutrals trying to come to terms on settlement deals. They turned a corner and came upon a glass-fronted room with large windows overlooking Seventh Avenue, and they each filed in. Judge Casey was already there, seated at the head of the conference table with a legal pad and some documents in front of him.

He rose now with a smile.

"Everybody, please come in," he said warmly, shaking everyone's hand, "have a seat and make yourselves comfortable."

He pointed to a credenza in the back of the room.

"There's coffee and pastries back there, and some fruit, so please help yourselves and then we'll get started."

Danny and Anzalone took seats on the far side of the room near the windows, and Ko and his team took the opposite side against the glass wall. Everyone ambled back and forth to the credenza, grabbing coffee and breakfast items, and Danny partook himself, filling a ceramic mug with black coffee. Anzalone sat and pulled some documents from her bag, paging through the papers. She waved off coffee, and in a few minutes everyone was settled in.

"Well, I first want to thank everyone for coming today," Judge Casey opened, "and Mr. Beers, let me also say to you that I'm very sorry for what happened to your daughter. I hope she is doing okay these days, and that you and your family are making out alright."

Danny nodded back without a word.

Casey was mid-70s but had a youthful and energetic appearance. He was tall and trim with a thick head of bright silver hair, cut tight in a military style. He wore dark-stemmed glasses and a navy bowtie over a bright white shirt, and right now his shirtsleeves were rolled up, his suit jacket hanging on a coat tree in the corner. Danny thought his greeting was sincere, and he noticed that his friendly reception took some tension out of the room.

"What I'd first like to do is make some introductions," he said, "because I think we will be here a while today. I'll begin – as you know, I'm George Casey, your mediator, and I'll ask that you please call me George. I'm hoping we can all go on a first-name basis today. Why don't we go around the room and introduce ourselves."

Each of the parties then made a short introduction, which Danny found unnecessary, because everyone in the room already knew one another from previous proceedings. The exception was the mid-40s woman with Ko and Corning, who introduced herself as Phyliss Tweed, a Senior Litigation Attorney at Gunther Home Products Corporation.

When it circled back to Casey, Danny realized the point of the introductions was to get everyone talking and to settle everyone's nerves. Judge Casey was doing a great job, Danny thought. He could see why he was in such high demand for these matters; his demeanor was welcoming and jovial, and he was creating an environment in which the parties could talk openly about the case and perhaps get something done.

"I also want to thank you for your mediation statements," Judge Casey added, "and the documents you provided. They were well prepared, and I found them to be very helpful."

Casey had both hands on a set of documents sitting in front of him. Anzalone had explained that several days prior to the meeting today each side had submitted a confidential "mediation statement" for Casey's review. Those statements, prepared by the lawyers, were only given to Casey and not to the other side. They privately informed him of what the case was about and the terms upon which each side was willing to settle. Without knowing what your adversary had submitted, the whole proceeding today was very much like a poker game, Danny thought.

"I know we have sophisticated and experienced lawyers here today," Casey went on, "but I always like to begin by stating how important these mediation sessions are to the judicial process and to the parties. This is a unique opportunity to resolve a very difficult case that everyone is very emotional about and very invested in. As we all know, everything we say in here today – to each other and privately to me – is completely confidential and cannot be used in the courtroom or at trial under any circumstances, should we find ourselves unable to come to terms. Therefore, we can all lay our cards on the table and have a candid discussion about the case and what we would each like to accomplish."

Casey rose and walked back to the credenza, continuing his introduction as he filled his coffee mug.

"As we all know, if you do not settle today, you will proceed to trial in about two weeks. And trials are risky and completely unpredictable. They will cost each side a lot of money, and of course after that you have appeals, which can add years to the process. But with mediation, everything can be resolved today – right here, right now. You achieve certainty and peace, and you do not leave your fate in the hands of six jurors who, let's be honest, know nothing about you, and you about them. So I urge you to go into these discussions today in the spirit of cooperation and compromise."

Casey plopped down into his seat, sipping from his coffee mug. He explained that he would soon break from the current joint session and meet privately with each side in "caucuses" to discuss where they stood on settlement. He said he was going to start with the plaintiffs – Anzalone and Danny – and that after that he would meet with the defendant and its lawyers. Anzalone had explained at breakfast that this "caucus" process was the same at every mediation – the mediator would first ask the plaintiff for a realistic "settlement demand," then talk to them about the basis for that number, and then he would speak separately with the defendant for a counter-offer. From there he would go back and forth, trying to narrow the gap and come to a final settlement number.

"Before we move to the private caucuses," Casey stated, "I typically like to give each side an opportunity to give a short statement about their case and speak directly and respectfully to the other side, in a confidential setting, so that we understand where each of us stands."

That all sounded very reasonable to Danny, but then Ko jumped in, leaning forward toward Judge Casey.

"Look, Judge, let me see if I can short circuit this. I think we all know what each other's case is about, so we don't see the need for any kind of opening statements. We've been at this for well over a year and we are basically on the courtroom steps for trial. So we want to see where this is going today, and to be frank, we are running out of patience."

Ko nodded at his two colleagues with a look of solidarity.

"Our position is clear," he continued. "The plaintiff here has no case and we are extremely confident about our prospects at trial. We are here to negotiate in good faith, of course, but despite that fact, as we sit here today, we still don't even have a settlement demand from Ms. Anzalone. Nothing will happen until we get that. If she is prepared to give that right now, we will respond, but if not, I suggest we get to the first caucus so we can get the ball rolling. And I can tell you if that if we don't hear something reasonable, and soon, that reflects the reality of their tanking lawsuit, we are walking, and this will be a very short meeting."

Danny looked across the room and saw that Corning and Tweed both had their arms crossed and their eyebrows lowered, in an all-business, combative posture. Casey tried to lighten the tone a bit, but Ko was insistent. In a few moments he and his two colleagues were retreating down the hallway to a nearby conference room, where they would be in a holding pattern while Casey spoke privately to Danny and Anzalone.

Once alone, Casey sat patiently with them and went over some points Anzalone had raised in the mediation statement. He pointed out some of the weaknesses in their case, and asked Anzalone if she had considered how the jury would react to those potential shortcomings. He also asked a lot of questions about Agnes, and her condition, and Danny did his best to address those inquiries.

In their favor, Anzalone pointed out that she would be bringing a now 11-year old child before a Bronx jury, that Agnes had been in a coma for a long time, and that there was no question in this case about medical causation – Gunther's product had clearly injured Agnes. Certainly, Gunther had to appreciate the risk it faced.

"I think they do," Casey said earnestly. "And that's why they're here today."

After about a half hour of discussion, Casey lifted his pen.

"Have you thought about an opening demand?" he asked.

Anzalone said they had. She told him about the discussions she had had with Ko, and that they were a long time removed from the $50 million demand she had made in their complaint. She explained the liens that the hospital and other healthcare providers would place on this settlement, and she took Casey through what her medical expert – Agnes's treating physician – would opine about the projected cost of Agnes's future medical care through her life. Based on all of that, Anzalone told Casey her client would open the negotiations today with a settlement demand of $650,000.

"But we have room," she said, letting him know that this was just an opening bid. "We're here to negotiate in good faith."

"I think that's very fair," Casey responded, jotting notes down on his pad. "Let me see what I can do."

Casey lifted his stack of papers and headed down the hallway.

Anzalone then told Danny that "now the waiting begins," as Casey tried to talk Gunther into a fair and reasonable counter-offer. Then he would come back into the room and present it to Danny's side. Casey could be with them for five minutes or an hour, you could never tell, she explained. From there, it would be up to Danny and Anzalone to counter with their own number, and then Casey would go back to the Gunther room. Anzalone described the process as "the dance," and said that the back and forth would likely take all day. But New York litigants loved Judge Casey, she explained, because he was very good at pushing parties to the middle, thereby finding the sweet spot that would settle the case.

She hadn't mentioned it to her client, but Anzalone was praying that at the end of the day Casey could get Ko and his team north of $400,000. With that result, after paying the liens and the experts, Anzalone would walk away with a little more than $70,000. It wasn't retirement money, but it would be a life savior. Financially, she was on fumes, as was her client.

They both needed this to happen.

WITHIN TEN MINUTES, Ko, Corning and Tweed came storming back into the conference room, with Judge Casey in tow. Casey was holding his legal pad tight against his chest as Ko and Corning quickly settled into their seats without a word. Tweed, on the other hand, began putting on her overcoat and stuffing her documents into her briefcase, shaking her head. It was obvious to Danny that she believed the meeting to be over.

Judge Casey placed his legal pad onto the conference table.

"Ms. Anzalone and Mr. Beers, my apologies, but it seems we've come to an impasse quicker than I thought we would today," he reported. "Mr. Ko would like to say something."

Ko looked directly at Anzalone.

"Ms. Anzalone," he said, his anger rising, "we came here today in good faith because we thought you understood our settlement position. I thought I made myself clear about the terms of this meeting. But I guess I didn't. Or you simply refused to hear me."

He placed his palms on the table.

"Your settlement demand of $650,000 is so far off the mark, so outrageous and delusional, that I seriously question whether we are even working on the same case. To be clear, your demand is rejected – categorically *rejected*. I made it very clear to you that we would settle this case only within the confines of our litigation costs, and now you come here with a number like that? You've wasted my time and my client's time, and we're not standing for it any longer."

Ko lifted his document stack and shoved it into his briefcase.

"So here's the deal," he said, still lasering in on Anzalone, "we will settle this case for $40,000 in exchange for complete general releases. That offer is non-negotiable and final and is valid until 5 pm today, and then it expires. We don't need any further negotiations, and we aren't interested in any more back and forth. We thank Judge Casey and we're sorry you wasted his time today as well. But in considering our offer, I want to say something else."

This time Ko turned toward Danny, and their eyes locked.

"If you reject our offer, *we will bury you*, do you understand?" he warned, pointing his finger. "If you force us to trial, we will bring the full resources of this law firm and our client down on you, and we will crush you before that jury. And when we obtain a complete defense verdict – and we *will* win – my client will come after you for our legal expenses and attorneys' fees, and we will chase you to the very corners of the Earth until you've paid every last dime. And even in the unlikely event that you can somehow pull off a victory here, which is impossible, we would tie you up in post-trial motions and appeals to make sure you won't see a penny for *years*."

Ko pulled his suit jacket off the back of a chair.

"I hope I'm making myself clear this time," he said. "This is the last discussion we will have with you on this matter."

Corning and Tweed were standing at the door, briefcases in hand, ready to beat a retreat to the elevators. Ko shook Judge Casey's hand, and then he turned to join his colleagues.

But then suddenly Danny stood.

His back was to the windows, and as Ko was pulling open the glass door, Danny yelled across the conference room.

"MR. KO!" he roared, and all heads in the room suddenly turned. Anzalone had already collected her documents and was placing them into her bag when she heard her client yell out her adversary's name. The sound startled her, and her eyes widened.

"Mr. Beers, please," was all she said, but Danny ignored her.

He walked around the head of the table and stood next to Judge Casey, who was still seated. When he was about four or five feet from Ko, he stopped and looked directly at him.

"We don't need until 5pm, you can have my answer right now."

"Oh yeah?" Ko asked dismissively, "what's that?"

"Screw you and your $40,000," Danny shot back. "Your offer is rejected. Categorically *rejected*. My daughter was in a coma for six months, sir, because she ate your client's product, and so $40,000 is an insult. Now *you* are wasting *my* time. But I will tell you this – my $650,000 demand just went up to a million dollars, okay? And you have until 4pm – not 5 – to accept it. A million dollars, and at 4pm sharp the offer expires, and we go to trial. And don't you ever point at me again."

Danny took one step closer.

"Do you understand *me*, sir?" he asked.

Ko stared at him a moment, and then he chuckled.

He looked over at Anzalone.

"You just made a very big mistake," he said. "See you at trial."

He turned and headed to the elevators.

CHAPTER 34

IT WAS BRIGHT ORANGE

FOR THE SECOND time in as many months, an unknown man in a trench coat unexpectedly approached a member of Danny's family.

This time it was Henry.

It was two days after the Beers mediation, on Saturday, and Henry was sitting at the bar at the Knights of Columbus, over on Sullivan Street, which jutted north from Route 25A across from a Jiffy Lube station. He was parked in front of a Coors Light draft and a shot of Jameson's, watching the Mets game along with a row of old-timers, cursing now as Noah Syndergaard had just given up a three-run homer, giving Pittsburgh a 4-3 lead.

"Ah, for Christ's sake!" Henry exclaimed, elbowing the man sitting next to him. "You believe this shit?"

Behind him, a short man with light olive skin walked into the bar. Sunlight washed over the room and then disappeared as the man opened and then shut the door to the bar. He was wrapped in a drab grey trench coat over a pair of jeans and sneakers, and had both hands stuffed into the pockets of the coat. He had dark eyes and a receding hairline, although his youthful expression told Henry he was no more than 35 or 36. Henry's police instincts kicked in – he knew right away the man was heading toward him.

Henry wheeled around and faced the man.

"You Henry Mahoney?" the man asked.

"Who the fuck are you?" Henry shot back. Then he stood, and the man suddenly was face to face with Henry's navel.

"Damn, man, they said you was big," he said, looking straight north, to the bottom of Henry's chin.

Henry pointed to the door.

"Private membership, pal. You either get lost on your own, or I help you to the door. Your choice."

The man pulled out a manila envelope from under hos trench coat and handed it to Henry.

"For your son-in-law," he said. "And *hombre,* I wouldn't wait."

The man promptly wheeled around and marched out the door.

Henry stood still for a moment, looking at the envelope in his hands. He quickly ripped it open and pulled out a document labeled "Final Report," but Henry had no time to read it. He rushed to the front door and pushed it open, letting it rest against his backside.

With a hand shielding the sun, Henry saw a sedan pulling out of the bluestone gravel driveway, the tires kicking up some stones. The man in the trench coat was sitting in the passenger seat. He couldn't see the driver's face, but under the afternoon sunshine he could clearly see the man's head, which Henry wouldn't forget.

It was bright orange.

CHAPTER 35

THE BUBBLES JUST STOPPED

May 3, 2019 – 3:00 am
Home, Ketchogue

Can't sleep – didn't sleep.

I was going to skip this, but I can't. I got so close the last time. This is really difficult for me to put down into words but I have to do it because I've been stuffing it down for well over a year and I have to let it out somehow. It's the middle of the night but at least I'll be done with it.

You know, it seems like it's never huge events that change your life, it's little things. Small insignificant decisions you make. Things you say and do in the normal course of your life because of who and what you are, and they lead you in a certain direction. You don't intend bad things, but they happen anyway. That's what I've learned.

So here's how it went down.

The day me and Paulie went to AC it was hot. I mean really hot. The sun felt like you were under a set of hot lamps, everywhere you went. And I will tell you that the day of Agnes's accident, that day at Turnberry, I walked outside the house that morning and waved to my neighbor and then I sat in my truck and looked up at the sky and had this eerie feeling. It was hot that day too, exactly the same kind of day, and it made me remember what happened with Deb.

Anyway, we got to AC and me and Paulie checked in to the Trop. We chucked our bags in the room and got changed and before I knew it we were drinking in a place called Tangos Lounge. We were just BSing and getting caught up and it was fun.

But I kept looking at my phone thinking about what a shitbomb I left Deb with and how she was probably sweating her ass off in that friggin' heat wave trying to lift Henry in and out of the car because he weighs about the same as Andre the Giant. Then Paulie pointed to my phone and said hey put that damn thing away you're like a teenage girl for God's sake, but I couldn't help it. I had this feeling I shouldn't be there, and it was tough to unwind thinking about it all. It was about ten past 4 and so I shot her a text.

I wrote, *"hey when are you leaving to get Grumps?"*

That was our nickname for Henry sometimes, instead of Gramps. I'd say it and Deb would laugh. I just wanted to know she was ok. I was wishing things were not that hairy for her. I wasn't really asking about what time she was leaving to get Henry. I didn't care one wit about when she was leaving. I was just checking in. I just wanted to hear from her. It was one simple text. I thumbed it out and clicked send. It took me no more than 10 seconds. And it only took those ten seconds for everything to change.

I sent the message and then right away I saw those bubbles. Those dots that tell you someone is writing back. See, Deb was getting back to me immediately, just like I had demanded all those times. That's my guess, that's what I figure she was doing, which was exactly what I asked, what I had been such a pain in the ass about. She was so selfless and thoughtful and because it bothered me she was responding as soon as she got it.

And then the bubbles just stopped.

Nothing came through.

I didn't give it a second thought.

About two hours later me and Paulie were at the blackjack table and I was up about $150 and my phone started buzzing. I grabbed it and saw that it was Will. I clicked the green button and said, hey. Will said, where the fuck are you. Just like that in a dead tone. Where are you Dan he said again.

I thought he was pissed we didn't invite him so I said I'm in AC with Paulie, we were gonna ask you to go but – and then Will interrupted and said you gotta get home. Like now. I stepped away from the table and covered my left ear and asked him what's the matter. I figured something went wrong with Henry's surgery but then it struck me that Deb would've called. He said you just gotta get home and I said Will what's wrong talk to me. I could tell by his voice. Then he told me – Deb was in an accident. It's bad Danny he said. We're at the hospital, me and Janet. Get here fast.

Well I didn't even say a word. I just clicked off the phone and grabbed Paulie by the shirt and we ran through the casino. I left every dollar and chip on the table and every article of clothing in the hotel room. We sprinted to the front entrance and told the valet guys it's an emergency and in a minute they had Paulie's car. I grabbed the keys and I drove 90 up the Garden State Parkway and through Staten Island and over the Verrazano Bridge and down the Belt Parkway until I got there. The whole time I'm on the phone with Will and Paulie was saying Jesus Christ hang up you're gonna kill us both. So I did. I don't even remember parking. I just remember me and Paulie ran into the hospital front entrance and the first person I saw was Janet. She was hysterical.

She was the one who told me.

Danny she's gone, she said. Deb's gone.

What happened after that was just mayhem. I went nuts and I grabbed a phone off one of the nurse's stations and I threw it against the wall. I kicked three or four chairs over and I was screaming at the top of my lungs. I started punching the wall and I put four holes through it and some police officers had to come and I was surrounded by all of them. I took a swing at one of the cops and before I knew it three more were there and they tackled me and sat on me until I calmed down and then I was frantic, screaming, kicking. The next few weeks I was just numb and then in the middle of all that we had the wake and the funeral and before I knew it she was buried and it was just me and the girls.

But the day after the accident, in the middle of all that mayhem, I got a call from the police station telling me I had to deal with the car because it had been towed from the scene and was in a lot over in Central Islip. They said there were some personal possessions that had to be picked up. Deb had taken Henry's Chevy Tahoe that day because there was no way Henry was fitting into the Prius and my first thought was to pass the message to Henry but I didn't want to deal with him and plus I wanted to see the car for myself. I just had to see it.

So I drove over there, met some guy with a long ponytail at the gate. There were smashed cars piled up all over the place inside this huge lot surrounded by a chain-link fence. Over in this booth they had a box with Deb's handbag in it and some other stuff of Henry's that they pulled from the Tahoe. Deb's purse was there, and the money was still in it, which I thought was a miracle.

Then I asked the guy, can I see the car. I just want to make sure there's nothing else in there. Thing's completely totaled boss he said, but yeah you can see it.

So he walked me over down this one section with all the cars piled up right and left of me and when I finally saw the Tahoe my heart stopped. A Tahoe is a big sturdy truck but this thing was a mess. It was completely destroyed. The thought that Deb was in that thing made my heart skip a beat. I stuck my head inside and I looked around and I don't know how they missed it but it was right there underneath the right rear passenger seat. It was Deb's phone. It was still powered up. I stuffed it in my pocket and grabbed that box and headed home.

But I just had to know the truth. So I typed in Deb's passcode, which I knew because it was our anniversary date. My text was right there – it came in at 4:11 pm.

hey when are you leaving to get Grumps?

And so was Deb's response:

On my way there no -

It was prompted there in the text box, but she never finished the sentence. She never sent the text.

I swallowed hard and then I deleted what Deb had started to write.

Sometime later I got a copy of the police report. It laid everything out pretty clearly. There is no question what happened. There was a security camera overlooking the parking lot of a tire shop and it caught the entire accident, which was described in gory detail in the report. Deb was driving about 45 mph down Route 106 and sure enough the video showed she had a phone in her hand. She veered off the road to the right and then did a massive overcorrection to the left. The Tahoe went onto the center median and then she tried to correct right again. But the median had a small ravine in the middle and the Tahoe flipped over six times. The report recorded the exact time of the accident because they got it from the security camera – 4:11 pm.

Exactly when I texted her.

Exactly when she was trying to respond.

So there you have it. I know that Deb died because of me. She only had her phone in her hand because that's what I insisted she do. That's what I imposed on her, and for what? Why? WHY? I should have figured she was driving. I shouldn't have been drinking in a bar when I had responsibilities back home. I should have stayed to help her out. If I did it would have been me picking up Henry and she would never have been in the goddamn car to begin with.

And I know this truth – if I never send that text message, if I never do that one single act – Deb would be alive, and she would have been there to stop Agnes from eating that shrimp. That's what I believe. So you can say it was me that killed her. I know it was an accident, and logic would tell you it was just a freak thing that happened, it was no one's fault, but I know the truth, I know what happened.

So I did what I did and I know what my role in the whole thing was and that's just not something you get away with in this life. You may think you do but you don't. That's just not the way it works. There are consequences for your actions, accountability.

Now in my heart I know that everything that happened with Agnes is punishment for what I did. That's the payback. The torment I feel now is my penance. There is no greater pain for me, there's nothing I fear more. Something else could have been done to me but doing it to my child is worse. Thing is, I know I've earned it, I deserve what's happening, by my daughter doesn't. I don't know why she has to be a part of this. I don't get it. But I do know that only I can make it right. So I've got to make my own redemption and it's got to start now.

See, over the last almost two years I have spent so much time with the woulda-shoulda-couldas over Deb's accident that's it become unhealthy. I've been wasting a lot of time feeling sorry for myself. I know I have to stop for the benefit of the girls. I have to find a way and that's what I'm gonna do. Nothing is going to stop me from getting things on the right track for them and then maybe in some small way I'll make up for what I did. Maybe one day I'll tell Gianna and Agnes what really happened to their Mom. Maybe, if I think it's important. And hopefully they will feel that their father is worthy of forgiveness.

In the meantime, we've got this trial coming up, and maybe, for the sake of the girls, something good will come out it. But who knows really, I am just keeping my fingers crossed.

Well, I'm gonna put this thing away now. It's really late and I'm drained. Just spent. But I got it out, said what I had to say, and I'm gonna try to sleep now.

And tomorrow is another day.

PART FIVE

TRIAL

CHAPTER 36

KING GEORGE

I F YOU HAD to select a place to try a case, there was nothing like the Bronx and the people who made up its jury pool. Regardless of what type of case she ever had up there, even when she was trying defense cases back in the day for Buckley Sullivan, Anzalone could always talk to these people on their terms. They were real, authentic men and women, and when you spoke honestly to them, they listened. Anzalone knew her case had major holes, but as the day of trial finally came Anzalone felt hopeful. She would speak to these people in a straightforward manner, tell her clients' story, and as Dan Beers kept saying, she would keep the faith.

Meanwhile, pursuant to an odd feature of New York practice, and by order of the administrative law judge, the matter of *Daniel X. Beers, et al. v. The Gunther Home Products Corporation, et al.*, case no. 18-67675, was assigned for trial to Justice Victor San Giorgio, rather than Elisa G. Fuentes, who had presided over the case from the beginning. This was because Justice San Giorgio was the next available jurist, and the wheels of justice waited for no person in this place. When Anzalone found out her case would be tried before Justice San Gorgio, she was delighted. He had a firm reputation as a plaintiff's judge, which made this Bronx courtroom the perfect venue as far as she was concerned. While she and Danny and the girls would seem right at home in this environment, the high-powered lawyers for Gunther would stick out like sore thumbs here. What with their 1200 dollar suits, their leather litigation bags engraved with their firm initials, the army of lawyers they would haul into the tiny Bronx courtroom, each dragging expensive exhibits and charts and blow-up demonstratives, all of which cost more than her client Dan Beers made in a year, well, they would simply be oozing money, wouldn't they.

Bleeding green, she hoped. Right in front of the jury.

If nothing else positive happened in this crazy trial, maybe they had that going for them.

Of course, there was a new development that had kept Anzalone up the last few nights. Mysteriously, someone had delivered an explosive scientific research report from the files of Gunther to her client's father-in-law, Henry Mahoney, who in turn had given it to Dan Beers. Her client then hand-delivered it to her, arriving at her office the next morning in a frenzy. He was so irate over it he wanted to go all the way to the White House, and Anzalone had to calm him down.

The document, meanwhile, was a bombshell. When Anzalone read it, she put two hands to her cheeks. It seemed to confirm that the Gunther Research Department had determined through scientific testing that sixteen batches of the Phillips frozen shrimp brand had been tainted with high levels of sulfites, and that the problem had occurred as a result of a mistake in their quality control processes. If this were true, it certainly explained a lot. But perhaps more significantly, the fact that Gunther had not turned this document over in discovery was unforgivable, and very illegal. If she had it in her possession during depositions, she could have made some serious progress.

Notwithstanding her initial excitement, there remained some legal problems with this document. First, it wasn't clear this corporate error, this manufacturing defect, caused Agnes's injuries. Was she even allergic to sulfites? There was no medical evidence supporting such a statement, and her father could not shed any light on that question. Also, did the Shop-Rite shrimp that the Brewers brought to Turnberry come from one of these tainted batches?

Under ordinary circumstances, Anzalone would file a motion with the court to re-open discovery, ask for sanctions and attorneys' fees, and take some depositions to discover what had happened. But that would only add time and money to the equation, and neither Anzalone nor Danny had either one of those commodities. They could go through the whole exercise only to find out that Agnes did not eat from a tainted bag, and then what?

In addition, there was also the added problem that the document was marked privileged, and likely had been stolen. Anzalone had no idea who delivered it to Henry Mahoney, she only knew that Gunther's privilege designation probably would never hold up in court. At the same time, when a privileged document fell into your hands accidentally, or inadvertently, you had an obligation under the rules to return it to your adversary, and not keep a copy. Here, the matter was entirely unclear. This was no accident – someone had delivered it to them intentionally – so did she have an obligation to inform Briggs and his team? It was questionable.

Factoring in all this information, Anzalone decided she would go forward with the trial. She would use the Report during cross-examination of their lead warnings expert, a man named Dr. Cory R. Filch, and hammer away at him about the obligation to warn about sulfite levels that exceeded FDA standards. Briggs would hit the roof over it, but fuck him, thought Anzalone. Let Gunther explain to Justice San Gorgio and a Bronx jury why they never turned the document over, and that Agnes did *not* eat from a tainted bag. Even if they could, Anzalone knew, the damage would be done. It would cause an explosion in the courtroom, and Anzalone couldn't wait.

Meanwhile, over the last three weeks, Anzalone and a very dedicated team – somehow, someway – made it through Gunther's document production. They slept about four hours a night, but with a lot of guts and determination they got it done. In the end they reviewed or skimmed nearly every document. Anzalone brought in her father, Carmine, and her mother, as well as her sister and her husband, and together they all reviewed paper for nearly twenty hours a day. Even Cassie stayed and helped. They ran search terms through the database, skipped over documents and files they knew were meaningless, found trends and followed them up. She created more search terms while reading certain files, and she ran those terms through again, finding even more documents. It was hell, but by some miracle, they finished. And Anzalone believed she had discovered some decent evidence to attack the Gunther witnesses.

But there was nothing like that Final Report.

There were a few more pre-trial developments. Two days earlier, Justice San Giorgio unfortunately had granted the motions for summary judgment from every non-Gunther defendant except for the Brewers, dismissing all of them from the lawsuit. The news of it sent Bruce Dixon – Danny heard – yelling through the town and arranging a celebration at Sullivan's Pub. Even Mayor Woody attended, according to social media reports. The Brewers were nowhere to be found, and so this meant that Anzalone was going to trial solely against Gunther. She received that news while reading the Final Report, so it landed with nothing more than a shrug of the shoulders. She had a trial and a defendant and an injured child to trot before a Bronx jury, and some fabulous new evidence to boot.

There was reason to be optimistic.

ON A WARM Monday morning in May, Anzalone stopped at a Dunkin' Donuts on East 161st Street, just down the street from the Yankee Stadium subway stop and grabbed herself an extra-large hazelnut coffee before meeting Danny on the steps of the courthouse. When she arrived, at just before 9 am, dragging a litigation bag on wheels, Danny was already there on the sidewalk, pacing back and forth with his own coffee in hand. He was dressed in khaki pants over an old pair of brown loafers, with a grey houndstooth sportscoat and a silver tie, one of those skinny Billy Idol ones that had to be hanging in his closet since the 1980s.

"How do I look?" he asked Anzalone, skipping pleasantries. He straightened his shoulders and adjusted the sportscoat.

"Perfect," Anzalone responded with a smile.

"You said we didn't need the girls today, right? If we do, my sister-in-law Janet can drive them in."

"Doubtful, Mr. Beers. First day of trial is jury selection, which could take all day and maybe even part of tomorrow. You ready?"

"Am I ready? I'm good, I just feel bad for you. I couldn't imagine doing this shit for a living."

Anzalone laughed.

"We'll be fine, Mr. Beers, let's head inside."

Danny and Anzalone ascended to the top steps of the courthouse just as two black Lincoln Towncars pulled to the curb on East 161st Street. They slowed to find a resting spot, but with all the parking spaces out front filled with employee cars pulled in backwards and facing the street, they proceeded to the corner, making a right turn onto Grand Concourse.

It was a sun-splashed spring morning, and from the top steps of the courthouse, Danny kept his eyes glued on the Towncars.

They came to a stop very close to the corner, right in front of a collection of blue wooden police horses arranged to drive foot traffic away from the courthouse. Almost on cue, two drivers exited and circled around to the passenger sides, pulling open the doors. Looking up East 161st Street, Danny watched as six dark suits emerged dragging litigation bags and bulky trial exhibits covered in brown paper wrapping.

"That's them, right?" Danny asked Anzalone. Dozens of people were now filing past them heading into the main entrance to the courthouse, all carrying newspapers and coffee containers and briefcases, ready to conduct the business of the courts.

"Yup, that's them," she answered. "Surprised?"

Danny was staring straight ahead, counting.

"One, two, three … ten, eleven and twelve. There's twelve of them, you see that? They have twelve lawyers there."

Anzalone smiled again. "I can count Mr. Beers."

"This look like a fair fight to you?"

Anzalone shrugged.

"This will be a one on one, me and Briggs. And I'm ready for him, I don't care how many bagmen he brought."

"Good, I like that."

"Plus, I think round one goes to us, Mr. Beers."

Anzalone nodded to sidewalk in front of the courthouse. It was filled with people moving in every direction, but mostly ascending the steps toward the revolving doors just behind them.

"You see those people," Anzalone said, leaning in to lower her voice, "turning their heads back to look at these hotshot lawyers?"

Danny looked where Anzalone was nodding. She was right. The people walking along the sidewalk and up the courthouse steps seemed to be looking curiously back toward the Towncars.

"Yeah, I see them," Danny whispered back. He was confused. So they were looking at the cars, what was the big deal?

"Jurors," Anzalone said. "Those people there, they are potential jurors. See the ones with the pink cards in their hands?"

Danny looked down to the corner of Grand Concourse where the vehicles had pulled over. He could see roughly two dozen people walking past them holding rectangular pink cards – jury summonses – which he recognized from having once received one out in Ketchogue.

"Oh yeah, the pink cards," he said.

"So let them see this mob of a legal team with their fancy limos and expensive charts, okay?" she said. "If I were a juror, making less than what it costs to gas one of those things up in a year, I'd guess these guys can afford to pay a judgment, wouldn't you?"

Danny laughed.

"Great point," said.

He turned his attention back to the Towncars again. An enormous man began to exit the rear passenger door of the second vehicle. He was dressed in a sharp navy-blue suit and red tie with a head so big he could barely push it through the door opening. Three of the other suits, younger lawyers it seemed, quickly ran to assist him, each taking an elbow just as his leg touched the pavement.

The man straightened up, threw a cigar butt to the floor, and then buttoned the front of his suit jacket as he began a deliberate march up the steps to the courthouse entrance. His pace was slow, measured, with his jaw jutting forward and his hands webbed together behind his back, as if he wanted everyone to stare at him, which they certainly were. He had a knowing grin on his face, a smile that revealed his comfort with these surroundings, as if he were silently declaring to the world that he was at home here, that this courtroom – his courtroom – was the place where he belonged, the place that he owned, as if no other human had any right to walk its hallways without his permission.

He looked like a king, Danny thought.

Like a President or something. Who the hell was this guy?

And just as he asked himself the question, the answer came to him in a flash. Danny could see about a dozen heads turning toward the man as he moved forward, and Danny recognized the face, having seen it so many times on television.

Anzalone and Danny then moved to the right, away from the entrance, as dozens of people pushed through the revolving doors.

"That's J. Hartwell Briggs," Danny said aloud. "That's him."

"The one and only," said Anzalone.

Danny watched as Briggs walked toward a side door adjacent to the electronic security machines. With his hands still behind his back, he entered the courthouse without having to be searched. Two guards held the door for him, one of them shaking his hand.

"And he's here for us, right?" Danny asked.

"That's right, Mr. Beers. For you, Debbie and the girls. Exactly where he ought to be."

Danny looked down at Anzalone.

"You always pick on the bullies, Ms. Anzalone?"

"Always, Mr. Beers," she said with a smile. "Let's get inside."

UNLIKE IN FEDERAL courts, only the lawyers conducted jury selection in New York City courthouses. The state judges stayed away and only got involved to referee arguments among the attorneys. To Anzalone, jury selection was her opportunity to connect with the jury pool before the trial even started, to look them in the eyes and introduce her client and talk to them like people, like neighbors, as if she were standing in line at the bagel store on a Saturday morning with a ticket number in her hand, waiting to be called. She would tell them a story and ask them questions and make them feel special. She'd let them speak their minds and offer their opinions and for once in their lives feel important.

Anzalone knew that this was what defense lawyers never seemed to understand about jury selection, because she had learned that lesson the hard way a few times, back at Buckley Sullivan. It was not so much as what you said to them as *how* you said it, because in her opinion the key to the whole damn thing was whether you connected with them right from the get-go. You needed to give them the feeling that they were there for a purpose bigger than themselves, and that if they only got on board with you during this case, that you and them together could make something special happen that really mattered to people, maybe changed their lives.

And whenever she made that connection, whether she was on the plaintiff's side or the defense team, Anzalone knew it was over. From the plaintiff's perspective, once that happened, she knew her client would be walking out of there with a little something extra in their pockets. The trial at that point, she would always say, was just a show.

Up in the Bronx, the lawyers conducted jury selection in a large open conference room on the first floor only a short distance from the security machines. Like the smaller courtrooms upstairs, the main jury room was filled only with two large fold-out conference tables and about two hundred individual metal chairs arranged in rows of about twelve. Other than a chalkboard behind the conference tables and an American flag posted in one of the corners, there was nothing else in the room at all.

Before they entered, Anzalone and Danny sat in the main lobby off the jury room sipping coffee, waiting for their case to be called. The army of lawyers from Foster Tuttle & Briggs stood in circles on the other side of the lobby, flipping through legal pads of notes and whispering in each other's ears.

Anzalone explained that the day would begin with a retired Judge speaking to the entire pool of assembled jurors.

"Here his name is Judge Pasquale Beninnati," Anzalone explained. "They give these jobs to retired judges because all they do is give the preliminary instructions before the lawyers take over."

"Preliminary instructions?" Danny asked.

"Yes, Beninnati will first thank the jurors for doing their civic duty and he'll lecture them about the importance of juror service," she answered. "Then he'll ask if anyone absolutely cannot serve because of a medical condition or a psychological disorder, or things of that nature. I love this part, because nearly every person in the room will approach him and ask off, using every conceivable excuse you can think of, and some you can't."

Anzalone laughed a bit, and then she continued.

"We'll be consulted, me and Briggs, but ultimately Beninnati decides who he'll let off and who he won't. I can tell you this though – unless you physically cannot do it, really can't do it, he sends them all back in. He's tough that way. I've seen it a thousand times."

Danny was fascinated by this talk, so foreign as it was to anything he did in his life. It was nothing like you see on TV. Plus, the conversation was easing his nerves a bit.

"Okay, then what happens?" he asked eagerly.

"Well, once Beninnati decides on the physically or emotionally unable cases, he basically turns the lawyers loose. He leaves, and then we go in. Each side will introduce themselves to the entire pool of jurors, tell them who their clients are. I'll introduce you by name, but I won't say anything else about you. Then the lawyers are permitted to tell them in very basic terms what your case is about. You are not permitted to argue your case at this point, and you need to be careful not to do it because you can risk having the entire pool struck, which is something we do not want. That happens, and we don't get another jury pool for six months."

"So, do you know what you're going to say?"

"I will keep it simple, believe me," Anzalone said. "And so will Briggs. He's supposed to be a master at this, and since everyone in the room knows who he is, there's not much he needs to say. Anyway, after the lawyers give those quick introductions, we go to the wheel."

Anzalone said this as if Danny knew what the wheel was, and she let the comment hang as she looked around the lobby and sipped her coffee again. Danny was past the point of being embarrassed by what he didn't know about this whole experience, so he asked her outright.

"Uh, what exactly is the wheel?"

"Oh, the wheel?" she said. "Well, that's how we pick jurors here. The wheel is nothing more than a round wooden box with a turn crank. For every person who received a jury notice and showed up and hasn't been let off by Beninnati, there is an index card with their names and addresses and some other information. The cards are all stuffed into a big wheel. For this case they sent out about sixty jury notices, because they know this case will go about two or three weeks, and they want to make sure there's enough alternates. I expect there will be about fifty people left when we enter, which means fifty index cards in the wheel."

"Is that a lot?"

"Biggest case I've ever had," she confessed. "Most of the time they notice about thirty. But anyway, Briggs and I will spin the wheel with the crank and then we'll reach in and pull out six random index cards. We'll call those people forward and sit them in the front row. Each side will examine their cards, take some notes, and then we get to ask those people questions. We'll go first because we are the plaintiffs. After we're done, Briggs and his team goes. When we both finish, then we go to the strikes."

Anzalone paused again, and Danny went on the offensive.

"You do realize I don't know what the strikes are, right?"

"Of course. I was just testing you."

"Please continue," Danny replied, smiling.

"Each side gets to exercise what we call strikes against any of the six jurors that are first selected," Anzalone explained. "Strikes means we get to kick them off the jury, to put it simple. But you don't get unlimited strikes. In civil cases like this, there are only two kinds. Strikes for cause, and another kind called peremptory strikes. Strikes for cause is when you strike a juror because you believe based on your questioning of that juror that he or she cannot in any way be fair and impartial during the trial and deliberations, or will not decide the case based on the evidence. There are no limits to the number of jurors you can strike for cause."

Danny was confused.

"But doesn't that mean you can just strike anyone you don't want," he asked, "which means we'll be here forever?"

"Actually no. Strikes for cause have to be explained to Judge Beninnati if the other side won't agree, and Beninnati will try everything in his power to rehabilitate that juror and get him or her to serve. All he needs to hear are the magic words 'fair and impartial,' and back they go. The truth is that it's very difficult to strike a juror for cause."

"I see," Danny said, following now. "And the other kind…"

"Peremptory strikes," Anzalone assisted. "We each get three of those. Those are strikes that each side gets to exercise without having to give an explanation. So, if we don't like a particular juror, we exercise a peremptory. We just say we're striking so and so and out they go."

"Well, how do you know who to strike and who not to?"

"Ahh," she answered, smiling brightly, "that's the million-dollar question. See, this is where the strategy comes in, the fun part. Me, I just go with my gut. I have some general rules, but I believe you need to assess each person individually and decide for yourself whether you think they will cast a vote for your client. Sometimes you're right, and sometimes you're wrong, but it's not something you can take out of a book."

Danny was a bit shaken now. He always thought this was more of a science than a fly by the seat of your pants kind of thing. The thought of having his fate decided by six people he had never met and didn't know but had somehow passed Anzalone's half-assed gut instinct test was wrenching the insides of his stomach. He recalled what Judge Casey said at the mediation and was beginning to understand now.

"I guess Briggs does it the same way?" he asked.

"Not exactly. See that grey suit standing next to Briggs?"

Anzalone pointed a pinky across the lobby. Danny looked and saw a tall, thin man with a large Adam's Apple perched atop a bright yellow bow tie flipping through a thick black binder and talking intently to Briggs. Briggs was listening and nodding.

"That's his jury consultant," Anzalone informed him. "He's from a company called VerdictNow. They run all kinds of fancy focus groups and mock trials and get paid obscene amounts of money to tell lawyers like Briggs exactly who should be on their juries. Over the last few months, Briggs and his team probably tried this case about a dozen times before different focus groups comprised of every conceivable demographic background imaginable. After that, VerdictNow likely ran all the information into a computer, which spits back all kinds of statistics twisted a thousand different ways. That's what's in his binder there. But as I said, it's all garbage in my opinion. People are human, Mr. Beers. The simple truth is that they do things and think things that computers can't predict."

"Anything else?" Danny asked.

"Well, there's a little more to the strategy part," she answered. "The key is, you don't want to burn all your peremptories during the first group of six, because then you'll have none during the second six, the third, and so on. You really need to be cautious. But you and I will have plenty of time to consult before we decide."

Danny was more confused than ever.

"The second six?" he asked.

"Yes, let's say we exercise one peremptory during the first group of six, and Briggs's team exercises two, but no one is struck for cause. That's three jurors kicked off. That leaves three remaining from the first group of six. The rule is that the three remaining automatically become juror numbers one, two and three for our trial. But we still need three more jurors to make out the six-person jury, and in this case Beninnati decided there will be four alternates.

So we would need to pick more people. Which means we go back to the wheel, call another group of six, and do the whole round of questioning and striking all over again. We keep going until – "

"We have ourselves a jury. Now I get it."

"See how easy?" Anzalone said, smiling again.

"Maybe for you," said Danny, stretching his back.

Danny looked across the lobby and saw J. Hartwell Briggs moving toward them. His massive jaw was jutting forward again with his hands behind his back, smiling as he neared where they were seated. As he approached, he stuck his right hand out toward Anzalone, who looked up at him but did not rise.

"Yew must be Miss Anzalone-y," said Briggs, his wide grin revealing a mouthful of yellow teeth. "Nice to finally put a face to the name."

Anzalone accepted his handshake while sitting, and Danny thought she looked confused. Her eyebrows wrinkled as she looked at him, and after pulling her hand back she placed her coffee cup on the floor and began wiping her palms with a napkin.

"The name's *Anzalone*," she said. "The –e on the end is silent."

"Ahh, yes, Anzalone," said Briggs. "Anyway, mighty nice to meet yew."

Anzalone peered around the lobby and saw no fewer than two dozen pairs of eyes on her. Briggs was towering over her with his paw extended down as she sat wiping her hands. Anzalone met all their stares, crossed one leg over the other, and looked back up toward this titan of the legal and political world.

"Can I, uh, help you with anything, Mr. … uh … well shit, I'm sorry," she said, "I didn't catch your name."

Danny's eyes widened at the comment. It took him a moment to realize that here was his lawyer, this tiny little tiger of a lady, giving shit to one of the most powerful lawyers in the world, right here in the Bronx County courthouse.

Danny covered his mouth with a fist and stifled a laugh. Briggs himself was taken aback as an awkward silence fell between them. After a moment or two his grin widened, and then he laughed loudly, pointing down at Anzalone.

Anzalone smiled and pointed right back at him.

"Well, okay, Ms. Anzalone-y!" Briggs chuckled, clapping his hands. "I guess we'll be seein' y'all inside. Good luck to yew!"

Briggs wheeled around and marched back to his group as Anzalone lifted her coffee cup again. She looked up at Danny, then smiled at him and winked.

BY 11:30 AM, Judge Beninnati had plowed through his instructions and had quietly assembled fifty-three jurors in the main conference room at the Bronx County courthouse. Danny and Anzalone sat together at the front of the room behind the right-side conference table. Briggs and three other lawyers sat behind the left. The jurors all sat facing forward in silence. They were sprinkled across six or seven rows, many reading books or shuffling newspapers, while the lawyers arranged notes and papers and documents, preparing to begin the process of selecting a six-person jury, with four alternates, in the case of *Beers vs. Gunther Home Products Corporation.*

For Danny's part, the stillness in the room was unnerving. If someone didn't speak soon, he was going to lose his mind. He quickly scanned his eyes across the faces of the fifty-something odd potential jurors and saw nothing but angry stares coming back at him, undoubtedly for having filed this godforsaken lawsuit. They clearly did not want to be here. There was not a smile or a warm gesture to be found, and those that weren't ogling him with crossed arms or twisted eyebrows had their heads buried in a newspaper, book or magazine, blowing frustrated sighs out as they crossed and re-crossed their legs.

What the hell was he doing here? How had his life taken such a turn as to place him in this courtroom?

Maybe he was misreading them, he hoped. Maybe this wasn't anger in their eyes. Perhaps this was just the simple look of irritation and annoyance that people feel when they are hauled down for jury duty, pulled away from their daily lives to resolve a dispute that was none of their business. Maybe this wasn't directed toward Danny or Anzalone at all, and maybe the final six people chosen would really listen to the evidence and treat him fairly. His lawyer would be asking these people for money, millions in fact.

Would they do justice? Give him a fair shake?

It was all he asked.

Danny reached down and rubbed his stomach, trying to rid himself of a burning sensation he had felt all day, one that had woken him before the alarm that morning. Then he shot a glance over at Anzalone, silently begging her to begin the proceedings.

"Well, Ms. Anzalone-y," Briggs finally said, turning to her and Danny. He was seated at the far-right side of his table, with Ko and two other lawyers next to him. Briggs held a thick black binder.

"Y'all ready to begin?" he asked.

"I'm ready when you are, Mr. Briggs," Anzalone said.

Danny swallowed hard. This was it – finally, Agnes's trial. His family could tell their story and beg for help, and maybe these people would assist. Maybe they had compassion in their hearts. Danny silently prayed, finding it difficult to catch his breath.

"Good then," Briggs replied. "Yew mind if I start?"

"Not at all," said Anzalone.

Briggs then stood and faced the jury pool.

"Good mornin', ladies and gentlemen, and thank yew for bein' here today," he said, standing tall. "The first thing we'd like to do today is to innerduce ourselves, which seems a good 'nuff place to start. My name is Hartwell Briggs, and I am pleased to be here today on behalf of the defendant, the Gunther Home Products Corporation. I'm with the law firm of Foster Tuttle & Briggs right here in New York City. This man here," he gestured to Ko, "is my partner, Yang Hsue Ko, and yew gone be hearin' from him as well."

Briggs then gave them all a huge smile.

"But even though I practice in New Yawk, y'all can probably tell from my accent that I'm a Tennessee man by birth."

He pointed to the jurors and winked.

"Now don't y'all hold that against me, ya hear?"

The room let go a nervous laugh, which Danny gladly joined. Finally, he saw some smiles on their aggravated faces, and it made Danny relax a bit, even though Briggs seemed to have scored an early point.

Briggs turned and gestured toward Anzalone.

"Ms. Anzalone-y?" he said, dropping into his chair.

Anzalone stood, with her diminutive frame barely rising above the conference room table. The difference between her and Briggs, a colossal man who seemed to fill the entire room, was so stark that Danny could hear some muffled laughter in the back of the room.

"Good morning, ladies and gentlemen," Anzalone began.

"My name is Nicole Anzalone and I represent the plaintiff in this matter, Mr. Daniel Beers, who is sitting right here next to me. I also represent his daughter, Agnes Beers, an 11-year-old child who you will meet very soon in this trial. Agnes recently emerged from a six-month long coma after eating a product sold by the defendant, the Gunther Home Products Corporation."

A cold silence fell upon the room. Whatever smiles Briggs had triggered quickly disappeared, causing the jurors to squirm in their seats. Anzalone had their attention, and she seized her opportunity.

"Ladies and gentlemen, I have my own law firm – I'm a solo practitioner – in a Long Island town called Ketchogue," she said. "I work on the second floor above a donut shop on Main Street."

Anzalone smiled and turned her head toward Briggs.

"Now don't y'all hold THAT against ME!" she said, and this time the room laughed heartily. She reached down and grabbed Danny by the forearm, still facing the jurors. Briggs was smiling too, and he nodded at Anzalone, acknowledging her jab.

When the laughter subsided, Anzalone stepped closer to the rows of jurors.

"What we're going to do first this morning," Anzalone explained, "is the following. Mr. Briggs is going to pull six index cards from the wheel over there and call out the names that are printed on them. As you can see, we've left the first row of seats open, and when we call your name, we ask that you come forward and sit in the first row. I will then ask you some questions, either individually or as a group, and ask that you give me honest and truthful answers. Then Mr. Briggs will ask you questions, and I would hope you will give him the same courtesies. Then we'll decide which of you will serve as jurors. Any questions so far?"

No hands were raised, and Anzalone turned toward Briggs.

"Good then," she said. "Mr. Briggs, please spin the wheel."

Anzalone sat, and Briggs rose from his seat. He buttoned his jacket and walked slowly over to the wheel, which sat on a separate small table near the corner where the flag stood. Danny watched as Briggs's strutted forward again, his hands behind his back, as always, looking very much like the king Danny saw entering the building a few hours before.

Danny wondered what these jurors must think of this great man, standing there before them. Everyone in the room knew who he was, that was a certainty. At the snap of a finger he could have been Governor of this State, and they certainly were aware of that fact. He wondered what they must feel like to have been given a jury summons and to have the luck of drawing this great and powerful lawyer, this bastion of the legal and political community, so respected, for their case. He wondered whether they understood, as Danny did, that world leaders from other nations made a point of visiting Briggs when they came to the United States. Danny scanned their faces and saw the awe that he himself felt. He wondered how it would be possible for Anzalone to convince them to rule against Briggs's client, regardless of what he and Agnes may ask of them.

Briggs stood next to the wheel and turned to the jury pool.

"Well, folks," he said, smiling again. "Here she goes."

Briggs grabbed the turn crank on the side of the wooden box and twisted it clockwise. The box began to spin with great speed. The index cards churned and flapped within the box, and then Briggs let go of the handle, until the box stopped spinning and came to rest. Then he pulled open a small door on the side and pulled out a white index card.

"Eastbrook, Jane!" Briggs bellowed.

All the names were printed on the cards with the last name appearing first, and then the first name after. Briggs read the first juror's name in that order, and then looked out toward the entire jury pool.

"Is Ms. Jane Eastbrook here?"

The collective heads of the jury pool began to twist and look at one another, until finally a red-haired 50-ish woman in the third row stood and raised her hand. She was thin and tall and wore a brown leather jacket, carrying her lunch in a plastic Foodtown bag. Like just about every other person, she had a small paperback tucked under her arm.

"Ahh, Ms. Eastbrook," Briggs said, "please, have a seat."

Ko and the two other lawyers accompanying Briggs were furiously scribbling notes, flipping through the pages of the black binders provided by the guy with the yellow bow tie, Danny noticed. The woman named Jane Eastbrook made her way forward and took the first seat in the row in front of the conference tables. Anzalone herself made a few notes on a legal pad, and then Briggs spun the wheel again.

The cards churned and flapped, and Briggs yanked out another one. "Provenzale, Paul!" he called out. "Provenzale, Paul. Is there a Mr. Provenzale here?"

Fifth row on the aisle. A short, stocky man, mid-30s, wearing blue jeans and a blue denim garage shirt with the name "Paul" stitched to the breast pocket. The man rose and stuck an index finger in the air.

"Right heah," Provenzale said, rolling his eyes.

Danny thought he heard him mutter the word "Christ" as he moved to the front row.

"Thank yew, Mr. Provenzale," Briggs said.

Danny noticed that Briggs smiled and looked each juror in the eye as they approached. Maybe he was making a connection with them, but who knew. Provenzale collapsed into the seat next to Eastbrook in a huff, and Briggs spun the wheel again.

"White, Yolanda!" Briggs then shouted. "White ... Yolanda!"

A black woman with a tight haircut and aviator style eyeglasses stood and started moving toward the aisle. Anzalone smiled, because this was a woman she had hoped would be called when the group first assembled. Anzalone got very good vibes from her, why she didn't know, her gut again she guessed, and sure enough when Yolanda White started moving toward her seat next to Provenzale, she looked directly at Anzalone and nodded before dropping into her chair.

Briggs waited for her to sit before turning back to the wheel.

"There you go, now thank yew, Ms. White," he said, grabbing the turn crank. "Righty then. Let's get ourselves to number four."

Danny could tell that Briggs was really enjoying this now. He was playing master of ceremonies to the book, smiling at each juror and dropping little comments and jokes here and there to keep things light. Danny felt the nervousness drain from his chest and stomach as Briggs went on, and he could see that the jurors were feeling more at ease themselves. Anzalone remained quiet, which unnerved Danny a little, but she did not appear uncomfortable or nervous and he knew that she would have her chance once the questioning began.

In the meantime, Briggs seemed to be rolling. The wheel came to a rest again, and Briggs reached in and pulled out a card.

"George, King!" Briggs yelled out.

He held the card in front of his face with a confused look, his eyebrows wrinkling a bit.

"George . . . King?" he yelled again, still staring at the card. This time it sounded like Briggs was asking a question.

Suddenly a gauntly thin old man rose from his seat in the very last row of the conference room. Danny surmised the man was at least eighty years old. He was hunched over when he rose, carrying a thin metal walking cane. His face was deeply black and leathery, with a small grey patch of hair spread across the top of his skull. There were thick ropey veins lining the back of his shaking hands, and he wore a light brown suit with a dark orange shirt and a maroon tie, looking like he was on his way to Church, Danny thought. His seat was in the middle of the row, and the people between him and the aisle rose to let him through, some of them taking him by the elbow to assist him as he shuffled slowly by.

When this frail elderly man finally reached the aisle, he turned to start his slow deliberate march toward the conference tables and the front row, where he would take the fourth seat next to Yolanda White. Before he started walking forward, however, Danny noticed that he grabbed the cane with two hands in front of him and threw his shoulders back as best he could, as if he didn't want anyone to see him hunched. He walked with his jaw pushed forward, a proud look on his face. His pace was slow, deliberate and painful, his steps short and plodding. As he moved forward Danny could see that his pants, in the area in front of his knees, were worn, as if the man had been wearing them while doing manual labor.

As the man got about a third of the way up the aisle, Danny saw Briggs still studying the index card. His confused stare seemed to be burning a hole in it, as if he were troubled by the way the name was written – "George, King" – with the comma between the first and last name. Danny wondered if Briggs thought there was something wrong with the name.

Sure enough, Briggs looked at the man, then back at the card.

"'Scuse me," he said, catching the attention of the room. The elderly man stopped in the center of the aisle and looked around, confused at first, but then his eyes landed on Briggs, who was smiling now.

"Mr. ... uh ... King?" Briggs asked, pointing at the index card.

"No suh," the man replied, shaking his head.

He looked at Briggs with his lips pursed and his chin extended forward again. The entire jury pool was now focused on this slight but very proud man, who seemed to be anticipating the next question. And now nobody was moving, not even the old man, who was standing alone halfway up the aisle. Briggs still held the index card out in front of him.

He looked at the card again and read aloud.

"Well then ... Mr. George is it?" Briggs said, smiling.

"Yes suh."

"So the name is ... King George? That right, sir?" Briggs asked again, this time with a wide grin spread across his face.

Danny could hear a few muffled laughs coming from the back of the room now. He squirmed in his chair a bit as the elderly man threw his shoulders back as far as he could, his chin jutting very far forward now, with a look of anger beginning to seep into the lines of his face. Briggs, however, still wore the grin. He looked at the entire pool as he asked his next question, like a game show host awaiting a laugh track.

"Sir? Am I correct that your name is ... King George?"

He held the index card behind his back.

"Yes suh," the man replied firmly.

"Well then," Briggs said loudly, "if Your Majesty would kindly take a seat, we will continue with the next juror!"

And with that the entire room exploded in laughter, everyone turning their heads and looking at one another.

Anzalone grabbed Danny by the forearm and squeezed, a pained look of caution spread across her face. She rose to her feet and noticed that King George was still staring forward at Briggs as the laughter rained down.

And then, just as it all began to subside, King George moved forward again in that slow, deliberate, plodding walk, heading down the aisle toward the conference tables.

As he approached the first row, and the laughter had all but dissipated, everyone in the room was fully expecting him to take a right hand turn into the row and take his seat next to Yolanda White, to be questioned as the fourth potential juror.

Except when he reached the bottom of the aisle, he turned left toward Briggs.

"Mr. George, if yew would please take ya seat now," Briggs said, gesturing toward the first row. But King George ignored him. He was still plodding forward, taking those short choppy steps, with his cane held in the two trembling hands in front of him. His face bore a blank expression, and he appeared to be concentrating on his steps, moving in a straight direction toward Briggs, a path that Danny could not help but notice.

"Mr. George, please. We do need yew to take ya seat, sir."

But once again King George ignored him, plodding forward, his brown shoes making a scraping sound on the linoleum-tiled floor. In a moment King George stood directly in front of Briggs, whose smile was now replaced with a confused stare, as if he were wondering whether the man simply didn't realize that the seat he was supposed to take was in the complete opposite direction of where he now stood.

Danny, however, saw something very different in King George's eyes. Something that he would not regard as confusion, not now, not ever. What Danny saw was determination, the look of a man who would not be humiliated. He wore an expression that made clear that what was about to transpire was going to take place no matter who J. Hartwell Briggs was, no matter what he had accomplished, and regardless of what these proceedings were supposed to represent.

And in that moment, a tremendous feeling of anticipation rose in Danny's chest, as if he knew something was about to happen, something significant that would change his life. In a flash that April day came back to him, the morning when all this started. The day at Turnberry Park when Agnes got sick. He saw an image of himself sitting in his pickup truck on his driveway and recalled that strange feeling of hopefulness as the sun beamed down on his face. And right now he had that same sense. He could feel the blood begin to pump through his veins and rush to his extremities, filling his feet and hands and warming his face.

He looked toward the center of the room and saw that King George now stood before Briggs, their faces about a foot apart.

Right there in front of Danny, King George raised his cane upright in his right hand, way up high behind his head, holding the tip of the handle so that the walking end was pointing straight in the air. A few jurors in the rear of the conference room slowly rose to their feet.

King George held the cane there for a moment, and then suddenly he dropped it. It fell to the floor behind him with a clanging thud. Now his right hand was empty and open, but he still held it up high behind his head, as if he were raising his hand to be called on in class. He stood there motionless, the hand over his head, fingers extended, staring straight into the eyes of the great J. Hartwell Briggs.

Briggs was looking forward at him as well, except that his jaw was now sunk low, the smile gone from his face. His forehead was wrinkled, and his mouth was agape, with his shoulders slumped and his hands dangling loosely at his side. Danny could see that the seemingly impenetrable confidence that Briggs wore when he arrived here that day was gone, replaced now with a grimace that simply could not hide its profound fear.

He looked like a condemned man about to be sentenced.

And then, in the blink of an eye, King George swung his trembling hand forward violently and smacked J. Hartwell Briggs directly in the face, the "thwack" of hand against flesh ringing loudly and bouncing off every wall of the conference room.

An audible gasp could be heard from the jurors.

"HELL YOU THINK YOU TALKIN' TO, BOY!" King George then roared, in a voice that completely shocked both Danny and Anzalone, the two of them wondering how it possibly had come from the body of this tiny, frail man. It filled the entire room, swallowing the silence that had descended upon all of them.

"Ain't nobody taught you NO RESPECT?!" King George yelled again, and then, after staring forward at Briggs for a long moment, a terribly awkward pause that felt like hours to the collective group, King George turned and reached down and yanked his cane from the floor. He straightened upright as best he could, with his shoulders pinned back, and then he turned and faced the rest of the jurors, none of whom were making a sound. He adjusted his jacket and tie and then continued his slow, plodding, chopped-stepped walk to his seat next to Yolanda White, the brown shoes scraping the linoleum again.

Yolanda White stood and helped him lower into the chair.

Danny was floored. He watched all of this as if it had been taking place in slow motion. When King George was finally in his seat, holding the cane with two fists and facing forward toward the conference tables, one leg crossed over the other, Danny looked over at Briggs, who hadn't made a move. He was now sitting in a chair next to the small table that held the wheel, with both palms on his knees, shoulders slumped, staring forward toward the floor, not saying a word. The grin, the jutted jaw, that aura of regal magnificence that made him look like a king – all of it – was gone now, as if it never existed to begin with, Danny thought.

Right now, no one in the room was moving a muscle.

"Mr. Briggs," Anzalone said.

Briggs didn't respond.

"MR. BRIGGS," she said again.

The room was still and silent.

"Uh, Ms. Anzalone?" Ko finally interrupted, rising to his feet.

He looked ashen and panicked.

And that was when Anzalone knew it was over.

She leaned down and whispered something in Danny's ear. Then she stood and turned to Ko.

"Yes sir, what can I do for?" she asked, knowingly.

"Can we take a short break for a moment?"

"Yes, why don't we do that," Anzalone responded.

She could not contain her smile.

"Let's take a short break."

CHAPTER 37

ONE DAY AT A TIME

ABOUT FIVE WEEKS later, Danny stood outside the donut shop on Ketchogue Terrace sipping from a container of black coffee. He took in the warm June air blowing south down Main Street and looked up at the cobalt blue sky. He smiled and then stole a glance at his watch. It was a few minutes before ten am, and he was dressed in his work blue jeans and construction boots, his F350 parked at a meter a few blocks away.

The next day, Danny would take the day off and bring the girls down to Fire Island for a day on the beach, but today he had some quick business with his lawyer. He took the last swig of his coffee and pitched the container into a garbage can on the street. Then he headed up the stairs to Anzalone's office, where she greeted him at the door with a smile. She was dressed in a dark blue suit because she had another court appearance that day, the business of her practice moving forward – upward and onward, as they say.

"Come in, Mr. Beers," she said warmly, "so good to see you."

"You too," Danny replied, "thanks for squeezing me in today."

Danny looked around and saw dozens of boxes piled up in the foyer and in the hallway leading to Anzalone's office. There was nothing on the walls either, and Danny saw that everything that had been hanging in frames was now wrapped in brown paper and stacked neatly on the floor. All the shelves had been cleaned out too. He peered into Anzalone's office and saw it was nearly empty.

"What's going on?" he asked Anzalone.

"We're moving!" she said cheerfully. "I took out some bigger office space down in Mineola, closer to the courts. The new digs are in a great corporate office building over there. Hired a few lawyers too. I'm gonna see if I can expand the business a little, make a go of it."

"Wow, that's great," Danny said. "Congrats."

"Thanks!" Anzalone responded.

Then she gestured to her office.

"Anyway, I have the envelope ready for you. Come on back and let me get you going. I know you have to get the girls."

"Hey, by the way, thank you so much for the gift," said Danny. "Don't even mention it."

Danny was so touched when Anzalone had dropped off a present for Gianna's birthday a few weeks earlier, and he wanted to thank her for that gesture. Anzalone settled the case with Gunther a few days after they jointly elected to end the jury selection on the afternoon of the first day, and so technically their case was over and he was no longer a client when she had delivered the present. It wasn't really a big deal, but it turned out his instinct about her was right on the money – she really did care. Today he was there to pick up his settlement check.

He entered her office and they chit-chatted about the weather for a few minutes, and then Danny got to a pressing matter.

"So, Ms. Anzalone," he said, "you mind if I ask you a question? There's something I've been curious about."

"Go right ahead."

"So, how did you know they would settle after what happened with King George that day?" Danny asked. "Did you really know right then and there? We never got to talk about that."

Anzalone pulled out a small business envelope from her desk drawer and handed it to Danny.

"Yes, I did," she responded. "See, thing is, after King George, Briggs and Gunther really had no choice but to move to strike the entire jury venire, which they did. In other words, they had to ask the Court to send all the jurors home and start over on the grounds they all had been infected by what King George did. And I knew that Judge Beninnati would never grant that motion in a million years, because Briggs had caused the problem himself. It would mean telling over sixty jurors that they could blow doors and split. Then they'd have to summon a hundred more. That is very expensive and would have taken over six months."

"So, Briggs was stuck with King George," Danny concluded.

"Exactly," said Anzalone. "And then they were screwed, because they absolutely had to exercise a peremptory strike and remove him, which they did. Under those circumstances, I would have done the same thing – any lawyer would have. What they didn't anticipate, though, what they couldn't have known, was the reaction of the jury pool to his removal."

Danny knew exactly what she meant. When Ko struck King George, there had been an audible gasp in the courtroom. The room of potential jurors shot darts at Briggs and Ko. They had fire in their eyes as the elderly man shuffled his way up the aisle and out the door. Danny thought there would be an outright rebellion right there in the jury room.

"See, King George had become the hero of that room," Anzalone confirmed, "you could see it. Maybe he represented every person there who ever wanted to stand up and fight The Man, you know, rail against the system, but whatever, he made them feel powerful. Standing up to Briggs like that was incredible. It made those jurors feel like they were capable of something that they themselves didn't even know about. Heck, I kind of felt that way myself. When they booted Mr. George from the jury, the rest of the pool was furious. Briggs knew it too, and that's why Gunther had no choice but to approach us. They could never go to trial with a jury like that. When they dethroned King George, it was over."

"Well, I was really surprised how quickly it got done, I have to tell you," Danny said.

"Well," Anzalone explained, "that's where the Final Report came in. Without that document, I'm confident we don't get a settlement."

"Wow," said Danny.

"When we met for settlement talks on the afternoon of the first day of jury selection," Anzalone went on, "Beninnati hadn't release the venire. There was a chance we could go right back in there and empanel that jury. That's when I pulled out the Final Report. I threw that document in Briggs's and Ko's face and I told them I would go to the press, the Disciplinary Board, drag them before Justice San Giorgio for gross discovery abuse, anything I had to do."

"My God," Danny said.

"I told them they were not going to get away with it, that they would pay for what they did. I made that clear to them. I gave them my new demand and told them they had until midnight. Ko kept a pretty good poker face, but in the end they caved, and they did so very quickly. They came back with a counter within hours, and we got the deal done."

"Incredible," Danny said, shaking his head.

"All of that convinced me that Agnes *did* in fact eat from a tainted bag, loaded with sulfites. And there was no way they could have kept the Final Report out of evidence, no way. Justice San Gorgio would have allowed it. Of course, if they had a defense and could prove that the shrimp was *not* from a tainted batch, they would have presented it. But they didn't. They knew this jury would have hammered them."

"So that report had that much impact?"

"Yes, combined with the potential press fallout, and the help of King George, well, I'm fairly certain that's why they capitulated."

"Well," said Danny, "what a story. I wouldn't have believed it if I didn't see it myself."

"Me too," said Anzalone.

"And now here we are," said Danny.

"Yes, here we are."

A moment later, Danny twisted open the small metal clasp on the envelope and pulled out a cashier's check made payable to Daniel X. Beers, as Parent and Guardian of Agnes Beers. He stared down at the number, right in the middle of the check, and his eyes glazed over:

EIGHT MILLION AND .00/ 100 DOLLARS

Just seeing it made him numb. It didn't seem real to him, and probably never would, because he would throw it in the bank and use to it to make sure he is around every day for his girls. Gunther had offered to pay it all to him over time, in something they called a structured settlement, but he turned them down and took it as a lump sum.

It felt like he was more in control that way.

"Will you keep working, Mr. Beers?"

"Yeah, I'm sure I will, but down south," Danny replied.

"Down south?" Anzalone asked, surprised.

"Yes, we're moving!" said Danny, throwing his arms up. "I'm listing the house, we're gonna re-locate. Maybe North Carolina,

South Carolina, anywhere warm, so that Agnes can be outside a lot. Haven't decided exactly where yet."

"Well how about that?" Anzalone said, smiling, "good for you."

"Anyway, there's a lot less pressure now, that's for sure. Once I get settled down there, I'll take the jobs I want and keep busy, make Christmas nice for the girls this year. From there, I'll just take things a day at a time."

Anzalone smiled at him.

"A day at a time," she said.

"Yup, a day at a time," Danny smiled back.

"Well, that's great Mr. Beers," she said, offering her hand. "If there's ever anything I can do for you, please don't hesitate to call."

"Well, there is one thing," Danny said.

"Oh yeah, what's that?" she asked.

"I was thinking maybe we could be on a first name basis now. You know, now that the case is over and everything. Whaddya think?"

Anzalone smiled and laughed.

"I'd like that a lot, Dan. You take care now."

"I definitely will, Nicole. See you around maybe."

CHAPTER 38

BOFEY QUINN'S PUBLIC HOUSE

THE WESTERN PART of County Clare contains some of the most breathtaking scenery you will ever see. There are miles upon miles of rolling green acres set out in a patchwork quilt, with single lane roads lined with rock walls that date back centuries. They cut majestically through the Irish landscape, interrupted only by tiny villages with single-story buildings, cozy pubs and quaint hotels.

O'Reilly and Tom had booked a room in the village of Lahinch, nestled up against the rugged shores of the Atlantic Ocean, at a place called McInerney's Sancta Maria Hotel. It was just a stone's throw from the Lahinch Golf Course, where the two had spent the last three August days spraying golf balls over every inch of the place. They cranked out thirty-six holes a day, and then they did nearly as much damage in the Lahinch pubs after sundown.

This afternoon they opted for a change of pace. They hopped in a rental car and decided to cruise through the Irish countryside. Tom drove. They left the hotel and jumped on the N67, Lahinch Road, heading east, cruising past the open greens and the clusters of sheep and cows, past the farms of Cloonaveige and on to the town of Ennistimon. From there they took the N85 heading southeast. Tom was plunked down in what would be the passenger seat in America, driving a manual transmission with his left hand, and on the left side of the road. O'Reilly was certain they would crash, and Tom just laughed. They rolled past Knockdramaugh, Ballyvraneen, Drumcullaun Lough, and then on to the village of Inagh, where they stopped off for a quick pint at a place called the Rambler's Rest.

Once freshly hydrated, the two then drove north on a single lane road numbered R460. The landscape was glorious. O'Reilly pressed the windows down and breathed in the cool August air. They drove up and down green rolling hills that seemed untouched by human hand. There were small farms and the occasional single-family homes, with views that ran for miles. Eventually they crossed a small bridge that spanned the River Fergus, and they found themselves in the village of Corofin. They drove slowly down Main Street, taking in the town, the shops, the pubs and the stores.

"Let's grab a bite here somewhere," Tom said cheerfully.

"Absolutely," agreed O'Reilly.

"This town is awesome."

"It really is."

Up on the left-hand side Tom saw an orange building with the words "BOFEY QUINN'S PUBLIC HOUSE" spread out on the front wall that faced the street. He said, "that's us, right there," and he pulled the car against the curb on the right side of the road. In a minute O'Reilly and Tom were inside. The pub contained a front room with some couches and a fireplace, and on the left side there was a bar. Behind that there were dinner tables, way in the back, and right now the place was about half full of customers.

Tom and O'Reilly grabbed two seats at the bar. A woman named Bridget greeted them warmly, and in no time they had two plates of lamb stew and a couple of pints of Guinness sitting in front of them. They chatted about their poor golf games, laughed about some events in the pubs over the last few nights, and then eventually the conversation turned to their respective jobs. Tom complained about the 81st Precinct and all the internal politics, and then he asked his brother about how everything had shaken loose at the "big fancy law firm."

O'Reilly took a swig of his Guinness, took a deep breath, and told Tom the entire story. He explained how he had left him at Clarita's Café, went home to his Park Slope studio, and then how he had boarded a train to Manhattan that very night. When O'Reilly had spilled his guts, and taken Tom through all of it, Tom pushed his plate forward.

"You have got to be shitting me," he said.

"I'm not."

"So, you're lying there on your back, under Lincoln's ass, and he sends this Ko guy to go get security?"

"That's right."

"Why didn't they just call?"

"Well, they tried, I think," said O'Reilly. "See, I was lying there on my back and when I heard him mention the water bottle, I thought I was gonna scream, so I covered my mouth, and then I looked to my right and saw the telephone cord plugged into the outlet. Right there on the wall next to me. So I pinched that little plastic thing and I yanked it."

"You 86'd the phone system?"

"I guess so."

"Holy shit. This is unbelievable."

"I know, it was just an instinct, but I guess it worked."

"Then what?"

"Well, I heard him pick up and then drop the phone, and then I heard Ko leave. Then Briggs opened the door and walked out. I don't know where he went – maybe he chased after Ko, who knows. But he locked the door behind him, I can tell you that. Course, it opens from the inside."

"Jesus Christ. So what did you do?"

"What did I do? I got the hell out of there!" said O'Reilly, taking a swig of his Guinness. "I jumped up and ran to the door. I stuck my head out and didn't see anyone in the hallway, so I sprinted to that archway near the bathrooms, and then I walked down 45 flights of stairs again. Or ran, is a better term. My calves and quads were sore for two weeks."

Tom chuckled and O'Reilly laughed with him, and then the two men threw their heads back and roared. They clinked their mugs of Guinness and O'Reilly explained how he had to crawl out through the loading dock again, avoiding the detection of the security cameras. Tom couldn't believe what he was hearing. But then the conversation turned serious again as O'Reilly explained how he and another FT&B employee had decided to get the document into the hands of a family member of the named plaintiff.

Tom listened attentively, and then he took a gulp of his beer and shook his head.

"You're something else, you know that little brother?"

"I felt it was the right thing to do."

"Which is your thing," said Tom, "I get it."

O'Reilly shrugged.

"You realize if they figure this shit out, if they learn it was you, you'll never be a lawyer, right? You're smoked."

"It was a chance I was willing to take."

"So now what?" Tom asked. "You going back there?"

"Nah, I'm not," said O'Reilly. "I politely declined, and they didn't put up much of a fight. I never really fit in there in the first place. I've got resumes out to a bunch of smaller firms, and I'll find my place. I'll land somewhere. I just gotta take my time and figure out where I want to be. But whatever I do, it's gotta be helping people, you know? I want to deal with human beings and their problems and see if I can make a difference."

"Right," said Tom. "So maybe we're not that much different after all."

O'Reilly smiled.

"That's what I've been trying to tell you, big brother."

Tom took a swig of his Guinness again.

"Hey, what about that dude Manny? What's up with him?"

"He left too. He's going to law school. I'm happy for him."

Tom shook his head and smiled. Then he punched his brother lightly in the chest.

"You know what? You really are a piece of work. What a story."

"Yeah, I know it," said O'Reilly.

Bridget wandered over, this time on the other side of the bar. She was cleaning a pint glass.

"Can I interest ye in two more Guinness, gentlemen?" she asked with a warm smile.

O'Reilly smiled right back at her.

"Does the Pope shit in the woods?"

EPILOGUE

December 24, 2019 – 11:42 pm
Christmas Eve, Prattleton, NC

One of the things me and Deb looked forward to when the girls were little was assembling all the toys and filling their stockings right after putting them to bed. It'd be Christmas Eve and we'd be so exhausted but excited at the same time because we knew how much fun the next day would bring. We'd finalize all the wrapping and I'd carry everything out from where we hid it and together me and Deb would arrange all the gifts and presents under the tree so it looked like Santa had dumped everything there in a rush. Then the girls would come in and wake us up at 5 in the morning. It was all so exciting and you wanted it to last forever.

So I just got done doing all that myself, and I have to tell you, even though Deb isn't here anymore I still feel like a little kid about it. I can't wait until tomorrow morning, so excited to see the look on the girls' faces. I went a little overboard this year but I have a few extra bucks now and I figured they deserved it after what they've been through. But it's little moments like this that make me miss Deb more than anything. You get the urge to tell her about it all and then when you realize you can't, well, that's where the hurt comes in.

One thing that's for sure is that Deb would not have believed what happened this past year, with the lawsuit and all. And of course, the move. Here we are in our first Christmas down here in North Carolina and I think the girls are adjusting well. I put the house up for sale in July about a month after I got the settlement money and I got full price in less than a week.

I had heard about this town down here and so I did some research about it and worked with a local realtor, a guy with a crazy southern accent named Winston. You don't get a lot of Winstons on Long Island but he's a great guy and he was very helpful and when I visited, he took me around the town and I fell in love with it. Great schools, warm weather, and a busy town center we can walk to filled with shops, cafes, breakfast places and some pretty cool restaurants. And nice and friendly people. We found a great home and wound up moving in early August and I was really glad I could get the girls all situated in their new schools in time for classes to start. They are both adjusting really well – Gianna has already made a ton of new friends and she loves the house especially the swimming pool and hot tub in the backyard. I call it a "dug-in," or a "ce-ment pond," and Gianna rolls her eyes. The house is nothing extravagant but it's a really nice place and roomy with a big open family room and kitchen and a nice spacious backyard. I didn't go nuts on a big house because I want to save all that money but I made sure the girls had their own bedrooms and bathrooms. I thought it would be a nice treat and that they would need the space as they got older. And of course, as you would expect, they both sleep in the same room and in the same bed most nights.

Anyway, I'll miss Ketchogue a lot and some of the friends I made there. I'll certainly miss the times I had there with Deb. It was so strange seeing the house completely empty with hundreds of boxes of our stuff piled up in the foyer and then loaded up into the moving van. So much time spent there, so many memories. I won't miss the last year and the horrible events of those months, but all that is behind us now and we are moving forward.

Soon after I got down here, I got a call from a guy named Jack Finnerty. I didn't even remember it, but I did a repair on a water sprinkler system for his brother Kevin one year and didn't charge him because it didn't take me but fifteen minutes, and Jack always really appreciated that he said. Anyway, Jack's wife works at the Ketchogue Boro School – Mrs. Finnerty – and Jack wanted to give me a head's up about something. He told me "off the record" that even after everything happened with Henry and the Bullying Director, that guy Mr. Nicholls decided to look into what happened with all that Twitter stuff with Gianna, which coincidentally just stopped after we settled the case. He told me that they found the culprit – it was a kid named Remy Wartham, the son of Regina Wartham, who was the President of the Rec Committee. The kid made a mistake and shot one of those tweets from the school library computer and they nailed him. But worse, he apparently sent a few from his mother's laptop, the investigation found, and Nicholls referred the matter to the local police, who believed Regina was involved too. Jack told me she then ratted out Moshe and Bruce Dixon, who were the ones who vandalized Moshe's OWN CAR! Over the last few weeks some arrests have been made and I understand they are all in a bit of trouble. But as I said, all of that is behind us now.

Meanwhile, we are settled down here now and it feels great. And Henry is here too. When I told him we were relocating he had his little townhome on the market practically the next day and he was already looking into places down here. "Fuck I need to be living on Long Island for?" he asked me, "I want to be around my granddaughters." He moved down in early November, he's only a mile away. He's already found a bunch of old-timers to play golf with and believe it or not there's a Knights of Columbus in a neighboring town. He goes there to drink beer and watch ball games sometimes and there are days I go with him. He sees the girls about four days a week and they love it. I have to tell you, since he's been down here walking around in the warm weather and soaking in the sunshine, hanging out with his grandkids, he's like a new man. I swear I actually saw him smile a few times; I think it's happened on at least half a dozen occasions. Honest to God. I joked with him about it and he told me to fuck off and leave him the hell alone, but he was smiling there's no question about it. It is great having him here and I'm delighted he made the move.

Thing is, though, I really miss Will and Janet and their kids. They were lifesavers for me over the last two years, and I don't think I would have survived without them. But more importantly, Will is my brother and my best friend and Janet is like a sister to me. It killed me to have to leave them, say goodbye. Family – that's what life is about when it comes right down to it. I wish to God they were down here but now I have the money to send us all back to visit whenever we want. And we're going to do that as often as we can.

Agnes meanwhile made great strides over the summer and even more so when we got her down here. Maybe it was the change of scenery, who knows, but she is walking really well and talking up a storm. Her speech is well formed now and even though I hired an aide to be with her in the classroom her teachers tell me that maybe in a year she won't even need one. Her strength and dexterity are nearly all back and we even had her play in a Rec soccer league this fall. She could only go in for a few minutes here and there and of course Gianna was there on the sideline cheering her brains out with Henry eyeballing the whole situation, making all the coaches and referees nervous as hell. But still, Agnes was out there. She is in physical and cognitive therapy three days a week and I have faith that she is going to make a complete recovery.

Back in October I got my business back on its feet and I sent out some business cards and flyers and advertising sheets giving notice that Beers Construction Company was open for hire in the great State of North Carolina. To my surprise I was busy in a matter of weeks. I am doing small jobs that I enjoy, and I do them mostly one at a time. When I get done with a job, I take on another one and I am working mostly by myself. I have a list of customers who want me and there doesn't seem to be a shortage of demand down here so that is all good. It keeps me busy but there's no pressure. I make sure I do a great job for my customers and I charge them a reasonable price and word seems to be getting out that I offer great services for modest cost. Hopefully things will keep going like this but if not, I think I'll be fine. They say that money doesn't cure all problems and I agree with that but let me tell you something - it sure as hell helps. Trust me on that one.

So right around that time, in October, I was at a Home Depot picking up a light fixture for a little old lady who lives near me and a nice-looking woman with a great smile came up and asked me if I knew what a junction box was. She was supposed to pick one up for a contractor doing work at her house. I explained it and then we struck up a conversation. I wound up standing in the electrical aisle BSing with her for over forty minutes. Her name is Christine. Dark hair, really athletic looking, likes to run, do yoga, and has lots of energy. She's a mom with two sons, she's in her early 40s, and it turns out her husband died about ten years ago from cancer. Sad.

Anyway, we've been dating about two months now, and I am really enjoying her company. She has a great sense of humor and she's very kind and we go out a lot in the town and hang out and laugh.

It felt very strange to me when it all got started and to be honest it was her that called me and asked to go to dinner. I was overwhelmed with guilt over it but I accepted. I called Will and asked him what he thought, told him I didn't think I could go through with it, and he told me I was nuts for even thinking that way and why wouldn't you go. And then Henry was over one day and I summoned up the nerve to ask him about it. I wanted to know if he thought it was alright. I told him I was thinking of canceling and he said to me, "Fuck is wrong with you? You gonna sit around here on your ass all by yourself the rest of your life?"

And so I went on that first date and I'm glad I did. Now Christine and I see each other a few days a week. It's casual but fun. We take walks through town and she's really great to talk to. We're getting to know each other and I know it will take some time. She has a ton of friends and I've met quite a few of them. We'll see where things go but I'm excited about it. Last week I told the girls about her and I couldn't believe how receptive they were. Christine came over and met them and the girls both gave her a hug and started pummeling her with questions. Funny thing is, I'd like to tell Deb about her because I think the two of them could have been friends. Isn't that crazy?

Anyway, even though I'm happy down here now there are times when I sit around this place and wonder how I got here. There were so many twists and turns that gave rise to everything, so many unexpected and random events that landed me here, but that's life, you know?

When I think back on all of it, when it came right down to it, when things were so bad and I didn't think we would survive, my family and I bounded together. We got each other through. I am really proud of that. Henry, Will, Janet, Gianna, and of course Agnes, we all became closer after all those events. We realized we could always rely on one another. As I told my lawyer, that wonderful woman named Nicole Anzalone, you have to have faith, right? There are so many things that can happen to you in this life, things you have no control over. But you love and trust in the people that are close to you, you do the best you can, and maybe things will work out. They won't always, of course, but if you stay positive, I think most times they will …

Well, I'm going to put this thing away now and get some sleep. Tomorrow is Christmas and I can't wait. Henry will be over first thing in the morning to open presents with us and then Will and Janet and the kids are flying in sometime around 1pm. We'll have a nice family Christmas dinner and then Christine and her boys are coming over for dessert and coffee later on in the night.

And I'm really looking forward to the day.

I can't wait for everyone to be together.

I'm excited about next year, and to my girls' futures.

I'm hopeful about what this crazy life will bring me.

I have faith that everything will be okay.

And that's everything if you ask me.

You know what I mean?

ACKNOWLEDGMENTS

I WROTE THE first few chapters of this book on New Jersey Transit trains while commuting back and forth each day from the Jersey Shore, where I live, to New York City, where I practice law. In that regard, I would first like to thank NJ Transit for its frequent train delays, which allowed me ample time to get this project off the ground. But it was the help and support of family and friends that helped me to complete this book, and for that I am eternally grateful. I could not have done it without them, and they all deserve my heartfelt appreciation.

First, a special and loving thank you to my wife Pam, children Patrick, Catie, Kelly and Brenna, my brothers Sean and Brendan, my sister Brianne, and my mother-in-law Terri Pinto, for all of their encouragement and support, and for patiently reading drafts of this book and giving invaluable feedback and insight into the characters, plot lines, book design, and everything else associated with the story. There's no way this book happens without them.

A special thank you goes to my daughter Catie, who is a better writer than I am and spent countless volunteer hours editing the final manuscript and correcting my funny English.

Eternal love, appreciation, gratitude and thanks also goes to my parents, Pat and Claire Bonner, for always encouraging and supporting my love of reading and writing. They would have gotten a big kick out of this whole thing.

I would also like to thank my dear friends Jack Menz and Nina Sankovitch, whose support and encouragement to push this project forward was more valued and appreciated than they probably know.

A nod must also go to The Organization (Peter Sutton, Bob Holland, Matt McLees and Peter Sicilian), for a lifetime of loyalty, friendship and laughs, all of which inspired the more comedic parts of this book.

And finally, a quick side note.

The story I told in the Prologue of this novel is based loosely on my own family. My grandfather (Danny's grandfather in the story) did in fact come to this country on the SS Caledonia from Ireland in 1927, and halfway through the voyage he decided he was going to live in Boston. But something changed his mind, and he chose New York instead.

He told me that story one day when I was in law school, and I never forgot it. He said that if he hadn't altered his plans that day, if he had settled in Boston and never met my grandmother, my father and I would not exist.

But you're here, he said, because the decision that one man makes on one day, no matter how trivial, can change everything. And that's all there is to it. You see?

Anyway, I tucked that little nugget away, and years later it gave me an idea. Hope you enjoyed it.

Patrick D. Bonner, Jr.
November 2020

Made in the USA
Middletown, DE
30 November 2020

25739648R00268